Also by Greg Barron

HarperCollins Publishers Australia
Rotten Gods
Savage Tide
Lethal Sky
Voodoo Dawn (short fiction)

Stories of Oz Publishing
The Hammer of Ramenskoye (short fiction)
Camp Leichhardt
Galloping Jones and Other True Stories from Australia's History
Whistler's Bones
Red Jack and the Ragged Thirteen
Outlaw: The Story of Joe Flick
The Time of Thunder
The Last Days of Dom Sebastian
Beyond the Big Bend

THE PEDESTRIAN

A NOVEL OF THE AGE OF STEAM

Greg Barron

First Edition, Stories of Oz Publishing 2023

storiesofoz.com

ozbookstore.com

admin@ozbookstore.com

ISBN: 978-0-6459925-0-2

Cover design: Angus Crowley

Cover Artwork: Angus Crowley

Editing: Brad Connors

Typeset in 12/16 Bembo and Noiseless Remington

To Catriona, who loves reading, mudlarking, and walking.

BOOK ONE

Chapter One

When Frederick Morton was a boy, the River Thames was his domain. He knew each waterman by sight, along with their colourful punts and skiffs. He could distinguish the individual pitches of the barge handlers' whistles and rattle off the names of most of the working steam-tugs, along with the yards that built them. He understood the river's antiquity – how it had snaked across the plains of south-eastern England through history – bearing antediluvian hunters in their coracles, Roman triremes, and the royal barges of kings and queens.

So intimately did he know the tides that he carried a month of tables in his head. He knew how seawater entered the Thames through the gaping mouth stretching from Southend-on-Sea to the Isle of Grain, boiled up through the bottleneck below Tilbury, reaching the deep bend of Greenwich, passing the Tower of London and Westminster, surging all the way upstream to Teddington Weir, where the tide reached its zenith.

He understood how the visiting waters began their ebb, the river dropping twenty feet in height from Twickenham to the Isle of Dogs and beyond, leaving vast banks of sand, gravel, chalk, and mud exposed under the sun and stars, along with a museum of relics; the skeletons of wrecked watercraft, dead cats, old rags, and occasionally, amongst the refuse, items of value.

These tidal flats were Frederick's hunting grounds. The realm of the mudlark.

★★★

One Tuesday morning late in the winter of 1848, Frederick, just nine years old, was ankle-deep in mud on the river's northern bank, between Victoria Wharf and the Limekiln Dock. It was so cold that a wafer of ice had formed on the crust. His feet were numb, but that did not stop him from delving through the rubble of old bricks, discarded iron, and rubbish.

By the time the tide had started to turn, the river waters were creeping back over ground already picked over by the army of mudlarks at work that morning, Frederick's trouser pockets contained a shoelace, a broken clay pipe, two copper nails and a bone knife handle. These finds, he supposed, were worth two pennies between them. Enough for a cheap loaf of bread made with flour and alum powder.

The rising waters forced Frederick up towards the embankment. Mercifully, the light rain stopped, and the sun appeared from behind a curtain of grey. Just to his left, he noticed a metallic flash under the surface. He took two quick paces to the spot and bent over, his hand darting through the water and closing on a hard, flat, round object that could only be a coin.

Frederick lifted his find, opening his hand, rubbing the mud away with his thumb. It *was* a coin – a silver crown – the closest thing to a fortune he had held in his life.

'Lucky little bugger,' grumbled a man who had been working nearby. He was a young fellow, or might have seemed so in better circumstances, with very light moustaches like the whiskers of a cat, teeth rotted to the gums, and eyes dull from dope or drink.

Realising that he had been incautious, Frederick closed his fist over the coin and started to trudge back through the mud towards the approaches to Chinnock's Wharf. The man followed, and

Frederick glanced back nervously. He was under no illusion that all mudlarks were honest. Some liked to steal from passing barges and many were opportunists with the potential for violence.

Not yet alarmed enough to run, however, he paused to wash his feet in a drainpipe that channelled stormwater down from the streets. It was freezing and foul, but it served to remove the mud well enough.

"'Ere, you,' said the man as he came up. 'Gi'us a look at what yez found.'

Frederick skipped up the wooden steps onto the wharf. At the top he waited with his back to the busy cart and foot traffic along Narrow Street, watching while the man climbed the stairs towards him.

'I an't going to steal it, lad, I just wants a butcher's at it.'

Frederick shook his head. The silver crown was the most valuable item he had ever found – not life-changing – but a lot of money, nonetheless. Far better even than the grey woollen seaman's cap he had picked up a few months earlier and now wore on his head.

This silver crown meant food for many weeks. A crown was worth five shillings, each shilling was twelve pence. Sixty pence in one coin. His stepfather would spend some of it on gin, but the rest would keep them fed for a month. A loaf of bread and a couple of potatoes each day. Meat off-cuts from the butcher twice a week. Buttermilk and cheese such as they rarely tasted.

The man, reaching the top of the stairs, flashed his dark eyes and sprang like a spider for the coin. Frederick darted out of the way, towards the street, but still he did not run.

'Ow, you little wretch,' cried the man. His eyes narrowed and up close his teeth appeared to be coated with brown slime. 'You are a bold, smart little bastard, aren't yer? I've seen you around. They say you are a clever boy, what can fix things with your 'ands.'

It was true. Frederick had the knack of making things work, and sometimes performed small repairs for money – weavers' looms, toy mechanisms, kitchen mincers and the like.

'I just does what I can to eat.'

But the man had not yet finished. 'I've seen yer, watchin' the trains comin' into Stepney; botherin' the engineers, pickin' their brains. But you'll never be anything. Like the rest of us oo was born in this 'ell you'll stay until you rot. There's those oo make sure that a man cannot rise from the cesspit to which he were birthed.' He made his face as kind as possible. 'Now gimme the coin. We'll take 'alf each, an' swear to look after each other. I'll like as not be able to 'elp you out meself within a week or two.' He started to walk towards Frederick with his hand out, eyes narrowed. 'Don't you know that the only way which us low-born folks can survive is to share our luck when we 'as it? Divide your special find with me, lad. Let us exchange it for lesser coinage – there's a shop just yonder. Then, when me own luck comes, I'll share wi' you.'

Frederick heard the desperation in the man's voice and saw how starved he was. His collarbone was marked with a sunken notch and his cheeks all but showed the bone through the skin. His hands shook and his nose was laced with red veins. He was a drinker, to be sure, perhaps even a frequenter of the opium dens on Gill Street near the causeway.

'We 'ave to work together, sonny. Drudgery! That's all you can expect from this life. It don't matter what you do – they'll find a way to grind you down.'

Frederick, deciding that there was nothing to be gained by prolonging the conversation, secured the coin in his pocket, then dashed across Narrow Street just behind a trundling wagon, sprinting towards the wide pool of the Limehouse Basin.

Veering into Horseferry Street, the Basin waters passed by on the right-hand side, and rows of busy potters' shops on the left, all of which catered to the seafaring trade. Up ahead a steam crane was unloading wooden crates from the hold of a schooner, and Frederick wished that he could stop to watch it work, but the heavy clump of mud-crusted boots told him that his pursuer had not yet given up. He knew the steam crane well. He'd studied the engine that drove it, had spoken to the engineer who maintained it, breathing in the lore of its design and maintenance.

Muddy water spattered from Frederick's feet to his trouser legs as he skirted South Quay, then the soda works. Passing through one of the grand arches supporting the railway viaduct, he hid behind a costermonger and his barrow, waiting and watching until he saw his pursuer stop, cough his lungs out, then turn back towards the river with a slump in his shoulders.

Feeling more secure now, Frederick walked from there, albeit at a brisk pace, along the Regent's Canal towpath. On this broad cobbled thoroughfare, he went on for a good half-mile, greeting the bargemen with their horses, avoiding fresh dung and other walkers. He crossed the canal on the Craven Bridge and diverted around the corner, where the tenements stood in grim rows. He was only a few blocks from home now, and he glanced back one last time to make sure that the desperate mudlark had not foxed him, and continued to follow.

Satisfied that this was not the case, he turned into Maroon Street. From up ahead he heard a roaring noise and saw a cloud of rising dust. Frederick paused, with his pulse pounding in his temple. It seemed to him that the earth itself was trembling. He walked forward slowly, stopping at the intersection with Southfield, shaking deep in his bones, for something terrifying was happening to this miserable glut of ramshackle terraces, built by shoddy tradesmen in the reign of King George III and neglected ever since: slums with one water tap and two privies per block – no sewers or system for the disposal of rubbish. Inhabitants of the upper floors tossed their waste onto the shingle roofs of lower storeys, while ground-floor dwellers threw rubbish out into the street, there to combine with manure, sawdust, rain and mud.

Frederick, having entered the street from the canal end, stared open-mouthed at the transformation that had taken place since he left home, back before the turn of the tide, seven or eight hours previously. Ranks of men were marching down the thoroughfare, one or two better-dressed individuals shouting orders at the others. Behind them came a giant, rumbling monster – a traction engine blasting coal smoke from its stack. It was an elephantine, heavy thing, shaking the earth as it moved, steam hissing from hidden apertures and blowing a whistle that near burst the ears. It had the word Forgill's painted on both sides.

Meanwhile, Frederick heard the hammering of fists on doors, and shouts of 'Everyone out! You 'ad yer warnings. It's too late now.' Groups of men, swishing thin canes, were forcing the occupants of the slums out of their homes to the street, where they stood in abject groups. At this point the savage herders began to direct them out towards Church Row and Saint Dunstan's.

Frederick looked towards home – the second floor of a three-storey tenement. Something almost beyond his imagination was happening. That monster of iron, a trundling terror, was backing up towards the ramshackle front steps.

Even then, he could not help but stare at the moving parts: the crankshaft and connecting rod – the chain that drove the wheels, registering how each component precipitated motion in the next. The beautiful simplicity. The endless potential of the work it could perform.

Four men dragged up heavy chains, connecting them to the foundations of the terrace. The traction engine started forward, the chains tightening. The engine beat rose to a clamour. A clot of dark smoke issued from the stack.

'Mama!' Frederick shouted, starting forward, before being collared by one of the swarming men.

'Stay back lad,' shouted the man. 'It's dangerous, can't you see?'

Frederick watched helplessly as the traction engine crawled on, the chain dislodging a pier. The structure toppled dangerously. Tears welled in Frederick's eyes.

Nearby, a gang of men advanced with sledgehammers and began to pound against the wall and shutters of one old place. It seemed to Frederick that they did their work with glee, smashing things with the sanction of owners and authorities, enjoying every moment.

'New housing, out with the old, in with somethin' better,' cried the man who made the mistake of loosening his grip on Frederick's jacket.

Free now, Frederick burst away, running towards the sagging door that led to the tenement stairs. Another man with a cane hurried to get ahead, blocking the lad's progress. He was tall, and very, very thin, dressed in a fox-skin coat, worn smooth down to the hide in places, but with fire still in the reddish glow of the fur.

'Get out of 'ere, these buildin's is coming down.'

'That's me own house. Ma and me stepfather are there, let me in.'

'They're gone.'

'Where?'

The very thin man pointed to the last of a line of heavily laden men, women, and children, disappearing into Salisbury Street. 'Gawd knows, but not 'ere. Now piss orf before youse are hurt.'

Frederick hesitated, and he was still processing this information, when he saw that a well-dressed boy, whose stovepipe hat made him appear tall, had followed him along the street, and now stood beside the very thin man with the cane. Frederick regarded the newcomer as if he were an alien creature.

Never had he seen a boy who was so clean and well-groomed – his eyes clear and skin free of vermin bites. The black of his tailcoat was pure ebony, and his shoes were the colour of coal with the shine of glass.

'What's this, Wilkins?' said the boy. 'A dirty goblin-child from the slums?'

'That's right, Master Percy. A gutter rat oo won't do as he's told.'

The very thin man's face became all pinched and ugly like Frederick's stepfather's when he was angry. He struck out with the cane, whipping it sideways so fast that it whistled in the air, striking Frederick on the backs of his calves.

Frederick howled and fell to his knees, in which position another blow landed across his forearm and side. It stung with an instant, burning pain.

'Now do as you're told,' said the very thin man. He clapped the boy he had called Master Percy on the back, and stepped away, returning his attention to the business of destruction.

Tears of pain filled Frederick's eyes, and he felt the silver crown come loose from his pocket and fall. He scrabbled for it desperately, finding it on the ground, grasping it, along with street grime and dirt.

'What have you got in your hand?' hissed the well-dressed boy.

Frederick tried to scamper to his feet, but before he could manage it the boy came forward and prised his fingers open, exposing the coin, gripping it between his thumb and forefinger.

Percy, as he seemed to be known, held the coin aloft. 'A crown. Where, I may well ask, did you steal it from?'

'I didn't steal it, I swear.'

'A goblin from the slums doesn't own silver crowns.'

'Give it back,' demanded Frederick, and he flew at the older boy, scratching and grappling desperately. He felt his universe explode as a knee came up hard, impacting the soft tissue of his nose.

Again, Frederick felt himself falling. Some of the men standing nearby laughed, while sledgehammers tore at rotting walls, and the traction engine huffed. The sun, meanwhile, blanketed by dust and the coal smoke that overlaid the city, sank behind the ruined tenements. By the time Frederick had recovered his feet, a flood of warm crimson dripping from his nostrils, Percy and the tall thin man were an impenetrable wall. The latter held his cane menacingly. 'I told you. Get out of here.'

When Frederick did not move, the man roared again. 'Go on.

Get.'

Frederick wiped at his nose with the sleeve of his jacket, then jabbed a finger at the well-dressed boy. 'He took me money.'

'Don't you lie, wicked boy,' said Wilkins, raising the stick and marching towards Frederick.

A loud, commanding voice rang out above the sound of striking hammers and even the traction engine. 'Percy, Wilkins, what on earth are you doing to the poor wretch?'

Frederick, realising that he was the wretch in question, looked up to see a gentleman wearing a top hat and tailcoat, walking with a determined stride towards them. This was a species of Londoner rarely seen in the slums of Stepney East.

'We're not doin' nothin' sir,' said the very thin man, his face hiding behind the collar of his fox-fur coat.

The gentleman harrumphed, 'That's not what it looks like.' With brown eyes turning kind and gentle he took a handkerchief from his pocket and passed it to Frederick. 'Here, hold this to your nose and the blood will stop.'

Frederick did so, regarding his benefactor with wary thanks. He was a tall man, with long grey sideburns and a dimple in his chin. His shoes shone with fresh polish, showing no trace of dust from the street. His eyes were at once wise and kind, and it occurred to Frederick, even then, that he was in the presence of a great man, one with the power to change his life.

Chapter Two

'What in Heaven's name happened to the lad's nose, Wilkins?' the gentleman asked.

The very thin man and Percy traded glances, and the former spoke up. 'It were an accident, sir. The lad was ravin', tryin' to run into the buildings what was being demolished, and in my concern I were a little rough. He fell over, he did.'

Wilkins's front teeth, Frederick noticed, were over-large, and now, as they rested on his lower lip, coupled with his bushy sideburns and fox-fur coat, he looked more like a mischievous squirrel than the dangerous man of a moment earlier.

'Now listen,' the gentleman said to Frederick. 'My name is Lord Forgill, and you must be honest with me. Is that how it happened? Did you fall over?'

Frederick nodded dumbly, eyes staring like puddles lit by a faraway dawn.

'What's your name lad?'

'Frederick, my lord.'

'I'm sorry if my employee's duty to keep you safe led to an injury.'

'This boy Percy sir, 'e took me money,' said Frederick. 'A silver crown.'

'Really?' demanded Lord Forgill, regarding his son balefully.

'No!' spat Percy, tossing his head when a glossy-clean lock of hair fell across his eyes. 'He's lying Papa. A cheating slum-boy he is, trying to get money from you. Where would a such-like person get a silver crown from?'

Lord Forgill looked thoughtful and turned back to Frederick. 'You can't find your family?'

'They're not 'ere sir.'

'Most of the former residents are down at Saint Dunstan's, but I'd like to take you home, get you cleaned up, and make sure that your nose doesn't start bleeding again. It's late in the day – tomorrow morning we'll find your family for you.'

The idea of being separated from his mother, even for one night, filled Frederick with dread. 'I want to find Mama now.'

'That would be very difficult, in the dark. We'll find her tomorrow. We'll take you home and get you clean and dressed – it's the least I can do. Tomorrow, in daylight, we'll find them sure enough.'

Percy scoffed, 'Father, really? You'll take this … person home to our house?'

'Yes. It pains me to have to explain to you that the creation of new housing has consequences for the former inhabitants. We have a responsibility to help where we can.' Then, to Frederick. 'Follow me.'

It was a command, not a request, and Frederick followed. As they walked into Salisbury Street, he could see a wagon drawn by two horses up ahead, both roan in colour and in full harness. A driver was attending to them with nose bags of oats.

Before they reached the conveyance, Lord Forgill dropped back from his son and said to Frederick, 'If Percy truly took a crown from you, I shall give you a new one before you join your family. First, please, do tell me where you obtained it from.'

'I likes to mudlark, an' I plucked it from the river this very day.

It were the best thing I did ever find, sir.'

Lord Forgill appeared to be trying to read Frederick's face, eyebrows angled like the barbs of a feather. At length he resumed walking and said, 'Very well then, you shall have your silver crown before we find your mother tomorrow.'

Percy Forgill glared at his father as the three of them entered the glossy black brougham carriage, with a crest embossed in gold on the side. The interior smelled of leather and varnish. Frederick sat gingerly on the edge of his seat as the vehicle ventured down towards the river, the wheels wandering in and out of ruts and channels in the surface, turning into White Horse Street, then joining the bustling traffic on Commercial Road.

'He stinks, father,' said Percy.

'Yes, of poverty,' said Lord Forgill. 'A condition which we are duty-bound to help alleviate.'

The Lord's son did not reply, and soon the sky turned dark. Frederick was now well beyond his own neighbourhood, and the unfamiliar sights and smells unsettled him. He started to regret embarking on this journey when he should have been looking for his mother.

After at least an hour on the road, Frederick saw Hyde Park on the left and on the right a precinct of homes so grand that they seemed like castles. The brougham paused, waiting while a liveried guard opened a gate, then moved onwards, entering a spacious compound enclosed by walls of lustrous Caen stone.

Gaslights atop columns along the drive illuminated sections of green lawn interspersed with beds of roses, geraniums, catmint, hollyhock and foxglove. The house itself came into view, seeming to possess a homely warmth despite its great size, constructed in more blocks of white stone, with a slate roof and three white balustrades at the front. Casement windows extended across two storeys. Stable boys came to unharness the horses and footmen opened the doors of the brougham.

Frederick got out when he was told, standing straight like a soldier on the gravel, waiting for instructions on what to do and where to go, watching the swirling dew and the snorting breath of the horses after the journey.

Yet Lord Forgill's philanthropy did not extend to admitting street-children to main entrances and marbled entryways. The lost child was admitted via a side-entrance into a network of kitchens, storerooms, and sculleries.

There, a housemaid drew a bath in a huge iron tub, and Frederick bathed and dressed in clean clothes – not new, but good plain garb. He was given a plate of potatoes, beans, and boiled meat.

In a pause between dinner and pudding Frederick heard Percy in a tantrum from another room, screaming at a servant who came back to the kitchen red faced, closing the door behind her. He had known members of his own class of a similar disposition. People to be avoided. People who lashed out. He hoped he would not encounter Percy Forgill again.

After supper a maid led Frederick to a room that must have been unused servant's quarters, for it was very small, though clean, with an iron bedstead and whitewashed walls. A single candle burned on a stand.

Ignoring the folded night gown under the pillow, Frederick climbed between the sheets in his new clothes and lay there, breathing in the smell of bleach and soap. He knew that it had been a mistake to come here, yet his belly was full, and Lord Forgill had been so commanding.

Letting the weight of his eyelids carry him off to sleep, Frederick dreamed of the heavy Forgill's machine – the traction engine – that he had seen pulling down buildings in the street, like the harbinger of a new age.

***

Frederick woke in the middle of the night to a heavy pounding that seemed to travel through the grain of the floorboards, into the base of his bed and into his spine. This was repeated three times, accompanied by a voice and rapid footsteps. When this was followed by the sound of screaming, Frederick was already out of bed and heading for the door. More screams came, penetrating his skull like knives.

Dressed now, Frederick turned the key, ran into the hallway then down a passage. There he saw Percy Forgill standing over something on the floor at the foot of the stairs, surrounded by a wide pool of a dark liquid.

Percy looked at Frederick. Strangely, all the hubris and aggression were gone from him. 'The wolf,' was all he said.

There was someone else too, hidden in the darkness at the top of the stairs. Frederick did not recognise what he saw there. More people were coming. More noise. Shouts of concern and running servants. Frederick's eyes moved back to the inert thing on the ground. He saw someone bending over it.

At length, while Frederick shivered in the background, withdrawing into a dream world that seemed like a nightmare, a doctor arrived, carrying a black bag. Lord Forgill took Frederick's arm and led him into a drawing room smelling of sandalwood and wax candles. Tears streamed down the gentleman's face. He was crying like a child, his chest racked with sobs. 'You must say nothing of what you saw here tonight. I will be kind to you, I will help you, but you must never say anything. Will you do that for me?'

Frederick felt a turmoil inside. 'Yes.'

'Please don't tell anyone. Not even your loved ones.'

'I won't say nothin'.'

'Very well, thank you. Now it's best that you should leave. Now.'

Frederick turned and ran from the house, twisting open the carved handles of the vast front doors. He ran blindly, imagining the wolf that Percy had spoken of making long bounds after him.

Running south at first, he oriented himself when he reached the railway line, slowing to a walk, continuing through the night, passing by the low-burning fires of the City's industrial heart. He saw figures huddled in blankets: the men, women and children of the streets, who stumbled from meal to meal, from cold to disease.

Frederick walked on. He had the talent of never growing physically tired. People marvelled at his ability to keep moving, and the night trek did not test him as it might have tested other boys.

Not long after dawn, Frederick recognised the blunt turret of Saint Dunstan's church and the smells of home. This was where, apparently, the refugees from the previous day's destruction had gathered. Many appeared to have camped in the grounds overnight.

Frederick searched the crowd, standing and sitting around the churchyard in sad groups. Girls clutched filthy rag dolls, and stripling lads play-wrestled on the pavement. Beyond them, the church graveyard lay under drooping elm and plane trees, broken-backed graves sunk into the earth and snaked over by creepers.

Still heavy at heart at the events of the previous night, Frederick gave the graves a wide berth. His progress was halted by two mastiffs in the preliminary stages of a fight. A moment later something struck him a mighty blow over the side of the head. He reeled back, then looked up to see his stepfather staring at him, eyes rimmed with red, and his breath foul from last night's gin.

Jack Price was tall for a Stepney man and broad shouldered, though thin, and you'd better not question his word or talk back, by God. He was a man's man, formerly earl of five yards by eight of squalor, now being pounded into ruins by man and machine.

'You little rascal, where ya been? An' where'd you get them new duds?'

Frederick caught sight of his mother, standing beside the pile of their belongings. She looked as forlorn as he had ever seen her. Her beautiful hair was covered in a cloth cap, her lips thin and white with worry. She called his name when she saw him, and opened her arms.

Nothing mattered then, for Frederick was in the one place he felt safe and loved: his mother's embrace, her lips on his forehead, both hands on the back of his head.

'Thanks be to the Lord God that you are here, and safe at last,' she said softly, pressing her lips to his clean hair.

Chapter Three

For sixpence a week the broken little group found a windowless room on Mile End Road. This place of rubble walls, leaking shingles and rancid air would be shared with another family, who were furious to find that their living space would be cut by half. They gave up every inch with spitting bile.

When the landlord led Jack Price, Mary and Frederick Morton into the room, the matriarch of the incumbent Govan family watched them come with hands on her apron-clad hips, 'There's no space for them, ya greedy bastard.'

'Shut yer hole,' said the landlord, 'or it's you I'll throw on the street, not them.'

Pip Govan had a mouth like a cannon, loaded with bitterness, spite and disappointment, firing salvos in wide arcs to all who crossed her path.

The families hung lengths of sacking on a rope to separate their domains. A single privy out the back serviced all three storeys and two more terraces. The queue was three or four deep from cock's crow to midnight. The room itself was crowded and raucous. There were arguments and lovemaking, flatulence and laughter. Frederick ignored most of it. He had a sleeping pallet to himself, and plenty enough to stay busy.

Frederick mudlarked through every daylight low tide, and his interest in steam engines continued unabated. As he scoured the Thames mud for trinkets, his eyes also sought out steam-powered boats as they passed, their paddlewheels churning, and dark smoke chuffing from the stacks.

The Stepney East train station became a favourite haunt, for the trains running on the London and Blackwall Railway were, at that time, not driven by locomotives, but were wound from station to station by seven-mile-long hemp cables, rolled onto giant drums by powerful, reversible, stationary steam engines.

Frederick climbed a fence to creep up close, watching the pistons cycle, the connecting rods turning the wheels that were geared to the drum. Every day was an engineering lesson. He learned to recognise the weaknesses in the system, the mayhem when a stretched cable broke, severed strands whipping through the air and the disconnected train rolling, occasionally derailing and crashing.

An engineer who performed maintenance on the railway engines taught him the basics – that steam expands to 1700 times the volume of the water it was formed from – that when confined it exerts a force that can work against a surface to create motion. Frederick, by then, understood how valves allowed steam to make a piston move both ways.

Tom Govan, the man in the adjoining half of the room, had a set of tools – files, spanners, and screwdrivers. His own hands were too affected by gin and arthritis to use them, and he was not averse to sharing with roommates, provided they were returned.

Frederick had been fixing things for a year or two, but with a full tool kit he was much more effective. He undertook minor repairs, for a pittance, on everything from kitchen devices to pushchair axles. It was an interesting training ground, and he understood that his first task was to work out how a particular machine functioned, then use this knowledge to discern which component had failed.

Occasionally the repair was beyond him, but most of the time he could find a way – filing a new, fabricated part, or using a spring cannibalised from a broken, similar machine. He began to collect stray bits and pieces that he found, either mudlarking or on the streets, and the extra income was appreciated.

★★★

Other forces were stirring, London was waking up to the power of education. Incited by the words of cultural leaders such as author Charles Dickens, Londoners were becoming aware that they had a generational issue with poverty and crime. How could London claim to be the greatest city in the world when a million of her people lived in squalor?

The 'Ragged Schools' movement, inspired by the work of tailor Thomas Cranfield, led to the formation of hundreds of new schools across England, built for the poorest and most 'raggedly clothed' children. In Stepney East, a young man of nineteen years, fired with idealism and armed with a rich sponsor – Lord Batholomew Forgill – purchased a solid terrace house, installed desks and blackboards, and placed a sign on the front porch.

> Stepney East Ragged School.
> Now instructing boys and girls in Reading, Writing and basic Arithmetic. No fees.

It wasn't Frederick who saw the sign first. It was his mother. There was a proud, hopeful cast to her lips and tears in her eyes when she walked with him down towards the canal on that first day. The proud carriage of her body, and shining eyes said that yes, they were dressed poorly, her son was as destitute as any lad could be, but he would be educated, and that meant hope for better things.

The number of enrolled girls was low, and their classes were held separately. Boys' sessions were held by day and evening. Frederick preferred the latter, as he still had time to mudlark. Students were given a supper of 'skilly and two' – oatmeal soup and two slices of bread, which they ate at their desks. The second slice Frederick would always button into his pocket to take home for his mother.

The teacher, nineteen-year-old Alexander Rawlings, wore good clothes, rumpled as winter clouds, rarely pressed, with a silk handkerchief hanging from his pocket, untidy and damp from his constant nose-blowing. The boys joked that their teacher's nose music put the shift whistle at the Gas Works between Johnson Street and Regent's Canal to shame. Rawlings spoke 'posh' English, but interspersed his words with multiple utterances and stammerings.

'Good morning, ah, erm, gentlemen. A good day to, er, begin with arithmetic. Take out your ah, er, erm ...'

The more impertinent students risked the impact of a whistling cane by calling their teacher, 'Wait-a-bit Rawlings,' and there were some hilarious interjections by well-practiced wags in the pauses between the beginnings of sentences and the endings.

The school occupied all three floors of the terrace, the classroom up top, equipped with rows of flip-top desks incorporating ink wells. There were fifty such desks in the room, with a teacher's lectern out front. There were also two chalkboards, a map of the British Isles, an abacus on a stand, and a portrait of Queen Victoria, who, it seemed to Frederick, ruled the entire world and would do so forever. The floors were of broad oak boards, so prone to creaking that it was impossible to stand without being heard.

Frederick chose a place on the left-hand side, with a view down Catherine Street to the sun of their solar system – Saint Dunstan's church, slowly greying away as the afternoon faded into evening and the scholars completed their exercises by gas light.

Mister Rawlings liked to pose problems derived from the real world of Stepney's streets, rubbing his hands together as if with excitement at sharing the exercise. 'Now, my ah, er clever scholars, if a street seller purchases um, one dozen nutmeg graters from a er tinsmith for a shilling, and sells them for ah, erm tuppence each, how much profit has he made?'

Often there were ethical dimensions to the questions: 'A woman, erm, makes her living as a tie maker. She, er rises from her bed at four in the ah morning and makes ten ties before erm going out into the street to sell them. At the end of the day, she has um, er gross earnings of two shillings. The materials cost ah one and sixpence.' He would then ask not only, 'How much profit would she erm make each week if she ah, worked six days?' But also, 'Do you ah think this is a fair recompense for her, erm labours?'

Frederick not only understood the basic unfairness of the lives being lived around him, but also had a brain capable of the arithmetic required to answer the question.

Within a few days, Wait-a-bit Rawlings was aware that he had a prodigy on his hands. 'You're a, um, ah quick one, Freddie. I expect er, big things from you.'

Lord Bartholomew Forgill, Mr Rawlings announced, was soon to arrive on one of his regular visits. 'Lord Forgill established this, um, school purely because of his kind heart,' the teacher explained, priming them for the visit. 'He has rebuilt many of the homes in this area and sits in the House of Lords. You must be very, ah polite, and speak respectfully if he ah invites you to.'

When Lord Forgill caught sight of Frederick, he reacted by pausing and resting his hand on the boy's shoulder. 'Frederick, isn't it?'

'Yes sir.'

The boy stared back in awe, for he now knew that Lord Forgill was the owner of a vast engine works in Wapping, one of the biggest such factories in London. The traction engine his men had used to topple buildings was still one of the most impressive and terrible things Frederick had seen – a prototype apparently, that had other engineering firms busy at their design boards trying to catch up.

'I recall our association from some time ago,' said Lord Forgill. 'I take it that you found your family without any trouble.'

'Yes sir, I did indeed.'

'Excellent, and have you been enjoying your studies?'

'I 'ave, thank you sir.'

'I'm glad you have been able to get an education at our little school.' He paused. 'Would you mind coming with me for a moment? I'd like to talk to you some more.'

Mister Rawlings's office was empty, and Frederick followed Lord Forgill there, the other children staring, wondering why he had been singled out. Normally an untidy, busy space, the office had been decluttered for the great man's visit, and the desk surface was clear. Invited to sit, Frederick did so, on the edge of a plain wooden chair.

'I just wanted to mention,' Lord Forgill said, 'the thing that happened on the night you stayed with us. What did you see?'

Frederick stared down at his feet. 'I don't rightly know sir.'

'There was an incident, were you aware of it?'

'I seen something on the floor sir.' Frederick blinked at the memory. 'An' a dark thing lurking, I think. Hairy and fearful it was.'

Lord Forgill shook his head. 'There was nothing lurking. That's just your imagination. Have you honoured your promise to say nothing of what you saw?'

'I 'ave, sir.'

Lord Forgill dug into his purse and took out a silver crown. 'This is what I promised you – and I will be monitoring your progress here. You are a bright one from all accounts and I may be able to assist.'

★★★

The windfall made a difference to their lives, for a time. The smell of cooking meat was a cruel test on neighbouring families, and Jack Price took his cronies on a bender. For a while there was always bread, and Frederick purchased the first few tools of his own, rusted old spanners from street vendors that he scrubbed back to shining steel.

Each night, after school, Frederick went home and told his mother what he had learned. He sat at the little table with a cheap candle burning, reading to her, or demonstrating how to calculate a three-digit quotient using long division. He brought pennies home from his mud-larking, while his stepfather drank and gambled, and Mary Morton laboured at mending clothing to be resold with new buttons and patched rips. Sometimes she worked for twelve hours straight until her hands were bent like claws and could not be straightened.

One day Jack had a fist fight with a stringy Welshman from a lower storey, out on the street. Everyone came to watch. Women screamed, children shrilled and men shouted encouragement as the combatants beat each other's faces with fists driven by muscles shrunk from malnutrition and their lungs scored by coal dust.

They were bored and frustrated, their minds weak from having nothing to do but find money for food and gin or ale. Frederick wished someone would stop them from fighting, but instead more men came, formed a ring and wagered pennies on the outcome.

When it was over Mary Morton sluiced the blood from her man's face and sewed a deep split in his lip, clicking her tongue at the ways of men and the meanness of life.

★★★

Percy Forgill, now and then, accompanied his father on his visits to the Ragged School. The young lord-in-waiting did not try to hide his disgust that his father should trouble himself to help such creatures as these children of the slums. Percy did not like them, and he made his prejudice plain. His dislike for Frederick ran deeper.

On one particular day, the schoolmaster had left a chalkboard scrawled with arithmetic for the boys to complete. Frederick was working his way through them, saving the more challenging sums for last, when Percy Forgill peered around the corner into the room, then marched in, coming alongside Frederick's desk, reaching out a hand to twist his ear until it burned with pain.

'You are gutter vermin. Don't ever forget that, will you?'

Frederick stared back dumbly. He did not make a sound, just plumbed the amber flecked depths of Percy Forgill's eyes at close range, not liking what he saw there one bit.

★★★

Early in the nineteenth century, the disease known as cholera took flight from its nursery deep in the Ganges Delta of India and was carried on ships across the sea. The first British epidemic killed tens of thousands. The second episode began in the late forties, sweeping through the slum suburbs of London, from Southwark to the East End, like a reaper's scythe. As with most institutions in the area, the Stepney East Ragged School closed its doors temporarily.

Frederick learned to step around bodies lying on the footpath, creeping past running-patterers reciting Coleridge on corners.

> Comes, black as a porpus. The diabolus ipse, call'd Cholery Morphus; Who with horns, hoofs, and tail, croaks for carrion to feed him, Tho' being a Devil, no one never has seed him!

Body carts rolled mournfully over cobblestones and mud, their maudlin operators mouthing morbid chants over the squeaking of the wheels. Preventative measures were adopted. It was well known that keeping the abdominal area very warm with woollen swaddling and blankets helped stave off the disease, as did eliminating foul smells.

The first tenants to be afflicted were Mrs Govan and her youngest daughter. The sound of their groans, and the stench of their emissions filled the little room night and day.

Government health officers walked the streets, inspecting yards and premises, looking for causes of the miasmas that were known to cause the disease – bad airs arising from rotten waste and creeping with the morning mists through the windows of families careless enough to leave them unshuttered, while a summer sun rose and baked and turned rooms into ovens where the sufferers groaned and died and were carried out.

For the next week of nerve-wracking days Frederick's family escaped infection, but one morning he woke with stomach cramps so severe it was like someone had taken his guts in the grip of huge pliers and was twisting mercilessly. In between the worst convulsions he seemed to be observing his prone body from afar.

Frederick would never forget the pain and discomfort of the cholera; how he streamed vile liquids, and the unslakable thirst. By the time he was on the mend his mother had been struck down also – crying out from her soiled bed, her lust for water so strong that whether delivered by the pint or the gallon it made no difference.

Frederick came to suspect that the cholera was the wolf in another guise. He saw its hunger, and ravening claws: the unfairness of the thing, for its discriminations were apparently random. This was a Biblical plague with no meaning; a filthy thing that took lives for sport.

He tried to keep his mother alive with the strength of his love, yet she faded hour by hour. Her skin lost its vibrancy and colour, and her eyes eroded into time-worn pebbles. Yet the light that had always seemed to shroud her never dimmed. Never! This inner light burned brighter than a star until the end.

★★★

At the epidemic's peak, most funerals involved little more ceremony than a prayer and a gentle heave into a mass grave. Jack Price, however, had enough love in him to borrow a shovel and, with Frederick at his side, carry Mary's body to the yard of Saint Dunstan's after midnight, where he began to dig down into the earth beside the grave of her daughter, Frederick's sister, who had arrived stillborn some two years earlier.

'Help, boy,' he ordered after a while, and Frederick took his turn on the shovel, shaking and looking wide-eyed around him.

'What are you frightened of?' asked Jack Price, the bowl of his clay pipe glowing red and illuminating his eyes like those of a demon.

Frederick said nothing, but of course he was stunned at the loss of his mother and afraid of what would happen now. In between strokes of the shovel, he searched the shadows beneath the trees, watchful for the breath of frightening things in the darkness.

Jack Price took his turn again at the shovel when Frederick grew tired. They struck a layer of sharp stones and progress slowed until they were through. Finally, however, they reached soft loam again, and the hole grew too deep to easily extract the spoil.

Now they laid Mary Morton's cold body down and filled the hole. Jack Price had preserved the top layer of turf, and he replaced it so an observer would not notice that the ground had been disturbed.

'At least it's done proper,' he said. 'She'll rest better 'ere.'

Then, on blurred cobblestones, his mind full of the sadness and tortured beauty of their prayers, Frederick followed his stepfather back to the half room they called home, there to huddle silently and wonder at why and how such a cataclysm could be lived through. How he could get up tomorrow and eat or breathe without her.

★★★

In the morning, dry of mouth and feeling like the world had finished, Frederick watched as his stepfather gathered his things.

'Where are you goin'?' Frederick asked at length.

'Away from disease, an' death. Somewhere else. Not 'ere.'

'Shan't I come with you?'

'No lad. I 'ave to start again, find a new woman, a new life, and a brat won't 'elp me chances.'

Frederick watched him go, then sat behind the jute curtains and considered the remains of his life. Later in the day Mrs Govan grasped the situation. She had buried two of her five children in the past three weeks.

'We'll take the space back,' she said flatly. 'An' you can have a corner to yerself. If you'll bring in sixpence a week I'll feed you once a day.'

Frederick felt weak with the realisation that he was as close to alone in the world as it is possible to get.

★★★

On the night after the departure of Frederick's stepfather, fourteen-year-old Lily Govan reached out in the darkness and took his hand, rubbing it with her thumb in silent compassion.

Over the next week Lily grew careless with closing the divider between her space and his. Through the breaks in the hanging jute he could see her undress; her small breasts, concave stomach and the bush of hair at the junction of her legs. He had recently sprouted a dark jungle there himself, and he was interested to find that females had the same growth.

Handholding was a gateway to more interesting pursuits. One night she dragged his hand closer and rubbed his knuckles across her pubis, then up across her chest.

When this was done, she carried out reciprocal explorations. Night after night they stayed in the safety of their own spaces, uttered not a sound, and educated each other on the delights of the opposite gender at a discreet arm's length. By day they scarcely spoke.

Frederick found himself looking forward to the smell of snuffed-out candles and Mrs Govan's mumbled bed-time prayers very much.

★★★

When the cholera threat diminished, school resumed, and Frederick went back to the mud banks to find the means to eat. Amongst the nails, belt buckles and buttons he found a leather satchel containing six exquisite ivory dice that he sold for three shillings. Two or three times a week he applied his skills with his growing tool kit for an extra penny or two.

At the same time, Frederick applied himself so conscientiously to his lessons at the Ragged School that Mr Rawlings gave him the task of instructing small groups of younger students. Frederick's particular talent was for mathematics, though he also had a flair for art, and turned in the finest roundhand script in the school.

The teacher, by then, had taken a strong interest in Frederick, and the death of his mother was common knowledge. The fact of the stepfather's departure, however, took some time to reach the teacher's ears.

'Where are you living?' asked Mr Rawlings.

'Same place, sir. Ma Govan feeds me dinner, and I 'as a corner all to meself.' He smiled, 'What with me tools and school things an' all, there ain't much space.'

'You have no um, family left at ah, all?'

'Not that I know of sir. Me mum was from up North somewhere.'

The teacher stopped his questions, but he appeared to be deep in thought.

★★★

A few days later Frederick was in the school room cutting a new quill when Mr Rawlings appeared. 'Freddie, would you erm, please come to my office?'

Frederick was surprised when he walked into the office, for Lord Forgill was there, standing to shake his hand. 'Good afternoon Freddie.'

'Good afternoon sir.'

'I have been watching your progress,' said the great man. 'You have made me pleased. Very pleased. And today I have a gift for you.'

Frederick remained silent, and Mr Rawlings prodded him in the back and whispered in his ear. 'Say something.'

'I'm sure I hain't worthy of no gift, Lord Forgill,' said Frederick.

'Well, Mr Rawlings and I believe that you are. How would you like to go to school?'

'Why, I already am going to school.'

'This modest institution has been a good starting point for you, but Mr Rawlings and I want you to take the next step, particularly in view of your talent for mathematics, and interest in engineering. I have approached the Headmaster of the Charterhouse School in Islington, one of the finest boys' schools in the land. My own son Percy is in First Form there.' With this piece of news Lord Forgill stopped, and searched Frederick's eyes for a moment before going on. 'I have made the necessary financial arrangements for you to begin your studies at the beginning of Michaelmas term, starting Monday, as a boarder. You will need new clothes in order to attend.'

Without being invited, Frederick sank into a chair, wiping his brow with his sleeve. 'Oh, bless me sir, but all this talk about clothes and fine schools, I don't quite ...' He looked up. 'Do you mean it sir?'

'Of course I mean it.' Forgill passed over a pamphlet, with a school crest embossed on the front, and an envelope. 'In here you'll find the necessary information. The envelope contains five pounds for the purchase of the gentleman's clothing you will need.'

'Five pounds? Oh goodness ... I don't know what to say sir,' said Frederick.

Lord Forgill clasped Frederick's hands in his own. 'Just say thank you. That will suffice for the moment.'

'Thank you, sir. You're the most generous man in the world.'

'I'm not, but if a man in my position can't change the world for the better what is the point? Justify my faith; fulfil your potential, and I'll be well satisfied.'

★★★

When Percy heard of this development, he was furious. He lurked downstairs until Frederick was on his way home, pushed his face against the nearest wall, then hissed into his ear. 'You dare show your face at my school and I'll punch you flat, do you understand? How much money did my father give you?'

'Five pounds.'

Percy's face turned white with rage. 'Show it to me.' Frederick took out the envelope and the other boy snatched it from his hand. 'Filthy goblins from the slums don't know what to do with so much cash.'

'Give it back,' demanded Frederick.

'Why should I? It's my money after all. One day it will all be mine.'

'I'll tell Mister Rawlings, and I'll tell Lord Forgill. He gave it to me, not you.'

Percy seized Frederick's arm and twisted it. 'If you do, I'll tell my father things. I'll make certain that he hates you.'

'You're a rotten bastard,' Frederick said. 'Cruel and mean and not like your father at all.'

Percy curled his lip and crossed his arms in front of his chest. 'I don't want to be like him. I plan to have a lot more fun than he does.'

Frederick watched helplessly as Percy opened the envelope. Five Bank of England one-pound notes disappeared into a waistcoat pocket, though he dropped the envelope and pamphlet to the ground.

Frederick scrambled to retrieve both items.

'Don't forget what I said,' warned Percy. 'If you dare to set one filthy foot in my school, you'll regret it.'

Chapter Four

On his way home Frederick read through the pamphlet, studying the section titled 'clothing.'

Only the Charterhouse scholarship students, better known as gownboys, merited full academic dress. Day boys and boarders were to wear 'gentleman's' attire. The pamphlet recommended that all fee-paying students would have on hand two pairs of trousers, two tailcoats, eight shirts, six pairs of worsted stockings, eight pairs of cotton stockings, six pocket handkerchiefs and a supply of books, quills and paper. The required shoes were referred to as 'gowsers.'

Frederick could not buy clothes without money. He could not go to school without gentleman's clothes. Yet he had an appreciation of just how rare an opportunity he had been given. He knew that grasping it would change his life.

★★★

At dawn Frederick collected his wicker basket and a wire rod, crept past the doors of the neighbours on each landing, reaching the street without even a penny for a pint of tea. He followed the towpath on the eastern bank, damp from the heavy fog, with rats scuttling in the shadows, and bargemen loading and readying their craft. At the Basin he walked along Narrow Street, taking the Ratcliff Cross stairs. On the way he passed an old man who had slipped and fallen. A lone policeman was attending to him. None of the slum-dwellers or canal people paid the situation any mind as they hurried by.

Reaching the riverbank, Frederick moved away from the other mudlarks who were already at work, setting out across the flats until his feet were caked in dark slime to the ankles.

In all his years of mudlarking, Frederick had never found an item worth more than the silver crown Percy had stolen. Now he needed to turn up something worth at least a pound. With one pound he could buy quality clothes second-hand, enough to get him by, along with the quills and inks he would need in the school room.

With fierce and unbroken concentration, he picked over the mud with his eyes, hands and rod. In the first hour he found one carved cherrywood pipe, worth at least sixpence, and hundreds of broken white clay fragments. In the second hour, he spotted a brass belt buckle amongst a thousand or more broken red bricks.

Then, as the tide started to rise again, pushing him back towards the embankment, Frederick searched with a growing sense of dismay. It wasn't possible to attend the Charterhouse School dressed in rags. Yet the afternoon produced nothing more. The tide rose until it lapped at the embankment. He gave up trying to probe, with dirty river water to his knees. He wandered up towards the canal, shivering and uncaring, stopping only to sell the pipe and brass buckle.

★★★

Sunday was Frederick's last chance. This time the best he could manage was a tin Apostle spoon before the river started to rise again. Despondency set in, and he sat on the edge of the embankment, watching the river and cursing his luck.

A compact steam side-wheeler drifted up in the current, scudding with the breeze to the starboard side, lacking power. Frederick heard the occupants swearing and complaining to each other. He saw a couple of figures inside the wheelhouse, along with two men and a woman on deck. One of the former, to judge from the coal dust on his face and arms, was the stoker. He and the other man were exchanging shouts.

The boat was about forty feet in length, with a beam of eight or nine. The paddlewheel on the starboard side, towards the stern, was immobile, though smoke was billowing from the stack.

Catching sight of Frederick, the man who appeared to be in charge grabbed a coiled rope. 'Here lad, catch this line an' make us fast ashore, will you?'

Frederick grasped the rope and threw a loop around a half-rotted pole on the shore. This done, he waded towards the boat, drawn by curiosity about the engine. It was, he saw, an inverted-vertical type, but very compact. The firebox glowed red through the door cracks.

'What's wrong with it?' Frederick asked, hanging on to the side.

'Rattles like a donkey-cart, twice each stroke an' no power. We need to be up at Nine Elms in two hours!'

They looked like ruffians both, but Frederick wasn't afraid. The woman started up on them. "Ow's this then, fer a turn out. You pair 'o fools couldn't organise a pie at a fair.'

'Let me look at the engine,' said Frederick.

The leader of the little crew laughed. 'An' what are you plannin' on doin' about it?'

Frederick broke in, 'Please lemme look. I know about engines, sir, an' I can fix things.'

'Let 'm look,' shrieked the woman. 'Anybody would 'ave to be of more use than you lot.'

'Just you shut yer trap, Eleanor,' said the leader, looking at the speaker balefully. Finally, however, he shrugged his wide shoulders. 'Well since I s'pose it can't do any 'arm, climb aboard, an' look all you want.'

The man leaned down with one arm, which Frederick used like a rope to clamber aboard. Reaching the deck, dripping filthy water from his legs and feet he walked aft and looked at the boiler. The glass showed a good level of water, and the pressure gauge was reading twenty-five pounds per square inch. His eyes moved to the engine itself.

'It looks like somethin's gorn pete in the valve, and there an't nothin' anyone can do wit'out an engineer,' said the stoker, leaning on his shovel.

'I can fix it,' said Frederick, with more confidence than he felt.

"Ow would you do that, matey?'

'Have you a spanner?'

'There're tools 'ere, sure enough,' said the stoker, reaching for a compact iron chest from under the gunnel, opening it within Frederick's reach.

Using first one spanner, then another, Frederick's hands were sure and nimble as he released the bolts that held the slide-valve chest cover. Delving inside, kneeling so he could look more closely, he studied the D-valve. This assembly, he had been shown by maintenance engineers on the railways, was held by two nuts, kept loose enough to allow the valve to move onto the face or off it, to prevent damage if water became trapped in the cylinder. A clip that had originally been fastened in place to stop these nuts from turning had rusted away, and both nuts had rattled loose.

'Bit of a mess,' commented the stoker, who seemed less than impressed that this grubby lad was so good with his tools.

"Tis indeed,' said Frederick. He used a rag from the kit to lay out the pieces as he removed the valve components from the valve chest. This done, he set about cleaning them, one by one. All the cleaned parts were then buffed with a rag and oiled before he started the assembly once more. He used a length of spring wire from the toolbox to create a new clip, bending and cutting with pliers and fitting the item several times before he was sure that the nuts would no longer move.

The slide-valve chest cover needed a new gasket to seal it, and Frederick looked around the boat for something suitable, finding nothing. With a flash of inspiration, he thought back to an old leather boot he had seen on the riverbed just an hour earlier.

'Hold on,' he said to his audience. 'I'll be back in a mo.'

He climbed over the side and sloshed through to where he had seen the boot during his earlier mudlarking. The tide had risen but he was able to feel around in knee-deep water and locate it. He washed the boot clean of mud and examined it. There was a large hole around the toe but the upper leathers were still good.

Back at the boat he threw the boot over the side and asked, 'A knife perchance?'

The leader produced a wicked looking dagger, and Frederick used the old, perished gasket as a template, trimming the leather to size. This done, he took a patch of sandpaper from the kit and used it to clean the gasket seat so the leather would fit more closely.

Now, while the stoker began to shovel fresh coal into the firebox, Frederick reattached the valve-chest cover bolts and tightened the nuts. Finally, he worked his way around the engine with an oil pot, lubricating and making adjustments, feeling the boiler's impatience; the deep rumbling as it stored up power.

'Do we 'ave working pressure?' Frederick called, parroting the 'real' engineers he had heard. Yet his heart was beating hard in his chest as he watched the stoker open the regulator and let the steam through. The engine stuttered at first, but then, a moment later, the paddlewheel began to churn.

The woman uttered such a squeal of delight that it almost overpowered the sound of the engine. 'You would 'ave to be the smartest li'l urchin in the world,' she said, then turned to the man beside her. 'Now give 'im somethin' for 'is trouble, Rupert. Poor young fellow 'as spent an hour 'elpin' us out.'

Frederick had not thought of being paid for helping. He wanted to say no, but he needed money badly, and his hand shook when the leader of the little band dug into his pocket and removed a gold sovereign – the most valuable coin of the realm – one whole pound.

'There you go, lad.'

Frederick took the money. It wasn't enough for all the gentleman's clothing on the list, but with careful perusal of the second-hand stores it would get him started. He felt a surge of excitement.

'Ah g'warn with you,' the woman said. 'Darn't be mingy, Rupert. Think of what would've 'appened if the deal didn't work out 'cos we was stranded 'ere.'

He dug out another sovereign, and if that wasn't enough, the pretty woman leaned down and kissed Frederick on the forehead. 'You're a grubby little bloke, but as clever as clever, an' I 'ope you does well.'

Rupert rolled his eyes. 'Ah Eleanor, anyone'd reckon you were sweet on the little bugger. Now come on, you're goin' ta get wet trousers lad, but if you'll push us off I'll call them sovereigns well an' truly earned.'

Frederick scrambled to leave the boat and untie the rope, watching as the stoker banked up the coals and again opened the regulator. The paddlewheel sped, pushing the little craft around the bend and out of sight. He sighed happily, and after washing the grease from his hands as best he could in the shallows, he set off for the clothing stalls up around Newark Street. The rest he would use to buy food – something special for Ma Govan to add to the pot.

★★★

After dark, Frederick moved closer to Lily. Two young people knowing that their paths were about to diverge forever, unable to articulate anything to help stave off the wound.

Lily was shaking with silent sobs. Frederick held her close and felt her heartbeat, absorbed her warmth and shared his courage. There was nothing else he could give her.

Months later, when Frederick had plucked up the courage to call in on the Govans, he learned that Lily had been sold into a ten-year labour contract with a leather factory in the West Midlands.

★★★

At seven o'clock on Monday morning, Frederick said goodbye to the family who had helped him to survive. He walked to Stepney East train station, stopping to buy a lump of bread a cheerful woman sold to him out of a sack. This he stowed in his new canvas satchel.

Frederick felt different in his new clothes, aware of the stares of those who knew him, watching from windows and doorways, too surprised to catcall or say a word. It was as if he was on a journey closed to them.

Finally, he boarded the train, held with restrained eagerness by the singing-tight cables that drew it towards the next station. He paid the conductor and sat down beside a businessman in a dark suit, a top hat on his lap.

The train journey alone was exciting enough, looking through windows at the slums of Whitechapel, the vast complex of the London Hospital, then Aldgate. Even after alighting from the carriage at Fenchurch Street, Frederick faced a long walk to the Charterhouse. Not daring to ask strangers for help, he managed to get himself lost, ending up at Barbican and having to backtrack.

Finally, however, he reached Charterhouse Square. There he faced the dark stone and brick of the twin arched school entrances, one large enough to admit a carriage, and the other sufficient for a man or woman on foot. Gaslights stood on black poles on either side, still burning in the fog, and candlelight shone from the three windows above.

Taking a deep breath, Frederick walked on inside. There, amongst the fifteenth century buildings, he felt so out of place that he hid in the cloisters. Half an hour passed before the usher spotted him, and gentled him up to the schoolmaster's office, where his enrolment was confirmed. A comment was made, suggesting that he smelled.

After being made to bathe in a long, leaden trough, Frederick was taken to the school doctor, who subjected him to the first medical examination of his life, peering into his open mouth, tapping his joints with a rubber hammer and listening to his heartbeat. 'You're half starved, you poor boy, but your teeth aren't too bad and your wind is good.'

Within an hour Frederick was officially a student at the school, enrolled in the first form, better known as the 'under petties.' His inaugural class took place in a vast room with forty other youths, arranged in three tiers. All were hunched over open textbooks filled with words Frederick had never seen before. He felt like the stupidest boy in the history of the world. The book was written in Latin and he could make nothing of it. Not only that, but his hard-won clothes looked dowdy next to the garb of his new classmates.

'Let us,' cried the master, a gentleman of Spanish descent known as Signor Machado, 'establish the *documentorum* of our newest scholar, Master Frederick Morton.'

The boy next to Frederick nudged his shoulder. 'Stand up.'

Frederick stood, his scrubbed face burning with a terrible heat. Shame mingled with the terrible certainty that he did not belong here.

'Would you please, Mr Morton, translate for me this phrase: *Et leo in cavea est ad circum.*'

'I'm very sorry sir, but I cannot understand it sir.'

'You're *wery sowwy*, but you cannot understand it?' the master mimicked.

The young gentlemen in the room laughed, and the teacher, encouraged, prattled on. 'Are you saying that you have presented at this school with no Latin? What kind of facility did you attend before?'

'A Ragged School, sir.'

The boys roared.

'A Ragged School? *Por favor salvame.* Good heavens, sit down, and see me after class. You have much catching up to do.'

★★★

When the luncheon bell pealed, the other boys filed into a dining hall to eat. Frederick was certain that such a privilege would not be his, so he bought a pint of tea for a penny from a barrow across from the square, then wandered in the sun of the Charterhouse gardens, nibbling at the bread he had purchased on the street before school.

Down past the 'green', where the boys played football between the cloisters, he entered a deep, extensive, and very old garden, where rose bushes grew from bases as thick as tree-stumps, and creepers rambled over patched and ancient walls. At length he found a corner with some dilapidated graves. He came to a halt there, reading the worn, almost indecipherable inscriptions on the stone faces of the markers. He had moved along to the largest of these, when he saw the tall shadow of the History Master. He was a gaunt fellow, with a long face and wiry beard, eating his lunch as he walked.

'You're the new boy, a protégé of Lord Forgill; correct?'

'Yes sir, my name is Frederick. Oos grave is that sir?'

'This,' said the History Master, 'is the grave of Saint John Houghton. Do you know who he was?'

'No sir? Were 'e a great man?'

'*Was* he a great man,' corrected the master. 'But yes, he was a great man indeed. He was Prior of the Carthusian monastery that occupied these very buildings in the late fifteenth century. Have you heard of the Carthusian Martyrs?'

'No sir.'

'Well, this is where they lived, on this very site. Saint John and his flock defied Henry the Eighth when he turned his back on the Catholic Church to marry Anne Boleyn. He was the first of many to be tried by Cromwell and put to death. They hung him, cut his body into pieces, and displayed those bloodied parts around London.' The master seemed to enjoy showing off his knowledge, using the balls of his feet like springs to lever himself up and down. 'When Cromwell's soldiers cut out Saint John's heart he famously cried, "O Jesus, what wouldst thou do with my heart?"'

Frederick, considering that rather distasteful image, said, 'Well thank you, sir. 'E truly was great, if King 'Enry went to so much trouble to dismember 'im.'

After a long pause the Master said, 'Well don't just stand here moping around – go and play sports with the other boys. I'm sure you'll soon make friends.' With those words he shoved the last of his cheese into his mouth, then strode off in the direction of the staff common room, presumably to obtain more lunch.

Frederick walked back to the 'green', where teams of boys were playing football. He quite liked ball games, and he was very fast on his feet, but in the past he had played only in alleys and streets, never on grass.

Percy Forgill was the goalkeeper, but he left that position when he spotted Frederick, bringing a small squad of his fellows with him. 'Enjoying your crusts, goblin?' He grinned at his peers. 'There's a plate waiting for him inside and he prefers to eat stale bread.'

Frederick stared up at Percy, hating his own ignorance, and one of the other boys chimed in, more kindly. 'He's a new-bug. Give him a chance.' Then, to Frederick. 'Listen you, all the boys eat in the dining room. Three meals a day is paid for with your fees.'

'Thank you,' said Frederick.

While the kind boy and most of the others ran off for their game, Percy and a couple of his cronies lingered.

'I hope you enjoyed your Latin lesson,' Percy said. 'When I relate the incident to Father, he will understand that you have no place here.'

Frederick said nothing, just continued to chew the tasteless bread.

'I don't agree with what my Father's doing, you know,' Percy went on. 'Your place is back in the fucking slums, selling corn cobs on the street or something.'

'Your father is a great man.'

Percy made a noise in his throat. 'Dragging dirty little goblins out of poverty and putting them in gentlemen's schools is not great. It's stupid.'

'This one's a rude little bugger,' one of the others said. 'He won't even look at you when you're talking to him.'

'He needs to learn respect,' said Percy.

The other boy danced around them. 'That's right. Respect for his betters, this hallowed ground, and we who knows the truth.'

Percy walked up closer to Frederick, right into his space, so close that his face was not six inches away. 'Hey goblin, do you remember the wolf?'

Frederick said nothing; but shivered at the memory.

'He lives here too. You can't escape him. Do you know that the Charterhouse was a burying ground during the Great Plague? Six hundred years ago. Bodies everywhere beneath our feet, and the shades of their departed souls prowl around and will cut your throat if you don't keep a lookout.'

Keeping his mouth shut, Frederick stared down at the grass at his feet. Percy Forgill took a bone from his pocket. No thicker than a rod, it was grub-grey in colour. He held it like a pencil between thumb and forefinger, whispered something in Latin, then reverted to English, 'If I give the word the wolf will be here, and the shades he commands will appear all around you. They'll follow you to your bed tonight, and in the darkness their bony hands will choke the life out of you.' Uttering a bloodcurdling cry, Percy jerked towards Frederick, the bone held like a dagger, while his friends doubled up with laughter.

★★★

The afternoon, it turned out, offered some hope. Trigonometry was a language Frederick could understand. He already knew many of the basics and the master complimented him at the end of his first lesson.

'An auspicious start, Mr Morton, but I went easy on you today. See me after class and I'll set you some catch-up exercises.'

'Yes, sir.'

At five o'clock, when the final bell sounded, Frederick was reeling at the new experiences of the day. Everything about the school was peculiar. Some children, such as Percy Forgill, were ordinary fee-paying students, from well-to-do homes, many of whom boarded from Monday to Friday. Then there were the gownboys, from lesser households but of deserving talent.

The hierarchies of this place did not stop there. The boarders, it seemed, had devised a system where the younger boys were forced to 'fag' for their elders. This involved scrubbing floors and tidying rooms for two hours before dinner.

As he worked, Frederick practiced speaking like a young gentleman, enunciating the letter 'h', not skipping ts, ending words like walking with 'ing' not 'in.' His accent, he had learned, was almost as important as his clothes.

That night Frederick lay down to sleep in the cleanest and softest bed of his life. Later, however, the dead of the black plague did indeed visit his bed. This took the form of boys dressed in sheets, holding bones and muttering incantations.

They pranced around his bed, at first uttering ethereal sounds and pointing their bones. Soon, however, they produced long socks filled with stones or dirt and they flicked these upwards so they contacted Frederick's body with a thump. It was theatre, but with deadly intent, and he could not prevent the tears of pain and fear that ran down his face, nor a soft moan that rose in pitch when the weapons struck his stomach, face or groin.

Eventually these 'spirits' melted away, until only one remained. Frederick sensed who it must be. The heavy sock flew out, aimed at his face, thumping into his lip. Blood filled his mouth. Frederick let loose a terrified wail. A hiss emanated from the sheeted apparition beside his head. The light of a candle appeared from the dormitory master's room. The sock landed one last painful time, then the boy who wielded it disappeared into the darkness.

Chapter Five

From the second day onwards, Frederick ate in the dining hall. Then, while the other boys played, he roamed the grounds, most usually while pursuing his new passion – the reading of novels from the school library – or some other distraction. On one occasion he armed himself with a glass protractor that the Mathematics Master let him borrow, measuring angles on everything from bricks to window arches, and estimating the heights of trees and walls.

A favourite site was just behind the chapel, sitting on the stone garden border in the sunlight. It was a quiet nook, from which he could see and avoid Percy or anyone else who came to bother him.

Frederick learned that he was not the only creature who favoured this area of the grounds. The spell of his reading was broken by the sound, as soft as a whisper, of fluffy paws on dry mulberry leaves. He looked across into the greenest pair of eyes he had ever seen.

Neither Frederick nor the cat made another sound. They just stared at each other. He made no effort to befriend it; no crooning or tongue-clicking. Their gaze was one of mutual interest. Two creatures in a dangerous environment.

Frederick saw the cat many times over those first months, and still he did not try to feed or touch it. He liked to look at the cat, however, and it liked looking back.

Meanwhile, diligent study was paying dividends. When Signor Machado boomed, 'Now which of you scholars would like to offer me your translation of the passage I set from Cicero's First Oration against Cataline?' Frederick raised his hand, and the rest of the class stared at him in shocked silence.

'I'd like to try sir.'

'Really, Morton? Well, how can I curb such enthusiasm. Share with us your translation.'

'With these omens, O Catiline.' He started timorously, but found voice as he went on. 'Be gone to your unjust war, to the great safety of the republic, to your own misfortune and injury, and to the death of those who have joined themselves to you in every wickedness and atrocity.'

'Well done, Morton. Some small errors, unjust should perhaps be impious, and death is not quite right. The word is *exitium*, more properly meaning destruction. But overall, good work. You've come a long way in a short time – from ragged school to scholar – and I commend you for it.'

'I cannot take all the credit, sir,' Frederick announced, with an up-thrust of his chin. 'It is the example of my good friend Percy Forgill what has helped me in this regard.'

'Oh,' said the master, moving his gaze to Percy. 'Well done Forgill. Nice to hear.'

Percy's face reddened, while the other boys sniggered around him. Frederick turned to look also, a sly smile stealing across his face. He was rewarded with a flash of confused hatred, for all bullies know when they have been outsmarted by their prey.

★★★

The Charterhouse gardens spilled over several acres, and exploring them required time. Further along from Frederick's favoured perch, still abutting the chapel's rear, there was an old access door no taller than a man's knees, made of very old but solid oak boards, with brass locks and hinges. Despite a screen of rose bushes and chrysanthemums, Frederick had noticed it on the second or third day, assuming that it provided access to the underfloor of the chapel altar. He had a well-developed sense of boundaries, however, and was aware that the door was not his to open.

One day, however, as Frederick wandered past, the hatch opened and half a dozen boys spilled out. Percy Forgill was the last in line. As he straightened up his eyes fell on Frederick.

'Are you spying on us, goblin?'

'No, I was just walking past.'

'I don't believe you. You want to see what's behind the door, don't you?'

'No ... I don't—'

'Come on in. I'll show you.'

One of the other boys demurred. 'Is that a good idea, Percy?'

'Yes it damned well is.' He raised his chin. 'Because I say it is.'

Percy shepherded Frederick through the hatch, and into the dark space beyond. There was scarcely room enough to crawl. All the boys followed. When they had settled, Percy intoned a Latin phrase and one of them lit a candle. Frederick saw that the stub was set inside the cranium of a human skull. Bones of all shapes and sizes lay in niches. Frederick felt claustrophobic – the ancient stonework above and on the sides of this tight space seemed to close in on him.

On an ancient foundation someone had painted the likeness of a wolf, its eyes dark slits and fangs white daggers. Red pastels decorated the teeth so they seemed to be dripping blood.

'Six hundred years ago,' said Percy, 'while the people of London cowered in their homes and waited for the plague to strike them down, this place was the dumping ground for the slain multitudes of the Black Death. The carters brought the bodies here, to be buried in great pits. Some weren't even quite dead, but they got picked up in any case, and tossed in, where they lay tortured amongst the corpses until death claimed them too.'

Frederick wanted to leave that mausoleum, very much. On hands and knees, he scrambled for the door, panting like a dog and heedless of the harsh scratching of the age-old earth on the skin of his knees and the filmy contact of cobwebs on his face.

The other boys laughed, but it was not until Frederick emerged into the sunlight that he could breathe again. An hour passed before his hands stopped trembling and the worst of the images were banished from his mind.

★★★

At least once each week, Percy Forgill and his acolytes forced Frederick through the access door. Each time he became less shocked by the ordeal, less desperate to run. He tried feigning boredom, stifling yawns, and not listening, hoping their game might start to pall.

At the same time, Frederick's Latin and mathematics improved so noticeably that the masters began to treat him as a protégé. Before long he could bisect an angle or conjugate a verb faster than most. His practice at masking his cockney accent was also paying off, and he attracted less attention. He imitated the swagger of the other boys: chest out, head upright, owning the ground on which he walked.

Percy, nursing his dislike, raised the stakes. One lunchtime in that underfloor mausoleum, while his acolytes kneeled in a long row to either side, Lord Forgill's son ordered Frederick to close his eyes.

The object they placed in his hands was soft, heavy, cold, and damp. He opened his eyes to discover that he was holding the remains of the garden cat, bloodied and quite dead. He wailed and dropped the feline corpse, trying to scamper for the door.

Laughing boys moved to block his way, until he became distressed, mouth open, hunting for breath. 'Let me out,' he cried.

Percy picked the cat's body up by the ruff and crawled after him, uttering a guttural hunting seal's bark that seemed to come from the bones and age of this terrible crypt.

Frederick cowered back against a pier while Percy swung the cat towards his face. Then, in a diving, desperate crawl, Frederick burrowed through Percy's minions, opening the hatch and heading outside, where he came to his feet and ran, around the corner, into the beckoning sunlight.

★★★

At the end of the year, when the final exam results were posted, Frederick placed third in mathematics, while Percy Forgill came in thirty-first. To cap off this success, at the last-day foot races Frederick ran second in his heat of the hundred-yard dash, and first in the three-mile endurance event.

It was at this sports day that Frederick saw Lord Forgill in the bleachers, with a girl of around thirteen years beside him. Her hair was hidden by a light blue bonnet, but her face was fair, her skin pale ivory. She held a parasol in her right hand.

In the final of the hundred-yard dash, Frederick was running first when he made the mistake of looking for Percy Forgill's sister in the stands. When his eyes fell on her it seemed to Frederick that she was looking directly at him. He stumbled a little, recovered, and came in fifth.

Three days later a card arrived from Lord Forgill, congratulating Frederick on his results, along with a gift in a large wooden case. It was a model steam engine, perfect in every detail, fuelled by a tiny paraffin burner. It was far and away the most wonderful thing Frederick had ever possessed, and he cried when it cycled for the first time.

Percy was not so magnanimous. He too had a gift for Frederick, but it was delivered in the deep-shadowed recesses of the gardens. The ordeal started with a cuff to the side of the head, then kicks and punches delivered to the body. Frederick tried to fight back, but there were three attackers in all.

'You're not wanted here,' Percy spat, chest heaving from the exertion of delivering the blows. 'You cheat in examinations. You smell and talk like a guttersnipe. Don't come back next term.'

★★★

Percy's warning was a vain one, for with no home to go to, Lord Forgill arranged for Frederick to remain at the Charterhouse through the break. Besides, the idea of giving up on that marvellous school; that life-changing place, was far more hurtful than any physical pain. Frederick spent the first few days of the break operating his model steam engine, and reading texts for the new term, including Shakespeare's tragedies. This was the beginning of a lifelong love of the Bard and the written word.

After the first truly fine Christmas dinner of his life, in the dining hall with the Charterhouse masters, Frederick discovered that he had some spare money from his allowance. He purchased a mechanical engineering text from Hatchards and caught a river ferry to the Kew pumping station, where some of the largest stationary engines in the country supplied London's water. These giant machines took Frederick's breath away – the colossal beams, the sheen of chrome in the piston shafts – the vast power. Machines, he was learning, could replace human hands. Machines could give people better lives; reduce the toll that constant manual labour wrought on the human body.

Even more exciting, Frederick was able to attend the International Exhibition in London, held in a monstrous pavilion alongside the Royal Horticultural Society Gardens in South Kensington. This event was held on an unimaginable scale, with millions of ticketholders passing through the doors. Frederick looked in awe on collections of diamonds from Golconda, India, and artworks describing life in the colonies. Most importantly, there were machines from all over the world – including working steam engines of all configurations. Frederick stayed until closing time, talking to the engineers and owners, reaping knowledge like a farmer reaps grain.

Day by day, week by week, the slum-boy's horizons broadened, and his self-belief grew along with it. The Spring term started well, with Percy Forgill and his torments seeming less important than they had been. Frederick had carved out his right to attend the school through hard work and talent.

Every now and then, at an awards day or concert, Frederick saw Percy's sister. So elegant, seeming to look back at him with an amused appraisal. He knew that she was as unattainable as a rare creature at the bottom of the ocean, but his experiences with Lily Govan had left him with a strong sensuality, and he desired Sophie Forgill with a desperate longing.

★★★

Sometimes on a Sunday, Frederick would catch the train or walk back to Stepney, to visit his mother's unmarked grave in the dank silence of Saint Dunstan's. Thereafter he'd head down to his old haunts, along Regent's Canal to the waterfront, then walk all the way back to school – four miles in a daze of wondering how he came to be wearing a good suit, speaking very much like a young gentleman, and knowing things he could never have known if he'd stayed in that world of slums, mud and water.

One day he ran into a woman on Narrow Street, ostentatiously dressed, with flowers in her hat, and a babe on her hip.

'Why hullo,' she said. 'You're the lad oo fixed the boat engine that day, when I was gettin' about with Rupert. Looks like you're doing well for yerself! Why lumme, look at the fancy duds, an' you're talking all posh now. What's yer name anyway, you never told us?'

'Frederick.'

'Frederick, eh? I'll call you Freddie. Mine's Eleanor. Eleanor Demsie.' She reached down and squeezed her daughter's cheek, who squirmed and turned inwards to her mother's legs.

'I'd better be off,' Frederick said, 'or I'll be late for supper.'

'We can't 'ave that,' said Eleanor, 'so off you go. But darn't be a stranger. Yer a good kid, and I remembers you well.'

★★★

One night, in third form, three of the older boys surround Frederick in his bed. He wakes as they wrap a rag around his head, forcing it into his mouth. Even if he were able to cry out, they know that the masters will not interfere, for Percy and his friends are now 'bloods' and therefore the unofficial leaders of the school.

Carrying jars of wine, they lead Frederick outside, where a cold and steady rain falls. They make him wait while they force their way into the gardener's store on the grounds. Armed with a lantern, shovels, hoes and crowbars, they assemble around the grave of Saint John Houghton.

Percy forces a shovel into Frederick's hands. 'Dig, goblin. Dig for the Saint.'

The ground is sodden and soft, and the hole fills with water as Frederick digs. He blows rain from between his lips, and glares at Percy between each stroke, his soul filling with memories of the night he buried his mother.

Slowly the hole deepens, until the shovel can no longer reach. Instead, he has to enlarge the hole and stand inside, delving deeper in the freezing rain while Percy stands close to the trunk of an elm tree.

Frederick hears and feels a thump as the shovel strikes something hard. 'Could be a rock,' says one of the boys, 'for there'd be no coffin after all this time.'

Percy advances from under the tree and lifts the lantern from its place on the gravestone to illuminate the hole. 'There'll be nothing left, but bone and teeth. Let go of the shovel and use your hands.'

Frederick releases the shovel and drops to his knees, delving in the muddy floor of the hole, then standing. 'They *are* bones down there. Don't make me touch them.'

'Bring them up,' snaps Percy.

'No, I won't do it.'

Percy leans down so his face is close, stretched tight like a mask. 'Bring up the damn bones.'

Giving in, Frederick hauls a handful of mud and bones, and dumps them on the ground, next to the grave. 'For the love of God, is that enough?'

'Get it all,' orders Percy, staring at the long leg bones, being washed clean by the rain. 'Bring it all up.'

The next load includes a pelvis, followed by rib bones. Finally, Frederick locates a skull, and he lays it beside the rest.

The yellow glow of candles shines out through windows now as people begin to stir, but Percy is too drunk to care. He uses the handle of a spade to break in the top of the cranium, then he fills it with wine from a flagon. He drinks down a deep draught and passes it to the next of the drunken boys.

Frederick climbs out of the grave, tears blending with the rain, his chest swelling and contracting from exertion.

Percy passes him the skull. 'Drink.'

Frederick uses a powerful swing of his arm to smash the grisly object from the older boy's hands. He runs through the rain, away from the grave, past the masters now arriving with their umbrellas and shocked, angry faces.

Chapter Six

In his final school year Frederick came third academically; first in mathematics, and Percy so far down the list that he was on the second page. As the former Stepney boy walked up onto the dais to collect his awards, the two boys exchanged a long glare, but in Percy's face there was something more – the understanding that Frederick was now a force to be reckoned with.

On the lawns afterwards, Lord Forgill suggested to Frederick that he might be interested in the London University College's mechanical engineering degree. 'And if you do well, as I'm sure you will, I hope you'll consider coming to work for me.'

Frederick understood that he was being offered the chance at a dream. 'My answer is yes, one thousand times over.'

A short time later he was standing back from the crowd, still thinking about what Lord Forgill had told him when he saw Sophie Forgill. At seventeen she was the most magnificent human being he had ever seen, with creamy skin, blue eyes, and blonde hair braided into an intricate pattern. In all the years of Frederick's association with the Forgill family they still had not exchanged one word.

Incredibly, she drifted towards him, 'I suppose I should congratulate you. I imagine that you must be very clever.'

Frederick shook his head, not knowing what to say.

'Cat got your tongue?' she asked.

Afraid that staying mute made him appear stupid, Frederick blurted, 'I think you're the most beautiful girl in the world.'

Lifting a mocking eyebrow she said, 'Well aren't you an impertinent fellow.'

Percy walked up and put his hand on Sophie's shoulder. 'Why are you talking to *him*, sis?'

She turned and smiled with those perfect lips, 'Freddie says that I'm the most beautiful girl in the world.'

They laughed until Frederick's cheeks reddened, and he could bear it no longer. He turned away. He had walked some distance when Percy caught up, gripping the loose material of his jacket below his right elbow.

'How dare you talk to my sister. You are not fit to breathe the same air as her, do you understand?'

Frederick could not breathe at all. He was drowning in shame.

★★★

Two years passed before he saw Sophie Forgill again. She was in the crowd when Frederick entered his first pedestrian race. It was a twenty-mile course, cross country, contested between young collegiates, fit of body and busy of mind. Frederick saw her near the starting line, with a trio of friends, all holding parasols to defeat the June sun, surrounded by a troop of eager escorts. Sophie's lips pursed strangely when she noticed him.

Frederick had not been near her since his school graduation day, and Percy, from what he had heard, was abroad – had been since the end of school. It made him breathe easier, knowing that Percy was out of the city, giving him the confidence to pursue university sports.

Pedestrianism – the art of walking – was a world-wide craze, and contests had been popular in England for more than a century. By now the rules of engagement were firm, with the participants vying for large purses. Already a useful runner, Frederick had learned a new gait – faster than a normal walk – with one foot remaining on the ground at all times.

This being his first race, Frederick had not known what to expect of himself. Within a mile or two, however, he was pleased to see that he was keeping pace with the main pack. Moreover, when a brief but chilly shower passed over at Becontree Heath on the outskirts of Romford, some of the competitors retired to the Golden Lion, adjacent to the town's market square, presumably to warm themselves with liquor.

At Brentwood, Frederick was still feeling fit, his legs not yet aching, only the ball of his right foot protesting against the constant and unaccustomed movement. There, he caught sight of Sophie Forgill once again. She ignored him as he passed, chatting to one of her companions instead.

It seemed to Frederick that a lifetime had passed since the girl of his dreams had cut his heart to pieces on the lawns of the Charterhouse. If he felt self-conscious it was from being dressed in his old school games clothes – a striped jersey, short pants and long striped socks.

He forged on past her, sticking to the side of the road, swinging his hips and using exaggerated movements of both arms to get along quite rapidly.

By nightfall he had all but forgotten Sophie, intent on keeping up with the leaders. After a meal, passed by volunteers to the walkers and eaten on the move, he overtook the slowest members of the front pack, some of whom were limping. With five miles remaining he was travelling well, powering along.

The walking track, Frederick discovered, was a place where he felt the equal of anyone. He no longer saw himself as a different species to these young gentlemen. He was just as good as them. His legs were as strong as theirs, his lungs as powerful.

He reached the finish line just after nine pm, with a faint and satisfying sense of having missed an opportunity. There was still strength in his legs. He wondered whether, if he had pushed harder towards the end, he might have placed in the top five, rather than twelfth.

'Good try Morton,' called one of the racers.

'You walk like there's something chasing you,' agreed one of the others.

Frederick did not tell them about the wolf. It was always following, always chasing, but he knew that they would not understand.

★★★

At London's University College, Frederick learned his trade under some of the most esteemed engineers in the world, including the world-famous Chair, William Pole, whose love of the theoretical was so strong that he spent his spare time authoring a twenty-volume text, *The Theory of Whist*.

'Engineering perfection,' Pole thundered at Frederick and his classmates, 'no matter how humble the application, is an admirable aim in itself. Whether you are designing and building a revolving pistol, a mince grinder, or a mighty ship, we must strive for the best machine we have the capacity to make.'

Frederick learned the names of steam engine parts and their functions until he could recite them by rote. Engineering plans, drawn by the great innovators, were works of art to Frederick. Newcomen was his Leonardo. Watt his Caravaggio.

Given the dismantled components of a modern, working steam engine, he drew blueprints from scratch. He learned the names of key patents, and the pivotal moments of the development of steam as an industrial power source. He learned how to assess the strength, lustre and malleability of various metals, the significance of bore and stroke, and the calorific rating of coals from different British mines.

Finally, after four solid years, with a newly-printed testamur in a frame on his mantlepiece, Frederick started at the Forgill Engine

Works as a junior engineer.

'Six pounds a month to begin with,' Lord Forgill said. 'But this will increase with seniority and experience.' He smiled, 'I'm pleased at how far you have come, but tell me, is this what you want?'

'I can't think of anything I'd rather do.'

★★★

Frederick could not even begin to articulate how he felt about this man who had changed his life. Most importantly, he knew in his heart that Lord Forgill believed in him. His fervent wish was to be worthy of that belief.

At the Forgill works in Wapping, eighteen draughtsmen, patternmakers and designing engineers occupied a second-floor room. It had long casement windows on the eastern and northern sides to admit light, with views taking in the warehouses lining London Docks, and across the water to Pennington Street. The floor beneath the desks throbbed and thrummed with the engines that powered the factory. The air reverberated with the clang of tools and the hiss of steam. The smell of coal smoke and molten iron permeated walls, floor, clothes, and skin.

The factory was a solid complex, yet it was ageing – bricks cracked into tiny veins like a foundryman's cheeks, impregnated with layers of coal dust. Smokestacks streamed dark lines of smoke and blasts of waving heat. A steam whistle blew the shift change and workers stamped to and from the warren of workers' flats, past courtyards stacked with pig iron, casting shops, furnaces, rolling mills and boring machines.

It was the most exciting place Frederick had ever seen, and by far the most interesting. In his first three months at Forgill's, Frederick ran errands and prepared copies of other men's designs. The chief engineer, Edwin J Moon, was a harsh master. For ten hours each day, Frederick and his fellow juniors suffered through desk inspections, tantrums at smudged pencil marks and timed toilet breaks. No short cuts were permitted. Tolerances for machinery parts were measured in fractions of inches, and an error in design or fabrication meant starting over, with a consequent loss in time and materials.

Frederick's first personal project was the *objectif général* of the time, a method of using exhaust gases to preheat water entering the boiler, thus saving on energy and reducing coal consumption. Any new design needed to overcome numerous hurdles, one being that the internal surfaces of heating tubes soon became coated with scale, reducing flow and efficiency. There was also the problem of sulphur forming on exterior surfaces and corroding cast iron pipes. A cleaning mechanism was necessary, as was a practical procedure for replacing tubes.

Frederick theorised that a flushing cycle with cold water would contract the pipes and release scale. He burned a series of candles down to stubs in his boarding house room working on the design, nervously submitting the finished diagram.

Four hours later Moon sent for him. 'You had assistance with this. Who was it?'

'No one helped me, sir, I did it myself.'

'We'll patent it,' said Moon, then dismissed Frederick with a wave of his hand.

★★★

Three weeks later, as an apparent reward, Frederick was sent to Northern England to perform routine maintenance and installation assessments. In Manchester and its satellite towns of Darwen, Burnley, Bury, Oldham and Todmorden, Frederick marvelled at the rows of towering mills. Each was six stories high, floors stacked like the decks of ships, an arrangement based around the driving force of the steam engine that was the beating heart, its power transmitted through each of the six storeys via line shafting. Frederick, with his acute powers of observation and agile mind, soon learned how the process worked. When the bales of cotton were unloaded by river and cart, the fibre entered the mixing room, followed by the willow and scutching machines. From there it was carded, then pushed through drawing, slabbing and stretching machines.

The mule spindle was the final stage for most yarns – possibly the single most important invention of the previous half-century, devised by a hairdresser called Richard Arkwright, and now responsible for the employment of around one million English men, women, and children. Each worker in a mill handled up to sixty spindles and worked a fifty-five-hour week for less than a pound in wages, all the while breathing air fouled with cotton tufts that floated through the factories like snowflakes.

Always, a steam engine cycled in the bowels of the mill, ropes on the flywheel turning dozens of shafts from which the machinery drew power. Most of these were made by northern manufacturers such as Robey, Hargraves, Galloways, Clayton and Fairbairn. This was a fact that Lord Forgill was eager to change, with his modern horizontal engines saving coal and maintenance time. To this end, a new sales office had just opened in the city that was now known as the 'cottonopolis' of the north.

Frederick returned to London brimming with ideas, and eager for work, spending his days sitting close to the sloping face of a drafting table, refining the machines that would make up a new 'assault' by Forgill's on the north.

In his free time, he attended industrial expositions, Sunday services at Saint John's in Wapping, and meetings of the Amalgamated Society of Engineers. When the opportunity arose, he played football, and competed in pedestrian races, some lasting for up to thirty-six hours, often on tracks behind 'sporting' pubs. This helped to compensate for the sedentary nature of his profession.

Living in a company boarding house in Wapping, Frederick courted three young women (consecutively not simultaneously), who ultimately chose other suitors.

Physically, Frederick grew broader in the shoulders, and his face strengthened – his jawline became more pronounced, with neatly-cut sideburns that glowed with a touch of ginger. His build was slim but strong, and he wore his waistcoat and dark trousers with some panache.

His best friend at the works was the foundry manager, Vic Jones, who was built like an iron trolley. He was also one of the most competent men Frederick had ever met.

They both agreed that Forgill's was a great place to work, but that it would remain so only while the old man remained in charge. 'It'll all change when he hands over to Percy,' Jones said one day as they ate cold sausage and bread in the lunchroom. 'I've no time for Forgill junior. He was a twin, did you know?'

Frederick shook his head.

'Yes, a twin – the other was the eldest by a few minutes, but he was never well.'

'Where is he now?'

Jones shrugged his shoulders. 'Died, many years back.' He scratched at his chin. 'I often wonder if he might have had a better temperament than Percy – who'll be back in the country next year, I'm told. Hope he stays away from here is all.'

Frederick went back to the work room, his mind filled with memories of a night so long ago, and a blood stain at the foot of the stairs. Nothing Jones had said made any sense at all.

★★★

In July 1866, Lord Forgill summoned his protégé to the company's Bow Street offices via an embossed card with the words, 'Please come and meet the board', along with a time and date.

When the day came, Frederick was wearing a new suit, and shoes that had been polished until they reflected his face. The board room was dominated by a vast mahogany table, the chairs occupied by an interesting collection of aristocrats and industrialists.

'Freddie, Isaac Simons is retiring at the end of the year,' Lord Forgill said.

'I heard the news,' said Frederick. 'Simons will be a big loss to the company.' The rumour mill had already informed him of this change. Sixty-eight-year-old Simons was Deputy Chief Engineer at the Forgill works. He spent much of his time away undertaking site assessments and completing technical sales quotes, often travelling abroad in order to do so.

'We would like you to take his place. It would mean a pay rise, and a company house – along with travel commitments. I believe that broader real-world experience will lead you to even greater things at the design table – which is, after all, your paramount skill.'

For Frederick it was an unexpected honour. After all, he was not yet twenty-five. 'I am filled with … nothing short of wonderment that you and the board would consider me sir.'

'Of course you are,' smiled Lord Forgill. 'But will you accept?'

'I will,' said Frederick. 'With everything I have – heart and soul.'

The next Sunday, as he had many times before, Frederick left his lodgings, attended the local church service, then took the train to Stepney. First, he visited the graveyard at Saint Dunstan's. He then walked to Southfield Street, where Lord Forgill's new tenements had obliterated all trace of the slums that had been on the site. The street now was a winding and seamless block of light brown brick, with a wrought-iron fence running along the front boundaries. There was scarcely a yard of ground wasted, and the men, women, and children he saw there were far better dressed than he and his neighbours had been, a decade and a half earlier.

A film of tears covering his eyes at the poignancy of his memories, Frederick cut down to the Regents Canal towpath, wandering the half mile alongside the canal to Narrow Street, then the Old Sun Wharf. With the river at low tide, he could feel the pull of the muddy flats with their hidden treasures.

Afterwards, he walked back up onto Broad Street, heading for the station. Passing a series of poor tenements, he saw a woman in a grubby dress, smoking a cheap clay pipe. With her was a girl of twelve or thirteen years. The lass was attempting to pet a fluffy ginger cat, which was arching its back on a brick fence.

Frederick was almost alongside when he again recognised Eleanor – the woman from the boat. She had lost teeth since he saw her last, and she must now be forty or so. Her daughter avoided looking at Frederick, seeming shy and gawkish.

'Hello Eleanor,' said Frederick.

Eleanor was staring at him, 'Oh, hullo Freddie,' she said, as if they had last spoken the day before. She reached out for her daughter's hand.

'This is Juliet, pretty li'l thing now hain't she?'

Frederick leaned over. 'Hello Juliet.'

Eleanor took a pull on her pipe, then cocked her head at him. 'Are you in a profession now then?'

'Yes, I'm an engineer with Forgills.'

'Well, ain't it a curious thing? Like the river tide itself, your star does rise and rise.' Eleanor shook her head as if in wonder. 'Does you enjoy your work then, Freddie?'

'I do,' he said.

'Then you're blessed, lad. Truly blessed an' I wish you good fortune.'

'Are things well for you, Eleanor?'

Removing the pipe, she sucked in her lips. 'Life 'as been 'ard for us, lately, oh lumme it 'as. But there's a new chance aroun' the corner. I know there is.'

'I'm glad to hear that. Well goodbye.'

'Bye Freddie. Me an' Juliet wishes you the very best.'

When he had walked a hundred paces and turned back to look, Eleanor Demsie was staring after him with a wistful expression on her face.

Chapter Seven

Percy Forgill swaggered back into London in the year of Frederick's promotion, arriving at Southampton inbound from Georgetown, Jamaica, with tanned skin and a piratical air. A month had passed since his twenty-fifth birthday, at which point an endowment of more than a thousand pounds a year had come into his possession.

In a brief meeting at home, Lord Forgill suggested that his second-born son might now consider a career in law, or at least become a clerk in the family company and work his way up. Instead, Percy took the opportunity to present a series of invoices that needed settling, principally gambling debts, and installed himself in a Chelsea flat, which he furnished in style. He wasted no time in announcing himself as a player at several private casinos.

Travelling had at first been enough for Percy, but when gambling and animal fights in exotic locations began to pall, he invested some of his limited funds, not to mention his personal safety, in an arms shipment from Santo Domingo to the hard-pressed confederacy of South Carolina. The camaraderie and excitement of life on board a three-masted brigantine, sailing in under the noses of union ironclads, appealed to Percy, as did the adrenalin-fuelled excitement of off-loading crates on a Chechessee River mudflat on a slack tide at midnight, accompanied by the sound of distant gunfire and flashes on the horizon.

In the Gulf of Venezuela, he had chewed coca leaves in a fishing village, and bought a bed-partner outright, for as long as he wanted her, for the price of a good cigar. In a Jamaican shanty an *obeah* woman showed him her tiny occult dolls, and he had watched her kill a chicken with a sharp knife, reading his future in the entrails. She told him to beware of the tides that rose and fell, in the rivers and the sea.

London's attractions might have seemed tame, after these experiences, yet apart from gambling there were many things in this great city to entertain him. Penny gaffs abounded, some offering freak shows, or entertainments such as bickering clowns and patterers. Yet, it was the now-illegal, but still common sport of cock-fighting that Percy enjoyed most. In those first weeks back in the country, he took ownership of the first of many cocks.

This specimen was two feet high, with short legs to plant its weight firmly in the ring. He was a huge individual of the classic old English game breed, with white feathers cascading down his heavy neck to a body plumage of green feathers, fading to dark grey, almost black. He had cost Percy ten guineas, and within a month earned back twice his purchase price.

This bloody and pleasing sequence came undone with a meeting against a specimen belonging to the Asil breed – a feisty cock with a blazing red head, wickedly curved spurs, not to mention speed and a thirst for blood.

While Percy's own bird lay bleeding and dying on the floor of the ring, he was already approaching the owner of the victorious cock, offering to purchase it. Before long he was following the birds back to the source, locating breeders, buying cocks scarcely weeks old, paying the best 'feeders', as trainers were called, to raise and house his fancies.

He loved the gore, the killing, and there was money to be made. The illegality was part of the game by then, and sympathetic bobbies were paid off. There were nights when Percy made significant cash, both prize money and inside bets, and this posed a security problem.

One night Percy was walking back through a Lambeth alley with more than a hundred pounds in coins, gold and notes weighing down his jacket pocket. He was coming up to a gate when he saw two men lurking in the shadows on either side. He turned, looking for an escape route, but another man appeared behind him.

The boldest of the three stepped onto the path with a pistol levelled at Percy's heart. 'Hand us your purse mate, and you'll live to kiss yer missus tonight.'

When Percy protested, the pistol butt came down on the side of his head, laying him low, and the three men joined forces to kick him on the ground. They took all the money, his shoes, his hat and coat. He walked home, over Vauxhall Bridge, freezing near to death.

On that cold and frightening journey, Percy realised that he needed help. He needed muscle. It was no point making money if it was at the mercy of every scoundrel with a firearm. Men could be paid, certainly, but money did not buy loyalty – the kind of loyalty that Frederick Morton had for Percy's father. The loyalty of a starving dog for the man who rescues and feeds him.

Percy knew that Frederick Morton had been promoted beyond his years at his father's factory. Not only that, but his father had several other protégés attending expensive schools. This program of sponsoring and mentoring underprivileged children gave Percy an idea, one that he mulled over for several days before taking action.

The following Monday, Percy requested and received an interview at the Willis-Monk Home for Incorrigible Boys and arranged to speak with the director. This personage was as bald as a desert on top of his head, but retained vigorous growth on the sides and back. One of his ears had been damaged in some accident or other, leaving a brown scar and an uneven lobe.

'I would like to assist some of your boys,' Percy began.

'Certainly, Mister Forgill, we have several boys with fine qualities who might excel—'

'Not them,' Percy said. 'I want to help those boys who have outgrown this place, who might be able to leave with the right sponsor – given guaranteed employment. I am talking about the incorrigibles. The violent. The unteachables.'

The director raised his eyebrows, 'There are some like that certainly, but why?'

Percy shook his head. 'Not your concern, sir. Not your concern at all. Bring me the worst of them now, and I'll be the judge of his suitability.'

The lad that the director ushered into the office wore a surly leer like a badge, and a wisp of a moustache on his fourteen-year-old upper lip.

'What's your name?' Percy asked.

'Craven. Peter Craven.' Still standing, the lad appeared to sniff the air, then regard Percy with a baleful eye. 'Cripes, look at the duds on you! Be worth a guinea or two, I'd wager.'

Percy ignored the comment. 'Tell me about yourself.'

'I grew up in Tower 'Amlets. There ain't much else to tell, but that I done a few wicked things and this place is one step from jail.'

'What wicked things?'

Craven glanced at the director, then, 'I was adept sir, in placin' me 'ands in gennelman's pockets an' extractin' the contents.'

The director sneered. 'Craven was a thief who preyed on the 'omeless and the infirm. He's a nasty piece of work, born under a bad sign, aren't you, Craven?'

The lad grinned crookedly, and looked at his potential new benefactor as if to say, *I am what I am. Do what you will about it.*

'My name is Percy Forgill, and I would like to hire some assistants to undertake, er, various duties. How would you like to leave this place, have your own lodgings in the city and work for me?'

Craven narrowed his eyes and folded his arms in front of his chest. 'What does I need to do in exchange?'

'Whatever I tell you to do.'

★★★

That evening, once the lad was settled in a room in a decrepit building Percy had purchased in Queen Street, deep in the slum area known as Seven Dials, Percy gave him his instructions. 'There's room for cock-stalls in the basement. There'll be more cocks coming. Your first job is to feed them, and care for them. I'll have someone to help you in a few weeks.'

And sure enough, before the end of the month there was another lad of around the same age, and then a third. The three of them soon earned a reputation around the area, and they took to the work like they were born to it.

By then there were always ten or twelve cocks in the basement, and one or two fighting terriers as well. At least once a week Percy would come to the house and ask to see the animals. After each cock fight, his boys, armed with small daggers, always escorted him to his carriage, or all the way home. Sometimes he went back to Queen Street with them to drink rum, and occasionally he paid for a prostitute for them.

Percy enjoyed the company of 'his' boys. They were rough and crude and thought nothing of any authority in the world. In some ways he wanted to be like them, to re-cast his own youth to theirs. He encouraged them to branch out into buying stolen goods from pickpockets, carriers and wharf men alike. He cultivated higher-end channels, usually pawn shop owners, to convert items of value into cash. He liked to imagine that his Queen Street premises, now becoming known as the Rookery, might rival the infamy of the nearby Rat's Castle – a den of thieves he wanted to emulate.

'I'll tell you a secret,' Percy said to them around the Rookery table. 'I wasn't born alone. There was another as did share my mother's womb—'

★★★

Frederick's first overseas assignment was to the United States, leaving from Euston Road railway station and travelling overland to Liverpool, where he boarded one of the world's biggest steamships. On board the *Umbria* he suffered a week of seasickness that kept him, mostly, confined to his cabin.

Alone on the wide Atlantic Ocean, the *Umbria* lost all perspective of size, but then, steaming into the main channel of the Hudson River, she towered above the tugs that shepherded her into the docks off 14th Street. The hull dwarfed the ant-like men readying lines, standing on the heavy timbers of the wharf. Even against the Manhattan skyline she was impressive.

That evening, Frederick settled into the Hotel Albert in Greenwich Village. Like all the accommodation arranged by the Forgill's factory, it was good value, not ostentatious.

Frederick had been working, by then, in the role of Deputy Chief Engineer for some six months, now living in a company terrace in Aldgate. Yet the nature of his new job meant that he was rarely home. A key aspect of his role was to travel – investigate markets and write quotations. Most of the last month, before the voyage for New York, had been spent in Manchester.

The line up of business meetings was exciting and rewarding. With the ashes of the Civil War barely cool, industrialists from the Northern States were turning to new, peacetime products and processes. 'You caught us at a good time,' said Davis Johnson of the Steele Machinery Group. Johnson had one of those ruddy, handsome faces, tanned from winters on the ski slopes of the Catskill Mountains, and summers racing sloops out of the New York Yacht Club's base on Shelter Island. 'We're fitting out machine shops from Queens to New Jersey. Each and every one needs an engine to spin the line-shafting.'

After a week in New York Frederick purchased a ticket on a west-bound train, and this experience further honed his freshly whetted love of travel. The dining car was first rate, and the Pullman sleeper made by craftsmen, with varnished oak panels and brass fittings. The rattle of the iron wheels, and the whistle and puff of the locomotive, was at once soothing and exciting. The scenery was first a verdant green with many of the trees familiar from home: elms, oak and poplars, their leaves like flakes of red and yellow gold. Yet, by the second morning the country was drier and flatter, with fields of corn, sugar beet, and grains, impressing on Frederick the immense richness of America's food belt.

When the train arrived in Chicago, he caught a cab to the Hilton Hotel ahead of a series of meetings. The first was with the Chicago Tribune, one of the country's highest circulation newspapers, their Hoe Eight Cylinder printing press powered by a compound steam engine that had seen better days.

'We can put sixteen thousand sheets an hour through this baby,' said the chief engineer. 'But with an engine like the Forgill's F-Class – if it's as good as the spec sheets say it is – we might add another five thousand. Even then we'll scarcely keep pace with circulation.'

'At the same time, we'll reduce your coal expenditure,' said Frederick. 'That means not only more profit, but cleaner air.' Air quality was a much talked about issue in Chicago, Frederick had discovered, even more so than in New York. Industrial emissions here, when combined with morning fog off Lake Michigan, produced a peasouper almost as thick as London's.

In the next three days Frederick met with textile mill owners, steel fabricators and tool makers. These were potentially big contracts, few or none of which might come through, but Frederick was armed with the facts and figures he needed, and he took the time to learn what these managers and owners needed for their businesses.

One heavy manufacturing outfit was controlled by an heiress. Impressed by Frederick's passion for his subject, she suggested dinner at one of Chicago's best restaurants, Schlogl's on Wells Street, not far from the Tribune's offices.

Frederick was far too polite and inexperienced to pick up on the obvious cues she was streaming out like pennants behind the fast skiffs on Lake Michigan. He went back to his hotel alone, wondering why she had seemed to have cooled towards him after the tiny glass of dessert wine with which they finished the evening.

★★★

The next day Frederick crossed the Missouri River, en route to Iowa. On his arrival there, a group of conservatively dressed men and women met him at the station, then whisked him onto a carriage heading out of town to one of the biggest corn mills in the state, still under construction, and in need of five or six hundred horsepower.

That evening, staying in a ground floor hotel, he slipped on short pants and a shirt, then jogged along a dead-straight track through the prairie, with tall yellow grass waving, and warm air rushing to meet his face.

Frederick felt a sense of pride in the muscles in his legs. Exercising had always been good for his mind, and his thoughts came thick and fast, along with meadowlarks and butterflies.

In Omaha, Nebraska, he visited the site where water for the growing population was drawn from wells deep under the dry surface, extracted by Cornish-style pump engines. They were gorgeous examples of 1790s engineering, all brass and oiled steel. But they were showing their age.

'These old engines,' said the city engineer, 'are costing us in maintenance and downtime. We're about to put out a tender for replacements, and with the coal savings your engines are promising, they're mighty attractive.'

Finally, the big Baldwin locomotive drew the train across the line into California. Every corner of this state spoke of progress, and of enterprise. In San Francisco, Frederick sent his suits down to be pressed and became a tourist for a day, familiarising himself with the city, finding that it was unlike any he had seen before: brash, new, and full of promise. The bay itself was glittering and bright, one of the most beautiful sights the former slum-boy had ever hoped to see.

He met with the owner of a light manufacturing complex in the Napa Valley, who had invented a powered grape press, and needed a compact engine to run it. 'I'm even thinking of commissioning a mobile unit that can be towed by horse team around the smaller wineries. What can you offer me?'

'Forgills have several engines that will do the job,' said Frederick. 'I can give you a specification sheet and quotation if you like.'

Frederick wrote so many quotes he lost track of them, yet few decision-makers would commit. Americans were a patriotic bunch, and locally built engines were strong competition. At first Frederick's strategy had been to pinpoint weaknesses in US-made machines, but this had backfired. Putting down the local products made his potential clients bristle.

It was better, he found, to focus on the Forgill engines as if there was no competition. 'We use only Bessemer mild steel – the best in the world. Our safety valves are the most reliable in the business, in fact, there has not been a serious explosion from a Forgill's boiler in our history.'

'What about spare parts?'

'We keep every nut and bearing in stock, and with modern transport we can have them delivered anywhere in the United States. If sales go as well as we're hoping, a dedicated parts warehouse on the east coast is part of the plan.'

In a San Francisco bookshop he purchased a copy of Herman Melville's *Moby Dick*, and on the way back East he immersed himself in the text, reading slowly and savouring each chapter. In this manner, the rather long volume took him all the way back to New York and onto the steamer, where Melville's descriptions of life on board the *Pequod* were easy to imagine against the backdrop of the grey Atlantic Ocean.

Chapter Eight

The voyage home to England was made notable by the unexpected presence, on board, of Sophie Forgill and her husband. News of their recent wedding had come to Frederick's notice as he flicked through the *Tattler* column in the Times. The sight of her face, after all these years, retained the capacity to make him blush.

Frederick ran into the couple at the docks before departure, and it was not possible for Sophie to ignore her father's deputy chief engineer. Still, after an introduction to her husband, Edward, who scarcely looked at Frederick, they parted ways for boarding, and did not see each other again until the meal that night.

Observing the couple over the next day or two, it seemed to Frederick that Sophie's husband was rarely in her presence on board. Frederick visited the promenade deck often enough to see him playing baccarat or whist in preference to being at her side.

On the second night out from New York, Sophie and Edward were placed at the same table as Frederick in the dining saloon. Edward engrossed himself in digging lobster meat from an expertly halved tail while next to him, Sophie ate very little. Instead, she was engaged in a conversation with a young American sitting opposite her.

Frederick tried to ignore the exchange, repelled by her

coquettish laughter at the man's attempts at humour. The American was very good looking, Frederick realised, but at least three or four years her junior. Sophie was not flirting merely to wound her husband, Frederick realised – this performance was for his benefit as well.

The arrival of a waiter, refilling glasses, endowed Edward with an opportunity to attempt to distract his wife. He dabbed at his lips with a napkin. 'I say, that was a superb thermidor.'

'The lobsters are fresh from the coast of Maine, sir.'

'Gosh, how in blazes do you keep them fresh for so long?'

'Ingeniously sir, we keep them alive in a tank until they are to appear on the menu.'

Edward turned to his wife and touched her forearm just above her glove. 'Did you hear that, Sophie? How awfully clever of them.'

'Awfully clever,' she repeated, but she was smiling, chin resting on one slim wrist, at the young American.

'What's your friend's name?' Edward asked Sophie. 'I don't think we have been introduced.'

The American responded by standing and leaning over the table with his hand outstretched. 'My name is Richard Waverley, pleased to meet you sir.'

Edward ignored both man and hand, instead picking at scraps on his plate between thumb and forefinger.

'I was just going to suggest that we call for another bottle of wine,' said Sophie.

'Excellent idea,' said her husband, attracting the attention of a waiter, who hurried over. 'Excuse me, you have the Chateau d'Yquem Sauvignon Blanc on the list, but I do wonder if you happen to have a bottle of the '84 vintage?'

'I will check, sir?'

After the waiter had gone Edward looked at the young engineer, who was back in his seat, looking wounded. 'I do so love wines from the Sauternes region. Wouldn't you agree?'

The American smiled politely, then looked away. Edward made a face and regarded Frederick as if he were the last hope. 'What about you?'

Sophie slapped her husband's wrist gently. 'What are you asking him for? Freddie wouldn't know a good wine from horse's piss.'

Frederick felt a flush grow in his chest, spreading up his neck. The mouthful of beef steak turned bitter in his mouth, and it was all he could do to stay in his seat, not to stand, and pull out his chair and leave.

The waiter returned with a bottle and poured a mouthful into Edward's glass.

'Excellent,' he said, after a delicate sniff. 'Please look after my guests first.'

Frederick's silent protest at the performance was to place his hand over the glass and refuse the offer.

The waiter hovered, addressing Edward. 'Will there be anything else, sir?'

Edward dug in his pocket, removing a silver half-crown and passing it to the waiter. 'Yes there is, as a matter of fact.' He pointed to the object of Sophie's flirtation, on the other side of the table. 'Can you please ensure that I am not seated near to that ill-bred cad at any future meal?'

The request was made in a loud, clear voice. Conversation stopped across three or four tables. The waiter himself made a noise in the back of his throat, about to say something, but then decided that his best course of action was to pocket the coin and withdraw.

Sophie reached across the table and touched the American's arm. 'I apologise for my husband's rudeness.'

Edward glared across at the American. 'No apology required. My wife has been making eyes at you all evening, and if you think I'll sit here and watch it happen you're both mistaken.'

The American stood, straightening his jacket. He bowed a farewell to Frederick, then to Sophie and withdrew from the table.

★★★

One pleasant feature of the return trip to England was the fine weather and calm seas, which allowed Frederick to keep his seasickness at bay, and enjoy time reading or just meandering around the deck in the sun. Returning from one of these excursions, he rounded a corridor in time to hear the raised voices of Sophie and her husband. He withdrew silently, not wanting to get stuck in the middle of another argument. He had lived too many years in the slums, with the barest levels of privacy, to be ignorant of marital warfare. He had seen it all, from sulks, to one-sided battery and full-blown fights.

The situation worsened. On the last night before the steamer's scheduled arrival in Liverpool, Frederick could not sleep, and long after midnight he was out on the deserted boat deck, enjoying the moon over the water. A quarter hour of solitude had passed when Sophie appeared, swigging from the neck of a bottle of Dom Perignon.

Seeing him, she stopped. 'Freddie?'

When he did not answer she stumbled closer. Her upper body, however, seemed to be moving with more intent than her feet and she stumbled. He hurried forwards in time to catch her.

Sophie's beautiful face was just inches away from his. He smelled the wine on her breath, and a faint sickly odour. For a moment they said nothing, but he felt her breathing change. Her arms were still twined with his, but they moved to encircle his chest, like the tentacles of an octopus, trying to pull him closer.

'Take me to your cabin,' she said, staring into his eyes so he could see the peril beyond.

'The only place you are going,' he said, 'is *your* cabin.' Yet the wanton invitation shocked him, made his groin swell.

'I know you want to. I've seen how you've looked at me, for all these years.'

'That was before I realised that you are cruel and selfish,' said Frederick.

Sophie disentangled herself, struggling to gain her balance. 'You turd of a man. Don't you dare tell anyone what just happened, or I will destroy you. My father likes you, it is true, but he won't when I've finished with you if you dare to cross me again.'

Frederick watched her go, his momentary arousal fading as fast as it had grown, and he did not feel hurt at all – only pity.

★★★

'In your opinion, why is the American market so hard to crack?'

Lord Forgill asked the question, having arrived at the factory in the late afternoon, where Frederick had been conferring with Vic Jones, the production manager. An impromptu meeting on the factory floor followed.

'Their needs are changing sir,' said Frederick. 'The Americans want smaller, lighter engines that use less coal and produce minimal smoke. Many of our English customers are still sold on large plodding engines running at low pressure. I do believe though, that they would also be interested in a new type of engine if we could make one.'

Lord Forgill looked thoughtful. 'What kinds of pressures are we talking about?'

'Well over a hundred psi. Even more maybe – I don't know until I've done all the calculations.'

'The Steam Manufacturers Association won't certify a boiler that produces more than fifty-five.'

'I know sir, but they will need to adapt to the future sooner or later. As you know, a boiler is stored power, and the higher the pressure the higher the work potential.'

'So to put forward an example, in an engine with the same footprint as our Z Class, how much horsepower can we produce by increasing input pressures to those levels?'

'Probably four hundred, more if we superheat the steam.'

Lord Forgill frowned, but Frederick could tell that he was thinking the idea over. Superheated steam was a concept that had not yet been commercialised.

'I know I've asked you to go to France in the Spring,' Lord Forgill said finally, 'but perhaps over the next few months you could do some preliminary designs – at least some solid concepts.'

'I'd like that, sir, thanks very much.'

★★★

For the next fifteen weeks Frederick laboured in the drafting room, with Moon furious that his junior was preparing a design that had bypassed the usual chain of command. On short notice Frederick travelled to Dortmund, Germany, to consult with an engineer called Wilhelm Schmidt, who had been working in the superheater field and was inclined to share information. Returning ten days later, Frederick made subtle changes to his blueprints.

The engine he was designing was revolutionary in some respects, but in others it was a traditional compound engine. The use of superheated steam was the main feature, along with dramatic input steam pressures approaching two-hundred psi, which would make the first, second and third cylinders work much harder.

Mathematics lay behind most of the work: calculations of cylinder volumes, flywheel size and cylinder spacings relative to valve openings. The estimated work per cycle, together with revolutions per minute, allowed a final estimation of brake horsepower.

The superheater was not a new concept, but it had never been successfully applied to a stationary engine. Superheaters used boiler heat to bring steam in tubes up to heretofore unheard of temperatures, with a resulting increase in efficiency.

Yet, the technical barriers were immense. Apart from the design of the superheater assembly, and the positioning of steam take-off and ingress tubes to the cylinder, there was an issue related to the fact that white-hot dry steam provides no lubrication of moving parts.

There were always ways to circumvent problems, and Frederick set about finding them. Quite apart from the work he completed at the drafting desk, he conferred with patternmakers, and consulted with Jones about the viability of casting or machining components.

★★★

After long days at the design table, Frederick took pleasure in returning to his company terrace house in Aldgate. Situated in one of the many housing estates Lord Forgill had developed, this, like all the construction projects associated with his name, was well-made from thoughtful plans.

It was a palatial home for one man, with three narrow storeys, accessed via a narrow staircase. The backyard was paved with Northumberland flagstones and furnished with a wrought iron table. The rear fence was covered with deep green creepers, moist and cool and somewhat protected in summer.

One evening, deep in the worst of winter's chill, Frederick had almost finished a late-night supper after a very long day, when he heard a knock. He wiped the last of the gravy from his plate and went to open the door. A woman stood in the entrance, with a blanket over her shoulder, and raggedy clothes underneath. Her eyes were hollow, and it took him some time to recognise her.

'Eleanor, is that you?'

Her voice was thick and heavy. 'Allo Freddie, I reckoned it were time I paid you a visit.'

Seeing how unsteady she was on her feet, Frederick hurried to catch her as she toppled through the threshold. He picked her up bodily, heading to the basement and the empty maid's room, where a single bed, unused since his arrival, sat unmade, and there he laid her down.

Eleanor Demsie, once so glamorous, had livid red rat-bites on her legs and arms. Her hair was mostly white now, and there were bald patches around her ears. Worst of all was the uncaring pallor of her eyes. This, Frederick realised, was a woman in deep distress.

Leaving the door open so the warmth from the fire could fill the room, Frederick hurried through to the kitchen and put the kettle on. This done, he slipped out through the front door, over a low paling fence, and knocked on the neighbour's door: the family of a foreman from the factory. There he paid one of the lads a penny to fetch the doctor.

This accomplished, he carried in a mug of tea for Eleanor, and sat on the edge of the bed. 'It's good to see you, but I'm sorry you're not well.'

'Oh, it's good to see you too,' said Eleanor. 'But they's been 'ard years since I seen you last.'

'I can see that. Where on earth have you been living?'

'Not good places, not good at all. Rats an' vermin' an' bad people … cold too. So bleedin' cold.'

When the doctor arrived, he examined Eleanor, then spoke to Frederick out in the hallway. 'The woman is malnourished, and her liver is distended. She's an alcoholic in the early stages of cirrhosis. May I ask why you are taking such an interest in her?'

'She did me a good turn once, many years ago,' said Frederick.

'Feed her, keep her away from gin and make sure that she gets plenty of rest. She needs a good hot bath and nourishing food as much as anything now.'

When Frederick told Eleanor that she could stay at the house until her health improved, she started to cry. 'Oh bless you, darlin' Freddie. I knowed you was a gentleman an' would not abandon old frien's. You won't regret it.' She shook her head in wonder. 'Ain't life the strangest thing? There we was, all them years ago. Me in the spring a' life, girlfrien' of one of the flashest rogues in the city a' London, and you were a filthy urchin grubbin' in the river for pennies an' shoelaces. Now, I'm damn near a wreck and you're takin' me in.'

Frederick hurried to reassure her, 'You're a long way from a wreck.' Something occurred to him then, and he almost dared not ask. His concern, however, soon got the better of his reticence. 'Where is your daughter, Juliet?'

Eleanor covered her eyes. '*They* took her. Ah lumme, but they've got 'er now and I know that I'll never get 'er back.'

'Good gracious,' said Frederick. 'What on earth do you mean? Is she in danger?'

But Eleanor had sailed off into unconsciousness, and was unable to reply.

★★★

Two days later, almost as soon as Eleanor had begun to look somewhat better, Frederick came home from work to find her raging around the house, destructive and furious at the world, looking for gin or the money to buy it, having already found and swallowed a pint of sherry.

It took Frederick an hour to calm her, sitting next to her on the lounge holding her wrists, and gently resisting her when she tried to get up.

'You are not strong enough,' he said, 'not for drink, or your old wild ways. Please, just sit with me and calm down.'

Strangely, this approach seemed to work. After a time, Eleanor relaxed, and eventually it was she who stood up and made a pot of tea, at which point there were tears in her eyes and she begged for his forgiveness.

'I do forgive you,' Frederick said. 'With all my heart. But something is upsetting you. Is it about Juliet? You still haven't told me where she is.'

Eleanor showed her teeth. 'They've took her, is all, and she won't be comin' back.'

'Is she in peril?'

'Well, not to her physical self. But the worst kind of peril if you arksed me.'

'Do you want me to help get her back?'

Eleanor folded her arms across her chest and shook her head resolutely. 'No. It's 'er own choice. Be damned if I'll be the one to interfere.'

★★★

In gentler times, Eleanor began to do much of the cooking and cleaning, hunting the maid who Frederick shared with two other single men in the block away when she appeared in the early afternoon for her stint at the house. The older woman was also good company, knowing so much about the city's underbelly – the dockside workers and their unions – street gangs and social politics. She had hundreds of stories, many second or third hand, but always interesting.

'Did I tell you 'bout the time the New Cut Boys kidnapped the Lord Mayor of all London?'

'I don't think you did.'

'Well, it were 'ushed up, a'course – it bein' embarrassin' an' all. Let me tell you what 'appened—' And Eleanor charged up her clay pipe, lit it with an ember from the grate, and launched into the yarn.

That Sunday, however, when Frederick tried to prevail on his guest to attend church with him she flew into a rage. 'A church? You won't see me prostrate meself before an altar for all the gold in Westminster Abbey. They can keep their weepin' saints, their melancholic ways … and the stone mausoleums where they sprouts their nonsense.' And when he returned from the service Eleanor was dead drunk.

This cycle of calm and rabid desire for drink lasted for twenty days, and on the twenty-first she was gone. Frederick returned home from work and she was no longer there. He felt responsible for her welfare. Somehow, in a way he didn't understand, their fates were bound up, and she was important to him.

The following weekend he went looking for her in the riverside taverns, down as far as the Limehouse Basin. He repeated the search the following weekend. Walking the wild streets, Frederick saw the young man that he himself might have become in the costermongers and labourers spending their earnings pissing in corners, chatting up tarts dressed in red and adorned with peacock feathers. Yet, Frederick was so busy with the new design that after a few weeks Eleanor slipped from his mind. His next overseas foray was looming and he had only weeks left to deliver concept plans for a remarkable new engine. He worked late into the evenings, and even did some test castings in partnership with Jones, the factory manager.

On the second last day of May 1867, he delivered draft blueprints for a world-first superheated steam engine to Lord Forgill at the Bow Street company offices, then went home to pack his bags. The packet-boat that would take him to Calais was by then warming its boilers in Dover.

★★★

The waters of the channel were limpid white, segueing into a colourless sky, so the firmament was a continuous pale shade – the same colour as the cliffs that reared behind Frederick as he walked up the gangway and onto the ship.

Chapter Nine

France, Frederick decided as he strolled towards a café appointment along the Passage Jouffroy, was very much to his liking. The passage offered an array of specialty shops, many of which seized his interest as he walked.

The young engineer was in a fine mood. His journeys, over the past few days, through the French industrial strongholds in Alsace and Rouen had gone well, and Paris suited his temperament. His schoolboy grasp of the French language had been a boon in his meetings with mill owners. They were an interesting lot, and British machinery was already in wide use. Many of the owners in Rouen were running old Boulton and Watt engines so there was no need to impress on them the quality of machinery from across the Channel. It was merely a matter of proving that upgrading would, over time, save them money.

'Coal is expensive in France, yes,' one of the owners had told him. 'We are paying seventy or eighty francs per ton, depending on the season. The extra economy you are telling us about will result in savings, yet I am torn.' He had gestured at the huffing, gentle machine in its stone housing. 'This engine has served us well for forty years. My father purchased it.'

Being based in the city allowed Frederick to meet with managing directors in the head offices of France's economic hub, and to sample life, Parisian style. Since his arrival he had been staying at the boutique Hôtel Familial, the usual billet for travellers from Forgill's, and he appreciated the hotel's economy, anonymity, and its proximity to the bustling Boulevard Montmartre. He loved the central location, surrounded as it was by cafes and small galleries. He was able to walk to most business meetings during the day, enjoying the sight of beautiful Frenchwomen strolling or shopping. The gently sloping streets were ideal for walking or running, and the parks for a new regime of press-ups, sit-ups and other floor exercises. At night he dined and drank in the Passages or along the Rue du Faubourg Montmartre.

Now, as he opened the mahogany and glass door of the café, near the entrance to the nearby Passage Verdeau, the maître d'hôtel approached, a neat and compact Frenchman with trimmed moustaches.

'I am here to meet a Monsieur du Brice,' said Frederick, looking around. It was a quiet, dark space of round tables and pretty waitresses.

The waiter shook his head. 'Not monsieur, but rather mademoiselle,' he said, then led the Englishman to a table with two seats. The other was occupied by one of the most attractive young women Frederick had seen in a city of attractive young women. Her eyes were light grey, and very large. Her pale blonde hair was partially enclosed by a jaunty beret. A smattering of light freckles on and around her nose made her seem girlish. She wore a figure-hugging dress, decorated with rosettes of silk.

'You must be Monsieur Morton,' she said. Then, seeing his expression, 'You look troubled.'

'I am here for a meeting. The card said M du Brice. So I was expecting a man.'

'Please do sit down. I may not be a man, but I am most certainly here to see you. Have you heard of my family, the du Brices?'

Frederick took the chair, still trying to recover his equilibrium. 'No, I'm sorry, but I haven't.'

The young woman raised her eyebrows, 'Then you have not researched your meeting satisfactorily.'

He splayed his hands, surrendering the point. 'I'm sorry.'

'My family is in business. We have extensive agricultural operations, but also processing and industrial interests. Most of these are centred around the town of Saint Laurent in Normandy.'

They settled in, ordering coffees and tasty éclairs. Once the cups were on the table Frederick said, 'It's nice to talk to someone who speaks English so well.'

'Oh, I regard myself as half English. I spent many of my school years there, at Badminton. My father decided that it would be advantageous for me to have a foot in each country, so to speak.' She took a long sip of her drink then said, 'But let's get down to business. My family is preparing several new installations requiring stationary engines. When can you come to Saint Laurent to do a site assessment?'

Frederick raised his eyebrows. The chance to sell not one, but several engines was an unusual opportunity. 'I have some appointments on Thursday and Friday, but I could possibly travel down on Sunday, assuming there is a train, and visit the site Monday morning?'

'There is a train, and that would be a convenient fixture for us also.'

Frederick listened to the music of her voice, feeling a long and liquid warmth, as if he were hearing a sound that he had been missing all his life. He slipped a hand inside his jacket pocket and removed a slim notebook and a pencil. 'Now, would you indulge me by telling me everything you can about your requirements? I'd like to be as well prepared as I can.'

There was a commotion out in the passage, then the sound of men's voices. Frederick swivelled his head to see a small group of

French army officers, two junior men and one at least a major, judging from his epaulettes. The more senior officer was quite a short man, but with a powerful build. A sword swung from a scabbard at his belt. His occupation trumpeted itself with gold, brocade, and self-belief. He peered into the café next door, then this one.

Mademoiselle du Brice saw the direction of Frederick's eyes, 'This man is my fiancé, Charles. I told him I'd be in the Passages meeting with an English businessman. He gets very jealous.'

The door opened, and the smell of tobacco wafted in with the major, who clicked his heels and beamed down at Mademoiselle du Brice.

'Hello Charles,' the young woman said, rising to allow the newcomer to kiss her cheek. 'This is Frederick Morton. He's going to quote for my father on some special new steam engines.'

'Very good,' the major said in English. 'Now, if you will dispense with your business, I wish to take you shopping, then dancing.' He extended his hand for Frederick, who had stood politely, to shake.

Mademoiselle du Brice touched Frederick's shoulder lightly. 'I'm afraid that the details will have to wait until you arrive on-site.' She smiled at the officer, then at Frederick. 'It is not possible to delay where Charles is concerned. I'm staying at the Hotel Crillon. When you have made your travel arrangements could you please send me a note with the itinerary?'

Frederick bowed in acquiescence, then watched as she took up her bag, and sauntered down the passage with her man. He could hear the major's voice rising as they walked away. The meeting with Frederick appeared to be the cause of his discontent.

★★★

Four days later, leaving the hotel on foot in the dawn, Frederick didn't bother trying to hail a cab, carrying his Gladstone bag easily. The walk of some eight blocks was not arduous, and he enjoyed the burn in his calf muscles from the gentle incline, greeting sweepers and cleaners with a soft 'bonjour' as he passed.

The Gare du Norde station was quiet when he arrived, and he was seated in his carriage thirty minutes before the scheduled departure time. The other passengers appeared to be mainly Saint Laurent families and their sons and daughters; affluent country people who had, Frederick supposed, spent the weekend in their city apartments.

Frederick sat alone on the journey, the empty seat next to him useful to hold his folded copy of the Times and a slim edition of Joseph Conrad's *Heart of Darkness*. With these distractions, and the view of green fields interspersed with villages, each with a church steeple like a tall forest tree amongst lesser roofs, the journey passed pleasantly enough.

Mademoiselle du Brice met him at the station, with no sign of her fiancé, or any chaperone, apart from the driver, who was dressed in a black wool coat with glass buttons and ribbon piping. The *volante* carriage that carried them was all dark leather and ebony. Gold gleamed on the fittings. If Frederick had any doubts as to the wealth of this family, they were fast being dispelled, and he sensed something more – sheer style – a commodity which can't be bought, but is always assisted by access to money.

'I'm so glad you are here, Monsieur Morton,' the young woman said, her accent playing a song with the words.

'The pleasure is mine,' he said, watching the driver stow his bags and return to his box to order the pair of horses to walk off, with a word of French and no recourse to whip or rein. In a moment, they were trotting down a narrow lane, fringed with white stones, and tall plane trees on either side, the sun filmy-green through the leaves and Mademoiselle du Brice's laugh like tinkling water beside him.

They reached a drive, flanked by columns of oak, crossed a stone bridge, and the du Brice mansion rose out of a green hillside like a dream.

'That's not the factory, I take it,' said Frederick.

More laughter. 'No, certainly not. First you need to be shown some hospitality. We'll get down to business tomorrow. For now, luncheon is much more important.'

Not generally given to small talk and pleasantries, Frederick met the rest of the family with interest. Madam du Brice was an older and more demonstrative version of her daughter – very tactile – squeezing Frederick's bicep as they were introduced, then resting a hand on his shoulder as they walked through to the drawing room to meet her husband. A man of smaller stature than either of the two women in the household, he had quick, alert eyes and his handshake was firm.

'Very good to meet you, Monsieur Morton. I have heard interesting things about Forgill's engines. Let's hope we can do business together.'

'Let's hope,' agreed Frederick.

They ate on a porch overlooking the garden, and after the meal Frederick's young hostess insisted that they take a couple of horses out to view the estates. He said nothing until they were halfway to the stables. Then, 'I'm embarrassed to admit that I can't ride.'

'You've never ridden?' she asked.

'No.'

'Then you will easily learn. I have a well-behaved mare who will treat you well.'

Frederick liked the horse straight off, and he mounted without difficulty. A smiling groom leaned on his garden fork to watch, making suggestions in French.

'Just ignore him,' said Clare. 'It's simple. If you say "*marcher*" she will walk, and "*arrêter*" she will stop. Hold the reins loosely and she will follow along with me and my mount. Don't lean forward too far or she might think you want to canter. Easy enough?'

'I hope so,' grinned Frederick. He liked the feeling of being so high above the ground, and the instructions seemed simple enough. The horse, it soon proved, was both quiet and compliant.

Yet, after an hour Frederick's backside had begun to ache like it was on fire, and his crotch was feeling the pressure of strained trousers and constant bumping, but Clare was only just getting started. They rode down scenic laneways fringed with rows of grapes and other crops, pausing at a small lake to sit on a bench and watch wigeons and mallards swim in graceful family groups. Frederick smiled to himself, sitting with his elbow on his knee and chin cupped in his hand.

'What are you thinking, Monsieur Morton?'

'That I would never have believed any one family could own such an … empire.'

'You have not seen it all yet,' she said seriously. 'Not by any means.'

'I come from … low beginnings,' he said.

Clare stared at him for a moment, as if trying to decide if this was a hostile statement. 'We — the du Brice's — are not noble,' she said. 'This estate, and others like it, were once owned by the aristocracy, until the French Revolution when they were separated from their fortunes, their estates, and most often their heads. My grandfather came from peasant stock, and through sheer hard work he built much of our business. My father has continued the expansion. We are a mercantile family, and birth counts for nothing in our eyes.' She took Frederick's hand slyly, and gave it a little squeeze, 'We are not so very different, you and I.'

★★★

Dinner that night was held in a dining room — more properly described as a banquet hall. The other guests were the owners of neighbouring estates, and Frederick's suit, though good quality, seemed drab beside the finest Paris-weave tailcoats of the gentlemen guests.

The Englishman was treated, in the main, with some interest, more by wives than husbands, for he was the youngest male there, and stood out with his athletic build and manly bearing. There was no doubt, however, that he was an outsider, and he felt more of an observer than a participant.

The food was challenging and delicious, snails served with strange spoons, and shiny tools that he assumed were some kind of nutcracker. Mademoiselle du Brice, seated on his left, whispered in his ear. 'The tongs are used to hold the shell, *cheri*. Then use the spoon to extract the snail. Look at me!'

Frederick watched as the young woman held the snail shell expertly with the tongs, dug inside the shell with the spoon, and slipped the garlic-scented morsel between her lips. Their eyes locked, and there was a hint of indulgence and liking in her gaze. He tried for himself, surprised at how much he enjoyed the taste.

She squeezed his forearm. 'Very good. We'll make a Frenchman of you yet.'

Later, the women left the table for the drawing room, and after a few polite questions in English the conversation reverted to French. They talked politics and business, for Frederick recognised names – Napoleon III, Robert Gascoyne-Cecil and Disraeli were all mentioned, but most of the conversation was closed to him.

At ten o'clock the guests left as if on a pre-arranged schedule, and Frederick went to bed, without seeing the young mademoiselle again. This fact unsettled him – and he was surprised at how much he had missed her company, having found the company of autocratic Frenchmen more than a little tedious.

★★★

The following morning the grand house was busy early, a bell ringing for breakfast when Frederick's pocket watch showed just seven-thirty. He was dressed and on his way downstairs shortly afterwards.

Breakfast had been set on the rear porch in the sunshine, overlooking a vast lawn bordered with beds of gladioli, impatiens, pansies and chrysanthemums. A classical-style monument sat in the middle, complete with fishpond and fountain. A valet ushered Frederick to a seat, and supplied him with coffee, croissants, fresh butter, and local honey.

'Did you sleep well?' asked Mademoiselle du Brice.

'Very soundly, thank you,' said Frederick. 'You must have retired early. I didn't see you again after supper.'

'You poor thing,' she said. 'I neglected you. I went to visit a friend – I grew up here and I know many girls – we like to get together to drink a little wine and gossip.'

The family were more relaxed without company in numbers, and Frederick ate hungrily, surprised by the quality of the food, and the rich taste and aroma of the coffee. A hint of bitterness. A touch of chocolate-like strength. It was like no coffee he had tasted.

Mademoiselle du Brice and her mother soon began talking about her upcoming wedding to the major, Charles Villon. The grand event would be held, apparently, on the lawns here. There would be a band, marquee tents, and hundreds of guests.

Frederick half-listened as he ate, sneaking glances at the young Frenchwoman. There, in the sunshine, he decided that she was even more beautiful than the made-up version of the evening before and he marvelled at the way his heart was thrumming like the strings of a harp.

Finally, while he enjoyed a second coffee, she turned to him. 'I'm so sorry, Monsieur Morton, I have been ignoring you again. But then, we have lots to do today – all business. Can you be ready in thirty minutes?'

'I'm quite ready now.'

'Then I will meet you out the front presently.'

★★★

The du Brice factory complex covered five acres and was almost as well laid out as the chateau farmland. Sitting next to Frederick in the open volante, Mademoiselle du Brice insisted that they drop the formalities.

'We have a big day ahead of us. Please call me Clare from now on, and I will refer to you as Frederick.'

Yet, having lowered this barrier, he was surprised how quickly she switched the banter to business, becoming an informative hostess, with a deep knowledge of the processes taking place in that huge compound.

'It's very unusual,' said Frederick, 'for a—'

'A woman to understand her family's business? Perhaps in England, but here it is not so strange.'

They left the conveyance, then set off on a walking tour. The focus of the factory operation was food production: corn milling, mixing, and canning.

'We also operate several wineries,' she said, 'but they are at a different site.'

They toured the warehousing sections, where a line of heavy wagons, drawn by immense Percheron horses came and went, bringing raw materials and leaving with finished produce. Frederick and Clare entered the cannery itself, with its mingled smells of cooking food and hot metals.

As a finale to the tour Clare took Frederick to three brand new buildings that were recognisable to him as textile mills.

'Flax?' he asked.

Clare clapped her hands softly. 'Correct. How did you know?'

'I saw it growing in the fields all around here as we came in. Most of the British production comes from Ireland, but I have seen it around Tayside in Scotland.'

Clare took over smoothly, 'There have been flax producers in this region of Southern Normandy for at least five hundred years, but we haven't been involved until now. After five years in the industry, we have three thousand acres planted, and are bringing in share farmers to add to the total. As soon as these mills are finished, we hope to be sending out thousands of bales of spun fibre each day.'

Frederick followed Clare into the buildings, rich with the smell of sawn wood. Like everything else the family were involved in, the craftsmanship and materials were of the finest quality. These mills were built to last.

After an inspection of all three storeys, Clare took him down to the lowest level, to a pit prepared for the steam engine that would one day drive the mill.

'My father,' she said, 'likes to use the best quality equipment. That's why he's so interested in the Forgill engines. The lower running costs are a strong inducement – though your company is not the only one manufacturing engines to that standard. I must warn you that we are also talking to a German machinery company.' She moved closer to him, so he could feel her breath on his breastbone through his open shirt and smell her perfume.

'These three facilities are just the beginning. If the profits are high enough, we'll build ten more mills – ten more engines. My father does not play with these things, he pursues profit. If he wants something, he takes it.' She paused then, 'I am a little the same.'

★★★

That night the door to Frederick's room clicked open. He sat up in bed to see Clare silhouetted in the opening, the moonlight glowing through the curtains. She closed the door without turning and glided across the floor.

Frederick's tongue felt like a strip of leather. 'What are you doing?' was all he could manage.

Clare slid in beside him. He felt the bed move with her weight, her fragrance perfuming the air. 'I'm here,' she whispered, 'to visit you.'

'Please. I think you should go.'

'Really, Frederick? You want me to go? You've been making love to me with your eyes all day. It made me wonder how it would be if you had the opportunity. Soon I will be married, who can blame me for wanting a taste of wild fruit? Yet, if you want me to go, of course I will, and please accept my apologies.'

'Wait,' he said. 'I think that I … want you to stay.'

'Go? Stay? You should make up your mind.'

Frederick took her hand, gripping it fiercely. 'I'm sorry,' he whispered. 'Please don't think badly of me but … horses are not the only things I have not yet ridden.'

'You are a virgin?'

The word virgin, to a boy or a man, is a schoolyard taunt, that cuts to the bone. Frederick had heard it a thousand times at the Charterhouse, especially in the senior years when the other boys were already visiting brothels or pressuring poor girls into taking off their clothes for money and favours.

'Yes,' he admitted.

No taunt came, and instead Clare threw her arms around him, laughing into his neck.

'What's so funny?' he asked, now thoroughly confused.

'Oh Frederick, I am a virgin too.'

He said nothing, lying back on the mattress now, the tension dissipating, the most incredible young woman he had ever met, with her mouth on his neck, her breath as hot as steam from a vent, the touch of her body more comforting and pleasurable than anything he had known.

'I thought that someone as urbane as you would be experienced,' she said into his ear. 'I hoped you might help me to learn a little of what to expect, how to please a man. I'm scared of what will happen, and how. I'm sorry, but you must think that I'm very immature.'

'No.'

She slid a hand over his chest until it reached his left shoulder, using it to manipulate him so they lay close, face-to-face in the bed. She pressed her lips to his, opening them just far enough to tantalise him.

'Do you want to see me – what I look like with no clothes on?'

she asked.

'Yes,' he croaked.

Clare swung out of bed and opened the curtains, revealing a night thick with mist, and a fluorescent moon. Then, standing beside the bed, she lifted her night dress over her head, revealing the body of an unselfconscious Venus: long legs, a trim waist, and breasts tipped with a darker shade.

Again, she climbed between the sheets, snuggling her naked body into him. His left hand moved to her neck, feeling the goosebumps the cool air had raised on her skin.

'You have kissed a woman before, have you not, *cheri*?'

'Yes, a few.' *Oh, but never a woman like you.*

'Then we know how to start,' she said, then kissed him more deeply than he had believed possible. When she took his wrist and led his hand to her breast, it was the beginning of a wondrous exploration, heightened by the moonlight shining on her body in every exquisite curve.

For the next hour, Frederick fell into a new experience, something beyond calculation, deeper than an abyss, fresher than dewfall. New emotion followed new sensation, and when it was over, with her head on his chest, hair spilling, tickling his neck, he wanted to stay like that; preserve the moment, for the rest of his life.

Clare traced his ribs with her forefinger. 'If you had not told me you were a virgin I would never have known. You took control – I liked it.'

Frederick smiled to himself. As a steam engineer, he knew more about how pistons and cylinders worked together than most men would ever know.

Chapter Ten

Back in Paris, Frederick spent two days preparing his quotation for the du Brice family. He had always had a fair hand, and the document was beautifully presented, with installation diagrams and projected operating expenditure based on local coal prices.

Finally, with the thin sheaf of paper packed up into a very large envelope, he left his hotel en route to the office of the Maître des Postes.

Quietly pleased with his work, and still somewhat preoccupied with the memory of his night with the beautiful Clare du Brice, he was surprised when he exited the Passages onto Rue de Montmartre and encountered the erect figure of Major Charles Villon, standing with a baton under his arm like a toy soldier, a deep frown on his face.

'Bonjour,' said Frederick in passing, continuing to walk, assuming that this was an accidental meeting.

'Wait,' cried the strident voice. 'You do not have the courage to face me like a man? *Non?* Stop walking, I command you.'

Frederick stopped, then turned back towards Villon. Awareness bloomed inside him that this meeting was not accidental. The French major had waited for him.

'I know what you have done,' Villon said. 'You have made love with my fiancé.' Outrage reddened his face like a flare.

Frederick stopped, his face immobile, wishing that he had kept walking. 'I beg your pardon?'

'Clare told me so herself, so don't try to hide the truth,' Villon went on.

Frederick felt the skin of his face burn, wondering why Clare would have made such an admission. 'Yes, it's true, but I did not pursue her.'

'Fight me.'

Frederick's brow creased with confusion, this excursion had altered from a pleasant walk into a confrontation. 'Do you mean it? Here and now?'

'No, not here. At a place and time of my choosing. With the sword.'

Frederick did not make the mistake of disbelieving or underestimating Villon. The major's eye was steady and sincere. He looked strong in the legs, arms and shoulders, and had probably been practising with the heavy, French short sword for half his life. 'And if I refuse?'

Charles Villon spat on the paved stone of the footpath. 'Then you will leave this city today, on your belly, without honour. I will see that you do so.'

Frederick had no desire to face this angry man with a blade in his hands. Yet, how could he walk away? He had already reported to London about the potential du Brice contract. Leaving it unresolved would raise questions. Not only that, but he had two other meetings involving possible sales. These he would not abandon.

'Since I don't intend to leave Paris today,' he said at last. 'I imagine that I will have to fight you.'

The major grimaced – as if to signal his satisfaction. 'My second will be in touch with the details.' He paused, as if for dramatic effect, then raised his chin. 'I suggest you obtain a weapon forthwith, and practise, for we fight until one man begs for quarter, or to the death.'

Frederick raised his eyebrows. Either the major was serious or he was blustering. Perhaps a bit of both. He turned and walked away, continuing his errand, now not quite so enamoured of the day.

★★★

With no idea of how long the process of organising a fight would take, Frederick decided that it was best to start practicing, no matter how ridiculous the situation seemed. He purchased his weapon at the House of Souzy Aîné, on the Boulevard Voltaire. The showroom had hundreds of edged and practice weapons – racks of foils and sabres varying from cheap and plain to heavily decorated. Some were almost as valuable as their own weight in gold.

The salesman, a willow-built young man who sported an oversized moustache, seemed unimpressed that Frederick was to fight a duel – as if it were nothing out of the ordinary. Yet, he spent some time matching the length and weight of the weapon with Frederick's physique, explaining his reasoning in quite reasonable English.

'You have very strong arms and shoulders,' the salesman said, 'and you are tall, so you can effectively wield a blade as long as seventy-three centimetres.'

The weapon was more expensive than Frederick had anticipated, but he couldn't resist the shining steel, perfect balance, and feel of the leather grip in his right hand. After all, perfection in engineering of all kinds appealed to him.

'Being an English businessman,' the salesman said, 'I imagine that you do not have many friends in this country?'

'True,' said Frederick, loving the sound of the blade swishing in the air as it moved. 'I know scarcely anyone.'

'Do you have a second, for the duel, monsieur?'

'Not yet.'

The salesman bowed. 'I am happy to act as your second. I'll give you my private address and you can tell your challenger where to find me.' He extended his hand. 'My name is Antonin Bonnefoy.'

Frederick was surprised and pleased, 'I'm Frederick Morton, and I appreciate your offer very much.'

Back in his hotel room, he ran the weapon through its paces for the first time. He had done some fencing in his school days, and the weapon felt good, like an extension of his arm. The balance was perfect. Even so, he still could not believe that the duel would proceed.

The blood of Colonel Charles de Brie was up, however, and he was ready to fight. Frederick was stepping from the Hôtel Familial into the passage one afternoon when Antonin hailed him.

'Monsieur Morton, I have news for you.'

Frederick led his new friend up to his room, where he opened the curtains and indicated a chair at the small table. 'Take a seat,' he said, then fetched two glasses of water and sat down himself. 'What news?'

'I had a visit from your challenger's second. The fight will be on Saturday the third of June, at eight in the morning, beside the pond near the Park of Saint Joan.' His brow furrowed. 'Less than two weeks from now. I must say that I'm a little worried. I did not realise that your man was a military officer – he will have spent his life swinging the steel, and has probably fought many duels in the past. Have you thought of withdrawing?'

Frederick considered the idea. 'No, I don't think I can withdraw.'

'Very well, then I will have to train you, but even more importantly, have you sent a written jibe – *la moquerie*, to your opponent?'

'No, what do you mean by that?'

'You need to compose a sentence or two, promising what you will do to him in the fight, or poking fun at his skills. It's very important.' Antonin looked at Frederick's face. 'Here, I will help you. Bring paper, quickly, while my inspiration is fresh.'

Frederick brought paper and a quill, watching while his new

friend inscribed his opponent's name as the salutation in near perfect copperplate. Then, he looked up. 'Now I understand that you made love to this man's fiancé.'

'That's correct.'

'Then how about this. "I enjoyed plundering the sweet flesh of the beauty whom we both desire. I possessed her fully, and will do so again, just as my sword tip will soon invade your chest and pierce your heart. The prize will then be mine forever.'

Frederick threw his head back and laughed, 'People write such things?'

'Oui, of course they do. Or how about, "After your death I will ravish her sweet body on your grave."'

Still amused, Frederick shook his head, 'Please don't write that. How about, "I hope to give a good account of myself in the fight and may the best man win."'

Antonin wrinkled his nose as if to an unpleasant smell. 'I suppose that will do as a starting point. May I add some embellishments?'

'As long as they are reasonable.'

While Antonin wrote his message and sealed the letter in an envelope, Frederick put the sword through its paces in the cramped room.

'It's lucky you are not fighting a duel in a hotel room,' commented Antonin. 'Your use of space is poor.'

Frederick stopped, a little crestfallen, but his new friend was already pushing back his chair and reaching for the bag of foils he had set down near the door.

'Come, let us try somewhere with room to move.'

★★★

Just a few blocks down the Rue de Richelieu, they turned into the Square Louvois, heading for a grassed area between flower beds and immature plane trees. The square was dominated by a fountain – a huge basin supported by statues of four beautiful women, each representing one of the great rivers of France: the Seine, the Garonne, the Loire, and the Saône. Across the road the grand National Library dominated the background so fully that Frederick had to blink his way out of an architectural-inspired trance when Antonin opened the bag of foils and threw one into the air.

Frederick caught it by the hilt, then, moving over the grass, they began to spar. After a few minutes Antonin lowered his weapon.

'You know the basic moves. I, however, will teach you some of the more sophisticated attacks that your opponent might use. He is a short man, oui?'

'Yes. Probably about five-feet-five or six, but with a solid build.'

'Feet?'

Frederick did a calculation in his head – having often needed to convert imperial measurements to metric in the course of his work, this wasn't hard. 'About one-hundred-and-sixty-five centimetres.'

Antonin flexed his shoulders, swinging back his arms while still holding the foil. 'Short and strong, yes? Such men can be dangerous, yet a swordsman who knows how to use his height to advantage can be likewise, and you have strength and speed to match. *En garde*! Let us begin the journey of making you a lion Major Villon will wish he had not awoken.'

★★★

In the middle of the week Frederick was dressing for a luncheon meeting when he answered a knock on the door to find Antonin in the threshold, holding aloft an envelope. 'We have had a reply from Colonel Charles de Brie.'

'Oh Antonin I'm sorry,' said Frederick. 'I'm late for an engagement.'

'That can wait, my friend, this is much more important – I've walked all the way here on my lunch break to read it to you.'

Frederick consulted his fob. 'I suppose five minutes won't matter. What does he say?'

Antonin cleared his throat and struck a pose like a king's messenger. 'You know not what you have done. Your sordid act will lead to the steel of my sword being embedded in your neck. The force of my lunge, the solidity of my balance on my right foot is famous in the ranks of the 24th Regiment. I give you this warning of my skills, and I look forward to bathing in your blood.'

Frederick found, strangely, that the words did not frighten him, but merely made him dislike Villon a little more. 'So do we reply again?'

'But of course. What would you like me to say?'

Frederick shrugged. 'Whatever you like, but with restraint. I must go.'

'Wait,' said Antonin. 'Let me suggest that we read between the lines of your challenger's text. He makes a lot of his lunge off the right foot. Does this mean that it's his weakness? Is he setting you up to expect this manner of attack, while he intends to launch his assault from the other side?'

Frederick thought for a moment, never having previously considered that to fight a duel required a series of pre-emptive mind games. 'Or he could be trying to make us think that way, and he truly is a master of the method he mentions.'

Antonin twisted the tips of his moustache. 'Perhaps.'

'Now,' said Frederick. 'I really do have to go. Will you meet me in the park this evening?'

'Oui. There is much to do. I should be finished work at five-thirty.'

★★★

That afternoon a letter arrived from Saint Laurent arranging a meeting the next day with Monsieur du Brice and his daughter in a conference room at the Hotel Crillon.

When the time came, Frederick was coldly furious with Clare, and in consequence he focussed most of his attention on her father.

She must have known that her decision to tell her fiancé of their union would bring conflict. How could it do otherwise?

'Your quotation is well presented and erudite,' Monsieur du Brice began. 'But before we proceed any further, I must ask some questions.'

Thirty minutes of interrogation followed, and at such times Frederick showed that he was not a mere salesperson, but an engineer with deep knowledge of the engines the company he worked for produced. Du Brice's questions were both penetrating and astute.

Frederick's only chance to talk to the young Frenchwoman alone came afterwards, when she escorted him to a cab.

'I heard about the duel,' she said, 'and Charles has let me read some of the amusing discourse between the two of you. I am flattered that you told him you'd rather see your entrails wound like rope around another man's sword than to live without me.'

Frederick's eyes enlarged. 'I did not write that, my overenthusiastic second did. More importantly, why did you tell your fiancé that we … were together, down at your estate?'

'I'm sorry *cheri*. I had a fit of guilt, and I decided that Charles and I should not start our lives together with a lie.' She paused. 'Shall you and I dine together tonight?'

'Are you mad? I'm already supposed to fight a duel with your fiancé for what we did last time – a duel to the death I might add, and you want to go out to dinner with me?'

'Charles is always fighting duels – and I have never heard of anyone being killed in them.' She widened her eyes. 'Besides, if you already have to fight to the death over me, we can't make things any worse, can we?' Clare gripped his upper arm gently. 'Charles's regiment was mobilised and sent to our border with Alsace yesterday. He is out of town for at least a week – returning in time for the duel. Where shall we meet?'

Frederick felt a leap of excitement. 'Name the place and I'll be there.'

★★★

The following morning, with sunlight streaming in through the shuttered windows, Frederick looked at Clare's sleeping form, the silk sheets arranged around her body as if by an artist. He used the water closet, then came back and sat on a chair, smoking one of her cigarettes experimentally, not enjoying the bite of the smoke in his mouth enough to draw it down into his lungs.

Finally, she opened her eyes. 'Put that down and come back to bed.'

'You're going to get me killed,' he said, but did as he was told, stubbing the cigarette out in an ash tray and slipping back between the sheets.

'Yes, *mon cheri*, but isn't it worthwhile? We must make the most of our little affair. Today you and I will walk hand in hand on the Champs Elysees, eat at a tiny cafe in the Latin quarter and make love on this bed as many times as we can.

With one hand on each of his shoulders she began to sing, touching his nose as if as a punctuation point.

> Dans un sommeil que charmait ton image Je rêvais le bonheur, ardent mirage,
> Tes yeux étaint plus doux, ta voix pure et sonore,
> Tu rayonnais comme un ciel éclairé par l'aurore.

Her voice was as clean as silken thread, and Frederick couldn't help but embrace a surge of happiness filling his heart. 'That's beautiful, what's the song?'

'It's called *Après un Reve*, by Gabriel Fauré,' she said. 'It means *After a Dream*. Would you like me to sing it in English?'

'Anything to hear you keep singing.'

Clare tilted her head to one side and made her eyes more loving than the rhymes of Ovid, rounder and greener than the hills of Saint Laurent.

In sleep made sweet by a vision of you
I dreamed of happiness, fervent illusion,
Your eyes were softer, your voice pure and ringing,
You shone like a sky that was lit by the dawn;

You called me and I departed the earth,
To flee with you toward the light,
The heavens parted their clouds for us,
We glimpsed unknown splendours; celestial fires.

A tear came to Frederick's eyes, and the hairs on his arms were standing proud, as he repeated the final line: 'We glimpsed unknown splendours; celestial fires.'

★★★

The days went by, and Frederick, for the first time in his life, did little work, but instead indulged himself in a world that a slum boy from Stepney should never have known.

On the third day after the meeting at the Hotel Crillon, he sent a telegram to the factory manager.

REQUEST TWO WEEKS VACATION LEAVE FRM ENDS

He had more than a month owing, so he wasn't sure why he felt guilty, but he did.

The answer came back from the factory manager.

VACATION APPROVED STOP MORE NOTICE NEXT
TIME ENDS

Frederick and Clare ate coq au vin in street cafes, with a glass of sauterne. They talked late, or sat in the bath together; watched stage shows and opera. This was Frederick's first experience of a true, all-encompassing affair of the heart.

In between times he wandered in a love-sick daze, or sparred with Antonin in one of many venues, at times with the shorter, heavier sword, so his wrists and biceps could learn to handle the greater weight, and his mind the lesser reach.

Those days could not last forever. One afternoon when they were lying on his bed, sweat from their exertions still on their foreheads, Clare drew a curtain on the affair. She sat up abruptly, and perched herself on the edge of the bed. In that position she tied her hair up, while he reached out and idly traced the knuckles of her spine where they appeared in the middle of her back. Next she arranged pillows around herself, drew up the sheet, and slipped one hand around his neck.

'I have two lots of news,' she said. 'One is very good for you, and the other is not so good. Which would you prefer to hear first?'

Frederick mused for a moment. 'The good news first, please.'

'My father has decided to purchase three Forgill's engines.'

Frederick sat up, 'That's fabulous news.'

'Yes, but I can tell you – it was a very close thing. We were in discussion with a German firm and your compatriots, Robey and Company. I do have to warn you that there will still be some negotiating ahead. Father thinks that your deposits are exorbitant, and he wants staged payments – to his own schedule.'

'I'm sure we can work out the details.'

'Of course we can,' she said. And for a moment they simply enjoyed looking into each other's eyes.

'Now what's the not-so-good news?' Frederick asked.

'Charles will arrive back in Paris tomorrow.'

Frederick's high spirits sank. 'And he insists on pursuing this senseless duel?'

'You do not understand Frenchmen, *cheri*. Honour is much more important than logic. His friends will all be looking forward to watching. As am I.'

'You want to watch me fight your fiancé, with a sword?'

'Isn't it every woman's dream?'

'Few people fight duels in England these days.'

'They do in France.' She squeezed his bicep and got up from the bed, beginning to dress. 'Charles is very fond of contests of all kinds. He would have been back in Paris yesterday, but he has got himself involved in a silly pedestrian competition with another officer – they have a wager as to who can walk from Strasbourg to Épinal. This is not such a great distance for Charles – about one hundred and thirty kilometres altogether.'

'Your fiancé is a pedestrian?' Frederick asked.

'Oui, apart from fighting it is Charles's favourite activity. Are you one of them also?' Clare delved in her bag and moved in front of the mirror.

'I entered quite a few races back when I had the time. If only your fiancé had challenged me to a pedestrian contest instead of a duel! He was born with a sword in his hand, I have no such advantage.'

Clare was doing something with her lips, and he realised that it was an artifice to spread some kind of cosmetic. 'Counter challenge him,' she said. 'To a pedestrian contest. I doubt he'd refuse if you do it publicly.'

'That's an idea. Do you really think he'd accept?'

'If you make it a big one – something challenging. The drama would appeal to him.'

'Have you any ideas for a route?'

Clare cocked her head at an angle. 'How about here, Paris, to a little seaside village called Saint Nazaire. My family have a villa there.' Her eyes danced mischievously, 'where I can comfort the winner.'

'How far?'

'I'm not sure exactly; three, perhaps four hundred kilometres?'

'A very long way to walk,' said Frederick. 'But it's better than a sword through my heart.'

Clare moved back to the bed and placed her hand across his pectoral muscles. 'I like your heart the way it is,' she said. 'Beating. Preferably next to mine.'

Chapter Eleven

Despite the confidence that he had expressed to Clare, Frederick had only a few pedestrian wins to his credit, and none for some years. He studied Clare's suggestion. From Paris to Saint Nazaire was 440 kilometres in all, or 270 English miles. It seemed like a staggering distance, but pedestrianism had long pushed the boundaries of ordinary human endurance. The greatest feats were common knowledge – Foster Powell had walked from London to York and back again, a distance of four hundred and thirty miles, after a sporting friend wagered one hundred guineas that he couldn't do it. Or John Batty, who managed seven hundred miles in two weeks of near-ceaseless walking. Frederick recalled also that a Captain Howe had accepted a two hundred guinea bet to walk further in twenty-four hours than a fellow officer, Captain Hewetson. Howe beat his opponent easily, covering eighty miles in the allotted period, more than most people could have managed on horseback.

These were near-insane feats of perseverance, but pedestrianism was a recognisably insane activity – a quality that helped make it one of the great spectator sports of the age.

Frederick placed a new advertisement in the Le Figaro newspaper, translated into French with Clare's assistance.

I, Frederick Morton, repudiate previous challenges and

hereby issue a counter challenge to Major Charles Villon of the 24th Regiment. I invite him, at the hour of eight ante meridian on the day of Saturday, June 10, to walk, within the rules of pedestrianism, from the Arc de Triomph, Paris, to the village of St Nazaire on the western coast. The first man to wet his face in the ocean waters there will be judged the rightful winner and the better man.

The following day's edition carried a reply.

I, Major Charles Villon, accept the challenge as issued: at the hour of eight ante meridian on the day of Saturday, June 10, to walk, within the rules of pedestrianism, from the Arc de Triomph, Paris, to the village of St Nazaire on the western coast. I look forward to the taste of salt on my lips, many hours before my competitor.

An article on page five suggested that the English challenger was foolhardy in the extreme to take on the seasoned pedestrian Major Charles Villon. Frederick chuckled to himself when he read it, having sought the hotel receptionist's assistance in the translation.

Whatever his chances, Frederick preferred to fail at a walking race than in a duel with the sword.

'I think that you will win,' Clare encouraged him, at a brief, clandestine meeting, 'but for the sake of my marriage I must appear to be on Charles's side. You won't feel hurt when you see me with him, will you?'

Frederick offered no answer. He didn't want to see her with Charles at all.

★★★

The pale limestone of the Arc de Triomphe shone in the morning light – the grandest of all venues – situated at the junction of twelve radiating avenues. Major Charles Villon stood nearby, surrounded by a knot of his fellow officers, all bescarfed and wearing great coats, drinking from hip flasks of cognac, in scorn of the morning chill.

Clare was also nearby, playing the dutiful fiancé, and once or twice she caught Frederick's eye, shooting him an amused smile. Behind the knot of Villon's well-wishers, at the Champs-Elysées end, was a two-in-hand wagonette, drawn by elegant grey horses. Stocks of cheeses, wine and food were in the process of being stowed aboard. This, Frederick realised, was the Villon camp's victualling wagon.

Frederick, for his part, had an old army rucksack he had picked up in a second-hand shop in the passages. Inside was a raincoat, a loaf of bread, a map, cheese, some sweetmeats, jerky, a bottle of water and a flask of port wine. His clothing was basic but practical – cut-off breeches, a striped shirt of subdued shades, and a stoker's cap such as he had occasionally worn on the job back at Forgill's.

Villon upheld the idiosyncratic dress code of the pedestrian, most particularly with a pair of oversized short pants revealing muscular and hairy legs. His jersey was white with embroidered red stripes, and he wore a peasant's cap sardonically. In one hand he held a goblet of red wine. Seeing Frederick watching, he raised the pewter receptacle with a bitter challenge in the cast of his lips.

A journalist was at his side, scribbling in a note pad. The press interest had been extraordinary. *La Figaro* had published an article which described the journey as a near-impossible task, only within reach of an 'indomitable son of France' like Villon, who was likely to leave his English adversary as a 'melted puddle on the roadside.'

Frederick did not mind that the race had become something of a nationalist affair and was bemused by the enthusiastic crowd of Parisians who had turned out to watch, including a somewhat disappointed Antonin. Many held tiny cups of coffee, and several bookmakers appeared to be taking money and exchanging written scrips with punters.

A few minutes before nine, one of Villon's officer friends produced a pistol and announced that the start was imminent. The crowd made of themselves a corridor, with the two pedestrians inside. It had seemed to Frederick that he was alone in this endeavour, while his adversary had a tribe of supporters. Now, however, with the starting gun being carefully loaded, sans lead ball, a small group of Britishers made themselves known.

'Good luck mate,' one called.

'Win it for old Queen Vicky, eh,' said another.

'Where you from, mate?' asked another.

'Aldgate,' said Frederick.

'Well, I'm from Shoreditch, so we're just about neighbours. Most of us are over here working for the Frenchies but peel off our coats and there's a Union Jack underneath. Good luck mate, God speed, and be sure to teach this little cock a lesson.'

Villon, whose English was very good, bristled at this last statement, but with a shake of his head as if to slough away the insult he continued to warm his body with comical leg shakes and mock-sensual shivers.

The start was imminent when Clare, seeing that Charles was busy with his warm-up exercises, managed to get close to Frederick. 'You have your match,' she said softly. 'All you have to do is win.'

Frederick took her words as encouragement. Her presence made him brim with energy. To him she was all the freshness and beauty of youth distilled into one slim figure. 'I'll win,' he said softly. 'Put a few francs on me – it will help your father pay for the marvellous engines from Forgill's.' Clare pressed her lips to her fingertips, which she then reached out to touch against his cheek so briefly that few people would have noticed. She withdrew, just as the starter cocked the hammer of his pistol and called for the two competitors to get set.

'*Partir*,' he cried, and the pistol discharged with a gush of smoke and blast of sound. Frederick was relieved. The awkward wait was over, and the shouts of those few vocal British supporters were loud in his ears.

Only two hundred and seventy miles to go, Frederick said to himself as he crossed the many lanes of horse and vehicle traffic, with some well-wishers clearing the way.

★★★

While the route through Paris, and the entire journey for that matter, was up to the participants to decide, both men had studied the maps and chose to head down the broad Avenue Victor Hugo, walking with that peculiar pedestrian gait at a crisp pace, each taking one side of the street as if by agreement. Villon's crew of fellow officers filled the support wagonette, which rolled along nearby, hanging half in and half out, calling on their champion to hurry, drinking and laughing as they went.

Villon seemed determined to stay at the front, in those early stages, as if it were a matter of honour, and Frederick did not contest the lead. Instead, he held back by some fifty paces, not hurrying, yet careful not to let the Frenchman out of his sight. This was Villon's city, and if there were short-cuts to be had, he would know them.

★★★

The first day of the race was a pleasure, with the sun shining, the Englishman fielding curious stares from Parisians spilling out of cafés. Yet the two competitors were out of the city by late morning, and soon the smell of fresh fields enlivened the air.

The Englishman was pleased with his gait: an easy transfer of weight, with a slight movement of the hips to slide the foot behind. He felt good in the knees, strong in the thighs and he looked forward to the rest of the contest.

Passing through the first village, Pailaseau, Frederick noticed that three girls of seventeen or eighteen years were watching him from out the front of a milliner's shop. They whispered together; giggled at a shared joke. Surely on a dare, one ran forward to intercept Frederick, and thereupon kissed him on the cheek. Her friends whistled and applauded as she returned to the huddle.

Frederick threw back his head and laughed at the sense of fun behind the act. Brimming with pleasure, he turned for a moment, walking part-backwards, raising a hand to hail them before continuing on his way.

★★★

Having chosen the date of the contest partly for the moon phase, Frederick was not surprised when, having just passed through the village of Ablis, the moon rose from behind his shoulders, casting a ghostly shadow on the road, and throwing the surrounding small-town architecture into relief.

At this point, neither of the walkers had stopped to rest, but finally, Frederick saw, in a field beside a river, that Major Villon's entourage had set up a trestle table lit with lanterns and a repast of cooked fowl, cheeses and wine.

Frederick looked curiously as he passed by, and Villon, it seemed, was watching for him to come, for he called out, 'Enjoy the lead, Englishman. You will not maintain it for long.' He then lifted his wine, and shouted, 'Bon appetit!' to rapturous cheers from his supporters. Several were young women, one hanging on to his arm. This more physical segment of his support team did not seem to include Clare.

Gaining the lead felt good to Frederick, and after a half-mile he swung his rucksack off, still walking as he did so, and removed a hunk of bread and some cheese. Washed down with first some water, then two or three big mouthfuls of port-wine, renewed strength flowed into his muscles. He did not feel like stopping, and with the moon rising to the summit of its luminous arc he walked on and on into the night.

Chartres was the first substantial city of the walk, and Frederick concentrated on the signs for Le Mans, the next big centre, using these to navigate through while the last restaurant-goers and bar patrons emerged to stare at the young Englishman as he hurried past. Deeper into the town, he was confronted with the growing silhouette of one of the most massive and magnificent cathedrals he had ever seen, even by moonlight discernible as being of great antiquity.

When the moon was about to set, glowing large in the west over fields of wheat, he finally stopped, moved to the side of the road, shed his coat, spread it on the grass and curled up to sleep, more fatigued than he knew.

★★★

The next morning Frederick did not know whether he was behind or in front, but after consulting the folded map he carried in the rucksack he strode off down the road, working the knots out of his muscles as he went. It seemed to him that he must have covered at least sixty miles of the trip, one quarter of the full distance.

At that time, the walk seemed like an impossible task. Frederick was aching in his calves and thighs, sore in the arches of his feet, and was wondering just how well the new shoes he had purchased for the occasion truly fitted.

He was also, apart from the endless delights of the scenery, a little bored with his own company. It pleased him, therefore, when upon entering a small village, a young man strode briskly out and began to keep pace beside him.

'Bonjour,' said Frederick, a little surprised.

'Bonjour, Monsieur Morton,' said the youth. 'Forgive me, but I read of your race in the newspaper, and I wish to walk with you for a time. My name is Michel, and I am at university, studying English language and literature. I thought it would be nice to converse with a native speaker – especially one so daring and adventurous.'

'You are welcome,' said Frederick, and in truth it was a pleasure. Michel was a brilliant young man, with a curious intellect; laughing as Frederick told the story of how the race had come to pass, then related some of his own romantic failures. Even a brief rain squall, a column of grey marching over the green fields with spread arms streaming curtains of rain, could not dampen their enjoyment of each other's company.

'The young woman in question is Mademoiselle Clare du Brice, then?' asked the young man.

'That's correct.'

'Then you are lucky to know her, from what I have heard. My cousin is from the village of Saint Laurent, where there was an outbreak of plague some three or four years ago. From what I have heard young Mademoiselle du Brice nursed many of the villagers tirelessly, heedless of her own health, saving the lives of many.'

'She has a good heart,' said Frederick, and there were tears in his eyes as he articulated the thought: *but she is not mine.*

For twenty miles, all the morning and into the afternoon they walked on, and Charles Villon was all but forgotten. When Frederick's new walking companion took his leave, having arranged to catch a train back to his home, the Englishman was sad to see him go.

★★★

The first blisters began to form late on the second day, on the outer sides of Frederick's big toes, then his instep, and all the smaller toes. By the third day most had matured and burst, removing the skin as effectively as a burn. Pain accompanied every step, no matter how he tried to spread his weight.

(She is not mine, said the rhythm of his feet).

The hinge of his left knee was like a strip of leather creased too many times until it started to tear. The right was holding up, but the hip on that side felt like it had a blunt nail buried deep in the joint. His lips were dry like parchment, with flakes of skin peeling away, leaving small bleeding cracks.

After dark, he began to imagine things in the shadows, envisioned the wolf padding along behind him, and he quickened his pace considerably, despite the pain, walking with nervous energy and a breathless fear. He heard its breath hiss in his ear and swivelled his head often to catch sight of it; always too late by an instant.

By midnight this panic subsided, leaving him well-placed, but fatigued. He began looking for a nook to spread his coat for two or three hours, to fend off the exhaustion that might otherwise overwhelm him. As far as he could calculate, he needed another thirteen to fourteen hours of hard walking to reach the finish, and that wasn't possible without rest.

Yet a suitable place had not appeared, and he was stuck in a machine-like compulsion that he knew he must break out of or burn out. Still, he plodded on, one step after the other, hypnotised by his own pain. He might have gone on until he fell, but for a loud call from a street-front house as he passed through a village. An elderly man was standing in a doorway, framed with red-painted timbers, and smelling of wine, coffee and garlic.

'*Ingles*, come in – you are welcome, welcome.'

This, finally, broke the spell. Frederick stopped walking and turned to look at the speaker numbly. Even then he might have stumbled back into motion, but the man emerged from the doorway and took his arm.

'Come in, come in. My daughter in Le Mans saw you there yesterday and sent a letter with a coachman. She says that your opponent has a travelling support group to cater for his every need and you have nothing. My dear wife has been cooking for you, while I waited and watched for you to arrive.'

Frederick went into the warmth gratefully. The first pleasure was a steaming bath, more luxurious than anything he could remember, followed by hot beef broth. While he ate, the Frenchman sat on a stool opposite him, tending to his blisters with small bandages made of clean rags.

After three hours of blessed sleep, on a bed into which he sank like a stone into water, the Frenchman woke him up with two cups of black, gritty coffee, and hot bread with olive oil and pickled meat.

Last of all, Frederick dressed again in clean clothes, donning two pairs of knitted socks that the Frenchwoman supplied.

When Frederick walked out onto the street, he was still aching all over, but his heart filled with joy at the human kindness he had just experienced. His determination hardened to win from here.

Yet, he did not know if Villon was behind or in front.

★★★

An hour after dawn, Frederick found himself winding down from gentle hills towards the sea. From there he could see the sparkling ocean, and a village in the distance that must surely be Saint Nazaire. He was beyond exhaustion, each movement of his legs an effort, and the bandaged blisters were again stinging.

Still, the end was now in sight, and the first scent of sea air in his nostrils was a powerful stimulant. It had rained recently, and the lane was covered by manure and mud. The occupants of a row of houses surrounded by farmland turned out to watch, and Frederick barely had the energy to smile.

As he rounded the next bend, Villon came into view. He was ahead by perhaps a kilometre. Yet, even from that distance it was obvious that the Frenchman was limping, his gait forced. With the downward slope helping to propel his body onward, Frederick prepared for a final effort.

Over the next hour, he gained little ground, but he did not falter either, not even when Villon's support wagon dropped back to taunt him, a moustached and humourless man sitting on the edge of the tray as they circled back.

'You cannot win from here, Englishman. Give up. Stop now.'

Another voice called out in French from a supine position in the wagon. '*Regarde le tomber.*'

This, Frederick realised, meant something along the lines of 'Watch him fall over.' The comment only made his resolution to win strengthen, as did the ragged laughter when the wagon rolled on.

The final leg of the route was primarily downhill, and at times the road wound along the sides of ridges, rising into green foothills. At one stage, when the track zig-zagged and looped back, Frederick found himself looking down on his opponent. Villon gave a cheery wave, a greeting intended to show his *savoir faire* and patent lack of fatigue.

Frederick did his best to reply in kind, then felt a strange and penetrating stab of jealousy. The man ahead of him was engaged to marry Clare. Winning this race would not change that fact. All Frederick was doing was proving a ridiculous matter of honour, which might more easily have been managed with a couple of swords and some minor bloodshed.

Pointless, he spat at himself. Villon was already the winner. Clare would be at the finish line, she would take her fiancé back to the villa she had mentioned and pamper him. Frederick did not even know how he would get transport back to Paris.

Idiot. He wasn't even being used – he was torturing himself. He should be selling engines, meeting with business owners and managers, not here, half dead, near lame, on a track winding down to a remote stretch of the French coast, all for the sake of a young woman so kind, sophisticated and beautiful that she could never be his.

(She is not mine. She is not mine).

When the strange fit of rage passed, Frederick came back to himself. He had wandered to the middle of the road, with a farmer on his wagon behind, shouting at him to make way. Villon, moreover, was now just a few hundred paces ahead.

Frederick moved over to the verge to let the wagon pass and stared ahead. The road to the seaside village was almost straight now, flat off the last of the hills, surrounded by a carpet of green. The sea was so close that Frederick could discern the white caps on the breeze-sculpted waves.

As he neared his opponent, Frederick could see the shake in his legs, a favouring of the right as if to compensate for pain or injury to his left. Ankle, Frederick supposed.

Yet even though Villon was obviously pulling out reserves from somewhere, Frederick was still gaining ground.

They entered the village of Saint Nazaire with Frederick fifty yards behind, passing villagers lined up on either side in their coloured jerseys, caps, and voluminous dresses. Carts and wagons had stopped at the kerb, people clapping when they saw the extremes the contestants had been reduced to. Both men had lost many pounds in weight over the last days, but Frederick more so than his opponent.

At the end of the road was a beach, lapped by small waves. Frederick summoned every cell, grunting with effort as he drove himself on. Then, there on the right, was Clare, standing beside one of the exquisite conveyances her family travelled around in. Frederick heard her cheers, and her eyes met his. That look held every kiss they had shared, the congress of skin, and the new doorways of pleasure they had explored together. It held promise, sadness, but regret most of all.

In recognition he raised a clenched fist and limped on towards the beach, past a couple of reporters from the French press, then a line of fishing boats drawn up on the sand. Villon was still ahead, stumbling across the beach, close to the water, when Frederick's shoes first crunched on coarse sand. He felt a premature ache of defeat. He was going to lose, there was no way to catch his rival now.

After almost falling in a hollow he steadied himself. Villon had reached the water, dropping to his knees in the shallows, and lifting a handful of seawater to his face. Frederick saw the waves curling onto the beach, and finally, he too felt the cool liquid meet his tortured feet.

A wave came rushing to meet him, barrelling along the sand, wetting him to the knees. On he blundered – waist then stomach high – the waves pushing him forwards and tugging him back, the freezing water stinging into his blisters. Now Frederick allowed himself to fall back into the sea, letting it soothe his damaged body.

He had lost the race. It felt like a calamity. Scarcely able to move for several moments, he finally stood and turned to see Clare with her arms around the victor, kissing him, heedless of the water foaming around them.

Bitterness writhed and twisted in his gut. Somehow, he rose to his feet and started to walk out of the water and away. He didn't care where. He felt a hand on his shoulder as Clare caught up to him. 'I haven't congratulated you yet. You almost won. You were so close.'

He said nothing, just let the tears fall from his eyes, down his face and onto his chest, joining the salty Atlantic wetness there.

'Please Frederick,' she whispered. 'He's my fiancé. You have known from the start that I am going to marry him.'

He walked on, away from her, bleeding so deeply in his heart that he felt as if he would never recover.

Chapter Twelve

The following winter was one of the coldest in living memory, with frost on the paths and ice fogs leaving stalactites hanging from the leaves of trees. Many of the River Thames's tributaries: the Lea, Ravensbourne, Beam, Tyburn and Effra froze over for several weeks, with only the forceful tides of the main river keeping the channels clear.

Meanwhile, any further moves towards the production of Frederick's new superheated engine stalled. The chief engineer, Moon, argued against the design, and he had convinced several board members to oppose production. Lord Forgill, meanwhile, was busy with other projects.

'Low pressure is safe,' Moon said repeatedly. 'This engine would be an expensive mistake.' And his disapproval was so strong that he scarcely spoke to Frederick.

While the board argued, Frederick's primary responsibility continued to be in sales and undertaking site quotations. He spent much of his time travelling between Manchester and London, fitting out mills, giving advice, then taking his place back on the designing floor, engineering improvements to current machines.

In March of the following year, Lord Forgill informed Frederick of a developing market for steam engines in the West Anatolia region of Turkey. A consortium of producers and processors, some with British links, had approached the company for prices and specifications.

'They're growing cotton,' said the great man. 'They need power for the gins and it's worth a visit if you're up for it.'

'I am,' said Frederick. 'When shall I leave?'

'As soon as you can.'

In the dying days of that terrible winter, Frederick decided that he had to find Eleanor before he went. After a weekend of fruitless searching, acting on a report from a river boatman, he found the ailing woman in a dosshouse on High Street, Stepney. These institutions were the worst of all accommodation options – crowded and dirty – all occupants thrown out at ten each morning so a new influx could be admitted, priced at demand.

Eleanor was haggard and drawn, and Frederick surmised that she had been drinking gin for many days without pause. He took her to lunch at a nearby pub, the Old Ship, and watched her devour a steak and kidney pie.

'I've been looking for you everywhere,' he said.

'Buggered why you would – best you leave me to the grog, an' rough mates. When the Reaper wants to blunten his scythe on me leathery old neck 'e knows where I am.'

Frederick planted an elbow on the table and cupped his chin reflectively. 'That's true, no doubt, Eleanor, but I have a problem.'

'Well, I 'ave enough of them to fill a ballroom, I doesn't need yours as well.'

'Please, Eleanor, all I need is your advice.'

She screwed her eyes up suspiciously. 'What advice?'

'I'm going overseas, on a long trip – a couple of months. I'm wondering what might happen when I lock up my house and leave it.'

Eleanor made a sound with her lips, as if to dismiss his fussing, then took a gulp of her cider. 'Well, you might 'ave a few rodents move in – one or two for a start, but they does like to breed. Everythink in London likes to breed, come ter think of it, from the 'ouse mouse to the 'ouse wife.'

'But what else, dear Eleanor? A good little terrace house like mine, when people see the grass grow un-cut, and no candlelight shine through the window at night?'

Eleanor folded her arms, and tilted her head to the side a little, itching at her temple with the stem of her pipe. 'I s'pose it might attract certain low fellows oo like to break through other people's doors an' take things.' She peered at him suspiciously, 'Why are yer asking me all this?'

'There's a loose flagstone on the front path. I'll leave a key under it and tell the neighbours to expect you. Will you go to my place and stay there while I'm away? I'll leave money in a jar in the pantry for you to buy food. Stay there, be safe and healthy – look after everything for me. Perhaps when I come back, you'll live there with me? After all, you're a far better cook than the latest one I've had.'

Eleanor stared back at him, as if she did not understand a word.

'Please, Eleanor, consider my request. I would appreciate it so very much.'

'I'll consider it,' she agreed. 'But no promises Freddie.' Her chin jutted. 'An' don't start thinkin' I'm too dull to know what you're about.' With that she broke down into a short fit of weeping.

★★★

As a boy, Frederick had dreamed of adventure, in a rat-infested home on a street where the sun scarcely shone through the miasma of coal and wood smoke at midday, while hunger pangs gnawed like snakes and the winter cold penetrated to his bones. He had listened to care-worn old seamen telling stories for penny tips at markets, evoking the salt, sand and sun of the South Seas; of beautiful island girls, elephant hunts and the whirling dervish dancers of Arabia.

Now, Frederick discovered that real-life adventures have shades of dark as well as light. In those first weeks he gazed up at the glorious facets of the Rock of Gibraltar, watched a marching line of waterspouts off the coast of Crete, spent nights clutching his belly, stricken by seasickness, and shouted greetings to the occupants of a pleasure boat out of Greece, packed with laughing men and women who seemed happier and more carefree than any human beings he had seen in his life.

With so many lonely hours, he thought far too much about Clare, and he started and abandoned letters to her three times. Sometimes, out on the deck at night, he could almost hear her voice in the sigh of small Mediterranean waves striking the islands or feel her beside him in the narrow bed. When these thoughts became too real, he had to banish her image from his mind, and concentrate on the work still to come.

On the coast of Western Anatolia, the steamer docked at the picturesque port of Smyrna, or Izmir as the Turks preferred to call it. This four-millennia-old port city was the burgeoning textiles-manufacturing centre of the Ottoman Empire, and machinery was at a premium. Traditional animal-powered gins, and the pressing of cotton fibre into bales by human feet, were now being supplanted by steam powered cotton gins, mostly under British ownership.

The harbour was busy with thousands of dhows and ships of all sizes as Frederick gripped the rail, looking out at the imposing Konak Square. The jetty swarmed with porters and cabs drawn by stout donkeys, and within a few minutes of landing Frederick was on his way to the Hotel Kraemer Palace, just back from the broad quay, where thousands of small boats bobbed and swung at anchor.

The hotel seemed to be a popular destination for non-Muslims, with a bar and restaurant on the ground floor. Lord Forgill had written to the British consul before Frederick's arrival, and the concierge handed him a dinner invitation for the following evening.

It was there, at a long dining table with the Consul resplendent at the head, along with his interesting, philanthropic wife and some local movers and shakers that Frederick learned much of what he needed to know about the local cotton industry. Essentially driven by British investors, beginning with cotton-shortages caused by the American Civil War, when the factories of England's north were screaming for fibre, vast areas on the banks of the Hermus and Meander rivers had been planted to cotton.

Between them the British gin-owners employed dozens of brokers who visited villages, advancing money for the presale of entire cotton crops. At harvest time the brokers were on hand to take delivery of the fibre and transport it by wagon and railway car to Smyrna.

Many of the factories were nominally owned by Turkish frontmen, in order to keep the authorities happy and to discourage anti-English feeling. Even then, care had to be taken – one British-owned factory had been burned to the ground by locals for the simple reason that the chimney seemed to them to mock the appearance of a minaret.

The Consul had placed Frederick on his left side, and took every opportunity to whisper asides in Frederick's ear. 'I should tell you, old boy, that between them these fellows at the table run three thousand cotton gins in a hundred odd factories – along with dozens of hydraulic presses. Some of the factories have split roles so their steam engines power cotton gins in season, and flour mills when the wheat harvest comes in.'

'Very clever,' said Frederick, and he was daunted by the fashionable Englishmen at that fine table, where the diners were attended by an army of servants. Yet, when he stood to speak, he fell naturally into his role as an evangelist for Forgill's engines. Numbers and specifications were at his fingertips, and more importantly his passion was contagious.

Those of the group who were planning on expanding, or replacing an existing engine, arranged for Frederick to tour their factory and speak to their on-site engineers.

'Our engines are from Middletons,' said one of the men. 'I've been quite happy with them.'

'Middleton's make fine engines,' agreed Frederick. 'But they are old technology compared to ours.'

The time in Anatolia was not all hard work, however, with invitations to several receptions, dinners and even an opera sung in Turkish by an exotically beautiful soprano. This was Frederick's first experience of this art form and he promised himself that it would not be his last.

Even better, on his last day in the country, Frederick stood at the ancient ruins of Pergamon and felt gooseflesh brush over his arms. In that silent and majestic place, he experienced a moment when life and death seemed to fuse into an inscrutable whole.

This melancholy, deepened by the certainty that he had lost Clare – a woman he could have loved for every breath of his life, lasted until he boarded the ship for home, and for every hour of the journey across the Mediterranean. It grew worse as they rounded the Pillars of Hercules; Abyla and Calpe. From there on, the rearing seas made his appetite diminish and his innards roil.

The feeling lingered until the moment, off the coast of Portugal, when he opened an English newspaper at breakfast, and saw one terrible phrase staring back at him. Melancholy became despair.

Leaving his coffee half drunk, and his kipper uneaten, Frederick left the saloon, and hurried outside, walking to the rail, still carrying the newspaper.

The sea was dark grey, flecked with white. Lines of squalls danced in the offing, and the railings were spattered with rain. Deep in the guts of the ship a forge-hammer steam engine turned the paddle wheel that was driving the ironclad hull home to London.

Frederick opened the paper again, but the words had not changed. They stared back at him with authority.

LORD BARTHOLOMEW FORGILL DEAD AT SIXTY-
EIGHT

Now he continued to read, searching for reasons why it might not be true. The third paragraph disclosed that Lord Forgill had been ill for some time, a fact known only to his family.

Frederick's seasickness, the loneliness of business travel, and the pain of lost love faded into insignificance. The death of Lord Forgill was a tower toppling to the ground, an earthquake leaving his world in ruins. Apart from his personal grief and shock, the ramifications for his life were incalculable.

According to the article, the great man's funeral would be held on the seventeenth, just three days off. Putting all other considerations aside, Frederick decided that attending the service would be his aim. It was something to hold onto in a moment so shocking he could scarcely see past it.

With the newspaper rolled up and gripped hard in his hand Frederick crossed the deck and returned to his cabin. In that storm-tossed enclosure, dark and cold, Frederick became fearful of the future: as afraid as he had been since the hard years of his childhood.

★★★

Many hours, perhaps a hundred, after he had retired to his bunk, the motion of the ship changed and Frederick heard the rap of a steward on the door. 'Dockin' at Soufampton in a quarter hour. Please 'ave your belongings ready.'

With only the thought of the following day's funeral giving him any sense of purpose, Frederick packed up his things and joined the throng on deck in time to watch the steamer come alongside the Queen Victoria Pier in a treacherous following sea, with a backdrop of tumbling black clouds. Steady, cold rain fell as a gang of seamen caught the lines and wound them around the bollards.

Frederick collected his luggage and hurried to the train station, where he attempted to book a seat on the first train back to London.

'No train this afternoon or tonight, sorry,' cried the

stationmaster. 'The line's blocked by a fallen tree near Shapley 'Eath. 'Twill be mid-morning before she gets through.'

With most of the passengers pressing five to a room into local accommodation, Frederick dressed in a jersey and shorts, and charged a luggage clerk with getting his suitcases away on the first train that made it through the next day.

'But sir, 'ow are you getting back to London?'

'I'll walk,' replied Frederick.

'Cripes sir, it's eighty miles!'

'Nevertheless, that's what I intend to do.'

The clerk's eyes remained wide, and an anxious smile tugged at his lips, as if he couldn't wait to tell his fellow staff members about this young Londoner being so anxious to get home that he would walk a ridiculous distance in the rain.

By the time Frederick set off there was a curious crowd arrayed to watch him go, but he was so numbed by the death of his benefactor and mentor that he scarcely noticed them. Lord Forgill was dead, and Percy would take control. Everything Frederick had was at risk. His career. His home. His future.

Leaving Southampton Port, he set off to the north, past hotels and long rows of houses. He walked at a good pace but with no energy; sodden and miserable. Reaching the outskirts of town he began to weep in the freezing rain, his only comfort the strength of his legs.

By the time it grew dark he could feel the wolf walking behind him, but he forced himself not to turn and look. He passed through Winchester in the night, reaching Basingstoke as the moon rose.

Hour after hour, he walked, pursued as he was by that slavering thing: a symbol of the worst of himself and his kind, with no thought or desire to stop or rest. The sun rose and grew higher though he scarcely noticed. By Twickenham he could smell old and familiar London smells, brimming with commingled emotions, including an awareness of the empty terror of his life, of the great vacancy that

Lord Forgill's death had left in him.

★★★

It was mid-afternoon when Frederick crossed the Thames on the Kew Bridge, paying his toll and ignoring the costermongers and beggars. On the other side, he headed towards Kensington, asking strangers for directions to the West London and Westminster Cemetery.

As soon as he passed through the cemetery gates Frederick felt his mood change. There, amongst the resting places of the dead, a sense of timelessness settles most deeply on the psyche; an appreciation of the cycle of birth, life and death.

In full appreciation of this, Frederick's eyes roved over the headstones, almost all of them facing east, positioned to see the second coming of the Lord, inscribed with hundreds of names, dates, ages; stone and concrete spattered with lichens and moss, especially on the more porous of the stones. Older headstones had crumbled and sunken into the earth – and some even more ancient graves lay in deep hollows as if they were being sucked towards Hades.

Lord Forgill's burial service was impossible to miss, hundreds of people standing, wearing hats and glossy coats, while a vicar, from his central position, droned words of solace and ceremony. Frederick had hardly slept in thirty hours, and he had walked eighty miles without eating. Controlling his emotions was not possible.

Tears dripped from his chin and onto his shirtfront as he approached. The rearmost rows of standing mourners parted as he shuffled through towards the front rank. A sob broke from his throat when he saw the coffin, with its gold fittings and polished timber face. It sat beside a hole in the black soil, square sided and seemingly as deep as hell itself. Again, Frederick could not prevent a catch of breath and a low moan.

The vicar stopped speaking, and a hum of disapproval ran through the crowd. Percy Forgill left the family group, closest to the vicar, and walked towards the interloper. With a wink and twist of his head he summoned two young men from the crowd, and they moved to their master's flanks.

'Get him out of here,' Percy hissed. They grabbed an arm each and began to drag Frederick away. At a distance of fifty yards they dropped him to the ground. Percy, who had trailed them all the way, stared down at Frederick with pitiless eyes. 'First off you were obviously misguided enough to think that you would be welcome at Father's funeral, but to come here dressed like a schoolboy at a football game and make an exhibition of yourself? Disgusting behaviour.'

Frederick saw that Sophie Forgill had left the group and was standing halfway from the graveside crowd to her brother. 'Just leave him,' she called out. 'He's not worth bothering about.'

Frederick stared at Percy. 'You didn't even love your own father.'

'That's none of your business,' said Percy. 'But I want you to understand something. I am now Lord Forgill. I am taking control of my father's real estate interests and the factory. You'd better start looking for new employment – and most of the members of the Steam Manufacturers Association are standing over there – I doubt they'll think very highly of you after this display. Don't go crawling to them for work.'

Frederick stared. He had expected Percy to wreak havoc on his life but hearing it in words was painful beyond bearing – the dreams of all those years, snatched away.

'You will also need to find somewhere else to live,' continued Percy, 'since you are currently occupying a house that belongs to me. You have until nine on Monday morning to get out. Do you understand?'

Frederick, cringing as if under fire from a shower of stones, had risen to his aching legs and already shuffling away.

'It's only fitting, don't you think Morton?' Percy called after him.

'That you are leaving now, the way my father found you, with nothing. You can go back to digging around on the riverbank for toothbrushes and nails, living in the slums where you belong.'

★★★

Frederick walked on as far as Covent Garden, before grief and fear of the future built to a level that he could not control. His life was unravelling. How had he ever thought that he was good enough to go to a fine school, or to be an engineer at all? It was as if Percy Forgill had exposed him for the fraud he was.

Wandering, he passed the welcoming doors of the Lamb and Flag. Frederick had never been much of a drinker, but he knew well enough how efficiently liquor can take one's troubles away. Invariably they come back redoubled the following day, but the process, as every good drunk knows, can easily be repeated.

Taking a stool, Frederick caught the attention of a barmaid in a burgundy dress and white bonnet, with showy, puffed sleeves and a gold-toothed smile.

"Allo there love,' she said. 'What'll it be?'

Frederick started with a stemmed glass full of Gordon's best gin and a ceramic pint mug of dark ale to chase it down.

Six hours later he passed out on the northern bank of the river, the fires and sparks of the factory chimneys on the far side glowing on the surface of the river like a reflection of Armageddon.

He woke in light rain. Somewhere, behind the city, there was a new dawn. The sunrise itself was not visible here. There was just a gradual increase in light.

Frederick tried to spit the taste of drink out of his mouth, then felt in his pockets. His pocketbook was gone, and he had a raw graze on his shoulder where someone or something had struck him.

Without money for train fare, Frederick had no choice but to walk on aching legs in fitful rain, east towards Aldgate. It was only a few miles but it seemed like many more. No one looked at him, or paid him any mind as he walked. The weather, at least, had improved, but he was now very hungry, the smell of roasted chestnuts from street barrows not helping.

It was mid-morning when Frederick staggered down Leadenhall Street and into his home suburb. The rain had moved on now, revealing a pale sky, but even the change of weather could not lift the feeling of doom that pervaded his consciousness.

Opening his gate, Frederick caught the scent of strangeness. The front door of his house was wide open, and it took a moment for him to realise that Eleanor must have taken up his offer to stay in the house. If not, had it been burgled?

With these thoughts competing for space in his head, he walked the three steps to the landing and inside. From the kitchen he saw that the door to the back yard was also open, and he walked through to the paved area outside.

He heard singing, and to his surprise a very small child appeared on the path. She was just a toddler, still unsteady in tiny blue buckle-up shoes. She had curly blonde hair tied with ribbons. Her hands and cheeks looked grubby, but her eyes were a sapphiric shade of blue. When the child saw him, she retreated back around the wall.

Frederick was so surprised that he at first rationalised the little girl as a neighbour's child who had strayed into his yard. He followed her, just as the sun poured forth a golden ray of light.

Sitting in chairs at the cast-iron table in the middle of the yard were two women. One was Eleanor, looking much healthier than she had been the last time they met.

The other woman was, to Frederick's eyes, as beautiful as the image he held in his memory. He watched her take the toddler in her arms, pausing in the act of kissing the crown of her head to look around for the newcomer.

Yet still Frederick's mind could not make the jump from then to now. The things he was seeing were not possible, yet here they were in front of his eyes.

'Clare? Is it you?'

'Of course it's me, *cheri*,' she said. 'You have finally decided to come home.'

The little girl disentangled herself, then took a couple of unsteady steps towards Frederick, staring up at him, curiosity overcoming caution.

Clare came to her feet, and walked forward to take her daughter's hand, squatting beside her. '*Regardez*, May. This beautiful man is your papa.' Then to Frederick. 'You look different – tanned, and sad.'

Frederick moved back and sat down on the step, taking deep breaths, mouth open. This silence, the time required to take in the facts of this beguiling young creature's existence, to process this new information in the cogs and gears of his engineer's mind, seemed to stretch on eternally.

Ah those tides, and how they change. This, however, was not a reversal of the flow, but a doubling of the river's strength, the current reaching; filling him; eddying; steadying; carrying all before it. A life event as pivotal as death – the day in which a man or woman becomes responsible for the life of their offspring.

The force of the realisation was so strong that Frederick sagged as if under a new weight, now at eye level with the child walking towards him, hand in hand with her mother. He said to May: 'Please forgive me, for being so confused. You see, I didn't know I had a daughter until just this moment.'

Eleanor called out from her chair, 'I told them you'd be back, Freddie,' she said, 'an' that you never forgets those oo are strong in your life. A kind gentleman, you are, and I'm gladder than words can say to see yer face again.'

BOOK TWO

Chapter Thirteen

The day of Clare's arrival, with Frederick's own daughter, he would later remember as the most intense and joyous of his life. Yet, there was still much to know, and a new sense of responsibility made him earnest. That first evening he asked few questions, and Clare waited until May was asleep and they were alone in the drawing room before she gave him any explanation at all.

'Charles cheated, *cheri*, in the pedestrian race. Can you believe that he rode on the wagon in the middle of the night instead of walking on his own two feet? Is that not the most despicable form of cheating possible?'

'He rode in the wagon?' Frederick said, incredulous, for the idea had not occurred to him. 'How do you know?'

'One of his so-called friends was very drunk one night and he told me everything. It was like he was proud of it – wanted me to think they were so very clever.'

'You cancelled your wedding because Charles beat me unfairly in a pedestrian race?'

'Yes, but also because I was pregnant with your child and I told him so. He called me a slut and a whore, slapped me across the face with his gloves as if I were a man who had insulted him at one of their silly barracks dinners.' She lowered her voice. 'He went to see my father and made a scene – my mother weeping and complaining of how her reputation was ruined – of how she would have to write to three hundred wedding guests and admit my infidelity.' Clare pretended to fan her face, and mimicked her mother's voice, '"Oh the shame. It will kill me. You must go to a doctor who can take care of such things. Surely you can do that for the sake of your future and the family name?"'

Clare's eyes were like stones as she went on. 'Words passed between us. Words that cannot be taken back. I left with nothing but a suitcase and my father's shouts ringing in my ears.' She raised a hand. 'Don't fret. My parents and I are in contact, and they know where I am. They want me to come home and discuss the situation again but I am not ready to forgive them just yet. I have a small annuity of my own, from my grandmother, so I am not destitute. I gave birth to May in Paris, but it was lonely there. I missed you and came to find you. Kind Eleanor was here and allowed me to stay.'

That first night a new strangeness infused their relationship, and Clare slept in the room she had been sharing with May. The romantic connection between Frederick and the Frenchwoman needed to be reconstructed brick by brick. More importantly, he needed to find new accommodation. There were too many imponderables. Diving back into the pleasures of their Paris love affair was not possible. Not yet.

Before retiring, Frederick kissed his daughter on her forehead and stroked her soft hair.

Then, after six hours of deep slumber he rose and woke Eleanor, who slept in a small, former maid's room upstairs.

'I need your help,' he said.

★★★

By eight in the morning they had most of Frederick's belongings out the front of the terrace, sitting in a pile, some in trunks and some not. He had also whistled up a neighbour's lad, and sent him to the nearby carrier firm of Wright, Dowling and Henderson, asking for a wagon and driver on an hourly rate.

'I can't believe that you arrived home yesterday and now we have to move,' said Clare, after he had explained the situation.

'It's not what I had hoped for,' said Frederick. 'I couldn't say anything last night – I was worried that I might frighten you away.'

'Where will we go?' she asked, lifting May onto her lap.

'Leave it to me,' he said. But in truth, he didn't have a clue.

A little before nine, a group of four men marched down the street from Aldgate Station. Wilkins, the very thin man, led the way, his long fox-fur coat flapping around his knees. This distinctive-looking character slowed, consulted a sheet of paper on a clipboard, then came to the door and knocked.

It was not a grey morning, Frederick saw as he opened the door, but a white one, with fog hanging between the rows of houses. This backdrop gave the malignant figures on the step an eerie presence. Studying the man on the stoop, Frederick dredged up a memory of a long-ago street in disarray, and a cruel man with a stick, and very long, bony limbs.

'It's a long time since I saw you last,' said Frederick, 'and my memories of the day are unpleasant.'

Wilkins ignored him, 'Do you have the place cleared an' a key for me?'

'Not quite yet.'

'If you can't do this yourself, then our instructions are simple: we will do it for you.' Wilkins held the clipboard up so Frederick could read it. 'This is an eviction order. Read it all you like, but the gist is that you must vacate this premise by nine o'clock. I also 'ave an official notice of termination of yer employment with Forgill's.' He took out his fob watch and dangled it close to Frederick's eyes. 'We intend to remove you an' your possessions, take your key an' lock the doors behind you.'

Frederick hurried inside, ahead of Percy Forgill's men, trying to control the desperation he felt. The wagon had not yet arrived. Until now the dreadful reality of being forced from his home had not fully dawned on him. Percy Forgill must have his house, thought Frederick miserably. He must visit more humiliation upon the boy he had once dismissed as a goblin from the slums.

The packing-up of the house was almost finished when the bells of the Church of St George tolled nine chimes, and Frederick walked down the steps to watch, while Wilkins ticked off the condition of every item of furniture that belonged to Forgill's and must remain with the house. This included the dining room table, desks, and some chairs.

Everything else they carried out to join the growing pile, while a crowd from the terraces, most of them the families of Frederick's former co-workers, gathered on the footpath to watch it happen. This was not merely embarrassing; it was public evisceration. To these others, it was also a lesson from the new regime.

'There is one last thing,' declared Wilkins. 'Lord Percy Forgill demands that you surrender to myself any designs or blueprints of an industrial nature you may've made during your time working at the factory. Do you 'ave any such things?'

Frederick said, 'No, I do not. My work was done at the factory.'

'Are you certain? The new Lord Forgill was very insistent on this point.'

'I'm certain. Now leave me in peace.'

Wilkins demanded the key and locked the house behind him, before walking away down the street with his assistants. When they had gone, Frederick stood in a forlorn huddle with Clare, Eleanor and May. The fog had cleared a little, but it was impossible to tell where the mist ended and the sky began, and the cold numbed the fingers.

Frederick took out his watch and studied it. The wagon was supposed to be here at nine, yet, in daylight hours, London's streets were jam-packed with carriages, horse traffic, barrows and more, and nothing reliant on London traffic ever quite ran on time.

Holding his daughter in his arms, Frederick wavered between numbing embarrassment and outright fear at what on earth he might do now. He knew that Wright, Dowling and Henderson, the owners of the wagon he had ordered, offered warehouse space for hire, and they would store his things. This would be their initial destination, but after that, he wasn't sure. Without employment, even a cheap hotel, for all four of them, would quickly stretch his savings.

These thoughts filled his mind until just before ten, when the wagon arrived, drawn by four stout shire horses. The driver and his mate, both strapping men, loaded up the tray, piling Frederick's trunks and furniture high, tying them down with hemp ropes and hitches while Eleanor stood on the wagon edge with her hands on her hips, and May grizzled in Clare's arms.

'Look after them things, you oafs,' snapped Eleanor. 'There must be nothin' scratched or you'll 'ave me to deal with.' Having delivered this warning she procured herself a seat on the box, presumably so as to keep an eye on proceedings.

While the load was readied for travel, the postman arrived, looking confused at the sight of the householder and his possessions on a wagon out in the street. Frederick whistled to him, 'Hi, Tom, anything for me?'

The postman looked with surprise then hurried across. 'What's 'appened, Freddie, where are you going?'

'Somewhere new. With Lord Forgill having passed away, I'm no longer part of the company.'

'Oh, I'm sorry to 'ear that. Do you 'ave a forwarding address?'

'Not yet, but when I do, I'll make sure to let Her Majesty's Mail know.'

'Very well, best of luck. And 'ere, there is one small package for you.'

'Are we reaadee?' boomed the driver.

'Just a minute,' called Frederick, while the postman handed

across a thick letter. It felt like there was at least one folded paper and something hard inside. With this in hand, Frederick settled down in the back of the cart with Clare beside him and May on her lap.

'Ready when you are,' he yelled.

With a word from the driver, the wagon eased into motion, soon finding a steady pace, with a squeak in the offside wheel synchronising with the clop of the horses' hooves.

The heels of Frederick's black shoes skimmed a few inches above the street, and he felt better, being on the move. He did not open the envelope, but looked back at the terrace that had been his home these last five or six years, while the wheels turned and the cart rolled onwards.

'I no longer have a job,' he said to Clare.

'That's their loss,' she said. 'There'll be other jobs. Now, are you going to open that letter?'

Once they had turned the corner he prised open the flap on the envelope, scarcely breathing as he recognised the name atop the return address. The realisation that the letter was from a dead man – the departed Lord Forgill – gave him a chill. It seemed that the letter had taken some days to be delivered. Someone must have despatched it *post mortem*. But why?

Frederick held his breath as he read, straight through from beginning to end. For a minute or two he sat in stunned silence, absorbing the contents of the ever-so-important missive. Finished, he delved into the envelope again, removing a pair of brass keys, aged and scratched, full of symbolism and possibility.

Clare watched him guardedly as he half stood on the trunk, leaning on the iron leg of his upside-down drafting desk, looking ahead to the four muscular horses and the busy streets as they manoeuvred westwards.

'Ahoy driver,' he called.

'Yes guv?'

'I have a new destination for you.'

'An' where might that be?' asked the driver.

'Across the river and down to Lewisham.'

'It'll cost you a shilling extra.'

'Then so be it,' said Frederick. 'Let it cost one more shilling.'

Sitting back down, he read the letter again, then folded it into the envelope. The pair of keys he held for some time, running his fingers over them, before secreting them deep in his side pocket.

'What's happened?' asked Clare. 'Who is the letter from and what does it mean to us?'

'It's from a very kind man, who I had the great fortune to know.' Frederick passed the paper to her, and watched her read the words, smile and grip his hand hard in hers. Closing his eyes, head lolling with the movement of the cart, he thanked the man who had loomed over his life like a God, while his daughter clambered from her mother's lap to his.

Before long the wagon trundled onto the crowded approaches of the Tower Bridge. Frederick looked up at the Tower of London on the right, and St Katharine's docks on the left, giving way to warehouses and the Irongate Wharf.

The sights and sounds of this route gave Frederick pleasure, and as the wagon crossed the bridge, he heard the costermongers calling, with the smells of cooking meats wafting up from stalls and barrows. It was low tide, and down on the river he could see exposed banks and the mudlarks at work, scrabbling for cast-off items worth the price of a meal.

As the wheels met the stony street surface on the other side of the bridge, they passed the Horselydown stairs and more warehouses back from the river. The traffic thinned as they crossed the network of tracks on the Southeast London Railway, and turned onto Old Kent Road.

Frederick stood up on one of the trunks so he could peer ahead now, also calling out to the driver with their precise destination. They were getting close. And now at least, they had somewhere to go.

Finally, deep into the afternoon, the wagon rolled into Lewisham. Frederick inhaled the scent of a new way of life. The air was clearer here, with a country tang that was more than just the appearance of a few fields.

The people they passed looked purposeful and friendly, and the gardens neatly kept. High Street was crowded with shops, a police station and the impressive Saint Mary the Virgin church, with its fortress-like tower and huddled trees sheltering a yard filled with grey headstones.

Further on a few blocks, past alms houses and a union workhouse, the driver turned to the right. Masons looked up from their hammers, and children stopped playing with their home-sewn dolls and wooden swords to stare at the man, two women and a child so rudely arrayed on the wagon with all their possessions.

Finally, down another side-street, the wagon driver cried 'Hup, whoa,' and the team came to a halt outside an iron gate. Frederick peered through at the knee-high grass and a residence beyond. It was a two-storey place with twin gables, whitewashed walls, gothic windows, and a fine brick chimney. Frederick had never in his life seen anything so unkempt yet full of promise.

As if to again confirm the truth of what now lay before his eyes, Frederick looked down at the letter he held open in his hand.

My Dear Frederick

When you read this, I will no longer dwell in this world. My physicians try to reassure me, but I can see in their eyes and hear enough of their whispers to know that the end is nigh. I am sorry to have kept my illness from you, but there are many vultures in the world of finance, and I had much to do before word leaked out.

I wish that you and my Percy could be allies in the years ahead. Yet I know in my heart what species of men you are. I am bound by the law of the land which compels me to leave my title and wealth to my son.

I know Percy will take from you much of what I bestowed,

and I have one last gift for you. It is a house, at 5 Poplar Street, Lewisham. It once belonged to one of my uncles, and it has fallen into disrepair. Yet, it is a good-sized abode and was solidly built. I give it to you unreservedly (my lawyers, Dykes and Summers, who will post this letter, will also have the deeds ready for you to collect). It is the least I can do for a young man who has given me as much in return as you have.

My legal advice is that this transaction is best done in this way – quite separately to my will, which could be contested. My lawyers assure me that there are no legal grounds for anyone to oppose a gift freely made, so you may move in with confidence.

From the day I first met you, I believed not only in your talent, but in your intrinsic goodness. I sense that you will one day do great things as an engineer, and come to make a difference to the world. Circumstances may conspire against you and make that difficult, but now you have a start.

Finally, I will rest easy in my heart to know that certain matters we agreed would remain a secret will continue to be so. I have trusted you for all these years and I continue to do so.

May your life be long, and full of joy.

Farewell

Bartholomew Forgill

Frederick folded the letter into his pocket and hopped down from the wagon. He used one of the two keys from the envelope on the Yale padlock. The mechanism was rusted, and he needed all the strength in his fingers to twist the key and pull the hasp. The hinges were also unwilling to move at first, and he had to heave open the gate, dragging it through the gravel of the drive.

Waving the wagon onwards, Frederick walked along behind, staring in wonder at the three stately elms on either side of the drive, then the house itself. For a moment he felt as if the edifice was a mirage that might soon disappear, but as the wagon came to a halt in the gravelled space near the front door, he accepted that it was a real, bricks and mortar house, and it belonged to him.

While the wagoners looked to a hand-pump out the back to

water the horses, Frederick approached the front door, itself a handsome construction of timber and etched glass. After a moment's worry that the key would not fit, he unlocked the door and walked inside, finding himself within a well-lit and commodious entry space, tiled in black and white. There were arched entry-ways to left and right, and a staircase directly ahead.

Clare came up beside Frederick, and he accepted May from her arms. Eleanor was still hanging back, and he waved her onwards.

'This place is yours now?' asked Clare.

'Yes. Ours, not mine.'

'It needs some work, but is it not beautiful?'

Walking to the right they found a parlour, the fireplace yawning dark and empty. Back the other way was a room that must surely be an office, then a dining room, and a kitchen and pantry. Their exploration of the lower floor complete, the staircase drew the little family upwards. This was itself an impressive feature, sweeping up towards a stained-glass window, then curving left to the upper floor, the bannisters carved into writhing serpents, supported by similarly decorated poles, and a crimson *fleur-de-lis* carpet fixed to each step with brass rods.

At the top was a long corridor, and a row of doors. The rooms, revealed one by one, showed signs of long vacancy – spider webs on the window frames, and dust gritty beneath his leather soles. The master bedroom was at the end of the row, a spacious area full of light and old love.

'Oh my,' said Clare. 'This place is a treasure.'

Finally, back downstairs, the wagon driver gave Frederick an impatient look. It was time to unload, a process that took close to an hour, partly due to the staircase, the wagoners sweating and puffing as they manoeuvred Frederick's belongings inside.

When everything had been placed in roughly the correct room, and the wagon had moved off, Frederick stood at the foot of the stairs, staring at a six-foot-tall floor clock that filled an alcove on the left – a masterpiece of design and function. The main face showed the time, and four smaller ones the date, month, moon phase, and best of all the tides at Greenwich Pier.

Frederick placed the key in the mechanism, wound the clock, and set the time and date. The pendulum began to swing, then the hand to tick, surprisingly loudly, the metallic sound echoing from the plaster walls. He could see in his mind the precision of its movement; the cogs and gears that made it function. It was fascinating, brilliant, and quite the most amazing thing about the entire house.

★★★

After an evening spent with Clare on the sofa, talking about the possibilities of a new life here, Frederick retired to his room alone. On his knees beside the bed, he said a long prayer of gratitude to his maker for the unimaginable gifts of the day. But then, in a silent whisper, he thanked the departed soul of Lord Forgill even more. This new house, Frederick decided, would be their Pemberley, and their Thornfield Hall. It was nowhere near as grand, nor as large as either, but it was an unimaginably fine place to live for a lad who grew up in a slum.

Even as he drifted off to sleep the house creaked and groaned as it cooled. The clock ticked audibly from the alcove. Frederick imagined that the house was speaking to him, welcoming him, and this thought comforted him through the first night, while the moon shone benevolently through his window from outside.

Chapter Fourteen

Frederick stirred before dawn, waking with a sense of wonder and burgeoning delight. He took his robe from the cupboard, slipped it around his shoulders, then walked down the corridor to May's room. Opening the door, he stood watching her small body, curled in sleep.

Two days earlier he had felt surprised and overwhelmed. Now he was exhilarated. He studied May's closed eyes, the plumpness of her cheeks, and the tousled beauty of her hair. At length he closed the door, walked downstairs and made tea before dressing. Glancing at the time on the clock as he went, he hurried outside, walking at a fast clip towards High Street.

The jeweller's shop was at number forty-three, beside an emporium. A CLOSED sign, calligraphed in blue ink, sat in the window. Frederick looked up, above the shop to where the family lived. The curtains were drawn and there were no sounds from inside.

Frederick knocked on the door, and after some delay a voice announced from the other side, 'I'm sorry sir, but the shop is closed. We open at ten o'clock.'

'I need help with a ring – it's an emergency.'

The sound of a key in a lock followed, and an elderly jeweller in his dressing gown appeared at the door. 'This is the first time I've heard the word emergency in relation to marriage from a man who isn't standing out here with a shotgun and pregnant daughter. Do you have cash to pay?'

'Yes, I do.'

The jeweller led Frederick into the store, pausing to open the curtains, endowing the room with light. The morning rays struck gold, silver, and diamonds, sending beams of colour to play on the walls and ceiling.

In ten minutes flat Frederick chose a gold band, set with a beautiful but not ostentatious diamond, not caring one whit about the damage to his savings. This was life, far more important than money. He hailed a hansom cab, scarcely able to control his impatience as it carried him down into Ladywell and towards the house.

'Would you wait here, please?' he asked the driver. Then, as an afterthought, 'May I borrow your pocketknife?'

With this implement in hand, he walked to the overgrown rose garden, past the beds of primroses, violets and daisies. Then, mindful of the thorns, he trimmed off half a dozen classic red roses, then interspersed them with pink John Hopper blooms.

Then, taking the knife back to the driver, he walked in the front door, where he found Clare and May in the process of walking out to meet him. Frederick fell to his knees in the threshold, almost at Clare's feet. This seemed to May to be a delightful game, and she clapped her hands and beamed.

After a pause to kiss his daughter on the forehead, Frederick looked up at Clare. 'I was wondering,' he said, 'if you would do me the honour of marrying me?'

Clare took the roses, lifting them to her nose, while Frederick fumbled with his free hand and withdrew the ring and its diamond. It was the first time he had seen the young Frenchwoman cry, a fact that only deepened May's appreciation of the moment.

Clare stared at the ring. 'You really want to marry me?' she asked.

'You're not taking pity on a poor unwed mother from the French Provinces?'

'I do, yes, and no I'm not. Now! This minute! I have a cab waiting so we can go and see the Vicar. What's your answer?'

'My answer is yes,' she said.

Frederick took Clare in his arms and kissed her on the lips, with May an interested participant in the huddle. Eleanor arrived at the door from the kitchen.

'Eleanor,' said Frederick. 'I've asked Clare to marry me.'

'Then at least you 'as not totally lost yer wits,' she said.

'We're going to see the Vicar now. Will you look after May while we're gone?'

May, however, was intelligent enough to know when something pivotal was going on. She clung to her mother's leg and refused to budge.

'Let her come,' said Frederick. 'This is important to her too, and it's best that we are honest about our situation to the Vicar.'

It seemed logical for Eleanor to come along also, in case they needed a witness, so all four of them took seats in the cab. At the church they found the Vicar talking to a couple of parishioners just outside the Priory Farm. He caught Frederick's eye, indicating with a nod and wave of his arm that they should wait.

Eleanor walked with the little girl in the graveyard, under the shadowy trees, while Frederick clutched Clare's hand as if with the sinews of his heart. Finally, the Vicar was free, and Frederick hurried forward to introduce himself.

'Hello, my name is Frederick Morton, and I have just moved here to Lewisham. This is my fiancée, Clare.'

'Indeed,' said the Vicar. 'Now let me guess. You would like to get married?'

'That's correct.'

He looked across at the little girl and her minder, then addressed Clare. 'And I take it that this little treasure is yours?'

'Yes, she is ours,' said Frederick.

'Can you tell me the circumstances please?'

Frederick summarised their affair, and the long separation that followed. He was emphatic about their commitment to be with each other.

'All very understandable. Such things do happen. When would you like the happy event to take place?'

'Now?' asked Clare, taking May in her arms, while Eleanor hung back, listening to every word.

'That's not possible I'm afraid,' said the Vicar, smiling. 'In most circumstances I would read the marriage banns for three Sundays prior to the wedding.'

Frederick could not hide his disappointment. 'I don't think we can wait that long, Father.'

'We do provide for more precipitous weddings. Such a marriage requires a special licence from the Bishop.'

'Is that hard to get?' Frederick asked. 'I mean ... can we get married tomorrow?'

The Vicar patted May on the head. 'It won't be difficult to get a special licence in a case such as this, but tomorrow is too soon. We can read the banns after the night service tomorrow evening, and again on Thursday. Then, if I can satisfy myself that you are both free to marry, and of proper Christian purpose, I could send a messenger to the Bishop. Saturday is the earliest possible date – I do have another wedding at eleven am, but I can squeeze you in early if it all works out.'

Frederick took Clare's hand. 'Saturday would be wonderful.'

There was humour in the Vicar's eyes when he said, 'The fee is normally five guineas, but urgency costs a little more. Seven guineas.'

Frederick reached for his pocketbook, and when the fee was paid they walked back to the cab, holding hands and swinging arms like schoolchildren.

Frederick suspected that, sooner or later, Percy Forgill would learn of his father's gift and respond with characteristic spite. He listened, now and then, for the sounds of horses or men on the street and at intervals watched through gaps between the curtains.

For most of the morning he hefted the scythe that he had found in an outhouse in the back yard. After a few minutes with a file, the blade sheared hairs from the back of his forearm as cleanly as a straight razor, and the implement proved to be efficacious against the nearest stand of mixed sedges, brome and grasses. Frederick loved to move his body and apply his muscles. The mechanics came easily to him, and before long he felt that he had the motion right.

When the lawns were tidy, Frederick dusted the old shelves in the downstairs room that would be his office, and there he set up his drafting table. He also found a small office desk in the old butler's room. It was plain, but stout, and he cleaned it fastidiously.

With more thought than speed, Frederick began to go through his boxes, placing items on the shelves. He had never dreamed of having so much space for his books – some had been stored after their initial reading. Most were scholarly works on engineering and design. Yet, there was also Dickens, Austen, Thackeray and Defoe, as well as his old school texts.

Frederick hated to forget a skill. At least once a week he liked to read a few pages of Latin, translating in his head as he went, imagining how his old masters at the Charterhouse would appreciate the crisp English rendition.

Books were not the only items competing for shelf space. There were also iron, brass and steel engine parts along with several sets of scales. The wooden box containing his working model of a steam engine – that pivotal gift from Lord Forgill – went inside a glass-fronted case.

When he had finished, Frederick moved to the desk, placing a sheet of notepaper on the surface. At the top, in pencil, he wrote the heading: Potential Employers.

There were several contenders. It was important that they be London-based. He had no idea whether any or all were hiring at the present time or not, but he needed work. Owning a house was one thing, running one was another.

There were a few specialist stationary steam engine manufacturers in and around London: Forgill's, Willans and Robinson down in Surrey, and Maudslays in Lambeth, though the latter had diversified into marine engines. Higginbottom's were a small company, makers of traditional beam engines.

The industry-leading James Watt and Company, orphan child of the illustrious Boulton and Watt, had an office in London, mainly as engineering consultants, but the factory was up at Smethwick, near Birmingham. The biggest players were located in the northern industrial cities: Hargraves, Robeys, Clayton, William Fairbairn and Sons, Galloways, B. Hick and Sons, and dozens of others.

Frederick sighed to himself. There was little point in taking possession of a house then moving two hundred miles away for work. That left just three local firms, four counting the unlikely possibility of James Watt taking him on as a consulting engineer in London.

He tailored his letters of introduction to each company, knowing their specialties and requirements. In two of the four cases he underlined his previous dealings with the company, involvement in trade fairs and industry conferences. It wasn't much, admittedly, but his list of professional experience looked brief in dashed sentences at the bottom – after ten years in the profession he'd worked for only one employer.

By the middle of the afternoon Frederick had written notes to James Watt, Maudsleys, Higginbottom's, and Willans and Robinson. In each, he requested consideration for any employment opportunities that might be available and asked for an appointment in which to press his case in person at the earliest convenience.

Clare did not just clean the house, she took control, declared cobwebs, dust, and grime to be the enemy, and with Eleanor's assistance went into battle on multiple fronts. The young Frenchwoman sang as she worked, and the clear tone of her voice filled the empty rooms and brought warmth to the house.

When the sun went down, the last glow shining through clean windows onto waxed boards, Frederick treated his little family to supper at the Joiner's Arms. Upon their arrival, the landlord gave him a quick briefing on the available beers. 'We brew a dark ale, a golden ale, an India pale and a sorghum beer – the latter is very much an acquired taste I might add.'

'I'll start with the Pale,' Frederick said, then moved his gaze to Clare.

'A sloe gin if you please,' she said.

'Eleanor?'

'Just a small cider for me,' she said, with a guilty glance at Frederick. She had, apparently, foresworn hard grog.

Having fetched the drinks from the bar, they sat in booth seats with sticky tables and ordered sausages stuffed with bacon and steamed cod, while the barmaid, a young woman with a round middle and a smile to match, joked with the regulars.

Frederick raised his glass, 'Here's to a new home and we who dwell in her.'

Eleanor started to cry, and May looked at her curiously, but before they could ask what was wrong the tears stopped. Then the food arrived. By the time they had finished eating Eleanor had a twinkle in her eye and had returned to her role of raconteur.

"Ave I ever told you about the time an 'andsome young bloke – Ned Easil were 'is name – took me to the Strand Theatre – a private box an' all – and oo should be in the very box next door, but Prince Bertie an' a beautiful young lass ...?'

The trio walked home after the meal, May riding on Frederick's shoulders. He was in a different state than he had been a few days earlier, merry from the ale and content with the bloom of a new kind of love.

Later, when Eleanor and May were both in bed, Frederick told Clare about Juliet, beginning with the few times he had seen her, in the slums around Limehouse, in her mother's arms, and as a small girl.

'We have to do something to help,' said Clare, her eyes creased with worry.

'At this stage, Eleanor doesn't want us to,' said Frederick, 'but I agree. It's a terrible sadness for her, whatever happened.'

★★★

The following morning, a sound woke Frederick at dawn, though at first he did not recognise it as something unwelcome. In Aldgate the predawn had been noisy with the sounds of night-carters, dogs, and babes crying. Lewisham was a quiet place. The tick of the clock downstairs was audible, but apart from that there was only the odd creak of the building coping with the morning chill.

When he heard the soft bray of a horse out on the street, the roll of a wheel on the gravel, and the click of a gate, Frederick felt the hairs on his arms and scalp stand erect and prickle against the sheets. Then, something else, a man's voice, out the front of the house, rising and falling in a monologue. Frederick pulled on trousers and a jacket and hurried downstairs.

Eleanor was already out of bed, still in her dressing gown, watching through a lower storey window. Frederick stood beside her and looked outside, where a pearl-shell fog was rolling off the Quaggy, closing in the unkempt garden, like one of those toy landscapes that exist within a glass sphere.

There was a man out on the drive, strolling back and forth on the gravel. He wore a top hat and fine clothes, yet he was dishevelled, as if he had been up all night. In one hand he held a gentleman's drinking flask. In the other was a brass-headed cane.

'Oo is he?' asked Eleanor.

'It's Percy Forgill, and he is unwelcome. You stay here.' Frederick walked to the front door, opening it and heading outside into the cool air, where the interloper turned and fixed his eyes on him.

'So it's true,' said Percy Forgill, spitting out his words with a drunken overworking of each syllable. 'My dear departed father left you a house, and you have the effrontery ... the sheer bloody effrontery to think you can keep it.'

There was movement at the carriage out the front, and two young men – youths, really – climbed out through the doors, coming to stand just inside the gate. One had a pistol in his belt, but his smirk, to Frederick, was more dangerous than the gun.

Frederick recognised the pair from Lord Forgill's funeral, when they had manhandled him away from the grave. This was different now, he had a home, a wife, and a child to protect. He subdued the stretched-tight fear in his gut and walked closer to Percy, stopping at a distance of a few paces. 'You are correct in only one thing. This is now my property, and I want you to leave.'

'Damn you, Freddie Morton. I have every right to be here.'

Frederick felt his own anger rise. 'Leave me, and my family, alone.'

'Family?' mumbled Percy. 'I heard about your French slut and the old bitch ...'

Frederick's fist was balled as hard as bone, and he cocked his arm, ready to throw a punch. At the last moment he controlled himself, not launching the blow, but instead pushing at the other man's sternum with the flat of both hands, knocking him down onto his rear end.

Rolling himself up onto his knees Percy let out a grunt and his face turned a pale shade. The two young men from the coach stepped forward, helping their fallen lord to his feet and flanking him. The one with the smirk drew his pistol and pointed it in Frederick's direction.

'You'll pay for that,' Percy said.

Frederick had not yet spent his surge of defiance. He was tired of a lifetime of Percy's lashing out. 'If you come here again, I'll inform the police.'

Percy stared at Frederick, moving his lips as if swishing something unpleasant around in his mouth. 'Back to the carriage,' he said to his boys, and when they did so he followed, his eyes never leaving Frederick, muttering in his drunken fussy manner into the fog that came to fullness with the dawn.

At the last moment, Percy, one hand on the rear door of his vehicle, pointed his finger at Frederick, before the carriage launched into motion and moved off down the road.

When Frederick reached the house, Clare was also downstairs. 'Who was that horrible drunken man? And those others, they appeared to be thugs.'

'He was my former employer,' Frederick said.

'Why did you push him?'

'Because he had no right to be here, and he's a bully. He's always been a bully.'

'There's more to it than that, surely?'

Frederick sighed, 'Yes, of course there is.'

★★★

Eleanor made tea, and they sat at the kitchen table, while Frederick told Clare everything that had happened, starting with the night in the Park Lane house all those years ago. 'I don't know who it was on the ground at the foot of the stairs,' he said. 'Perhaps it was Sophie, I just don't know. Vic Jones at the factory says that Percy had a twin, but I've heard other things too, some or none of which may be true.'

'There would be a record, if something serious happened,' Clare said. 'I could try the Times office – read the old newspapers.'

'No.'

'Why not?'

'Because I promised Lord Forgill that I would not tell. And … it's not important.'

Clare draped her left arm around his shoulders. 'Dear Frederick. We have just had armed and angry men here on our doorstep at dawn. That makes the situation important, does it not?'

Frederick hesitated at first, then, 'You're right. It does.' Yet still he did not want to break his promise.

Chapter Fifteen

In Wednesday afternoon's mail, Frederick received the first return letter from his initial round of job applications. Surprisingly, it was from the company he had considered to be the least likely to respond.

Sidney Risecroft, of James Watt and Company, requested that Frederick attend the company offices in Bond Street the following day at ten in the morning. It was a good start, and he enjoyed rising and dressing as if for work – mornings had always exerted a powerful pull on Frederick. It seemed ridiculous to be sitting around the house in a dressing gown, when other men were already busy at their desks and workbenches all over the city.

Today, however, Frederick had a good reason to resume his old ritual. He dressed as he had for all those years at the Forgill factory – a three-piece suit, and polished black leather shoes so soft and creased that they fitted his feet like a second skin. His cuff links shone with sterling silver, and he added a smear of Macassar Oil to his hair.

Walking to High Street, Frederick joined the commuters on the tramway down to Greenwich Station. From there, the seven-thirty express took him across the Cannon Street Bridge, where he alighted and hailed a hansom cab.

Still too early to head towards the city for the meeting, Frederick directed the driver down along Lower Thames Street, past the

Tower, and into Wapping. He felt a strange tightness in his chest as the cab turned into Old Gravel Lane towards the factory he had attended every weekday morning, all his adult life. He told himself that he just wanted to look, but as the cab driver pulled up on the opposite side of the lane, he found himself yearning for his old familiar work room.

Yet, the Forgill's factory looked more austere and less welcoming than Frederick remembered it. The dark smoke from the stacks seemed somehow malignant as it joined the mingled fog and pollutants that crowned the city day and night – a miasma he had scarcely noticed until he had breathed the cleaner air down at Lewisham for a few days.

'Are we gettin' orf mate?' asked the cabbie impatiently, while the horse lowered his head and rested gratefully.

'Not yet. Would you wait, please?'

Lord Percy Forgill, Frederick saw, was just then walking out from the factory, through the gate, looking very tall in his top hat. He was impossible to miss, with his arrogant stride. Wilkins and half a dozen of the senior factory staff followed, escorting the new owner out to his coach as they had always done for Lord Forgill senior.

While Frederick watched, and the cabbie harrumphed and consulted his pocket watch, Lord Forgill stepped into his carriage and the conveyance pulled away. One of the men in the group caught Frederick's eye, waved, then hurried across the street towards the cab. It was Vic Jones, the factory foreman, with his thinning cap of red hair. Frederick left the cab to greet him.

'Freddie, it does my heart good to see you.' Jones pumped Frederick's hand, then lowered his eyes. 'It must have hurt to have been dismissed so cruelly … I'm sorry I didn't stand up for you, but I have a wife and ankle-biters. What could I do?'

Frederick choked up in the back of his throat. 'I understand.'

'I know they miss your talent in the designing room, though Moon would never admit it.' Jones coughed, a little embarrassed, but ploughed on; 'There's many who say, very quietly mind you, that you're one of the great steam engineers in the country. They say that one day you might be up there with Watt and Trescothick – but Moon takes all the credit.'

'Thank you, but that's not true.'

'Anyways, I need to get back to work,' Jones said. Then, 'Have you been able to find a position somewhere?'

Frederick gripped the lapels of his coat. 'I'm working on it. In fact, that's where I'm off to this morning.'

'Well, best of luck,' said Jones, and they shook hands again before he turned away.

Frederick watched his friend go, then climbed back into his seat. 'We can set off now,' he said to the cabbie, 'Leadenhall Street.' He then looked away so the driver would not be able to see his eyes and plumb his feelings.

★★★

Frederick's next stop was not a factory, but a building, the London office of the once great and still significant James Watt and Company. A national institution, the office occupied an upper floor a few doors from the grand East India House.

Alighting from the cab a few blocks before his destination to soak up some time, Frederick was forced to wait due to an incident on the street. A carriage had run up onto the footpath. The horses were tangled and kicking, and a gentleman had been knocked to the ground. Two passers-by had pillowed his head on a jacket and were talking urgently to him. A uniformed bobby and the coachman were arguing as the latter attempted to deflect blame for the mess.

While Frederick waited, two businessmen came up beside him. They were affluent, well-fed, dressed and groomed; one in his fifties with long, grey sideburns, but very suave and fit. The other was much younger and a little plump. The men caught Frederick's attention, first because of the sheer glowing prosperity that surrounded them like an aura, then by the topic of conversation.

'Don't talk to me about Percy Forgill,' spat the older man. 'I can't stand the bastard – tried to get a slice of the action in the Manchester canal business – very pushy from all accounts.'

'You're exaggerating, Neddy, I'm sure, but I know what you mean,' said the other. 'He's not half the man his father was.'

'He's a puffed-up weasel, with no style or substance – better known for his successes in the cock pit than the stock market.'

Frederick smiled to himself. Still early for his appointment, once the carriage had been cleared from the path, he followed the pair as they walked around the corner to Bishopsgate, entering the Barings Bank offices at Number Eight. Frederick realised that he had been standing next to Ned Baring himself, one of the best-known financiers in the land. The thought that such an important man had no time for Percy Forgill gave him hope. It was nice to know that other people shared his feelings.

Yet, Frederick was far too preoccupied with the quest for employment to give the matter much thought, and after a short walk, he arrived at the Watt and Company rooms. Sidney Risecroft invited him into his office, and had tea brought on a tray. He and Frederick had met before, at trade shows and exhibitions.

'I like your work, I always have,' said Risecroft, 'and I know that Bartholomew spoke very highly of you – which is one of the reasons I wanted to grant you the courtesy of an interview. Yet we don't have any openings here in London.' He grimaced and wrung his hands. 'If you are willing to move to Birmingham, however, we'd happily find a position for an engineer of your calibre.'

'Moving north isn't my preference right now.'

'In that case I can only promise to let you know if we have a vacancy.'

Frederick shook the man's hand and expressed his gratitude for the consideration. Effectively dismissed, he moved to the door and closed it behind him, aware that the chances of working in this

London office without a good chunk of experience in the Watt factory were as likely as the English Channel freezing over.

★★★

In the following days Frederick received polite letters from both the Maudslay and Higginbottom's Engine Works. Both letters said, 'No, thank you,' in longwinded fashion. The receipt of those firm but friendly notes marked the moment that Frederick began to doubt he might gain employment in his chosen field at all.

Again, the prospect of having to move north for work hovered over him. It was true that he now had a house to sell, to fund a move. Yet, the house was Lord Forgill's gift, how could he be so mercenary as to sell it off like some chattel?

The final chance landed with a letter that the postman dropped in while Frederick was out walking, a pastime that helped him deal with the long hours of unemployment. The letter was from Antony Grimmen, of Willans and Robinson out at Thames Dalton in Surrey.

Grimmen had been a year below Frederick at the University College, and they had met several times since, becoming strong acquaintances with a fair measure of mutual respect.

Yet, Grimmen, when Frederick arrived, was guarded. A long tour of the site seemed like a strategy to delay any serious discussion. Always interested in the manufacturing process, Frederick traipsed from the foundry to design room, through the assembly areas, exchanging friendly nods with staff of all levels. The workers were content, he realised, and there was a warm and easy familiarity between them and their manager.

Afterwards, Grimmen dashed any hopes that Frederick had built up during the tour.

'I'll be honest,' the factory manager said. 'I, and many others, think you are a gifted engineer, and you would most certainly be an asset here, but I cannot employ you.'

'Please—'

'Freddie, don't make this harder than it jolly well is. Lord Forgill Senior was the President of the Steam Manufacturers' Association. Percy is acting in the role for at least the next eight months, until the next General Meeting comes around. I have to stay on-side with him. He has made it known, in subtle terms, that anyone who employs you will be viewed unfavourably.'

Frederick felt the breath sag from his lungs. 'Watts offered me a position, if I was willing to move to Birmingham, which I'm not.'

'Watt and Co are big and prestigious enough not to care what Percy Forgill thinks. We, unfortunately, are not … I wanted to pay you the compliment of a meeting, but I can't lie. The industry is closed to you unless you move up north.'

'Thank you for your time, and please let me know if the situation changes.'

Grimmen rasped at the stubble on his chin with the ball of his thumb. 'So, what will you do?'

Frederick paused in the act of standing. 'I've applied so far only for jobs within the stationary engine industry – and I'll admit that's where my passion lies, but there are still marine and locomotive engine companies to explore.'

'That's not your speciality.'

'No, but I believe I could make the change – I know the Steam Engine Factory at Woolwich Dockyard are developing new engines. Fryth and Collins are innovators seeking clever designers and Penn's …'

'Penn's won't hire engineers without marine engine experience,' said Grimmen. 'I know that for a fact.'

Frederick felt a sour taste in his mouth. 'I'll just have to try.'

The other man folded his arms. 'One of the bigger textile mills, sawmills or factories might employ you as a maintenance engineer. It depends on how much you want to work, doesn't it?'

Frederick said nothing. His savings were disappearing. He needed something to stem the flow, and very soon.

Frederick and Clare uttered their solemn vows of holy matrimony at Saint Mary the Virgin at nine in the morning on Saturday. Eleanor sat in the third pew with May and watched, misty eyed, as the ceremony began.

Clare wore a gown of white satin, with no hint of a train, that she had purchased in a salon in Marylebone. When they left the church she shed a tear.

'What's wrong?' asked Frederick.

'I wish Maman and Papa were here to see me in my gown.'

When it was over, Frederick took Clare home as his wife, and a new joyousness seemed to fill the house. In the evening, once May was settled, Clare walked critically around Frederick's room before saying, 'I'm sorry, *cheri*, but there will be some changes in here. How you can sleep in such an ugly bed is beyond my understanding.'

Frederick felt a mild affront. 'I made the head and base myself.'

Clare clasped her arm around his middle. 'And I'm sure that it is very solid, from an engineering point of view, but it does not, I'm sorry to say, have style.'

'Whatever you wish to do is fine with me.'

'Right now,' she said, 'there are many things I wish to do, and for the first of them you must help me out of this dress.'

Just holding her was a delight and pleasure. Making love to her was a gift. Her mouth pressed against his ear, and warm, moist air floated like mist into his being. Her fingers crept over his skin and made it come alive. He found it incredible that a woman could be both strong and soft at the same time, with secret curves within curves, places that are strangely pliant, with scents deepening like the coming of a storm and the healing power of the sun in the aftermath.

Frederick recognised his wife as a natural creation, a friend, and a soul. When it was over, he lay back, her head on his chest, hair spilling out, her hand flat on his stomach.

'I'm going to be good to you,' he said.
'I know. You already are.'

Chapter Sixteen

On Monday, while Frederick stayed at home with Eleanor and May, Clare buttoned a green striped casaque over a sensible dress and strode to Ladywell Station, soothing her husband's protestations.

'Percy Forgill has expelled you from your job and your home in Aldgate. He has brought armed men to this house. Pushing him to the ground has not solved anything, apart from making him angrier. He remains a threat to this family and we need to know more about how and why that is the case.'

It was late in the afternoon when she returned, pink around the eyes and grateful to drop into a lounge chair in the drawing room with a glass of soda flavoured with lemon juice.

'I went to the Times office and read more newspapers than I have in my life,' she said.

'Did you find out anything of interest?'

'A little. Something to pique your interest. Vic Jones was correct. Percy Forgill was born a twin.' She rummaged in her handbag for a notebook, opened it up and read, '"Born today, to Lord Bartholomew Forgill and Lady Forgill, two boys, twins, Montgomery and Percival. March 15 1837." The question now is not whether there was a twin, but what happened to him.'

Frederick said, 'We must be careful. If Percy finds out that we're looking into this—'

Clare made a face. 'It can hardly create any more animosity than there is already – especially after you pushed him onto his *derriere*.'

'I also promised his father that I would keep matters to myself.'

'Lord Forgill is dead, and he asked that you keep the things you saw confidential. That doesn't stop me from doing some digging.' Again she rummaged in her bag and withdrew a folded sheet, printed with bold and attention-seeking type. 'On to something more immediate. I was given this handbill as I passed the Coach and Horses.' She passed it over to Frederick.

The headline read: PEDESTRIANS WANTED. He read through the fine print, which detailed some of the rules and the fact that there was a fifty-pound purse. Still, he laid the page aside. 'You think I should enter?'

'Why not? The prize money would be welcome.'

'My chances of winning are very low. I'm better off concentrating on finding work, don't you think?'

'Perhaps,' said Clare, 'but it would be good for you to participate in a race where others are not cheating. You might be better than you know.'

Frederick shook his head again. 'I still don't think so.'

Unperturbed, Clare took the sheet from him, laid it flat then pinned it to the kitchen wall.

★★★

Becoming increasingly anxious about his fruitless search for work over the coming days, Frederick's regular perusal of the Morning Standard brought more bad news. An article, on page thirty-two, detailed an accident at Forgill's Engine Works, resulting in the amputation of a man's lower leg. Frederick was shocked to see the victim's name, V. N. Jones.

Within an hour he was on his way by train to London Hospital in Whitechapel. There, he found Jones in a ward of fifty or more open cots, with nurses moving through, one of whom had just brought the injured man a cup of tea.

'It's not too bad,' Jones said, white as a ghost, sitting up against a bank of pillows. 'The tea here's better than it is at work. At Forgill's, nowadays, they brew three pots with the same leaves.' He stared blankly then said, 'Oh Freddie, they've taken my leg below the knee.'

'How did it happen?'

'Too few men doing the work of many. Half a length of tube steel rolled on me. Crushed my calf so it looked like a pancake.'

'Oh dear Jesus. I'm so sorry.'

Vic lowered his voice, 'Forgill's under the leadership of Percy Forgill is a dark and lonely place. You can almost hear the change in the engines – they used to run smoothly. Now it's as if they are protesting, squealing with every turn. Cheaper iron, shorter breaks. It's a tight ship, yet a miserable ship. Even the rats are starving.' He looked down again at his leg, and lost the thread of his thoughts. 'Now I'm fucked and no mistake.'

★★★

Resigned to seeking a role as something other than a design engineer working on new stationary steam engines, Frederick set his sights on the next tier of opportunities. On Thursday morning, he dressed neatly, made sure he had his union card, and kissed Clare and May goodbye.

London, Frederick knew better than most, can be the friendliest city in the world or one of the most frightening. It has deep underground roots, the memories of hundreds of generations of men and women buried in churchyards and long-forgotten cemeteries, the ruins of the old city walls like the buried backbone of a dinosaur. And all the time the tides on the river Thames cycle, in and out, marking the passage of time just as surely as the clock in Frederick's alcove, at the foot of the stairs.

Frederick took the tramway down to Greenwich. Within a few miles of that station were countless factories and premises that might hire an engineer, most of them centred on Woolwich and Deptford. His first stop was the office of the Amalgamated Society of Engineers, Greenwich Branch, where he displayed his card and asked if they knew of any opportunities.

'There's work around,' said the clerk, 'but it's mostly marine. 'Umphrey an' Tennant was lookin' for a designing engineer but the vacancy may 'ave been filled by now. I can give you a note if you'd like.'

By noon Frederick learned that there was an acute snobbery in the marine engineering sector. A post as a maintenance engineer appeared to be the best he could hope for. The salary for such a role, even if he was able to find a position, would be half of what he had earned at Forgill's under its founder.

***

The Steam Engine Company at Deptford employed over one thousand men of all trades and boasted a dedicated recruitment office. Being a unionised workplace the clerk in charge first asked for Frederick's card, then scanned through his resume.

'Impressive, but we just don't have any work for an engineer of your standin' at the moment.'

'What about lesser positions?'

'Well, it's a matter of skills, sir. I can't put you on as a machinist, as you don't 'ave the trainin' for that sir. You could do maintenance engineer work, a' course, but there are no vacancies of that type.'

Frederick walked on, visiting enormous factories with broad assembly and foundry bays, their stacks belching black smoke and a cloud of fine black dust settling on everything. He inquired at Maudsley's, Humphrey and Tennant, Fryth and Collins and even Penn's. They sympathised, and took his name, but sadly, had no positions available.

Finally, losing heart and inspiration, Frederick stopped by the river. He took the bread and cheese he had brought along and ate it silently, watching the water churn upstream, feeling an empty yawing fear in his guts.

★★★

Walking back to Lewisham to save on tram fare, Frederick paused on High Street when he saw a 'Position Available' sign on a wall, just beneath a brass plaque embedded in the stones of the front façade.

James Benson, Esq
Agents d'procurement viz real estate, livestock and general.
Special needs assisted, and discretion guaranteed.

As Frederick took the stairs to the top floor a peculiar kind of smoke cut its way, sharp as a knife, up each of his nostrils. The smell strengthened as he walked through an open door and into a quiet office, where a clerk, manning the front counter, was deeply involved in his letters.

A cloud of this strange-smelling smoke came through from the other room, and Frederick found it overpowering. A man walked through. He was at least forty, with large dull eyes, a clipped moustache and a strange cigar, rolled from yellow-brown leaves between his lips. A boater hat sat low down on his forehead, seemingly a permanent fixture.

'Cloves,' said the man, in thin, nasal tones.

'Ah, what?'

'The smell is of burning cloves. Hartisans in the Spice Islands, far away in the heastern seas roll them into cigars and smoke 'em. I picked up the 'abit in me navy days.' He stepped forwards, arm outstretched. 'The name is James Benson, better known as the Bosun. Tell me 'ow can I 'elp a young fellow like yeself?'

'The sign out the front suggests that you may be able to offer employment opportunities?'

Benson sighed and perched himself on the edge of his clerk's desk. 'Hemployment hopportunities? Now that's a question.'

Frederick burned with impatience, 'Well of course it's a question. Do you have any salaried positions I might apply for?'

'P'raps. But the honly hemployment hopportunities we 'ave at present is a nightwatchman position, a temporary one at that.'

'Any job will do. May I please apply sir?'

Benson took a deep puff of his cigar, expelled an evil-smelling stream of smoke then screwed up his eyes. 'Happlication haccepted. But the pay ain't much, fer night work.'

'Anything will do at the moment.'

'Can ye start tonight?'

'I can't think of any reason why not,' said Frederick. 'What time?'

Benson consulted an enormous fob watch on a chain. 'It'll be dark in three hours. Pop 'ome for some grub then come back at six an' I'll give ye the details.'

★★★

Gas lamps shone yellow light into the dark mist rising from the drains as Frederick walked with a strong rhythm. In his right hand was the comforting weight of a baton. He was thinking about Clare, and how this new job meant that he would be sleeping in the daytime. It wasn't ideal, but it would have to do for the moment.

Sighing, Frederick continued on, through that old industrial precinct along the River Ravensbourne, close to where it became Deptford Creek, which emptied into the Thames.

'The owner wants the factory site sold,' Bosun Benson had said. 'And there's been low-life scum gettin' in and squattin'; lightin' fires and makin' mess. It's up to you to stop it.'

As Frederick reached the address shown on a scrap of paper, a rat scuttled across his path and disappeared into a pile of scrap iron. He stopped, eyes hardening. He was far too intelligent and creative to let the job get tedious. Moving back to the roadway, he filled his pockets with stones, before resuming his beat. At the first opportunity he let fly. He missed the rat by a whisker, the stone slamming into the iron with a clang.

His gaze moved to a cluster of solid buildings, while old coke crunched underfoot. A faded sign told the story of the previous owner. 'Thomas and Sons Pump Works.' So, he thought to himself, this premise was an old manufacturing plant.

A smell reached his nostrils, something he knew well from Forgill's. It was stale and old, but it was the smell of a cast iron part, fresh from the foundry. The smell was so intoxicating that, in a trance, he walked up close to the front façade.

The factory office was built of brick, along with the main foundry and assembly house. The manufacturing bays were of brick, solid and well-built. Signs across the fenced enclosure verified the availability of the site.

FOR SALE
PRIME HEAVY MANUFACTURING JAMES BENSON ESQ, AGENT.
47a LEWISHAM HIGH STREET

In a separate building, he could see the unmistakable form of an old beam engine, possibly a Boulton and Watt original. Even if it were sixty or eighty years old, Frederick didn't doubt that it would still run. With such power at the source, he knew, anything could be accomplished in those premises.

As Frederick started to move on, another rat appeared against one of the nearby buildings. He took a stone from his pocket and threw with perfect accuracy. The rat squealed, scuttled a pace or two more then fell sideways.

Frederick fingered his rock supply, but his mind was on the buildings and their potential.

★★★

Back at home for breakfast Frederick ate eggs on toast while he told Clare about the premises. 'It's an old pump works – it shares some of the installations we used at Forgills.' He paused, barely able to articulate something that he knew to be a fact. 'With the right equipment and a skilled workforce I could build engines there.'

'In that case you should find out the asking price,' she said. 'It won't hurt to do so.'

'It'll be far too much money for us,' he said.

Clare patted his wrist. 'Yet, this is the first time I have seen your eyes sparkling with excitement since you started looking for a new job.'

★★★

On Saturday and Sunday, at work, in the garden, and on a pew at St Mary the Virgin church, Frederick gave the matter a good deal of thought. He even lingered after the Sunday service to speak with the Vicar, taking a seat with that kindly soul in the sun, in view of the Priory Farm, to discuss this new vision.

On Monday morning, after another long night of walking his beat around the facility, outfitting a factory in his mind and throwing stones at rats, he went home for a long slumber. Awaking after midday he walked up to see Bosun Benson, braving the swirls of clove smoke at the top of the stairwell.

'What news, young Frederick?' asked the Bosun. 'It ain't pay day yet.'

Frederick felt tongue tied, but he managed to communicate that he wished to discuss the sale terms of the factory he had become nightwatchman for.

'Ho then, a business discussion,' cried the other man, rubbing his hands together like a bowler about to start his over. 'Do ye like rum?'

'I've been known to knock back a peg or two, but I usually wait until evening.'

'What does the time matter? Let's 'ave one together.'

They walked three blocks to the Rising Sun, down at Loampit Vale, where Benson ordered the drinks and Frederick paid.

'The old pump works I've been looking after,' Frederick said when they were settled. 'What would a place like that be worth?'

Bosun swirled a mouthful of rum through his teeth then swallowed. 'Not as much as when the owner left it, an' lesser each day as it becomes more bedraggled. 'E'll be grinnin' if 'e gets eight 'undred pounds for it now.'

Frederick widened his eyes at the sheer immensity of that sum of money. 'What about a lease?'

The Bosun looked at Frederick with new eyes. 'Them premises is for sale, not lease. The owner 'as moved north and is keen to wash 'is 'ands of the place.'

Frederick thanked the agent for the intelligence. He could not raise more than a small fraction of the sale price, whereas the prospect of a lease might have given him hope.

'Just between you and me,' Benson said, 'at this stage 'e'd most likely take seven 'undred, prime street and riverfront land an' all.' He crinkled his eyes in curiosity, 'What would you want with such a place?'

Frederick finished his rum, 'Nothing really. It's out of my reach, I'm afraid.'

★★★

As he walked home, Frederick felt deflated. Seven hundred pounds to purchase a decrepit factory – it might as well be a million.

Back at the house, however, he could not shake the idea. He sat in the back yard, under the spreading London sycamore, adjacent to the disused stables, while May played in the leaf litter. His mind ran through the engines that he could build in such a place. He couldn't help it. He was an engineer, and he was trained to design and build engines.

The idea of making these under his own name filled him with excitement, yet, even if he had seven hundred pounds, he would need at least twice that amount to tool up for heavy manufacturing, let alone run a factory, pay wages and raw materials, through the long process of producing the first engines for sale.

The idea, however, had taken hold, and would not let go.

'It's a silly idea,' he told Clare. 'I would just forget it – except that it's such a wonderful place to set up a factory.'

'Now you are fighting – taking control. I like it.'

'But I do not have enough money. I can scarcely raise fifty pounds now – this move has been very expensive.'

'I have about the same until my annuity comes through next March. One hundred between us.' She paused. 'There's always the pedestrian contest up at the Coach and Horses.'

'Even in the unlikely event that I won, we'd still only have one hundred and fifty pounds altogether. Not enough.'

'To start your own business, you will need to borrow money. To do that it's best to have as much of your own cash as possible. Fifty pounds in prize money is more than you can earn in months of being a nightwatchman.'

'Let's be practical,' Frederick warned. 'I won't come first, and second prize is only ten quid. I entered a few smaller races as a young man, but as a pedestrian I've been in only two very long competitions. One was a university road event, which I did not win, and the other was simply a way of avoiding being impaled by your boyfriend – which I did not win.'

'He cheated. You won.'

Frederick smiled to himself and said nothing more. Arguing with Clare, he had learned, was a waste of time.

Chapter Seventeen

Two days later, after returning from his nightwatchman duties, Frederick picked up May, sat her on his lap and ate a breakfast of fried eggs and bacon.

'I think I will go in the pedestrian race after all,' he said. 'Fifty pounds is fifty pounds.'

Clare smiled knowingly. 'Good thinking,' she said, then came behind him to massage his shoulders gently. 'I for one am confident that you can win.'

Frederick began training, walking three miles down to Greenwich and back each day after he rose from a morning slumber, then walking most of the night for his salaried duties, breaking off occasionally to chase small groups of drifters away from the premises he was guarding. All the while he coached himself in the correct gait, for the rules of pedestrianism dictated that one foot must always remain on the ground, and judges at such an event would be quick to disqualify transgressors.

When the designated Wednesday evening rolled around, Frederick had arranged for a stand-in to carry out his nightwatchman duties. He felt as fit as he had for many years, dressed in short pants and jersey, standing with the starting crowd at the pavilion behind the Coach and Horses. Clare was present, along with Eleanor and

May.

The arena was packed for the event, and around fifty participants paraded at the starting line, wearing an assortment of striped jerseys, flannel shirts, lamb's wool stockings, various caps and felt or leather shoes. All had numbers sewn onto braids draped across one shoulder.

'Why did they have to give me the number thirteen?' Frederick complained to Clare. 'As if I'm not quite up against it enough!'

She laughed, 'I didn't know you were superstitious.'

'I'm not, but you never know.'

Frederick had paid his entry fee of one pound, along with another pound that he had placed with a bookmaker, backing himself to win, at twenty-to-one odds.

'Lucky this is a short bout,' said Frederick. 'Some of these contests go for seven days.'

'I don't think I have the patience to be a spectator for that long,' said Clare. 'Let alone walk night and day like some kind of machine.'

In preparation for the start Frederick drank half a gallon of water, filled his pockets with boiled sweets, then hurried off to the starting line with the other pedestrians.

'Welcome, ladies and gentlemen,' cried the compère, resplendent in a red hat and silver jacket. His voice was puppet-hall pompous, matching his plump and rosy cheeks. 'Thanks for attending this tasty exhibition of the venerable art of pedestrianism, that most pure art of endurance and body strength. When my whistle blows, the event will begin, and our competitors will walk laps of this track. Each lap will be recorded, and whomsoever completes the most laps before ten of the clock on Friday evening will be declared the winner. As you all know, the contestants may sleep and eat as much as they wish … even get blind drunk if that is their desire.' He paused while the audience laughed, then went on rapidly. 'Yet, our winner must pass the post more times than anyone else, under their own steam and within the rules of pedestrianism, before ten Friday evening. Now, contestants, are you ready?'

The answer a resounding yes, the compère raised the whistle to his lips and blew, the sound almost drowned out by the roar and chatter of the crowd. More bets changed hands. Unlike the footraces Frederick had participated in, however, there was no initial jostling towards the front. It was an almost leisurely start, with plenty of time to check out the other racers.

Frederick understood that the idiosyncratic gaits of the competitors added to the spectacle. Some quite lounged along, scarcely lifting their feet from the track. Others walked with their arms held close to their chests, affecting a kind of shuffle. Still more swung their arms enthusiastically, giving the appearance of hurrying. Some smiled, others maintained a fierce grimace. Some would rely on speed and rest more often, others on economy of movement and spend less time in their tent.

The great sport of pedestrianism was one of individualism, style, courage and persistence. No wonder then that London, and much of the world, had been in love with it for more than a century. After the first lap, while keen punters on the spectators' benches assessed their fancies, there was another rush to the bookmakers, whose voices rose and fell through the arena as they offered odds and issued scripts.

Clare, with May in her arms, was on the edge of the track as Frederick came around for the first lap, calling out, 'Go my love! You are as good as any of these men.'

Midnight passed, and a good proportion of the crowd ebbed away, including Frederick's own small group of supporters. By one in the morning some competitors had retired to their tents to sleep. Frederick understood that there were many different strategies at play – some exponents held that many short rests was the best recipe, others preferred to push on to near-exhaustion.

Frederick's plan was simple – to muddle around the track to the best of his ability and rest when he had to.

At six in the morning Clare, Eleanor and May arrived with a basket containing a whole cooked fowl, cheese, and a bottle of ale, arranging the meal on a camp table. Frederick was still on the track, looking haggard and deep-eyed, but in better condition than many of the others. Seeing his entourage, he hurried out back to the privies, then came to the tent to eat, noticing that a new crowd of spectators were beginning to arrive.

'Have you slept yet?' Clare asked.

'No, but I'm in front.'

'Of course you are, silly, but now they are rested and you are not.'

Frederick saw the worry in her eyes. 'Please don't fret about it. I'll take an hour or two to sleep now, once I've eaten, and by Jove I'm starved.' He tore at the chicken like a raptor and downed the ale in a few gulps.

Finished, he took May in his arms while Clare tidied up the plates. 'We'll be back with lunch at noon,' she said. 'You get some sleep – I'll arrange for someone to wake you.'

Frederick settled into the blankets in the tent. 'Just an hour,' he said. 'I don't want the others to catch me.'

In no time at all, Clare saw, Frederick's eyes had closed, and his breathing was even and low. Leaving him, with May's hand in hers, she walked across to one of several errand boys who hung around the course, offering services including procuring foodstuffs or drinks, carrying messages, or waking sleeping competitors at specific times.

'Excuse me, will you wake number thirteen in two hours, at nine o'clock?'

'Sure thing missus. It'll cost you tuppence, an' pay me now.'

★★★

After spending the morning at home, Clare hurried to the bakery and grocers for bread and cheese.

Back at the arena, she was surprised not to see Frederick out on the track. A prickle of worry became suspicion as she hurried to his sleeping tent. Clare knew that Frederick was capable of deep repose when he needed it. But this was … madness. What did he think he was doing? What happened to the boy who was supposed to wake him? A glance at the leaderboard, rendered in chalk next to the counting table, confirmed her suspicions. Heart racing now, she parted the tent flap to find Frederick lying on his side, eyes closed, in heavy slumber.

'My darling. Get up!' she cried. When his eyes still did not open, she slapped his face gently.

Frederick sat up, then opened his eyes. 'Damnation! What time is it?'

'After twelve. I said to have a sleep, but not for six hours. You're coming last, *cheri*.'

'Oh curses, give me water, and I'll eat on the track.'

'Don't panic. There are two days still to go and you're well rested. Take the time to drink, eat, and use the privy. Then get on the track. You'll catch up, I have faith in you.'

It was true, for with Frederick fed and refreshed, he was soon walking again, stiffly at first, then resuming his previous fluid motion. Clare blew him a kiss and stayed to watch from the front stand. After Frederick's third or fourth lap, however, she spotted the lad she had paid to wake him. The boy tried to duck off into the crowd, but within a few paces Clare caught up and grabbed his arm.

'I paid you to wake Number Thirteen!'

'I know ya did, but a sporting gennelmen paid me sixpence not to wake him – must see him 'as a threat – just the way this business goes. Tell your man not to eat foodstuffs anyone gives 'im or it'll come wi' a load a' Epsom salts.'

Clare raised her eyes heavenwards, 'Give me my tuppence back.'

'I already spent it, missus, now let me go.' The lad started to struggle, and Clare released him, managing a light cuff on his ear before he'd weaved off into the crowd.

***

The cramps in Frederick's leg started after the second day. As soon
as he sat to eat, his calves would lock into hard boards like sawn
timber. Clare brought known antidotes – pickled eels and salted
plums, and these foods provided some relief. The crowd, by then,
were getting vocal, cheering on their fancies, and shouting 'huzzah!'
as the leaders passed the counting table each time. With just twenty-
four hours to go, the tally board was a matter of intense interest, the
betting favourites coming to the fore.

Clare rubbed Frederick's legs down with oil and brought thick
meaty broth. She hoped it was enough.

It wasn't, but Frederick was no ordinary walker. On the last day,
when his mind's defences were as weak as those of his body, he began
to imagine a familiar shape: dark, furred and long-fanged, on the
track behind him. The alchemist of fear rattled his test tubes and filled
Frederick with strength.

Breathing jerkily, shaking through the trunk of his body to his
feet, Frederick walked on past the bulk of his competitors, five steps
ahead of the wolf, with its frightening tread and pitiless eyes.

***

On Friday evening, with three hours to go, Frederick was coming
second overall – just two laps behind the leading pedestrian, who had
not slept in some nineteen hours. The man, whose name, Bill
Wiseman, had been adapted by the press to Billy the Flash, was a
professional, thirty-nine years old, who had once walked from
London to Glasgow in seven days. His support crew ran out at
intervals with lumps of bread soaked in Madeira, fortifying him for a
final effort. Spectators in the stands stamped their feet on the boards
to a brisk rhythm, adding to the tension.

Every muscle on Frederick's face was visible, the veins on the side of his neck bulging like cables. Around and around he went, though his walk became more of a hobble, and the crowd was watching him in awe; the story of his big first-morning sleep-in doing the rounds as if it were some kind of secret technique.

Yet, Frederick was close to all-out. It was the inspiration of his little family on the sidelines – including Eleanor – calling out his name, that kept him going – along with the money. Fifty pounds – seventy including his side bet, would be a big help in raising finance for his dream. He could not afford to lose.

With ten minutes to go, both he and his only serious rival had completed one hundred and thirty-two miles, one-thousand-and-fifty-six laps of the track. It was neck and neck, but by the final curve Frederick got his arms working, cycling back and forth, and off he went, overtaking his rival and reaching the finish line to a few exasperated shouts of disgust, but an overwhelming cheer at this heroic effort.

'I'm so proud of you, so very, very proud,' said Clare, throwing her arms around his neck.

Frederick choked for breath, 'Please just tell me that I don't have to walk home.'

'I've got a cabbie waiting out the front.'

With seventy crisp English pounds in his possession, Frederick surrendered to the care of the woman he loved, and the potential for sleep.

Chapter Eighteen

Frederick had never borrowed a substantial sum of money in his life, and the local High Street branch of the Bank of England, to which he had recently moved his account, seemed like the best place to start. It was a brick building on a street of weatherboard, with few windows and fewer doors. Inside was all dark panels and cherrywood trim, a layer of tobacco smoke residue on every surface and floorboards blotched with old wax.

Approaching the teller Frederick said, 'Excuse me, I'd like to talk to someone about borrowing money – taking out a loan that is.' It was strange how the very request made him feel nervous.

'Your name, sir?' asked an earnest voice.

'Frederick Morton.'

The teller left his cubicle, returning a few minutes later via an access door. 'Come with me, please sir. I'll take you to Mister Batherton, the manager.'

Frederick padded along behind, down a narrow and very dark corridor, through a door of embossed mahogany, and into a room lit by a north-facing bay window. This grimy pane of glass offered a view of an ash-strewn dumping-ground for broken wagonettes and traps. The window was open by a crack, the only escape-route for the pipe-smoke that the manager seemed to breathe in preference to oxygen. The desk was adorned with a framed lithograph of a very tall woman in a voluminous dress.

Horace Batherton held a rubber stamp poised in the air as he looked up at Frederick. He was a rotund man with an inflated neck, and a cavernous dimple on his chin.

'You are looking for a loan?' he asked.

'That's correct. A substantial business loan.'

The rubber stamp struck like a locomotive coupling to a carriage.

'Go on,' said Batherton. He harrumphed a few times as Frederick explained how he had found a site with potential and would like to turn it into a factory. There he would build stationary steam engines to his own design.

Horace Batherton had heard similar stories before. He had been around. He moved in rarefied circles compared to Frederick and he knew it. Batherton liked to lend money to equals, and in short, he had in less than a minute conceived several prejudices against Frederick. One was that he talked like an East Ender who was trying not to talk like an East Ender. Also, his clothes, while neat, were of an out-of-date style. Most importantly, in Horace Batherton's opinion, Frederick was not, by birth, a gentleman.

The teller returned with a thin file. This he placed on the desk before withdrawing silently. It was Frederick's account file, and Batherton skimmed it swiftly. He found nothing therein that contradicted his initial assessment of the man.

'Excuse me, sir,' he said. 'But you're an unemployed draughtsman—'

'Engineer,' Frederick corrected.

'Very well then, you're an unemployed engineer, who was jolly lucky to inherit a house – and a decrepit old place at that. You have some savings, but nothing substantial … I urge you to give up on the idea. You are not the kind of man who builds factories. Get a good job and I'm sure you'll do well.'

'Are you saying that I'm not of the right social class to own a factory?'

The manager ignored the question. 'No bank will lend you money unless you can persuade a person of substantial means to guarantee the loan.'

Frederick regarded the man with a level gaze. 'The answer is no?'

The bank manager's pipe had stopped drawing, and he tapped the bowl into a tray. The smoke-smell turned an even more evil shade of stale. 'That's correct. The answer is no.'

'I'll see myself out,' said Frederick, but the manager kept on fiddling with his pipe, ignoring him.

Clare, patrolling the footpath with May, listened to Frederick's report of the conversation gravely. 'He sounds like a pig of a man,' she said.

'I'm afraid that I have to agree,' said Frederick. He sighed, 'I don't feel like giving up, even though it seems hopeless.'

'One attempt does not mean hopeless,' she said, gripping his hand with hers.

★★★

That afternoon, attempting to sleep on the lounge in preparation for another night shift at the old pump works, Frederick remembered a chance conversation on a London street.

Percy Forgill? I can't stand the bastard.

Ned Baring, more properly known as Baron Revelstoke. The banker. Was the enemy of Frederick's enemy his friend?

'You are very restless,' Clare said from her chair, where she was reading a French novel, occasionally wiping tears away from her eyes.

'I am, yes. But I have an idea.' He sat up and told her about the chance meeting with Ned Baring.

'Not exactly an introduction,' said Clare, 'but it's a start. I could go with you – I know and understand these tycoons of the world of business, and they will have heard of my family. I might be of help – at least with the first step, which is to get him to talk to you.' She squeezed his arm. 'Now go back to sleep, and we'll try to see him tomorrow.'

Frederick did fall asleep, yet his repose was troubled. From the moment he first saw the premises and the idea came to him of turning it into a factory, he had been caught between two voices in his head. One was ambition and drive, the other was a stronger, whining voice, telling him that he was not good enough, that men like Freddie Morton from Stepney did not own factories, and any such attempt would end in disaster.

Now, dozing on the lounge, this voice manifested itself into a nightmare. There was Percy Forgill in his father's graveyard, leaning with one hand on the tomb itself, swigging from a silver flask held in the other, his face made ugly with drink.

'You'll always be a goblin from the slums,' he said. 'I hate you. I'll bring you down.'

There too was Horace Batherton, smoke curling from the bowl of his pipe and trickling from his lips. 'Men like you don't own factories,' he said. 'You're not a gentleman.'

'Go North,' said Sidney Risecroft from Boulton and Watt.

Even Sophie Forgill made an appearance in the dream, cackling at every word her brother uttered. They were a team, taunting him together, a savage reminder of his lowly beginnings – frightening caricatures – their features exaggerated, nails long and sharp, faces fleshless and impassive.

When he woke, Frederick lay on his back and stared up at the ceiling, and after a while Clare appeared beside him. 'What's wrong? You were calling out.'

'We shouldn't waste our time with this factory idea. It can't happen.'

Clare squeezed his hand. 'You must learn to believe in yourself.

Haven't you ever heard of Dick Whittington, the slum boy who sold his cat and went on to make a fortune and become Lord Mayor of London?'

'I have no cat,' Frederick pointed out.

'You have talent, and that's more important. You can do this thing, and I will help you.'

★★★

The next morning, Frederick and Clare travelled by tram and train into the city. The day was near perfect, with a rare breeze blowing from the east, leaving the sky clear of coal-smoke and other pollutants – a day in which to dream of the impossible. At Number Eight Bishopsgate the doorman swung the door open, admitting the petitioners to a broad wood-panelled lobby. Men in stove-pipe hats sat on sofa chairs alongside a woman with a chubby dachshund on a lead sitting meekly beside her. Clerks bustled behind the reception desk.

Frederick acknowledged the waiting room with a polite nod as he entered with Clare. He took her arms as they walked together to the main desk. He saw eyes turn to appraise her – she had taken pains with her appearance, wearing a magenta dress with silver embroidery that had appeared in her wardrobe as if from thin air.

Even with Clare, beautiful and assured, beside him, Frederick's tread faltered, as if he only then understood the monumental presumption he had shown in coming here, to one of England's most successful merchant banks. Still, there was no chance of backing out now – the nearest clerk had already cocked an eyebrow at him.

'I'd like to see Mr Baring, please,' Frederick said.

The clerk had a kind face, but he looked somewhat pained by the request. 'Mr Baring doesn't generally see members of the public. We're a merchant bank – business loans, governments, major projects, that kind of thing. Do you understand what I mean?'

Frederick did not reply or turn to leave. Instead, he shared a long look with Clare, seeing his own feelings reflected there. In their brief meeting, he had sensed a quality in Ned Baring that very few men have, and Lord Bartholomew Forgill had showed – a greatness of manner. Frederick had a feeling that Ned Baring dealt in miracles, a commodity he was in need of.

Addressing the clerk once more he said, 'If you don't mind, I insist on seeing Baron Revelstoke. You see, the proposition my wife and I are here about is actually business related.'

Clare butted in, exaggerating her accent a little. 'Do you know who I am? My maiden name is du Brice. You might know of the Saint Laurent du Brices?'

Fortuitously Ned Baring himself appeared, walking into the reception area with an impatient frown on his face and waving a sheet of paper in one hand. This was the second time Frederick had seen the famous banker and here, in his element, he looked formidable. It wasn't just his height, German Lane suit, or the deeply-set eyes – an expression that was at once serious and thoughtful: but a combination of all those things. Ned Baring, Baron Revelstoke, was a man in control of his world.

The banker stopped when he saw Frederick, and the clerk broke the silence. 'Sir, this is ah, Frederick Morton, and his wife Clare, of the French industrialist family du Brice.'

'Ah, good morning,' said Baring. Then, his eyes resting on Frederick, he narrowed his eyes. 'Don't I know you?'

'No, sir, well that is to say … we were standing next to each other on the pavement one morning, several weeks ago. A carriage had crashed—'

'Ah, so that's why I recognise you. What brings you here then?' Frederick took a deep breath, and what seemed like the biggest risk of his life. 'I understood from what you said to your companion that you are no friend of Lord Percival Forgill.'

Ned Baring took a moment to register the comment. 'That's certainly true, but it's jolly impertinent of you to listen to a private conversation.'

'I am not a friend of Percy Forgill either. I need assistance – with a business proposal.'

Baring sighed, 'Well come on in and let's hear what you have to say.'

Frederick and Clare exchanged an encouraging glance. They followed the banker past a series of open doors, all connecting to a single large and windowless workroom, fitted with hundreds of desks, all with clerks hunched over with bent backs like drab whales in an ocean. Skylights up high in the tall ceilings struggled to admit sufficient light, and on each desk burned one or two candles.

Next, they passed a door with a brass plate identifying it as the Partners' Room. Inside Frederick could see a fire burning in a grate, marble fittings, and vast mahogany desks. Portraits lined the walls and the spines of books showed from deep and substantial shelves.

By now wondering how he had been so arrogant as to walk into this bastion of financial aristocracy, Frederick followed his host and his wife through a final door bearing a plaque made of brass that read: 'Baron Revelstoke.'

Inside, teak panels stretched from the floor to one-third of the wall height. Above this was fine plaster work, with four rosettes on the ceiling, and two enormous windows, admitting ample light to the interior.

Baring held a leather-upholstered seat for Clare, then waved Frederick to another. This done, he sat in the throne behind his desk. 'I apologise for my clerk, but it is unusual for us to see new faces in this bank.' Then, to Clare. 'So, you are a daughter of Jean Paul du Brice?'

'Yes, I am.'

'Please give him my regards. He is a man I admire very much.' His warm but calculating eyes moved to Frederick. 'Now, how can I help you?'

Frederick sighed, 'I am a steam engineer and I want to set up my own factory.'

Baring looked sceptical. 'A real engineer? University educated?'

'Yes, London College, and ...' Frederick hesitated, he hated to stamp himself with the kinds of symbols that often served to grind him down, but he knew their importance ... 'Charterhouse School.'

'Ah, impressive,' said Baring. 'I'm a Rugby man myself. Were you a gownboy?'

'No, I was sponsored, by Lord Bartholomew Forgill, a great man.'

'He was indeed a great man,' said Baring, 'unlike his son. He must have believed in you.'

Frederick paused, exhaled, and allowed himself to agree. 'I worked as a designing engineer for six years and became Deputy Chief Engineer. When Percy Forgill took over I parted ways with the company. I plan to go out on my own. I've found the premises, but I need capital.'

'Do you have collateral?'

'Yes. A house in Lewisham – also given to me by Lord Forgill.'

'Tell me your story,' said Baring. 'I have the feeling that there is more to this than meets the eye.'

Frederick presented a thoughtful ten-minute summary, showing himself in a positive light, but also as humble. It did not seem rehearsed, as indeed it wasn't. When he finished the story with the inheritance of the house, then the serendipitous location of the old foundry, Ned Baring threw back his head and laughed. 'I admire you, Frederick Morton, for having the pluck to try to tool up in opposition to Forgill's after being sacked by that overgrown cock-rooster Percy. Now, tell me, what would you manufacture in this factory of yours?'

'I would start with a general static engine suitable for small operations, yet the real money is in textile mill power plants. I did some work on a superheated, high-pressure engine a few years back. I'd like to build this one – right now it would be the most advanced engine in the world.'

'That's all the detail you can give me?'

'At this stage, yes.'

'Your slate is clean – you've never been bankrupt?'

'Never. I worked for Lord Forgill all those years.'

'You have some cash savings?'

'Some, yes.'

Baring folded his arms. 'I'm sympathetic, particularly since you can offer collateral, but am nowhere near convinced. You need a business plan. Projections. How many of these engines can you manufacture? How soon can the first of these be made? How much profit will there be in each one? How will you market your engines?'

Frederick felt a little deflated. 'Oh. Well of course—'

'Cheer up, old boy,' said Baring. 'You're an engineer, not yet a businessman. You need to learn. I'll hazard a guess that you don't even have a clear idea of the amount of money you need to borrow?'

Frederick shook his head. 'No, not really, not yet, but I need at least seven hundred pounds for the premises.'

'The purchase price is just a start. From the very beginning, long before you sell your first engine and see a return, you will need to pay wages, buy raw materials, coal, paper to draw your blueprints on.' He paused. 'Have you a name in mind for your company?'

'I have some ideas,' said Clare, and Frederick glanced at her. He was a little surprised by the question. He hadn't thought about a name for the factory, and was beginning to feel foolish.

Ned Baring sighed and regarded Frederick, frowning. 'Running a business is hard. It requires boundless energy and forethought. Are you certain you want to take that step?'

Frederick stared back, not daring to say anything.

'Companies do not succeed right away,' Baring went on. 'They start with an idea – a genesis that may go on for years, perhaps half a lifetime. Careful planning follows, then things get started. Beginnings are easy enough, but in the second phase a business needs to grow, and to do this you will work harder than you have ever worked in your life. You will do whatever it takes, and usually that means not only producing the best jolly product it is possible to make, but also by forcing your way into new markets. If you're lucky enough to have built a good business, you might eventually be able to consolidate with steady growth. Eventually, however, most businesses are forced to evolve or decline, and the best of the best outgrow their founder.' Baring smiled mischievously. 'You'll know you've succeeded when your company doesn't need you anymore.'

Frederick enjoyed the manner in which the banker conjured castles in the sky, then let them fall. 'I'll remember that,' he said.

'Come back to me,' said Ned Baring, planting both elbows on the desk with his hands folded over the top, 'with proof of your desire and commitment. Come back with a striking company name; and a business plan that includes concept drawings and specifications of the engines you plan to build, financial projections, and a list of the machinery and tools you will need to purchase, down to the last hammer.'

'How do I put everything you've just said into a plan?'

'Business is about gumption, finding out and doing. I'm not going to spoon feed you.'

'Very well,' said Frederick. 'I'll do what you ask – whatever it takes.'

Clare curtsied deferentially, and the two men shook hands. It was a strange thing, but they liked each other – the engineer who had come from East London's slums and the numbers man who had moved in the highest levels of society all his life. It was a fast and instinctive bond, and the handshake sealed it.

Chapter Nineteen

Ned Baring's request for a business plan was a revelation to Frederick. The more he thought about it, the more he understood that planning a business was not so different to designing a machine. The plan was a type of blueprint, he realised, and a successful business could hardly be created without one.

On the way home on the train, while Clare enthused about the opportunity, Frederick made notes, sketched diagrams, drafted tables and made lists in a notebook. He did not have the knowledge to order these thoughts, but he knew what he needed to get a factory started. He knew engines and manufacturing.

Back at home, he hurried in as powerfully as a ship-of-the-line, heading for his office, where Clare forced him to articulate all the steps necessary in developing the business plan, and identifying the aspects for which he would need help.

'You are not an accountant,' she said, 'and while I did some book-keeping for my father, neither am I. We will need to find a good one – my first task for tomorrow.' She narrowed her eyes. 'Now please remember that you need to sleep – you can't work all day and all night.'

'I know, but I am a little bit excited.'

'Of course you are, *cheri*. So am I.'

Within two hours, Frederick had rough-sketched three engines. The first was a portable steam engine, integrated with a boiler similar to a traction engine but without wheels, in a format known as an 'overtype.' Delivering eighteen brake horsepower, it could be used to drive a threshing machine in Salisbury, a printing press in Durham, artisanal silk mills in Lewisham, or potters' wheels in Staffordshire, all from a belt tensioned around the flywheel.

The second would be a powerhouse designed for mills, using a cross-compound horizontal configuration with two hundred pounds per square inch of superheated steam driving three cylinders. A heavy flywheel, twelve feet in diameter, would be grooved to accept the ropes that would drive each floor of a textile mill, though it could just as easily adapt itself to a brewery or flour mill.

The third engine was barely a concept. This, Frederick decided, would be a revolutionary engine for high-speed applications such as electricity generation. This was possible using gearing, but the best engineers in the business were investigating other means, including very fast single-acting engines.

When Clare loomed over his shoulder she made appreciative noises. 'The second one would be perfect for my father's flax mills,' she said. Even these initial sketches challenged the imagination, the engines seeming almost real.

'I'll call them Models I, II and III,' Frederick said.

'No, *cheri*. Why would you give your creations such tedious names? Think again, be romantic, and when the time comes to market these engines you'll capture peoples' hearts as well as their chequebooks.'

***

That night, as Frederick went about his duties at the factory premises, his mind was not idle. He continued the design of his three engines in his head.

The first was a standard configuration, though combining many desirable elements, and would not present too many challenges. The second, despite his previous work for Lord Forgill, would not be an easy machine to perfect, for the barriers to using superheated steam in a stationary engine were substantial. Overcoming those barriers occupied Frederick's thoughts.

It was a strange thing, but his mind threw up a single word from his schoolboy studies of Latin. The word was *fortis*, meaning brave. The superheated mill engine would be a brave engine to make. And in the morning, when he returned home, thirty minutes with his old copy of Thomas K. Arnold's *Practical Introduction to Latin Prose Composition* gave him names for the other two models.

'I have names for my engines,' he said to Clare proudly. 'The first will be the Mobilis – the mobile engine. The second will be the Fortis – the brave, and the third will be the Imperium, the authority. What do you think?'

'Dramatic,' she said, 'perhaps a little too much so, yet customers love to buy drama and colour. I think it's perfect.'

★★★

While Frederick and Clare pursued the creation of a business plan, much of the care of May fell to Eleanor. By now they had an intuitive bond, that curious child, and the much older woman who was fiercely intelligent, despite never having seen the inside of a school room.

Woman and child had a suite of games and activities, and the questions never ceased. 'What's gin, Eleanor?' asked the little girl.

'It's fer pourin' down yer gullet. Makes a person's mind go all fuzzy.'

'Why do people drink it then?'

Eleanor ruffled her hair. 'Because it makes some things that grown-ups 'ave to put up with easier to bear, darlin'.'

'Why do you smoke a pipe?'

'To make me voice all nice an' growly. So's I can scare cats and dogs.'

May loved to walk out to meet the postman as he sidled up with his leather satchel over one shoulder.

'An' here's me girl,' he'd say, and pass the mail to May, who would examine the salutations as if she could read them. In fact, she had learned the difference between her mother's name and her father's, by the shape and length of the words.

Three days after Frederick's meeting with Ned Baring, the postman passed three envelopes into May's hand, and she studied them carefully. 'For Papa,' she said, 'and Papa again.' Then, looking at the third envelope she stopped cold, with such a look of consternation that both Eleanor and the postman laughed.

'What's wrong, little one?' asked Eleanor at length.

'This one isn't for Maman, and not Papa either.'

Eleanor took the envelope from May's little fingers and looked at it. It was folded from home-made rag paper, as cheap as anything around, but it was not the paper that caught her attention. There were many words printed in ink on the front, and to her great surprise she recognised one of them. She turned it over, and on the back she saw another word that she knew. She froze, her breath cold in her throat.

'What?' asked May.

'Oh, nothin' much really. But this letter is for me, I'm thinkin'.' Still not trusting her own skills, however, she called the postman back, for he had just moved ahead, continuing on his rounds.

'"Scuse me, Trev,' she called.

'Yes?' He wandered back, and Eleanor held out the envelope, her thumb aimed towards her name. 'This says Eleanor, right?'

'Indeed it does Miss.'

She turned the envelope over. 'An' on the back 'ere it says Juliet, don't it?'

'Yes.' With compassion he said, 'If you open it, I'll read the whole thing for you?'

Eleanor shook her head, and snatched the letter away. 'No need,' she said. 'But many thanks for bringin' it.'

When they turned back towards the house, May said, 'Why is your hand trembling so?'

★★★

The accountant Clare selected had an office on High Street, with an imposing brass plaque on the building's stone face. He was an older man, with whiskers that looked like the worn-out strands of a wire brush, fibres straying in all directions. He did, however, have a good mind for figures, and he kept beautiful ledgers.

The accountant asked hundreds of questions, demanding evidence of pricing for everything from Bessemer steel, pig iron, and lubrication oils. He wanted to know how rapidly Frederick could take an engine from concept to finished product.

Frederick was confident that they could manufacture and assemble the first Mobilis engine in twelve months and have it tested and ready for production in fourteen. The superheated Fortis would take two more years to produce in prototype.

The most vexing problem would be the sourcing and development of a high-temperature lubricating oil. All steam engines require unique lubricants, necessary to negate friction in pistons, slide valves and cylinder walls. Oils needed to mix with steam, and therein lay the problem: water displaces most types, with the exception of animal oils.

For that reason, most early steam engines were lubricated by pure animal fat, manufactured through the boiling down of carcasses, most often sheep. The next problem, as far as the Fortis engine was concerned, was that at high temperatures, these oils turned rancid and failed to work. This lack of a suitable oil was the single largest hurdle to the successful design of the Fortis engine, and financial projections had to take into account the time needed to source the right substance.

The third engine, the Imperium, had even more imponderables and unknowns. The accountant advised that they should incorporate it into the plan only as a future direction. It played no part in sales projections and running costs.

The Lewisham accountant's assistance was invaluable. Frederick was amazed to see how rising expenditure was rolled back by sales at the beginning of Year Three – and the relationship between marketing, income and expenditure.

Frederick spent hours at union offices in Greenwich and Woolwich, discovering exactly what salaries he would be required to pay various workers in his still quite theoretical factory. He started with the Steam Engine Makers' Society, where a clerk sporting a thick black moustache opened a book, ran a forefinger through the index, then consulted a page midway through. After more searching, he found a listing and read it out.

'Factory cleaners: two shillings and eight pence per day. Moulders, iron-founders, brass founders, vice men, filers: three shillings ... planers: three shillings and sixpence ... shall I make a list for you?'

Determined to be thorough, Frederick also visited the Amalgamated Society of Engineers, the Ironfounders' Society and finally the High Order of Friendly Boilermakers of the London Unity.

Returning to the house, Frederick cross-referenced similar roles from across the unions, and chose the highest rate applicable. These made up the final fair-copy list that he added to the business plan. He also set up meetings in the City, pricing machinery and scheduling delivery lead times. The plan was progressing well, but costs were building up, and Frederick had not considered the prospect of competition for the premises.

★★★

That week, when Frederick called in on the Bosun for his pay cheque, the agent was shaking hands with another businessman at the threshold of his office.

'Ah Frederick,' said the Bosun. 'You'll be after your wages. I'm afraid this good fellow 'as just put ye out of a job.'

'How so?' asked Frederick.

'He's purchased the old factory premises as you've been nightwatchman at for these last weeks.'

Frederick looked at the stranger searchingly. He was dressed in a standard trade suit, jacket and bowler, and the ends of his moustache waxed and twisted.

'Has the deal been finalised?' Frederick asked.

'Not yet, but the offer 'as been made and I will communicate it to the vendor by letter – I expect a response within a few days. My feeling is that the owner will jump at it.' Bosun went to his desk and scribbled a cheque, passing it to Frederick with a flourish. 'Here's your wages, in any case.'

Frederick lingered in the office, an odd tremor in his chest as the Bosun walked the visitor down the stairs, returning a few minutes later, raising his eyebrows to see Frederick still there. 'Can I 'elp ye with anything else, young Frederick?'

'I'm just a little disappointed. I was hoping to make an offer on the place soon.'

'Well, we'd discussed that,' said the Bosun. 'But ye hintimated at the time that ye doesn't 'ave the funds. That's the rub, bless ye Frederick. Ye either 'as the funds or ye don't. The fellow you just met 'as the funds.'

'I am in the process of applying for a business loan, but it will take a few more days. May I ask how much the other fellow has offered for the premises?'

'Ye can arks sir, but that does not mean I will hanswer. Let's just say that while not quite the arksing price it is more than the low figure you an' me discussed.'

'Very well,' said Frederick. 'Thanks for being so forthcoming with me.'

★★★

'There are other sites, surely,' Clare consoled her husband in the back yard under the sycamore. They were eating corned beef and pickle sandwiches on fresh-sliced knotted white bread still smelling of flour and warm crust, while Eleanor sat with May, an array of small dolls, involved in some intrigue, in various poses on the ground between them.

'There may be,' said Frederick, 'but not nearby … I've kept my eyes out, and I doubt we'll find anything so closely matching the facilities we need.' He compressed his lips reflectively. There was also the Boulton and Watt beam engine in its stone housing. He had to admit that this engine had a talisman-like symbolism to him.

'If you think you need that particular premise then you have to do something about it,' said Clare.

'How?'

'Offer more than the other man.'

'But if they accept my offer I'll need to pay a ten per cent deposit – if Barings don't come through with the funding then we'll lose the money – anything up to eighty pounds – that's about all I can raise now without dipping into your funds. The accountant needs to be paid and our living expenses are higher than my wages have been.'

Clare looked a little exasperated, 'You have to decide which course of action is right, then proceed boldly.'

'To be certain of winning the bid I'd have to offer full price, or at least very close – by tomorrow morning to be safe.'

Clare gripped Frederick's hand and looked at him intently. 'Eighty pounds is a lot of money to us, but we will survive – we have our special little house and each other. I am not incapable of earning money if it becomes necessary. Do what feels right to you.'

Frederick took another sandwich and knitted his brows

reflectively. He told himself it was a relief – matters had been taken out of his hands.

★★★

That night the dreams came again. The setting was the same as the last. Percy Forgill, Horace Batherton, and even Bosun Benson were the players, with Lord Forgill overlooking them like a god on high.

'You should have known,' said Percy. 'You're not of the right class to own a factory.'

Batherton and Benson were sitting at a table together, clinking glasses and smiling, as if running some underhanded deal of their own, the mingled smells of clove and tobacco smoke forming a miasma in that graveyard world.

Then, the scene changed, growing darker still. Percy changed, going back through the years to a younger form, standing over something at the foot of the stairs.

'The wolf,' he was saying. 'It will come for you.'

Frederick saw it in his dream, the white teeth and fearsome, powerful jaws. He blinked awake, thankful that reality was not quite so frightening. Careful not to disturb Clare, he turned on his side, cold fear filling his heart.

★★★

The following morning, Frederick called on Bosun Benson with a written offer for the premises of seven hundred and thirty pounds.

'Oh I'm sorry,' said the Bosun, 'but it turns out that the vendor is currently in London, and in fact, I dined with 'im this evenin' last. 'E's accepted the other party's offer. The premises is sold. There's to be a meetin' in an hour's time between the vendor an' the buyer, at which occasion the deposit will be furnished an' paperwork signed.' He paused. 'Come see me tomorrow an' we'll have a squiz at what else is havailable.'

Frederick couldn't hide his disappointment. 'There's nothing else that would be so perfect for me.'

The bosun clasped his shoulder. 'Bad luck, old fellow.'

'What if I offered a higher price?'

'Well that kind of thing is done, 'ere and there, a gazumpin' it's called, but the offer were very close to the asking price, and for twenty quid or so it's not worth the blow to the prestige of me business, so to speak, so let's not consider that, eh?'

★★★

Frederick walked home, feeling bereft. It seemed that he had lost an important opportunity. He started trying to add up what it might cost to have a factory premises built from scratch – foundry, assembly bays and offices – many thousands, certainly.

He sat in his office for an hour, then walked back to town for a meeting with the accountant, where he admitted that the plan had hit a snag.

'Unfortunately, another party has beaten us to the premises. It's been sold.'

'Is there anything similar around?'

'Not that I've seen so far. There are empty factory buildings, but nothing designed for heavy manufacturing.'

'So before you even start you'll need to build purpose-built areas – that means an architect in consultation with a civil engineer to draw up plans. Then a couple of builders to quote on the construction.'

'And a steam engine to run the machinery – ironic since that's what we're going to build.'

The accountant sat down, laid his beautifully prepared figures aside and took a fresh leaf of paper. 'Let's have a look at the numbers.'

At the end of an hour he tallied up the position of the company. 'The bottom line depends on how much interest you'll be paying on the principal, but I'm not sure that the enterprise is worthwhile – without suitable premises you'll need to borrow three times as much money – you need to sell many, many engines to make it pay. Look at this … by the end of Year Five you are still behind.'

Frederick left, the euphoria of just a few days ago unravelling. He needed consolation. He needed to connect with his purpose, and there was only one man who came to mind.

★★★

Instead of heading home, Frederick took a train from Ladywell Station. More than an hour passed before he stepped off again, a sad and lonely time indeed. From Earl's Court he walked to the West London and Westminster Cemetery.

Lord Forgill's tomb was of tasteful white marble, in the shape of a classical temple, with hollows containing twelve Grecian columns on each side. Quotes from Plato, Aristotle, and Thomas More were etched in gold leaf.

Frederick hadn't expected such a grand monument to be in place so quickly, though he supposed that Percy Forgill had been more than eager to put his father to rest and let him be forgotten.

Kneeling, a tear sprang to Frederick's eyes. He felt the need to speak but could not yet find the words. In the silence, a robin flew to a branch nearby and chattered like a child to the empty air. Strangely, Frederick drew comfort from this, as if it were a sign that something in the universe was listening, at least.

'Dear Lord Forgill. I … wish to thank you for the gift of the house. It has saved me from homelessness, and given me a chance, perhaps, to do some of the things I feel that I was born to do.'

In low tones, stopping when anyone passed by, Frederick talked of the failed attempt to obtain the old pump works, Ned Baring's involvement, and the preparation of the business plan. 'I don't think it's going to work out for me this time. I might need to move up north – that means selling the Lewisham house. I'm sorry, but I can't see any other way forward for my family.'

He had not expected an answer, but those empty moments seemed crushing. Lord Forgill could not help and guide him any longer. His destiny was in God's hands, and his own.

Frederick came to his feet and looked around at the surrounding gravestones. Even from there he could see the name Forgill, over and over. There were generations of them here, in this family plot.

Without conscious thought, he began to walk around the area, running his eyes over the old inscriptions. Some of the graves were over a century old, and the newest dated back a decade or two.

Strangely, there was no sign of the resting place of a Montgomery Forgill. It was as if the twin had never existed. Unremembered, unmentioned and unmarked. It seemed to Frederick to be a sad fate, if he had lived at all, for surely if Percy's twin had existed and passed away his grave would be here.

★★★

On High Street the following Saturday morning, wandering the Lewisham markets with Clare, Frederick happened to run into the Bosun, who confirmed that the contract signing and deposit payment had gone through without a hitch.

The agent placed a gentle hand on Frederick's shoulder. 'Sorry things didn't go your way. I've got me eyes peeled for somethin' that might suit ye, don't worry.'

Yet the moment, to Frederick, seemed to have passed — all the momentum he had built had come to a halt and there was no longer an exciting way forward. He needed to find another job, no matter what field. Clare had suggested that he could set himself up as a repairman, for there were plenty of engines in the silk mills and factories along the Thames and in Lewisham itself.

'Fifty pounds worth of specialist tools is all I'll need,' he agreed, but repair work was not what he wanted to do, and it would never be more than a stopgap. He raised the option of moving northwards, probably Manchester or Birmingham, with Eleanor and Clare that evening. 'I can get a good job up there,' he said, 'and housing will be less expensive. I believe that we can sell here and buy something quite liveable in the North.'

Clare dropped her fork cold. 'I understand what you're saying, and May and I go where you go, but selling this house? How could you even think about it?'

He turned his face to Eleanor, who stared for a moment, before tears started welling in her eyes and a choking sob broke out from her lips. In a trice she was uttering a full-blown wail. May, obviously confused by this, began to cry also.

'What's wrong?' Frederick asked, while Clare positioned herself to wrap an arm around Eleanor's back.

'Me Juliet! That's what's wrong. I can't leave 'er and go so far away. We, uh, uh, ain't 'ardly 'ad a minute together since she went to *them.*'

Frederick looked pained. 'Where is she, Eleanor? Can you please tell me?'

'I got a letter, an' it says 'er name on the back – but I can't bloody read it, so I dunno, I really don't.'

'How long have you had this letter?'

'A few days, Freddie. I 'aven't wanted to trouble anyone wif it.' She looked down. 'I've been 'opin' to learn the trick of readin' but it just won't come to me.'

'Would you fetch the letter?' asked Frederick.

Eleanor took a balled-up handkerchief from the pocket of her pinafore, blew her nose and dried each of her eyes in turn, then went to her room for the letter.

When she returned, Frederick took the envelope from her hands and examined the address, unsurprisingly made out to Eleanor Demsie, care of a dosshouse in Stepney, with several addresses crossed out and new ones scrawled above or below. *Try Poplar Street Lewisham*, someone had written.

'May I?' he asked.

'Go on then,' said Eleanor, yet the skin of her face had turned as white as the feathers of a turtle dove.

Frederick opened the envelope and unfolded the page. He was surprised. The paper was clean and the script quite well rendered – not the kind of message to be expected from the terrible and nefarious persons who had apparently taken Eleanor's daughter.

Starting at the beginning, he began to read aloud.

> Dear Mother,
>
> It has been several years now since we were parted and even then not on such good terms. I have almost learned to write proper as you can see. This is my own hand writing, tho Sister Perrin is helping me with some words what are hard.
>
> I want to say that I have finished my novitiate, and have taken vows in the Sisterhood of Saint Peter. I am happy and am writing now to tell you where I am so you might visit. Once I had agreed with Father Hunt that I might join the good sisters of the Church ...

Frederick stopped reading and stared at Eleanor. 'Juliet has joined a nunnery? You made out that she had been kidnapped by a gang of pimps or worse. This is what you've been so upset about?'

Eleanor crossed her arms in front of her chest, but she could not hide the pleased smile on her face from hearing her daughter's words. 'I've no love for the church, an' they seduced me own daughter an' stole 'er away. Why would I be 'appy for them to do that?'

Frederick shook his head in consternation and continued to read.

> We live and work at a new convent at Kilburn, just a little way out of London, where we nurse convalescent patients too well for hospital and too sick to return home.
>
> We have just twelve beds so far, but there are plans for more. It is a good life. I would love to see you. It would mean so much.
>
> Sister Joan (that is what I am called now)

Frederick looked inquiringly at Clare, who read his thoughts like a fortune-teller reads tea leaves. He turned back to Eleanor. 'We'll go tomorrow and find her. All of us.'

Chapter Twenty

Kilburn was not the easiest place to get to from Lewisham, though it was slowly being swallowed by the outward spread of Greater London. The trip necessitated arriving at Ladywell Station not long after daybreak, and two line changes. It was almost eleven when the three adults and one wide-eyed child stepped off the train and onto the platform at their destination.

The hire of an old-style hackney coach, arranged by the station master, took only a few minutes before they were heading out towards Mortimer Road. The convent itself, when they reached it, was not much to look at. It was a stone building, decorated with creepers, with a tall fence and some outbuildings. A sign beside the door identified the occupants as the Sisters of the Community of St Peter.

As Frederick opened the gate for Clare and Eleanor, he spotted a nun assisting a young man to walk on the lawns, his prosthetic lower leg flexing as he stumbled and cursed. He had the bearing of a soldier, and Frederick wondered in which far-flung corner of the empire he had lost his lower leg.

'You'll do the talkin' won't you Freddie?' Eleanor whispered suddenly, clutching his arm.

'I will, if you want me to.'

Frederick almost came to regret this, for not only did they have to hunt for the mother superior from office to chapel, to hen house and pantry, before cornering her outside the twelve-bed convalescent home, but she was a fierce and energetic leader, who made it plain that visitors to the convent were an annoyance.

'I'm sorry to bother you,' Frederick said, 'but this good woman here is the mother of one of your nuns. Sister Joan is her name.'

The mother superior turned and studied Eleanor. 'You're no good woman as far as I've heard, but a gin-soaked tart.'

Frederick would have protested, but Eleanor crossed her arms over her chest. 'I was that once, I'll admit, but no more. Now I wants to see me own daughter, oo invited me 'ere.'

'Very well then, I know that Sister Joan is keen to see you. She is coming along well, for a girl of such a ... er ... background.' The mother superior's expression softened, for she had caught sight of May, and reached out to take her little hand. 'Good day, little one!' she said. 'What's your name?'

'May.'

'How delightful!'

There was a sudden exclamation from behind, and the party turned to see a very young woman, pushing a pale, middle-aged convalescent in a wheelchair. Frederick recognised in her the little girl he had last seen on a street in a slum, attempting to pet a cat.

Leaving the chair and the woman in it, the young nun advanced on Eleanor. 'Mumma?'

'That's me, darlin',' she said, opening her arms.

The mother superior watched them for a moment, with her hands on her hips, 'You can have one hour,' she said to Juliet, 'after you push poor Missus Ryckman back to her room.'

★★★

For all that time, Frederick and Clare strolled in the sun, while May played with leaves and shadowed ravens across the lawns. Eleanor and her daughter sat hand in hand, at a table beside a clothesline strung with white hospital nightshirts and bed linen. Even when a light shower passed overhead, the pair did not seek shelter.

The hour had long expired when the mother superior arrived to chivvy her young charge back to work – an order that was delayed while mother and daughter embraced fiercely, and a smiling Eleanor came back and took Clare's arm.

'Let's go now,' she said. 'We might 'ave time for a pie at the station – I did see a good barrow there, didn't I?'

'I think you did,' said Frederick, 'and so did I.'

They were back at the station, brushing the last of the crumbs from their shirts when Eleanor announced, 'If you wishes to move north, Freddie, then I'll be honoured to come along as your cook and maid. Juliet is well, and she is 'appy. That's all I needs to know.'

Frederick squeezed her hand, 'Thank you, but nothing is settled yet.'

★★★

It was a long trip home, with Eleanor looking out the window dreamily as they went, her head resting on the glass. Frederick sat close to Clare, the warmth of her thigh and shoulder against his, letting her handle the tickets and changes, allowing himself to spend time thinking about the future.

It was after three when they arrived home, taking a cab from the station and arriving to find a carriage drawn up at the front, all but blocking the gate, with a driver seeing to the horses and looking inside impatiently. Bosun Benson and another gentleman were standing in the drive.

Frederick paid off the cab driver, and helped the two women down, before approaching their visitors. 'Good afternoon, Bosun. To what do I owe the honour of this call?'

'Well Frederick, dear Mister Morton sir, this is Tom Thomas. He is the owner of the factory premises you was so interested in acquiring in recent times.'

The two men shook hands, and Frederick felt alive with curiosity as to the purpose of this visit.

'What would you say?' asked the stranger, 'if my premises were available for sale again?'

Frederick felt a jolt of excitement, 'Well I'd be surprised, and pleased. I thought the sale had gone through?'

There, standing on the edge of the street with the wagon parked out from the kerb, they created somewhat of an obstruction, and a heavy wagon stacked with general goods in cases and barrels had to slow to a crawl to squeeze past. One of the horses reared, necessitating a move into the drive, where Eleanor, Clare and May were watching curiously.

'I 'ave to explain something,' Benson cut in. 'The contract for the sale of the factory premises 'ad a hanti-competition clause – the new owner must not "use said facility to build machines of a nature resembling products manufactured by the Thomas and Sons Pumping Works Ltd." The man oo 'as contracted to buy the factory 'as grossly misrepresented himself. In fact 'e was a lawyer paid by a rival firm oo might 'ave done just that thing. The contract 'as therefore been terminated under the terms just iterated.'

Frederick scarcely dared breathe. 'So the premises is free again?'

'That's correct.'

'Then I am very, very interested.'

'You intend to build stationary steam engines?' the owner asked.

'Those and only those,' said Frederick.

'Then you would be a suitable buyer.'

'That's wonderful news.' Frederick went on to explain his situation, working on the business plan and waiting for funding.

The vendor exchanged glances with his agent. 'If you like I could give you an option for seven days, for a small deposit. That will allow time to get your finance in place.'

'Perfect! Thank you.'

They shook hands on the deal, and Frederick looked down to see May wrapping her arms around his leg. He lifted her up and held her close to him.

'We'll let ye get in,' said the Bosun. 'Come up tomorrow an' we'll sort out the option.'

'Thank you,' said Frederick. 'It's such wonderful news.' And as the carriage rolled away towards Lewisham, he kissed May in the centre of her soft cheek.

★★★

The next morning Frederick was at Bosun Benson's office at nine, where he wrote a deposit cheque and signed the option. Then, with the seeming force of one of his own, as yet unbuilt steam engines, he headed for the accountant's office.

'Back to the original plan,' he announced. 'We're in business, providing Barings will approve the loan.'

That night Frederick sat with Clare, Eleanor and May at the Joiner's Arms with a list of possible business names, crossing out and adding.

'How about the Lewisham Machinery Company?' Clare suggested.

'There's already a Lewisham Agricultural Machinery Company, I checked,' said Frederick.

Eleanor took a sip of her stout, ''Ows about something happy, like the Goodluck Steam Engine Company?'

'I like the idea,' said Frederick. 'But I'm not sure that it sounds quite professional enough.'

May, who had just finished eating a pork sausage cut into tiny squares, let out a squawk that cut through the sounds of the drinkers at the tables, and Frederick laughed. 'May's suggestion might be the best one yet,' he said.

'Simple is always best,' said Clare. 'Perhaps you should use your own name, and a couple of words to describe the business.'

The next day, Clare took a fresh sheet of paper, and in her best roundhand script wrote: The Morton Steam Power Company – Business Plan. Then, over twelve intense hours she crafted the final fair copy so that the document was beautiful as well as informative.

Frederick and Clare dropped the plan in to Ned Baring's Bishopsgate office the following morning, then walked the streets, and sipped tea at tea-houses, returning at noon. The banker was out at lunch, and they killed time in the waiting room. Frederick was thinking that he had never wanted anything in his life as much as he wanted this, except perhaps for the woman who now sat beside him.

Ned Baring arrived back in the office at half past one, smelling of good brandy. 'Ah, you're here, good, it saves me writing to you. Come in.' Once in the office, settled into chairs, Baring added, 'I'll need to send someone around to provide a valuation on the house, and to look over these premises you've decided on. I can also help with the legal requirements … incorporation etcetera. If it all comes together, I'll get a business funding proposal drawn up.'

Frederick felt a flood of excitement, fear, and grateful joy, all at the same time. 'You'll lend us the money?'

'If the valuations come in at anything reasonable, the answer is yes. I propose that the bank funds your company in two ways. One loan for the purchase of the factory property along with plant and equipment to get things going. That will mean a mortgage over both the facility itself and your house. The other would be a line of credit, administered through your local bank, but covered by us. We'd set an expenditure limit, with the terms renegotiated every twelve months.' He passed across a part-printed, part-handwritten sheet. 'These are the basics of the deal I'm offering.'

Frederick took the sheet and stared down at the figures. His accountant's costings had warned him that interest on the loan would add up to an exorbitant sum, but he had not understood until then how a five-thousand-pound loan would cost almost eight thousand pounds, over the seven-year term of the proposal.

Baring watched him reading through. 'At the end of the seven years, all being well, you'll want to expand, and we'll renegotiate.' He paused, 'I'm not a young man, but I can assure you that the bank will act in good faith whether I am still active or not.'

'Thank you ... beyond words,' said Frederick.

'How can I resist? We can embarrass Percy Forgill and manufacture the best stationary steam engines in the world, perhaps even make some money, all at the same time.' He paused. 'Lord Forgill senior started something in making you his protégé, and someone needs to finish off the job. It might as well be me.'

★★★

Taking possession of the new factory site had to wait for the registration and incorporation of the company, then the drawing up and exchange of contracts, which took some days.

Another crucial task was the opening of a new business account at a local bank through which the funds from Barings would be disbursed. Almost reluctantly, still smarting a little at the manner in which the manager, Horace Batherton, had rejected his initial approach for a loan, Frederick decided to go with the local Bank of London branch, arranging chequing facilities and the Barings-funded overdraft. The manager seemed surprised, and even a little put out, that Frederick had managed to obtain a business loan, and affected an air of indulging a child who had been given far too many toys.

The company chequebook soon arrived, embossed and stamped, and to Frederick this was an important moment in his transition from employee to owner, part of the journey of becoming a man who controlled his own future.

Finally, on the day of the handover, Frederick was up at dawn, arriving at the premises with Clare while ice still shone white on the pavement. Opening the main door with a flourish, he was soon overcome with a sense of the enormity of what he was about to do. The empty bays that had before seemed so full of promise, now looked filthy and decrepit.

The first eight employees had all been hired through the respective union offices – four boilermakers and a smith with a solid record in a foundry. The others were machinists, with some all-round skills, and a sheet-metal worker. Frederick assembled this paltry workforce, talking to them of his first steps in turning these empty spaces into a first-class factory, and enjoying the ragged applause of his new men as he attempted to fill them with his own sense of purpose.

Then, no matter what their trade or speciality, for all staff, the first hours of the Morton Steam Power Company's existence involved the wielding of brooms, dustpans and damp rags, along with the filling of hired wagons with scrap and rubbish. Frederick appreciated the work ethic and skills he had hired with these men but was aware that staffing the factory with specialists remained his single most pressing problem. Skilled stationary-engine workers worked mostly up north, and London-based men were in strong demand.

Carriers arrived at the front loading-bay, delivering lathes and other machines. These were manoeuvred inside on rollers, snigged into place with the overhead gantries built into each bay.

Clare, with May's assistance, was already cleaning out the office, and arranging the cabinets and desks – that would be her domain. Eleanor, meanwhile, was sweeping as effectively as any of the men and gave back any cheek they cared to offer her.

In the early afternoon, a sign writer arrived to paint the newly registered company name on the face of the factory building, on both sides, facing street and waterfront. By then the general layout was beginning to take shape. The three main work bays, each some one hundred and twenty feet long, had been allocated a specific purpose. Bay One was the tool room and machine shop. Bay Two the foundry and forging plant. Bay Three would be used for assembly and despatch. There was also an open space at the junction of all three bays that would one day, Frederick decided, act as a show room.

★★★

Later in the day, Frederick's focus shifted to the classic powerhouse that would drive the factory – run every lathe, grinder and drill on the premises through line shafting – as well as the power-hungry hydraulic accumulator and the huge Sturtevant blower that would blast air into the furnace.

The engine was located in a dedicated housing on the river side. The maker's plate identified it as a Boulton and Watt – one of the original marvels designed by the genius himself. The beam was a shaft of solid oak, infused with the heat, oil and smoke of half a century of factory life.

Frederick laid a hand on the huge cylinder, struck by the thought that, for the first time in his life, he owned a full-sized steam engine.

'You and I,' he said, 'are going to be friends. I will look after you, and you after me, until we get the job done.' And he set about polishing every square inch of her surfaces, shovelling near-fossilised ash and rust from her firebox and cleaning up her boiler with a wire brush. The factory sheet metal worker was allocated the task of fabricating new ash pans.

The next morning, with the engine glistening, Frederick took on the role of stoker, warming the firebox with timber before adding the first shovelfuls of coal. A little after noon, he opened the governor, and steam pushed into the cylinder for the first time in many years. The engine turned reluctantly at first, but Frederick felt the first stroke in his bones, and the peculiar satisfaction that it was he who had built the pressure in the boiler, and thereby caused this miracle to happen.

★★★

Late on the second afternoon, Wilkins, the Thin Man in his fox-fur coat, came along North Road on a bicycle. He stopped and looked at the factory, seeing smoke rising from the stack and hearing industrious sounds emanating from inside. His eyes fell on the glistening new paint that spelled out 'The Morton Steam Power Company.'

The Thin Man sneered. It was one thing to paint a sign on a wall, and another to create sophisticated machinery from a vacuum.

With this thought in mind, he mounted his bicycle and rode away.

Chapter Twenty-one

Percy Forgill carried the Purdey sixteen-gauge double shotgun at the balance point, with the stock between his elbow and upper body as he followed the line across mixed meadow and woods, with brambles away to the left and brookside trees to the right. Ahead he could hear the sounds of beaters working through the brush.

One of Percy's great pleasures, upon the demise of his father, was taking possession of the family's country estate – two thousand acres and a manor house in Surrey. Just three miles from the village of Bromley Heath, it lay at the end of a lane lined with stone fences and gorse.

Lord Bartholomew Forgill's penny-pinching ways, and the extent of his saved wealth had surprised Percy. Why would a man not live life to excess when he had the means to do so? Of course, it had been here that Lady Forgill, their mother, had been pulled from the pond all those years ago, and their father had avoided the place ever since. A shame, in Percy's opinion, for it was a magnificent property.

The house had been large but Spartan, cold and dreary, and not to Percy's taste at all. A small army of tradesmen had been working on rectifying that fact, and the stables were now twice as large as they had been.

'Coming up behind,' called a voice, and Percy swivelled to see the lanky form of Wilkins. The pair had always got on well, and now that his father was gone, the Thin Man was invaluable – a strategic thinker for whom intelligence gathering came naturally.

'Good morning, Lord Forgill,' said Wilkins, reaching his side.

Percy ignored the greeting. 'You should be careful wearing that mangy old coat of yours. Someone might mistake you for a fox and take a shot at you.' He paused then, 'You have no gun?'

'I'm not a sporting man, sir.'

'It's an easy enough thing to learn.' Percy sensed the impatience of the other man. 'You teach yourself not to flinch from the kick of the gun, nor indeed from the blood of the bird.'

'I don't mind the gore of a killed animal, or the recoil of hard walnut against me shoulder,' said Wilkins, 'but I am London bred, sir, an' don't find comfort in the country outdoors.' He looked down at his feet. 'Even now, the wet grass on the caps of these fine shoes is not to me taste.'

Percy huffed, 'You said in your message that you have information on Morton's activities.'

'I do. The rumours are true. Morton 'as begun 'is own engine works.'

'I don't understand,' blurted Percy, 'how Morton has the capacity to do that. Was Father so soft in the head that he gave the man money as well as the damned house?'

'We have found no evidence of that. Morton managed to raise finance from a merchant bank – Barings, actually. Given that he has a house as collateral, he would not have had much difficulty raising capital.'

'And Ned Baring would be happy enough to finance anyone setting up in opposition to me.'

A pair of pigeons burst from the woods, climbing almost vertically. Percy swivelled the gun and fired twice. The first shot missed, but the second winged the slower of the birds. It did not drop, but fluttered to the ground, where it made vain attempts to fly. Percy walked to the spot, picked up the bird and wrung its neck. 'One to me,' he said, then broke open the gun to load fresh cartridges from the belt around his waist.

The Thin Man raised an eyebrow. 'It might 'ave been better to have kept Morton on as an employee so you could watch the bastard.'

Percy Forgill's eyes glittered a deep shade of blue. 'I do not require your advice, just your observations.'

'Right sir, I apologise.'

'Now tell me everything you know.'

The Thin Man took a notepad from his pocket and scanned the neat lines of script. 'The premises was formerly a pump works. Morton 'as purchased the site outright, with frontage to Deptford Creek an' the street. A powerful, albeit very old Boulton and Watt steam engine is operatin', and several different types of lathes and other machinery 'as been delivered. As far as I can ascertain, Morton 'as, at this point, about ten employees.'

Percy laughed, 'I fail to see how he can build one engine, let alone a business, with ten employees.'

'It is an 'umble start, but Frederick Morton is very … industrious.'

'Yes, you're right,' Percy hissed. 'I know he is, damn him.' He paused. 'Now look out, the beaters are almost through. Go back to the house and we'll talk again at luncheon.'

As Wilkins walked away Percy spotted a third pigeon – darting out of cover down low. He fitted the shotgun to his shoulder and fired. This time the tight-packed number-eight shot struck the bird squarely and it fell to the ground in a puff of feathers. He smiled to himself. Two. Not a bad start.

★★★

After the hunt, the guests gathered on the back lawns of the estate, where trestles covered with white linen displayed a variety of food, and a covey of liveried waiters distributed wine. Later, in a pit screened by trees, a bull terrier belonging to Percy would engage in mortal combat with a champion dog of the American fighting breed.

Percy sighed with pleasure. This was the kind of life he had been born to lead, far removed from the austerity of his father's tenure. He sipped at his drink, watching as his sister Sophie walked across to him.

'What did Wilkins want?'

'Not much. Morton is starting up a factory in some decrepit works in Deptford.'

'The cheek of him. He needs to be brought down.'

'I know he does. Bear in mind, however, that we don't know what he knows, or what promises he made to Pater.'

Sophie regarded her brother at length. 'You must be subtle. You are rich, and powerful. You can destroy him at arms' length. Where is he getting the money? That would be a good place to start.'

Percy looked at his sister. Her eyes were bright and clear, her face beautiful. Now, separated from her first husband, she was as popular as any young woman in the capital. She had many sexual partners, some married, often at these weekend parties, but he didn't care. The thought, in fact, excited him.

An esoteric figure came out of the doorway to join them. He was perhaps forty years old, with a long beard, wearing robes like those of a priest. His name was Eugene Vintras. He took Sophie's hand and spoke in heavily-accented English.

'Oh, beloved of Ovid,' he cried, 'lead me to the wine.' As other rich men might invite poets or artists to their table, so did Percy like to sprinkle his gatherings with people of interest. Vintras, however, was no poet, but a French devil-worshipper. He had fled to London to escape persecution in his homeland, and he preached a dark gospel that found receptive ears in the Forgill siblings.

The voices in Vintras's head, apparently, came from the Prophet

Elijah, and the Virgin Mary. He inhabited a world of spirits that provided for Percy a distraction from the affairs of the Forgill business empire.

Percy hesitated for a moment. He wanted to participate in whatever activities Vintras might devise for the afternoon but was more than a little inspired by Sophie's suggestions for nipping Morton's aspirations in the bud.

It would be best, he decided, to dispose of all business matters before moving on for the day. 'Excuse me for a moment,' he said, then went across to find Wilkins, who was sipping a sloe gin on his own.

'I would have thought that even you could have some fun here,' Percy said.

An insect settled near the Thin Man's nose and he seized it in his palm with a flick of his wrist. This done, he crushed and dropped the insect to the grass. 'I'm watchin' and listenin',' he said. 'That's entertainment to me.'

Percy took a vacant chair. 'My sister just made a suggestion. How do you think we might exert influence over the bank that is funding Morton?'

Wilkins thought for a moment. 'The best way would be to find an' recruit a clerk at Barings. If I could identify someone oo values money more than loyalty, they might sooner or later provide information what we can use against the bank.'

Percy removed his gloves, placing them on his lap. 'You're right. And once we have information we can act.'

'The process may take some time,' warned Wilkins.

Percy had been reading a certain work of philosophy called *The Prince*, by a medieval Italian statesman called Niccolò Machiavelli. The wisdom therein had quite captured his imagination. One of Machiavelli's precepts was, *Never attempt to win by force what can be won by deception.* 'You're a natural, Wilkins,' he said. 'Please go ahead and find me this clerk.'

Towards evening, when the guns had been oiled and replaced in their cases, the luncheon tables folded and dishes washed by a small and overworked crew of servants – twelve of the guests, including Percy, Sophie and Vintras himself, sat at a table in the manor's library, where no doubt long-dead earls and their children had lost themselves in the texts that lined the shelves.

The table occupied the centre of the room, a powerful placement that Vintras had insisted on. The surface, polished by decades of elbows, books and hands, was of solid oak, a rich and lustrous brown with strong dark grains running along the face.

The Ouija board was on the surface of the table, and Vintras had his eyes closed. 'I sense guilt,' he cried, 'and death. I smell it in my nostrils.'

Percy closed his eyes and smiled to himself. He could almost smell his old friend the wolf loping along the beaten pathway to his door.

★★★

Despite working ten to fourteen hours each day, gearing the factory up to produce its first engine parts, Frederick found time to get across to London Hospital to visit Jones, usually carrying a parcel of delicacies baked by Clare or Eleanor. On the fourth or fifth such visit he saw from his friend's face, even as he approached the bed, that something had changed.

'The stump is healing well,' Vic explained, 'and they'll be trying me out with a pegleg tomorrow.'

'That's good news,' said Frederick. 'Yet you look despondent – and God knows you have reason to be.'

'I'm sorry. I can't help it. Elfard, the factory manager, came in here yesterday with his pet physician – old Williams – who examined me and said I'd be unfit for factory work. Elfard sacked me on the spot. I got two week's wages and a ten-pound injury payment. After twenty years on the job, they treat me like this—' He coughed, then, 'They say that I won't be mobile enough on my pegleg to do the job.'

'The bastards.'

'I don't know what I'm going to do – they're supposed to be discharging me on the weekend. I've got four kids still at home, and rent to pay – we'll have enough, with my severance pay for a month or two, and after that—'

'How much was Forgill paying you?'

'Fourteen pounds a month.'

Frederick did some quick figures in his head. It was a lot of money, but the benefits of having such an experienced man on the floor were enormous. 'I'll pay you fifteen, for a start. Can you begin next week?'

'You'll employ me, with my leg half gone, hobbling around like an old man?'

'How could I miss the opportunity to hire one of the best men in the industry.'

Tears flooded Jones's eyes, 'Oh, thank you.' Then, 'Percy Forgill will be shouting mad.'

'He's shouting mad anyway. He'll see my little operation here as a threat, but he can't hurt me now.'

'I wouldn't be too sure of that,' said Jones. 'But in any case, I'll gladly accept your kind offer.' He grinned widely. 'I can hardly wait to tell dear Allie that we're not all for the dosshouse after all.'

★★★

Central to the process of producing high-performance steam engines was boiler making. Frederick had studied the work of an engineer called Woolf, who had introduced precision into the process, including the steam-powered punching of rivet holes. Boiler designs were many, and Frederick developed his own variation of the elongated-barrel-shaped Lancashire style. This decision was encouraged by the fact that there were no current patents protecting this design.

The new Mobilis engine would have the boiler incorporated into the frame, much like a traction engine, while the whole machine would be mounted on an iron chassis, or heavy cast wheels, depending on customer preferences.

To manufacture each component of the Mobilis, then assemble it into a working machine, the Morton Works, as it was soon nicknamed, used scaled down versions of all the areas Frederick knew well from the Forgill's plant, distributed through the three bays. There was no dedicated drafting room, as Frederick handled all the design tasks himself, often working late into the night in his office at home.

When Jones arrived for his first day at work, Frederick felt a renewed faith that his little enterprise was in with a chance. The sound of the peg leg clapping on the floor became a great comfort, and within a week of Jones's arrival, nine skilled workers from Forgill's had applied for work at Morton's, and Frederick had taken them on.

Jones supervised the casting of parts in loam, and green and dry sand. Turners rubbed shoulders with assemblers. Machinists bent over lathes and measured parts in thousandths of an inch while Frederick modified designs and lent a hand wherever it was required.

Nothing in his experience had prepared him for the joy of seeing his own designs rise from sheets of flat paper into molten iron, cooling to become near-unbreakable parts. Long hours, often for Clare as well as himself, became an imperative, and one of the few personal purchases he made was a small trap and two horses to draw it. This made the journey to and from the factory less of an ordeal.

Building the first Mobilis engine took twelve months, and when the day came, the crew assembled the prototype on the central floor space, and burnished it to a brilliant shine. A general announcement summoned all the factory workers to come and watch the test.

'Fire her up,' called Frederick. 'Let's see our creation run.'

The stoker started with scrap wood for the initial heating, as coal burned at too high a temperature to start a cold boiler. As the wood flared, he used a long rake to distribute heat through the firebox.

Frederick paced the concrete floor, watching every step. The engine was a thing of beauty, all gleaming chrome and bright paint. The assembly sat beneath the boiler, bolted to the bedplate casting. It utilised two high-pressure cylinders, with the feed-pump eccentric on the crankshaft.

With the fireboxes warm at last, the stoker started adding coal. Heat radiated from the boiler, and the ashpans glowed. Frederick himself checked gauges and filled oil cups.

A shining carriage arrived out the front of the factory, and Ned Baring himself, in glossy black tails, and his wife Louisa, stepped down to the ash-strewn roadway, there to watch the new Mobilis machine exit the womb, take its first breaths and cry on its own. Even Jones, looking dapper with his cane and pegleg, could scarcely hold back tears at the magnificent, huffing machine that they had made in those once-decrepit factory bays.

Frederick shook Ned Baring's hand. 'I'm so glad you could come.'

'I wouldn't have missed it.'

There were others too – Clare and Eleanor – even Horace Batherton from the bank and Bosun Benson smoking his clove cigarettes, waxing lyrical about the age of steam now being able to visit every farmhouse, and backyard factory.

Finally, the boiler reached working pressure, and Frederick, grinning like a child, watched the piston cycle for the first time. The eccentric turned, and the slide valve caused steam to feed into alternating ends of the cylinder.

Ned Baring's eyes were fixed on the revolving flywheel. 'You're a miracle worker,' he said. But Frederick took a notepad and pencil stub from his top pocket and was soon busy writing notes. The machine was almost perfect, but not quite.

Afterwards, in a private room at the Joiner's Arms on High Street, frothy china pots of ale were lined up on the bar. Louisa Baring held her champagne as carefully as a rose stem and looked askance at the rough factory workers who were imbibing happily of the free-flowing beer.

Ned Baring raised his beverage. 'Here's to a new engine that is lighter, more transportable, simpler and easier to operate than anything else on the market.'

Jones drank deeply, heedless of the foam falling back over his wrists, then slammed the empty pot down on the bar, accepting a new one from the barman, who watched proceedings with a very long clay pipe between his lips. 'Another toast,' he cried. 'To the finest engineer in all England.'

'Hear, hear,' cried the assembled gang on both sides of the table.

'To the captain of a factory bettered by none in all of London, and a crew as able as any on the high seas,' came the toast from Bosun Benson.

Clare too, proposed a toast, 'To Ned Baring and his bank that made the factory possible.'

'So very true,' cried Frederick, to the accompaniment of men seconding the motion and liquid pouring down throats like miniature waterfalls.

'So, what now?' Louisa Baring asked.

'We start work on the Fortis,' Frederick replied.

'To the Fortis,' someone repeated, and they all drank again.

Frederick joined in the shouts and enthusiasm, but husbanded his beer carefully, drinking just two pints throughout the evening. Back home by eleven, he went to his desk and sharpened his pencil. Changes were necessary if the Mobilis engine was to be faultless.

Chapter Twenty-two

With the factory beginning production, Frederick understood that it was time to start marketing. After all, the business plan called for initial sales of two units per month. To this end Frederick hung his workshop overalls on their peg, donned a hat and dark jacket, and set off to tell the marketplace why they needed this new engine.

He visited dozens of civic and rural machinery distributors, offering attractive commissions. He took out half-page advertisements in twenty or more regional newspapers. He spoke until he was hoarse, of the simplicity and miserly fuel consumption of the unit, and reduced the price to £210 as an introductory offer, marginally cheaper than his closest competitor in these markets, the Robey and Company's 'Undertype.'

'The Mobilis burns only forty pounds of coal each hour,' Frederick said many times, in many different ways. 'Maintenance is a simple matter, and we are keeping every part down to the tiniest spring in stock and ready for despatch.'

When, after two weeks away, Frederick arrived back on the train, he found the house faultlessly clean, mostly due to Eleanor's tireless efforts, and the factory's three bays running smoothly, directed by Vic Jones, his disability no impediment to keeping a watchful eye on all areas of the plant.

Clare, however, took her work on the company books seriously, and accosted Frederick almost as soon as he walked in the door. 'We are low on cash – purchasing raw materials for the ordered engines is eating up our reserves. The next payment from Barings is spoken for, and we have some suppliers at sixty days.'

'I suppose we'll just have to build the engines faster.'

'Possibly,' said Clare, 'but you'd need to hire more staff or pay overtime. I have another idea.'

★★★

Pregnant with their second child, Clare found sitting uncomfortable; at that time dealing with back pain and a pinched sciatic nerve. Even so, she maintained her usual high-energy routine. On an excursion to the City with May, she saw and souvenired a playbill advertising a pedestrian contest, the title wrapped across the top in giant bold letters.

PEDESTRIANS WANTED. LONDON TO LEEDS. 200 MILES FOR A 200 POUND PURSE

Frederick read through the fine print before putting the page aside. 'I don't have time to be a pedestrian as well as running a fledgling business.'

'That may be true, but two hundred pounds is a lot of money. You are not the one doing the books – I spend much of my day juggling creditors. Two hundred pounds would make a serious difference.'

'It will only make a difference if I win the race, and second prize is just twenty-five.'

'Getting out of the factory would do you good. This race will generate publicity. Perhaps we could have a jersey made, with MORTON STEAM POWER on the back.' Clare walked over to him, tilted his chin with her thumb and forefinger and picked a speck of cotton waste from his jacket. 'You are the most determined man

I have ever met. I don't believe anyone can stop you from achieving what you genuinely wish to do.'

'Let's talk no more of it. I want to be here with you and May, not away racing other fellows on lonely roads.' His words sounded unconvincing, even to his own ears. He liked the thought of putting aside the world of business for a few days, to compete in the open air, with other men. They both knew it.

Clare grinned at him. 'Two hundred pounds,' was all she said, the last word with emphasis.

★★★

It was the lure of the money that saw him mailing in his five-guinea participation fee. Two hundred pounds was enough to buy the iron to build four Mobilis engines. Enough to pay wages for several weeks. Besides, the race started on a Saturday, and Jones could run the factory on Monday and Tuesday.

'I still don't think I'll win,' Frederick said.

'Maybe not,' said Clare. 'But you are very good at this walking business, so why shouldn't you give it a try?'

★★★

The Thin Man sent a brief note, scheduling a meeting in Hyde Park within walking distance of Percy's Park Lane abode. The chosen place was a green nook amongst the trees, out of sight of strolling lords and ladies in top hats.

On Percy's way to the meeting, the weather was turning, a blustery wind howling in over his back. Even the ravens and squirrels were off finding shelter where they could. Percy wore a heavy coat and woollen scarf draped twice around his neck. He strolled down past the Speakers' Corner, ignoring the self-styled philosophers and their small crowds of listeners.

The Thin Man was there early, the bicycle propped up in the usual place. He stubbed out his cigarette as Percy approached and brushed the latest fall of leaves from the chair. Yet he did not stand for his master's arrival. It was not their way. To an observer they would be equals. Old friends in a park.

'What's the news?' Percy asked. He did not waste time with pleasantries.

Wilkins lit a cigarette and drew deeply. 'Morton has paid the entry fee for a pedestrian contest – a lucrative one.'

'How do you find out such trivial information as that?' asked Percy.

'I 'ave me ear to the ground, and a web of contacts that the Yard would envy. I simply let it be known oo I've an interest in, and the intelligence trickles in.' He paused. 'I thought you might be more interested.'

'I *am* interested, somewhat. Obviously, Morton needs money. What's the route?'

'London to Leeds. For a purse of two hundred pounds sterling.'

'A desperate man indeed,' commented Percy.

The Thin Man raised a sly eyebrow, knowing that his next statement would pique his employer's interest. 'From what I understand 'e'll be wearin' a shirt with the words, "The Morton Steam Power Company" on the back.'

'Like a sponsor, eh?'

'Yes sir.'

'Is he likely to win?'

'Conventional wisdom would say no, but Morton is not a conventional man. As we have observed before today, he is very determined.'

Percy Forgill removed his cigarette case, fitted one of the paper tubes to a holder, then struck a vesta and lit it. 'I wonder who is currently the best pedestrian racer in the country?'

'I'm not sure, sir.'

'Find out, would you please?'

'Of course, sir.'

'By tonight, if you can, we have arrangements to make.'

'Very well sir.'

★★★

The race start took place on the following Saturday morning, at London Fields, Hackney. The competitors and their supporters milled like fish in a pond waiting to be fed. Behind the crowd, near a copse of swaying trees, a herd of cattle grazed, unperturbed by the commotion, their lowing just audible under the hum of conversation.

Frederick looked around at the other eighty-seven participants, all male but for three or four. He noted their colourful jerseys, stockings or breeches, hats and trousers, some performing superstitious rituals like drinking green tea or looking for good-luck charms such as feathers on the ground. Others gathered near the pub, across a sweep of green lawn, throwing down a final ale before the start. They were of a delightful array of body shapes, some very tall, some short and wiry, but in general they were lean or even gaunt. Studying them, Frederick's assessment of his own chances plunged.

In all, Frederick found this a more intimidating experience than his cross-country event in Paris, or even the pub bout when he had first moved to Lewisham. The numbers of well-wishers made it seem like a carnival. Clare, May and Eleanor had travelled across the river for the occasion, waving at him from behind a rope barrier, while Vic Jones and half a dozen workers from the factory clutched beer mugs, cheering and talking.

Frederick wore the white jersey Clare had made for him, with the words 'MORTON STEAM POWER' appliquéd across the back, just as some of the other competitors had done for their sponsors. He also wore a brand-new pair of walking shoes, another gift from Clare. He had worn them everywhere for days, letting them meld to his feet ready for the race.

Ignoring the bravado of those who insisted on elbowing their way to the front of the pack, Frederick was happy to find a place towards the back. 'Idiots,' said the fellow next to him. 'As if a couple of yards is going to make a difference over two hundred miles.'

Frederick smiled back, then listened as the race patron ran through the rules, a list that included not only the proper gait, but also covered such misdemeanours as tripping, spitting and sledging. Finally, the starter took control, producing a cap and ball revolver which he pointed skywards and fired with a puff of black powder smoke. The walkers hurried out in a bunch, bustling like worker ants out of the hive at daybreak. Once again Frederick did not rush, but gathered himself some space in which to move, waving one last time to Vic and the factory workers, then blowing a kiss to Clare, who was holding May in her arms so she could see her father. The pair hurried along the ropes to wave, until a shrub blocked Clare's forward progress and she was forced to stop.

Frederick waved one last time, loving them both, before the mass of pedestrians carried him away. He was part of the movement that saw the body of racers metamorphose from a blob of men to a line, filing from the park pathway to the first of many narrow streets.

Frederick understood that this contest would be conducted very differently to his unofficial bout with Charles Villon, where the route was a matter of choice. Even so, he was surprised to see race marshals standing at strategic intervals as he set off on the first leg, west across the city to Canonbury and East Finchley.

Light rain started to fall as the snaking line of pedestrians coiled to the right and headed northwards, but Frederick did not mind the tiny droplets dampening his hat and shoulders or clinging to his lashes. He was finding his feet, assessing the bodies and temperaments of those ahead, not yet ready to begin any move towards the front, but planning to do so when the time was right.

As he went his feet made a rhythm that became a mantra in his head.

Every mile, if I win, is worth one pound.

By mid-afternoon they had passed through Chiswell Green then Luton, on the road to the North. The rain came and went, and Frederick thought himself to be in good shape.

★★★

Night fell before the strange procession reached Leicester, and by then Frederick shared the road with a spread-out line of walkers. The next man was some two hundred yards ahead, and a pair were so close behind that he could hear them converse in breathy sentences. Night, it seemed, was a time for holding position, and steady walking.

Now and then competitors could be seen either heading to a support wagon, drawn up alongside the road, or finding a quiet spot in a handy park to get some sleep.

Frederick had planned his breaks, and with relief he spotted his own wagon waiting for him beyond Leicester. The driver they had hired for the occasion was called Jenkins, who had a nice steady attitude. Not a tall man, Jenkins was very heavy in the shoulders and thighs, with scarcely any neck at all, thinning ginger hair and pale blue eyes. He had an air of reliability about him, and the welcoming smile was genuine.

'Allow me three hours sleep, please,' Frederick said, after he had eaten. 'No more.'

The wagon was an indulgence, but necessary for a race such as this – if Frederick was to have any hope of winning the money, he needed every advantage – a safe and reliable place to rest, good food, and clean clothes.

Frederick fell into sleep, and in no time, it seemed, Jenkins was shaking his shoulder and bringing him out of a deep slumber. After a hurried bite to eat and copious water he was up and walking, but he felt brittle from sleep, and the darkness was unsettling.

His pace was fast, almost too fast, and the hair on the back of his neck was standing erect. His old walking companion, it seemed, was close behind. That lupine shape trailed like a nightmare, insatiable and as forlorn as it was frightening. Even though Frederick could articulate to himself the impossibility of this, adrenaline continued to spur his legs, and he passed many other racers before dawn, when the sun rose and the wolf slunk away.

Frederick's plan, that morning, was to begin moving up through the pack, using the good weather and his well-rested state. The road was amenable to rapid walking – thirty feet wide in all, with a macadamised surface laid as level as any London street, with a fall of a few inches from the centre to the edges.

He studied other racers as he passed them. They were, he decided, an interesting bunch of athletes, as was the changing scenery. Even the road surface didn't remain static. Near Sheffield it began to incorporate ironworks slag, giving it a crunching firmness that more effectively shed water from occasional light rain.

Just after midday, having overtaken more of the faltering pedestrians, Frederick noted a distinctive figure up ahead. He was a tall fellow, and Frederick understood that he was different from most of the others. He was not merely holding his place, but like Frederick he was accelerating, overtaking others, walking to a plan.

Frederick did not mean to speed up, but he wanted to catch that one man – he was no run-of-the mill competitor performing above himself – but someone planning to win.

It took Frederick almost an hour to get close to his target, and it was then that he saw something that both intrigued and troubled him. Printed across the back of the man's jersey were the words – FORGILL'S ENGINE WORKS.

Frederick realised that he could not, no matter what the odds, allow this man to beat him to Leeds.

★★★

At the base of a hill this human-machine turned to see Frederick on his tail, dogged and gaining. Alarmed, he adopted a pace that seemed to be impossible to match. Frederick's legs were on fire as he tackled the slope, armed with a growing understanding of just how hard he was going to have to work to win this race.

Heading into the night, now less than fifty miles from Leeds, Frederick watched the leader step off the road to a waiting wagon for food and sleep. This gave him a strange feeling – momentarily at least, he no longer had a serious competitor in the race.

Still following the itinerary that he and Clare had mapped out, Frederick staggered on, desperate for sleep, towards the town of Barnsley, where his own wagon was waiting. He goaded himself with the knowledge that on the morrow he would see both Clare and May, who were catching the train up to Leeds for the finish.

Jenkins was waiting with a pot of chicken broth, a plate of buttered bread and a quart of brandy. Frederick ate hungrily, listening to his driver's summary of the race progress. 'So far as I'm concerned, Mister Morton sir, there's only two men in the race – you and the string bean of a bloke.'

'Not much of a prize for third,' said Frederick, 'so I'd better keep with him.'

After the meal he took off his shoes and socks, and examined his toes, pleased to see no sign of blisters.

'How long will you sleep for?' asked the driver.

'Two hours tonight,' said Frederick, moving to the straw-tick mattress and pulling the blanket up over his body. Closing his eyes, and blocking out the stabbing pain in his legs, Frederick invoked sleep as if it were some back-country god. Unconsciousness came not stealthily, but like a sledge-hammer blow to the head. At first this repose was dreamless, and then his mind roved far from his exhausted body. Later, after the first abyss-like sleep, he became conscious of a rounded belly, and soft breasts pressed against his back; hot breath tingling on his neck.

Waking to the touch of lips to his ear, he felt himself becoming energised in a new way. He turned as far as the encircling arms allowed him. 'Clare?'

'Yes, it's me. I gave Jenkins some money to go and sleep in the tavern there.'

'You have a way of surprising me.'

'You have a way of making me miss you. Now before you start worrying, May is at our hotel in Leeds with Eleanor. I'll catch the train back again at five in the morning. So we have a few minutes together, my darling.' Clare snuggled into him, massaged the hard and battered muscles of his thighs, 'You are in a good position, *cheri*. There is just that one man who will be hard to beat.'

'I know. And I suspect that Percy Forgill only sponsored him to get at me.'

'I suspect that you are right.' Clare made a snorting sound. 'I have been doing some research into his past activities. But first you must remember that he is competing only for money, not with a passion. His name is Rufus Johnson. He has won many, many races. Bristol to London in nine hours. Portsea to Edinburgh in three days.'

'Impressive.'

'Yet, he is ten years older than you, and he likes to win a little too much – he has been known to alter his gait when hard pressed.'

Frederick raised an eyebrow, 'You mean sneak in a little run?'

'Yes – he might be a little too keen to collect whatever reward Percy Forgill has promised him for winning. You must press him hard, my darling. You have won against a cheat before.'

★★★

Clare and Jenkins were correct – for the last twenty miles there were only two men in the race. Later Frederick would read in the Leeds Times' gleeful puns about the 'men of iron' representing steam engine manufacturers and their 'desperate battle' for a winning position.

When Frederick entered the northern city's first calm streets a little after dawn, the wolf was hard on his tail, and Rufus Johnson was some hundred yards ahead. A significant number of spectators had left their homes to watch the racers come in. Their gentle clapping was testament to the physical extremes they could see on the faces of the leaders, and Frederick inclined his head to acknowledge it. He was still not resigned to second place. It seemed, for the first time, that he had gained some ground against the leader. The money was now immaterial, it was a man-to-man contest. They had both left lesser competitors in their wake, most either straggling or dropped out along the way. Frederick felt himself to be on the brink of something very special indeed.

As they passed an immense wool-processing factory, the smell of lanolin thickening the air, a commotion broke out in the crowd around a bend up ahead; some catcalls and jeers. At first Frederick thought that the other man had won – and they were cheering him. Yet these were more jeers than cheers, and the race was not due to end until they reached Roundhay Park. This area was still industrial in nature.

The sound soon died off and Frederick pushed all contemplation away, moving his muscles in that mechanical yet fluid pedestrian gait. Despite his efforts, when he rounded the bend, with the park now in view, he was surprised to see his adversary a little further ahead.

When Frederick girded himself for a final effort, he found very little in the way of reserves. His legs worked of their own volition now, not responding to the urgings of his mind. Finally, entering the park at last, he could see the town's famous drinking fountain with its bronze cups, and the thought of water made him swoon.

Only a few hundred yards to go now, and his tall competitor was still ahead. Frederick realised that even if he found renewed vigour, even if he took flight like a bird, it was no longer possible to catch the man.

The irony struck him. His second long-distance cross-country pedestrian race, and again he would take second place. All this work, all these preparations, for so little return. Second place was worth just twenty-five pounds, a figure Frederick had spent on preparations, travel, and the wagon. It wasn't enough, and he realised just how badly he had wanted to win.

As Frederick closed in on the rope, he saw Clare with May, there behind the barriers, walking along with him as he stumbled slowly to the end, easily keeping pace with his reduced rate of travel. He wanted to respond to their urgings, but he could not do so. He had nothing left. Besides, it was all over. The Forgill's Man had just breasted the final tape to a chorus of cheers.

Frederick staggered on, past the finish line, as if his legs did not know how to stop. Clare resolved this senseless motion by taking him in her arms. He offered no resistance when she helped him to the ground, where he spread like a dropped towel. May tried to hug him from his prone position, confused at his physical condition, talking to him in her matter-of-fact way.

The confusion in her words combined with his disappointment to crush his spirit. 'So close,' Clare was saying. 'I'm proud of you.'

Yet, Frederick felt only shame, that he had side-tracked himself into a contest he had not won, when he should have been at the factory making engines.

A race helper placed a cool glass of lemonade in his right hand. This he drained very quickly, feeling each sugary droplet move through his body, revitalising and awakening. His left hand was held firmly by May, while she pointed around the park and asked the same questions over and over.

Frederick was conscious of a crowd around the winning pedestrian, and there was some gesticulating. 'What's going on there?' he grunted.

'I don't know,' said Clare. 'There's some kind of commotion going on ... one of the marshals is over with the judges, and there appears to be a small crowd of angry people.'

Frederick walked closer to the group, finishing his drink and lifting May up to his hip. The little meeting, it seemed, was over. To his dismay Frederick became the focus of attention.

The race marshal, flanked by his assistants, picked him out and walked towards him. 'Excuse me,' said the marshal. 'The fellow who crossed the line first has been disqualified. You are the winner.'

'How?'

'It has been confirmed that Mister Johnson broke into a jog, sir.'

'The poor man,' groaned Frederick. 'He's the winner, jog or no jog.'

'You should be very happy sir.'

'I am, but that's a terrible way to lose a very long race.'

★★★

Later, in their room at the Smithfield Hotel on North Street, Clare insisted on champagne − a '69 Renaudin-Bollinger that tasted of oyster-shell and walnut, the bubbles enlivening Frederick's tired mind, at least for a while.

'Two cross-country races,' Clare enthused, 'and both times you were beaten by cheats − meaning that you won both of them.'

'I feel sorry for the man,' said Frederick. 'He is a far better pedestrian than I, whether he cheated or not.'

'Two hundred pounds,' she said, 'is a big windfall for us and the company.'

'Breathing space,' he agreed, 'for several weeks. Yet I can't keep entering pedestrian contests.'

Chapter Twenty-three

Wilkins found that 'buying' an insider at Barings Bank was no simple task. Despite the number of clerks who worked there, most were happy and loyal. Finding one who was interested in betraying his employer took time. In fact, two years passed before a young clerk who had only lately accepted employment with the company joined Wilkins for a meal at the Stag and Hounds in Shoreditch. After the meal the young man agreed to another pint, supplied by Wilkins, and suggested that he could do with earning a few quid, what with getting married and all – life was expensive these days and getting worse.

The Thin Man, still wearing his fox-skin coat, sailed into Percy Forgill's offices the following morning and waited fifteen minutes for his employer to be free.

'I've found a man at Barings oo will help us.'

'How senior is he?'

'Just a clerk, sir, but he is a charmin' type, oo will swiftly rise. My guess is he'll be worth every penny we can invest in him. I've arranged for a meetin' today in his lunch hour, if you can manage it.

'That was presumptuous of you, but I will make the time if I can.'

★★★

The meeting took place in a coffee house in Spital Square, an unfashionable establishment used by wagoneers and sales people rather than the members of upper echelon society who might recognise Lord Percy Forgill.

Percy dressed down for the occasion, wearing a plain business suit, albeit tailor-made, and with a homburg hat that made him look more like a jobber from the stock market than a Lord of the Realm.

The Thin Man was there with the clerk when Percy sat down, ordered a coffee and appraised his potential informant. The clerk had a tidy figure, with those very fine whiskers that require shaving only once or twice a week. His eyes were a washed-out blue behind thick wire-framed specs, and his hair had been tossed by the wind into wispy blonde curls.

'How long have you been working for Barings?' Percy asked.

'Five months, sir.'

'And you're willing to betray him for a few pounds?'

The clerk looked miserable. 'Not just a few, sir. I'll need a retainer. Twenty guineas per annum.'

'And you will meet with me say twice each year, and brief me on the bank's activities?'

'Yes.'

'You have a deal then.' Percy rose to leave and turned to Wilkins. 'Make arrangements for the man to be paid please.' He said nothing more, just collected his hat and coat and walked away. The whole plan had, at first, seemed interesting and clever, but now it irked him that it was so slow.

★★★

Despite Frederick's work on a high-pressure, superheated stationary engine for his benefactor, Forgill's had never taken any steps towards building one. The chief engineer's opposition to the concept, it seemed, had influenced the board. Even now, under Percy's ownership, the company was focussing on building larger, traditional horizontal engines.

Several years had passed since Frederick had drawn up those first concept drawings, and technology had moved on. The superheated engine that he now designed was a vastly improved version of the last, with his experience at manufacturing, and recent developments in the field informing his pencil.

'It's time to build the Fortis,' he told Clare.

'The brave,' she said. 'Just like you.'

★★★

Steam engine design did not begin with lathes and milling machines, but with a slide rule and tables. Once the basic engine type had been decided upon, the engineer would settle on the number of horsepower the engine was required to produce. Then, in order to determine the area of the piston in square inches, it was necessary to know the piston speed and steam pressures.

With those values in mind, a number of design decisions needed to be made – such as whether the piston body, or spider as it was known, would be of solid or cellular design, what use would be made of cylinder lagging and which materials would be used.

The Fortis was, in some ways, a revolutionary engine, and in others, a traditional horizontal compound engine. The superheater was the main feature that would set it apart, making dramatic input steam pressures approaching two-hundred psi achievable.

Mathematics lay behind much of the work: calculations of cylinder volumes, flywheel size and cylinder spacings relative to valve openings; flow values, and pressures required in the first and secondary cylinders. The estimated work per cycle, together with revolutions per minute, allowed a final estimation of brake horsepower. By the time the first parts were cast, the drawings filled a cabinet.

The superheater was not a new concept, but it had never been applied to a stationary engine. Superheaters used boiler heat to bring steam in tubes up to heretofore unheard-of temperatures, with a resulting increase in efficiency.

'Gentlemen,' Frederick addressed a meeting of his staff, standing and sitting with arms folded on their chests, or wiping hands on oily rags, 'two hundred degrees of superheat will mean a twenty-five per cent reduction in fuel expenditure, along with a dramatic boost in horsepower from the same engine footprint, and a vast reduction in thermal waste.'

There was silence for a moment, then, 'Mister Morton, one of the barriers to this type of engine is a high temperature lubricating oil? Do we have access to a suitable source?'

'Not yet, but we will find one. We'll also need to work on a new kind of piston packing – current types would burn in the kinds of temperatures we're proposing. From this point onwards I do not want to hear the words "We can't," or "It won't work." Do we all understand each other?'

★★★

In the following months, prototype superheaters were assembled and tested – tubes made of a special alloy with one-hundred-and-eighty-degree bends, sized to fit under the header drum of a specially designed boiler.

Refining the design continued, while new Mobilis engines rolled out of the Bay Three assembly areas. Frederick found ways to improve the Fortis, increasing the theoretical boiler steaming capacity, measured in pounds per hour, until even his own workers whistled in surprise.

More parts emerged from the foundry, the biggest of them some eight hundred pounds in weight, and meanwhile the hunt went on for a special lubricating oil. An article in an engineering periodical helped narrow the search down to a well near Oil Springs, Ontario, Canada, that had produced samples with remarkable abilities not to degrade at high temperatures – upwards of three-hundred-degrees

Fahrenheit. Three weeks later, eighteen gallons of these new oils arrived, becoming the subject of testing in the factory.

★★★

Early in 1873, Clare gave birth to a boy, Denley, soon shortened to Denny, and sixteen months later, Matthew. They were, in their parents' eyes at least, perfect, constantly-evolving personalities, and although this was a time when Frederick felt that he needed to work harder – more days than not he hurried home from the factory at five or six in the evening to be with his family.

Despite the addition of a full-time maid, Eleanor, in those days, was both cook and nanny, an important part of family life, with her lips like the two halves of a mussel shell, gripping the stem of her clay pipe, though Clare had long banned her from smoking in the drawing room. The children liked the older woman very much, and together they spent many hours in the back yard, where Eleanor was free to smoke, and the siblings to roam.

Clare loved to dine out, and she insisted that they patronise the new restaurants that were springing up around Lewisham and Ladywell. Not decadently expensive like Verrey's or Rules in the City, the local establishments were dining houses more in line with the family's budget.

As for child-rearing, Clare was like no mother Frederick had imagined. She talked to her young charges as if they were adults, asked rhetorical questions, and when she found a word or action that made them laugh, she repeated it, until none of them could control their mirth.

Even on the frostiest mornings, Clare would install Matthew in the pushchair and stroll footpaths outside blocks of brown-brick homes, with Denny holding hands with May, making their way along uneven cobbles, past frozen puddles and robins whistling from the elms.

Bath time was a noisy affair, completed with splashing –

sometimes tears, as Clare insisted that every grain of dirt be removed from each child. When Frederick performed this duty, the children saw him as a soft-touch, and lulled him into singing to them instead of scrubbing harshly.

Now and then a letter would arrive from Saint Laurent, France, and Clare would read it and exclaim. 'Pah! They want us to visit, but surely my father can understand what it's like for us to be building a business – and a family.'

Believing that it was never too early to expose her children to culture in the form of museums and galleries, Clare began monthly excursions into the City with both she and her children dressed fashionably for the occasion. Clare's four-year-old Paris frocks were still fresh enough in London. May always had new dresses, and the boys suits of bright colours and dashing cut. Most of the time they would return with bags of fresh vegetables or small treasures gleaned from the markets of Covent Garden, and always a story or two to tell about the day. This, it seemed to Frederick, was a marvellous environment for his children to grow in, and scarcely a week went by that there would not be a new addition in the drawing room, bedroom, or entry: a lamp shade, a hat stand or, in keeping with Clare's increasing interest in indoor plants, a fern or brass pot.

Over those years she threw herself into the Victorian mania for indoor fern-growing, the more exotic the better, and her terrariums, arranged through the hallways and drawing room, were filled with bright green plants from Madagascar, Africa and the Antipodes.

Meanwhile, May grew tomboyish, Denny carefree, and Matthew thoughtful.

★★★

When May was seven years old, she was presented with the younger sister she had always wanted, a fair-haired babe they called Harriet. Keeping the infant happy became May's chief occupation; a task she took quite seriously.

One Sunday afternoon, not long after Harriet had taken her first, much-applauded step, May appeared in the garden when Frederick was enjoying some spadework and watering – an activity that had become one of his practical delights – particularly nurturing Clare's roses. His daughter paused at five paces and watched him blend compost into a pot of soil.

'Father, may I please use your toolbox?'

Frederick finished the pot he was filling, then turned to his daughter – loving the deep seriousness of her dark eyes, the spray of freckles across her nose, and the proud planes of her cheeks. 'Why would that be?'

'Harriet's music box is broken. I want to fix it.'

Frederick raised his eyebrows, 'Of course you can.' He watched her go indulgently. She always put things back in their place, and instinctively grasped the importance of doing just that.

Once she had gone, Frederick continued his work. One of the patternmakers at the factory had given him some daffodil bulbs, and he began to plant them out in some terracotta pots that had become vacant. He planted three on each side of the stone porch. Once this was done, he spent a pleasant half hour pulling weeds from the lawn, and was surprised when May came through the door, tears streaming down her cheeks.

'What on earth is wrong?' Frederick asked.

'I tried,' she said. 'But I can't fix it.'

'The music box?'

May dabbed at her eyes and nose with a handkerchief. 'Yes.'

'Do you want me to help?'

'Yes please.'

'Then so I shall. Just give me a moment to take off my boots and wash my hands.'

★★★

Inside, Frederick opened the curtains to admit light, then took a seat at the drawing room table where May had disassembled the music box. He examined each of the pieces minutely, then held the drum between thumb and forefinger.

'This looks like a toy,' he said, 'but it's not.'

'What is it then?' May asked, her eyes drying, thrilled by the sight of her father's big fingers holding the tiny parts.

'It's quite sophisticated engineering. Every component has a task. Some are more or less important than others, but all play their part.' He turned to look at her, smiling. 'First lesson. If ever you take something unfamiliar apart, draw a diagram as you go. Deconstruct. Try to understand how it works.'

May, hearing these words as a challenge, leaned over, picked up the bar of tines and clipped one with her fingernail, making it chime dully. 'Each one of these plays a note,' she said. 'There are five tines because there are only five notes in the song. When the drum rotates, the little bumps lift the tines at the correct moment, and that plays the song.'

'Yet, the drum can't sit in mid-air like that, can it?' Frederick asked.

'No,' said May. She reached out and touched a tube of steel not much thicker than a toothpick. 'It needs an axle like this to spin around on.' Again she delved in the pile of parts. 'And mounts to hold the axle in place.'

'Very good.'

But May was not finished yet; 'The clockwork turns the drum through this cog.'

'Yes, the clockwork is the engine that drives everything along. Now let's see if we can deduce what the problem with the music box is. Is the clockwork winding?'

'Yes, it seems to wind.'

'Will it turn once it has been wound?'

'It's turning now, very slowly, I can see it.'

'What happens when we connect it to the cog?'

May glanced at him, as if for permission, then fitted the clockwork assembly back into the box, followed by the tiny gears. She looked up again, 'It stops.'

'Then there's a problem in the gear. Is there some grit, perhaps?'

May's face was a study in concentration as she lifted and examined the tiny steel cogs, trying to spin one by hand.

'Oh look,' she said at last. 'This axle has made the housing bigger – perhaps now the cog's teeth won't sit properly.'

Frederick took the part from her and examined it. 'You're right – the gears aren't meshing together. Can you think of a way to fix it?'

May thought for a moment, smiling now, then shook her head.

'The force on these parts is not very great,' said Frederick. 'I believe that we can solder over the old mount and drill a new hole for the axle to occupy. What do you think?'

May nodded vehemently. 'Yes, that's what we should do.'

Chapter Twenty-four

Slowly, over these full and busy years, the prototype Fortis was built, modified, and rebuilt at the Deptford Creek factory. With some sadness, the old Boulton and Watt beam engine that powered the Morton factory was sold and removed, and the prototype superheated Fortis assembled in its place – to minimise down-time this operation was completed in just four days of round-the-clock labour.

The new engine was then launched to a full factory celebration. The Fortis would lead the industry, and while it was aimed at the textile mills of Northern England, it could be lifted by steam crane onto a barge on the waters of Deptford Creek, behind the factory, towed to one of London's many docks and loaded on a ship bound for any port in the world. The brand-new engineering marvel was nineteen feet long, and eight feet high. It was more like a streamlined monster than an engine, assembled on a fabricated base so it could be snigged with chains, lifted or floated from place to place. It had a bore of six inches and stroke of seven and one half, with the second and third cylinders larger again. It produced a maximum of four-hundred brake horsepower.

Small groups moved outside to inspect the boiler house, with its tall stack streaming smoke into the air. The boiler itself, while being of traditional Lancashire design, had a longer than usual smokebox to accommodate the superheater.

The firebox was glowing, the boiler hot, while Frederick performed the engineer's role of 'oiling round' for the first time, lubricating everything from the main cylinders, with that special new oil, to the bearings, and some thirty other points besides, while a stoker laboured over the shovel, adjusted the damper, and watched the water 'glass' and pressure gauge.

Finally, the stoker reported a full head of steam, and Frederick opened the regulator. The assembled crowd watched the flywheel turn for the first time, but Frederick was oblivious to them, feeling the engine's movement as if it were his own body, watching the cylinder drains for condensate, before closing them off, hearing the resultant boost in power as he did so.

The engine sounded smooth and quiet, but with an underlying hum of indefatigable power, just like the tides on the river. This was an engine that the world must take seriously: years ahead of its time.

As with the Mobilis, an inspector from the Steam Manufacturers' Association scheduled a visit to certify the boiler. The inspector happily passed the beautifully constructed boiler as fit for sale, and when the engine ran he shook his head in wonder.

'You sir,' he said to Frederick, 'are a most remarkable engineer.'

★★★

Throughout the conception, birth, and growth of Morton children and Morton engines, Clare had never lost her interest in finding the truth of Percy Forgill and his twin, though she had little opportunity to pursue the matter. One day in the mid-'eighties, however, she attended the funeral of the mother of an old Badminton school friend, at St James's Parish church on Piccadilly.

At the conclusion of the ceremony the crowd moved to the graveside, where the body was interred. Afterwards, knowing only a very few of the mourners, Clare wandered around the graves. She had not even articulated the thought that she was looking for anything in particular, but running her eyes over the headstones and their inscriptions passed the time before she knew she must head inside to the hall for tea and scones. At times she paused to touch mossy stone, tracing faded letters and names, placing her feet carefully to avoid standing on ground occupied by a body below.

Some minutes later, up towards the back corner, her eyes fell on the grave of Montgomery Forgill. The epitaph included no cause of death, but the dates confirmed his age: ten years old at the time of his death.

The find surprised her. From Frederick she already knew that most of the Forgill family were buried at the West London and Westminster cemetery. Casting around the area, however, she did find some much older Forgill memorials, the most recent of which was an Augustus Forgill from the mid-eighteenth century, his wife Ellen, along with the grave of an infant who had passed at the age of just three months.

Making a decision to delay her arrival at the wake for the moment, Clare eyed off the Parish office, adjoining the block of church buildings. Perhaps, she decided, it was worth making a discreet enquiry while she was here.

When Clare ascended the steps and entered the office, a woman in her mid-sixties with heavy trunk and shoulders was in attendance, along with a youthful but very serious clerk trimming a new quill.

Clare waited at some length for a response, then cleared her throat, followed by a polite, 'Good morning.'

The woman looked up, 'If you're after Father Henry he's had to rush off after the funeral just now. He'll be with the bishop down at Westminster until Evensong.'

'You might be able to help me – do you have the Parish records here?'

'We have most of the registers, dating back a century and a half,' she paused. 'You're French. Do you have relatives here?'

'I regard myself as English now, but it's another family I'm looking into.'

'Births, deaths, weddings?'

'A birth, well two actually.'

'What date?'

'March 15, 1837.'

'Please wait while I fetch the ledger.'

The woman disappeared for at least five minutes, then returned with a dusty volume. Clare felt the urge to sneeze but held it off as the woman turned pages, finally slowing and arriving at the desired page.

'Some of the handwriting of these people, priests and clerks alike was indescribable, bless them,' she said, running her finger along the page. 'What name were you after?'

'Forgill.'

'May I ask what business it is of a Frenchwoman off the street to be asking after the records of a great family and good friends of this church.'

Clare considered inventing a cover story, but she was quite sure that the woman had no legal standing to refuse her the information. 'My reasons are my own. Those are public records and I have a right to see them.'

The woman turned to the young clerk, and the two of them shared a long glance. 'Perhaps I should ask Father Henry,' she said at last.

Clare stood her ground. 'It is not a matter for Father Henry. These are legal records and I am entitled to view them.'

'Very well then,' said the woman. 'On March 15, 1837. The births of twin boys, to the late Lord Forgill and Lady Forgill. Montgomery and Percival, who as I'm sure you're aware now holds the family title.'

'It is Montgomery I am interested in. Is there any record of his death? On January the twentieth 1848?'

'Yes, Montgomery died around then – he's buried here, as I'm sure you noticed, judging by the questions.' The woman snapped the ledger shut. 'That is as far as I can or will help you. You delve in matters that are none of your business. If you wish to return at some point and ask Father Henry, I know you'll get short shrift from him.'

'How did Montgomery die?' Clare asked.

'If I tell you, will you leave us in peace?'

'Yes.'

The woman pursed her lips, 'The lad was an epileptic. He died of a seizure.'

'Very well then, thank you.'

★★★

Forgill's had commenced building a new engine to Moon's personal design, and the prototype was four months behind schedule – not helped by the bleeding of staff to the Morton factory.

Slowly, however, under Percy's ceaseless haranguing, the machine was nearing completion. It was a horizontal compound engine, and he was invited to see it working on a chilly Thursday afternoon, a day so cold that the spectators huddled as close as they dared to the massive boiler.

The engine itself was a vast affair, filling the test floor, monstrous in scale, the iron finished with a new process that made it appear almost black. The pistons moved in their cylinders slowly but with great power.

Percy loved the eye-glow of red in the furnace, the black iron, and the cycling of the huge engine. To his eyes it was a thing from hell, such as might be made in the workshops of the underworld.

After an hour of watching the great engine run, with a representative of the *Times* on hand to record the moment, Percy felt some satisfaction. Yet, back in the factory office afterwards, he questioned each department, and the answers displeased him. 'How soon can we get these engines into full production?' he asked the floor supervisor.

'We're low on skilled staff sir, we've lost ten key men to Morton's factory in the last few years. And Vic Jones is there also – he's a hard man to do without.'

Then, to the sales department. 'How are the advance orders coming along?'

'I'm sorry, sir, but many of our regulars are holding off on us – the Morton factory have just released a superheated model with a smaller footprint, better economy and more power.'

Percy turned his attention to Moon, glaring at him. 'You told me that the superheated engine would not work?'

Moon raised his nose in the air. 'Not quite. I told you, rather, that superheaters are dangerous and unnecessary. An explosion will occur sooner or later, but obviously Morton has convinced some people that they are safe.'

Marshalling his forces, Percy obtained a specifications sheet for the Fortis engine, through the Steam Manufacturers Association. He had Moon study the design over several days, comparing it to the original plans Frederick had drawn up while working at the factory.

Thomas Brachard, of Donald and Associates, an expert on company and patent law, sat in the chair of Percy's office and studied the two documents while Percy explained; 'Morton is making an engine, ostensibly the same as the one he designed for my father at Forgill's, whilst in our employ. Can I do anything about it?'

'There are similarities,' Brachard said at length. 'Just as Mister Moon has pointed out – but we'd need a consulting engineer to give an independent opinion. There were no patents applied for?'

'No, damn it, we've checked. But—' Percy hissed, 'Morton designed it on our account, while being paid by my family, at my father's express command.'

Brachard shook his head slowly. 'There's a concept called "shop rights" which means that anything designed by an employee, all else being equal, belongs to the company. Yet, if every idea contained in the design is in the public domain, not protected by patents, and might reasonably be arrived at by a competent engineer, then I can't see a legal action succeeding. You could try, but most likely you would lose, with costs.'

'I could beggar him in the meantime – keep the action going until he has no money left to pay.'

Both men knew that civil cases in the British legal system could be stretched out for years without judgement.

'A case would only be worthwhile if you could get an injunction on the manufacture and sale of the engine in question, and that's unlikely under current laws. You also mentioned that Ned Baring has funded the venture. Morton might not have deep pockets, but Barings does. If Baron Revelstoke decides to fund a defence – well, the strategy will not work.'

★★★

Percy called for his carriage and a footman arrived at the door to escort him through. Bartholomew Forgill's old carriage was very fine, but stodgy with its thick panelling and heavy wrought iron, and Percy had replaced it with a modern French-inspired brougham made by Gideons of Birmingham, with ebony inlays, solid-silver fittings and the family coat of arms rendered in gold paint on the doors.

Shortly afterwards, Percy alighted from the carriage at Pall Mall, leaving the driver to park the vehicle and wait. The sun was shining through Saint James Square as he set off towards the fine corner building, formed from Caen stone, that made up the Carlton Club.

At the threshold Percy scarcely acknowledged the doorman who, recognising him, opened the iron-studded teak doors. Inside was a haven of tradition and decorum, away from the hubbub of the streets. The Carlton Club was a Conservative Party stronghold, and Percy strode in, passing several well-known politicians and their puppet masters in the corridors, many of whom he was acquainted with.

Quite apart from fine chefs, and deferential, solicitous waiters, the club was also famous for the facilitation of deals, the generation of conspiracies, and as a stepping-stone to less salubrious, though very expensive, premises in the area.

Leaving his coat, hat and walking stick at the desk, Percy ascended a flight of stairs, then entered a vast upstairs dining space where dozens of well-dressed men were smoking pipes, eating from fine bone-china plates, and sipping from crystal glasses. On the eastern wall, near the window, was a table with twelve chairs. This was Percy's table – a table that never ran out of diners. Most but not all, were old Carthusians. Some carried titles. All were rich. They were a club within a club. Insiders within insiders; the kinds of men with whom Percy felt most at home. Men in velvet jackets, dark ties and coloured waistcoats. Their blood was, in the main, not quite as blue as Percy's own, but the ability to use corporate and titular power to bludgeon, control, amass fortunes and build empires came naturally to them just the same.

Percy took note of the current occupants of those chairs, seven in all. A shipping magnate; a developer puffing on a vast cigar; a small-arms manufacturer; a financial adviser; a stockbroker; a shipping magnate; an army-captain-turned-company-manager; a housing developer and a banker.

The end seat of the table was always reserved for Percy. He was the highest-ranking member of their little group. He took the chair and sat down.

When a waiter brought him a menu he waved it away. 'No food,' he said. 'Bring me a brandy, that's all, and be quick about it.' Over the next hour he nursed a succession of brandies, participating in the conversation around him. Many of the group were having union trouble: industrial action and stop-work meetings.

'Marxists proliferating like flies,' said the Small-arms Manufacturer. 'I'd squash the whole bally lot of them if I could.'

They discussed ways to break the strikes, to target organisers and their families. Some of the suggestions were comical, some practical, and others downright nefarious.

'What's wrong today, Percy? You seem very low,' said the Banker.

'It's that damned Frederick Morton.'

'Freddie Morton from school?'

'The very same: a slum-boy from Stepney who my father took pity on and educated. Morton is a low-grade engineer at best – not talented enough to keep employment at our factory. He most certainly does not belong in the ranks of industrialists. I now believe that he spent his years at my factory executing his own private designs. Even worse, he doesn't understand how the labour market works – he's offering higher wages, and now some kind of blasted health fund for the families of his workers. He must be stopped, or all the labouring class will begin to demand such conditions – the contagion of discontent will flow beyond London, and ever northwards.'

A grumble of agreement passed through the company. They all knew how any flame was soon fanned by agitators in the workforce. Once offered somewhere, it wasn't long before a concession would be demanded by all.

'You never did like Morton,' said the Stockbroker.

'Why would I? My father plucked him from the slums and elevated him above me – his own son. In return, Morton gave us trickery and lies. Now, much more seriously, he is doing us all a genuine wrong.'

'How can we help?'

'We can all begin a quiet campaign against the institution that is funding him – namely Barings Bank.'

The conversation stalled when a waiter arrived with more drinks, then resumed. The mood intensified after the meal and several glasses of port wine, and by three o'clock the company had resolved to take several steps against the Morton concern, including finding ways to make Ned Baring aware that he had picked the wrong man to champion.

Percy seethed. It wasn't enough. The slow revenge was proving to be too slow. The snail's pace of retribution had allowed Frederick Morton to grow stronger, and the clerk at Barings was yet to deliver one snippet of useful information.

At the concierge's desk Percy scribbled a note addressed to Wilkins and had it dispatched immediately.

★★★

When Percy called for his carriage he was wobbling on his feet, and while he waited for his footman to appear Wilkins materialised from the crowd across the square. He led his employer to a quiet space out of earshot.

Percy lit the stub of a cigar and stared. 'You look smug, like you know something I'm not going to like.'

'I'm not smug sir, but I have learned some information that will not be to your likin'. Clare Forgill was at Saint James in the Fields a couple of days ago, askin' questions about you an' your er, deceased twin brother. She wanted to see the register. She asked Anne Giles if she knew his cause of death.'

Percy looked across to where the footman was now waiting at a discreet distance to lead him to the carriage. Rage filled his lungs with air hotter than a furnace. 'The French bitch,' he hissed. 'He put her up to it. He will try to bring me down.' For a moment he had to pause, his mind working furiously, knowing it was past time that he took decisive action against his enemy. 'Go to Seven Dials,' he spat, 'and prepare my boys for a devious night's work too long delayed.'

'What exactly do you want done, sir?'

★★★

It was after midnight when Frederick woke to the sound of horses on the drive, followed by the hammering of a man at the door. He hurried down the stairs to see the face of Bosun Benson in the night, a tight expression on his face and his demeanour suggesting a man who had woken hurriedly and dressed with haste.

'Your factory,' said the Bosun, 'it's afire.'

'I'll dress,' said Frederick. 'Give me a minute.'

He was as good as his word, pausing only to strike a Vesta to light a candle, then don trousers, shirt and jacket over his nightclothes, pull on shoes without socks and hurry down again. Clare was only just waking, promising to follow at all speed.

As Bosun's carriage turned onto Blackheath Road, they saw a flaming glow in the sky, and Frederick felt himself tear inside. It was an Armageddon. A glimpse of hell.

The fire brigade was already there – out of the three bays only one was visibly aflame, but there were families from nearby residences watching from the street, and a burned man, wrapped in rags, had just been loaded into a wagon and driven away to hospital.

Frederick ran for the factory's main door, despite the smoke that was pouring out. Moving through and inside, he surveyed the ruins of his factory. The reception area was chaos, drawers emptied all over the floor, chairs smashed. Clare's desk lay on its side, her meticulous filing cabinets emptied. His own office was worse, cupboards emptied of folios and papers, now a jumbled mess. The gas lights were broken, the fittings destroyed, and ink poured all over the desktop.

It was the factory floor that made his heart sink, the violated feeling growing as it combined with the certainty of financial ruin. The third bay was impassable, with a wall of firefighters and their hoses. Elsewhere Frederick saw carefully arranged tools either thrown in all directions, ruined or missing. Patterns torn and strewn around, sensitive equipment such as expensive Brown and Sharpe micrometers had been smashed against anvils with sledgehammers.

Fluids such as hydraulic and lubricating oil had been poured from drums. Any items of recognisable value were gone, including ingots of copper, worth sixty pounds per ton. Good leather gloves and protective aprons had a ready market, and the best of these were gone too.

★★★

While Frederick surveyed the damage and thanked God that the fire was under control, the acolyte Peter Craven, burned horribly doing the bidding of his master, held skinless hands to a fleshless face and wailed in pain, curled in the back of a wagon.

Percy Forgill lay awake, alone in his bed with brandy singing through his blood, wondering how the foray had gone, imagining that the attack was not just on a factory, but on Morton himself, with clubs rising and falling, leaving him broken and bleeding. The feeling of power enlivened him: the thought that these men – his tame wolves – could be unleashed with a word.

★★★

At Saint Thomas's hospital two orderlies used a stretcher to carry Craven inside, where his scorched clothing was removed, and the doctor whispered to his nurses that the poor fellow might die.

Craven shivered with pain as the nurses peeled off the melted, pasted remnants of his shirt, pricked the vesicles of fluid that lined his skin with needles, then lowered him into a bath of warm water, his livid skin scarlet – raw flesh in places. He passed out and had to be supported.

Meanwhile, Wilkins took his remaining charges back over the river towards home, subdued now, each of them still full of bravado, but secretly hoping that the law would find no thread to connect them with the crime.

Chapter Twenty-five

Over the following days, the families of Frederick's workers arrived, some assisting the carpenter to replace burned beams and battens. Others took up brooms and hoses to clean the mess, and sort out the scattered supplies and tools. Even the Vicar and several members of the church committee arrived to help. The general opinion was that only the stout brick construction of the factory bays had kept the fire from destroying the place utterly – most of the flames had been from a timber store, accelerants, and the roof support timbers.

Jenkins, who Frederick had kept on since the last pedestrian race as a part-time driver, now also took on a role as nightwatchman, and with his taciturn manner, sturdy build and double-barrelled eight-gauge shotgun Frederick did not expect further trouble.

In the ruined factory, the smell of flame and ruination in her nostrils, Clare turned on Frederick. 'That man has to be stopped.'

'Percy Forgill might not be to blame.'

'You don't think so? This kind of attack will keep happening until he is dealt with. It's not fair on us, your workers and their families, nor even Ned Baring who put up the money for the factory in good faith.'

'What do you mean "dealt with"? I can't challenge him to a sword fight, or a race. It's not so simple.'

'You didn't even mention him to the policeman.'

'I have no proof. If I tell the constable that a lord of the realm arranged to have my factory smashed to pieces and almost burned down, he'd laugh at me.'

'The problem is that you still don't understand your own worth,' said Clare. 'You think this little princeling is better than you because he was born in a big house with a title. We know he did something terrible to his brother, and we know he's a sneaky vindictive coward. You have to do something, my love, before this man destroys us, and if you don't, I will.'

***

Inside his heart, Frederick *was* worried. Five days after the burning of the factory he travelled into the city, first to discuss the fire with Ned Baring, then moving onto the sales office of Asquith lathes, looking into replacement parts for the two machines that had been all but wrecked.

When this business was complete, on his way to the station he diverted past the store front of the famous sword and firearm manufacturers, Wilkinson and Sons. Frederick stared through the glass at rows of fine infantry swords, very different to the shorter French version he still owned and kept deep in his closet. It was not the bladed weapons that held his interest, however but a series of pistols on display, some of which were craftsman-made cap and ball duelling weapons. Others, however, were more modern – single and double action revolvers.

His eyes fell on an under/over type, with twin bores like dark tunnels. It was a simple but brutal-looking piece of engineering, and Frederick found himself deconstructing it in his mind.

The question of personal protection, for Frederick and his family, had been on his mind. The enemy he faced was unhinged, and the next crisis could not be easily predicted. Inclining his head at the doorman, he walked inside, admiring the displays of swords in racks, and firearms of all types.

After a brisk greeting he had a salesman scurrying to the window display, bringing the double-barrelled handgun to the counter, where he broke the action and checked it. Now Frederick could see the filigree work on the blued metal.

'This sir,' said the salesman, 'is from our own works. It fires the state-of-the-art .476 Enfield cartridge, one in each barrel, with two separate triggers. Assuming that you would want this handgun for protection, sir, I can assure you – it's accurate enough to strike a man at twenty paces, and leave him incapacitated or dead. It is also small enough to be concealed.

'May I hold it?' asked Frederick.

'I would not expect you to buy it without doing so.'

Frederick took the weapon and hefted it. Concealable yes, but heavy for its size, and the fine engineering was obvious.

'How much is it?' he asked, already knowing that the price was too high for a man with a ruined factory in the process of rebuilding.

'Forty-two guineas, sir.'

'That seems like a lot.'

'The filigree work took one man almost a week. It's a work of art.'

'Indeed, it is,' said Frederick, placing the weapon on the counter but keeping one hand on it. 'Would you be able to loan me a screwdriver for a moment?'

The salesman frowned, but turned, lifted a small screwdriver from a shelf and passed it across, his frown deepening as Frederick began to unfasten the screw that fixed the receiver to the wooden stock.

'Oh dear, no sir, you mustn't do that.'

But Frederick had already removed the first screw, and was now working on the small bolt that fixed a plate to the side of the receiver. Even as he worked, he lifted his eyes to the salesman.

'Now how does one buy cartridges for this pistol?'

'We supply them in tins of fifty, sir. Three pounds two shillings.'

'Then be so good as to fetch me a tin.'

By the time the salesman returned, Frederick had disassembled the weapon, and was testing spring strength between his fingers. This caught the attention of a more senior man.

'Excuse me sir, you must desist at once.'

'I told him that,' said the salesman.

Frederick stopped for a moment, laying down the screwdriver. 'If you don't interrupt me, I'll have it together again in a moment.' He opened his pocketbook and laid a five-pound note on the counter. 'Now please find me some change and wrap those cartridges for me.'

The senior man and the salesman watched Frederick's nimble fingers reassemble the pistol, taking it from his hands as soon as he was finished.

'This is most irregular,' harrumphed the senior man. 'If you have broken anything you will have to pay for repairs.'

Frederick waited while the man cocked and test-fired the pistol, pointing it at the ground as he did so.

'You'll find no mark on it, please satisfy yourselves of that, and I'll bid you good day,' said Frederick. Then, leaving the screwdriver on the counter, and taking his change along with the wrapped tin of cartridges, he left the store.

★★★

Back at the factory that afternoon, Frederick borrowed an undamaged micrometer from the workshop then took one pistol cartridge from the tin. He measured the case diameter as .476 of an inch while that of the projectile was .455.

With these details carefully noted he went to his drafting desk, and on a fresh sheet, sketched the moving parts of the double-barrelled handgun. In the evening he sent Clare a message that he would be home late, and when he was alone, he used the only working lathe to drill two .450 diameter barrels into a blank of carbon steel, slightly larger for the first inch at the chamber end to accommodate the case.

Over succeeding evenings, he made the thirty-seven parts that made up the handgun, though for the handgrip he had to take the factory carpenter into his confidence. This beautifully finished walnut piece, hand-chequered for grip, was completed two days later. The finished handgun resembled the Wilkinson original in every respect except that there was no filigree work, and the barrel was smooth rather than rifled, meaning a loss of accuracy over distance. Up close, however, the lethality of the weapon would be unaffected.

Only one task remained: to test this lethal creation. To this end, the following Saturday, Frederick drove himself down past Catford, where open acres of farmland rolled out beyond the River Pool.

Frederick secured his horse and walked to a nearby copse, where he loaded his little weapon with two of the fat .476 cartridges, raised his arm, aimed at a tree some ten paces away and squeezed the first trigger. A clot of black powder smoke flew from the gun. Frederick's ears rang from the discharge, and his wrist felt like it was broken. Even so, once the smoke cleared, he could see a fresh white scar the size of a shilling in the middle of the trunk.

Ignoring the pain of his wrist and the ringing in his ears, Frederick raised the pistol again, firing the second barrel with another cloud of smoke and harsh impact on his ears. This time the projectile skidded along the side of the trunk, and made a noticeable dimple in the ground some distance behind it. When he opened the breech the barrel was warm, but the ejector lugs did their work, presenting the cases for extraction. Frederick placed them in his pocket and walked back towards the cart and his anxious horse. If nothing else would stop Percy Forgill, he decided, as a very last resort, this would do it.

From that day, the pistol lived in a recess of the leather case that he carried to and from work every day. Amongst his papers he scarcely noticed the extra weight of the gun, along with ten cartridges. It made him feel a little better.

★★★

Eight weeks after the attack on the premises, two Mobilis engines were despatched, bound for a flour mill in the Midlands. Despite a Herculean effort to repair the damaged factory the order was more than a month behind schedule, but the purchasing company understood the situation and maintained their patience.

With the factory returning to normal, and gearing up for full production of the Fortis, Frederick began an intense marketing effort. His first focus was the silk mills of Lewisham, concentrated on the Ravensbourne downstream from the weir and Elmira Street. After a successful information evening he was able to take a deposit on a Fortis to be installed in one of the biggest mills, whose previous engine, from another manufacturer, had been plagued with maintenance problems. It was a big win, to be able to install one of the new machines so close to the factory – one that could be used to demonstrate the efficacy of the new model to prospective purchasers.

With the factory business in desperate need of more cash sales, Frederick set off on a journey – to sell his Fortis into the textile mills of Northern England.

'Every order is a tick on the balance sheet,' said Ned Baring. 'You're a good salesman – see what you can do.'

Apologising to Jones for leaving him in charge, with Clare in the office when family routines allowed, Frederick travelled by train to Manchester, installing himself at a good but economical hotel. In his pocket was a stack of business cards, and freshly printed brochures filled his briefcase.

Armed with a set of specifications, and exhaustive running figures, Frederick set out to convince mill owners to take a chance on a new machine. Many of these mills were running Boulton and Watt engines with flywheels that measured thirty feet in diameter.

Some still turned oaken line shafting, and bull-headed mill owners with Yorkshire accents baulked at suggestions that these might be replaced with cast-iron at the same time as the engine.

'T'ose shafts've served us well since my Da built t'is mill for'y year ago.'

'Of course they have,' said Frederick, 'and they're beautiful. But they are not as efficient. You can repay the purchase cost in five years with the coal savings.'

Men in suits began hailing Frederick on the street and enquiring if they might learn a little more.'

'Will t'is engine run my mill?'

'Well that depends how many spindles you run.'

'Thir'y t'ousand.'

'We work on a rule of thumb of one hundred spindles per horsepower. With four-hundred horsepower on hand this machine will more than run your mill – it'll leave you with reserve capacity in case you expand.'

'Worth t'inking about,' the man would reply, rubbing his chin thoughtfully. Later there might be a letter asking for a site visit. Frederick's original two-week sales trip became four weeks, with Clare, May, Denny, Matthew and Harriet joining him for the latter part of that time because he could not bear to be away from them any longer.

Finally, when the family caught the train homewards, Frederick felt much more confident about the future. The Fortis was a success – the right engine at the right time, and he had a feeling in his bones that his little factory was about to start paying its way.

★★★

Eleanor, former first lady of the London Docks, knows better than most people how information travels on the streets of London, through the alleys and lanes, in the air and under viaducts, across tables and over bars in the taverns; across marital beds, between the seats of night trains, in the dim kitchens of dosshouses and the boats of smugglers. How, once seen, an act of criminality becomes 'news' and of interest to lips fond of flapping and minds desiring entertainment.

Eleanor knows how and where to place her ear to hear such whispers, and how to follow a trail to its source.

Secure in the family's absence, Eleanor locks the front door of the Lewisham house, and sets out to prowl her old haunts. By tram she reaches Greenwich, the centre of time, where her old mate the Lineyham plies his oars, and for a penny, rows her along the river.

Her aim is to listen to the secrets of the streets, of the underground world that does its work in closed rooms, and traffics in thievery and violence, profits from curiosity, the gambling of money and the pursuit of pleasure; the counterfeiting of notes, the theft of gold, the sale of goods procured by the pickpocket's art.

The Lineyham has a scarred and weathered face, with lines like current marks, and he swings the oars like it's no effort at all. 'So you 'as been well?' he asks.

'Oh well enough – a good quiet life.'

'An' little Juliet?'

'Don't tease me, old man. You know they seduced her with their 'oly rituals and took her far away. But yes, I recently seen her, an' she is well.'

'You never did love the church, did yer?'

Eleanor shakes her head firmly, then, after a pause of twenty strokes or more. 'Just by the by, do you know oo Lord Forgill is?'

'I've 'eard tell of 'im – an e's an odd cove. Makes 'is money on 'igh Street as well as on the cross. I know e' used t' run cocks an' dogs, though hush these days, now e's 'spectable. But there are other unsavoury things that 'e gets 'imself involved in.'

'Do you know anyone oo works f 'rim?'

The Lineyham shakes his head, still not missing a stroke. 'Not as such, though I can arks aroun'.'

Eleanor points ahead to the Commonwealth Docks Pier off Swing Bridge Road, looming up on the left bank, busy with lighters and small steam freighters. 'Just drop's at the stairs there ol' friend, and you've earned your coin well and true.'

★★★

An hour later, having passed the docks and ponds, and skirted Southwark Park, she walks the streets with her ears tuned. She wears a nondescript grey dress, the kind of thing an off-duty maid might wear, when heading out for a mug of tea and a cake. At tavern after tavern she sits with a watered gin and listens, watches, then follows one or two small groups that pique her interest. Along the canals and docks she tunes her ear to the banter of the bargemen.

Late in the day she catches an omnibus across the river on London Bridge, and as night falls is already delving into the East End towards Bethnal Green, once taking a lift with a wagon driver and his load of scrap iron.

Eleanor plays the drunken biddy, bantering with the landlord and play-flirting with the drinkers, while keeping her senses alive to any reference that might pertain to Lord Forgill and the attack on the factory. The first night she stays at the Golden Lion at Mile End, sleeping on a bug-ridden mattress, determined to see the mission through.

On her fourth day in the City, Eleanor takes a table at the Gray Horse in Shoreditch. After an hour she is about to move on when two flash rogues swing in from the street, with stove-pipe hats of different shades and satin waist coats. They order mugs of ale and sit nearby. At the bar they are loud, joking with the landlord who is well known to them. But when they take a table they talk in guarded tones, consulting fob watches like gentlemen.

'If Craven weren't burned so bad …'

'They say 'e'll be out of Saint Thomas's in a week …'

'The skin of 'is face looks like roast pork.'

'Careless of him, e' almost ruined the whole caper.'

The other grins, 'We turned the damned factory inside out, shame Craven 'ad to injure 'imself so.'

A moment later they upend their mugs and leave. Eleanor walks to the barman. 'Excuse me sir, but can you tell me the names of those two young coves oo just left?'

The barman spits on the floor. 'None of yer business, hag. Me lips are closed.'

Eleanor hurries out to follow but the streets are thick with pedestrian and vehicle traffic.

★★★

Even so, she has learned enough. She finds Craven at St Thomas's Hospital, where, the nurses explain, he has contracted an infection and fever. Eleanor sits on the bed and feels a wave of genuine compassion. Peter Craven is a sight, trussed up in bandages and the visible skin around his eyes and lips red and raw. He raves and raves, seeming to understand that someone is with him, but not who.

'Oo's this 'ere,' he mutters as if to himself. 'What livin' soul 'as come to pity me? Is it you mother?'

'No, it's yer dear sister,' says Eleanor.

'Oh strike me,' he says. 'But the pain … the pain … I wish I could peel me skin away and take it all ta hell an' be et by a fireball made by the devil 'imself.'

Eleanor says nothing, just lets him continue, and as time goes on his raving grows wilder. 'I never took the damned watch,' he shouts once. 'You've mislaid it sir.' Then his voice turns low and mournful. 'They blames me for everything, even what I 'ain't done. Even when I tell the truth they think I'm lying, oh mother, don't die – oh the pain, it stings so sharp.'

Eleanor reaches for his unburned hand and squeezes it. For a while he seems to sleep, but at length his eyes snap open, and he looks at Eleanor with a seeming clear gaze.

'Oo are you?' he asks. 'You ain't me dear sister Nellie.'

Eleanor squeezes his hand harder. 'No indeed I ain't. I'm your enemy. A good friend o' the man your boss Lord Percy Forgill wants to destroy. I know what you done, and I'll see you punished for it.'

The burned man babbled for at least a minute, his head thrashing from one side to the other. 'Lord Percy,' he says. 'done bad things too, but I must never tell a soul – he 'as our trust and we 'as 'is. I shouldn't've used the bloody kerosene, damn Wilkins.'

'Did you get burned when you set afire Freddie Morton's factory?'

'Yes, yes, we was promised ten guineas extra each. T'wasn't worth it, so things turn out.'

'Lord Forgill promised you?' she prompts.

'Yes, Lord Percy always keeps 'is word.' He stops and stares at Eleanor. 'Is it Saturday?'

'I believe it is.'

'Then today's the day they do that sodding thing they do – where they worships with the mad Frenchman.'

'Where do they go?' Eleanor asks.

Three times she asks before he whispers an address, just in time before the nurses return and ask her to leave.

★★★

By the time Eleanor leaves, Craven appears to have forgotten her. She hurries from the hospital, wondering if she will have missed this strange ritual that Lord Percy Forgill apparently follows every Saturday.

Over the river again, finding the place is not easy, for Eleanor's close knowledge of the city ends somewhere around Holborn. Finally, however, she approaches the door and hears singing. She slips inside, finding herself in a very large room, like a guild hall, yet she sees that it has been converted to some strange kind of church.

The far wall is adorned with an upside-down cross. A man

occupies the stage, and he wears a robe shaped like a toga. Some of the congregation are scantily clad or bare-skinned. Percy Forgill is there, and Sophie too, their eyes closed in rapture.

The sermon is in accented English, echoing from the damp walls. A goblet of wine passes from hand to hand, and spills down the chests of participants. The scene makes Eleanor's flesh crawl.

When she can stand it no longer, she slips from the room, knowing that she will have to protect Frederick – she and Clare together will need to join forces to destroy Percy Forgill, for he, and these others, are evil and appear to revel in it.

★★★

When Frederick returns from his journey, he listens to the facts that Eleanor has learned. But when she begs him to take the information she has gleaned from Craven to the police he shakes his head. 'Do you think they would accept the ravings of a fevered burn victim as evidence against a lord of the realm?'

Eleanor thrusts out her chin. 'What about this devil worship? It's evil.'

'It's not illegal,' says Frederick. 'I've read about it in the Times. They call themselves the Hermetic Society of the Golden Dawn. The cult seems to attract writers and crack-pots – Conan Doyle is one, Yeats the poet, and Percy Forgill.'

Clare's eyes widen in frustration. 'You surely cannot feel that this is a good thing.'

Frederick shakes his head sadly. 'Nothing we know about Percy Forgill could be regarded as evidence. Making it public will do nothing but make him angry. At the moment I would rather rebuild and get on with our lives. One day things might change, but now is not the time.'

'I think we should keep digging,' says Clare. 'This Craven man told Eleanor that Percy admitted to doing something bad himself – perhaps the things you saw that night in Park Lane.'

Frederick turns to her fiercely, 'Have you considered that looking into Percy Forgill's past might have precipitated the attack on our factory?' She says nothing, and Frederick goes on. 'From now on, we leave him alone, and pray that he will respond in kind.'

Chapter Twenty-six

Matthew was never robust. At the age of four he developed a mild cough and complained of sleeplessness. When his youthful muscles melted away from his limbs Clare sent for the doctor. An hour later he arrived, a stout little man with his black bag up on the box beside him.

Everyone knew that Lewisham's Doctor Ellis had problems of his own – an infant with a wasting illness. Frederick had seen the man with his wife at the market with the poor little mite, who was not expected to live beyond a few months, in a pushchair. Ellis, however, was a kind man – always willing to travel to sick patients, and not too concerned with payment. He sat on the church committee and his pew was rarely empty on Sundays.

The doctor examined Matthew, making him take off his shirt and trousers and lie on the bed in his undershorts, bony ribs pushing against white skin while the doctor probed and pressed into his abdomen, using his stethoscope several times in different places.

The prognosis, unfortunately, was grim. 'The boy has consumption – tuberculosis, I'm sorry to say,' said Dr Ellis after he had packed up his things.

Frederick looked away, hiding the pain in his eyes. Tuberculosis killed half of all those infected.

Nights of broken sleep tending to the afflicted child followed. Frederick and Clare took turns to get up, sit Matthew upright in his bed; to hold his hands while he shook with a strange palsy that may or may not have been a side-effect of the disease.

Thankfully, in Matthew's case, his lungs cleared, though the malicious disease had not finished with him. It manifested itself most seriously in the bones of his legs.

Two years of regular hospitalisations followed, during which time Matthew read his way through books as if to vicariously live the life of a normal, active boy.

For the first time in some years, Frederick saw a bleak side to his vision of the future.

★★★

An envelope arrived at the factory, postmarked from Saint Laurent, France. The letter inside had been produced with the aid of a typing machine, like the Smith Premier that had recently arrived in the Morton Steam Power Company office. Frederick first scanned down to the signature line, where he recognised his father-in-law's name, then read it from the beginning.

Dear Frederick

I realise that much time has passed since our last meeting. I have several things to ask of you, but I will begin this letter on a business footing.

We are now building more flax mills, and I am interested in six Fortis engines, to be delivered prior to Summer. As a business matter, I would like you to come and view the installation, and discuss the best possible configuration for these engines.

Finally, I must get personal. I beg you, with all my heart, to ask Clare to accompany you, along with your children. Our crimes are great, but I beg you to allow us a chance to reunite. I need you to take a chance on us as I once did on you.

Yours sincerely

M. du Brice

When Frederick read the letter aloud in the drawing room that evening, Clare made a face. 'He's trying to buy my love.'

Frederick stopped. 'Six Fortis engines is a significant sale for Morton Steam, but that's not the most important thing.' He lowered his voice. 'I think it's time you reunited with your parents – for our children's sakes. I know you want to.'

Clare put aside the napkins she had been folding, smiled wanly, looking away from him.

★★★

With Eleanor remaining at home to look after the house, the family travelled by packet-ship to Le Havre and were met by a brougham almost as grand as Lord Forgill's.

While Frederick presented his quotation for six Fortis engines, priced keenly in deference to the family connections, Harriet entranced her grandparents with occasional forthright observations, delivered without the aid of front teeth. Denny spent every spare minute at the stables, and May impressed them with her knowledge of the Morton business, rattling off the parts of a stationary steam engine like any other girl might describe the compartments of her doll house.

The visit was, overall, a success, and Frederick blushed to see the bedroom where he and Clare had first made love. She insisted on celebrating the moment by repeating the act. It was spring, and there were flowers in the air, and the fourteen days they spent at Saint Laurent were like a dream.

They returned home a happier, more closely-knit family, and a deposit cheque for six Fortis engines made the feeling sweeter.

★★★

Over the years the Barings Clerk justified Percy Forgill's retainer with small titbits of information, none of which proved to be of much import, but enough to make it clear to Percy that he was worth the money.

Importantly, too, just as Wilkins had projected, the man was on an upwards trajectory, and in 1887 he was appointed assistant commercial loan manager for North and South America. Of course, life for Percy too was marching on. He had married a young socialite, though the marriage was limping into irrelevance. One late autumn morning Wilkins sent a handwritten message, with a date and time for another secret meeting with the banker.

In their usual meeting place, deep in Hyde Park, Wilkins occupied a bench in a sea of leaves that had fallen from the plane trees above. The clerk sat beside him, looking very nervous indeed.

Without preamble or a word of greeting, Percy took a seat beside the Baring's man, his feet sinking into the bronze and yellow drifts of leaves.

'Mr Wilkins says that you have some information for me,' said Percy.

'Yes, Lord Forgill.'

'What is it?'

The clerk, obviously nervous, removed his spectacles, wiped his eyes, then replaced the instrument on his ears and nose. 'Not to put too fine a point on it, sir. I think that the information I have in my possession is worth a bonus.'

'Tell me and I'll assess it's worth.'

The clerk thought for a moment. 'I want another fifty pounds ... I could lose my job for this.'

Percy snarled, 'I'll give you twenty-five, but only if I think your disclosure justifies the sum.'

The clerk sighed deeply. 'Very well then. Twenty-five. Now this is all a big secret, but there's been a disaster for Barings in Argentina sir.'

'Go on.'

The clerk dabbed at his brow with a pocket handkerchief. 'We

– Barings that is – are acting as underwriters for a two-million-pound share issue – a public float for what looked like a promising outfit called the Buenos Aires Water Supply and Drainage Company. Barings supplied the funds but, with all the political unrest, very few of the shares sold. It was a financial disaster. Barings is losing a great deal of money – millions of pounds in fact.'

Percy leaned back in his chair and grilled the clerk for twenty minutes, as if the man were a witness on the stand, until he had gleaned every possible detail, and was satisfied with the veracity of the information. 'Pay the man,' he said to Wilkins at last, then he stood up and left.

★★★

Within an hour Percy had been home, dressed in more appropriate attire, and sent a letter by courier to his friend Jack Wilson, the newspaper owner, part of his little luncheon group, to make sure he would be in attendance. Soon afterwards he arrived at the Carlton Club for the meeting.

Arriving at the upstairs dining room, he was pleased to see that Wilson was already in attendance. With the offer to share a bottle of Château Haut-Batailley, Percy led him to a booth overlooking Pall Mall.

'Are you abreast of events in Argentina?' Percy asked.

Wilson shrugged, 'Like every tin pot country in the world, they're heavily in debt. *El Presidente* Miguel Celman is corrupt, as are all such leaders, and the poor downtrodden people remain restless. Their champions in this case, Aristóbulo del Valle and Leandro Alem and the rest of their Civic Union, are likely to try to do something about the situation very soon.'

'Revolution on the way?' asked Percy.

'Perhaps, but more likely a bloodless coup.'

'Your newspaper has not been reporting this situation very thoroughly.'

Wilson flared his nostrils, as if on the scent of a story. 'Oh, I don't know,' he said. 'We've been keeping the public informed.'

'Are you aware of the London financial perspective to this? One of our large merchant banks – Barings to be precise – is exposed in Argentina and is involved in a disastrous public share offer. They stand to lose millions.'

Wilson's mouth opened like a fish gulping for air at the surface of a pond. Barings was one of the most successful and highly regarded financial institutions in the city of London. Trouble there would have serious ramifications. He shifted in his seat. 'Tell me more.'

Percy lifted the wine glass to his lips, deciding that the Haut-Batailley was a vintage worthy of the occasion. 'Listen carefully,' he said.

Chapter Twenty-seven

Something miraculous happened in the mid and late 'eighties. The Morton works, with its pared down, efficient operation, sold as many Fortis engines as they could make. This meant changes for the family. Good things, that they could scarcely believe were possible. Best of all, Matthew survived his illness, albeit with a limp, and his older brother Denny grew into a robust specimen, disinterested in school, who was apprenticed to the foundry in his teens.

Athletic in all fields, Denny had been the open boxing and wrestling champion in his final year at the Lewisham School, despite being three or four years younger than most of the other contenders. This physical strength was a boon in the tough manual labour of the factory, and his already impressive frame grew only more sturdy.

With his regular salary from the factory, Denny was able to purchase a fifteen-hand gelding with spirit and an urge to run. Within a few weeks he'd obtained a new leather saddle and bridle, and before long he was galloping 'like a hussar' as Frederick liked to say, up and down the street.

Much of his spare time was taken up with developing his riding skills, and many times the family were called outside for an exhibition. These were usually trumpeted by a tremendous clatter of hooves out on the drive, then a series of shouts from Denny.

'Father, Matthew … come see what I've taught Racer to do now.'

The whole family, including Eleanor, would file outside to watch Denny as he backed his horse up along the narrow path, his black eyes narrowed with concentration, or induced his mount to stand on its hind legs for a an instant or two.

The small audience would clap enthusiastically, then wander back inside.

★★★

Evenings at the Lewisham house were lively and interesting, for the factory carpenter had, years earlier, crafted a dining table from oak boards that had once formed part of the Lewisham Priory. It was big enough for ten, twelve at a pinch, for there were extra guests at least once or twice a week, whether friends of the children or a visiting business contact.

Clare encouraged her family to discuss politics and culture at the table. Oftentimes debates continued long after the plates had been cleared, washed and dried. Visitors were picked clean of information about their travels and occupations by the voracious minds of the Morton children, their opinions questioned and dissected.

Later, most evenings, Frederick and Clare retired to the sofa, where one of the children might read a few stanzas of poetry, or practice on the piano that now occupied one corner. Otherwise, the couple would engross themselves in novels or memoirs, discuss the business of the day or play hearts and old maid on the coffee table. These were good times, that all members of the family would recall fondly.

★★★

While Denny had left school and May, now in the fourth form, was intent on completing her education at Lewisham, Frederick and Clare decided that they had the means to elevate their younger children to 'better' schools. At the conclusion of her primary education, Harriet was enrolled in Saint Catherine's Girls' College in Bramley, Surrey, and Matthew at the new Godalming campus of Frederick's alma mater, Charterhouse School. These two facilities were a couple of miles away from each other, to the southwest of Lewisham.

On an ensuing Saturday morning, Harriet and Matthew were packed up and ready to leave, sitting up high in the trap, not long after dawn. Harriet was by then blonde and pretty, with an irresistible smile and expressive blue eyes. Matthew had a lean build with an angular face – thin but handsome.

Even though Jenkins was now employed as a full-time driver, Frederick elected to take his two youngest on this important mission himself, while Clare fussed and kissed cheeks, shedding tears and swearing that her babies could surely not have grown up enough to go away to school.

It was a perfect spring morning, a day for happiness and laughter, with the horses plodding lazily, enjoying the sunshine as heartily as their passengers. They stopped for the night in Epsom, where Frederick pointed out how the London clay soils met those of chalk, characteristic of the Downs, and later the famous racecourse where the Derby had been run for more than one hundred years.

In an atmospheric old dining room in a local inn, the fire flaring in the grate, they ate mutton chops, gravy and potatoes, laughing at the adventure, while Frederick sipped a local ale and enjoyed the freshest mussels he had eaten in some time.

The next day, just before noon, the silhouette of Harriet's new school appeared through the trees and over fields, along with the spires of the Bramley church. Thirteen-year-old Harriet stood up on the box and stared at the vista, past the trees and meadow flowers that lined the lane. For some months she had been calling herself a socialist, and now she made a note of disapproval in her throat.

'It looks like a bastion of wealth and privilege,' she said.

'That may be so,' said Frederick. 'But it offers the best education available. There will be adjustments you need to make, but you are here to learn, and not just from books.'

Soon afterwards, as they walked through the hedge-lined entrance and into the school quadrangle, Harriet decided that she had never seen so many well-dressed girls in her life.

The head mistress met them in the vestibule. 'Good morning,' she said, 'I am Miss Franklin.'

Miss Franklin was at least fifty, Harriet decided, with her grey hair tied in a bun, and sun-spots on her skin that grew striking follicles of their own.

Harriet folded her arms and gave her new superior a look, clearly saying, 'You don't impress me.' Frederick prodded his daughter in the back of her ankle with the toe of his shoe. She took the hint and curtsied, earning a trace of a smile from the headmistress's dour lips.

A tour followed, Matthew looking at the ground when groups of girls stared and giggled as he limped by. Harriet did her best to appear oblivious to them. 'I haven't seen anyone so much as looking at a book since we arrived here,' she observed.

'Since that's all of ten minutes,' said Frederick, 'I suspect you might need to give it a little longer.'

The school students were divided into various houses, each presided over by a woman of formidable morals and far-reaching good sense. Harriet's new abode had been chosen based on her age and background, and it was only upon entering the grand old house that she began to see the value of what was happening to her. The house mistress was no more than twenty-five, well-groomed and attractive in a shirtwaist and matching skirt of pale lilac.

Harriet liked Miss Bromley from the start, and they talked with lively animation, while Frederick and Matthew helped the porters carry in her trunks. Harriet unpacked her books onto the shelves before so much as a scarf landed in one of the drawers.

When both father and brother had gone, and Miss Bromley came into her room, the young housemistress caught sight of *The Communist Manifesto* on Harriet's bookshelf. She exclaimed, 'Oh Harriet, you've read Marx?'

'Yes, Miss Bromley.'

'Is it your first Marxist book?'

'No, I've read others – I just haven't unpacked them yet.'

Miss Bromley fell to her knees and examined the other titles. 'So many plays! You are an admirer of the theatre?'

'It's my passion,' said Harriet simply.

Miss Bromley clasped her hands together with excitement. 'You, young lady, have come to the right place. We will be friends,' she declared.

When the room was tidy and organised to Harriet's satisfaction she sat down and wrote a letter to Miss Franklin, listing five suggestions for improvements to school procedures and organisation. These changes had occurred to her as having the potential to improve the establishment of Saint Catherine's, particularly in the eyes of new girls.

★★★

The journey on to Matthew's school, the relocated Charterhouse at Godalming, was much quieter than the first part of the trip. Frederick's middle child kept his nose glued to Stephen Crane's *The Red Badge of Courage* and seemed somewhat anxious when they reached the green Surrey farms and market gardens along Peperharow Road, breasting a hill to look down on the monastic-inspired sandstone school buildings, with the River Wye snaking along behind them.

'I'm an old boy, as you know,' mused Frederick, 'back when the school was still in London.'

Matthew glanced up from his book. 'Did you enjoy school, Father?'

Frederick made a face, wry and thoughtful. 'I loved to learn, and

I felt privileged to be there. The other boys were the trouble, and I fear that it will be the same for you also.'

★★★

The sixth-former who had been delegated to show Matthew the school grounds was the very image of public-school refinement — taking Matthew and his father on a tour of his new home at the *Verites* house with good cheer and polite words of welcome. This charade lasted only until Frederick and his horses had disappeared down the lane. Soon thereafter, Matthew had his first lesson on what it was like to be a junior at an English public school.

Two more sixth formers appeared — dressed stylishly in flannel trousers, and shirts with butterfly collars. They picked Matthew up, then carried him, inverted, to the furthest of the school's houses. There he was slammed into a room strewn with dirty clothes, plates and schoolbooks.

'Clean it up,' he was told.

That night, by the time Matthew had discovered where his bed was located, and retrieved his luggage from behind the chapel, he had missed supper, and lights-out was looming. He spent his only free minute writing to his father, begging him to come back and collect him with all possible speed. The letter was snatched from him by another sixth-former, one of the sporting elite known as 'bloods' who appeared to rule the school.

Matthew's letter home was produced as 'evidence' of 'treason' and read aloud at a mock court martial, beginning at midnight, the upshot of which was that the new boy was ordered to rise at five each day to empty the chamber pots of his tormentors. When, finally, Matthew reached his bed, he found that someone had poured water over his sheets and blankets, the temperature of which was now close to freezing.

By the time Matthew fronted a classroom, at eight the next morning, he was sick with misery, and convinced that he would not survive more than a week at the Charterhouse School.

Interestingly, though, the master dropped a slip of paper on Matthew's school desk – a printed list of activities such as stamp collecting, sport, games, chess and singing. These were weekly clubs, pursued every Friday afternoon. Matthew selected chess, and for two hours a week he escaped into a world of intellectual warfare with like-minded students.

The chess club was one of his few pleasures, for Matthew was already a member of another club – one that convened after lights-out, and on the weekends after the obligatory game of rugger on the ovals.

This club was not of his choosing. Admittance, for a boy of his quiet demeanour and crippled leg, was automatic. The rules were subject to the whims of the bullies in the crowd, who fed their developing egotism with the infliction of torments and pain.

One game, introduced to Matthew on the first Saturday after he started at the school, was called 'Fox and Hounds.'

Matthew was the fox.

The game began after luncheon, when the boys sent the limping boy into the yellow broom and gorse bushes adjacent to the school to hide, while they spread out in a ragged line and someone counted to one hundred. When they came looking Matthew heard them calling to each other across the breeze. They avoided sending their scents down-wind as if they were hunting an animal.

Matthew's heart was soon charged with adrenalin, his pulse pounding in his forehead. His runs were short and awkward, his left leg weak, leaving him no chance to beat these bloods and aspiring bloods with outright speed.

'There he is,' someone yelled, pitched high, and a stone flew from a cocked arm, striking Matthew in the back of the neck, leaving a stinging red welt. Trying not to cry out he blundered away in the other direction, the sounds of the boys' mutual congratulations following him in muffled bursts.

'You got him good, Jackson. Nice throw.'

'Where's that damned fox gone?'

'Over there.'

'Nice work, gentlemen, Morrow and Carter will head him off – he won't get far.'

Matthew struggled on, trying to put as much distance as possible between himself and the sounds of pursuit. He ducked through a patch of blackberry, the thorns tearing at his clothes, then tramped through a narrow vale of mud. He came to a small lake in the woods, the mirror surface reflecting the sky, a pair of foraging ducks waddling away as he approached.

The pain from the stone impact grew, and Matthew felt mucus form in his throat, running down around his lips to his chin. His breath was hacking now, and another boy appeared on the far side of the pond, racing around to cut him off, coming into range and letting fly with another stone. The first missed, but the second scored his cheek just under one eye.

'Got him!' came the shout from behind, and there were more footfalls in the undergrowth; more excited chatter. Through it all, Matthew's sense of fair play was as wounded as his body. If they were supposed to be hounds, why were they throwing stones?

Three boys in a file came around the other side of the pond, their reflections in the pond distorted – foreshortened – so they seemed like animals.

Feeling a new chill. Matthew left the pond, veering to the left, down a narrow drain, more mud splashing, then he dragged his bad leg up and towards a clearing where the sun had just broken though.

Again, they were closing in, and their voices came to resemble the snarling yelps of hounds knowing their prey was close; knowing that soon they would taste blood.

Matthew understood that they had become a pack. He wished he could suddenly be the massive, muscled Queequeg, from Moby Dick, with his harpoon. Or brave Ivanhoe, returning from the Holy

Land in his armour. But he wasn't. He was plain Matthew Morton, and he could not be a hero, not here today in any case.

In acceptance of this fact, he sat down on the ground, and when he heard them come up, he folded himself into a ball. Stones thumped against his back. Worse, he could feel their hatred, for he had spoiled their game by not fighting to the death, like a real fox would. For several minutes they stayed, throwing stones and insults, then wandered away to find a new game.

That was how a searching party of masters and prefects from Matthew's house found him, just on dark, when they formed a party to look. He had not moved in all that time.

Chapter Twenty-eight

While his factory workers cast iron, machined parts and assembled components in double shifts to keep pace with orders, Frederick completed the design of an ingenious winding gear and drum that would couple to the Fortis, opening up a new range of applications for the engine.

The design featured the ability to select reverse, forward slow and forward rapid, by moving a lever. Within weeks of the patternmakers putting his designs into practice, the first castings were emerging from the foundry.

Frederick also completed work on a ball bearing for 'reducing friction from the handling of spinning shafts', for which he applied for a royal patent. He was convinced that if cotton-mill-shafts ran through these bearings, a huge boost in efficiency would result.

The factory was so busy that Frederick was forced to leave much of the day-to-day supervision to Jones. Thus, at times he missed small changes that he might otherwise have noticed. One Saturday morning he walked onto the factory floor, surprised to find a slim figure in a cap and blue overalls, leaning over a work bench.

Strangely, Frederick did not recognise the man, and he hired all workers personally. Yet this person had a slide valve assembly in pieces on the work bench and seemed to know his business.

Frederick cleared his throat. 'Excuse me sir, but may I ask what you are doing here?'

The cap came off, and hair fell past the worker's shoulders. The face became familiar. 'Why Father, I do believe that I am not only your daughter, but a shareholder in the company. I have every right to be here.' It was May, he realised with a start, her hands dirty with grease, and a streak of the same substance down one side of her face.

Frederick was so surprised that he did not say anything for a moment or two. Of course, she had long been hanging around the factory after school, but seeing her out on the floor was quite a shock.

'She's pretty handy with the tools,' said Jones, proudly coming up behind her. 'Yesterday she had a governor in parts, and back together again in record time.'

Frederick couldn't resist feeling pleased, but he had never envisaged his daughter doing such work, and was it proper for her to do so? 'I know we've been short-handed, but isn't it better that you concentrate on your schoolwork, and keep your hands clean?'

'Why?' asked May innocently. 'I'm already top of my class. Can't I do this as well?'

Frederick looked at her eyes, then down at the capable hands that gripped the valve housing. Pride won over any sense of propriety. 'Of course, you can,' he said. 'Perhaps we could start paying you a part-time wage, if Jones thinks that you are useful.'

'I do,' said Jones. 'She's a real talent.'

★★★

Frederick met with Ned Baring rarely in those days, and thus, when a letter arrived with an invitation to call on the financier in his London office, Frederick arranged with Jenkins to leave after lunch.

All the possible permutations of the forthcoming talk occupied Frederick's mind through the morning and on the long journey into the City. When he arrived at Bishopsgate, it was a little before the hour, and he was forced to wait until Ned appeared, escorting an elderly man in a coarse woollen jacket and black cap from the office.

Baring shook hands with enthusiasm, but he looked thinner than last time, and as he escorted Frederick to his office the engineer sensed an air of nervousness that he had not noticed in the past.

'Have a seat, please Freddie, and thanks so much for coming in to see me at such short notice.'

'My pleasure.'

Ned breathed noisily through his nostrils. 'What do you know about a South American country by the name of Argentina?'

Frederick's eyes widened in surprise. 'Not a great deal. I know about the Revolution of the Park – the uprising against President Celman. I know that the Vice-President,' he paused, 'I think his name was Pellegrini, took office.'

'Do you know why the uprising took place?'

Frederick shrugged, 'Corruption and greed on the part of the elite. The usual.'

'Close enough to the truth at this stage. Now, investment banks like Barings tend to concentrate on a particular country, establish political connections – find worthy projects to support.'

'Sounds logical,' said Frederick.

'Well, while the Australian colonies, India and South Africa have been the mainstay of other banks, Argentina, and to a lesser extent Ecuador, has, in recent years been *our* country. On paper, it is perfect. Massive natural resources, a go-ahead government.' Ned paused to open a wooden cigar box and select one from the row, holding it to his nose to inhale the strong tobacco smell, cutting the tip with a pair of scissors then holding it unlit in his hand. 'Anyway, to cut a long story short, a few years ago we acted as underwriters for a two-million-pound share issue – which failed spectacularly. We lost a great deal of money.'

'A great deal?'

'Two million pounds is a lot of money, wouldn't you agree?'

'I would,' Frederick said, trying not to look as miserable as he felt.

'But that's not the full extent of the problem. I am telling you this, because we may not be in a position to honour our commitment to you if things go as badly as I expect they might.'

'In what way?'

Baring cleared his throat, as if to be certain that nothing he said could be misconstrued. 'Our regular payments aligned with your line of credit may be in jeopardy in the coming months. Please don't panic – we should be able to operate more or less as usual until September. After that I just can't guarantee anything.'

Frederick stared blankly. 'I understand.'

'There's also the issue of the main capital loan. I may have to look at finding someone to take over your debt.'

'This is bad timing,' said Frederick. 'We are just about to start designing the new Imperium.'

Ned Baring delved in his desk drawer for a match, and used it to light his cigar. 'I'm sorry – it never occurred to me that such a cataclysm could befall this company, and you have my sincerest apologies that it must affect your business as well.'

★★★

Weekly clubs were also a feature of Harriet's new school, although unlike the Charterhouse, the clubs at Saint Catherine's were organised by the students themselves.

Harriet had been attracted to the school because, apparently, plays and performances were held annually. In these she hoped to participate, and thereby hone her skills as a thespian. The school literature had mentioned a drama club. This, Harriet decided, would be her spiritual home.

The drama club was controlled, Harriet soon learned, by a girl called Sapphire Peters. Tall and regal, she floated around the school with two close friends who trailed from her like dinghies from a river boat. They were, it seemed to Harriet, more co-conspirators than friends, for the three seemed to always be in earnest discussion. At every opportunity Harriet took time to study these drama club girls. They were in their own world, always picking flowers for each other and pinning them behind ears, whispering and telling secrets, reading poetry and lines from Shakespeare's tragedies aloud.

Harriet asked one of the girls in her house why this clique were so reserved and exclusive. 'It's just a drama club thing,' was the answer. 'You won't get in, so don't bother trying.'

This response filled Harriet with mingled indignation and excitement. The drama club was exactly where she needed to be. 'Why on earth not?'

'Because they're firmly cloistered. Just about nobody gets in.'

When the lists came around for school clubs that Friday, Harriet put her name down for the drama club as her first choice. After luncheon, one of the girls she had seen with Sapphire Peters approached her.

'You're Harriet Morton?'

'That's me.'

'Well, we don't accept girls into the drama club without a reading.'

Harriet felt a surge of hope. 'I'm happy to do a reading. When?'

'You'll be told when the auditions are on. I'd advise you to choose your piece wisely, and practice. Our standards are very high.'

Dawdling back to the dormitory house that afternoon, hugging her books to her chest, Harriet tried to decide on the best choice of play to read for her audition. Her mother, and father when possible, had taken all four children to the theatre as far afield as the West End, but most of the shows she had attended were local melodramas or productions of Shakespeare's more popular works. To compensate for the lack Harriet devoured the scripts of plays she could only dream of seeing.

One of her favourites was called *Armand, the Child of the People,* the work of French-born American playwright and actress, Anna

Cora Mowatt. It appealed to her partly because it had been written by a woman, one of the few amongst thousands of plays by men, and also because of the romantic setting – the court of Louis XV.

On Friday, when the drama club convened for the purpose of hearing readings by prospective members, Harriet was last in line of a roster of girls, only two of whom had so far been accepted into the group. It was a nerve-wracking process, with nothing in the way of encouragement being offered by the drama club incumbents, who sat with their legs crossed, supported by cushions, taking notes on lined pads.

Harriet ascended the stage and cleared her throat. 'I will read from, *Armand, the Child of the People,* by Anna Cora Mowatt. This is the final scene, set in the court of Louis the Fifteenth, Paris.'

'Very well,' said Sapphire Peters. 'Please begin when you are ready.'

After taking a moment to compose herself, Harriet cried: 'My child! Remember thou art not thine own to give. Nay, I know what thou wouldst say. First bow thy knee to one who claims thy reverence and love. Behold thy mother's sire. I was thy lover – I am now thy King! We claim the right to wed thee as we will. Nay, traitress – no rebellion, for thy sire sanctions our choice. Armand, more chary hold our second gift than thou hast done the first.' Harriet clasped the hilt of an imaginary sword at her waist, then finished the speech with a tremor in her voice; 'No more of that. We pardon, Blanche is thine. My cup is brimming over, speak thou my Blanche, my long-lost bride, tell me thy happiness hath reached the blessed zenith of mine.'

She came to a stop, looking blankly out at the panel of judges with her heart hammering, trying to read their reaction on their faces.

'Stilted,' said Sapphire Peters. 'Dripping with mock sentimentality and insincerity.' She stood up from her chair and ascended the side steps onto the stage. 'Do you have the script with you?'

Harriet walked to where she had left her bag and withdrew the slim book, passing it to Sapphire Peters, who flicked through, locating a passage at random, reading it a couple of times before striking a pose. 'And these flowers that in unconscious sweetness,' she cried, 'bloomed in her death-cold hand, and that shall now wither upon my breast as she has withered. But dwell there as she dwells in spite of death. All, all, with blended voices, strangely real. Would seem to bid me stay! Would chain me here. As though with cords invisible they bound me still to hope and her! Away! Away! My nature grows too soft. Farewell for aye. My early dreams – farewell my ideal world. Peopled by joy and hope – farewell for ever!'

Harriet looked at Sapphire in shock. Real tears were falling from her eyes, now rimmed with red, her voice racked with emotion.

Sapphire handed the book back to Harriet. 'If you want to act, you have to learn to feel, you have to *be* the character.'

Harriet felt an aching disappointment in her throat. 'But how can I learn if you won't let me join the drama club?'

Sapphire Peters dabbed at her eyes with a handkerchief, before resuming her usual breezy demeanour. 'Lessons would be a good start. Learn how to act first, then you may join the drama club.'

***

If learning to act on the stage is like climbing a mountain, Harriet was born with all the necessary tools; all she needed was a guide to show her the passes leading to the peaks. Her chosen *sherpa* was a twenty-eight-year-old from Godalming village who had been a promising West End leading man until he had developed a polyp in his throat that made professional acting impossible. He was kindly, spoke in a hoarse whisper, and was very giving of his skills.

Through Rowan Borger, Harriet learned that the art of acting is not a mirror, but rather a deep pool with depths only the brave and dedicated can explore. She learned the magic of provoking feeling, letting your heart show in your face, of inhabiting another person's soul. Borger instructed her in the art of modulating and projecting her voice, learning lines, the importance of detail; of divining how a character would have thought, acted and spoken. Most of all she learned that the magic is in inviting the audience to share the moment, to be part of the scene.

'Do your research,' Berg advised. 'Find out what you can. If you are playing the part of a Scottish maidservant, interview a maid and discover her likes and dislikes, how she came to work where she works, her secret hopes and dreams. Find out how she talked – not just a generic accent – every district has its own dialect, learn what it is and practice. That knowledge will not only make you convincing when you come to the stage, but give you confidence in playing the role. A professional leaves nothing to chance.'

For two school terms Harriet learned and rehearsed. Then, with her tutor's encouragement, she decided it was time to audition again for the Drama Club.

For her second audition Harriet chose a current hit, a revival of the Watts Phillips play, *The Dead Heart*, then playing at the Lyceum, starring one of the most celebrated actors of the day, Henry Irving.

She took care with her costume, and again chose a dramatic final scene, playing the French Countess. Her accent was perfect, honed by years of listening to her mother, and noting the nuances of the speech carefully.

With Sapphire and her friends having arranged themselves on cushions, Harriet began the reading. 'Citizen Valerie is free,' she cried, 'I but await the passport to see you through the barriers. What is it that has blanched your face? What do you fear? You point to the guillotine! You speak not. I see a man mounting the scaffold. His back is towards us! Now he turns this way – he waves his hand.' Harriet closed her eyes, shaking with emotion, and screamed, 'ROBERT LANDRY!'

Having uttered these words, she fell to the floor, in as complete a faint as if these had been real events, and she had been the real countess.

When Harriet raised her head at last, Sapphire Peters and her friends were on their feet. They were applauding.

★★★

Denny's best friend was a lad his own age called Sam. Both youths were game for just about any outdoor activity, from fishing to shooting, and camping out in the woods when the opportunity presented itself. Sam knew every bird known to frequent the middle reaches of the Thames, and the countryside all the way to Surrey Hills and southeast to the Kent Downs. He loved nothing better than stumbling on an unexplored section of stream, or a hill that needed climbing. He was enthusiastic, emotional and sensitive.

Sam worked as a clerk for a Lewisham solicitor and had been a constant in Denny's life since their school days. Shorter in stature, with a chunkier build than Denny, Sam carried a pipe everywhere he went – his tobacco addiction stretched back to his thirteenth year.

If one of the pair found themselves in a misunderstanding at the Joiner's Arms on a Saturday night, the other was at his side in an instant. Most times this was enough to force an aggressive party to back down, but on the occasions that it wasn't enough, Sam could acquit himself well, though he lacked Denny's work-hardened musculature.

Sam was fond of an ale, good food and a hearty laugh. He collected jokes to be dispensed at the right moment, often late at night around a fire lit on the bank of the Ravensbourne.

One afternoon Denny walked down the lane with a fishing pole over his shoulder, stopping at Sam's house. It was an old place, overgrown by shade trees, but neatly kept, nonetheless. On the verandah a black cat was busy abrading itself against one of the timber supports.

Sam came through the door, and his sister followed, wearing a pale-lavender dress and white bonnet. She carried a basket containing a book, and cloth-wrapped items that smelled like freshly baked scones. Sam waved his tweed cap at his sister, 'Eadie wants to come down with us and just sit on the riverbank and read. Is that fine with you?'

'I promise I won't talk or make noise,' she added.

Denny grinned back, feeling a strange little tingle. 'Of course, come along.'

The two youths walked neck-and-neck as Eadie followed along behind. Ignoring her to all appearances, Denny focussed his senses on the sounds of her shoes on the macadam, and her occasional stops to draw scent from daisies and pansies growing on the sides of the road.

They clambered down the banks of the River Quaggy, choosing a favourite deep hole. Pausing on the short green grass on the bank, Eadie took a rug from her basket and spread it. Sitting with arranged skirts, Eadie opened her book and began to read, attended by butterflies, and a cheeky red squirrel that showed himself at intervals from behind a willow trunk, his tail held high as he flowed from place to place. Denny chose his stand, a little apart from his friend so they would not tangle or get in each other's way, and cast his worm for the first time. Sam took a flask of whisky from his pocket, drank down a generous measure and offered to throw it across for him.

'Not yet,' said Denny. 'Not until I've earned a thirst.'

As he fished, he could not resist swivelling his neck and looking back towards Eadie. Every time he did, she was looking down at her book, but sometimes, while his bait was sinking through the brown water, he felt a burning sensation in the back of his neck, as if she was watching him.

True to her promise, however, she said scarcely a word from the time they arrived, at least until Sam's willow pole began twitching and he struck hard.

'Have you got one, Sam?' Eadie called.

'Sure have,' he grinned, and after a short fight he lifted a healthy roach to the bank. Ten minutes later he added another. After an hour, Sam had two roach and a trout. When Denny hooked one, he heard an emphatic and feminine, 'Oh, well done,' from behind him.

Later, in the gloaming, Eadie surprised Denny by putting down her book, producing a knife and cleaning all the fish, washing the gut cavity of each in the stream as if from long practice.

'I'm impressed,' said Denny.

'Amazing, isn't she?' said Sam. 'Looks like I've out fished you this afternoon, by the way.'

Denny was about to reply, but instead he caught Eadie's eye. Not only was she beautiful, but youth, love-of-life and mischief were all three dancing behind her eyes.

'It doesn't matter,' Denny said. 'I had fun anyway.'

'It was a fine afternoon to be on the water, and that's for sure,' said Sam, and the three of them gathered up their gear and walked home, this time together in a ragged little line.

When they parted out the front of Sam's house, Eadie reached out and touched Denny's arm, more of a swipe than a touch, but it shocked him with its warmth.

'Goodbye,' she said. 'Hopefully we'll see you again soon.'

'Here's hoping,' he said, and when he turned and looked towards home, she watched him go, arms folded across her chest.

Chapter Twenty-nine

Barings Bank had always been a successful institution, one of the most important merchant banks in England. Yet financial ruin can be as swift as any flood or fire, and just as merciless.

Day by day Frederick read news of the bank's demise – how a consortium headed by the Bank of England's former governor, Henry Gibbs, was trying to patch together a rescue plan, while forcing a restructure and liquidating Ned Baring's personal fortune.

As the true extent of Baring's Bank's losses became known, Ned became one of the most sought-after men in London, and he was too canny to remain at his Mayfair mansion. Then, when his creditors and the press wised up to his presence at his country estate, Membland in Devon, he moved to a room at the brand-new Savoy hotel.

Yet, the Barings offices were still manned, and according to the loans manager now reporting to Percy Forgill, the fugitive sometimes appeared there, working at his desk in short stints, entering and leaving with a scarf around his neck and hat tilted low over his eyes. Ever resourceful, Wilkins instructed the clerk on Forgill's pay roll to send a runner – an urchin paid to wait on stand-by, down to Bow Street – if Baron Revelstoke happened to arrive at the premises. A few days later this messenger burst into Percy's office, carrying a folded paper, his face red and streaming sweat from his exertions. Still, he had the gall to insist on a shilling when he had been promised sixpence, and Percy was impatient enough to give it to him.

Knowing that Ned Baring's presence might be fleeting, Percy had his coachman out the front in just minutes. Reaching Number Eight, Bishopsgate, he bustled his way through the entrance and fronted reception, battering through the protestations of underlings that their boss was not there, using his impeccable dress and obvious status to roll like a Thames barge over them.

Ned Baring was at his desk, sorting through documents in a folio when the door opened.

'I'm sorry Mister Baring, I couldn't stop him,' cried one of two clerks that fluttered around the visitor.

'What in the devil's name do *you* want?' said Ned.

'I've been waiting to catch you here,' said Percy. 'I heard that you've been hiding like a rat.' Percy paused to light a cheroot, and sprayed smoke around him as if to fumigate the air. 'But I knew you'd come back to clean out your nest.'

'You'd better state your business, or I'll have you removed.'

'Strangely, I'm here to tell you something that might assist in your cause. I know you are not fond of me, and I don't particularly like you either, but at the present time you need all the help you can get. I'd like to purchase the Morton debt.'

The look in Baring's face was hard to read. Relief, but sadness also. The look of a man taking his best friend's desirable wife to his bed. The knowledge that this gift came with the price of betraying a man who trusted him. 'Very generous of you. Why?'

'I have my reasons.'

'You know that I can't say no, don't you?'

'All men must make their own decisions.'

Percy Forgill took his cheque book from his coat pocket and sat it on the desk. 'Bring the loan documents and deeds to the property, and I'll pay the loan out now.'

Ned called for a clerk, and within a few minutes he had the necessary documents in his hands. 'There are two separate loans – one is unsecured, but the instalment loan includes a mortgage over the Lewisham house as well as the premises themselves. The line of credit ballooned out after two years and we refinanced the instalment loan. The loan stands at a little over four thousand pounds, and the line of credit at just shy of nine hundred. The total comes to £4938 10" 6'. Are you prepared to part with that amount of money?'

'I am.'

'Those agreements are binding,' Ned pointed out. 'You can't foreclose on Frederick Morton unless he falls into arrears, and he is not, and nor has he ever been, in arrears.'

'That's true, but I note that the annual line of credit expires in three week's time, at which point it must be renegotiated.'

'Technically, yes, 'though I do hope you will adhere to the spirit of the agreement.'

When Percy had written the cheque, he held it just out of reach. 'One last thing, Morton is not to be informed. Not yet.'

'That's not fair – I have a responsibility to my client ...'

'Abide by my wishes, or the deal is off.'

'You've got Freddie wrong,' said Ned, 'he's a good man, and he deserves to succeed. But yes, I have no choice but to agree.'

Percy said nothing, just allowed Ned Baring to take the cheque, then left the room, holding the title deeds and loan agreements in his right hand.

★★★

The first Frederick knew of a practical issue was, at the end of the month, when he was waiting for the delivery of the week's payroll from the bank.

His mood was low, for the postman had just arrived with a sheaf of invoices from suppliers of iron, tools and coal. Then, much worse, Horace Batherton from the bank sent a note, explaining that the payroll could not be delivered, and would Frederick please call on him immediately.

Shortly afterwards, as Frederick strode down High Street with his workshop apron off, and his suit brushed, he had a feeling of dread, a wave of bile washing at the back of his throat.

Horace Batherton met Frederick at the door of the bank, led him past the cashiers in their booths of jointed teak, organised tea, and ushered him into his office.

Dropping into a chair, upholstered with velvet, Batherton took a sip of tea, his forefinger hooked in the handle of his cup. There was a gleam of pride in his expression of concern, as if he had now been proven right in surmising that Frederick was not the right kind of man to run a business.

'Mister Morton, Barings Bank is no longer covering your overdraft, and there are not enough funds in your account to meet this week's wages bill.'

Frederick frowned, 'Barings are no longer honouring the line of credit?'

'No, I'm afraid. Your account, in fact, is overdrawn.' He lifted a ledger from the desk and examined a row of figures through a monocle. 'Forty pounds. May I ask how soon you may return it to a credit position?'

'Tomorrow, I would think. I'll speak with Barings and find out what's happened with this month's payment, I'm sure it's just an oversight.'

★★★

That evening Frederick excused himself after dinner and walked past the clock in the alcove to his office. There he poured himself a glass of single malt whisky. This was an existential moment, and he knew it. His funding had been taken away, and there was no safety net. Everything he had built was at risk.

Taking a sip, savouring the flavour on his tongue, he walked to one of the cupboards, from which he removed a wooden case, blowing off the dust and unlatching it on the desk. Inside was a working model of a separate-condenser Watt engine, that childhood gift from Lord Forgill.

It was many, many years since he had last fired up the miniature boiler, made of copper plate, rendered in perfect detail, down to the last tiny rivet. Equipping himself with a flask of paraffin and a pitcher of water, Frederick filled the boiler, then the spirit burner. He lit the wick, placed it under the boiler, then waited with one hand under his chin, the years falling away like a dropped curtain.

The engine was a thing of beauty, despite the tarnish and verdigris left by the passing years. Dormant for so long, there was an element of suspense in waiting for it to work. Frederick had always seen the power of steam as a miracle, a gift that had changed the world. His greatest fear was that one day the magic would fail.

Over patient minutes the boiler pressure built. Frederick, grinning like a child, watched as the weight of the beam lifted the piston upwards, in the process opening a number of unseen valves, allowing steam to push through a tiny copper pipe and into the foot of the piston. Meanwhile, the water pump cycled, forcing water into the condenser.

As the steam piston reached the top of its stroke, one valve closed and another opened. The upper piston chamber was invaded by steam from the boiler. Steam from under the piston rushed into the condenser. The piston was drawn into the vacuum.

The first stroke complete, a puff escaped from the vent, and the cycle repeated. Now the flywheel started to revolve, driven by the sun and planet gears. The engine was almost alive now – a replica of a machine that had proved to have a working life of a century or more. Engineered to keep working indefinitely, day and night, to replace the labours of hundreds of thousands of humans.

There was a knock at the door and Clare entered. Seeing the expression on his face she went to him and draped her arms around his shoulders, almost as fascinated by the working model as he was. Her love, to Frederick, combined with the seriousness of the moment – his understanding of his place in the world, and the way his talents must be used.

The steam engine changed lives, made the impossible possible, altered the face of society. It was the driving force of a future. The beginning of an age, and the end of an age. Steam was the core element of Frederick Morton's life. He could not let the failure of Barings bring it all crashing down.

At length, when the water in the boiler was almost exhausted, he removed the burner, blew out the flame and let the boiler cool until the piston stopped moving.

'What will you do next?' Clare asked.

'I'll need to borrow money from somewhere.'

'We could ask Papa.'

'No,' said Frederick. 'I can't ask him. There will be other options.' He sighed. 'First I need to hear the facts from Ned.'

★★★

Dressed and breakfasted by seven in the morning, Frederick took the train from Ladywell Station and across to the City. He saw everything with fresh eyes – the parade of monuments, broad streets with hurrying businessmen, flower girls with their bunches of primroses, but most of all the beggars, knowing for a fact that there, but for the grace of God, go all men and women.

Taking the Eastern Line to Bishopsgate, Frederick alighted at the station below the viaduct and hurried down to the Barings office. The front door was open, and the seats filled with disgruntled looking men and women. The clerk was agitated and out of sorts.

'I need to see Mister Baring, as soon as possible,' Frederick said.

'I'm sorry,' said the clerk, waving an arm at the assemblage, 'but you're not the only one with a problem.' Then, lowering his voice, 'He's out of town for a few days. You'd understand Mr Morton, he's been under ever so much pressure. He'll be back soon, but until then he's uncontactable.'

Frederick stood his ground. 'Barings is not honouring its funding commitments to my company.'

The clerk closed his eyes for a moment, then reopened them. 'Your debt has been sold, sir, several weeks ago.'

'Who to?'

'Lord Percy Forgill, and I believe that your Line of Credit was due for annual renegotiation – perhaps that's the hold up. I'm sure you merely need to speak to him.'

Frederick felt a chill, as if cold water had been poured down his spine. 'Sold to … Lord Forgill?'

'Yes, Mr Morton. I carried the documents into the office myself, sir.'

Frederick recalled the agreement pertaining to the line of credit. It was true that the terms were supposed to be renegotiated annually. He thought out loud; 'Mister Baring never worried about it. He just increased the funding amount if it was necessary. But Percy Forgill is another matter – he won't give me an inch.'

The clerk shrugged, 'Can your bank provide you with an emergency loan?'

Frederick thought of Horace Batherton. 'Unlikely.'

The clerk sighed. 'I feel for you. Men of the ruling class would simply ask around at their club and the problem would be solved.' He took up a piece of paper and a quill, writing down a name and address on the sheet. 'If your bank won't come to the party try this lot. They're your best bet, I'm afraid.'

As Frederick left the building, the ramifications of Percy Forgill becoming his creditor rammed themselves home. He stood on the pavement, his face enveloped in a cold sweat. The line of credit was not his only problem. The entire capital loan agreement had already been extended once or twice. He couldn't quite remember, but it seemed to Frederick that it would expire again within a year or two.

There, on one of London's busiest streets, where snarling drivers swore and cracked their whips, Frederick's anger rose like pressure in a boiler. Clare had been right, Percy Forgill would not stop until he had ground the man he still saw as beneath him into the dirt.

Frederick realised that it was time for a confrontation. He hailed a cab and nursed his anger through the chaos of Piccadilly Circus, and down to Bow Street. Before he'd met Clare he had believed himself to be a lesser human than those who flounced through the city in their fine clothes, and lived softly from others living hard. But Clare had changed all that.

Seeing Percy Forgill – standing up to him on his own ground – was now an imperative. Frederick could barely control his voice when the cab stopped outside the Forgill office, and he turned to the driver, delivering a curt instruction. 'Wait here please.'

Inside, Percy Forgill's clerks manned the ramparts – the first line of defence. They were a mean-looking lot, underfed and over-employed like badly managed hunting dogs, taught to compete with each other for scraps of their master's favour.

Frederick placed both of his big work-forged hands on the counter. 'I need to see Percy Forgill immediately.' He could not bring himself to use the honorific 'Lord.'

'I'm sorry sir, but he is not to be disturbed.'

'Rubbish,' growled Frederick, and he marched through the office, heedless of the clerks. Down a corridor, he continued past an ornate boardroom. It was easy to see which door led to Percy's office, for the handle was plated with gold.

Frederick opened the door and hurried through without knocking. Percy Forgill had been leaning back, smoking and reading from a sheaf of paper, his posture changing dramatically as Frederick entered.

'What on earth do you want?' he asked. 'And what gives you the right to come bursting in here?'

'I have every right to confront you,' said Frederick. 'How dare you become my creditor by stealth? To place me in your power once more by exploiting a good man, Ned Baring, when he was down. Did you make it a condition of the sale that he could not inform me?'

Percy regained his *savoir faire*. 'It's me who is setting the terms here. Not you. The renegotiation date for your Line of Credit expired some ten days ago. It has therefore been cancelled and is payable in full immediately.' He shuffled through a pile of papers on his desk and selected one. 'I also note that the monthly payment of your instalment loan falls due at month's end, which is tomorrow. The amount is £97. Please ensure that these payments are made in a timely manner. In short, I require that £940 is received at my office within twenty-four hours or you will be regarded as being in default and I will take steps to reclaim the funds.'

'Why do you have to destroy me?'

'It is a business imperative that you and your type are eradicated. How dare you steal my workers, then encourage them to get above themselves, just as you have done?'

'I will fight for what I have built.'

Percy shrugged. 'Fight all you like, so long as it starts with nine-hundred-and-forty pounds by tomorrow afternoon. If you can't, I'll have the sheriff at your door, your factory will be closed, and I will take the house you should never have been given.'

When Frederick re-joined the driver at the cab, climbing up beside him, he opened the folded paper the clerk at Barings had given him. He gave the driver the address and watched with blurry eyes as the horses clumped towards the commercial district of Cheapside. The driver dropped him at a corner, then waited while he climbed three flights off the street to the offices of a firm of financiers called Bischoffsheim and Goldschmidt.

The front room was panelled in mahogany and walnut, with a Chippendale sideboard standing against one wall. The art adorning the walls was recognisably significant. This was a haven of old money

– continental money. The kind of money that changed hands behind the scenes, unrecognised, destroying and building, making men rich or leaving them bankrupt.

Bischoffsheim was a little younger than Frederick himself. He was not ostentatiously dressed, and neither was Adolphe Goldschmidt, who was sitting beside him. They discussed the business of the day. More Irish troubles, and difficulties with the new County Boroughs.

Raphael Bischoffsheim spoke with a strong German accent. 'Now, I take it that you are here to ask for a loan?'

'Yes, I am.'

'Has the ah, Barings situation precipitated these liquidity problems?'

'In the main part, yes. My company has been trading quite well and I'm sure that I have no black marks to my name.'

Goldschmidt, after a glance at the more senior Bischoffsheim, took over. 'Mr Morton, your personal integrity is not in question. But when a man who carries substantial debt comes to ask for a further loan it behoves us to think very carefully.'

The two financiers looked at each other, then Bischoffsheim said, 'How much do you need?'

'One and a half thousand – a payment owing to Lord Forgill, and operating expenses for several weeks.'

'Pounds or guineas?'

'Pounds.'

'Please leave us for a moment and we will discuss the matter.'

Frederick withdrew to the waiting room, sitting on a fine upholstered chair, reminded again of the gulf that exists between those who have money and those who don't. Somehow, through the kindness of others, hard work and imagination he had joined those on the other side. Now, it seemed, he had fallen back – as helpless as a beggar, worse, because his own family and dozens of others depended on him to stock their larders and pay their rents.

Ten, twenty, thirty minutes passed. Finally, the door opened, and Bischoffsheim appeared. 'Come in please, Mister Morton, and take a seat.

Frederick did as he was asked.

'I'm very sorry, but you are too much of a risk – and Lord Forgill is, let's say, a hostile creditor. He will not give you an inch and he may make it difficult for us to get our money back if the uh, worst happens.'

'That's your last word on the matter?' Frederick asked, but he was already buttoning his jacket.

'Yes it is. I'm very sorry.'

Chapter Thirty

Frederick and Clare's bedroom was a haven, tastefully furnished, a space where passing years did not matter, where they were still a young couple in the spring of their lives, making love in the sunshine of a Paris morning. It smelled of potpourri and clean sheets, the curtains hung artfully, and the floor spotless.

The bedroom had rules that were strictly enforced. Clothes were not left draped over chairs, but were always folded. The contents of pockets were not emptied onto side tables. The bed was made each morning when they rose, not left for Eleanor to do.

The bedroom was a place in which to read, it was a place for love, and pleasant talk, and rarely did business matters intrude. That night, however, after struggling to comprehend two pages of *The Brothers Karamazov*, Frederick gave in to his thoughts.

'Today was a hard day to swallow,' he said. 'Nearly one thousand pounds by tomorrow evening – it's such a lot of money. How have we gone from running a successful business to near penury in a couple of months?'

Clare lowered her own novel and regarded him seriously. 'We know that Percy Forgill was behind the raid on the factory. Isn't it time to go to the police?'

'That won't help us now, it's all too long ago.' He let out a long sigh. 'Letting Percy have this property would kill me.'

'Let me wire Papa and ask him for the money.'

Frederick closed his eyes. 'No, we can't ask him. We could sell things.'

Clare reached down and gripped his hand. 'I would do anything to keep the business going. I would sell jewellery – even clothes to pay wages, but I will not do so for the extortion of that man.'

'Engines perhaps,' said Frederick. 'There's a working Mobilis that we use as a demonstrator, but the sale price is less than three hundred pounds. We'll have another Fortis ready by the twenty-ninth to go down to the new Empress Mill, the final payment will be about nine hundred pounds. But that's too far away.'

'Call Forgill's bluff. Don't pay the money,' Clare said.

'And let him walk in and take the company?'

'You still have twenty-four hours. Get some legal advice – Denny's friend Sam works for a lawyer, perhaps he will see you tomorrow. Does Percy have the right to rescind your line of credit because it wasn't renegotiated? Doesn't the previous agreement still stand? Percy Forgill might not be acting within the law.'

Frederick rolled onto his side and took her in his arms. 'You're right,' he said into her ear. 'I'll dig out the loan agreements and get some advice.'

★★★

The following morning, Denny hurried off after breakfast to find Sam. He was back a little after eight, breathless and red-faced. 'Father, Sam's boss Mr Wallace will see you at ten this morning. Sam said to warn you that he charges five quid for a consultation.'

'Understood,' said Frederick, 'please thank Sam for me.'

'I already have,' grinned Denny. 'Now I'd best get down to the factory.'

Strangely, Frederick was feeling upbeat, and this emotion propelled him all the way to High Street, where he was fifteen minutes early for his meeting.

★★★

Jonathan Wallace, attorney at law, was a man of at least sixty, with a clean-shaven face and an amiable manner. He used two pairs of eyeglasses, one sitting over the other, to study the fine text of Frederick's loan agreement. This process occupied a quarter hour during which he inked his quill and made notes, often producing small noises in the back of his throat.

When he was done the lawyer looked across at Frederick. 'So the debt was purchased by this Lord Forgill without your knowledge or consent?'

'That's correct.'

'Well, the law does allow for that sort of thing, but this failure to renegotiate a new agreement for the line of credit does *not* mean that the full amount falls due, though I imagine Lord Forgill has lawyers who would argue that case. The word negotiate implies that two parties are involved in discussing the matter. Not one.'

'So what should I do?'

'How much is the normal instalment on the line of credit, and any arrears on the principal loan?'

'There are no arrears, but the amount falling due today would be ninety-seven pounds.'

'Can you leave me a cheque for that amount, made out to Lord Forgill?'

Frederick thought quickly. His account was forty pounds overdrawn, but he knew that between unbanked cheques and cash on hand they should be able to raise and bank around one hundred and fifty pounds. 'If that will help.'

'Yes, it will. Then I'll write Forgill a letter, as your representative, stating that you expect the same arrangements as were made with Mr Baring to continue, that he has no grounds to demand full repayment.' The lawyer raised his eyebrows. 'Make no mistake,

I expect to hear back from his own counsel, and this will cost money in fees, but I don't bully easily, and there is nothing in those agreements that makes his actions just.' He paused. 'May I ask why a Lord of the realm would act in such a manner?'

'We went to school together, and we are not friends.'

'I see,' said the lawyer. 'Now here's the rub. I may be able to prevent him foreclosing on you but getting him to honour the spirit of the line of credit – forwarding funds into your working bank account each week will be much harder. It may not happen at all.'

'Stopping the foreclosure is the first issue,' said Frederick, and as he wrote the cheque for the instalment, the lawyer added, 'While you're at it, my initial consultation fee is five pounds, and another five for the letter and response. A cheque for ten pounds will get the ball rolling, so to speak.'

Frederick shrugged and wrote the second cheque. A few minutes later, when he left the office, it seemed that he had just made a valuable ally, albeit an expensive one.

★★★

At seven o'clock that evening, Frederick had just returned from a long day at the factory, worried sick at what might have happened on the legal front – whether Percy Forgill might be already making plans to shut him down. He had changed and was on his way down the stairs when a fatigued-looking Wallace knocked on the door of the Lewisham house.

'I have quite a bit of news for you – I've been in the city, meeting with Forgill's solicitors. We've got them – at least for the moment. There will be no line of credit, but you may continue to pay off the outstanding amount at the agreed rate.'

'I'm surprised they made concessions.'

'They had no choice. Percy Forgill overstepped the mark. He had no grounds for calling in the loan – you just need to keep your payments up to date.'

That would be difficult, Frederick knew, without the credit facility he had relied on through all the years of the company's operation, but at least he had breathing space.

'Would you join me in a brandy?' he asked. 'My wife buys it for me – she is French and has impeccable taste.'

'Just a very quick one,' said Wallace. 'How can I resist?'

★★★

After the halcyon days of a few years before, the Morton Steam Power Company entered a new phase of frugality. Regular payments kept Percy Forgill at bay, yet the end of each month was a fretful time.

Frederick's hair began to turn a shade of grey, and it thinned on top. With the help of his accountant he prepared yet another business plan, based on new realities. Horace Batherton agreed, in the end, that his bank would provide a small overdraft facility, but it was not enough for the vagaries of steel prices and seasonal sales difficulties, and it was a battle to keep everything afloat.

'Percy Forgill is waiting for us to slip up,' he said to Clare.

She pursed her lips. 'We must not let it happen,' she said. 'Morton Steam Power is the engine that drives our family. It pays for the education of our children, our clothes, and every aspect of our lifestyle. I am tired of that man and his jealousies looming over us.'

★★★

In the early 'nineties – with the great innovators Tesla and Edison at work – one of the most important tasks in the industrial world was the generation of electricity. Needing a way forward, Frederick threw everything into the design of the Imperium engine – determined that it would spin an alternator faster and more efficiently than any other engine on the market.

Frederick's genius was to simplify many of the theoretical models that had been kicking around for centuries, starting with

Hero of Alexandria's two-thousand-year-old aeolipile. Turbines had the advantage that circular movement was inherent in the design without any need for cams or quaint but effective sun-and-planet gears to impart that motion. There were problems: all turbine prototypes made to date produced an infernal racket, and had proved to be a maintenance nightmare, with frequent downtime. In addition, it was not easy to regulate the speed of any turbine yet built.

At the Inventions Exhibition in London, 1885, Frederick had stopped, open-mouthed, watching a turbine model constructed by an engineer called Parsons. The turbine was spinning at an incredible 18,000 revolutions per minute. It was a fascinating machine, worthy of an hour or more of Frederick's attention, but at the time it had seemed to be too fast, not practical for general industrial applications.

George Westinghouse, Frederick was aware, had also built a prototype turbine – with more efficient blade shapes, and a unique nozzle. Yet, it seemed to Frederick that neither Parson's design, nor that of Westinghouse, was quite right. Work still needed to be done on the shape of the turbine blades and the method of steam ingress.

Frederick spent increasing time in the machine shop at the factory, borrowing one of the sheet-metal workers to help him fashion turbine blades, mounting these on a central bearing and using a steam nozzle to spin them, calculating speeds and making adjustments to angles and blade shapes.

Over months of experimentation, Frederick systematically solved the issues that previous innovators had experienced with turbines, working on the assumption that the basis of good engineering was to reduce the number of working parts, thereby easing friction, costs, and tooling. The Imperium, in fact, had fewer components than the Fortis, for the turbine was an ingeniously simple design. Yet, for the high-speed work of spinning a power-generating alternator, it was the perfect machine, economical and smooth.

★★★

At first seeming like a long stretch in Dante's nine circles of hell, Matthew's time at the Charterhouse School passed without mortal injury or irreconcilable trauma. Those years would remain in his mind as a scroll of memories – athletics days, with the four great sporting houses sprawled over the grassy verges of the oval – shouting their war cries to the tortured runners. He would always remember examinations in the great hall, so quiet that the echoes of a pencil falling to a desk blurred the meaning on the page for minutes to come.

He remembered degradation, small triumphs, and moments of despair. Enduring the mock sentiment of his last days in sixth form; traditional farewells; the boys to men speeches, and handshakes with the masters who had secretly disliked him, partly because he was better read than they were.

In his final year Matthew took on the role of editor of the school newspaper, the Carthusian, wreaking sarcasm on arrogant 'bloods', and even the solemn traditions of the school itself, without either party knowing it. In this way he earned the respect of most of the 'pros', as keen scholars were known. He was awarded the title of 'bard of the year', after the publication of a poem assembled from the unhappiness of those years. Through it all, the limping, studious, quiet boy obtained one of the best classical educations available, while growing into a handsome young man, with very serious brown eyes.

Matthew's entry to Magdalen College, Oxford, saw him, once again, at the bottom of the pecking order, though overall this new establishment was much more to his taste. Hero-worshipping various dons, infatuations with new authors and friendships with like-minded students were the highlights of those years.

Life at Oxford was eccentric and interesting. And his nights were still enriched with the clash of Achilles's sword, the flutter of sails in the South Seas, and the fictional human dramas of the milieu.

The main event of his freshman year, before family circumstances tore him away from his new place of learning, was meeting a young woman with whom he fell in love. Not having experienced this emotion before, he found this experience both unnerving and exciting.

The fateful meeting occurred at a garden party. This party was memorable because Oscar Wilde, himself an alumnus of Magdalen College, was in attendance. Matthew was star-struck, experiencing an almost dream-like moment when the great man turned from a conversation and smiled at him.

Yet, that instance in itself was not to be the most memorable of the day. That distinction belonged to Matthew's first sight of a woman he believed to be the most arresting he had seen in all his days.

When she caught his eye she was surrounded by young men so that he had to move to get a better view of her face. Her skin was white, her neck slim and she was wearing a gown of peach, a string of pearls hanging low. Apart from her looks, he was impressed by the way she talked to the fellows around her as equals, with none of the self-effacing flattery employed by other women he knew.

Matthew was in conversation with his Latin tutor, who noticed his wandering eyes. 'Her name is Miss Pattinson. She's very bright – it's likely that she will graduate with first-class honours next year.'

Matthew acted as if that information was of marginal interest, but soon made his excuses and attempted to inveigle himself into the group surrounding Miss Pattinson.

Up close she was even more attractive, her lips bright with lipstick, and her hair braided into a complicated arrangement. It took a few minutes for Matthew to overcome his nerves at being so close to her, and he then had to wait for a gap in the conversation long enough for him to exploit.

Wracking his brains for an opening gambit, he settled on that standard, pedestrian, but very safe path of asking her what she was studying.

'History,' she said, 'and Renaissance literature. And you?'

'Modern literature.'

'Excellent, who's your favourite?'

Matthew screwed up his eyes. 'Probably George Eliot, or Flaubert.'

'You lean towards the realists then?'

'I do.'

'I like the way you speak,' she said, 'a little of Southeast London, a little Public School. The blend is interesting.'

The other young men, feeling themselves excluded, melted away, and after half an hour of talking Miss Pattinson touched Matthew's shoulder, gripping it lightly for a moment. 'I must head off, I'm afraid.'

'Must you?' asked Matthew, and before he could stop himself, he burst out, 'when can I see you again?'

The silence was thunderous, and Matthew imagined how gauche and shallow she must think him. Instead, oblivious to his unease, she adjusted her bag over her shoulder. 'I'm at Somerville College, why don't you come around one afternoon and we'll take a stroll? I'm sure that we have plenty more to talk about.'

'I know we do,' said Matthew, and he could scarcely contain his anticipation.

★★★

Ten days passed before Oxford was blessed with one of those perfect mornings that showed the town at its golden best. After luncheon, Matthew presented himself at Somerville College, and asked for Miss Pattinson.

The wait was interminable. Holding his hat by the rim, and rotating it gently, he amused himself by picking off a speck or two as it turned. When he tired of this, he refastened one shoelace, then removed and refolded the white kerchief that protruded from his top pocket.

Finally, he heard the sound of laughing and two young women appeared: Miss Pattinson and one other. Matthew stood, more than a little flustered.

'Good afternoon, Mr Morton,' said the object of his affections. 'This is my friend, Miss Taylor.'

Matthew clicked his heels together and bowed. 'Good afternoon Miss Taylor, will you be joining us on our stroll?'

'Oh no, I wouldn't dare intrude, besides, I have an appointment with my German professor.' She touched her friend's hand, winked, then hurried out ahead of them.

Miss Pattinson did not offer her hand to be kissed, or her arm to be taken, instead she smiled naturally. 'Thanks awfully for coming over. I've been cramming all morning and need some air. Where would you like to go?'

Matthew shrugged, 'Boars Hill isn't too far is it?'

'I'm up for it if you are.'

Miss Pattinson soon proved to be more of a strider than a stroller, and Matthew found himself working hard to keep up with her. Most of the clever conversational prompts he had thought up over the last few days seemed unnecessary in this much more vibrant exercise than he had foreseen.

'Your limp,' she asked. 'Is it permanent?'

'Yes, I had consumption as a child and it spread to my legs.'

'I'm sorry,' she said. I didn't mean to wound you. You move very well. Do you like walking?'

'You could say that it runs in the family. My father won quite a few pedestrian contests in his younger days.'

'But you're more of a reader?'

'Yes. I've always loved reading.'

From the top of Boar's Hill the town looked picture-perfect in its hollow: with church spires like tall grasses in a field, the cloisters of New College, the rowers on the river and the students in groups outside, many affecting the ostentatious Oxford dress code that would look outrageous anywhere else in England.

On the way back down Matthew grew bold enough to ask if he might write to Miss Pattinson over the summer break.

'If you'd like to,' she said graciously. 'I'm sure that your letters will be interesting: I must say that you are proving to be not as stultifying as some of your peers.'

'I'd better polish my prose style then,' he said.

★★★

That night Matthew could scarcely sleep without thinking of her, picturing her face, hearing the perfection of her voice in his head. She was unfathomably out of his league, he suspected, but that seemed not to matter.

Chapter Thirty-one

When Eugene Vintras returned to his native Lyons and died soon afterwards, Percy felt rudderless for the next few years. The church he had co-founded, the Hermetic Society of the Golden Dawn, was still operating, yet without the compelling Frenchman Percy felt a waning passion for the group. He was still married, yet childless, and his wife lived, most of the time, in her own place in Belgrave Square.

Percy saw himself as a businessman, a modern Demiurge. He loved to go to the factory and watch the black iron of his engines as they came into being. He still enjoyed cock fights, and his country weekends remained legendary amongst the sporting nobility.

His proteges, at the Rookery, not only lent him a violent arm when required, but were helping to grow an illicit business empire. The Rookery was now infamous – a honeycomb of rooms used for the illicit generation of cash. Stolen goods were funnelled through its front and side doors, and nothing was off the table. The 'boys' ran a cadre of pimps at arm's length, offering a steady source of girls sourced from the same kinds of institutions as the boys had themselves attended.

Trading on a tradition of excellence over many years, the continued success of the Forgill's factory supported Percy's belief that he was a better man than Frederick, though Sophie was of the belief that her brother was allowing the man to grow like a weed unrestrained.

'You're weak,' spat Sophie, who had married again, but was already drifting away from her new husband. 'You play at hating him. Do I have to do the dirty work for you again?'

★★★

Percy had been only three years old when the wolf came loping through the nursery door and into the bed of his twin, leaving a trail of saliva and blood. The wolf was epilepsy, and it dragged him to the floor, his limbs jerking wildly.

Six months later the eldest brother's thrashing body scattered toy soldiers and rainbow-coloured blocks. The governess was weeping when the doctor arrived. From then onward a hired nurse stayed close by, day and night.

By the age of seven Percy's twin had been in the surgeries of five different physicians and he was suffering an episode monthly. One doctor, at a distinguished clinic in Harley Street, tested him for allergies to common foods. The second measured electrical impulses from his brain, the next bound him in bandages and a fourth attempted hypnosis. The fifth and last travelled all the way from Edinburgh to burn incense sticks and hunt down noxious odours in the Park Lane house.

The three children tried to prepare themselves for the wolf 's arrival. It started innocently, a child's bow and arrow behind the door. There was never time to nock an arrow and draw the weapon. He came unbidden; with eyes of candle-flame yellow. Sterner measures were needed. Sophie and Percy laid their plans. Had done what they thought they had to do. But it was all wrong. They had not counted on the blood, and the shame and guilt.

Even so, that night would have remained a family secret except that little Freddie Morton – who had been plucked off the street and into their fine home – had seen what happened.

Freddie Morton knew.

Percy Forgill wanted to obliterate him from the earth. He always had.

Scarcely a day passed without Percy looking for opportunities to grind Frederick down. He dreamed of cutting his throat, but instead contented himself with vetoing Frederick's membership of the Steam Manufacturer's Association. He would not give an inch on debt payments due, and now and then he scoured the financial contracts in search of a loophole the lawyers had missed.

An article in the Times about the new legal concept of 'Industrial Property,' formulated into policy at the multi-nation Paris Agreement, prompted Percy to call for his legal team one afternoon. They filed in, dour and besuited. Percy did not like having a foreign tongue translated for him, and the law was a murky, alien language.

'I would like to revisit the idea of suing Frederick Morton for breach of Industrial Property,' he announced. He did not go on to say that even if the suit did not succeed, the legal fight would bleed funds from Morton, who was scarcely able to meet payments as it was.

'I agree sir,' said his plump lead counsel, a partner in the firm of Howitt and Newcombe. 'There have been changes to the law since the Paris Agreement that will give our suit a better chance.'

'That's what I'm banking on,' said Percy. 'See to it, and as quickly as you can.'

★★★

The bedroom was still dark when Harriet stirred, striking a match and touching it to the wick of a bedside candle.

Her clothes were laid out on the foot of the bed; plain, practical things. She dressed quickly, then picked up a valise that she had filled the previous night with an elegant gown, fresh underclothing and even a small case of makeup. Hefting this she went down to boil the kettle and find some bread and cheese for breakfast.

Outside, Jenkins was waiting with the trap, horses steaming and snorting in the morning cold. If he was unhappy at being asked to rise so early in the day he gave no sign.

"Op up, we've a long run, even at this hour, so I do 'ope you 'as dressed warmly.'

Harriet sat on the box while Jenkins clicked his tongue and flicked the reins. With surprising energy, the pair of horses drew them out through the drive, into Lewisham and onto the Old Kent Road towards Southwark.

The sun had not yet risen as they neared the river, though the fog glowed fluorescent white with the coming dawn. At Lambeth Marsh the smells started to change: deeply rotten in the low-lying areas, where ditches were filled with black, polluted water. Open, warming fires burned on road verges and desperate faces looked up as they passed.

Harriet was flushed with excitement. Having just finished school she was finding the trappings of adulthood of great interest. Her strong interest in the equalisation of wealth had led her to joining Mrs Bromley and her philanthropic friends in operating their irregular but well-organised summer-soup kitchens in the slums. But that was not the only cause for the deep sense of anticipation.

On this particular day, as the horses carried them into Tanswell Street, in the New Cut area of Lambeth Marsh, Harriet had another reason to be excited. At two o'clock that afternoon she had a meeting with a theatrical agent – someone who might land her a role in a real production. The appointment had been arranged after Harriet, in her leaving year, stole the show as Ophelia in a school production of *Hamlet*.

After the show she had been given a card by a man from the audience who had sauntered into the backstage area. 'You're a real talent,' he had said. 'A good friend of mine is an agent, and he's always looking for new stars.'

The appointment had then required several letters, backwards and forwards, and today, after the soup kitchen was done, she would arrive at the house and offices of Thomas Jensen, theatrical agent. Before that, she reminded herself, there was work to be done.

The New Cut, Harriet reflected as she approached, was one of the worst slums in London, where six thousand people huddled in and around seven hundred crumbling terrace houses. The street was littered with people sleeping rough, broken windows, burned wagons and general litter.

Leaving the wagon, and taking her leave of Jenkins, Harriet took her valise and set off to help Miss Bromley and her friends as they set up the trestles and lit gas rings. They talked of books and theatre. Harriet loved the energy of the bustling little group. A sparkling, intellectual conversation kept their minds busy as they worked.

'Miss Bromley,' said Harriet. 'I finished reading Proudhon's *Philosophie de la Misère.*'

'I applaud you, did you learn much from the work?'

'I did indeed. Such ideas! I do believe that I'll read it two or three times before I understand more than a quarter of it all.'

The excitable house mistress leaned forward from the cauldron of oats she was preparing to plant a kiss on Harriet's forehead. 'Well done!'

There was soon no time to talk, for as an apprehensive sun filtered into a world of coal smoke, fog and poverty, people began to wander up, hungry but hesitant. One or two young men shouted ribald comments at the young ladies bustling over pots and plates, others just stared.

The children came first, round-eyed, grubby and thankful. Many were so hungry they ate with their hands, cramming porridge into their mouths and licking the bowls clean.

The men wandered up. Unemployed or underpaid. Many had not washed for months or years. Some had lice hanging from their hair, others had visible sores. Some took the food boldly, as if they were deserving of nothing less than being served breakfast by upper middle-class women. Others were resentful, that they should be so abased as to have to be fed like this.

The women came last, red in the hands and faces from morning chores. Drawn but hopeful. And there was something in those eyes that Harriet knew in herself. The things females everywhere know. There was an occasional barbed comment about rich girls slumming for their own reasons, but gratitude was the most common emotion.

By mid-morning the day was growing hot, and the crowd thickened. Word had spread, and even Miss Bromley removed her bonnet, dabbing at the sweat on her indomitable brow. 'Another hour or two and we'll have nothing left to serve,' she said proudly.

The ladles were scraping on the bottoms of the pots when Miss Bromley clasped Harriet's arm. 'You'd better go and meet your agent. But would you come for dinner afterwards? I want to hear all about your appointment, and I'd love you to meet some of my friends.'

'That would be marvellous,' said Harriet, then she lifted her valise and hurried away.

★★★

Harriet changed in the bathrooms at Piccadilly Station, using the mirror to apply lipstick and face powder. She left her valise in a locker. She was thus unencumbered apart from a slim folder of scripts and a business card embossed with the name Thomas Jensen Esq., Theatrical Agent, as she walked towards the address on Albemarle Street.

Approaching a nondescript terrace Harriet knocked on the door. She was admitted to a drawing room by a man who she assumed to be a butler. There was a squalid air to the room. Male sweat, gin, tobacco. She did not sit down. Instead, she waited, on her feet, studying the photographs of famous stage actors and opera singers on the walls – many of them her idols, all signed to Thomas Jensen with love and gratitude. Even the great Adelina Patti was there.

The agent appeared from a side room, looking as if he had just risen from sleep. His sharp features were blurred from a dark stubble and puffiness around his eyes.

'Well, aren't you a beauty,' he said. 'Did Jacob Richards send you?'

'Yes, that was his name.'

'You must be the schoolgirl from Lewisham, then?'

'No longer a schoolgirl, but yes, I'm Harriet Morton, sir. I brought a script or two,' she said, if you'd like me to do a reading.'

'Scripts?' he said. 'I have thousands of those. Have a seat and let's talk.' He led her to a leather lounge, and sat opposite. 'What kinds of roles do you see yourself playing?'

'Anything, but I like roles where women are agents of change, where they make a difference.'

'Oh, I'm sure we can find such roles for you.' He leaned out and traced the line of her jaw with his forefinger. 'You will view well on the stage.'

Harriet tried not to shiver from the way his touch made her feel. 'Thank you,' she said at last.

'Now, we need to put together a portfolio for you – that means a list of shows to your credit – parts you've played and all that kind of thing. We also need some photographs to go with it.'

'Oh, I didn't bring any, sorry.'

Jensen produced a devilish grin, 'No we'll take them upstairs in our little studio. I'll fetch you some paper and a pencil, and you can write down your credits first.

And while Harriet entered the details of her plays to date in her neatest script, along with the types of productions she would like to be in, she glanced regularly at the prints on the walls, feeling that she was taking the first step to the same level of success.

When it was done Jensen led her upstairs to a room. It was set up with an Eastman box camera on a tripod, a pair of bright gas lights, and a red couch at the other end. On a small table stood a bottle of champagne and a glass.

'Have a glass of bubbles,' Jensen said. 'It'll help you to relax.'

Harriet accepted the glass, and sipped deeply, finding that it did not make her relax. It made her feel more distinctly alive. The little girl she used to be was outside on the street. Having passed through the door she had grown into something new.

When the glass was empty Jensen took it from her hands and invited her to sit on the couch. The flash puffed for the first time. Jensen asked for a change in the way she was sitting. Three, four times, the flash seared her eyes again.

Soon Jensen suggested another glass of champagne. By then, her head was swimming. They did some standing shots, some by the window. Harriet felt that she looked sophisticated and assured.

'Now Harriet, this might be hard for you, but directors often want to see a little more than a girl in a dress – they will consult with costume designers – and remember – you have to be grown up about this – do whatever it takes. For the next couple of shots I need you to take off your dress.'

Harriet felt too sleepy to respond, and Jensen came forward to unbutton the back of her dress, letting it slip down to the floor. She stepped away, still in her slip.

'Very good,' Jensen applauded.

When she tried to sleep, he slapped her face and sat her up. Twice more the flash seared her eyes.

Then he was taking off the rest of her clothes. Harriet tried to stop him.

'Lean down that way. Toss your hair to one side. Hands on your hips. Now sit down. Don't cross your legs.'

Harriet Morton was a beautiful young woman. Her eyes were blue chips of sapphire and her hair the colour of sunlit grasslands. Adored by adults, and beloved at school, now she was learning that beauty can be a curse as well as a gift. That beauty was not lost on the darker side of society and new ways to make money had arrived with the magic of photography.

★★★

Harriet woke on the lounge, with her clothes on, but uncomfortable. Someone had dressed her inexpertly. Jensen let her out the front door and promised that he would be in touch. Half a block down she leaned on a fence and was sick into someone's garden. She did not go to Miss Bromley's place as she had promised, but rather she walked to the train station and straight home, still feeling sick to her stomach.

Chapter Thirty-two

The clouds rolled away to the west, revealing a sunny day with a warm easterly breeze. Sam, Denny and Eadie went picnicking on horseback, with Eadie riding astride behind Sam, the two horses picking their way along Ladywell Fields, on the west bank of the Ravensbourne.

Arriving at an agreeable picnic site, on a scenic bend of the river, they let the horses graze on long halter ropes, while Denny skipped stones across the water. Eadie, meanwhile, took off her shoes, lifted her dress and paddled to her knees, singing divinely while she did so. Sam walked his horse in, splashed him all over then retired a little way off in the sun to brush him. With a blush, Denny realised that he was alone with Eadie.

Spreading a blanket, and sitting down demurely, she patted the place next to her. 'Come and talk to me.'

Denny did as he asked, sitting on his feet with his knees extended, not daring to look at her from up so close. He rested his wrists on his knees, fidgeting with his hands, while Eadie lay with her hands behind her back, looking upwards.

'Some people like to find shapes in the clouds,' she said, 'but I enjoy the sky itself. It's so deep and mystical, like looking at forever.'

'It's a beautiful colour today,' he replied. 'As blue as a certain person's eyes.'

Eadie chuckled, 'My eyes aren't that shade at all, in fact they're a watery blue, like the sea down at Folkestone.'

Sam, having finished brushing his horse, mounted up bareback and trotted away. With his friend out of sight, Denny changed position, kneeling to take Eadie in his arms. He kissed her lips, all rubbery pliant and damp. In between kisses he held her close, too respectful of her to give in to his passion, the warm sun on his shoulders and thinking that life could never be more perfect.

★★★

The Sheriff of Lewisham was, in those days, an imposing man. He drove a black wagonette, and both he and his driver wore Webley revolvers in side holsters. The Sheriff had the power to seize and confiscate. He served writs, and wore a grey hat like a rain cloud. Few doubted that he served a necessary purpose, but no one drank ale or ate cheese with the Sheriff of Lewisham.

Sheriff knew that rising early was the best way to catch his prey at their workplaces, or at their homes. Seizing goods was his speciality, and it was rumoured that the official's own house was furnished with the very best that thirty years of Lewisham's debtors could provide.

Frederick, arriving in his trap one morning, saw the sheriff and his grey hat haunting the front entrance of the factory. He stepped down and walked towards the visitor, arms folded across his chest.

'Are you Frederick Morton, director of the Morton Steam Power Company?' asked the Sheriff. His teeth were yellow, and set in a cave of a mouth.

'Yes, I am.'

'Then you and I have business, of a not so pleasant nature.'

'How so?' asked Frederick.

'I 'ave a writ, sir, a legal document that I must serve on you, lodged with the Chancery Division of the High Court.' With a flourish he produced a square of paper. "'That the machine titled the Fortis does breach Industrial Property held by the Forgill Engine Works Limited and registered under the terms of the Paris Convention for the Protection of Industrial Property." To paraphrase the remainder of this lengthy document, sir, you are not permitted to sell the Fortis machine until you negotiate a licensing fee or successfully defend the suit.'

There was so much to be dismayed about in those few sentences that Frederick was at first struck quite dumb. 'We have to sell engines,' he said finally, 'we need the cash flow.'

'That,' said the sheriff, 'is your problem.'

★★★

An hour later, up on High Street, Jonathan Wallace read the document at length before commenting. 'It seems that Forgill's have registered a design for a superheated engine, submitted to their company by you, many years ago – only this week, mind you, and now allege that your Fortis infringes their industrial property.' He paused, 'Is it true that the engines are substantively the same?'

Frederick shook his head vehemently. 'No, they're not. They share many design elements, but not patentable ones, which is why nothing was registered back then.'

He exhaled deeply. 'What can we do? I need to sell my engines.'

'Have you a couple of hours available now?'

'I have nothing more worthwhile to do than to sort this out.'

'Indeed. Let's prepare a defence, and if you can lend me your trap and driver I'll petition the judge who signed this document that an order stopping you from selling is an unfair restraint on your business – with luck we can have the order lifted right away.'

★★★

Preparing the defence took three hours, and at midday Frederick sent Jenkins to drive the lawyer into the city. The pair did not return until sometime after eight in the evening, by which time Frederick was watching for them out the window.

'I'm sorry,' said Wallace. 'I tried my best, but the order holds. You cannot sell a Fortis engine on British soil.' He paused. 'The judge has accepted the defence. There'll be an initial hearing on February ninth.'

'That's three months away,' said Frederick.

'The wheels of the justice system turn slowly, but there's not much more we can do until then, apart from continuing to strengthen our defence.'

Frederick shook the man's hand. 'You tried your best, I can't ask for more than that.' Then, to Jenkins. 'Take Mr Wallace home, if you will, and thanks to both of you for a big day.'

***

The next morning there was an article in the Times about the suit. After he had read the page Frederick passed it to Clare. She smacked the paper with the back of her hand, right over the artist's rendition of Percy Forgill's face. 'That smug man, oh God how I hate him.'

Yet, she calmed down and read the story from beginning to end. 'This still doesn't affect our other engine, the Mobilis, does it?'

'No, we can continue to make and sell the Mobilis, but the Fortis is worth five times as much per unit, and it's unique, no one else has anything like it.'

'You can still sell them in France?'

'Apparently so.'

'I'll ask my father if any of his business friends has a need for engines. He loves the Fortis, and he raves about them in every letter.'

'Anything will help,' said Frederick. Yet he knew such a step would not be enough, and the next payment would fall due in two weeks.

***

The days that had once winged by like migrating pigeons, now seemed to slow to a crawl, and the routine of waking, dressing, eating, working seemed like drudgery for the first time in Frederick's life. How could he work for the factory's future when it seemed to have no future?

While hope ebbed away, something momentous happened. One evening Frederick came home from the factory to find Ned Baring in the drawing room, with Clare having let him in and provided tea. Harriet was playing the piano and singing upstairs, and Eleanor was wringing her hands in the kitchen, unable to believe that a real Baron was in the house, wondering what on earth she would feed him should he stay for supper.

As for Frederick, he didn't know how to react. He was not sure how he now felt about the once dashing banker – still grateful to the man for giving him the start he needed, and his advice had always been incisive. Yet, the bank's collapse, along with the sale of Frederick's debt to Percy Forgill had chipped away at the relationship.

Baring's dress-code was, as always, fine enough for entrance to any club in the City – a black frock coat and top hat sat on the stand in the entry, and he remained, despite his fall from grace, a mighty person to descend on that humble Lewisham home. He looked much older, however, with the last of his hair now white, clinging to the back of his scalp as if for dear life.

'Ned,' Frederick began. 'This is such a surprise. I heard that you were back at Membland.'

'Yes, it's my home now – one of the few assets I was able to keep. It's also handy to get away from the damned press and to give my family some peace. My so-called benefactors have taken everything I owned, apart from the Devon estate, as part of the bail-out terms. We've been able to resurrect the business as Baring Brothers and Co, and while it's nothing like it was, we're still in the game and I have a modest salary to live on. Louisa and I are renting in Kensington while we're in town. Things could be worse.'

'Still, it's terribly hard for you … I'm very sorry,' said Frederick.

'No. I'm the one who's sorry. That's why I'm here – I saw the article in the newspaper this morning – Forgill seems to have you over a damned barrel. I landed you in it, and I intend to make amends.'

Frederick lifted his empty teacup, then turned to Clare. 'Do you think we might have something stronger?'

'Of course. Cognac or sherry?'

'I'll take sherry, please,' said Baring.

'The same for me,' said Frederick, sharing a smile with Clare as she walked off.

'I'm so sorry for what I did,' Baring said. 'Selling your debt to that caddish Forgill was an act of bastardry. In my defence I can only plead genuine desperation – every pound helped at the time.' He paused as Clare arrived with the drinks, taking a small but appreciative sip. 'The bloody man is determined to destroy you, isn't he?'

'Yes, it seems so.'

'A friend of mine was talking to a sub-editor at the Financial News. Apparently Forgill and some of his cronies from the Carlton Club were giving out titbits of information to the press – obtained God knows where and how – whipping up hysteria about the Argentinian situation – the situation that helped lead to the downfall of my bank.'

Frederick tugged at his collar, desperate for air. 'Then the fall of Barings was partly because of me.'

'No, it is not. The blame is mine. I overexposed the bank to a flailing economy, and a disastrous float, and all Forgill did was draw attention to it. On the other hand, though, that kind of malevolence does make my blood boil, so we must pay him back in kind. If Forgill's aim is to destroy you and your company, we must fight him tooth and nail.' He paused. 'I don't want to be indelicate, but how bad is the financial situation with Morton Steam?'

'Difficult,' said Frederick, 'and without Fortis sales it will become impossible. Not only that, but the term of our capital loan ends in a couple of years – like a cliff looming up on us.'

Baring scratched his chin between thumb and forefinger, 'I know. Technically speaking the full residual of the loan will fall due.'

'We'll be finished then, if not before,' said Frederick. 'I can't come up with three or four thousand pounds, or whatever the residue is. Percy will take the house – and the factory.'

'Not if I can help it,' said Ned. 'I have an idea – still in its infancy – but I wanted to run it past you – a way in which you would be out of Percy Forgill's grip forever. I have lost my fortune, but I still have considerable influence and the new Baring Brothers entity is a platform, at least. I'd like to help get you out of trouble and enjoy some sweet vengeance on Forgill for what he did to me – to both of us.'

'Sounds interesting,' said Frederick. 'What's the plan?'

The dinner bell tinkled from the kitchen, and the little family assembled at the dining table – including Eleanor, who snuck occasional glances at the guest. If it seemed strange to Baron Revelstoke that the cook might join the family at the table, he said nothing.

He did, however, compliment them on the meal – loin mutton chops done in the grill, cooked so the fat had turned golden yellow. Potatoes baked so crisp that they exploded with flavour. Supper was followed by a raisin pudding.

Then, when the plates had been cleared, Baring asked for a sheet of cartridge paper and a pencil. When Frederick had procured the items, he wrote boldly at the top of the sheet, 'THE MORTON STEAM COMPANY LIMITED.'

'What does the limited mean?' asked Frederick.

'It signifies a publicly traded company. My dear Frederick, I propose that we float your little company on the London Stock Exchange, and thereby turn it into a big company. You and your family will retain say thirty per cent of the issued shares, while we offer the rest to the public, in the process raising something like a hundred thousand pounds. With part of the money, you pay Lord Percy Forgill out and never owe him another penny. The rest will allow you to expand and consolidate. Provided everything goes to plan and we can interest shareholders in the company.'

Frederick's brows moved busily. It sounded too good to be true. 'Could I also issue some shares to my workers? They've been so loyal.'

'Good idea. Make them all small shareholders if you like. We can also invite some of the most august and well-regarded members of the financial world to sit on the board – men and women who not even Percy Forgill would dare cross.'

'Would they do it?'

Ned smiled, 'Oh yes, everyone loves sitting on a company board. Why wouldn't they? You get paid a nice retainer, just to go to a meeting once a month.'

'There's one problem,' said Frederick. 'How do I keep everything going in the meantime? I can't sell the Fortis, my most profitable engine.'

The visitor was silent for a moment, the wheels turning in his head, 'Correction, you can't sell the Fortis engine in the United Kingdom. The court can't legally stop you from selling them overseas.' He looked at Frederick seriously. 'You also have to defeat Percy Forgill's suit in court, and soon. A legal case hanging over the company's head will make a float much more difficult. Let your trade creditors ride out to sixty or even ninety days – convince them to keep backing you. You have a new engine on the drawing board, don't you?'

'Yes I do, but I can't afford to build it.'

'You have to – the markets love new technology. Build a prototype at least.' He regarded Frederick seriously. 'I know that you are naturally conservative, and you dislike being in debt, but you must risk everything. If you are to fail, let it be a spectacular failure.'

'It's a big risk,' sighed Frederick, 'to go deeper into debt. That could mean a debtors prison for me.'

'Unlikely, but possible. The economy is flat at the moment, and if we can't impress investors the offer might fail to subscribe, and we'll fall flat on our faces. But if it works you will be free of debt and riding high. So, what do you say?'

'What would we need to do for this to happen?'

'Establish Morton Steam overseas. Sell engines there, and get your Imperium off paper and into steel.'

Frederick raised his eyebrows at Clare, asking the question without words. She nodded in response. He turned back to the banker. 'We say an emphatic yes.'

'Good. I've already discussed the concept with a broker friend of mine, John Lievere. I'll set up a meeting, for tomorrow afternoon if possible. Would you be able to travel into the city then?'

'Yes, whenever you need me to.'

'Then let's drink to the success of the enterprise.'

★★★

A little later, Frederick asked Eleanor to fetch his leather case from his office. It was half open and the contents spilled onto the deck when she picked it up.

Eleanor stared, seeing the gun nestled amongst the papers, deadly and precisely machined like everything that Frederick made. She closed her hand around the grip and lifted it, surprised at the weight.

'A gun made to kill Percy Forgill,' she mumbled to herself. Then, she carefully repacked Frederick's things into the case, and took it to him as she had been asked.

★★★

While Frederick, with a renewed sense of purpose, travelled to the factory and then to the meeting in the city, Clare and Eleanor held a council of war at the kitchen table. Their weapons were steaming cups of tea.

Eleanor was in her sixties by then, with her skin lined and wrinkled from the years, and puckered around the lips from the stem of her pipe. Her hands were yellowed from nicotine, and the skin of her arms loose around those bony limbs.

Clare, on the other hand, was growing more striking with her years, and determined, with a defined jaw and steely eyes. Today there was no humour in her eyes.

'My husband, and my family are in peril from that horrible man,' she said.

Eleanor showed her perfect row of false teeth. 'I'm with you. 'E's a ruiner, a jealous dog.'

'We have to stop Percy Forgill before he destroys us,' said Clare. 'He will not let the float proceed – we know he won't. Frederick refuses to pursue him, so it's time for you and I to do what needs to be done. Together we must learn the truth of this man's past and bring him down.'

Eleanor grimaced, 'We'll bring the bastard down alright.'

The two women joined hands, and together clenched them into a single fist, but still Eleanor did not mention the gun in the briefcase.

★★★

Harriet was sitting on the edge of her bed, a letter from Thomas Jensen, theatrical agent, open in her hands.

> Dearest Harriet,
>
> While I have not yet found a suitable part for you I have made considerable progress and may have good news for you soon. In the meantime I wonder if you would consider some work as a hostess. Saturday next is a gathering of certain army officers of fine breeding to celebrate the impending marriage of a young major in the Royal Fusiliers. They wish to have the presence of several attractive young women and you came to mind … the fee would be twenty guineas for the evening.

Harriet felt a dark slide in her gut, and she tore the letter, once, twice, and many times, until tiny strips of cheap paper littered the floor.

★★★

In the early hours of the following morning, the faint ticking of the clock, audible throughout the Lewisham house, ceased. The clock that had kept time so reliably since the day the family moved in, stopped cold.

Frederick had been half asleep, dozing between bouts of worry over the future. The abrupt cessation of the ticking noise, however, had him out of bed in his night shirt and sleeping cap, creeping down the stairs to where the clock had indeed stopped, the small hand just shy of the number two.

Frederick stared at the face, knowing that he had wound it himself just that evening. He walked up close and peered through the glass at the pendulum hanging motionless inside the clock, almost as if he were willing it to move. He stepped backwards, and at almost the same moment, there was an audible click and the clock swung back into motion.

Watching the pendulum, Frederick felt his own heartbeat fall into step with it. He felt the rhythm of the tides in the river and of the Fortis engine at the factory all align in one thrilling moment that confused and elated him.

As Frederick climbed back up the stairs, he felt a sense of relief, but also a heightened awareness. Lying awake, between then and dawn, he made plans for exactly how he was going to proceed.

BOOK THREE

Chapter Thirty-three

On Whitsunday eve, in the year 1893, the Morton family gathered. May, Denny, Matthew and Harriet had each received a written invitation to an 'important meeting of the family,' and it would not do to be late.

The boys wore stiff suits, and their sisters dresses with uncomfortable but fashionable bustles – walking briskly along the ragstone paths lined with hedges – past creepers that scaled walls and haunted lower-storey windows. They walked down a corridor lined with rugs and adorned with new paintings. They passed Clare's fernery, and dozens of potted plants, from a Chinese primrose, to a Central American monstera.

They passed the clock in its niche beside the staircase, just as it chimed the hour of ten. One after the other they entered the room that had, for more than twenty years, been Frederick Morton's office. Inside, they took seats on the smoke-darkened leather of the couch. Behind them the spines of countless books lined the shelves like the ribcage of an elephant. Some of these were the famous works of great thinkers and historians. Others were engineering texts from three centuries of innovators.

The collection of brass, iron and chromium engine parts had grown over the years, occupying every spare niche, along with burnished tools, and scale models representing the birth and development of steam, from Cornish pumps to traction engines.

Frederick used his desk chair like a throne, his hair now grey and almost bare on top, yet his eyes were as vital and interested as they had always been. Clare sat beside him, and even old Eleanor found a place near the door.

Frederick cleared his throat then moved his eyes in an arc, a sweeping glance that encompassed each of his children in turn. 'I know you are all wondering why a family meeting is necessary. Let me assure you that momentous events have brought us together. Today, I am sorry to say, the life we all lead is in peril.'

The siblings looked at each other, expressions of surprise on their faces.

'Since the loss of the support of Barings Bank we, as a company, have struggled. For many years we relied on a continuous line of credit, and the loss of this facility has created many difficulties. We relied on Barings. And now legal action by the Forgill's company means that we cannot sell our Fortis engine in the United Kingdom. We are also faced with the expiry of capital loans provided by Barings, in two years from now – a debt we cannot hope to pay.'

'We have been thrown one lifeline. On the advice of Baron Revelstoke, your mother and I have made the decision to float Morton Steam Power on the London, Sydney, New York and Johannesburg Stock Exchanges, with the reorganised Baring Brothers company underwriting the issue.

'The float will not be easy. This is a difficult economic climate. Morton Steam Power is not truly ready to take this step. We are working on a prospectus that will attract investors from all branches of society, yet, to gain their trust our order books must be full, and the factory at peak production. Everything we own: our reputation and our lifestyle, now depends on the float. It will take place in twelve months from now. If the float goes well, we will become one of England's most important industrial companies. If we fail, we lose everything, even … this very house.'

There were blank looks, and an even deeper silence as the words sunk in.

'At this hour of need I call on you to help save our family business. The company must expand overseas, partly for the extra gravitas that an international presence will give us in the market, but also because, to maintain some cash flow and repay development costs we have to sell Fortis engines overseas, as many as we can.

'I would like to set up branches in Sydney, Australia, and Cape Town, South Africa. The first step is to acquire office space, then warehousing that can be used for receiving and assembling engines as they arrive by ship.'

His eyes moved to the eldest child. 'Dearest May, I need your help here, at the factory, where you will soon, hopefully, begin your engineering studies. Between us, you and I will look at the American situation – we will open negotiations for a company to distribute our engines there.' His eyes rolled onwards. 'Denny?'

The eldest son's eyes were shining. 'Yes Father?'

'You are an invaluable man at the factory, but we all know of your love of adventure, and I therefore send you the farthest. I'd like you to serve our interests in a country where you might also find time to pursue your passions. I would like you to personally inaugurate an Australian office, with an eye to the Far East.'

Denny's face showed surprise, then excitement. 'Thank you, sir. That's well … quite exciting.'

'I am hoping that your friend Sam might accompany you, as a secretary and assistant, but you will have to ask him yourself.'

'I'll ask him, most assuredly.'

'Now Matthew. You are a dreamer, your interest in books and literature is a credit to you, but I ask you to put your learning aside in our time of need. You will sail to Cape Town to oversee our African interests.'

'You mean, leave my studies at Oxford?'

'Yes, I'm sorry, that will be necessary for the time being.'

'I understand, Father.' Yet the younger son looked stunned as Frederick moved on.

'Harriet. You are so very young, barely seventeen, and your mother and I have discussed this at length. 'Would you travel with Matthew, and assist him with his task? Can you delay your ambitions in the theatre for the sake of us all?'

No ripple crossed her face. 'I will.'

'Travel arrangements are being made for all of you. A representative of the Thomas Cook company will be here later in the day to discuss booking and ticketing. My only stipulation is that you make yourselves ready to leave within ten days, some of which will be taken up with training.' He turned and took Clare's hand.

A moment later, strangely, the children started to clap. It was an expression of emotion that no one could quite articulate. It was a brave new adventure for them all – and a desperate fight for survival.

★★★

Denny pulled at his collar with two fingers to relieve the stuffy feeling, brought on by the close quarters of the office and the gravitas of the meeting. Heading first to his bedroom to change into moleskins and loose shirt, he headed down the stairs, and past the kitchen, taking an apple from a bowl as he passed.

Outside, he passed under the ivy-covered trellis to where Sam was waiting with two horses, one black and one grey, both tacked up with English hunting saddles and stamping impatiently.

'I thought you'd never get here,' said Sam. 'Racer is anxious to run.'

'Sorry, I got held up.'

Without a word Denny took the reins from Sam's hand, smiling when the gelding nuzzled at his armpit. 'Well he's pleased to see me, that's all.' He slipped his left foot into the stirrup, took a grip on the horse's neck and mounted smoothly. Sam did the same.

Setting off with a clap of his heels, Denny was content to keep his gelding to a demure trot past the stables, through the gate and into the street.

Once down between the rows of street-side trees and onto the recreation ground, he relaxed at last. He was most at home on horseback, and amongst open fields rather than houses.

'What was the family meeting all about, anyways?' Sam asked.

'I'll tell you in a moment. But first I'm going to beat you to the bridge.

Denny clicked his tongue, transferred his weight smoothly forward and pressed in with his heels. His mount responded with a surge of power off the hind legs. Both horses loved a gallop, and with the wind in Denny's face he felt the stuffiness dissipate. Finally, on the bridge itself, looking down on the dark but flowing waters of the Ravensbourne, they pulled up, energised from the run.

'So now are you going to tell me what's happening?' Sam asked.

'Family business,' Denny said slyly.

'What kind of family business?'

'Well. Guess where I'm going.'

'Salisbury?'

'No.'

'Edinburgh?'

'No.' Denny paused for effect. 'Australia.'

'That's just daft, Denny. Australia's ten thousand miles away – might as well be Allycomfee!'

'Maybe so, but Australia is where I'm going. You're looking at the new Australian and Far East manager for the Morton Steam Power Company.'

'Well strike me. It must be true, because you never could look me in the eye when you tell a lie. What brought this on?'

'I can't say too much, but Father has been forced to arrange a public float on the stock exchange. He needs our help to sell engines overseas. So I'm off to Australia. Matthew has to leave Oxford and head to Africa. Harriet is going with him. The big question is, would you like to come with me? Father said that he'll match your monthly salary.'

'You want me to come too?'

'Why not? It wouldn't seem right to go off on an adventure like that without you, and I could do with a right-hand man.'

Sam shook his head as if trying to wake from a dream. 'By all the stars, you are serious.'

'I am. We'll be leaving in ten days, so you'd best start packing.

'Well I s'pose I'd better.' Sam paused. 'But there's one person I know who's not goin' to like hearing this.'

'Who?'

'My little sister, Eadie.'

'Why, she won't miss you that much, will she?'

Sam gave Denny a sideways glance, long and meaningful.

★★★

Before the meeting, Matthew Morton had been lost in the poetry of Wordsworth, floating on clouds of imagery and finely tuned adjectives, imagining himself and the beautiful Miss Pattinson on a summer's day by a Northern lake, fingers twined in clover leaves and walking through fields of wild daffodils. Now he had been asked to travel half-way across the globe.

Matthew's first thought was to head to the library, and to this end he climbed the stairs and padded down the corridor, all bare squeaking boards but for a carpet runner patterned with roses. Opening the library door, the smell of must and cool air met him. Against the papered walls sat glass-fronted cabinets of burr walnut. Rows of open mahogany bookshelves filled the centre. A chaise lounge, cane-backed library chairs and a writing desk sat near the windows to take advantage of natural light.

This room had been a sanctum to Matthew for all of his life. Now he had an urgent need to think and to research.

Africa! The dark continent.

Matthew's excitement was tempered by worry that the family business was in such dire straits. Yet surely the more he could learn from books, the better the job he could do? It was difficult, however, to know just where to start.

The library was organised according to the whims of family members, with books grouped into loose associations. Matthew, however, understood the system intimately.

Livingstone's *Missionary Travels and Researches in South Africa* came to Matthew's hand, then Ryder Haggard's; *King Solomon's Mines* and *Nada the Lily*. Who was the female author, writing about Africa, he had heard good things about up at Oxford? Olive Schreiner? He paused to place his bounty on a table, before steaming down the shelves, soon locating a copy of Rand McNally's *Atlas of the World*. When, at length, he left the library, he had eight volumes, thick and thin, piled up in his arms, and had to call out to the maid, who happened to be walking his way with a cleaning trolley. 'Would you mind awfully closing the door for me, Gloria.'

The maid smiled indulgently. 'Of course. Do you want me to help carry those?'

'Oh, I'll be right, thank you.'

Reaching his room, Matthew opened the blinds and arranged his pillows. He had already decided to approach the books in chronological order of publishing year, so he left the others on his desk and opened the first of Livingstone's books that came to hand, inhaling the smell of pages unturned for ten or more years. With the only sound the cooing of pigeons on the window eaves, he began to read.

After working through the frontpages he was into the foreword. A knock on the door went unnoticed at first, but then persisted into a heavy banging. 'Come in,' he called.

The door opened, and May pushed into the room. 'I see, baby brother, that you've wasted no time gathering some reading matter on your destination.'

Matthew flicked his eyes up from the page. 'As William Shakespeare stated so divinely: "To pore upon a book, to seek the light of truth …" I think, under the circumstances, it behoves me to do so.'

'And well you might. He also said that, "A beggar's book outworths a noble's blood."'

'Ah, Henry the Eighth. Well done.'

'I did go to school, you know – a mere government school perhaps, but they did teach us a few things.'

'Any news on your application to the University College?' Matthew asked.

'Not yet,' she said. 'But fingers crossed – third time lucky.'

Matthew knew that she had applied to study engineering for the two previous years, unsuccessfully both times. 'I hope you get in, I really do, but please, if you don't have anything more to say, pray run along and let me read.'

May placed her hands on her hips. 'Don't you want to talk? You've just been told that you won't be going back up to Oxford in the new term, and that you have to go abroad and try to do something you've never done in your life before, namely, work. Aren't you frightened?'

'I'm a little overcome,' he admitted at last.

'I am too,' she said at last, 'to lose you all overseas like this. And if they don't let me into their dashed university I'll be furious.'

★★★

On Monday morning, Denny and Matthew were both at the factory by nine, with Vic Jones running them through their paces. 'Three days, boys,' said Jones. 'And you're going to know every important fact: sizing, specifications, prices, site requirements and coal consumption for every machine in every conceivable application.'

Much of the tour was aimed at Matthew, who had never worked

in the factory, apart from some general assistance on his holidays. Denny was a fully-fledged foundryman now, but this was the first time he had studied the premises with the eyes of an owner – the molten iron in the foundry, watching the parts appear from the moulds, before being machined to exacting tolerances in the machine shop. Together the two brothers watched the parts being assembled by craftsmen into working engines, which were then tested and prepared for dispatch.

On the showroom floor of the factory complex, Frederick took over, 'Watt's condenser steam engine was the mainstay of industry for a century, but those engines were so heavy and hungry for coal they could scarce be used away from a coal mine head – drawing water from shafts was their forte. It took a succession of geniuses to take us to the high-pressure light steam engines of today. Trevithick, Blenkinsop, Stephenson. The cities of Northern England and their steam-driven cotton mills clothed the world. In the year eighteen-hundred, one third of all the world's shipping traffic was passing through Liverpool, on the river Mersey.

'This Fortis machine is a very special beast. It can be installed anywhere in the world, supplying power far in excess of what its footprint would suggest. Your main aim is to get sales for Fortis engines since we can't sell them here. The supply chain is proven, the lead time is minimal, and we can rapidly gear up to make as many as we need.'

Vic Jones interjected, 'You boys don't understand the achievement you see right there. This Fortis machine would not have been possible without your Da's design genius, and his drive and determination. There is nothing else like it anywhere.'

The brothers touched the gleaming shaft, the gold maker's plate, the bright paint, and the precisely machined components.

'It's as mobile an engine as can be made today,' Frederick went on. 'Shipped on an iron base, able to be lifted on and off rail cars or barges via crane. It can power factories, pumping stations and lighting plants. There are many, many mills running on fifty-year-old low-pressure steam engines. Our imperative must be for them to update. Less coal, less water, more profit. You young gents are going out into the world to sell these units, all our futures depend on your success. These are undeveloped markets but they will not remain so – the world is industrialising at a rapid pace and steam is powering the process. You need to sell engines to businesses who don't even know they need them yet.'

On the third day, Frederick and Vic Jones took turns to grill the boys on specifications, running costs, pricing, delivery lead times and everything else they could think of.

Frederick hoped and prayed that they were ready.

Chapter Thirty-four

On Thursday, with his business education complete and a free day to pack, Denny sat on his bed with a map of Australia laid out on the covers, marked with rivers, mountains, deserts, towns and cities. The map had been an insert into a copy of 'The Boys' Own Paper' some years earlier. Denny unfolded it on the bed, using his forefinger to trace future and imaginary travels over the continent. Deeply immersed, he heard a gentle knock. The door opened, and Gloria called through. 'Excuse me, Master Denny. Young Eadie is here to see you.'

'Oh, right. Thanks.' Denny stood up and walked downstairs. She was waiting in the foyer, wearing a white dress and blue checked apron. Both suited her neat figure.

'Hullo Eadie. Good to see you.' Denny pecked her cheek.

'Are you packed yet? Sam has, pretty much.' She lifted the basket. 'I brung you some things for your journey. Look, there's the chutney you like, and pickled onions.'

'And gherkins,' he said. 'Thank you. My favourite.'

'I trust you'll have room for them in your luggage.'

'You bet I will.' He grinned, 'I'll leave all those wretched suits and things behind to make room.'

'Oh well then,' she said, beaming. 'I'd best be heading back.'

'I'll walk you down, if you like. I could do with stretching my legs.'

He stacked the jars on the entry table and stuck his head down the corridor. 'Oh Gloria, would you mind taking these up to my room for me. I'm going to walk Miss Eadie home.'

'Right away, Master Denny.' She paused, 'And good morning, dear Eadie. Did you make these?'

'Yes Mrs Buchanan.'

'I hope they turned out. You always forget something, don't you love?'

Eadie's face glowed red, and she tried not to look at Denny. 'Sometimes I do. But not this time.'

'Bless you, Eadie. How is your Ma?'

'She's well enough, thank you, Mrs Buchanan.'

'Tell her I'll be 'round for a cuppa soon.'

'She and Da are at my aunt's down in Brighton. She's very sick and also they're hoping that the sea air will help shake Da's ague.'

'My best to them then,' said the maid.

Once he had walked Eadie outside Denny wasn't sure what to say, at first, but led the way onto the footpath, enjoying the feel of the sun on his face.

'Are you happy to be going off, so far away?' Eadie asked.

'It's exciting,' he said, 'though I must admit to some nerves.'

'I'm glad Sam is going with you,' she said. 'I know you'll look after each other.'

'We've been friends for a long time.'

Eadie, with a flash of her dark eyes said, 'You and me have been friends for a long time too.'

'That we have.'

'I'll miss you,' she said. Denny looked at her sharply and she coloured. 'I'll miss both of you. I'm used to having you around is all.'

'Me too. Anyway, we're going to have dinner together – all of us – before we go, you'll be invited too.'

He looked away for a moment, and when he turned back she had burst into tears. 'What's wrong Eadie, what did I say?'

She shook her head and dabbed at her eyes with a white handkerchief. 'I'm just sad that you're going, is all. I felt like … something with you and me—'

Denny wrapped his arm around her. 'I know what you mean, but this doesn't have to be the end of it.'

'No?'

'I'll be gone for more than a year, but if you'll wait—'

'Of course I'll wait, silly,' she said.

They had reached her house, and Eadie leaned up and kissed him once on the lips. 'Go and pack,' she said, 'and don't worry about me.'

As Eadie walked down the path to her front door she said to herself, *He asked me to wait. That's kind of like being engaged.*

★★★

Matthew was packing the last of his clothes, making folded piles on his bed. Gloria had ensured that everything was ironed, and it should have been a simple matter to decide what needed to be taken or left behind.

For the second-youngest Morton, however, it wasn't so simple. Through research he had learned that Africa was a continent of extremes, stretching from the Tropic of Cancer to the Tropic of Capricorn, then down past the thirtieth parallel. Cairo would be very hot, at this time of year, while Cape Town might be cool.

After spending five minutes trying to choose between a light corduroy and lambskin jacket, he added them both to the trunk, on the floor beside a smaller but stouter version, already packed with books.

Other neat piles followed – breeches, underwear, rough and ready dungarees, one by one, until the trunk was packed full and the lid would not quite close. Matthew sighed, and decided that he was deserving of a distraction.

Moving to the desk, he picked up the notepad on which he had written the latest version of his letter to Miss Pattinson. The sixth or seventh draft. He had quite lost count. He started to read.

> Dear Miss Pattinson,
>
> What a lovely day we had on Boar's Hill! Certainly one of the most memorable of my time at Oxford so far. Even more memorable than seeing Oscar Wilde at the reception where you and I met, and hearing you tell me that I was 'not quite as stultifying' as most of my peers.

Matthew stopped, lifting his quill. Did his effort so far have substance? Was it witty and interesting? He closed his eyes until he saw the girl again in his mind. Her fearless intelligence. A passion for history and the written word. She was certain to be one of the first female History students to graduate with first class honours, and Matthew now felt a proprietary pride in her, especially when his fellow male students found themselves threatened by her abilities and near-perfect grades. The next section he had added in the last few days, and he was far from happy at the construction.

> Now I must become your personal Hermes and bear some news. I will be working abroad, probably for the next twelve months, and unfortunately it will be at least that long before I return to my studies at Olympus, sorry of course I mean Oxford. The Chancellor has, benevolently, granted me a leave of absence. In the meantime, however, I am keen to receive any correspondence you care to write and ...

Matthew clicked his tongue and waved his pencil like a bobby's baton. It just wasn't quite there. For the hundredth time he wrestled with whether he was worthy to write to the fair Miss Pattinson at all. Just keeping up with her current abode was a struggle, requiring diligent research through a network of acquaintances. Right now, she was in Prague, visiting relatives. He had addressed an envelope in perfect copperplate, ready and waiting for the day he could finish the letter and post it.

★★★

The night before the steamer was to depart from Tilbury, the Morton family dined together at the house. It was quite the most exciting occasion anyone could remember. The dining table was large. Yet, with Jon Wallace, Bosun Benson, Eadie, Vic Jones, and a couple of close friends of the youngest Morton children present, two more seats were required, so Harriet and Matthew were squeezed into corners. Eleanor, with Clare's assistance, had been in the kitchen since dawn.

The crush mattered little, for the table was lively, and the wine bottle rarely rested for long. Frederick carved the pheasant, along with a ham worthy of Christmas. The potatoes had been par-boiled before being roasted in the wood oven to crisp perfection.

Harriet sat beside May while they ate, 'You don't feel left out, do you? With the rest of us rushing off around the world?'

'No, but I'll miss you. I have to help Father make beautiful engines for you to sell, and I'm still waiting for my letter from the university. Have you heard from your new agent?'

Harriet made a face, 'I have, but not for a role. He sent me a letter inviting me to a party next Saturday night.'

'Well, that's nice, though I suppose you won't be able to go now.'

'I wouldn't have gone anyway,' said Harriet. 'I was to be paid, apparently, twenty pounds, to flatter and entertain a bunch of senior army officers – like some kind of courtesan.'

May stared, 'Truly?'

'I'm beginning to think that Mister Jensen is a creature.'

'Sounds like it. Don't tell Denny or he'll go around and punch him on the nose.'

'I certainly won't be telling him.'

After the main course, Frederick came to his feet and the diners fell silent. He spoke of new beginnings, of courage to do what needed to be done, of how much he and Clare would miss their children, and how proud they were of the challenge they had taken on.

'Hear, hear,' said the Bosun, already with a tipsy twinkle in his eye.

It was a wonderful evening, with adventure and the hope of a new life for the family business in the offing. Clare shed a tear, here and there, and Frederick took her hand and squeezed it, knowing the difficulty of the moment, for it was no small thing to send two sons and a daughter across the seas in vulnerable ships, there to perform a task for which they were generally unprepared.

Yet there was a feeling in that room, of a wonderful future within reach – that they were friends and comrades as well as family. Above all, there was hope.

★★★

Later, while Matthew sat in his room, agonising over his letter to Miss Pattinson, and the dinner still raged in the dining room, Denny walked Eadie home. At the entry table she found a packet of vestas and a candle, lighting it and turning to face him.

'Close the door and come with me.'

Eadie led him down the corridor, upstairs and into her bedroom. She placed the candle on the sideboard. 'Now that you are going away I want to make no demands of you. Only that we give of ourselves to each other now.' She stood up, walked to him, leaned up to kiss him, then took his right hand and held it to her breast. 'We must not take too long or you will be missed.'

Denny said nothing, but moved his lips along the line of her jaw to the side of her neck.

★★★

Percy Forgill was beginning to feel as if the forty-two rooms of the family home in Park Lane had loosened like dry moss from his father's memory and pledged allegiance to the next generation. Looking up at the western facade now from outside, the branches of the cherry trees stood stark against the creeper-covered exterior, having died since the old man took ill. The grounds were extensive, with a tennis court and croquet lawn.

Percy left the gate and crossed the road into the park. At the usual place the Thin Man waited on a bench under a spreading plane tree. Percy sat beside him.

Wilkins was no longer young and had grown gaunt with his advancing years. The fox-fur coat he had once worn had become threadbare with age, and had been replaced with a dark woollen version.

'This is the situation,' Wilkins was saying. 'I have information that The Morton Steam Power Company intends to incorporate as a Limited Company in a float on the stock exchange at the end of the year. Their preparations for this are extensive. Morton's two sons and one of his daughters are bein' despatched in the capacity of salespersons, with responsibilities for Africa and Australasia.'

Percy hated how bold and forthright the Morton plan sounded. He cleared his throat. 'This is a concern. There is a well-established system with which we do business overseas – franchises and dealerships. Direct sales undermine everything this company, led by my father, has achieved in the last sixty years. My agent in Cairo, Maurice Gray, will be warned in no uncertain terms about what to expect.' Percy's words came faster as his agitation grew. 'Apart from the fact that Morton has blatantly stolen ideas formulated in our own factory, then poached some of our best staff, I believe that he and his factory present an existential threat. The problem is not only what Frederick Morton does, but what every upstart working-class engineer starts doing – ignoring traditional sales structures, and undercutting our trusted dealers. Right now Forgill's has pending sales in Egypt, New South Wales and the Witwatersrand. I do not want interference.' He regarded Wilkins seriously, 'I want to send out one of my boys – prepared to harry and disrupt when the opportunity presents itself. Barden, do you think?'

Wilkins coughed, 'Craven would be the best, but since the fire – with his scars – he can't blend in. P'raps Crydley would be best. 'E works well on his own.'

'You're right,' Percy agreed. 'Can you start thinking about how he might be employed in harrowing and disrupting?'

'That I will, sir, and I'll let you know within a day or two. Of Morton's two sons, Denny is the greater danger sir, an' 'e should be dealt with first. Matthew is a scholarly type, and shouldn't present much of a problem – Gray will sort him out in Cairo and we shouldn't have to worry about him again.'

'I agree, send Crydley after Denny Morton then, and I'll talk to Maurice Gray.'

Chapter Thirty-five

Not only did the Vicar make a fuss of the Mortons who were about to head overseas at their final Sunday service, but an enthusiastic party of well-wishers travelled down to Tilbury for their departure. Frederick, Clare, May, Eleanor and Eadie were all present, along with Sam's employer, Jonathan Wallace and his wife Jayne.

The mood was sombre, and when May commented that it was like sending her brothers and sister away to war no one disagreed. Denny had a barely-contained energy thrumming in his every moment, Matthew subdued and serious, and Harriet quieter than usual.

The first stage of the journey to Tilbury was a train to Fenchurch Street, then another down along the northern bank of the Thames to the new port complex, not far from the low but menacing fortifications that dated back to King Henry VIII, the cannons still aiming down along the channel where the river widened, beginning the transition from estuary to sea.

The RMS *Ormuz*, the steamer that would carry Denny, Matthew, Harriet and Sam into Eastern seas, was almost five hundred feet long, and of six thousand tons displacement, with twin funnels, and four masts. Lying alongside the Number Three Dock at Tilbury, she looked as big as an industrial street-block, tethered by hemp cables as thick as tree trunks to the bollards. Seamen scuttled on deck, or climbed spider-like in the rigging, their cries mingling with those of the birds and the never-ceasing thump of engines.

Boarding was undertaken in the late evening for a dawn departure. Frederick watched the ship being prepared in silence, electric lights providing a fair-like gaiety.

'I'm looking forward to the sea journey,' enthused Denny.

'Perhaps you are,' said his father, 'but you'll soon tire of it, I suspect.

Clare did her best to embrace all three of her departing offspring at the same time, and it didn't matter that she ran out of hands and arms for she was, at least, close to them for the last time in what she knew would be a long while. 'Your natural charm will win out, will it not?' she said, and they laughed together over the first boarding call from the gangway.

'Well, all that remains now is to wish you all well.' Frederick shook hands with both the boys. 'I am already proud of the spirit in which you have taken this assignment.' Matthew looked proud and there was a new tilt to his shoulders that even his mother noticed.

No one was surprised when Denny led Eadie a small distance away from the group and they huddled closely for as much time as they could get. When they returned Eadie's cheeks were shining wet where she had wiped away her tears.

Frederick embraced Harriet, then, with a hand on either side of her face looked into her eyes. 'I believe in you, Harriet, I really do. There's something very special about you.'

Harriet buried her face into her father's shoulder.

★★★

Frederick, Clare, Eadie and May stayed the night at the grand new Tilbury Hotel, with window views over the complex and the river. They rose early to wave off the tiny figures on the rail, steaming out into the brown tide of the Thames.

To Frederick and Clare it was as if part of their shared heart was sailing off into a new and unknown world. It was their last hope of saving the business, yet both wished that this drastic step had not been necessary.

'Well they're gone,' said Frederick as the *Ormuz* was lost to view. He was unsurprised to see that Clare was weeping, for his own vision was made opaque by tears.

★★★

On returning to the Lewisham house, late in the day, May found a much-anticipated envelope in the letter box. This she clutched to her heart, taking it to her bedroom, where she laid it on the bed fearfully. Three times she had applied to study engineering at the London University College. Twice she had been informed that classes were full and her application had been rejected. This day had already been an emotional one, and another rejection seemed to be too much.

Be kind to me, she whispered down to the envelope, *I have every right to study at your university – as much right as any young man in the world.*

Finally, steeling herself once more, she opened the letter.

> Dear Miss Morton
>
> The Chancellor invites you to attend a formal interview to discuss your application to study a Bachelor of Engineering at the University College, London.

The letter was signed by Sir Hudson Beare, the Chair of Engineering. May read it twice right through to make sure she was missing nothing, then burst into tears.

★★★

The following morning, trying to ignore the infectious excitement of her parents, May changed her clothes twice before hurrying out to the carriage. She wanted to look serious but refused to try to make herself seem mannish or to mask her gender. She was tired, for she had been up past midnight reading the life and work of Sir Hudson Beare, or at least what was available in the journals of the British Engineer's Association, one of the many periodicals her father subscribed to. Feeling indomitable, she made her way out to the drive, where Jenkins was ready and huffing impatiently.

'We'll need to make 'aste, Miss May, if you're to keep yer appointment.'

'Well, I'm ready,' she said. 'So why are we standing around talking?'

'Quite right Miss, we'll be off then.'

May's sense of indomitability lasted all the way across London Bridge, through Cheapside and Holborn Road. It lasted as she looked out at the fine shops along New Oxford and as they passed the magnificence of the British Museum. It lasted up Cower Street when May first spotted the ornate main dome of the University College's Octagon Building, wavered a little when she passed through the gates, and weakened further as she walked inside, feeling very gauche and small beneath the beauty of the high galleries.

The University College was no ancient seat of learning like Oxford and Cambridge, but a secular institution – a youthful sixty years of age – yet it had a frightening gravitas that sent her confidence crawling away into the shadows. Directed to wait on a hard chair May chided herself for needless stress. She knew that female students had been admitted to the faculties of Arts and Science since the late seventies, though Medicine and Engineering had only recently followed suit.

Finally, a clerk called May's name, and she walked into an office with dark panelled walls, that smelled of old pipe smoke. Every horizontal surface was filled with piles of rocks, some of which had been chiselled into rough shapes, others in their natural form.

An interesting machine – some kind of manual press – stood

against one wall, and various scales sat on tables. A mortar and pestle lay haphazardly on the floor where a less observant visitor might have tripped over it.

At the desk sat Sir Thomas Hudson Beare, the Chair of Engineering, wearing his robes with aplomb. It did not seem appropriate to move too close, so May waited at a distance of ten feet, amusing herself by looking at the rocks and related paraphernalia.

For the first few minutes after she entered the office, Sir Hudson did not speak to her at all, but continued to write. When he did look up it was to glare at her until she dropped her eyes, at which point he went back to writing. This pattern was repeated several times, until she regained some of the reckless courage she had felt before leaving home.

'Would you prefer that I waited outside?'

Beare continued to ignore her.

'Am I so abhorrent, sir, that you can't bring yourself to speak to me?'

The Chair of Engineering gave no sign of hearing her, aside from a lift of his chin. May continued to study him. His moustache and eyebrows were perfect matches, the latter being miniature versions of the former.

'I imagine that you find the weather here quite cold, after summers in your homeland, South Australia,' May said.

Finally, the pen stopped moving. 'You've made some enquiries about me?'

'History tells me that it is good practice to prepare before a battle.'

He exhaled slowly, 'This is not a battle: I asked to meet you, didn't I? Still, allow me to advise you with all candour: engineering is a profession for men. You should reconsider your choice and engage in Arts, Science or History, not engineering.'

'But engineering is the field in which I wish to study and work.

My family business is engineering – it's where my interests lie.'

Beare coughed. 'I don't want to put this indelicately, but even in Arts and Science, the few women we do have are from the very best schools—'

'Are you telling me that I am not intelligent, because I went to a government school?' She stepped forward to the desk, opened the portfolio she carried and dropped a sheaf of papers onto the desk. 'Those are my school reports. You should look at them.'

Beare sighed, put down his quill, and lifted the reports. May watched his eyes move over each, one by one, his expression unchanged. Finally, he passed them back and said, 'Come. Take a look at what I do, and we'll see if you can make head or tail of it.'

May followed the professor out of the building, across a lawn, and into another wing of the institution, keeping pace with his hurried stride. Already she could hear the hum of moving machinery, and this sound deepened as Beare opened a door and led her into a vast room. The bulk of this space was dominated by a machine, but like nothing she had seen before. Shaped like a diamond laying on its side, it was at least ten paces long, and made of polished steel. Pipes entered at each end, and screw-type arrangements entered at top and bottom. The humming sound emanated from what looked like a gas-powered pump, which fed one of the pipes.

May moved her attention to dozens of cubes, arranged in order around the room, all of which were topped with a thin layer of plaster of Paris.

Further on, she saw iron industrial bins filled with crushed stone down to a size of several inches. Some were flooded with water.

'This room is my world, at the moment,' said Beare. He smiled, as if privy to a secret she could never guess. 'Have you the faintest idea what I am doing?'

May did not answer straight away, but rather she walked one complete circuit of the room. This done, she looked up at the eminent Sir Hudson, and pointed to the storage bins.

'Those are stones,' she said, 'crushed to a standard size of roughly two and a half inches. There are four discrete areas containing bins, and they appear to me to be categorised according to the four major stone types: dolomite, sandstone, granites and limestones. I note that each bin is labelled with locality names, for example Lightcliffe, Monks Park and Aberdeenshire. It seems to me that these would be the names of specific quarries from which the stones were obtained. Am I right?'

'Correct, so far,' said Beare, smiling. 'But what of the cubes?'

May walked closer to the nearest of these. 'Inside the cubes are samples of various rocks, covered with a layer of plaster of Paris, and probably lead sheet. Some of the rocks have been subject to inundation, and others are tested dry.'

'Tested?'

'Yes,' said May, then pointed at the machine that dominated the room. 'The machine we have here is a Greenwood and Bratley load-testing machine—'

'How on earth did you know the manufacturer's name?' asked Beare.

May pointed. 'The maker's plate is on the mounts. I may be a mere girl who attended a government school, but I can read, and I know where to look for such things.'

'You might as well finish the story,' said Beare. 'What's this all about?'

'The cubes are placed inside the machine, and the resistance to pressure measured. In short, I believe you are measuring the load bearing and impact strength of all the commonly-quarried rocks in Great Britain – a worthy task, and I'm sure that many bridge builders will appreciate the data you produce.'

Sir Hudson clapped. 'Bravo.' He was smiling now. 'I'm impressed. Your real interest is in mechanical engineering, I take it?'

'Yes.'

'I have a meeting in an hour with my professors and I'm quite sure they will agree with my recommendation that you be admitted as a student of engineering at this college.'

'Thank you,' she said, feeling a warm glow suffuse through her body.

'I am impressed with your impromptu analysis of my work.'

'Thank you,' said May. Then to herself, *I read your journal articles. It's as simple as that.*

★★★

The house in Lewisham was a silent place without Denny, Matthew and Harriet, and Clare grieved for their absence. Yet her determination to keep the family safe had only strengthened, and she and Eleanor held frequent whispered conferences.

The older woman had set out to find what had happened to the burned man, Peter Craven. After weeks of inquiries, she had found him in a rambling house known as the Rookery, in the district known as Seven Dials. "E seems to be spending most of his time tending to cocks in the cellar – they come to and fro from Percy Forgill's country place. 'E looks a sight, oh lumme 'e does, with his skin all raised and scarred on 'is neck an' arms.'

It was a solid first step, but Clare was still determined to pursue official records pertaining to Percy's twin. To this end, the day after May's successful interview with Sir Hudson Beare, Clare and Eleanor set off together for Ladywell Station, travelling by rail across Southwark and Lambeth, changing at Waterloo for Charing Cross.

The General Registry Office was located in the North Wing of Somerset House, close to Waterloo Bridge, and fronting the Strand. Clare and Eleanor walked through Lowther's Arcade, then crossed the ashen quadrangle. Reaching the entrance to the office Clare smiled politely at the liveried officer who guarded the entrance.

Inside they found a long expanse of reflective tile surface, patterned in a kaleidoscope of black and white, and Clare's heels echoed as she walked towards the reception desk. There were three clerks at work, and she approached the nearest of them.

'I'd like to view a death certificate, please.'

'Which year?'

'1848.'

The young man made a face, 'You're fortunate. We formalised the collection of birth and death certificates in 1837, so the one you want will be in one of the registers. What borough, please?'

'Westminster, I believe.'

'Do you have a name and date?'

Clare took a slip of paper from her handbag and passed it across the table.

The clerk glanced at it. 'And what are your names?'

'Clare Morton, and Eleanor Demsie.'

'Thank you. If you'll take a seat, I'll call you when I've found it.'

Ten, then fifteen minutes passed. Clare made a desultory attempt at a small embroidery, then gave up to study the room and the people in it.

Finally, the clerk returned with leather folder, and waved them across to a vacant reading desk on the other side of the room. There he opened the folder, revealing a handwritten form. 'That's what you want, isn't it? Montgomery Forgill, eight years old.' He raised his eyebrows. 'You didn't mention that the family are noble?'

Clare scanned the entry. The handwriting was beautiful and flowing, but not easily decipherable. *Parents: Lord Batholomew and Lady Forgill.* The cause of death began with a capital G but Clare could not quite read it.

'Grand mal seizure and fall,' said the clerk. 'I'm used to reading these registers. There was no inquest by the way – that's what the N in that column means.'

'Can you read the name of the doctor who wrote this?'

'Oh dear,' said the clerk, 'that's a tough one – and not a name I've noticed before – let me get a glass and I'll try.'

The clerk walked off, and Clare heard the sound of a drawer

opening. A moment later he was back with a magnifying glass that he settled over the entry. 'I believe the name is Dr A Howgan, or perhaps Horgan.' He turned to one of the other clerks, moving back towards the desk. 'Here, Peter, you have a good eye for these things – what do you believe is this name here.'

The other man came over without a word, dropped his eye down close to the register. 'Horrigan,' he said.

'I do believe you're right,' said the original clerk, then turned back to Clare. 'There you go. Dr A Horrigan.'

'Thank you very much,' said Clare. 'Can I please have a minute to note down these details?'

'Take as long as you need and let me know when you are done.'

Chapter Thirty-six

The spirits of the Morton siblings were buoyed with a sense of relief from worry, adventure, and companionship as the *Ormuz* glided down the Thames, through Gravesend and Hope Reach, past the broad Southend saltings and into the sea.

Over the following days, while the coasts of France, Portugal then Spain lay low on the horizon, Denny, Sam, Matthew and Harriet took every opportunity available to them.

They toured the engine room at the invitation of the ship's engineer, awed at the sheer size of the ten-thousand horsepower behemoth that drove the ship, admiring how the piston rods ran straight into the cylinders, with the crankshaft below. This, Denny recognised as a type of engine known as a forge-hammer, a vertical design with three cylinders. It was an admirable piece of engineering, designed for simplicity and ease of maintenance, developing more power than ten railway locomotives.

The four travellers ate in the second-saloon dining room, with wine and entertainment afterwards. Denny was, as usual, the ringleader, but Matthew was in the process of emerging into something new, conceived at Oxford and born on the open seas.

At Gibraltar, the famous Rock filled the landscape, bare and stark and roughly hewn as if it were the work of giant stonemasons. The city below was lined with jetties that thrust into the water like stiffly held fingers.

The *Ormuz* slowed, waddling in the wash of sea traffic. European skiffs, schooners and brigantines contrasted with beautiful dhows, their fore-and-aft sails making triangles of pillow-white against the sea.

The Morton entourage braved the crowded boat deck to get a better view, as the *Ormuz* came alongside the docks to take on coal and discharge passengers. The outermost five yards of the ship provided the only clear space, apart from the partly-covered promenade deck, to stroll and observe the sea, for the rest was a maze of ventilator pipes, masts, and rigging.

'How long are we staying here?' asked Sam.

'Just long enough to coal her up – a few hours, I believe,' said Denny. He turned to Matthew. 'You'll be in Cairo in a matter of days,' he said. 'Are you excited?'

Matthew shrugged. 'Reading Livingstone and Haggard has exaggerated the dangers, and I'd rather be up at Oxford, but yes, one can't help but feel a flutter of anticipation – partly because I'm worried that I won't be very good at selling engines – and Father is counting on us.'

Denny clapped his shoulder. 'I have a feeling you'll be better than any of us – all those big words and fancy phrases. And you never know, you might find yourself caught up in just such an adventure as you've read about in books.'

A shudder transmitted through the deck as the hull made contact with the jetty, bruising against the fenders while seamen coiled ropes and wound them around bollards. Shouted instructions went down the pipes, ringing with steel in tight echoes.

'I will do my best to avoid any such thing,' said Matthew. 'I have other plans.'

Denny had seen the trunk of books Matthew had brought along, now safely in the holds. No doubt the titles had been carefully selected from the family library and Hatchards booksellers of London. A feast of Defoe, Collins, Macaulay, Gaskell, Bronte, Dickinson, Melville, Thoreau and Whitman. Denny suspected that Matthew intended to find a way of marketing the Morton engines while spending a good chunk of his time reading through the contents of the trunk.

Turning to share a smile with Harriet, he guessed that they were thinking the same thoughts at the same time. He'd been surprised that their Father had decided to send her along with Matthew to Africa, but it was wonderful for them to be together for the first leg of this great adventure.

Harriet joined in, 'Where's your sense of fun, Matty? You can't tell me you'd rather be sitting around with a bunch of snotty friends at Oxford than at the rail of a ship sailing into the Mediterranean Sea?'

A shout and an outburst of conversation further along the deck caught their attention. The siblings turned to look, but Matthew replied passionately. 'You don't understand what's happening at Oxford right now. I feel like I'm part of a movement; a brave new way of thinking. Being away from that is a little frustrating. Make no mistake, I'll do the best I can for the family, but hopefully I'll soon be back in the common room, reading, drinking wine and arguing about whether Dickens or Thackeray best portrayed Victorian England.'

'Sounds pointless to me.' Denny said. Yet he was distracted. The commotion down along the deck had resumed and his curiosity get the better of him. He locked eyes with Sam. 'Come on, let's see what's happening.'

A crowd was gathering, and it was necessary for the Morton party to push their way through. The captain himself was there, with two crewmen gripping a bearded man by his arms. The captain was holding a small revolver in his left hand, pointed down for safety.

Denny turned to the passenger standing beside him, a rural type in his thirties, dressed in a tweed coat like he was off for a walk on the moors. 'What's going on?'

'One of the passengers noticed a bulge under that man's jacket. Turns out he has a holster with a revolver underneath. The captain isn't impressed. Listen.'

'I will not,' lectured the captain, 'have firearms carried by persons aboard my ship. You may have your weapon back at the end of the voyage, and until then it will remain in the Chief Steward's safe. Do you understand?'

'Yes, Captain Murphy. Am I to be detained?' There was a mocking quality to his voice, suggesting that he might well walk on the wrong side of the law.

'Not unless you give me further reason to do so,' said the captain. Then, to the two seamen who held the offender. 'Let him go.'

★★★

Harriet had been standing next to a fair-haired man of forty or so, who had turned to look at her several times. She was used to men staring, but this one's eyes were like probes, stripping the clothes from her body.

'Excuse me,' she said finally. 'Have we met?'

'Not personally,' he said, with a lift of his eyebrows. 'But let's just say ... I've seen a lot of you. Would you care for a drink later? This voyage might not be so tedious after all.'

The words, as they filtered into her mind, seemed to emanate from another world. That sordid room in London, not the dramatic beauty of Gibraltar. The feeling of escape evaporated. 'I don't think I would care for a drink, and I am not the slightest bit sure about what you're talking about,' she said.

'Oh I think you do.' His eyes slid down from her face, to her neck, then her bosom. 'You're quite the photograph album star – on sale in London shops that specialise in such things.'

Harriet felt a surge of anger, pressing her lips together so hard they turned inwards. One or two of Denny's choice swear words came into her head and it was all she could do not to say them aloud.

She turned and walked towards the companionway, halfway there before Denny caught up with her. 'Hey sis, what did that rude bastard say to you?'

Harriet looked away. Her brother's blood was up, the last thing she needed was a punch-up. 'Nothing at all, just pleasantries. The press of people just got a bit much for me.'

Denny looked unconvinced. 'I don't like the look of that fellow. If he approaches you again, please tell me, and I'll give him something to think about.'

★★★

Harriet, however, was determined to stop this poison herself. She watched for the man who had approached her, noted where he sat at dinner that evening. Saw him with his wife, son and two daughters.

The following day, seeing her at the rail alone, he came up beside her and slid his hand over the curve of her waist. 'I've been thinking about you,' he said thickly.

Harriet spun out of his grasp and away. He followed, striding after her.

Then, out of earshot of other passengers, she turned on him. 'Now you listen to me. If you tell anyone about those damned pictures, or follow me again, touch me, or even look at me, I will tell your wife about the things you've said to me. I will tell her about the kind of photographs you like to look at, and I will do it in front of as many people as I can. Those pictures were taken by trickery, and if they are for sale somewhere, it is not with my permission. Do you understand?'

He stepped backwards, then lifted the palms of both hands like flags of surrender. 'I was just kidding, settle down.'

'You weren't. Now get away from me.'

Scowling darkly, he turned on his heel and walked away.

★★★

Five days of sailing across the Mediterranean followed, finishing with the Suez Canal, a two-day ordeal in feverish heat. Most of the first and second saloon passengers availed themselves of a daily salt-water bath, then spent every spare moment on the promenade deck, rather than in the library or smoking rooms below.

Mail came aboard at Port Said, and for many of the travellers reading and replying helped fill the time. Frederick and Clare had both written to each of their children. Frederick's letters were somewhat formal, but they were treasured.

Sam received mail from his mother and sister. He looked at Denny, who already had a letter open, and was nose-deep in the pages.

'I recognise the handwriting. You got a letter from Eadie too?'

'That I did. Does it bother you?'

'Not one whit. She likes you and you like her, that's a good thing.'

Denny smiled to himself. It was indeed.

Chapter Thirty-seven

At Suez, the siblings parted ways. Matthew and Harriet boarded a train for Cairo, drawn by an old Stephenson locomotive, while Denny and Sam had a few hours in port before the *Ormuz* sailed on for the East. It was yet another heartfelt farewell, but Matthew found, to his surprise, that he was keen to get down to the business of selling engines.

Sam, as he and Denny were preparing to reboard the ship, noticed the bearded man watching them – the man whose revolver had been confiscated by the captain. He mentioned the sighting as he and Denny headed down to their berths.

For Denny, however, the man's presence meant little, and scared him not at all. This was the beginning of a great adventure – their stops on the way to Australia sounded exciting: Aden, Colombo and Singapore. A bearded man down in third was not enough to stem this flood of enthusiasm.

★★★

Cairo, with the Nile winding as wide as an English lake through the centre, defied first impressions or prejudice. It was a sprawling organism of a city. One cab driver told the travellers that the city had boasted half a million souls way back in the Dark Ages, when Saladin himself had been Vizier.

'A bit ridiculously grand!' said Harriet as she and Matthew arrived at the famous Shepheard's Hotel.

'Very much so,' agreed Matthew. 'But Anthony Trollope mentions this hotel in his story *An Unprotected Female at the Pyramids* so I'm rather excited to be staying here.'

Porters arrived, scurrying to the rear of the coach where Matthew took control of the unloading and distribution, then followed along as Harriet walked inside.

The Shepheard Hotel's interior featured bars, marbled bathrooms, ballrooms and gilt skirtings. In keeping with the necessity of avoiding extravagance, their rooms were on the first floor rather than the second, but they proved to be opulent and were serviced by an army of porters and servants.

Later, the siblings enjoyed a dinner so lavish that in London only royalty, the very rich and the peerage might have experienced it. Each diner was assigned his own waiter, who stood at their elbow, filling glasses after every sip, and the food arrived in waves, each dish more intricate than the last.

Retiring to his room, Matthew stayed up late, taking his compendium from his luggage and rereading his letter to Miss Pattinson in its entirety before adding a few paragraphs about Cairo.

Today my sister Harriet and I arrived in Cairo, staying at the famous Shepheard's Hotel, no less. What a bustling city, steeped with the spicy scents of desert sands and the river Nile. The sense of history is overwhelming here, present in the voices of hawkers, hagglers, beggars, snake charmers and musicians.

With your love of history I know that you would adore how the city sinks into the ruins of earlier times while the new layers are built again on top. It's like a living story, being told before one's eyes.

Five more days and then Harriet and I will board a steamer bound for southern Africa ...

His quill moving as if of his own volition, he wrote three solid pages before he closed the lid on his inkpot and retired for the night.

★★★

The next day, armed with a map, and a knowledgeable driver, Matthew and Harriet journeyed deep into the delta, where they spotted flocks of the revered ibis out foraging on irrigated fields. Harriet pleaded for a stop so she could walk towards them, a smile of pleasure spreading across her face, and for Matthew the lost time was worthwhile to see her so absorbed and happy.

Around the city of Mahla they found that a second phase of industrialisation was taking place. Cotton production here had peaked during the American Civil War, when the flood of cheap product from the Deep South became a trickle. Long-staple Nile River cotton, renowned for its softness, filled the gap, and fortunes were made. British fortunes. Made at the expense of feudal-style peasant labourers, whose position was so dire that many would poke out an eye or otherwise self-mutilate to escape their servitude.

At the coalface of the industry – small rural cotton gins, Matthew saw an opportunity, providing Mobilis machines to help these artisan-level operations make money. He presented his sales pitch so many times he learned it by heart, most of the time employing the services of an interpreter.

The gin owners were, in general, Egyptians, but with some British-born businessmen amongst them. They were a guarded lot, and Matthew made little headway at first.

'Unlike your old engines,' Matthew said more times than he could count, 'our fireboxes are designed to burn both bituminous coal and anthracite – your mines of the North Sinai produce only bituminous coal. Much of your anthracite is imported – you must be paying exorbitant prices.'

'That's true *efendim*. Yet we cannot afford a new engine when the old one still runs.'

The growing success of the visit was soured by an unpleasant encounter on the evening of their fourth day in Egypt. Matthew and Harriet had just finished eating at the hotel restaurant, capping the meal off with a treacle tart, when the maître d'hôtel approached, a man who had the art of making eye contact without seeming to do so. 'Excuse me, *efendim*, one of our guests has asked if you would join him in a drink at the bar.'

Matthew raised his eyebrows, 'Could you tell us his name, please?'

'Yes, *efendim*, he is a businessman by the name of Maurice Gray.'

'We'd be delighted to join the man, since he seems to know us,' said Matthew, but with a wary note in his voice. He had heard Maurice Gray's name spoken several times since their arrival in the city.

With Harriet in tow, Matthew followed the maître d'hôtel to the bar, where an Englishman was sitting on a mahogany barstool equipped with deep red cushions. A silver watch chain hung from a side pocket of his tailored suit. His eyes were shaded with deep pockets of skin, and his lashes were excessively dark. Two very tall Egyptian men, with the protective air of bodyguards, sat on stools at a respectful distance.

The Englishman stood to shake hands, addressing the maître d'hôtel. 'Fetch my new friends another glass of whatever they fancy.' Then, to Harriet and Matthew. 'Please, sit down.'

Once they were all settled on stools and the drinks had arrived, delivered as if by a click of the fingers, the Englishman spoke again, 'My name is Maurice Gray, and I own the largest stationary engine franchise in this city. I trust your journey has thus far been pleasant.'

'Pleasant indeed,' said Matthew. 'And Cairo is a fascinating city. It's very nice to make your acquaintance – I'd like to know more about the industrial sector here and how we can help service it.'

'That's just the thing – my company is the official distributor for three fine British machinery firms – Higginbottom's, Maudsley's and Forgill's. We don't want competition from newcomers.'

Matthew knew he should say something, but Harriet beat him to it. 'We have every right to come here and introduce our family's engines to the marketplace.'

'I hate to be the bearer of inconvenient news, but that's not the case. Neither you, nor your engines are welcome. Please feel free to visit the pyramids and take a boat journey on the river Nile, but the factories and mills of this city are out of bounds. I will not let upstarts threaten the livelihoods of those who have been in the industry for decades. You can't just arrive in a country and ignore the existing network of dealerships and agencies. I've spent twenty years building my portfolio, nurturing my customers and supplying them with stationary engines that serve them very well indeed.'

Harriet turned to look at Matthew, whose face had turned scarlet with shock.

Matthew's heart was beating fast, knowing for a fact that his brother Denny would have told this man something witty but confrontational – to take a running jump off the nearest pyramid or something like that. He wanted to stand, puff out his chest and tell the man just that, but instead he sat miserably. He felt worse when Harriet was the one to answer back.

'We have something new to sell,' she said, 'and we believe that the factories of Cairo can benefit. This overrides your self-interest, and if the other factories you represent can offer the same, let them try.'

'At your peril,' said Gray. 'I won't warn you twice.'

As they walked away from the bar, heading towards the stairs, Harriet said to Matthew. 'You are going to have to learn to stand up for yourself.'

Matthew's active mind never tired of creating scenarios where he could act like a hero, kill the dragon, joust with the evil knight. Yet, when the moment arose adrenaline filled his bloodstream, weakening not only his body, but his mind, immobilising him. This, however, passed quickly when the danger was over.

'I will,' he said to Harriet, feeling better already. 'I just didn't think a restaurant bar was the right place to do it. Wait and see, I'll make Maurice Gray regret that he spoke to us in such a way.'

★★★

Over the following days Matthew gathered information about Maurice Gray like a swallow gathers mud and grass. He started with the British Consul, then questioned everyone he encountered who had some involvement in the industry.

Gray, it seemed, added a thirty-per-cent premium on London prices for steam engines, over and above the cost of freight, and charged twice the going rate for spare parts. He used a network of bullies to enforce service agreements and eliminate competitors. An alumnus of Eton School, his supply of funds was assured by his London contacts.

With his mind weighed down by this information, Matthew scheduled a day off to climb the great pyramid at Giza with Harriet.

Their knees shook with the vertigo-inducing heights, and the awe-inspiring touch of history to the present. As they climbed, the view became dizzying, so the lesser monuments surrounding them looked like children's toys. The vista was of unrelenting drab dun, and the hot desert breeze grew stronger as they neared the summit.

At the frightening, giddying summit, Harriet confided in her brother, telling him the story of the theatrical agent, and the photographs that had ended up on sale in grimy stores selling albums filled with photographs of unclad women.

Matthew built himself into a mood of bloody-minded anger. 'Oh how dare he?' he muttered. 'If you'd told Denny he would have gone around and taken the bastard's head off.'

Harriet took his hand. 'I didn't want that, and I still don't. It was a stupid and naive mistake. And now we have an important job to do. We have to play our part.'

'You're right,' said Matthew. 'One bully at a time.' At the

summit of the most famous human-made structure on earth, he decided to make Maurice Gray his nemesis, figuring that if he could do one positive thing for Egyptian industry, it would be to expose how Gray was taking advantage of them.

★★★

The following evening, in a meeting room spread with cushions in the suburb of Heliopolis, in the north-east of Cairo, Matthew drank dark ground coffee spiced with cardamom and addressed a consortium of local owners of cotton gins, textile mills, flour mills, corn mills and carpet weaving factories.

There was no alcohol, but some of the men smoked strong tobacco cigarettes, so that the smoke swirled in the gas light, the smell mingling with the aromatic tang of burning sticks in holders, spread with dry resin that Matthew supposed must be frankincense. When it was his time to speak, he paused after each sentence while his interpreter translated. He studied the faces of the men in the room. They were of a wide range of ages, from youthful to silvered, or even near bald. Some appeared to be sceptical, others angry.

The talk went on for around an hour, while Matthew laid out the economics of supply and delivery from London to Cairo. He then took questions from the floor, some in halting English, others through the translator.

'It's very convenient,' said one man, 'that you, Mister Morton, should make these charges against your competitors, then conveniently have less expensive engines for us to buy – unproven engines – ones we have never seen. Self-interest, no?'

Matthew shrugged, 'It may seem so. But in London our engines are more expensive than the Forgill's models you have been purchasing. It's only when the local agent inflates the price that they cost more. It's important for you to know that, whether you buy from us or not.'

'Would you travel to my humble mill tomorrow and tell me

what I need?'

'Yes, with pleasure,' said Matthew.

★★★

The following evening an Egyptian man with a thick moustache and stocky build approached Harriet and Matthew on the street outside their hotel as they waited for their driver. 'I have a message for you from Mister Gray. He wishes you to know that this is Africa, not London, and Egypt is still not formally part of the Empire. Things can happen to outsiders who meddle. You have twelve hours to leave this city.' He added a final, whispered sentence, 'After that, there will be consequences.'

Ignoring the ultimatum, Harriet and Matthew again set out on their sales work. The harassment began later that day, starting with the appearance of hard-looking men sitting near to them at cafés and in public conveyances. These same men haunted the hotel lobby, folding their newspapers and following as Harriet and Matthew came down the stairs and went about their business.

Having initially made inroads, Matthew soon found door after door closed to him.

'I'm sorry, *efendim*, but we are no longer interested.'

'You have been warned off by Gray and his men?''

'Sorry. Not interested.'

Finally, after taking a deposit for just one Mobilis engine, Matthew and Harriet came home to find their room ransacked, trunks emptied. Their cash and vital documents were locked in the hotel safe, but it was a confronting moment, nonetheless.

Later, returning from a restaurant past the opera house, amongst the general traffic came the thunder of hooves, Matthew turned to see a two-in-hand wagon bearing down at a full gallop, hooves flying and dust rising.

'Hey,' he shouted, but there was no change in direction. The wagon, it seemed, was heading diabolically towards them.

Matthew turned to see the driver swathed in black cloth, close enough to see his pitiless eyes. Reaching out desperately, he grappled for Harriet's hand and together they ran for the kerb, with the carriage following them every step of the way.

Finally the vehicle thundered on past, and a crowd of passers-by hurried towards the guests.

'Are you injured?'

'Not a scratch.' Matthew looked back the way the carriage had disappeared. 'No thanks to the scoundrel who tried to run us down.'

★★★

There was a five-year-old copy of the venerable Post Office London Directory at the factory, and Clare brought it home after a three-hour stint at her book-keeping duties.

'What on earth do you want that for?' Frederick asked as he saw her heading out the door with the volume.

'Just a few addresses to find,' she lied, and no sooner had she arrived home, but she and Eleanor were flicking pages, looking for a certain doctor who had attended the death of Montgomery Forgill. Eleanor's reading skills were poor, but she liked to be involved, and Clare liked having her there beside her.

The directory, Clare understood, did not attempt to list the entire population of London, but only those of some 'note'. Traders, merchants, bankers, professionals, tradespeople, retail and wholesale businesses, councillors, commissioners, and health practitioners.

Finding a Doctor A Horrigan, to Clare's relief, took just a few minutes. The address was in Pimlico, and Clare wrote it down, wondering if the best course of action was to write to him first or simply travel into the city again and knock on his door.

'Just go in an' see him,' said Eleanor. 'No point fussin' about with it.'

'You're right. I'll go in tomorrow,' said Clare. 'Will you come?' Eleanor seemed to consider for a moment, studying the address carefully. 'That's a nob's street. You'll do better there without the likes of me.'

★★★

The residence listed in the Post Office directory was in Duke's Lane, Pimlico, a narrow but genteel strip of identical two-storey terraces, the tiny front yards of which were fortified with heavy cast iron fences.

Clare stopped at number thirty-two, opened a gate, and climbed three steps adorned with geometric tiles, reaching a green door equipped with a letter plate and surrounded by a clever spiral of stained glass windows. There she lifted the knocker and rapped firmly, the smell of broiling fish drifting through the keyhole and gaps in the jamb.

The door opened promptly, and the woman who stood in the entry way was about Clare's own age, but with lank hair and thick spectacles, her eyes blinking as if she were surprised by everything.

'Hello? Can I help you?'

'I'm looking for Doctor Horrigan?'

'I'm sorry, but my father passed away, this last winter.'

Clare's heart sank. 'Oh, I'm very sorry to hear that.'

'Are you French?'

'Originally, yes.'

'May I ask why you wish to see him?'

Honesty, it seemed to Clare, would be the best policy. 'It's a long story.'

'I understand. Would you come in and have a cup of tea?'

'I'd like that, thank you.'

Thirty minutes later, her nostrils, and even her clothes, it seemed, full of the odour of halibut boiling in a pan, Clare was on her way out of the door, carrying a bundle of calf-bound notebooks tied with string. These were the notes, jottings, and journals of Doctor Anthony Horrigan, that his daughter had pressed upon her. She had seemed eager to be rid of them.

Reading through those volumes, Clare realised, would take some time.

Chapter Thirty-eight

'It irks me,' said Percy Forgill, 'that Morton, for this month at least, has managed to obtain an extension on his line of credit from the bank. Next month will be more difficult for him. He is mortgaged to the hilt – he must make his loan repayments to us, and the bank also – not to mention paying his lawyer. Provided we prevent any inflow of money I do not see how he can survive until this supposed public share offer.'

Wilkins agreed. 'He is a resourceful bastard, but lack of cash will choke him. Gray in Cairo has reported that his son Matthew's continued to approach the mills and may have made some headway.'

'Incomprehensible!' spat Percy. 'Maurice has gone positively soft. 'So what are we doing to stop Morton's brats from ruining our overseas operations?'

Wilkins shrugged. 'Harryin' and disruptin' just like you told me.'

'Not enough,' said Percy. 'Where is Crydley?'

'Following the older son like we agreed. Don't worry, e'as a good plan.'

'That's all very well. But the harry and disrupt thing is not working well enough. Tell Crydley that from me.'

'What should be do?'

'More than harry. More than disrupt.'

★★★

When the RMS *Ormuz* docked at Aden, Yemen, to take on coal and passengers, Denny lifted his head from his pillow. No engine noise. No movement in the hull.

The strangeness of it saw Denny dress and head up on deck. He was just in time to see a party of seamen in a whaleboat alongside. On the decks he could see coils of cat-gut line and a bucketful of small fish.

'Hoy there,' said Denny. 'Where are you fellows off to?'

One of the boat's crew, a rascally looking able seaman not too much older than Denny, with a close-shaven face answered, 'On the cook's orders sir, we're off to catch a mess of fish for the first- and second-class kitchens sir. I imagine that it will be for your supper tonight.'

Bored as he was, this sounded like just the kind of adventure Denny needed. 'Aren't we sailing rather soon?'

'No sir, not until the top of the tide just after eleven. The captain issued his orders just now.'

'Have you room for two more?'

'I'd be glad to have two strong young backs, for it's a long row and it means we could take a spell, but I'm not sure if the captain would permit it sir.'

Denny looked towards the quarterdeck, 'He won't find out. And if he did I'll just say I insisted.'

The seaman doffed his cap. 'Welcome aboard then, sir. Sidney Peake at your service.'

Denny looked at him quizzically. 'Have I met you before, you seem familiar?'

'Not as far as I know sir,' the seaman said with a crooked grin. 'Must have been one of me twin brothers.'

'Alright then,' said Frederick. 'I'll just run down and get my companion.'

***

Denny and Sam had spent many a pleasant day plying a clinker dinghy on the broader pools of the Ravensbourne, and they took up this new challenge with energy, thrusting against a strong current, enjoying watching the spectacular shoreline pass by.

Aden Harbour was situated inside the rim of an ancient volcanic crater, surrounded by peaks, making it one of the safest ports in all the oceans. As soon as they were out of sight of anything resembling authority, Sidney Peake produced a flask of rum from under his sea jacket and offered it first to Denny, who took a hearty swig, whereupon the flask passed around to all hands.

'Don't tell a soul, I beg you sir,' said Peake. 'Tot-bottling is worth five strokes of the lash.'

As they rowed on, a steamer loomed out of the open sea, making for the inner harbour. Black smoke billowed from a single stack amidships. It was strange, Denny thought, to watch it grow larger, turning bow-on until he started to worry for their safety.

'Don't fret, sir,' said Peake. 'He'll alter to starboard within a chain or two now.'

The seaman was right, for the steamer adjusted its course, and looked to pass safely, albeit within a few hundred yards. Passengers lined the rails, enjoying the view and fresh air.

'She's a Dutchman,' said one of the seamen. 'The *Meermin* she's called. On the Java run.'

By this time Sid Peake's flask was empty and one belonging to another seaman had been opened. The levels of mirth and boyish fun increased with the consumption of alcohol.

'Alright boys,' shouted Peake. 'Let's give the Dutch madams something to think about.'

Grinning like schoolboys, the three sailors perched themselves atop the thwart seats, backs to the steamer.

'On the count of three,' called Peake.

Denny shot Sam a look, rolling his eyes as if to say that their shipmates were insane.

'One ... two ... three.' On that count the three seamen dropped their trousers to their ankles and extended their posteriors over the ocean, while the others howled with mirth. Shouts of anger and dismay carried across the water from the passengers on the steamer, but she was moving at a good clip, and had soon passed on.

Minutes later, just outside the protective arms of the harbour, Peake ordered a course change. They rowed perilously close to the rocks, tossed by jagged ocean swells.

'Lay up here,' shouted Peake, less than a chain's length away from a bombora, breaking the surface with weathered stone, waves surging over and around. He gripped Denny's shirt to get his attention, laughing at the salt spray on his lips and hair. 'Just here, in the lee of the bommie, there's an 'ole deeper than Southwark Sal's crinkum-crankum. That's where we'll catch our fish. We 'ave no anchor, so we take it in turns to lean on the oars to keep us in place. The cook needs a good quantity of fish, and it's up to us to get them.'

The bucket the seamen had brought was full of yellowtail scad they had caught back at the *Ormuz's* berth. These finger-length fish were hooked through the tail and dropped down to the depths, borne by lead weights, on heavy handlines strung with catgut.

Denny's bait had scarcely struck the bottom when something down in the deep grabbed it, and he was forced to give line before starting the retrieve, muscles knotting up in his forearms, biceps and shoulders.

'Good grief,' he cried. 'What in all creation is this thing?'

'Bit bigger than a Quaggy roach,' Sam laughed, but a moment later, his line too was seized by some underwater beast and he was stretched trying to bring it in. The first fish to hit the deck was at the hands of one of the burly, experienced seamen. It was a yard long, armoured with reddish gold scales, flapping, huge and beautiful in the morning light.

'What is it?' cried Denny.

'Red emperor, sir,' said one of the seamen. 'And mighty fine on the fork they are too.'

Denny brought his fish to the surface, lifting it aboard, laughing with enjoyment at the hard physical activity. But there was no time to pause, as soon as he'd unhooked his catch he was sending a new bait back down into the depths, readying himself for the powerful bite and run from the deep.

Not every drop brought results. At times the bait was stolen by a canny fish, and on one occasion the line itself was snipped by sharp teeth. Even so, the fish continued to come aboard: flapping, bleeding and dying on the deck: emperor, snapper, sweetlip and a huge mackerel, until there was scarcely room for their feet.

Sid grinned, 'Not all of these beauties will go to the first-class lounge. We'll eat well below decks tonight.'

But the swell was building also, and the freeboard on the boat decreasing with the load. 'That'll do lads,' said Peake, 'let's turn tail for our beloved bitch, the *Ormuz*, while this tub can still float.'

And on the way back, someone started up a sea shanty from the days when sail was king, before steamships took control of the seas.

> Alof there, alof!' our jolly boatswain cries,
> Blow high, blow low, and so sailed we;
> 'Look ahead, look astern, look aweather and alee,
> Look along down the coast of the High Barbaree.
>
> There's nought upon the stern, there's nought upon the lee,
> Blow high, blow low, and so sailed we;
> But there's a lofty ship to windward, and she's sailing fast and free,
> Sailing down along the coast of the High Barbaree.

Still singing, three men scaled and eviscerated the fish while others rowed. The bow-on silhouette of another steamer became visible ahead, steaming towards them, billowing a steam of black smoke into the sky.

'There's another big one coming out,' said Sam. 'That's strange, I didn't see a third ship berthed.'

The steamer gathered pace, soon showing more and more of her port side as she headed for the open sea.

Denny stared, 'I'll be damned, but it looks like the *Ormuz* to me.'

'It is,' said Sam, 'and they're going without us.' He stood up and began to wave madly. A few of the passengers enjoying the view from the rail waved back.

Denny turned to the man who had called himself Sid, 'Why are you just sitting there? That's our ship, leaving us behind. What are you going to do about it?'

One of the 'seamen' dug his mate in the ribs, then they all burst into laughter. 'I've got another question for you, Mister Denny Morton,' said the man who identified himself as Sid. 'What are you going to do with all these fucking fish?'

Standing, Denny formed his hands into a speaking horn, and shouted at the disappearing ship. Then, to the men on board the rowboat. 'We've been set up. You're not seamen from the *Ormuz* at all.' He looked at the ringleader. 'Your name is not Sid. I knew I'd seen you before – you're the one who had the gun – the captain confiscated it – you've shaved your beard and that's what threw me off.'

'Oh in Heaven's name,' said Sam. 'I had my thoughts, damn me for keeping them to myself.'

The mask of bonhomie disappeared, replaced with a snarl as 'Sid' reached for a cutlass hidden under the thwart and pointed it at Denny's heart. 'A regular Sherlock 'Olmes we have 'ere fellas, the game is up, well an' truly. I wish I had me revolver but sadly it's still locked in a safe on board the ship. This 'ere blade will 'ave to do. Now, Master Denny Morton, row quietly and we'll take you to shore. Cause any problems and we'll dump you overboard right here. And my name ain't Sid, it's Tommy Crydley, of Seven Dials, London. These men are the hoariest scoundrels ever to 'ang around the Port 'o Aden – unemployed able seamen with a nose fer mischief who I met last night and paid a fiver each to back me up an' 'ave some fun besides.'

Denny went to make a stroke on the oar, but in his agitation the rowlock lifted from its socket and the oar came free. Without conscious thought he continued the motion, lifting it from the seat. He swung the oar with a cry of rage, and struck the cutlass-wielding man a heavy blow on the side of the head. Crydley dropped the weapon and lay on his side, stunned.

Snatching up the cutlass Denny took position, threatening the other two seamen. 'Take up the oars and start rowing like blazes. We'll catch up to our steamer or you'll suffer for it.'

As the two scoundrels acknowledged that the tables had turned and began to row, Denny waved his free arm at the fast-moving steamer, but it moved regally on, unconscious of the pursuit.

★★★

Harriet had decided, even before the near-miss with the wagon, that she was going to have to take action to protect both her brother and the family's business interests in Egypt. The exact nature of her action was yet to be decided. When a possibility occurred to her, she was unable to proceed, as more information was required.

Harriet had learned, over their week in Cairo, that the well-to-do British expats of Cairo used the Shepheard's Hotel bar and restaurant like a clubhouse. She and Matthew had seen groups of them here every evening, dressed in London-bought finery, dancing, bullying the waiters and laughing like they owned the place.

Mid-morning the next day, Harriet pushed open the door of the empty restaurant, where a troop of waiters were wafting clean cloths into the air and onto tables, folding napkins and polishing silverware. She had hardly moved more than a few paces inside when the maître d'hôtel hurried across to intercept her.

He was a well-built Egyptian, with a cultured moustache and the required deferential manner. He had greeted she and Matthew on the two occasions they had dined there. Bowing his head, he said, 'Excuse me Miss Morton, but we are not opening until noon.'

Impressed that he had remembered her name, Harriet stopped walking, and touched his arm. 'Oh sir, I know that. But I wondered if I may have five minutes of your time?'

The Maître d'hôtel looked up at the clock, 'I can give you five minutes, Miss Morton.'

He led her to one of the unmade tables near the door and pulled the chair out for her. He took the opposite seat.

'Now how can I help you?'

'I want to talk to you about Effendi Gray?'

A guarded look came over his face, and Harriet grasped how she had to approach the situation. 'He is a good man, a great friend of the Hotel,' said the Maître d'hôtel, 'and he helps to bring prosperity to the Egyptian people.'

'No he doesn't,' said Harriet. 'He makes money at the *expense* of the Egyptian people. My brother and I represent a company that is fair and true. We can bring steam engines here that are cheaper, with no distributor growing fat from the profits. Maurice Gray has threatened us. He is trying to kill us.'

Harriet reached into her purse and took out a golden sovereign – part of an emergency fund she had saved from her own money. She placed it into the open right hand of the maître d'hôtel. 'I would like you to tell me everything you know about him.'

The maître d'hôtel looked down at the coin in his hand and frowned. 'I know a little. He went to Eton school. He is fond of collecting relics from the third dynasty.'

'Is he married?'

'Yes, and he has three children – all away in England attending boarding schools.'

'Tell me about his wife,' said Harriet.

'Her name is Emma, she is a very fine lady, and is the president of several charities. I know that Mister Gray worships the ground she walks on.'

'Is she involved in her husband's business affairs?'

'No, not at all. That would be very unusual.' The servile manner seemed to disappear from his face, and he lowered his voice. 'Let me be frank with you. The British businessmen of this city strip it bare, and their wives know very little of what they do. Many of them spend much of their time in charitable works, assisting orphans and the very poor. I believe that the good British wives of Cairo would be appalled if they knew how their husbands conducted their business.'

'Where would I find Emma Gray, do you think, on a Thursday afternoon?'

The maître d'hôtel took the coin previously given to him by Harriet and returned it to her hand. 'I do not need payment to help a good person such as yourself. I will tell you because you deserve to be helped.'

★★★

At three o'clock that afternoon Harriet slipped into the Ali Sharaf Women's Bathhouse in nearby El-Bagour Street, not far from the shining dome of the Tawhid mosque. She had left Matthew at the hotel, dividing his time between writing business quotations and personal letters.

Harriet recalled her brother's lack of enthusiasm for her plan to visit a local bathhouse. 'There's a perfectly good bath here,' he had said.

'But dear Matthew, I wish to learn something of the culture. It will be exciting and interesting for me.'

'Won't you have to ... take off your clothes?'

'That is the usual thing when people are bathing ... I have it on good authority that this is the place the local English people use, so it can't be too much of a den of iniquity, can it?'

Matthew had tried to insist on escorting her to the street outside, at least, but he finally accepted her argument that with a headscarf in place, and thus anonymous, she would be safer alone.

Moving inside, Harriet paid sixpence to the attendant – a dark-haired young woman with an olive complexion and almond-shaped eyes with heavy lids – almost too sophisticated a face for one so young.

'Do you speak English?' Harriet asked.

'Yes.'

'What is your name?'

'Safaa, but the English ladies like to call me Sophie.'

'Thank you Safaa. Do you know a woman called Emma Gray?'

'Yes, she is a regular, and I expect to see her here soon.'

'I would like to meet her, will you let me know when she arrives?'

'As you wish miss. Now I will help you to … disrobe.'

As the young woman unbuttoned the back of her dress, Harriet recalled the last time she had undressed in front of another person. Now there was no shame. It seemed natural. Naked, she walked on into the steam room, where the heat was both intense and pleasurable.

Two other women were there, also without clothing. Both were middle-aged, with old scars and stretchmarks displayed unashamedly. They conversed in Egyptian, eyes flitting Harriet's way now and then. She was quite sure that they were discussing her, but there was no sense of hostility, and the heat induced in her a torpor.

After what must have been ten minutes the two women stood up and opened the door, saying something in Egyptian to Harriet. Assuming that they meant well she stood and followed them through into a room in which there was one smaller pool, and one much larger. The three women plunged into the first. The temperature was barely tepid, and was meant only for a brief plunge.

The larger pool held very warm water, and there were already half a dozen women luxuriating there, many leaning on the sides and talking. Harriet followed the others down the steps, then floated on her back for a time, genuinely enjoying the sensation.

Two older matrons arrived, their bodies strangely beautiful to Harriet. She had learned the trick of observation. She listened to their voices, tried to sense their fears and needs, these people who lived like queens so far from home.

The young attendant entered the bath house by a side door and approached Harriet, who had moved to one corner. She leaned down close and whispered. 'Mrs Gray is in the steam room now, she will come here soon.'

A quarter of an hour later a very beautiful British woman entered the bathhouse. Harriet put her age at around thirty-five, at least twenty years younger than her husband,

As the woman entered the water, plunged in fully and came up with slicked-back hair, Harriet leaned on the edge, head lying on the meat of her bicep, weeping softly.

The woman ignored her for a moment or two, then swam closer. 'What is wrong, dear?'

'It's nothing,' said Harriet, all her skills uniting for the performance. 'Please, just leave me alone.'

'Oh but I cannot do that. What's wrong?'

Harriet moved her head to the other side, as if to avoid the woman's gaze. 'I'm just so far from Mother and Father, and things have become so horrid.'

'Please, tell me what has happened?'

'Well, my family is in the business of steam engines, and my brother and I have come here to market them, but it's impossible. There are horrible men here, who are … oh I don't wish to smear anyone's name.'

'No, tell me.'

'There are men who charge unfair premiums on the engines they sell, and they don't want us marketing direct here. There have been threats, and even an attempt to run us down with a wagon and kill us.'

'Oh my dear, who are these men?'

'What's the point? You can't help.'

'Please, tell me?'

Harriet sniffed and turned to look at the woman. 'The worst of them is called Maurice Gray. He has been horrible to us.'

The woman's face flashed from anger, to affront.

'Leave this to me, dear. Where are you staying?'

***

Later, when Harriet was back at the hotel there was a knock on the door.

When she saw that it was Maurice Gray and his wife, Harriet feigned surprise as artfully as if the drama club were judging her performance. She offered tea and made a fuss of how interesting it had been to meet up in the bath house.

'I have come to apologise,' said Gray. 'There is room for all of us here. You may do the business you need to do, and I will not hinder you.'

Harriet enjoyed watching Matthew's face most of all, as it changed from astonishment to pleasure.

When Maurice and Emma Gray had taken their leave Harriet smirked at her brother, more than a little pleased with herself. 'We've only got two days left before we must embark for Cape Town. Let's see how many orders we can get in that time.'

***

When finally, they boarded a return train to Suez, there to meet the SS *Kailmeer* they had done well enough to merit a congratulatory telegram from Frederick.

EVERY SALE HELPS PROUD OF YOU LOVE F

Chapter Thirty-nine

Doctor Horrigan, it seemed to Clare, was in the habit of writing in the tiniest and untidiest of scripts. He had not followed a chronological protocol in his journals, making the reading of them a Herculean labour. Clare now understood why the man's daughter had insisted that she needed to take the books with her.

'I dunno 'ow you can make head nor tail of 'em,' said Eleanor.

'I haven't yet,' agreed Clare. 'It's not easy.'

These were not, strictly diaries, but an amalgam of thoughts, financial records, recollections, ideas, and sketches, some of them anatomical. There were very few dates, and the doctor had not used the notebooks consecutively, but two or three concurrently.

After obtaining the journals, both on the train and at home, Clare had spent hours flicking through without result. Days had followed without free time to return to the task. The following Sunday after church, however, instead of going into the garden, Clare set herself up on the drawing room table with the books fanned out and slips of paper cut as markers. Now she began to methodically search for the Forgill name.

The first entry was dated 1837, when the doctor attended the home of Lord Bartholomew Forgill to examine the nobleman's pregnant wife. An hour passed before she found the second, which related to the birth.

It was not until late in the afternoon, her eyes strained from searching pages of close-written script, that she saw the Forgill name again. She began to read aloud, for Eleanor's benefit.

> I fear that my long association with the Forgill family may be at an end, after the events that transpired in the small hours of this day.
>
> If it is what I fear, then a terrible crime was committed. I was called to try to save the boy, which was not possible. His blunt trauma injuries were obvious, though I cannot rule out the possibility that a seizure caused him to fall down the stairs of his own account.
>
> I hope young Percival can live with the consequences if he was indeed the cause of these injuries.
>
> With the death of the elder child he has just made himself the inheritor of a title. I sense those calculations behind his eyes. Yet Lord Bartholomew begged me to ignore the obvious. And it is true that the boy suffered Grand Mal seizures. Either way my association with the family has ended. I will carry this as a secret to my grave, but my suspicious mind screams at me that the boy is guilty of fratricide.

Eleanor stared back at Clare. 'What in the name of 'eaven can we do now?'

★★★

The *Ormuz* was growing smaller as it veered out of the harbour and gathered pace. Denny knew that they could not hope to reach it, but he had a way of blocking the impossible from his psyche. His way was to believe that determination, hard work and persistence could overcome any odds.

'Row, you curs,' he shouted.

'Fool! We can't catch a bleeding steamship,' groaned Crydley. Having recovered a little, he was holding his head where Denny's blow had landed, with a bitter curl to his lips.

'We can try, and we'll be a hell of a lot faster without your dead weight. When we pass the harbour entrance up there, I'll go as close as I dare, and you can all get out and swim.'

'What if we'd rather stay with the boat?'

'You don't have a choice. Jump out yourselves, or I'll prod you out with the cudgel.'

As soon as they were alongside the tongue of rocky land that came down to meet the sea, Denny yelled, 'Now, go.'

Only Crydley managed to leap ashore without getting wet, but by the time Sam and Denny had stroked their way past the point, the three men were safe on the dry rock wall, staring after them with angry and embarrassed expressions on their faces.

'With this breeze at our backs we'd have a chance,' said Sam, 'if only we had a sail. We have to catch her before she reaches the open ocean. I'd say right now she's doing about six knots, but when she reaches deep water it will be at least twice that.'

Denny worked his oar powerfully. 'We got outsmarted back there,' he said. 'I feel like an idiot. We knew when the ship was sailing.'

'Without making a joke of it,' Sam said, 'we were taken in, hook, line and sinker. Our English friend, presumably a tool of your father's enemies, knew that we wouldn't be able to resist getting off the damn steamer and heading out to catch fish – he looked different with his beard shaved – but he's the same one who's been dogging us all along.'

'Very clever little plot,' agreed Denny, 'but at least we're leaving him behind in Aden. If we can catch the *Ormuz* we'll be out of reach.'

Sam went silent. 'She'll start to pick up speed as soon as she's out of the roadstead.'

'Then we do our best,' Denny said. 'All our things are on that boat, another steamer will be weeks away.'

'Hey look to starboard,' called Sam.

Denny looked, still continuing to row. Coming up behind them was a beautiful Arabic *batils*, rigged with a single triangular sail, but with a streamlined shape. Perhaps, Denny mused, the plaything of some rich Yemeni merchant. It was poetry to watch, the hull cleaving the water like a shark's fin.

Denny let go of the oars and began to wave.

'Keep going. He's seen us. Yes, he's altering course,' said Sam.

The sailboat came alongside, her gorgeous lines even more noticeable up close. She was at least forty feet long and the young master, moustached and suave, stood in bare feet on the fo'c'sle. 'Hello, hello,' he called.

Denny pointed to the steamer. 'See the steamer, the *Ormuz*. We're supposed to be on board. They went without us. Can you help us to catch them?'

The man narrowed his eyes. 'For English pounds? Yes.'

Denny had a fifty-pound emergency fund sewn into the hem of his shirt.

'Fifty pounds, and that's all the money we have, but we have fish,' shouted Denny, pointing down at the deck. 'Look, big fish.'

'And the boat,' added Sam. 'You can have the boat.'

The master helped them aboard, issuing orders that the boat be secured by a painter. Then, with the sails rising up, the dhow began to leap ahead through the waves.

'Do you think we'll make it?' Denny asked.

The young master shrugged his shoulder, but the steely look in his eyes showed that he was going to give it a damned good try.

'Look at the wake!' cried Denny. 'We must be making ten, twelve knots, and that's faster than them right now. We've got a chance.'

Then, as if responding to his words, the wind became fitful, and the sails luffed.

'Come on,' growled Denny. 'Blow, damn you, blow.'

A gust came off the port bow, a confused little moment before it died away again, and their spirits with it. Then, like a miracle it came back, steady and strong.

'That's better,' Denny noted.

'They're putting on steam,' cried Sam.

Denny saw that his friend was right, the black smoke streaming from the stack was increasing, and the wake rising. He began to pray. He couldn't begin to imagine having to telegraph his father that he had been left stranded by a clever trick, with very little money and only the clothes he was standing up in.

But the steamer was taking time to accelerate, and the wind was picking up again. The master flashed his white teeth. He was enjoying himself, Denny decided, robes flowing with the same breeze as was pushing them through the water.

'Good Lord, we're going to catch them,' said Denny as they loomed up from behind, keeping to the calm water in the centre of the wake.

In response to the helm, the sailing vessel swung out from the wake, and yard by yard, began to come alongside the huge craft.

'Wave,' cried Denny. And there were people on the rails, waving back. Even an officer, peering down at them.

'They're not stopping,' said Sam.

'They have to, surely.'

'They probably think we're pirates or something. This part of the Arabian Sea is apparently alive with them. How can we convince the steamer to stop?'

The young Arab seaman seemed to understand the problem. He passed the tiller to one of his men, and hurried below, returning a moment later with a folded Union Jack.

'You clever man,' cried Denny. 'Here, Sam, take one end.'

Together, standing at the rail, they held out the flag. The crowd at the rails started clapping.

'God's teeth, how thick are they?' cried Denny, but then, the huge iron ship began to slow. The sense of relief was so strong that a tear formed at the corner of his eye.

Denny tore the hem on his shirt, withdrew the fifty pounds and passed it to the master.

'You are one hell of a seaman, I wish I had more to give you.'

★★★

Matthew and Harriet had travelled from Port Said on the SS *Kailmeer*, via Mogadishu, Lamu, Zanzibar, Durban, and Port Elizabeth. For all that distance the steamer's engine huffed and wheezed, driving a wooden paddle wheel patched with rusted iron.

Even so, she managed a solid six knots, hour after hour.

Matthew had found himself a quiet square of shade on deck and settled down with Thackeray and Dickens. Harriet, meanwhile, distracted herself with games of whist, lectures, passably fine dining and reading scripts to the waves from the stern rail, sometimes attracting a small audience.

Within forty-eight hours of arriving in Cape Town, while Matthew slept off a bad flu he had caught on board, en route from Port Said, Harriet organised a long-term apartment for them at Mouille Point.

'I think you'll like it,' she told her brother when they checked out of the Grand Hotel and rode the tram, surrounded by trunks at their feet. 'It's out of the city, but it doesn't take long to get to and fro.'

'You're a marvel,' said Matthew. 'I can't believe you got our accommodation sorted all by yourself.'

'I'm here to help you. That doesn't only mean sitting around taking notes.'

★★★

Harriet was right, Matthew did like their apartment. How could he not? It sprawled over one whole floor of a three-storey structure, built of Saldanha Bay stone, with a view of the water and a white-painted lighthouse from the balcony. The interior was papered in cool grape leaves and twisting vines, writhing over and around the window frames, and furnished in a style Matthew recognised as Arts and Crafts.

After unpacking the contents of their trunks they spent much of the afternoon strolling the nature strip above the beaches and rocks. Then, in the evening when the sun dropped, and the moon hung low over the water, they took chairs out onto the balcony and watched the fishing boats hunting for shoals of katonkel tuna in the bay.

The maid, a pleasant African woman called Betts, served a feast of cut meats and cheeses, and a bottle of local Newlands lager.

'So the next thing we need to do is find an office,' said Matthew.

Harriet lifted the copy of the Cape Town Times that was sitting on the table. 'I've circled our three best prospects, but I think we should hire a coach and have a look around the town first.'

'I agree, that's a good plan.'

When the beer was gone and the meal finished, Matthew kissed Harriet on the forehead and went off to his own room. Somehow though, he didn't feel like sleep. His eyes fell on the desk that faced the drawn curtains. A simple design, with three drawers, a sloping face, and some fine decorative work on either side. His compendium sat ready on the shelf above, where he had unpacked it.

On impulse he sat down at the chair, wiggled his bottom a little until he felt comfortable, then opened the compendium. He took the letter to Miss Pattinson out and reread every word. For the first time it did not make him cringe. As soon as he had finished, he took up some new paper, and continued on from where he had left off.

I do hope you will forgive the disjointed nature of this letter, but I have much to tell you. It all started on a steamer off the coast of Africa. She was barely worthy of the name, just a few hundred tons, with coal-smudged sides and a captain such a man of the sea that the skin of his face all but had barnacles growing on it.

He finished the paragraph then started another, his quill flying across the page. An hour passed before he was done. His only agony was at the end, when he could not quite decide between, Yours Truly, or Faithfully Yours. In the end he settled on simply Yours.

Without any rereading, he folded the letter in its entirety, placed it in the envelope and sealed it. Life, he had learned on his journey thus far, was not to be wasted by being excessively cautious.

★★★

Betts was able to provide an introduction to a driver willing to take the siblings on a tour of Cape Town. His name was Roundhead Jimmy, and he proved to be a knowledgeable guide to the city, driving with both lines in one hand in the English style. Matthew and Harriet sat perched atop the spring cart, passers-by casting admiring glances at the handsome brother and sister and their regal driver.

Matthew needed to despatch his letter, and he asked the driver to stop opposite the post office on Adderton Street, where he paid for sufficient stamps to carry his letter off to Prague. He slipped the letter into the iron slot with a final indrawn breath of fear at what Miss Pattinson might think of his correspondence. Yet he felt curiously free and excited.

When he joined Harriet she was more than a little curious. 'Who was the letter to?'

'None of your business,' he said, but there was a twinkle in his eye as they set off again into the morning traffic of provedore wagons, carriages, traps and carts.

'I think I know,' she said smugly.

'No you don't.'

'It's a girl, though, isn't it?'

Matthew shook his head. The idea of calling someone as smart and sophisticated as Miss Pattinson a mere girl was laughable.

'No,' he said.

With the letter on its way Matthew gave himself up to enjoying

Cape Town. He was stunned at the grandeur of the city – the combination of Dutch and British architecture. St George's Cathedral was the centrepiece, along with Parliament House and the shops of Heerengracht.

'I didn't expect Cape Town to be so beautiful,' said Matthew, gazing past the buildings to the dark-blue silhouettes of distant mountains.

'That's Devil's Hill,' explained their driver. 'Then Lion's Head, and the last, to the east, is Lion's Rump.'

Harriet said, 'Such imaginative names ... I can see how they came about. Take us closer please, I'd love a better view.'

As they continued out of town towards Devil's Hill, the quality of housing degenerated. Finally, a shanty town hove into view. The driver moved his hand to the left to begin a turn down a side-road and away.

'Why aren't you taking us there?' Harriet asked.

'Young lady,' said Jimmy. 'You do not want to see such a place, It's just Woodstock. Poor coloured people live there.'

'Take us, please.'

The driver looked at Matthew, who agreed with his sister. 'Yes, do continue.'

They passed by meagre shacks, and running, thin children, pregnant women with small children; open water troughs and dwellings made of cast-off materials. Here and there were piggeries or factories too filthy for the better parts of town – small scale smelters of iron – a knackery, and tallow works.

Harriet felt tears prick at her eyes, and the beauty of the day became insignificant. This place seemed, somehow, even worse than the most squalid slums of London. 'I could not have imagined that such a place existed,' she said.

Roundhead Jimmy turned around. 'Most of the fine gents 'n' ladies of Cape Town pretend Woodstock aren't there at all. They can be driven right past an' not see anything.'

'Doesn't anyone help these people?' Harriet asked.

Jimmy shook his head, and grinned, showing off a missing front tooth. 'All the gentle folk just pretends it not there, like I said.'

Up ahead there was a crowd on the road. Two groups appeared to be arguing. 'I think that's far enough,' said Matthew. 'Take us back to town, please.'

★★★

When Jimmy left them with a Long Street real estate agent they spent three hours viewing four different premises before finding the right place. It was a second-storey nook, stained a little from mould and smelling of bleach, but was fully furnished. There was an office with a desk for Matthew, and even a rosewood cigar box.

'I'll keep my pens in it,' he said.

A small meeting room was perfect for discussions with potential customers and a cubicle for Harriet was located alongside, equipped with timber filing cabinets and a typewriter.

'We'll take it,' said Matthew. 'Can we have the key now?'

Chapter Forty

The hearing was held in the Chancery Division of the High Court, in the Old Hall at Lincoln's Inn in the City. It was a room of significant age, steeped in tradition and smelling of generations of furniture wax.

The judge was a powerful presence, with a stout frame, a formal wig, and the cheek and jowls of a pale British bulldog. He used the kind of verdant vocabulary that Frederick had not encountered since stumbling into an English literature class by accident in his first week of college.

Frederick took a seat next to his lawyer, noticing that Forgill's legal team formed a veritable army rank. Percy Forgill was not present. In the gallery Ned Baring sat beside Clare, Eleanor and May, and a few interested young lawyers.

The case started with the judge reading the suit, and taking a long look at Frederick, as if to soak up his personality and ethics in a glance. Following this, the case was underway; Jonathan Wallace summed up the Morton company's defence neatly, and this was refuted by the opposition.

At significant expense – money he could not afford – Frederick had hired the best consulting engineer in the business – Sidney Risecroft from Boulton and Watt, who had long ago offered

Frederick a position if he would move north to Birmingham. The company name still meant something. Everyone knew who they were, and they were too big to be bullied by Percy Forgill.

'Could you, sir,' asked the Forgill's lawyer, 'have designed the same engine, using engineering knowledge in the public domain?'

'Yes, I might possibly have done so, but without the flair that Mr Morton has shown in putting this engine together.'

The judge looked down at the Forgill team and said, 'Your case is starting to look a little tenuous sir.'

Wallace exchanged a glance with Frederick, but the Forgill's men were ready. 'We have several other potential witnesses,' said the lawyer, 'we would like to seek an adjournment while we contact them.'

'How long?'

'Six months please, your honour.'

'You can have two. No more.'

Wallace rose, 'I strenuously object. Will you please lift the no sale order on the engines in the meantime, so my client is not negatively impacted while the opposition seek to prepare a case.'

The lead on the other side was on his feet in a moment. 'Nay, sir. There is no point in the suit if the defending party is permitted to sell our designs as his own and profit from them.'

'Agreed,' said the judge, then looked down at Frederick. 'You need to successfully defend the suit, and then you can sell the engines.'

'Damn them,' hissed Frederick as they left the building. 'We have the case won and they know it.'

'Are you going to be able to survive for two months?' asked Wallace.

'Somehow we have to,' he breathed. 'If only I had the money to start building the Imperium in earnest. It's a completely new engine that Percy can't interfere with.'

While the *Ormuz*'s engines drove her onwards, the Indian Ocean stretched as far as the eye could see. Now, sightings of any vessel, even Arab dhows became unusual, and Denny spent his many spare hours making himself an expert on the kinds of Australian businesses that might be interested in the Morton engines.

With Sam assisting, he made lists of every type of operation from sawmills and shearing sheds to gold mines. Together the pair developed form letters that could be adapted to different applications. Sam's experience as a solicitor's clerk proved invaluable, and more than once he steered his friend into a better way of expressing himself, stressing the importance of observing the niceties of business communication.

'Dear Sir,' dictated Denny. 'I wish to draw your attention to the attributes of the Fortis stationary engine and what it can do for ...'

'Not like that,' Sam said, shaking his head.

'No?'

'If you are writing to someone you haven't met before it's better to introduce yourself at the beginning of the letter. Make them feel as if you are a new friend.'

'What do you suggest?'

'Perhaps something like, "Dear Sir. Please allow me to introduce myself. My name is Denny Morton and my family company has been engaged in the manufacture of steam engines since 1870."'

'Yes, yes,' said Denny. 'Let's write that.'

The pile of sealed envelopes grew, stacked in a box until the opportunity for posting presented itself.

Meanwhile, in the pursuit of physical fitness a program of running around the decks took place before breakfast, when the narrow corridor of free space was empty of idlers. The two men also enlisted the help of an officer, who purloined some rope from the ship's stores, along with some piping for uprights to string it through.

Then, after a serious discussion about the official dimensions of a boxing ring they measured out a space on the boat deck. The sparring sessions started the following day, with a dozen or more eager participants joining in at first. More than a few, however, found something else to do once they'd proved their mettle, or lack of, in the makeshift ring. Others took it as a handy opportunity to learn the noble art.

For Denny these activities were not just exercise for the sake of it, but part of his general desire to excel at physical sports.

The rumble of the engine, deep in the ship, was a presence night and day, like the distant beating of a heavy drum. It only changed when the wind fully served, and the sails were filled to the point where to save coal the boiler was allowed to cool, and the ship's beating heart fell silent.

This was rare, however, and Denny was conscious of any change. On the third day out of Aden the engine note changed, slowing down through a series of different frequencies of vibration until finally it settled at low revolutions.

Eager for any change or departure from the ordinary, Denny climbed the companionway with Sam behind him. Together they spilled out on to the boat deck to see that up ahead, rising and falling in the ocean swell, was a Chinese junk, of timber construction and some eighty feet in length. The single mast was all but gone; just the splintered end pointing skywards.

'Dashed if it doesn't look abandoned,' said Denny, and they hurried aft, past the belching smoke stacks, watching as a small boat was launched from the *Ormuz*, swinging off the davits to a string of commands.

'Turns for lowering,' shouted the midshipman in charge of the detail. 'Aaaand drop!'

Then, while the steamer lay dead in the water, they watched the longboat circumnavigate the junk, then return. All the time that the longboat was close to the junk, the bark of the loudhailer rose above the sounds of the sea on the hull and the murmur of conversation from the growing crowd on the steamer's deck.

When the small boat and her crew came back, more orders were shouted. These, it seemed to Denny, involved the fetching of a keg of paraffin from the holds. Curious, he hurried up to deck officer who was directing proceedings.

'What manner of ship is that? Where is the crew?'

'It's a death ship – most likely been drifting for days. We can't see anyone alive on her. Rather than let her be a navigation hazard we're going to put fire into her and be on our way.'

'How do you know there's not someone still alive on board? Nobody's even stepped aboard.'

'The first mate shouted most thoroughly; I can assure you.'

'You can't set fire to a ship when someone might be aboard.'

'They are Chinese sir, and I'll not risk one of my men for them.'

'I'll go,' Denny said, then turned to Sam for support. 'The two of us will go aboard, make certain that there are no survivors, then we can spread your paraffin around all the better.'

'You are passengers, it would be highly irregular—'

'We're volunteers in a good cause.'

At that moment the captain appeared, and the deck officer, looking relieved at not having to make a decision went off to confer with him.

'Very well then,' the officer said when he returned. 'You can go.' He shouted down to his crew, 'These two volunteers will check below decks for survivors, then spread the accelerant.'

Denny and Sam climbed down ropes and took their places in the long boat, where they were subject to some amused stares from the seamen at their oars. Denny turned to Sam, 'Sorry for dropping you in it.'

'I don't mind, anything to beat the boredom off.'

After a determined row across to the ship, the crew helped to roll the barrel of paraffin up onto the junk. Even before Denny set foot on deck, he could smell something gut-wrenchingly awful.

Together with Sam, he clambered up after the barrel, then set off towards the main cabin area. The stench worsened, and Denny recognised it as the smell of putrefaction.

Up close he could see the fine teak construction of the boat. There was no doubt in his mind that this vessel had once been the pride of some Shanghai magnate's fleet. Yet he experienced a sense of unreality as his eyes fell on the first body sprawled on the main deck. Three more lay nearby. Chinese characters had been scratched into the timbers around the third.

Denny was the first to enter a timber companionway. Eight steps, with each graduating to a deeper degree of darkness. There was carnage below. Just about every cabin bunk held a body covered by a blanket. The smell of rotting flesh was indescribable.

'Poor bastards,' Denny breathed.

'Let's get out of here,' hissed Sam. 'It's horrible.'

'In a minute. We have to make sure.'

They passed down another companionway, leading to a deck of stinking cubicles, where close-packed bodies lay.

Sam stopped cold, his face turning white.

'You check the left,' Denny said. 'I'll check the right.' A pause then, 'Come on—'

Sam lifted his shirt and held it over his nose and mouth with one hand, opening one door after another, peering into the gloomy interiors. He was about to close the door on the last of these when he heard a rhythmic rising and falling. The egress and ingress of air into a pair of lungs. Yet how could that be in this place of death?

Sam felt each hair on his head stiffen, and even the backs of his arms bristled as if covered by needles. Forcing himself to step inside the room, he saw the body of what appeared to be an old woman on a cot, brown skin stretched over a skeletal form, but the bony chest was rising and falling. He took a step closer, within the darkness of the tiny cabin, terror already clawing at his heart, when her hand came out like a striking cobra and took his wrist in an iron grip.

She began to speak, so soft it was like a forest bird scratching though leaves. The words were in her own language and meant nothing to Sam, but each was like a knife-thrust towards his heart.

'Let me go,' he hissed.

The old woman fell silent as he sprang back, tearing his wrist free, turning once to see her head lolling back onto the bed, then ran from the cabin, slamming the door behind him.

He was outside when Denny called out. 'Anyone down there? I thought I heard voices.'

'No, it was just me. They're all dead. Let's burn this piece of filth and get on our way.'

With paraffin spread all over the deck, the two men rowed back to the ship, where the bosun used a Verey pistol to send a flare into the heart of the junk. It burned with a towering flame that danced on the surface of the sea. The *Ormuz*'s passengers and crew lined the rail to watch, strangely silent.

'Poor bastards,' said Denny, and when Sam laid his head down that night his head was filled with dreams of starved corpses and an old woman, living flesh and hair burning up in a paraffin-fuelled fire.

***

The arrival of the *Ormuz* at the port of Colombo, Ceylon, meant not only that Denny was able to dispatch mail, but also to collect personal letters and telegrams.

There were letters from Frederick, Edward and Eadie, and a farrier's bill in an unmarked envelope that had inadvertently been redirected. Denny tore through the first two letters but was not about to read Eadie's in front of Sam, so he waited for a quiet moment in the evening when he walked to the rail and took out the envelope, holding the letter to his nose, inhaling the scent of the woman he loved as if she were sitting next to him.

Dearest Denny

What a time I've had back here in Lewisham. Mother and Da are still in Brighton, but according to their letters he is ever so much better, which is a great relief, and my aunt has also taken a pleasing turn. Otherwise, things have gone on much as before. They should be back before winter.

I have been working and saving money and work at the mill has been no better or worse than usual.

My cat, (you will recall his name is Mister Sweep), was on the roof of Mrs Pickering's house, no doubt pursuing a rodent, when he fell clear through the thatch and into the poor old lady's kitchen. From what I hear both parties were equally surprised, especially as poor puss narrowly avoided landing on the pot belly stove.

When I arrived on the scene my dear neighbour was chasing Sweep out the door with a hot poker, and happy to escape he was too! It was all fine in the end except that I had to pay Jack Fletcher to restore the hole in the thatch.

I know you think my dreams are silly, but last night I dreamed about whales. Giant black beasts they were, and you were standing at the rail of a ship watching them spout and cavort …

Denny read on, and for those minutes in which he read the letter he was transported back to quiet, never-changing Lewisham, where everyone knows everyone, and most of their business besides. He saw blackberries, picked with purple-stained hands and the smell of them in pails, and the sweet pies that followed. He heard the robin's proud call from the trees, barking dogs and the cries of children playing.

Eadie had always had the ability to make him smile, and the letter, read at such remove from her sweet person, worked in the same way. When he had finished, he was surprised to feel a half-grown tear at the corner of each eye. It was not sadness that provoked them, just a wistful joy. He read the letter again, and despite his tiredness he returned to his cabin and placed a clean sheet of notepaper on his desk.

> Dear Eadie
>
> Thanks for your letter. I wish I had seen your poor cat fall through the roof. He's always seemed so cocky and foot-sure that I'd wager he's been sulky ever since.

Denny stopped writing and read his first paragraph over again. He frowned. Was he talking down to her? It was the kind of response he might have sent to a child. He didn't cross out what he had written, but he rubbed his quill between thumb and forefinger for a moment while he thought hard. Finally, he started writing again.

> Well, for my part, I'm still travelling. Sydney is a couple of weeks away now, and I can't wait to get off the ship. Sometimes I just want to dive off the bow and swim the rest of the way, but I know I can't. I long for the feeling of freedom on horseback or my own two feet. Perhaps in New South Wales I will have that feeling again.

He read through what he had written, then picked up the quill again. His candle had burned down to a stub before he had finished.

★★★

Over in his bunk, Sam was dealing with increasing guilt at leaving the old woman to die. He had not meant to do it. In his mind he ran over the things that he should have done. Called for a stretcher. Asked one of the medics to come across. They could have saved her life. He was no better than a murderer.

He had let her burn.

He wondered if the guilt would ever fade.

Chapter Forty-one

Clare was almost as keen a newspaper reader as Frederick, yet her interests were wide and she read the crime pages avidly – her interest fuelled by the novels of Conan Doyle and Stephenson. On the side of the law, the *Times* mentioned one man consistently, bringing this or that criminal to justice, keeping hangmen and gaolers busy with his indefatigable methods. The name of this real-life Sherlock was Inspector Gerard Hatfield, of Scotland Yard. A recent edition of the *London Illustrated News* included an artist's impression of the man, dimple chinned and square jawed, standing before a dejected criminal in the witness stand of the Old Bailey.

'He's our man,' she confided to Eleanor. 'I'll write to him – lay out the information we have, and take it from there.'

Eleanor closed her eyes, picturing Percy Forgill on the gallows, with Inspector Hatfield looking up at him as the trapdoor opened.

★★★

At the start of Hilary Term, May presented herself at the Robert L Gates practicum room for her first class in Electrical Engineering. She took a seat at the front, her interest focussed on a large metal object, bolted to a heavy table, with copper windings visible. Electrical leads, shielded in rubber, emerged from a plug on the wall.

Professor Ambrose Halburton arrived ten minutes late, his

academic gown seeming to follow him like a boiling black rain cloud. He was on the wings of late middle age, thin and spidery, with wispy hair like spiders' webs, in urgent need of cutting and tidying.

Catching sight of May he peered over his spectacles. 'Oh yes,' he said. 'I heard that *you* would be in the class.' He turned away from her, and addressed the rest of the class as if she were not there. 'Good morning gentlemen,' he said, ignoring the woman in his class. 'Welcome to the brave new world of electrical engineering. For small and medium industrial power utilisations, this is the future. Watch!'

The professor flicked a switch, and the motor came to life, spinning a fan blade coupled via a belt, that blew a gale of air out into the room, scattering papers, and provoking shouts of amazement and excitement.

Goosebumps rose on May's arms. The engine made a noise, a warm hum, but compared to a steam engine it was nothing. There were no emissions, just a sharp electrical smell.

The machine ran for some five minutes before the professor flicked off the switch.

'Have you heard,' he asked, 'of Nikola Tesla?'

There were some shakes of the head and a few affirmative grunts from around the room.

'Well, you all should have,' he said. 'Davenport invented the electric motor, but Tesla used alternating current to make it a viable proposition. In this class we will use his dynamos to generate electricity, and create step-up and step-down transformers. We will investigate his attempts to develop a coil that transmits electricity through air. We must count ourselves fortunate to live in the lifetime of such a genius.'

The excitable old man retrieved a pocket handkerchief from a coat pocket and used it to wipe a sheen of sweat from his face before going on. 'I envisage that AC induction motors will one day power light and medium industry across the world. In this class you will learn to design and build these motors. You will learn to design and build alternators.'

May was transfixed as the professor told them of the technology 'war' between Edison's DC current, and Westinghouse's AC. With a gleam in his eye he described how Edison's engineer, Harold Brown, had publicly electrified dogs to demonstrate the efficacy of their product.

He went on to show how and why AC current had emerged as the dominant system. 'It's better for fixed applications,' he said. 'We can transform voltage more easily, route the power for vast distances, and it's simpler to generate.'

May was aware that she had seen something life-changing, but it had not yet occurred to her that she had found her field. A visit to the College library yielded an armload of books, and she hurried home to begin reading, making notes as she went.

The following weeks were some of the most interesting of her life: devouring texts like a dragon devours knights. Her bedroom was soon littered with coils of wire, magnets, batteries made from discs of copper and zinc, saline solution, and rubber-coated leads.

Within a few days, she had convinced herself, and had started on Frederick, that not only should the Morton Company be creating and building their own alternators to couple with the Imperium, but that they should also start diversifying into electric industrial power.

'Let's build the new Imperium first,' he said. 'Then we'll talk again.'

★★★

The latter part of Denny and Sam's voyage passed slowly, with the impressive speeds reached by the *Ormuz* early in the journey slowing down to disappointing daily runs.

Denny asked the Chief Steward, who lowered his voice. 'We're going so slow because all our stokers are damned beginners and they're passing out from the heat. One even threatened to brain his supervisor with a shovel. The captain's had the poor man chained to the funnel shaft for the last two days.'

'That sounds ridiculous,' said Denny. 'Why would we have such an inexperienced crew?'

The Steward hesitated, then; 'It won't do any harm to tell you now. Just a day or two before we sailed from Tilbury, the stokers' union had a stoush with the Orient Steam Navigation Company. They pulled all their members off the ship. The management had no choice but to round up all the unemployed no-hopers they could find around the docks and offer them a shovel and a trip to the antipodes. 'Of course, having never done a day's work in their lives they work at half the pace of a real stoker.'

'I can understand the problem,' Denny said. 'Having shovelled my share of coal I can't think what it would be like down there in fearsome heat, while we sit around up here, sipping cocktails and complaining.'

Even at this pace, the miles passed by, and on the final leg of the voyage, in the blue water off the South Coast of New South Wales. Denny headed out on to the boat deck to take in some fresh air.

It was a beautiful day, with the water emerald blue, and Montague Island passing to starboard. He was deep in thought when one of the lookouts shouted, 'Whales ahoy!'

Denny swivelled his head to the port side. The whales were humpbacks, huge and black on their backs and fins. There were five or six individuals in the pod, heading north to their breeding grounds in the warm waters off Queensland. Fins spiralled out of the water, showing stark white bellies. Others tail-slapped with a sound audible even over the beat of the engines, others moved close to the ship as if it were a game.

One gargantuan whale breached fully, water jetting from its skin and falling in cascades as she flew, finally splashing back to her natural element with a burst of white spray.

Denny had been at the rail for ten minutes before he remembered

Eadie's dream.

... last night I dreamed about whales. Giant black beasts they were, and you were standing at the rail of a ship watching them spout and cavort.

'Your dream was right, dear Eadie,' he said aloud. With that thought came a pang of longing for the woman he loved, and for home, so strong he all but swooned. A longing for a time less complicated and laden with responsibility, sitting on the banks of the River Quaggy with the sweetest of all women.

★★★

Denny and Sam loved the city of Sydney from the moment the *Ormuz* docked, and they stepped onto the bustling Market Street docks. It was late winter in Australia, with warm days that sparkled on the harbour. Sydney boasted one of the world's biggest stores – Anthony Hordern's Palace Emporium in Haymarket – along with rows of specialty shops along George Street, interspersed with blacksmith's forges and foundries, signposted by sparks and fire and the whistle of steam escaping from pressure valves.

Sydney was a city of parks, blooms, and well-made roads, along with a steam tram network crisscrossing the city, making all areas accessible. A shared room had been reserved at the Belmont Family Club, a mid-range boarding house on Wynyard Square. The facility was neat and tidy, with forty rooms, many rented by long term residents, others by rural visitors and new arrivals.

Denny was lucky enough to sign a twelve-month lease for an office in the pastoral chambers at 375 George Street, a building shared with architects, surveyors, stock and station agents and a light machinery firm called Cranston and Co. Cranston was a cranky-looking fellow who frowned at everyone he passed on the dark timber stairwell that gave access to each of the floors.

The office itself consisted of a small foyer and two inner rooms.

A hired signwriter worked his magic with gold lettering on the front window, and Denny was proud to see it there.

> The Morton Steam Power Company. London. Cape Town. Sydney
> Mr Denley Morton, Australian Manager.

For three pounds a month they hired a capable local woman to run the desk, fetch mail and write letters. She had striking features and was a little formidable with her sun-browned face and blazing eyes, happy to speak her mind.

'We've had a number of leads already,' Sam said, looking down at the incoming mail spread on the table, ready to be opened sequentially.

One of the first return letters from their burst of activity on board ship, was an inquiry about a Fortis engine to power a machine sewing shop in West Botany. This was just a train ride away and a good place to start. Denny and Sam spent the Friday morning on a site visit, then set about preparing the quotation.

At a little after five, Denny put down his pencil and rubbed the stubble on his chin with the pad of his thumb. 'We've been walking past the pub down the road all week. I think it's time we sampled the local ale, don't you?'

'I've always reckoned on you as a genius,' said Sam. 'Lead the way.'

★★★

Prahlert's Hotel was a compact pub just two doors down from the boarding house. The front bar smelled of stale beer, sweat and tobacco smoke. The men scattered throughout were drinking from tall, clear glasses of various heights.

Denny fronted the bar, with Sam beside him, planting one elbow on the beer-steeped hardwood, reaching for his pocketbook with his free hand. 'We're new in town,' he said. 'What's the standard beer?'

The barman placed three glasses on the table, the biggest of which looked to be at least eighteen inches tall. 'This is a full pint, sir, and this one is thirteen fluid ounces – called a 'long-sleever', at fourpence and threepence a glass respectively. We also have these little ounce glasses – nobblers we call them, for a penny.'

'Thank you,' said Denny. 'We'll have two long-sleevers of your best ale.'

The barman operated the taps skilfully, then placed two of the frosted glasses on the bar towel, foam almost but not quite pouring over the rims.

'That's quite a drink,' said Denny, after the first sip slid coolly down his throat.

Sam agreed, 'Not quite the same as home. I doubt the barley grows so well in this climate, but it's a good drop nonetheless.'

A few of the men around the bar introduced themselves, and before long Denny and Sam found themselves at a table with a crew of affable strangers.

After Denny's initial 'shout' he found that the other men 'shouted' back, and the glasses emptied quickly, to be replaced just as fast. Denny started to enjoy the banter, along with exclamations of joy or disappointment as results from the day's races at a track to the south called Randwick came in.

Coming around to his turn to 'shout' again, Denny was heading back to the table with the last three long-sleevers when he tripped on the feet of a humourless young fellow who had been lounging in a chair, scribbling in a notebook. The man's oversized black leather shoes protruded from under the table, like a blunt reef waiting for an unsuspecting sea captain.

Only a small amount of beer was spilled, but the man put down his pencil and came to his feet, a dark and bushy moustache still touched with froth from his last sip of beer. 'Oh, heavens, sorry mate,' he said. 'That appears to have been my fault.'

'No problem,' Denny said. 'It was just a few drops.'

'Let me buy you a drink.'

'No need for that.'

'Just a yarn then. You look like you're fresh off the boat.'

'A "yarn" sounds good. I'll just take these beers over and I'll be back.'

The young Englishman was as good as his word, delivering the beers, then returning to the table, placing his long-sleever on the coaster and taking a seat. 'My name's Denny, by the way.'

The hand he shook was large and strong. 'Mine's Henry, journalist-at-large. What do you do for a crust?'

'I'm in business.'

'Ah, such a noble calling, the wheels of industry etcetera, etcetera.'

'Are you going to have another beer?' Denny asked, pointing at the man's now empty glass.

Henry took out his pocketbook and looked inside. 'Oh, I seem to be fresh out of cash. Damn, the banks are shut, otherwise I'd pop down for more.'

'I won't hear of it,' said Denny, digging in his pocket for a shilling, troubling the barman for another beer and placing the frothing glass in front of his new friend.

'Ah thank you, a true gentleman. You'll do well in this country, for there are too many of the other sort. Now, one good turn deserves another, I'll tell you anything you want to know. Are you planning on staying in the city or getting about out west?'

'Oh I'm planning on seeing the country, if I can. Our family business is in stationary steam engines, and I need to get out and talk to potential buyers myself, wherever possible.'

'So is it all about the almighty pound with you, or are you a starry-eyed soul dreaming of seeing the outback?'

Outback. It was the first time Denny had heard the word. It sounded odd, but somehow romantic. 'Outback?' he repeated. 'What on earth is that?'

Henry's moustache twitched like a squirrel's tail. 'It's the place that begins where everything civilised and normal ends. It's where the ground turns red, as red as a broken heart. I could describe for you, if we had the time, every dry riverbed I've crossed. Of lakes either brimming with water or lying bare, the surface of dry, cracked clay. Why, I've seen a million pelicans in a desert that became an inland sea.' Henry's eyes glazed over. It seemed to Denny that he had become wistful, with something of the mystic in his voice.

'It sounds beautiful.'

'The outback *is* beautiful, my friend. Beautiful and dangerous.'

'How do I get there?'

'Get on a horse and ride west.'

'How will I know when I arrive?'

'You'll know.'

Sam came over and rested a hand on Denny's shoulder. 'Mouse just "lost his shirt" on the last race of the day and he's as "mad as a gumtree full of galahs."' They both laughed at the idiom, before Sam went on, 'They're good fellows, are you coming back over?'

'Of course. Give me a moment,' said Denny, shaking hands and taking leave of his new acquaintance. 'I hope to see you again.'

'Likewise,' drawled Henry, then went back to scribbling in his pad.

Returning to his seat at the other table, Denny told Sam about the encounter.

Mouse heard what he said, laughed, and nudged the man next to him, 'The outback's not just down the road, you know. You've got no idea how bloody big this country is.'

Denny smiled at Sam, ignoring their mirth. 'Having just steamed along the entire underside of the place we do have some idea. As for the rest of it – there's one way to find out – and I intend to do that very soon.'

★★★

Later, when Sam and Denny left the pub, they encountered a gang of men coming down the street, arms linked, and chanting. The two Englishmen had no choice but to duck out of the way.

'Tomorrow, mates,' shouted someone from the midst of the troupe. 'Tomorrow we shut down the fucking city.' They paused in the middle of Wynyard Square. Two or three of them went into the pub, then came out with more men, including some of those who had been drinking with Denny and Sam.

Henry appeared also, writing in his pad as he watched events. Denny now understood the journalist's presence at the bar. Something was afoot; something big.

Another crowd approached from the far end of the square, joining in with the first, while more trickled in from all sides. The assembly formed a hollow circle, and one man took the centre, shaking his fist as he spoke.

'The bosses think they can take food from the mouths of our families. They think they can crush us under the force of arms, and with their unjust laws. But we, my friends, have history and righteousness on our side.'

Loud cheers rang out. Denny felt himself moved. These were men hardened by physical labour, who spent the bulk of their waking hours making other men rich. His natural sympathies were with them.

'Get ready,' shouted the speaker. 'Every working man assembles at nine. The johnnies will be here, but we'll be ready for them.'

The crowd roared their approval and began to disperse, but two or three outliers from the group spotted Sam and Denny and headed across.

'You two blokes ...' one of them shouted. 'Bosses or workers?'

'I'm a foundryman,' Denny cried. 'So that makes me a worker.'

Coming close, the speaker grabbed Denny's hands and examined the palms, still callused from labouring at the factory. Satisfied, he turned to Sam searchingly.

'I'm a clerk,' said Sam.

Denny raised a clenched fist, 'I'm in the Foundryman's Union, Deptford Creek London. My mate and I'll be here tomorrow for solidarity.'

'Solidarity mate.' Then a respectful nod. 'You'll be welcome.'

★★★

In the early days of the Morton Steam Factory, Ned Baring had coached Frederick on the nature of business and money.

Cash flow, allied with overall profitability was king. If money was passing through the business, and takings outweighed costs, bills could be paid.

Now, with only a few sales coming in from overseas, and Fortis engines embargoed in the British Isles, cash flow slowed to a trickle. At the same time, the practicalities of the float meant that a certain largesse continued, and the foreign sales campaign needed funding.

It was a difficult time, and Frederick spent much of the night with the issues of the day running through his mind, over and over, like the cycling of an engine over which he had no control.

Chapter Forty-two

When the first written assignment was due, Professor Ambrose Halburton, one of the best-regarded electrical engineers in the United Kingdom, walked around the room collecting papers from the students, bypassing May. Holding back tears, she waited until the end of the lesson. When the others had gone, she walked to his desk.

'Why won't you take my paper?'

The professor gathered his things, not looking at her. 'Because I don't recognise you as part of the class.'

'Why not? Read my work and you'll find that it's as good as any of theirs.'

'I'll have to take your word for that.'

May followed him out the door, and down the corridor, where he reached the bottom of a set of steps. He paused and turned to face her, bottom lip quivering. 'Will you stop following me?'

'No, it's not fair. If you don't mark my work, I'll fail the subject.'

'Then withdraw. We both know why you're here, and it's not to learn. You're some kind of put-up job by the women's movement.'

'No,' she said. 'I'm … really interested.'

Making a face he turned and began to climb the staircase, with May following. After two flights he slowed, breathing heavily, sitting down on a step, placing the pile of papers beside him.

'What's wrong?' she asked. 'You're not well?'

'I'll be better in a minute, just leave me alone, for Heaven's sake.'

Two young men approached from below. May snapped, 'Please get the nurse, as fast as you can.' She sat next to the struggling old man, loosened his collar and waited while the nurse arrived with two orderlies. They gave him smelling salts, then assisted him to stand, directing him, at a very slow walk, towards the infirmary.

'He'll pull through,' said the nurse. 'He's had these turns before.'

'Thank you,' said May. 'Would it help if I took his things to his office?'

'That would be wonderful, thank you.'

May hefted the pile of documents and carried them to the Professor's office. Placing them onto the uncluttered surface of his desk, she arranged them so that her own assignment sat on top of the pile.

★★★

Three days later, the professor was back in front of the class, still refusing to acknowledge May. The next week, however, when he passed the marked papers back around the class, he dropped May's onto her desk. The grade B+ stood out in red ink on the front.

★★★

Eadie was bent over the bowl of the lavatory bucket, her knees aching from contact with the hard tiled floor. The nausea had begun a few days earlier, lingering from morning to noon, but she had not yet missed a shift at the silk mill, and she did not intend to.

When she felt a little better, she bathed, then dressed for work in a dark navy dress, with a fitted bodice and buttons at the front. Despite her growing repugnance for food, she forced herself to eat spoonfuls of porridge, sweetened with honey. Soon afterwards she walked up to High Street, joining some regulars along the way to the tram. It was still dark, and there was a camaraderie in this morning parade.

Arriving at the mill, she tied on her apron and set to work threading the spindles. If she slowed, the overseer, a cruel man of about thirty, filled with his own self-importance, was sure to let her know.

Yet, by nine in the morning Eadie had no choice but to run to the privy, then hurry back to the spindles. Glenys, one of several middle-aged women who worked alongside her, leaned forward and whispered, 'I 'ope your Denny is coming back soon to make it all legal.'

'What on earth do you mean?'

The other woman leaned close to her ear and whispered. 'I mean that from where I'm standin' it looks like yer havin' a baby.'

'That's ridiculous,' said Eadie.

'Of course it is,' mocked the other woman, winking lasciviously. 'Ridiculous! But every time I've seen a young woman turn green and run to the lav in the middle of the morning shift, her belly has started swellin' up soon after.'

'Please don't tell anyone,' Eadie said, eyes wide, and her heart quickening at this frightening, exhilarating news. On her way home after work, she called in at Doctor Evans's house, but he was out on his rounds. His wife promised to send him to her in the morning.

It was a long night, the bones of the house creaking with the cold. The heart of the place, it seemed, had departed with Sam, and Eadie wished he was home, even if she couldn't confide in him. They were close as only siblings could be, and she knew that her soul would not feel so chafed and raw if he were there.

First thing in the morning Eadie sent a message to the silk mill with a neighbour, pleading that she was too ill to work. Her pay would be docked but knowing the truth was important.

The doctor arrived just after nine: brisk, efficient and unsympathetic. 'When did your blood last run?'

'A little while ago, but I'm quite irregular.'

The doctor examined her, making her lie on the bed with her dress lifted up, while he probed and pressed into her abdomen, used his stethoscope several times in different places. 'I'm glad your mother's away,' he said finally.

'What do you mean?'

'I mean that you are not married, and you, Eadith, are going to have a baby. You might have thought through the consequences of certain actions beforehand. Your mother is a virtuous woman who will be horrified.' He pushed his stethoscope into his bag and closed it. 'Let me know if you need me to recommend a certain type of doctor – the kind who specialises in little sluts like you.'

'How can you talk to a person like that?' she asked. Tears appeared in both eyes, and trailed down her cheeks.

'You have abrogated your right to be treated as a lady, for you are not one. Oh, and that will be six shillings for the consultation, please do make sure it is received by the end of the week.'

The doctor left the house without another word. The door slammed behind him and Eadie burst into tears.

★★★

Not knowing what else to do, Eadie went to work, shunning Glenys and her knowing stares, performing tasks with single-minded efficiency, subduing the nausea as best she could. Three days passed, and her mood swung from believing that she was being punished for her wanton behaviour – to anger that any man could treat a human being with such callous and judgemental bile. Several times she took up paper to write to Denny but suitable words would not materialise.

Sometimes her hands crept to her belly and she tried to sense the tiny life-form growing inside there – a part of her and a part of Denny, imbued with his spirit and love of life. At these times a sense of well-being filled her heart.

★★★

The noise on Sydney's streets started just after the cock crowed in the boarding house yard. The sound of marching feet followed, then men talking and yelling.

Sam and Denny prepared themselves with a hearty breakfast of fresh bread topped with slabs of crispy bacon, smeared with runny yellow egg.

'Are you sure you want to do this?' asked Sam.

'They're my kind of people,' said Denny. 'We have to stand up for ourselves.'

As the two Englishmen walked off Wynyard Square and into George Street, they saw how the ranks were already forming, raggedly filling the street from left to right. At a whistle and a shout, then the first of many chants, they set off, with children running from the slum houses to shadow the men.

Just beyond the corner of George and King Streets, outside the pastoral chambers, a row of mounted police waited, filling the street from shop front to shop front, walking their horses down in direct opposition to the march. Each man wore a pith helmet, holding their reins in one hand, a stout billy club in the other. An officer in the centre shouted orders and encouragement.

'Keep the line there on the left. Close up, close up.'

'Special constables,' someone near to Denny growled. 'They've brought in hundreds of them.'

The two opposing forces met and struck, with the police horses working like hammered wedges through the ranks of workers, clubs attached to police wrists by leather lanyards rising and falling like gardener's scythes.

'Hold on,' said Sam. 'I'm not sure I feel strongly enough about this to cop a beating.'

'No,' said Denny, 'and Eadie would never forgive me if I led you into it – looks like it's the hard core clashing with the coppers. Most of the strikers are hanging back.'

It was true, only the more militant members of the march were engaging with the police, others were flowing down into King Street, using alleys, or diverting down to Pitt, in an effort to by-pass the police line. Denny found himself carried away in this direction. He noted that one of the marchers had stopped to put a rock through a windowpane, no doubt a store belonging to some loathsome employer.

A block down King Street, on the Pitt Street corner, the marchers were reforming, meeting up with another contingent of strikers heading in from the suburbs. This, decided Denny, was becoming a brutal affair, a genuine battle, with many of the strikers red faced and agitated.

Denny saw the journalist Henry, who he had met at the pub the night before, standing with a brick wall at his back, observing events, taking notes in his book. Next to him was a photographer bent over his tripod-supported machine.

Denny gave Henry a shout of greeting as he passed, and received a cheery wave in return. Just then, however, a fresh contingent of police on foot came pelting up from the Domain; at least a hundred of them, all armed similarly to their comrades on horseback.

A trio of men in uniform noticed the journalist and photographer, and they, while their fellows wedged their way into the main body of strikers, hurried over. One took hold of Henry's notebook, on which he still had a grip, and another seized the camera.

'Henry needs help,' Denny said to Sam, 'let's go.' Fighting their way through, they reached the scene. Denny barged into the camera-taker, snatching the instrument back.

The policeman who was engaged in the tug of war with Henry's notebook stepped back and fumbled at removing his baton from its scabbard. Sam looked at Denny, who nodded back. It was time to make a tactical withdrawal. Henry didn't need any urging, and together the group took to their heels, heading down along Pitt Street, in the direction they had come.

A brief pursuit was half-hearted, for the police were being hard pressed by the strikers back at the intersection. Chasing a couple of newsmen was not quite as urgent as joining the general melee.

Reaching Martin Place, the four stopped, breathing hard from the run. Denny placed the tripod and camera on the ground. 'I hope that nothing is broken.'

'It looks fine, thanks to you,' said the photographer.

Henry straightened his moustache, then, 'Seems like I owe you a favour. I've enough copy for an article and we got out with our equipment intact.'

'No problem,' said Denny. Then, spying a coffee house across the square he said, 'I don't think it's advisable for Sam and I to go back to the fray. Those constables will be keeping an eye out for us. How about we sit down for a quick beverage before we part ways?'

'Good idea,' said Henry.

The journalist had left his pocketbook at home, (always a good idea when heading off to a fracas like this, he said), and Denny was happy to shout, buying coffee for himself and the journalist, and tea for Sam and the photographer. Settled into their seats, Henry gave them a great deal of background information on the strikes. In Denny's mind it was more than enough to compensate him for a few pennies' worth of hot beverages.

'Now tell me about these engines of yours,' said Henry.

Denny gave the stranger a five-minute synopsis of the company, his father's role in founding it, and the coal-saving properties of the engines.

'You want to sell machinery?' Henry broke in. 'I'll tell you something. A friend of mine is one of the directors of a big mine out at Broken Hill.'

'Where's that?'

'In the middle of nowhere, almost at the border with South Australia.' He dropped his voice. 'A mountain of silver, the most valuable mine in the world. They're on the hunt for horsepower, masses of it, and I know for a fact that they've been talking to a big London firm. Would you like me to find out more?'

'I'd be so very grateful if you could,' said Denny.

Chapter Forty-three

In the days after the protest march Denny had some interesting Sydney meetings, one with a company called Crompton who were making a name in the burgeoning electrical lighting market. They needed reliable and affordable steam engines to drive their alternators.

'At the moment the Fortis will do the job,' Denny told the board. 'But in a few months we'll have a new engine, the Imperium, purpose made for power generation, ten years ahead of anything else in the field.'

Even more encouraging was an agreement with a Sydney manufacturer of ground-breaking centrifugal pumps. Their head office, conveniently, was just around in Hay Street. Denny worked with an engineer to, on paper at least, couple a Morton Fortis to a Tangyes pump, a high-end powerhouse that was best-in-market for the burgeoning irrigation industry.

The ink had scarcely dried in this agreement when a letter came from Frederick, six weeks old, but a lot had happened since Denny had parted from his siblings in Egypt.

Denny read the letter in their room, shaking his head as he learned of the dire financial position the family company was in, beginning with news of any resolution of the Forgill lawsuit being delayed for at least two months.

> We are trying to fill the very few orders that have resulted
> from our overseas expansion, but we need more.

The big sales were out there somewhere, Denny told himself. The newspapers were filled with stories of discoveries and development. Gold in Central Queensland and Western Australia. Silver in Broken Hill. Copper in Burra, South Australia. Pastoral properties pushing out west and north. Shearing sheds as big as Westminster Abbey. There was so much happening, over such a vast canvas, that Denny did not know where to start, until an unexpected letter arrived from Henry, the journalist he had met in the pub.

> Dear Mr Morton
>
> I promised you news of the Broken Hill Proprietary
> Company. I can confirm that they are negotiating the
> purchase of some twenty thousand pounds worth of
> stationary steam engines. Buxton and Thornley were a
> favoured tenderer but they are now out of the race. The
> company has thirty days to consider a quote from British
> firm Forgill's, of whom you may well know …

Denny read the name Forgill's out loud. It was a name that swam in complicated undercurrents of enmity, loyalty and hurt. Much of the history between Frederick Morton and the company remained a mystery to Denny, and the name was rarely spoken aloud by his family.

> The fellow you need to talk to is John Howell, the
> manager. I am also acquainted with George McCulloch,
> one of the founding partners. My suggestion is that you
> cable them forthwith.
>
> I also suggest that I no longer owe you a beer and a
> coffee. And if this works out, you owe me many beers.
>
> Yours, etc HA Lawson

Here was an opportunity to snatch a deal from his father's nemesis, yet only thirty days remained to exploit it! A mountain of silver; the most valuable mine in the world; a thousand miles away!

Denny turned to Sam. 'How good would it be if we could get this huge order ahead of Forgill's?'

The first thing Denny did was compose a reply by letter to Henry Lawson, thanking him for his help, and promising a river of beer if the deal came through. Then, over lunch, he discussed the situation with Sam.

'We can't do this by telegram,' he said. 'If we want to win this order, we need to go out there and seize it for ourselves.'

'What about the office?' Sam asked.

'Our receptionist, Mrs McCrae, can run the show on her own. Then we can deal with quotes when we get back.'

Sam shrugged. 'If you think it's worthwhile, I'm with you.'

Back at his desk, Denny wrote a telegram, addressed to Mr John Howell in Broken Hill.

> DEAR MR HOWELL I REPRESENT MORTON STEAM LATELY ARRIVED IN SYDNEY STOP WOULD LIKE TO MEET WITH YOU AT YOUR SITE SOONEST TO DISCUSS YOUR EQUIPMENT NEEDS STOP ABLE TO LEAVE FORTHWITH STOP I CAN PROMISE YOU THIRTY PER CENTUM COAL SAVINGS OVER OUR COMPETITORS DF MORTON

Just three hours later a reply came back.

> PLEASED TO DISCUSS MORTON ENGINES ON SITE STOP ORDER MUST BE RESOLVED BY END OF MONTH TO MEET PLANNED PRODUCTION SCHEDULES STOP J HOWELL

Some excellent maps of the colony were available, and Denny sat with Sam late that night, planning routes and logistics. They'd brought saddles and outdoor clothing with them, but they still had a long list: everything from carbolic soap to flour; powdered egg, sauces and tonics; various polishes; borax, cream of tartar and tea.

Over the following days, their room became a storehouse. Lying in bed, Denny dreamed of the outback his friend Henry had so eloquently described.

One of their new drinking mates at Prahlert's, a man who hailed from Dubbo in the Central West, lent Denny a volume of poetry by one Adam Lindsay Gordon. He loved to read the rousing descriptions of bush scenes and the larrikin folk who lived there.

When Denny was told to try reading a journal called the Bulletin, he picked up a copy at a news stand. Standing in the sun he flicked through, then stared with a thump of his heart at the name Henry Lawson – the author of a story and several poems within those pages. At first he suspected that there must be two men of that name. An image of the wordsmith beside one of the poems removed all doubt.

'I know the man,' he told everyone in the pub who would listen. 'He was sitting over there. I bought him a beer, and he wrote me a letter.' He went on to tell how it was the poet himself who had also planted the seed of the idea to brave the outback and suggested that he approach the Broken Hill Proprietary Company in person. 'You're soft in the head,' said one of their drinking partners. 'Why would you leave merry Sydney, for that?' This last word, underlined with a finger pointing to the west, dismissed every square inch of Australia west of Parramatta as a wasteland.

THANKS FOR OPPORTUNITY STOP WILL ARRIVE SITE IN PERSON TO INVESTIGATE YOUR NEEDS AND QUOTE BEFORE CLOSE OCTOBER 31 STOP KINDEST REGARDS DF MORTON

The same day, when Sam went down to fetch the mail a letter arrived from the Mildura Progress Association requesting a quotation on some very large irrigation pumps and engines. This was a response from one of the letters that Denny had posted in Colombo.

'That's two big potential sales,' said Denny. 'Makes the trip even more worthwhile.'

★★★

Eadie took the tram down to Southwark, with the contents of her bank account folded into her purse. Leaving the station, she presented herself at the offices of the Thomas Cook Company, booking agents for the Orient and Steam Navigation Company. There she purchased a second-class ticket from Tilbury to Sydney, for a departure in seven days' time.

On the way back, she called in at the Morton Factory, where the last shift of the week was starting to wind down, and the building echoed with the clang of tools being cleaned, and shovels levering ash from fireboxes. Other gangs stacked material ready for the Monday morning shift.

Eadie found Frederick in his office, working at the design table, 'Oh hello,' she said. 'I'd tried to knock, but there's so much noise—'

'I'm so sorry,' he said, leaping to his feet. 'But it's good to see you.'

Eadie swallowed, wondering why this was so hard. 'I've come to tell you that I'm sailing for New South Wales in a week.'

Frederick looked surprised, but his voice remained steady. 'That's marvellous for you, thanks for coming to tell me.'

'I need to be with Sam ... and Denny.' She paused. 'The thing is, they don't know I'm coming – I'll write, but like as not I'll get there myself almost as fast as a letter. I wondered if you've been in contact with them – by telegram perhaps. Are they even in the country yet?' She paused, 'They both write to me, but the mail takes so long.'

'What a fool I am,' said Frederick. 'It was remiss of me not to let you know they'd arrived safely. They're both in Sydney now – getting things organised.'

'Will you let them know I'm coming?'

'I will, of course.' Frederick took her hand. 'Do you need assistance of any kind? You know I'll help where I can.'

Eadie shook her head, 'I have my ticket, and I've written to my parents. They'll be back here in week or two, and I know they'll be worried, but I need to do this.'

'I understand,' said Frederick, 'and I insist that you allow me to take you down to Tilbury.'

May appeared in the doorway, still with her college books in a shoulder bag. 'Oh hello Eadie, good to see you.'

Frederick looked up. 'Eadie's heading out to New South Wales to join Sam and Denny. You and I and Maman might take her down to Tilbury next Sunday?'

'With pleasure,' said May, putting her bag on the floor and taking the younger woman in her arms. 'What an adventure! I almost wish that I was coming with you.'

★★★

Prior to their departure for the western reaches of the colony, Denny was surprised to find some personal mail amongst the usual official correspondence. The envelope was square and formal, with an angled flap, on heavy paper.

Even Sam stopped his packing to watch Denny slit the envelope open with his pocket knife. 'What is it?' he asked.

'I'm not sure yet, but it looks like an invitation.'

'An invitation?'

The embossed card inside enquired if both Denny and Sam would attend a charity dinner and ball, at the newly completed Centennial Hall, with the aim of raising money for Sydney orphans. It had been forwarded from one of the proprietors of the Tangyes firm – Jim Sweetman. The cost was exorbitant – ten pounds each – an amount that would eat away a good portion of the money needed for their upcoming journey.

'Ten pounds each?' spat Sam. 'That's a fortune.'

'I'd like to support a good cause like that,' said Denny, 'but things are tight and we'll need every penny we have on the road.'

Sam stroked his chin – the beginnings of a goatee beard he had started growing a few days earlier. 'Yet it's the kind of event where you'll meet some of the leading lights of industry, and perhaps those from further afield. Maybe we should go.'

'You're right,' Denny grinned. 'It's a business imperative! Not to mention a chance to eat good food and drink nice grog. We'll have to get our dinner suits pressed and clean the dress shoes – then they can go into storage until we come back from our trip.

★★★

Denny had heard people talk of the brand-new Centennial Hall, named to commemorate one hundred years since the arrival of English mariners in Australia. Built as part of the Sydney Town Hall complex it was a grand venue, floored with the best of Australian hardwood timbers – golden tallowwood from the coastal hinterland, and blackwood from Victoria. The ceilings soared up seventy feet, supported by marble pillars, with stained glass windows near the peaks, each depicting a beautiful native plant.

It was a glittering night, with a band in full swing, liveried waiters moving through the throng with their silver trays.

'They're certainly doing their best for our ten quid,' whispered Sam, accepting a glass of champagne with one hand, and a Sydney rock oyster grilled in the shell with Worcestershire sauce and a dash of stout with the other.

At dinner the pair were seated beside Jim Sweetman, his wife Nella, and their two daughters. 'I'm so glad you boys could come,' said Sweetman, 'there's more than enough of us old fuddy-duddies.' He lowered his voice. 'And the girls will appreciate the dance partners.'

Pairing with Sweetman's daughters, Denny found, was no chore. Kate, the eldest, had long auburn hair, a full figure and a winning smile. Sam took her out waltzing before the introductions were complete. Agnes, the younger was slim and fair-haired, with sunny eyes. Denny warned her straight up that he was no expert on the dance floor. 'Please don't expect too much of me. I'm a working man, unused to this kind of thing.'

'I'll help you,' she said. 'I'm sure you'll have talent.'

They danced through two numbers, with Agnes's hands light on his shoulder, and his own wrist resting on her waist. All the while she whispered instructions in his ear, and he found that the basics were easy to master.

Back at the table, Denny fell into conversation with the girls' father, while a local admirer snatched Agnes up for a dance. He was an awkward kind of fellow, with big teeth and a fixed grin. Denny watched their progress around the dance floor while he sipped the champagne.

'I'm impressed with your company's engines,' Sweetman said. 'The Mobilis, particularly, is just what this country needs – portable and powerful.'

'I hope so – and my job is to find companies requiring just such a machine – particularly those with the money to buy it.'

'Before you go, duck in and see Fred Wolseley at his factory – he's manufacturing machinery to replace the old hand shears in shearing sheds – and he's just down the road here. You'll be out in sheep country, and if you're smart, you'll keep going all the way up into Queensland. The big sheds are all keen on mechanising, but they don't know who to talk to.' Asking a waiter for a pencil, Sweetman scribbled an address on the back of one of his own business cards.

'Thanks very much,' said Denny. 'We'll go and see him tomorrow. Queensland might have to wait for another trip, but I'm keen to explore all avenues.'

By then Agnes was back from a dance, standing by his shoulder, 'Talking business at a ball is so boring. Come on Denny!'

Sweetman laughed at his daughter's enthusiasm, and the young Englishman stood, taking the girl's hand and leading her back to the floor.

This time he relaxed, and Agnes noticed. 'That's better. You're getting the hang of it. A few lessons and you'll be marvellous.'

Denny grinned, 'I don't think I'll have time for that. We're heading out west in a few days.'

'Oh! Well Kate and I are going Home to London – our first experience. We'll be staying with my grandmother. You've lived there all your life, tell me about London.'

Denny considered the question. 'London is everything: traditional, modern, busy, lonely, lively, friendly, unfriendly, cold much of the time, very hot sometimes in July and August. It's so big, it has everything you could wish for and then some.'

'What's the one thing I should do in London while I'm there?'

'Saint Paul's Cathedral is very grand, and you'll probably like the Covent Garden markets – they have balls there too – far bigger than this one. The British Museum of course ... Madame Tussaud's if you like things a little spooky ... there are so many places I can't think of them all.'

'I'll go to those ones at least,' she said. 'I promise.'

Back at the table the senior Sweetmans had gone up to dance, while Sam and Kate were taking a rest, drinking champagne, but a little quietly, as was Sam's way. They moved chairs so the four of them were closer.

Agnes cocked her pretty face and peered at Denny minutely. 'So it's just you and Sam, on this trip. No wife?'

Deciding that he had drunk enough champagne, he placed his empty glass on a passing waiter's tray, and refused another. 'Just us, yes, and I have no wife – not yet, but that's going to change soon.' He looked at Sam and they shared a grin.

'Oh really, you're engaged?'

'Not officially, but we're going to marry just the same.'

'Who's the lucky girl?'

Sam broke in, 'A very special girl.'

'A lady then?'

'Very much a lady.'

'What's her name?' asked Kate, but Denny shook his head. He saw no need to traffic Eadie's personal details for these obvious gossips.

'I bet I can guess,' said Agnes. 'Is it Mary?'

Denny shook his head, 'Not even close.'

'Deborah?' tried Kate.

Her sister answered, 'Not Deborah, more likely Elizabeth or something like that.' She looked at Denny's face. 'That's it, isn't it?'

'Something like that,' agreed Denny, to end the conversation. 'Now Kate, would you care to dance? After Agnes's excellent tutelage I believe that I'm starting to get the idea.'

★★★

Later, as they walked home, Denny said, 'Twenty pounds well spent, I think.'

'Most certainly, I haven't had so much fun since we left home.'

'I think Kate liked you,' said Denny.

'I think so too,' agreed Sam. 'After all, she's human.'

Reaching the lobby of the boarding house the night clerk handed Denny a telegram. This he placed in his top pocket, waiting until he reached his room to read it.

Sitting on his bed, he thumbed the envelope open, read the slip, then grinned across at Sam. 'Guess what?'

'What?'

Denny read the message out loud, '"Eadie leaving for Sydney on *Vesuvius* FM." She's coming here! I don't know why, and how it came to be so, but she's coming.'

'Oh, that's wonderful news,' said Sam.

'We'll have to be back from our trip in time to meet her, but we can manage it, I'm sure.'

Denny's heart, as he climbed into bed, hummed with elation. This feeling had nothing to do with Agnes Sweetman. It was because he had articulated an intention that made his heart sing with delight; then, just hours later, learned that the person he was longing for, who he wanted to cleave to for the rest of his life, would soon be on her way.

Unwittingly, he had also set in train a misunderstanding that would come close to breaking him completely.

★★★

After several weeks of settling in and establishing the office, Matthew took a train to Johannesburg, leaving Harriet behind to keep the office running. Alighting from the platform in the city of gold he found a tent city stretching for miles, interspersed with mullock heaps and working shafts. Of interest to Matthew was the first of many stationary engines belching steam and coal smoke, powering the stamp batteries that crushed auriferous rock to powder so the gold could be extracted.

Johannesburg was a young town – scarcely four years old – centred on the vast Market Square – where bullock wagons and travellers' coaches outspanned on the bare dirt. Where tramways were under construction down the broad streets, and gangs of African workers sang rousing songs as their pickaxes rose and fell.

On the Eastern side of the square stood a series of imposing and brand-new public buildings – the Standard Bank, Natal Bank, Bank of England and Bank of Africa. On the streets Matthew heard the mingling of many accents: Cornish, Scots, Irish, German, Boer, and the singing of African hawkers.

All day and night the thump of batteries carried through to Matthew's room. Johannesburg was a city driven on steam, its wealth derived from labour-saving engines and their untiring capacity to work. Wagons of coal to feed these beasts arrived, one after the other, drawn by bullock and horse teams from the nearby Highveld Coalfields.

Matthew ate the evening meal at a restaurant, enjoying the company of a slim and beautiful American woman, a British army major and a bear-like new millionaire from the rush – an impressive man who had fought the Zulu impis at Rorke's Drift. Their mingled laughter and the roar of wild men drinking heavily at the bar was an exciting backdrop.

The next few days in the town were busy and productive, as Matthew brought news of the Fortis engine and its winding gear to mine owners and managers. He addressed Digger's Committees and other owner's groups, promising speedy delivery times and a reduction in coal usage. He inveigled his way into the exclusive Witwatersrand Club where decision-makers sniffed expensive wine corks and quaffed lobsters carried from Natal packed in straw and ice.

Matthew learned the names of the most significant mines and visited them all – Salisbury, Jumpers, Roodeport Central, Knights and Langlaate. Yet, he also found time for reading the cache of books he had brought on the adventure, along with unwinding and finding a taste for Cape wines and Johannesburg's cosmopolitan, if rough-around-the-edges fare. The town had dozens of bars and cafes – the Cafe Monaco, Albany and Phillip's Bar. He tried them all, and on Sunday he made his way to Saint Mary's church in Jeppestown for his first service in several weeks.

When every plausible sales channel in the Johannesburg area had been pursued, Matthew boarded a train bound for Kimberley on the Cape Western Line, over a route that had, according to legend, been charted by the Prime Minister of the day with a ruler and pencil.

The CGR Dubs and Company locomotive, with its fresh green paint, polished brass domes, and cow catcher sweeping low ahead of the wheels, puffed through the inclines, bridges and tunnels of the Hex River Mountains, then the stark arid plains of the Karoo Desert.

★★★

The town of Kimberley was no oasis, but a vast industrial domain, where mine headgear was more common than trees, and men walked by with jewelled cufflinks and dusty Cuban-heeled boots.

After years of conflict, the two great pioneers of the Kimberley fields – Cecil Rhodes and Barney Barnato, had recently joined forces to create the De Beers Consolidated Mines Company. Even so, many independent mines remained, some owned by consortiums of London businessmen. Surely, Matthew told himself, some would require new and efficient steam engines.

One grizzled old owner, an independent type who had been on the diggings since the Klip Drift rush, took Matthew under his wing, wangled him entrance to the Kimberley Club, where the elite drank Bollinger and played billiards, and there introduced him to all the owners and managers who were worth knowing.

Matthew's impromptu guide's name was 'Spider' Caldwell, who gave Matthew an uncut diamond of around a carat, along with a receipt to prove that it was legally obtained.

Meanwhile, through the Kimberley Club, Matthew was able to find two companies in the market for winding and hauling engines, and he was able to open negotiations with both. There were strong competitors – the British firm of Paxman had a firm foothold here, as did Forgill's, along with Fraser and Chalmers. Yet, the portability of the Fortis, and the clever coupling to the drum and gears was a talking point, along with the economic coal usage and engineering brilliance of the superheater. These men liked technology for its own sake. They liked fine things, and the cutting-edge nature of the Fortis was attractive.

Then, on what was meant to be Matthew's last day, returning dusty with sweat from a day negotiating with mine owners and managers, an incredible sight met his eyes over the town common. Filling, it seemed, half the sky, was one of the biggest hot-air balloons

Matthew had seen. The envelope was shaped like a bulbous, inverted tear drop. Blue, red and white stripes ran down the full length. A web-like arrangement of ropes covered the balloon, with strands hanging down to a wicker car beneath. Inside was a slim male figure, waving to miners and bullock drivers as he lowered an anchor to the ground and thereby pulled the contraption earthwards.

Walking across to investigate, Matthew heard a voice in French. This was a language he spoke well, from both his mother's example and tuition at school.

'Good afternoon,' Matthew called. 'What an amazing balloon.' Up close, he saw that the aeronaut was quite dark-skinned, and very handsome. 'I didn't expect a Frenchman to fall from the sky in the middle of the diamond fields.'

The newcomer narrowed his eyes to regard Matthew with a piercing look, 'And I did not expect to meet an Englishman with schoolboy French, either.' He thrust out a confident hand. 'My name is Jules D'Marnier, by the way, and I am attempting the first balloon traverse of Africa from north to south. As for tonight, I am waiting for the winds to change – and carry me south. I am also in need of a break from the journey. Can you recommend a good hotel?'

'I'm Matthew Morton, formerly of Lewisham, and I will lead you to an excellent hotel.'

★★★

That night they dined together, and Matthew asked many questions, satisfying his curiosity about the physics of travel by balloon.

'What,' he asked, 'makes it stay up?'

'It's filled with coal gas, which is lighter than air, and therefore it rises. The silk envelope is impregnated with gutta percha – which makes it almost air-tight, but not quite, so every few days I have to go down to the ground and make more gas.'

'How?'

'I'll show you tomorrow, it will be easier to explain the process at the balloon.'

'How do you steer?'

'True steerage is not possible. Yet breezes can sometimes blow from different directions at different levels, so I try to go to a height where I will get the most favourable breeze.'

Matthew delighted in having an intellectual conversationalist. The two young men talked of books and authors, from Flaubert to the Bronte sisters, until most of the other tables were empty and the waiters were no longer hurrying to refill their glasses.

'Your French is very good,' Jules commented.

'So is your English,' Matthew replied. 'And I am half French.' It was strange, but he had never seen himself in that light before. 'My mother grew up in Normandy and spoke to us in French quite a lot.'

'It shows,' said Jules. 'I also have mixed parentage.' There was a note of pride in his voice, his dark eyes flashing. 'My mother is from Algeria, of the Chenouis people, which is why my skin is quite dark. We live in a town in South-western France called Saint Sever. Have you heard of it?'

'No, sorry.'

'France has many small towns. Saint Sever has only a few thousands of people, though it is very old. My father is a schoolmaster, which is why I am good at English. Sometimes he makes our whole family speak English for a week, occasionally German, or even Latin, though I am not so good at that.'

'You did not wish to go to university?' Matthew asked.

'Not yet. I want to see the world first. It is so wide and exciting. My father and mother encourage me to go where my heart dares me to go. After all, if my father had not been adventuring in Algeria they would never have met, and I would not exist. This balloon, by the way, was made in our village to my father's design. He had been researching and testing prototypes for years.'

'I'm jealous,' Matthew declared.

'Of what?'

'That you can fly high in the air, and experience something so exciting.' He made a face. 'I was consumptive as a child, and I can't run as well as most people. The idea of moving fast, high above the earth seems bird-like and masterful to me.'

'I have an idea,' said Jules. 'I am waiting for the winds to change – would you like to come up in the balloon with me for a couple of days.'

Matthew ached with wanting to do such a thing. 'I'm supposed to catch the train back to Cape Town tomorrow.'

'Come with me instead. Life is to be lived. We will go north for a few days, then, when the wind changes I will take you all the way back to Cape Town.'

'That would save me time on the train.' Matthew cracked a grin, 'and would be marvellous fun besides.'

★★★

Percy Forgill paced back and forth in the office that had once been his father's. The room made him feel like a child again, a reminder that Lord Bartholomew Forgill had not ceased to tower over his life like some timeless colossus.

Progress reports of the Morton Steam Company's impending float were almost incomprehensible. Percy had thought the man was finished and taken his eye off him for a moment, yet here he was, trying to rise from what should have been ashes, again with the help of the infamous banking criminal Ned Baring and the considerable network at his disposal.

Not only that, but Morton's son Denny was apparently heading to Broken Hill to attempt to snatch a massive order that would otherwise almost certainly go to Forgill's.

Yes, Freddie Morton was barely afloat financially, but somehow the factory was operating at full capacity. It was time to finish him. How? Again his pacing took him to the wall beneath the elephant tusk and he stared upwards, stopped, and called for his secretary.

'Yes, sir?'

'I want those old things gone from this room today.' He waved an arm at the various trophies of his father's life, hanging on the walls and standing in corners or shelves. 'I want all of it gone.'

'Very well sir, but the walls will be rather bare. Shall I replace your father's things with something new?'

'If you would. Paintings – anything.'

The secretary bowed low. 'I'll make the arrangements, sir.'

Percy made a decision. 'Tell the driver that I wish to leave for Seven Dials in ten minutes.'

'Very well, sir.'

★★★

Peter Craven was the first of Percy's boys and the most trusted. The terrible burn scars that marred the young man's face pained the Lord to his heart, and he knew the anguish the disfigurement had caused.

They were sitting at the rookery, a bottle of brandy open on the table and two glasses half full. The house was busy with noise and intrigue as usual, cocks crowing from the ground floor, a snarling dog, and street sounds infiltrating through the windows.

'I believe that we sent the wrong man to deal with Denny Morton,' said Percy. 'Crydley has made a mess of it from start to finish.' He tapped his fingers on the table. 'He has reached New South Wales and will do what needs doing, but I need someone to sail out and join him – someone unafraid to do what needs doing.'

'What do you mean by "needs doing" guvnor? Can you tell me that much?'

'I want this overseas scheme of Mortons to fail. I want him to squirm and suffer and lose heart.'

Craven's shiny forehead creased, and he lowered his voice, 'You want me to break Denny Morton's legs?'

Percy said nothing, just stared back at his protégé.

Craven smiled, 'You want me to do him in, sir?'

Percy said nothing for a moment, his lips writhing together like mating snakes. 'If necessary damn it. Yes. It's a lot to ask, but I will reward you.'

Craven made no sound but nodded once.

Percy, seeming pleased at this signal, went on, 'When that is done I need you to go to South Africa, to stop the younger brother, who also appears to have found some success. I need someone reliable, who will not falter.'

Craven's scars seemed to glow crimson when he spoke. 'You know I will not fail you. Not while I 'ave breath in me lungs.'

'I know.' Percy stood. 'I will ask Wilkins to book your passage on the next available steamship.'

Chapter Forty-four

Getting packed up and catching a cab to the Sydney Railway Terminal at Redfern on time seemed like an impossible task, given that most of the previous day had been taken up with a visit to the Wolseley Shearing Machinery Factory.

This venture, run by Fred Wolseley and his manager Herb Austin, was a spirited and exciting business that reminded Denny of his own family company. By the end of the day, he had a firm idea of how the shearing machinery worked, and how perfectly the Fortis, or in small installations the Mobilis engine, would complement it.

Now, while their substantial luggage was loaded into the baggage car, Denny insisted on walking the full length of the train to the locomotive, pointing out the gold maker's plate on the glistening green and black engine with a high dome and a matching tender close behind.

'What a beauty!' said Sam.

'Isn't she just?' exclaimed Denny. 'One of the first condensing steam locos. Made by Beyer Peacock in Manchester. Father says that Charles Beyer was one of the great steam engineers.'

Satisfied with his inspection, Denny led the way to the second-class carriage that corresponded with their seat number, finding their designated places in a compartment equipped with facing seats and overhead luggage racks. After a series of whistles, and with the hiss of Westinghouse brakes, the train set off southwards at a spirited rate, past Mittagong by mid-morning, and into the Southern Highlands.

They reached Goulburn around noon, where the grass had dried in the sun to a pale grey-yellow, and ragged hills studded with blue-green trees rolled on into the distance. The train came to a halt at the station, and more passengers ambled aboard the carriage – a bushman in a battered cabbage-tree hat, a trio of young ladies and a family dressed in their Sunday best.

The vista changed as the day wore on, through the wild country of Gunning and Yass, the rounded hills of Bowning, then on into the southwest. 'A vast land indeed,' said Sam as they ate hot pies from the buffet car, washed down with bottles of beer.

★★★

Back in third class, Tommy Crydley nibbled at his own pie and nursed a glass of ale. The thought of being so close to Denny Morton filled him with rage. He hated the young foundryman for how he had overturned the situation in Aden. It had been embarrassing to wire London for more money for another steamer ticket.

He'd hated letting Lord Percy Forgill down, the man who had plucked him from a path that might have one day led him to an appointment with a noose. The man who had given him respect, had made him see life as more than just a filthy journey through the back streets of the world's most famous city.

He was angry. Now was his chance.

He had a telegram from Percy Forgill in his pocket. It said:

HAVE DESPATCHED P CRAVEN TO LEND ASSISTANCE
EST SEVEN WEEKS STOP IN MEANTIME YOU MUST
PREVENT DENNY MORTON FROM REACHING
BROKEN HILL BY ANY AND ALL POSSIBLE MEANS

Crydley was determined to do so.

By cable and letter, Frederick had been conducting negotiations with a potential New York distributor, hoping to sell his Fortis engines to the construction companies piling up skyscrapers in the blocks around City Hall Park. Now that the UK market was out of bounds for the Fortis, United States sales would be a boost to their chances of survival.

As part of the arrangements, the company agreed to send an engineer to look at the factory, and assess the suitability of the Fortis for elevator applications. Twenty-four hours after the man's arrival in Liverpool, May agreed to travel with Jenkins to Euston Road station to meet him.

May was expecting a grey-bearded, distinguished type, but the man who carried a neat Gladstone Bag down from the steamer at Tilbury was in his late twenties.

The American engineer greeted May with interested brown eyes. 'James Washington,' he said. 'You must be Miss Morton.'

'Yes, please call me May,' she said, then cocked an eyebrow. 'An American called Washington? I can't believe it, are you related to the great man?'

'Distantly perhaps, but in spite of my Ma's attempt to link us up, the connection is still a family mystery.'

May smiled, realising that the duty of showing James Washington around the Morton factory might not be as tedious as she had feared. On the journey home, with Jenkins at the reins, she took pleasure in pointing out the sights – everything from the Tower of London to the costermongers and their barrows.

When they arrived at the factory James Washington watched the Fortis running.

'You sir,' he said to Frederick. 'You designed this engine?'

'I did.'

'Congratulations … it's a work of art,' he said.

Then, as he sat with May afterwards, studying the specifications he asked, 'So what's your role in all this?'

'Here at the factory, I do a bit of everything, really, but in three years I'll be a qualified engineer.'

'Great, we'll be equals.'

May hid her face for a moment.

'Did I say something wrong?'

'No. You're just the very first person who didn't say, "But you're a woman. How can you be an engineer?"'

★★★

That night they ate at the Coach and Horses with Frederick, Clare, Vic Jones, and his wife Allie. The visiting American laughed at the sight of pie floaters and thick pasties, and enjoyed a hearty ale along with the other men.

They talked engines and the future – internal combustion and electricity – but mainly the design evolution of the three Morton engines.

Forty-eight hours later, the young engineer boarded the train for his return to New York. To May's surprise he kissed her on the cheek.

'Thank you,' he said. 'I've enjoyed your company ... and if ever you'd like to visit New York ... I'd be happy to return the favour.'

'I'm pretty busy with study and the factory, but you never know—'

The American grinned, 'No, you don't. But I'll be hoping.'

After finding his seat on the train he opened the window. 'Perhaps I can call a building after you,' he grinned. 'How does the Maytower sound?'

May smiled all the way back to the factory, but when her father called her into his office, she realised that those few days had been just a short respite. Things were growing difficult – creditors were pressing for payment. While spending had skyrocketed with the overseas expansion, orders had yet to compensate, and through it all Lord Forgill hovered like a vulture.

Frederick confided in May that it was time to do the unthinkable.

★★★

The decision to lay off staff came hard – it was such a terrible backward step. Frederick endured a sleepless night then set off for work early, trying to pretend that it was just a normal day. He greeted his workers as they arrived, smiling at the familiar sight of the men warming their hands at the furnaces, talking of the day's tasks before settling down to their work.

'Gentlemen, please,' Frederick said, walking through the facility and asking them to assemble. 'I must talk to you on a matter of both gravity and urgency.'

The word passed to those who hadn't heard, some not yet in their aprons and others already grimy from work. They gathered near the unfinished prototype Imperium engine, the machine that was both the company's crowning achievement and one of the reasons for the current cash flow crisis.

From youngest to oldest, Frederick felt the intensity of their relationship. Each face held a place in his heart, a story of their meeting, the challenges they had accepted and won through as employer and employee, and in many cases, friends. These men were family.

'I have some very bad news; I'm afraid to say that this is the last week in which I can be sure to pay the full complement of salaries. Therefore,' his voice cracked, 'I have no option but to let some of you go.'

The men stared, stony-faced back at Frederick, others cringed as if struck with a cane. One or two groaned.

'I will keep on just Mister Jones, two stokers to keep the engine going, Brown and Tarrant, and Mighell, Leigh and Druitt in the foundry. He went on and on in a monotone, area by area, seeing the slumping shoulders and shaking heads.

'Somehow we will try to fill the small number of orders we have – four in total – and perhaps, if more sales come in, we can start to hire once more.

'At the front office you will be able to collect your wages as usual, along with a small bonus – all I can manage to help tide you over while you find a new job.'

'I don't want a new job,' called one of the men. 'I want to work here.'

Frederick looked at the speaker. 'No one is more sorry than me, but I cannot let you work so much as one hour without pay.' He was not, in general, a bitter man, yet he could not help a flare of that emotion. The need to lay off staff was due to a combination of factors, none of which he had dreamed to be possible a few years ago. All could be blamed on Percy Forgill.

'What will happen to the factory, sir?' someone asked.

Sighing, Frederick opted for honesty and full disclosure. 'In three weeks' time a repayment will fall due, and we must somehow try to honour it. If we can't, there will be no public share offer. The Morton Steam Power Company will be no more.'

Frederick paid the last wage for most of the workers out himself, shaking each man by the hand and wishing them well.

When it was done he went to his office and sat in the chair that somehow, over the years, had seemed to mould itself to his back. It fitted like an old shoe. This factory had become part of him, and he part of it. Now it was all in vain. Soon he would have to speak to Ned Baring and cancel the float.

After a while, May came in and sat on the other side of his desk, and Jones followed. Both wore grim expressions.

'I've asked that we keep full steam while we see what we can do with a skeleton crew,' Jones said.

'Thanks, old friend,' said Frederick. 'A warning though, I might only be able to pay you for another week or two – to let you go would break my heart, but it wouldn't hurt for you to start looking around for other opportunities.'

May planted her elbows on the desk and looked at her father. 'Well at least you're stuck with me.'

'That's one of the few good things I can think of.'

'We still need to finish the Imperium,' she said. 'Can we do it?'

Frederick nodded sagely. 'Let's hope so. But your brothers and sister will need to sell some engines to give us breathing space.'

May reached across the desk to take her father's hand. 'We have to trust that they can get those sales for us.'

Frederick looked stricken. 'I should not have sent them overseas like this, particularly little Harriet.'

'Father,' said May. 'You underestimate them. They want to fight for this. I want to fight for this. The factory is our future too.'

★★★

At the break-of-gauge in Albury Denny and Sam transferred to a river boat for the next leg of the journey. The *Starling* was not the largest paddle steamer on the Murray River, but a grand vessel nonetheless, with three decks including a wheelhouse and promenade deck. A wood-burner like most of the river boats, her stack streamed dark smoke and sparks and her crew had a business-like air as they readied her for departure at the Albury jetty.

On board, Sam and Denny found themselves in a cabin shared with eight other men, furnished with floor-to-ceiling bunks and scarcely enough floor space to walk between them. It mattered little, for the passengers were soon on the generous top deck, dodging overhanging tree branches, watching the Albury wharf recede and the wondrous river beckon.

'I could get used to this,' said Sam, opening a bottle of beer and pouring two glasses. Over the coming days that sentiment proved to be true, for the majestic inland river flowed like silk through a unique landscape.

Sam used his binoculars to spot galahs and gang-gang cockatoos in the trees, and cormorants fishing in the shallows or drying their wings on branches of the dark-hued snags that lurked everywhere from alongside the banks to the middle of the stream.

Powerful and rhythmic, the *Starling*'s engines carried them through the narrows of the Barmah Choke, past the picturesque junction with the Goulburn River, then Echuca – the multi-layered dock complex of Victoria's second-busiest port. A quarter-mile of river was host to shipyards, freight and passenger agents, and dozens of large vessels. The jetties themselves were a three-storey network, braced by a scaffold of straight and diagonal logs.

Many of the passengers headed for one of the adjacent pubs, but Denny was content to sit on the promenade deck and watch this strange world, while the mate waxed lyrical about the 'Chicago of the Murray.'

Finally, with her holds full, the *Starling* slid back into the river, and the encircling arms of the river red gums. These grand old trees twisted and warped their way skywards, broad and pitted and gnarled and studded with boles so that each individual seemed to have won its place in a hard-fought battle. In alignment with these ancient beings, it seemed to Denny that the mad pace of life slowed, suddenly, into a magical rhythm, where time moved at the speed of two lazy paddlewheels and the steam engine that drove them.

★★★

Back in Albury, Crydley had waited until Denny Morton and his companion had boarded, then thrust his hands into his pockets and looked out along both jetties, searching through the many private boats that he could see alongside. Walking down and along the rows he found two men lounging on the dock adjacent to a fast-looking screw-driven launch.

'Hey there gents,' he said. 'Are you up for a charter?'

The older of the two scrambled to his feet. He was an interesting specimen, with a long snowy beard, yellow brown from pipe smoke around his lips. 'Depends on the colour of your money.'

Crydley dug into his pocketbook and extracted a Bank of New South Wales five-pound note. 'How's this for a start?'

The older man took the note, made a concertina of it, and snapped it hard. Satisfied, he stowed it in his pocket. 'Where do you want to go?'

Crydley swung his meagre swag into the boat and pointed downstream. 'That way. Probably at least to Mildura. Perhaps further.'

'That's five hunnert river miles, mate. I won't do it for less 'an ten quid – an' you'll need to be prepared to swing an axe with us when we run low on timber for the firebox.'

'Done,' said Crydley. 'Can we say an hour from now we cast off?'

'Make it two,' said the owner. 'It'll take us that long to provision an' get up a full 'ead of steam.'

★★★

Through days of gentle but steady breezes, Matthew and Jules drifted over the grasslands of Southern Africa, domain of the cattle-herders. Proud men and women stared upwards at the striped balloon as it sailed overhead. The cries of children carried over the soft whistle of wind in the cords and the moaning flap of the envelope as it moved and adjusted, catching the breeze in places, and shedding it in others.

They flew over lakes with hippos heaving from the water like living boulders, and dark crocodiles haunting the shallows. Matthew spotted lions resting around the gutted remnants of their kill, and hyenas lurking, waiting for the pride to move on.

The pair ate little and talked much, bringing the balloon down low over rivers or lakes to scoop water, using a bucket on a rope, or frantically gaining height to clear mountain ranges. Matthew had always thought of Africa's interior as some vast jungle, but the reality was that it changed constantly from grassy plains to the scattered shards of stone-cast hills, then distant mountain tops.

Several times each day, Jules would set the balloon down to answer calls of nature, and, on one occasion to barter for fresh, golden ears of corn and aromatic dried goat meat from terrified Bantu villagers. These gentle people fascinated Matthew with their striped cloaks, hair plastered with sheep's fat, and ebony disks set into their earlobes.

Less frequently, a more important ritual took place. Jules would bring the balloon down on a plain, looking carefully for possible hazards such as lions. Using a suitably sized anchor he would tether the craft, then unpack a box of equipment from the bottom of the basket. Working together, they would make more coal gas to keep their craft aloft. It was magical, Matthew always thought as he operated the foot-pump, to watch the envelope fill and become taut, straining at the tethering ropes as if it were alive.

The breezes carried them to the north as Jules had predicted. Sometimes they would spend an hour or more in silence. Later, Matthew would look back on these days as some of the happiest and least complicated of his life.

On the fifth day out of Kimberley the wind dropped, becoming the gentlest of zephyrs. There, hanging in the doldrums, they drifted over something so unexpected and dramatic that Matthew knew he would never see anything like it again.

'Look below,' cried Jules.

Matthew looked, and he saw that they were passing over a broad river, flowing like liquid silk, populated by hippopotami in their hundreds.

'This must be the Zambezi,' cried Jules. 'I've dreamed of this moment, and I was sorry I missed it on my way south.'

Then, in a gut-swooping sight, the huge river dropped, in a dozen separate streams, over a vast rift in the earth, with a mist of spray climbing to the heavens.

Matthew had goosebumps pricking at his skin as he clutched at the hemp cords of the balloon. It occurred to him that he and Jules might be the first humans to see this sight from the air – the great Victoria Falls in their entirety. The view was spectacular beyond words, and together they peered down through the spray and into the dark gorges below.

'Nothing else will ever compare to what I see right now,' said Matthew. 'This moment will stay with me forever, and I have you to thank for it.'

'New friends and new places,' said Jules.

'What could be better?' Matthew grinned, 'As Emily Dickinson stated so well, "My friends are my estate, forgive me then the avarice to hoard them."'

'Well put!' said Jules. 'Now do you recall Alexander Dumas's musings on the subject? "Friendship consists in forgetting what one gives and remembering what one receives."'

'I haven't read that one – but I shall next chance I get. Now here's one more. My father is a great fan of the American writer Mark Twain and often quotes him. He says, "Grief can take care of itself, but to get the full value of joy you must have somebody to divide it with."'

Jules repeated the words, a smile on his face, looking back so as not to miss one moment of the river dropping into a hole in the earth. Then, however, the balloon buffeted to a new wind, from a new direction.

'The wind is changing,' he cried. 'And now we're going to take you home to Cape Town.'

Chapter Forty-five

As if morning sickness wasn't enough, a new and virulent nausea hinted at its presence soon after the SS *Vesuvius* steamed out of the Thames. By the time the ship entered the North Sea and rounded the cliffs of the peninsular it had reached full voice. Off the coast of France Eadie lay in her cot, while other, unaffected passengers lined the deck to view the lights of Calais. Seasickness became her companion, her torment, and a bitter enemy.

The first week was uncomfortable, but from the fortieth parallel, when they steamed into the Mediterranean, the air grew balmy and hot, and Eadie's mind had far too many empty hours to fill with treacherous thoughts. Sweat dampening her forehead and cheeks, she worried about how Denny might receive her, imagined all the eligible young women he must have met in the colony of New South Wales.

Getting on a boat and going to Australia had seemed like a good idea. Now, particularly in the dark mornings with the ship pitching, it seemed like a horrendous mistake. What if he didn't want her anymore? The thought tortured her.

She wrote in her diary:

The woman on the waves,
The new life, the being who grows inside.
But would she be welcome in the antipodes,

when she saw him again?

The words gave her no solace, and the endless sea had no answers. Despite the hundreds of passengers who packed the dining saloon, and the company of the three other ladies who shared her cabin, she had never in her life felt more alone.

★★★

After hundreds of river miles lined with trees, then endless reed beds around Swan Hill, the *Starling* reached the Port of Mildura, where a deputation from the Progress Committee was waiting. This tidy little group was led by William Chaffey: a well-dressed and dapper gent with a Canadian accent. He had a sun-browned, somewhat lean face, with long, narrow sideburns and a neat moustache.

First on the agenda was a flying tour of the irrigation blocks surrounding the town. 'We've taken up a quarter of a million acres of riverfront land,' Chaffey explained. 'My brother Charles is cultivating a similar area downriver at Renmark, South Australia, and he's interested in what you have on offer, also.'

Denny found the rows of pine-log workers' houses, and vast blocks of red soil fascinating. Most particularly he liked the use of modern technology – giant traction engines pulling disc ploughs or scooping out irrigation channels. This was a major investment, demonstrating the kind of can-do attitude he loved to see and be part of.

Upriver, at Psyche Bend, Chaffey showed them a colossal stone pump house, where an equally colossal beam engine blasted water up into King's Billabong, from which it gravity-fed into the network of channels already in operation.

'I designed the pumps myself,' said Chaffey, 'and had them built, along with the engines, in Birmingham, but I have to admit that they're not efficient. If your company's Fortis engines can reduce coal consumption by thirty per cent, I'd be a fool not to consider them for this role, particularly if the installation is not as expensive as it was for these old girls.'

'We ship our Fortis engines complete,' Denny informed him. 'Installation requires a concrete slab, and shelter from the elements. For your application simply couple the engine to one of the excellent new centrifugal pumps made right here in Australia by the firm of Tangyes.'

'That's a powerful combination,' said one of Chaffey's managers. 'What kind of flow rate are we talking?'

The engineers at Tangyes had worked through the figures for just such a question. 'Well, let's say you couple our four-hundred-horsepower Fortis to a twenty-four-inch Tangyes centrifugal, and work on the assumption that it's sited with a suction lift of ten feet and a total head of fifty. With thirty-inch steel pipe installed you will deliver close to a million gallons of water every hour onto your farm.' Silence, then some slow whistles. 'And it will do it using thirty percent less coal than a Forgill's or Garrett engine.'

At the end of the meeting, William Chaffey requested a full set of schematic drawings to help him decide on the technical prowess of the machines, and Denny had the distinct feeling that the canny Canadian was interested in copying Morton and Tangyes technology, rather than handing over a deposit cheque.

★★★

Chaffey had rooms booked for Denny and Sam in Mildura's sprawling Coffee Palace, with its twenty odd rooms upstairs and a commodious café downstairs. In any other town there would have been five or six pubs nearby, but Mildura was, it was turning out, nothing less than a Chaffey company town – and temperance was a big part of the ethos.

'No grog!' complained Sam, 'not even a beer.'

'Not a drop in the town at all,' said Denny. 'The Chaffeys are abstainers, so they make the whole town follow suit.'

'A ridiculous idea,' said Sam. 'What in the name of blazes are they thinkin'?'

★★★

The next morning Denny stood with Sam on the heavy boards at the jetty's edge, looking upstream along a quarter mile of the broad Murray River, hoping for a glimpse of dark smoke from the stack of their new waterborne conveyance. Their luggage was piled on the docks beside them ready for loading, and the pleasant sound of a magpie carolling further up the embankment competed against the sounds of workers constructing a new jetty – chiselling mortises and boring holes in piles.

'Excuse me, Mister Morton,' came a voice from up towards the Harbour Master's office. Denny turned to see a man in a bowler hat, grubby dungarees and a grey suit jacket hurrying towards him, waving a slip of paper and slowing as he neared. 'Bad news, I'm afraid sir. I just received a telegram from the Harbour Master in Echuca. The *Florence Annie* won't be coming. She struck a snag near Robinvale and is in port for repairs.'

Denny turned to look at Sam, who had his pipe in his mouth, looking unamused. 'That's damned inconvenient. Are there any other steamers due? If we're to be in Broken Hill in five days, we need to disembark in Menindee in three at the most.'

The Harbour Master shook his head. 'Nothing more today sir – oh there are work boats, and perhaps a hawking steamer coming and going. One might take you up a few miles here and there, but it will be tortuous going and you'd be constantly stopping.'

While they were talking the pilot wandered across from the other side of the jetty, hands in his pockets. He cut a Bohemian figure at conservative Mildura, with his long hair tied back with a leather band. 'There was a fellow down here last night looking for crew for a run up the Darling past Wilcannia.'

The Harbour Master made a noise in his nostrils. 'Lew Grant, was it?'

'That's him.'

He turned to Denny. 'Lew's a partner in a couple of stations, one just downriver from here, and the other up the Darling. They use a paddle steamer to move stores between the two runs and for ferrying wool to market. Both the other partners – they're brothers – are married but Lew's a hard-bitten single man – not easy to get along with and I don't trust him, but … if you really want to get there.'

'Did he manage to find any crew?'

The harbourmaster shook his head. 'Nah, probably not. Lew doesn't like to pay rivermen's wages – working unsuspecting passengers to the bone is more his style. You thinking of giving him a try?'

'I might as far as Menindee,' said Denny. 'This Lew Grant could find some new men there perhaps?'

The pilot opened his hands, 'I'm happy to run you down to him in the launch if you feel inclined – the little boiler is hot. I had it ready to guide the *Florence Annie* in, if it were needed.'

Again, Denny looked inquiringly at Sam. They had been friends for so long that no words needed to pass between them. 'That would be much appreciated,' he said at last.

They both heard the sound of an engine coming from downriver, and a small steam-driven boat appeared around the furthest bend, still a quarter mile distant. Denny could just make out a figure standing in the bow, and he felt a chill. It was strange, but he could feel his father's enemies reaching out towards him, from ten thousand miles away. He turned to the harbourmaster.

'Would you do me a favour please?'

'Yes, anything in my power.'

'If a man on board that boat asks if you've seen me, please don't let on that I've been here.'

The harbourmaster looked surprised. 'If that's what you wish.'

'Thank you.' Denny picked up the handle of his nearest suitcase and followed the pilot across the jetty.

'What was that all about?' Sam asked as they walked.

'Just a hunch,' said Denny.

★★★

The pilot's launch was a twenty-six-footer, the engine spinning a bronze, three-bladed prop, the flat-bottomed hull drawing just thirty-six inches of water. With three men on board, it moved along at a crisp seven knots. The pilot knew every snag, every bar, and pointed out birds from shags to corellas. They passed station landings, many with skiffs or punts tied up alongside.

Finally, they came to a rough jetty dominated by one of the grandest river red gums Denny had seen, with a stately bird of prey occupying a high branch, gazing imperiously up and down the river.

'I believe it must be a white-breasted sea eagle,' said Sam, who had purchased a field guide to Australian birds before they left Sydney and thumbed through it at every opportunity.

'You're right sir,' said the pilot. 'That's what she is. Every day, like as not, you'll find her up on that same limb.'

Of more immediate interest to Denny was a curious vessel tied up at the jetty. It was a paddle steamer, but of an unusual type known as a stern-wheeler, with a single powered wheel aft, abutting the engine room. A hand-painted sign on the sides of the cabin read 'SPS *Tamar*.' The unofficial Murray River flag flew from the masthead – a red cross and three horizontal white bars.

The boiler, situated on the port beam, was a curious beast of a thing, of no recognisable design type, and oblong in shape. It was, nevertheless, building steam, with smoke pouring from the stack and a wave of heat haze emanating skywards, broiling the overhanging leaves and filling the air with a strong scent of eucalyptus.

Forward of the engine was a timber cabin with a wheelhouse above, surrounded by hundreds of square feet of deck space. An iron cage sat on the deck, and inside were six of the stateliest looking, albeit unsettled, merino rams Denny had seen since his arrival in the colony. A couple of men hurried here and there, loading the vessel up with equipment and provisions.

As the pilot cut the engine and glided the launch in towards the jetty, a man with the frame of an ageing welterweight, and muscled arms to match, hurried across. He cushioned the bow from striking the jetty timbers, manipulated the craft side-on with his hands, then lashed it to an iron bollard with a sheet.

'Good day there, Mister Preston,' he cried, feet braced wide apart.

'Mornin' Lew,' returned the pilot. 'You look like you're about ready to cast off.'

'Very close sir,' Lew returned. He was, Denny estimated, about forty-five, with a horseshoe moustache, and stubble on the remainder of his face. He kept a briar pipe in the corner of his mouth, and the smell of rough tobacco surrounded him like a cloud. His eyes were dark brown, gave the impression of missing nothing, and never left Denny and Sam throughout the exchange.

'You're taking livestock this trip?' asked the pilot.

'Yes sir, six beauties fresh from the saleyards, worth twenty guineas apiece and new blood for up at Wyehala.' His eyes rested on Denny and Sam in turn. 'Wyehala is our run up on the Darling. Those damn ewes won't know what hit them — never seen a fresher bunch of lads. We had to cage them last night to keep them out of a paddock of cull ewes we're holdin' near the homestead.'

'We've heard you need crew?' said Denny.

'It'd be preferable for this journey, yes, but you'd need to work — it aren't a free ride.'

'We don't mind work,' said Denny.

'Any experience?'

'Not much on board a boat,' said Denny, 'but I'm a foundryman in a stationary steam engine factory back home. I can feed a firebox as well as the next fellow and also perform basic maintenance. The trouble is that we can only stay with you as far as Menindee.'

'Menindee will be a good help anyhow. It shouldn't be hard to pick up some help for the last leg, and if we lay on a good store of wood before we lose you, Pedro and I might be able to manage.' He paused to puff away at his pipe. 'I don't mind sayin' that some engine skills will be advantageous.' Lew moved his gaze onto Sam. 'What about you?'

'I go where he goes,' said Sam.

Lew looked him up and down. 'You look a bit soft. Can yez swing an axe?'

'Well enough, I'd say,' said Sam.

Lew spat into the river. 'I can't afford to be choosy. Throw your gear aboard, both of yez.'

The pilot helped unload their belongings then took his leave. 'See you next time,' he said, then took the tiller and backed away from the jetty, out into the stream and away.

Lew watched the man go for a moment, arms folded across his chest, then called the other crew member over to meet them. This was a very slight, hollow-cheeked young man with an old arm injury, evidenced by scar tissue around his bicep, down past his elbow. Denny and Sam shook hands with him in turn.

'This is Pedro,' said Lew. 'If he don't do what yez tell 'im, clip 'im on the ear nice and firm.'

★★★

Apart from Lew's cabin, which was on the upper level adjacent to the wheelhouse, the sleeping quarters were shared – four cramped bunks in a cupboard-space below. Made of pit-sawn river red gum logs, it was a grimy space, and dark even in daylight.

'Top or bottom bunk?' Denny asked, tapping a straw mattress with the flat of his hand.

'Bottom if you don't mind,' said Sam. 'The closer to the ground – or should I say the waterline – the better as far as I'm concerned.'

Denny swung his things up onto the top bunk. 'No problem, I'll get a better view out the little window.'

Moving back out on deck, Denny had a look at the engine. It was a two-cylinder compound horizontal model of dubious ancestry – no maker's name cast in the iron, but it seemed sound enough. The drive for the paddle wheel was simple: a belt from the flywheel to a reduction pulley. The paddle wheel itself was situated within a cut-away section of deck. Denny had seen stern-wheelers on the Thames. There were some advantages over side-paddles, particularly when it came to narrow waterways, but they were less responsive to command, being steered with a rudder, and were not suitable for towing barges.

The firebox was burning very hot, for the boiler's seams were venting small quantities of steam. The needle was steady at a little under twenty-eight pounds per square inch and a sign – hand stamped on copper sheet in bold letters said, 'DO NOT EXCEED 30 PSI.'

Still, it seemed to be holding up, and judging from the state of the seams it was more likely to split than to explode, not that Denny wanted to be anywhere near such an event when and if it happened.

'Righto,' cracked Lew's voice from the wheelhouse. 'You, Denny, oil round and check the ash pans. Pedro, get in some wood. Sam! Stand by to throw off the lines.'

The crew hurried to their tasks and within a few minutes the *Tamar* was free and clear of the jetty, moving out into the centre of the stream and reaching full speed. The paddlewheel, being located so far aft, Denny found, had the effect of lifting the stern slightly, pushing the bow down and sloping the deck forwards. Lew's prize rams were not keen on the sensation, let alone being surrounded by water on the mighty Murray, and all six gave voice to their dissatisfaction.

The trim, it soon became obvious, was awry, with a list to starboard, and the first few hours were spent repositioning crates of stores to rectify the issue. The rams had to be supplied with hay and water, and the firebox with fuel. Denny had not seen a wood-fired boiler for some years, and he was astounded at the calorific energy of the dry river red gum logs. When he said as much to Pedro, the deckhand grinned a white-toothed grin. 'Good wood. Best wood.'

★★★

At the junction with the Darling River, Denny and Sam saw the two mighty rivers became one. Here, the clay-tinged outback tide of the flooded Darling met the cleaner, lighter Murray. The two colours, Denny saw, did not mix at first, but flowed side by side for some distance.

The entrance to the Darling was a true hairpin turn, guarded by a mud bank, and Lew used the rudder at full lock, allowing the stronger current of the Murray to push the aft end downstream before piling on the power so the stern-wheeler turned into the junction and entered the Darling. The town of Wentworth appeared on both banks of the river, and at the same time a sleek customs launch moved out to intercept them.

'Damn them,' shouted Lew. 'New South Bloody Wales Customs. Harrassin' me like every time.'

The cutter drew alongside, and a voice boomed out from a loudhailer. 'Heave to there, *Tamar*.'

Lew did as he was told, coming down from the wheelhouse to stand on the edge of the deck, hands on his hips and snarling at the customs men. 'I've told you vultures before. I don't carry goods for sale, we're stocking the damn station.'

'You're registered in the colony of Victoria, sir. We 'ave every right to search you.'

Despite Lew's protestations a uniformed and slouch-hatted officer stepped aboard and effected a search, looking for hidden trade goods, and making an official estimate of what products might be sold in the station store at the destination, calculating the colony's percentage share of the value then demanding payment of four pounds and ten shillings on the spot.

For ten miles afterwards Lew's mood was dark, shouting at Pedro to keep the firebox hot and at Sam for slouching in the shade. Within the hour, however, the captain picked up a bottle of rum from a fully stocked compartment that the customs officer had not found, and began to drink from a tooth glass, refilling constantly.

"Ere you,' he shouted at Denny. 'Take the 'elm.'

Denny climbed the ladder somewhat reluctantly. He had not, quite so soon, expected to find himself in control of a river boat – given that he was expected to operate the craft alone with no instruction. Still, the controls were simple enough, and it was only a matter of getting used to the handling. The view through the glass windows of the wheelhouse was superb, with snags visible at or just below the surface at fifty or more yards distance. The rudder, Denny found, was slow to steer the hull, and a movement of the wheel was needed well in advance of requirements for navigation.

At first, he was nervous, backing off the regulator, staring ahead, looking out for floating logs, snags and mud bars, but after a while he relaxed somewhat, and began to enjoy driving the boat, while the river and its surrounds entranced him.

The Darling had high sloping banks on either side, trees clinging to the muddy slopes with their roots exposed like skeletons. The layers of soil showed the aeons of time in which the river had flowed – different shades telling tales of past floods, fires and good seasons. The grand river red gums were populated with screeching white corellas, while the water itself flowed so slowly it seemed, to Denny's eyes, to stand completely still.

Twice, on the first day out of Mildura, they were overtaken by faster paddle steamers heading upstream. One was towing a barge loaded with farm machinery bound for the Port of Bourke. The seamen waved and shouted this information, and even a few ribald jokes that were doing the rounds as they passed.

'Hey boys,' cried one wag. 'Here's a joke for yez. Well, Mama catches her little boy with a shillin' coin. "Where did ya get that?" she asks. "Father Murphy," he says. "Well, I 'ope you remembered yer manners and thanked 'im."'

The joke teller stretched out the silence, broken only by the cycling of the engines, then delivered the punchline: "Well I didn't really thank 'im. I just promised I won't tell Pa that I seen you and 'im cuddlin' up naked in the vestibule."'

The other crew, as seemed to be a regular thing, kept up the laughter, jokes and news of the river ahead until distance made it impossible.

By the time it grew too dark for safe navigation, Lew, now thoroughly drunk, ordered a halt for the night. Pedro, with Sam's inexpert help, secured them, fore and aft, to snags near the western bank. The deckhand then cooked up a tasty stew, and afterwards threw his swag on the deck to give the two friends privacy in the cabin.

Sam, it seemed, was not so enamoured of their second steamboat, and disliked their little cabin with just a single small window on each side. He lit half a dozen candles to supplement the single slush lantern. 'This cabin is too dingy for my liking, he said. 'It reminds me of that horrible death ship out on the Indian Ocean.'

'Just relax,' said Denny. 'That was a very different time and place.'

'I know,' said Sam, 'but I still don't like it – and Lew's a bastard, isn't he?'

'Most definitely, but we can live with it for a few days, don't you think?'

Yet, there were ghosts here too, and even Denny could almost see them around the river that night. Outside on the deck the river was an eerie sight, with side-curtains of curling trees, the cloudless sky alive with stars, and the river a dark-purple pathway through the interior.

The next morning Sam became more cheerful as he took his first stint at the helm. Denny made coffee for all hands and carried a mug up to his friend.

'Are you handling it alright?'

Sam turned and grimaced, hands tight on the wheel. 'It's not too bad at this speed – still trying to get used to it.'

'Speed it up a bit will yeh?' called Lew from below.

Denny stood next to him, hands on the dash. 'Just try bumping the revolutions up slightly. You'll find that she handles better.'

★★★

At intervals throughout the day, they passed station jetties signposted with the names of the adjacent stations – Tapeo, Billabong, Parra, Illengary, and a dozen others. Occasionally people waved from the banks. Sometimes too, they saw camps of Aborigines, dressed in ragged old breeches and shirts, furs and plaited things, their wurlies made of bark and logs. Some carried spears or other implements and stared at the passing boat impassively.

Denny saw skiffs or dinghies drawn up on the banks, and at one, a thin dark-skinned boy was walking up the bank, dragging a river cod almost as big as a calf behind him.

In the mid-afternoon, spotting one of these camps, Lew beached the Tamar against a muddy bar, and dug some plug tobacco and a bottle of rum from one of his secret hatches. Thus equipped, he hopped down from the bow and sloshed ashore through the shallows. A full-bearded, gnarled white man, and several Aborigines came to the top bank to meet him.

The sounds of raised voices, haggling and arguing followed. Lew and the others faded from view. When they reappeared a few minutes later the *Tamar*'s skipper was holding the arm of a young Aboriginal woman, barefooted and wearing a cheap print dress. Lew lifted her up on to the bow with a grip around her middle, then followed, using the rail to raise himself.

'Pedro,' he called. 'Take the 'elm and point us north. As soon as I grab meself another bottle of rum I've got business in me cabin.'

Denny wandered around from where he had been sitting in the shade with Sam, looked at the young woman, who stood at the base of the ladder as the *Tamar* steamed away from the bank and turned upstream.

Tears flowed from her eyes, each of them as deep and brown as the river. Now and then she turned to look at the bank, where a young man of around her age was running, shadowing them along from the upper bank. With a nauseous plunge Denny realised that he was a brother or husband, obviously not complicit in whatever deal had just been done.

Denny turned to the captain as he returned with another bottle. 'You bought her?'

'I didn't buy her forever, just up to Wilcannia maybe, as long as I feel like it, or until I get another one. Not bad for a couple of plugs of baccy and a bottle of grog, eh?' He used a stained forefinger to raise her lip. 'Good teeth, too, for a lubra.'

'Let her go,' said Denny.

Lew spat. 'I will not.'

'Let her go,' the young Englishman repeated. 'I won't sit by while people are bought and sold.'

Lew took a swing at Denny, a bar-room haymaker that would have hurt if it connected. The intended target ducked, then drove his fist into the other man's solar plexus. Lew sank to the deck, a pained expression on his face.

Ignoring him now, Denny took the woman's hand, 'Can you swim?'

She stared back at him, without expression, then walked to the edge of the deck. From there she dived gracefully into the river. With relief Denny watched her swim to the bank, where she left the water and began to walk towards the man who had followed, not looking at the riverboat again.

The captain was coming to his feet, and Denny had no desire to continue the fight. 'I'll make good the cost of the tobacco and rum,' he said, 'but I won't sit by and see people treated like that.'

Lew scowled, 'Watch your back, Morton. I'll wait my chance.'

★★★

The next day, their third on the *Tamar*, it was almost eleven according to the wheelhouse chronometer when Denny, who had been re-stacking wood near the firebox, glanced astern and saw a smaller launch following. It was a screw-driven craft, with a chuff of steam and dark line of smoke from the stack. The man standing in the bow with a telescope looked familiar.

Denny walked forward to where Lew was supervising Sam in feeding hay to the rams. 'Look after the damn things,' the captain was shouting. 'Thirty guineas apiece they were.'

'You said twenty before,' Sam pointed out.

'None of your cheek now.'

'Excuse me,' Denny interrupted, 'but I think I'd better warn you. We may have a problem.'

'What?' Lew spat.

'There's a boat behind us – it seems like quite a fast one, and there's a man on board who looks like one who caused us some mischief in the Yemen.'

Lew said nothing at first, but walked drunkenly up the ladder to the wheelhouse, returning with a pair of brass Merz binoculars. Then, with Denny following he headed aft, standing at the rail beside the enclosed paddlewheel. From there he looked back through the twin optics.

'Who are they?'

'I don't know exactly. Business rivals. Can I have a look?' Denny took the instrument, held it to his eyes, and used the focus ring to make the image clear. The man he was looking at was a familiar one.

He noted the dark beard, that had regrown since Aden, but the heavy brows and boxer's crooked nose could not be disguised. 'It's him, alright – the one who tried to make fools of us in the Yemen. I can only assume that he means to do us harm. If you wish to put Sam and I ashore to take our chances I understand.'

'Oh, I wouldn't do that.' Lew made a sly grin and walked to the ladder, heading up into the wheelhouse. 'But they're goin' to a lot of trouble. They must want you real bad.'

While he was gone the *Tamar* rounded a bend, unfolding a wide straight stretch of smooth brown water and overhanging trees. Lew came back down the ladder holding a double-barrelled shotgun in his hands.

'No,' Denny said. 'Don't start some kind of shootout with them.'

Lew turned to him; his lips pushed together so hard he had a new dimple on his chin. 'Now why would I do that?' Instead, he levelled the weapon at Sam and Denny. 'I'd rather do some bargaining.' He called up to Pedro. 'Heave to,' he shouted, and a moment later the paddle wheel stopped turning. Then, to Denny and Sam. 'Sit down on deck, right there, both of you, and don't move a muscle.'

'What are you playing at?' asked Denny, but the skipper ignored him, waiting for the pursuing launch to come up, still holding the shotgun. The *Tamar* wallowed in the dying wake of both vessels as the launch came to a halt, some twenty yards off the starboard quarter.

'Are you looking for someone?' Lew shouted.

Tommy Crydley cupped his hands and replied. 'Yes, we want Morton, yonder. Pass him over to us and we'll be on our way.'

'What's your price?' Lew growled.

'What do you mean?'

'How much money is he worth to you? If you're not willing to pay, I'll take him with me. He's handy on board.'

Crydley whipped a revolver from a holster and levelled it across the water at Lew, who laughed it off and swung his shotgun to cover the man. 'I aren't scared of your little squirt. Try it and the fish will be eatin' bits of yer guts, all over the damned river.'

Denny noted, meanwhile, that the breeze was taking them towards the far bank. The players in this little drama, it seemed, were now oblivious to his presence – more worried that the other man might open fire. Finally, Crydley must have understood the weakness of his position. 'How much do you want?'

'Let's say twenty quid for both of them.'

'I only want Morton.'

'Fifteen quid then.'

One of the other men on the boat broke in. 'For fuck's sake pay 'im the money. We've come far enough as it is.'

'Alright, fifteen pounds, but bring him here before I pay you.'

Lew shook his head slowly. 'Nah. Money first. Show it to me.'

Crydley removed a pocketbook and counted out fifteen pounds in notes. 'Alright, we're coming in close now.'

A moment later the two hulls touched. Lew leaned forward to place his right foot on the launch's gunwale while retaining his balance on the *Tamar* with his left. Thus positioned, he reached out for the money.

The hull of the *Tamar*, still moving with the breeze, struck a snag, the impact of which caused it to shake from hull to mast. It wasn't much, but enough to throw Lew off balance, forcing him to step with his left foot down into the launch to stop himself from falling.

Denny didn't waste time thinking, just leapt to his feet and ran aft to the engine, and the manual regulator. It was connected by cable to the wheelhouse but was just as easily controlled from the engine end.

It was perhaps ten paces away, and he was halfway there when he saw Lew realise what was happening. The captain was still struggling for balance, however, seemingly unsure whether to fire off a round with the shotgun or get back on board.

Denny was nothing if not fast. He reached the regulator and

opened it all the way. The boiler was fully pressured, and the effect was immediate – the paddle wheel churned like one of the big Sturtevant blowers at the Morton factory, and the *Tamar* lurched forwards, making it even harder for Lew to regain his position. The paddle steamer's bow pushed against the snag at first, rearing out of the water until the sheer force broke the snag off with a crash and the *Tamar* surged towards the middle of the river, while shouts rang out and the shotgun boomed, a spurt of gun smoke punching up into the air. Pellets rattled into the steamer.

At fifty- or sixty-yards distance, Denny released the regulator and headed for the ladder, running up past a white-faced Sam and to the wheelhouse, where he was expecting to have to deal with Pedro.

What he found, rather, was the thin Spaniard laughing to himself, smiling and taking control of the *Tamar*, directing it upstream with all speed. 'You captain now,' he said.

'It seems so.' Denny grinned back.

'Good work. Lew bad. Good work.'

'Now listen Pedro, we have to try to outrun these people, as they are going to be after us, and two of them have guns.'

Pedro held up his forefinger, and Denny nodded agreement. Lew had fired one barrel of his shotgun and would only have one shell left. That, at least, was some comfort.

He went below as the paddle steamer inched up to full speed. Sam, it seemed, had recovered himself, and had moved back to the engine, feeding the firebox.

'We're playing a dangerous game,' warned Denny. 'It's on thirty-one psi now and God knows if the boiler will take any more.'

'Isn't this piracy?' Sam asked.

'I imagine so,' said Denny, 'but the alternative didn't seem too attractive.'

'Are we going to be able to outpace them?'

Denny looked back at the pursuing launch, then again at the boiler. Drops sprayed from the paddlewheel, struck the iron surface and hissed like snakes. 'I don't think so.'

'They're gaining on us,' said Sam.

'Yes, they are.'

'We just have to keep feeding the boiler and hope it holds.'

'They're coming, they're coming,' shouted Pedro from the wheelhouse as Denny hurried for more of the two-foot lengths of wood. 'More steam, hurry.'

As if to punctuate this urgent cry, a number of revolver shots flew around them, though Lew seemed to be conserving the one unfired shell in his shotgun. The rams up forward, in their cage, seemed to catch something of the urgency, bleating and crashing into the bars.

Denny was cramming wood into the firebox and turning the air flow up to maximum, watching the gauge continue to climb. Slowly, as the red gum blocks roared with heat, the needle reached thirty-four, then thirty-five psi.

Pedro gave a yelp of excitement from above as the paddle wheel started spinning faster than it had in many years. Yet, steam was hissing through seams and rivet holes. Denny prayed it would not erupt. Now, more closely matched in speed, the two vessels raced neck and neck. Again, gunshots rang out while Denny headed back up to the wheelhouse.

'There's nothing else we can try?' asked Sam.

Denny used his hand to smooth the sweat back from his forehead. None I can think of, except maybe jettisoning some cargo.'

Denny was considering this idea when Pedro gave a hoot of glee, and the *Tamar* shot towards one bank, in a manoeuvre preparatory to a wide turn.

'What in blazes are you doing?' asked Denny. The boat was rocking dangerously, catching a small snag on the turn and tilting to port. By the time it stabilised Pedro had finished with the turn, and was bearing down at speed on the launch, which was now, swathed with black smoke, attempting to take evasive action.

'No Pedro, don't,' but as Denny climbed the steps and reached for the wheel it was too late. Crydley fired some desultory shots towards them, then all three men on the launch jumped overboard before the *Tamar* struck the smaller craft and crunched it under the hull with a terrible tearing sound.

By then Denny had wrested control of the wheel and Sam had come up also. Pedro was laughing, clapping Denny on the back.

'You captain now,' he said.

They paused for long enough to make sure that their four erstwhile pursuers had reached the safety of a snag before Denny spun the *Tamar* around and headed upriver.

★★★

They do not see what happens next. Lew, furious, settles himself on the snag and points the shotgun, with its one loaded barrel, towards his own departing boat. The roar of the gun is a despairing one, for the range is too long for bird shot to accurately fly.

'You fool,' snarked Crydley, hanging on to the same half submerged branch as the former boat skipper. The others were already swimming towards the bank.

Lew lost control. Reversing the shotgun, he swung the butt down onto Crydley's temple, bashing him repeatedly, until the butt broke off the gun and the injured man, bleeding from several deep wounds in his head, released the snag and floated away in the current.

Chapter Forty-six

Occupying a new building on the Victoria Embankment, Scotland Yard was a Norman Shaw design, all rounded turrets and lines of white Portland stone running through the red brick. Big Ben loomed overhead in the distance.

Clare took a moment to admire the architecture as the brougham drew up at the main entrance. She was admitted to the waiting room by a helmeted bobby, and after proving her appointment with the letter in her hand, she was admitted to the office of Inspector Gerard Hatfield.

He waved her to a seat, then placed a pair of spectacles on his nose, armed with which, he appeared to study her. At length he settled back in the chair.

'Mrs Morton,' he began, 'how nice of you to travel so far to see me.'

'Thanks for agreeing to meet with me.'

'Now, getting straight to business. You raise the issue of a night long ago, almost half a century in fact, when you believe that a crime may have been committed – to wit, that Percy Forgill may have killed his brother, by pushing him down the stairs.'

'Yes,' said Clare, 'and I know there may be some reluctance to pursue this case given that they are a noble family—'

Hatfield cut her off with a wave of his hand. 'No Mrs Morton. No reluctance at all, I would arrest the Queen herself in the unlikely event that she committed a crime. The fact is, however, that this event has been investigated before, and the case closed – some thirty years ago, before my time. I have familiarised myself with the case files. Shall I enlighten you?'

Clare leaned forward. 'Please do.'

'A complaint was made by a former nurse, alleging that a criminal act was committed on the night in question. Are you aware of that?'

'No sir, I am not.'

'Very well then. Former staff and members of the family were interviewed, and in the end it was decided that there was not enough evidence to place charges for criminal behaviour, particularly since the possible offenders were underage at the time.'

Clare's eyebrows came together. 'You say offenders, not offender, why is that?'

'The nurse alleged that Percy and Sophie Forgill were both involved.'

Clare leaned back, a thoughtful expression on her face. 'I had not considered her involvement. What about the doctor who signed the death certificate? What did he say? I am in possession of his journals, and he too was struck with the possibility that Percy had at least caused the accident.'

'The Doctor, his name escapes me, was interviewed, and stuck to his story that the boy suffered a seizure on the stairs. This morning I had a chat to one of our older serving detectives, who was around at the time. There was some discussion, apparently, of exhuming the corpse and looking for corroboration, but the family put a stop to that.' He paused. 'I think, because of the amount of time between then and now, it's best to leave this investigation as it stands – they were just children and could scarcely be tried now for the crime.'

'At least they could be forced to acknowledge it,' said Clare.

'The evidence is not solid.'

'Will you tell me the name of the nurse and where she lives?'

'Her name is Eve Simpson,' Hatfield said. 'She lives at Leigh-on-Sea. As far as I know, she is still alive.'

★★★

In the glow of moonlight, occasionally consulting Lew's charts they motored the *Tamar* on all night, taking shifts to sleep between stoking and navigational duties. In the afternoon of the next day, with hundreds of miles between them and the boat's owner they nosed into the western bank north of Kinchega Station and prepared to abandon ship. Pedro had, some hours earlier, negotiated working passage on a steamer heading south, bound for Mannum, Lake Alexandrina and Goolwa.

'We can't leave those rams on board,' said Sam.

'Agreed,' said Denny. 'They've had a tough enough time as it is.' The two men wrestled the animals off the boat and into the muddy shallows, watching as they ran up the steep bank. Eager as they were to get away from the paddle steamer and the cage, the rams, nonetheless, appeared to be no worse for the trip.

With everything they needed, including their own luggage, now ashore, a naked Denny took the vessel out into the central channel and cut power, leaving it adrift so its owner, should he eventually find it, would not know where they had come ashore.

Swimming back to the bank using his efficient but unschooled stroke, Denny dressed in dry clothes. Heavily laden with luggage, the pair set off on foot for the town of Menindee, hoping to get some distance from the river before Lew found his vessel and started looking for them.

Kinchega Station, Denny had been told, had one of the few mechanised shearing sheds in Western New South Wales. He would have loved to divert from their path and have a look, but time was running out for the Broken Hill deal, and he wasn't keen on giving their position away so close to the river.

'The *Tamar*'s holds are empty of fuel,' said Denny. 'It'll take a day to chop a new supply. I don't think we'll have to worry about either Lew or Forgill's man again, and once we leave Menindee they'll never find us, even if they look.'

The semi-arid landscape, Denny found as they walked in from the bank, was fascinating. For the first few hundred paces, under the spell of the river red gums, they found a variety of green herbage, including tiny succulents. There were bird calls aplenty, from the pure song of a butcher bird to the harsher sounds of corellas, parrots and galahs squawking from their nests in tree hollows or from branches.

Beyond the heavily-wooded banks, Sam and Denny found their first taste of the true interior – white clay pans – arid vistas vanishing into heat haze, low scrub and salt bush. The silence was broken only by the dire caw of ravens, often unseen, but always present.

★★★

After two hours of walking, the pair reached Menindee – a thriving river town, lively with travellers. Three other paddle steamers were tied up down at the docks, while men rolled barrels and shifted cargo by hand and derrick.

Sam had wired ahead from Mildura a list of provisions for purchase, and these were ready for collection from one of two stores. They had also arranged horses and tack from a local stable with branches in Menindee, Wilcannia and Broken Hill, with collection and delivery at all three points.

Denny and Sam led the horses out of the way of the busy staff and began the work of tacking up horses and balancing packs. Heading back inside for some forgotten items, Denny also purchased a copy of the latest Bulletin magazine, featuring two poems from his friend Henry Lawson.

Then, with the packhorses loaded, they went out past the biggest of the lakes: Menindee then Pamamaroo, brimming full from the passage of recent floodwaters; as vast as inland oceans, and alive with water birds.

Denny entertained visions of what this land might one day become, 'I can see a city on the banks here – green fields irrigated from these waters stretching as far as the eye can see.'

'You've got a fine imagination,' said Sam. 'A bloke back in town was telling me that the lakes are dry as parchment, often as not.'

'Such problems can be overcome with modern engineering, my friend,' said Denny. 'Weirs; dams. Look at what they did with the Suez Canal!'

Before long they met a drover and his team heading towards town. The boss was easy to spot; a lean sun-browned man wearing dungarees, a loose Crimea shirt and the usual cabbage-tree stockman's hat. The horses were lean from work, but fine creatures, nevertheless.

The boss stopped alongside Denny. 'G'day there.'

'Hello.'

'Just arrived in the country?'

'Yes.'

'Well, you've got a nice seat on your horse.'

'Thank you,' said Denny. 'Is this where the outback starts?'

'That's a strange question, son. No one knows where it starts and ends. Keep ridin' northwest for a week or two and you'll see red sandhills like mountains.'

Denny thanked the man for his advice, then dug in his heels, riding on towards the setting sun. Once, when the going was slow and even, he looked in his saddle bags for the copy of the Bulletin featuring Henry Lawson's poetry. One stanza he read over and over.

Up Queensland way with cattle, he travelled regions vast;

And many months have vanished since homefolk saw him last.

He hums a song of someone, he hopes to marry soon;

> And hobble-chains and camp-ware keep jingling to the
> tune.

The landscape was essentially a vast plain, sometimes rounded into slow rises that could be called hills only in comparison to the flat vista all around. This, and some larger spiny ridges on the horizon were, according to a rough map the stable owner had drawn, known as Scrope's Range. The vegetation was scattered on dry earth of a pale pink hue. The dominant flora was saltbush – sometimes a moody deep blue, occasionally mauve, at other times dull grey. Here and there were clumps of white-flowered daisy bush and stands of mulga.

'Bloody drab if you ask me,' said Sam.

They had covered a pleasing twenty miles by late afternoon, and when they reached a broad sandy creek bed, with a small brown pool, Denny suggested a halt for the night.

'I'm a little sore,' he admitted. 'No point pushing things on the first day. We're soft from trains, coaches and boats. But by God it feels good to be out here, and this is as pretty a spot as we'll find.'

The dealer had supplied hobbles for the horses, and they had trouble fitting the leather bracelets around the front fetlocks for the first time. The horses sensed their nervousness, responding with irritated kicks and jerks.

'We'll keep a good eye on them,' said Denny, when it was done, but he couldn't stop smiling. This feeling of happiness was brought on by the combination of fresh air, and the dying sun glowering through the writhing branches of the gums.

The brand-new billy can was soon smudged with soot from the fire, and the camp oven was laden with spuds and lamb cutlets. The latter had already spoiled a little and would have to be well cooked. The sun gave a last intense wink as if to promise a return the following day, then slid down the horizon, dragging a curtain of darkness behind.

Even then it was not completely dark. A host of stars appeared, and the flames, fuelled with dry branches, leapt high, illuminating both men, and the nearest trees. Denny ate hungrily, then put his tin plate down with a clink. He walked over to the saddle bags, returning with a square-faced bottle of whisky. 'I think we should celebrate our first night on the road in a far country.'

He poured a generous peg into two mugs, then picked up the bottle to examine the label. 'I think you'll approve of this stuff. Single malt from a little distillery near Dunkeith – I picked it up in Sydney just for this day.'

Sam took a swig while Denny continued to enthuse about the future, of the possibilities out here in the bush. The fire burned down, with gaseous surges of orange and blue between the lava-glow of coals.

After a long silence Sam said, 'Why does it have to be so damned dark?'

'It's not dark, old friend. Look at these stars. Every single one is like a million candles … no, not candles … they're so yellow. The stars are intense – white light like it must be up in heaven itself.'

'I hear you, but I just don't like it.'

'Good God, Sam,' said Denny, reaching out to touch his friend's arm. 'You're shaking.'

'Don't touch me!' Sam shouted, raising his hand to his face. He made a moaning cry, 'I'm sorry, but I can see her burning face. Oh, sweet Jesus, she's burning.'

'No one's burning, Sam. Now just wait a moment, I'll build the fire up, so we can see better.'

Denny scrabbled to find handfuls of dry lignum, plentiful under the trees. Almost as soon as the flames leaped high again, Sam seemed to recover.

'I'm sorry, Denny, but it's such a blessed dark night – no moon at all.'

'No moon yet, but it'll be up in an hour or two. I'll keep the fire burning fiercely until then,' said Denny. 'That's no chore, and when we find a town again, we'll buy a couple of good slush lanterns and hang them on the trees all around. Then even if there's no moon, you'll have enough light to see.'

'Thank you, my friend, I'm not proving to be a good and brave companion for you, am I?'

'You're the best friend I could ever have, and always will be.'

★★★

Arriving at Cape Town at last, Jules and Matthew grounded the balloon to rapturous applause at the Company's Garden, in central Cape Town. After a ceremony certifying the first airborne crossing of Africa from North to South, Jules and Matthew went aloft again, the mayor's formal welcome still ringing in their ears. Near sunset, with the sea a vast plain of silver, they hovered around Mouille Point. Matthew could see Harriet on the balcony, watching the balloon as Jules dropped the anchor.

'My sister Harriet,' he said.

'That young woman is your sister?' Jules asked.

'Yes, that's her.'

'She,' said Jules softly, 'is magnifique. And is that wonderful place your apartment?'

'We're leasing it but yes, and you're welcome to stay here.'

'I won't stay,' said Jules, 'I'd prefer to be in the city – but if I could fold and store my balloon here, I'd appreciate it.'

'Of course,' said Matthew. 'I, and Harriet too, will help in any way we can.'

★★★

On the balcony that evening, Jules produced a bottle of excellent cognac from his luggage. 'I've brought this all the way from home. This is my moment,' he said. 'The first man to cross all of Africa – and the companion who made the last leg so much more pleasant.'

Matthew widened his eyes. 'I don't think Harriet should—'

'Drink brandy?' she scoffed. 'Surely if I'm old enough to come to Africa, and run our Cape Town office by myself, then I'm old enough to drink a little brandy.'

'Of course she's old enough,' cried Jules. 'My sister was permitted to drink brandy at thirteen. Don't be a spoilsport.'

'Very well then. To friends!' toasted Matthew.

'To reunions!' said Harriet.

'To living life to the full!' cried Jules.

After supper, when the two men had talked for a while, with Harriet relegated to the role of listening politely, she excused herself. 'I'll leave you two to your reminiscing. I'm accustomed to retire at this hour.'

Later, however, when Jules had departed for his hotel, Harriet was still reading by lamplight. Matthew knocked on the door.

'Come in.'

Entering sheepishly, a little drunk, he sat on the edge of the bed. 'I saw that your light was on.'

'Still reading – you know better than anyone how a book can get its claws into you.'

Matthew changed the subject. 'Isn't Jules the most amazing person?'

'He is amazing, yes, but also, may I say, a little vain.'

'Vain? Did you think so?'

'Just a little. Not one of my favourite traits.'

'Oh Harriet, you'll see much more of him while he's in Cape Town. I trust you'll change your mind.'

'I hope so, dear brother, but the main thing is that it's nice to have you back. Now get off to bed, you'll need a clear head in the morning.'

Matthew shook his head in amazement, 'You're a wonder, handling the office while I was away.'

'That's the job Father gave me. Now off you go. We can talk tomorrow.'

Chapter Forty-seven

By the third day out of Menindee one of the hired horses was lame and another too 'flat' to ride. While the landscape became increasingly arid, Denny and Sam were forced to walk through the heat of an outback day, leading their mounts, finally trudging into Broken Hill long after dark.

With a strong sense of relief at having reached the town before the Broken Hill Proprietary Company's deadline, they booked accommodation at the Australian Club Hotel, on Argent Street. The room was plain but clean and comfortable, with a view through a window across to the courthouse.

The bathroom was down the hall, and both men enjoyed a luxurious tub, before dressing for dinner. They ate ravenously at the busy dining room, with tankards of ale to wash down roast mutton and potatoes flooded with gravy.

'Well,' said Denny. 'Tomorrow's the deadline. We'd just better hope they've waited for us. I've a good feeling about this town. It's a go-ahead place if ever I've seen one.'

★★★

The next morning, after a solid nine hours of sleep, and well-fortified with breakfast, they sat atop a cab heading for the BHP Company offices. The town looked crisp in the morning cool, though later,

Denny had already learned, a curtain of dust would descend as mining operations reached their peak.

The shop fronts along Argent Street: Kibby's Drapery Store, an ironmonger, the Crystal Skating Rink and a brace of public houses, were already attracting foot traffic. The town had an air of alertness, of an almost religious zealotry, though the god being worshipped lay in grey, silver and black shades of ore beneath the surface.

The driver pointed out some new constructions, including a theatre and a Freemasons' Hall, then stopped outside a neat stone building with a sign over the door: Broken Hill Mining Proprietary Limited.

The company manager, a tall and lean man, with stern lips and a Californian drawl, met Denny and Sam at the door. 'You must be the Morton Steam representatives. Good to meet you, I'm John Howell.'

'Nice to meet you too,' said Denny. 'I'm Denny Morton, and this is our legal man, Sam Harris.' Sam flipped his friend a smile at this description.

With the offer of coffee or tea, Howell admitted them to a boardroom, the most impressive attribute of which was a wide table. A set of papers sat on the surface, and even as he walked in, Denny could see the Forgill's company letterhead on a written quotation on the desk.

Two more men stood up from the table while Howell introduced them. 'I'd like you to meet a couple more of our founding partners, George McCulloch and George Rasp.'

Denny summed them up – both well dressed and distinguished-looking, wearing short beards, dress coats and watch chains. George Rasp was quite bald on top, while McCulloch had a dusting of silver above each ear.

'I must admit that I had started to give up on you people getting here,' Howell said.

'Slow but steady,' agreed Denny. 'We came via Mildura and

Menindee.'

'Ah good work, the mighty Murray-Darling is a great start to seeing the Australian inland,' Howell said, taking a seat opposite Denny. 'Now, getting down to business, I have to say; we are impressed with the specifications of the Morton Fortis.' He cleared his throat. 'Yet we are also close to reaching agreement with one of your competitors.'

Two more men filed into the room, taking seats at the table. More introductions followed. An office boy bearing a tray asked each of the men for their preference of hot beverages.

'I'm not going to beg,' said Denny, conscious of the new faces in the room, 'but we'd appreciate a chance. We've been ten days getting here.'

Howell nodded his head. 'That's true enough, and we do appreciate your determination.'

'Our engines use less coal than any of our competitors,' said Denny. 'It must cost a fortune to bring supplies out here – a thousand miles from the Hunter Valley, correct?' We can save you thirty per cent off your coal bill, perhaps more. The Fortis is the only stationary engine in the world right now that uses superheated steam, and that means more power for less fuel.'

Howell sighed, then turned to address the board members now seated at the table. 'Our responsibility is to the shareholders of this company. We would be remiss if we did not investigate all the options available to us today.' The manager shuffled through some papers on the table, then passed across a handwritten list of engine sizes and configurations. 'We will require around eight-thousand horsepower in total – we're ditching shafts and moving to an open cut system – the way I've done things back in the States. We need power for draglines, cranes and processing. Unfortunately, however, we are fully stretched cash wise, and need to cover part of our investment with company stock.'

Denny shook his head sadly. 'That's a big order, but I'm not sure that company stock is going to be acceptable.'

'We have returned almost four million pounds to shareholders since we started four years ago. But,' Howell sighed, 'I understand that stock is always more of a risk than cash. Your reaction is natural.' He changed the subject artfully. 'Now tell me, how do you know Henry Lawson?'

The board listened with interest to the story of Denny meeting the poet in a Sydney pub. He was obviously a favourite here.

'I'll thank Henry when next I see him,' George McCulloch said at the end of the story. 'Normally, to investigate machinery options we are forced to travel. We have good reason to believe that we are sitting on the largest deposit of silver in the history of the world and are on the cusp of a major expansion. Now, we've seen the spec sheets you posted through, but I want to hear this from your own lips. Tell me about the Fortis. Why is it so special?'

Denny did as he was asked, starting with the way his father had incorporated Wilhelm Schmidt's work on superheaters, and the years needed to perfect the design. Of the decade-long lag between the new Morton engine and their nearest competitors.

The men in the room were captivated. Denny beamed back at them, knowing he had made a connection. Everyone admires success.

Howell handed across a sheaf of paper, on which was spelled out the company's exact requirements. 'Thank you for that fascinating summary. Now, as I said, we need to act swiftly. The Forgill company are pressing us for acceptance, and they have good engines – proven models that have a long history of usage around the world – not to mention a strong New South Wales agent who guarantees the provision of spare parts and engineering support. Can you have something indicative to us by four this afternoon?'

'I'll do my best,' said Denny.

'There's one last thing. We would like to send a consulting engineer to your factory to view the engine itself and give us his assessment.'

'Now?'

'As soon as possible.' Howell looked at his watch. 'Though it's late at night in London. First thing in the morning, if possible.'

'I'll cable the factory and arrange it, say nine am?'

'Make it eight,' Howell said. 'Our man is an early riser. Now, let's have a quick ride around the site and we'll let you get to work.'

★★★

They toured the site on borrowed horses, the size of the operation astounding the Englishmen. Sam whistled softly. 'I would never have believed that such riches would flow from this dry an' dusty ground.'

George Rasp pointed out the 'broken' hill itself and explained the discovery in a faint but crisp German accent. 'That's vere I made ze first find. I vasn't even certain it was silver, but—' he extended a finger like a lamppost. 'I had a copy of the miner's almanac, and everything tested just right. I vas a poor boundary rider … little did I know.'

'Last year,' said Howell, 'we extracted eighty-two thousand tons of ore from this site. From the ore we produced almost four million ounces of silver. We're planning on doubling our output within six months and are in the process of building five more fifty-ton smelters, making a total of thirteen.'

Denny was staggered at the scale of the operation, and all this development had taken place in a scarcely believable four years. 'I'll do some figures,' he said, 'and get back to you this afternoon.'

★★★

When the tour was over, Denny sent a telegram to London, preparing Frederick for the visiting engineer. He did not hint at the massive scale of the possible BHP order, warning only that it would be for more than one machine. Then, back at the hotel, with a pot of cold ale at his elbow, Denny sat, struggling with the quandary of accepting stock in the Broken Hill Company in lieu of cash in part-payment of this staggering order. It was a premium contract, yet even the deposit would be paid partly in stock.

The silver was coming in. He had seen the hoppers of ore with his own eyes, but their plans for expansion, along with the perils of operating in a remote area, were eating up capital.

'We need economies of scale,' Howell had said. 'We have to get bigger.'

Would his father take the risk of accepting stock in lieu of cash? Perhaps. The order would be worth it.

You gave me full autonomy, Denny mused to himself. *But how far does that go?*

The door slammed. It was Sam, back from collecting the mail, forwarded on from the Sydney office. 'One for you, Master Denny … and I do believe that my little sister writes to you more than me.'

'Pass it here, please Sam. I need a distraction.'

Denny felt a glow of pleasure at seeing Eadie's handwriting on the yellow envelope. Reading her letter would be a good way to calm him before preparing the quotation, even though it was written some two and a half months earlier, long before she decided to travel out to join he and Sam.

Dearest Denny,

It seems like aeons since I last heard your voice, and sometimes it feels like my letters take fight across the world, like aimless birds. Some may have missed you in their travels. Still, I write, and hope.

My black cat, Master Sweep, has been staying out late and fighting lately. The cause of this is a delicate little tabby belonging to Mrs Lowe. I'm hoping that there will be a litter of kittens early in the spring. I'm sure they will be ever such good mousers.

Denny closed his eyes, transported from the stark landscape around Broken Hill to the green fields of home, Eadie's black cat's green eyes staring back at him from its favourite perch, the lower branches of an elder tree in her yard.

> I know that you will soon be on the road in a new country, visiting the far-flung places where captains of industry might purchase those marvellous Morton engines.

She had also grasped the importance of what he and his siblings were attempting to do. Selling engines was the basis of everything. Orders, and the accompanying deposits, kept the factory operating, the workers paid. Once the engines were built, the transport network kicked in, and they arrived at their new homes, ready to pump water, operate mills, stamp ore or power machine shops.

Denny sighed and read on through the next two pages. The final sentences had him reading and re-reading.

> My heart tells me that you will do the right thing, wherever you go. I usually find that when something feels right, it is right.

Denny tapped his fingers on the desk reflectively. Eadie was wise. The Broken Hill Proprietary Company was peopled by good men of principle. They had their problems and limitations, but so did the Morton Steam company.

Grateful for Eadie's heart and insight, he continued to prepare the quotation with the engine spec sheets and price list at his elbow. He worked fast, knowing he had less than three hours to conjure an irresistible deal for Howell and the board, but also to make Morton Steam a lot of money. He made sure to point out in his preamble that the Morton Factory now had an office in the colony of New South Wales, not just an agency like its competitors.

At four-thirty pm he and Sam hand-delivered the quotation back to the company office.

'Thank you, sir,' said Howell, taking it from his hands. 'If you would call back tomorrow morning, we'll have an answer for you.'

★★★

Sam tried to keep Denny distracted as they wandered the town through the last few hours of daylight. They talked of home, and future plans as they strolled down and along the thoroughfares named after elements and minerals: Carbide Street, Sulphide Street, Wolfram Street and Chloride Street. On the many tailings piles they picked up rocks with shining lumps of galena or sparkling mica.

They ate back at the hotel, and retired early, encouraged by a return telegram from Frederick in London, reporting that the visit from the consulting engineer had gone well. He had, apparently, left the premises very impressed with the engine.

★★★

The next morning, when Denny and Sam returned to the Proprietary Company offices Howell greeted them at the door, and led them to the boardroom, where he invited them to sit.

'The board have had a difficult decision to make,' Howell said. 'We have considered the ongoing coal savings, but even more importantly, the matter of machine redundancy. We want engines that will still be state-of-the-art in ten years' time – and our London consulting engineer tell us that your engine is, shall I quote from his telegram, "a mighty feat of engineering that offers economy, longevity, and more power for the footprint than any competitor."'

'That's wonderful news,' said Denny.

'Accordingly, we have decided to go with the Morton quotation. The cost was higher, overall, per horsepower, yet we believe that the Morton engines are a better fit for our business.'

Denny had rehearsed this moment in his mind. He had planned on being reserved and professional, 'Oh thank you, sir. That's stupendous news and I cannot thank you enough.'

The board, however, seemed to appreciate his enthusiasm, while Sam produced company contracts gravely, and prepared them for signing. When it was all done, Denny accepted a larger cheque than he had dreamed of holding in his life and authorised the transfer of shares into the Morton company name.

'You won't regret this,' said Howell when they shook hands outside. 'I've seen a lot of mines in a lot of places, but that darn hill is almost solid silver. Now, I know it's not worth as much as it used to be before Western nations started abandoning the silver standard in favour of gold, but new coins are appearing every day. A good proportion of them need silver.'

★★★

'Congratulations! You got the order and well-deserved too,' said Sam, as they walked towards the Commercial Bank of Sydney on Argent Street, there to arrange the deposit of a very large cheque. Denny felt better already. The three thousand pounds of cash deposit would have strong benefits for the company. Manufacturing the engines would cost much more than that, but there was a time to take risks, and this was it.

After the bank, the pair visited the telegraph office where Denny composed a message home.

MAJOR CONTRACT SIGNED WITH BROKEN HILL PROPRIETARY COMPANY STOP 3000 POUNDS DEPOSIT STOP FOURTEEN FORTIS ENGINES STOP DETAILS TO FOLLOW BY MAIL DM

The two friends did not set out to celebrate, but that night they let themselves go. It was Friday night and Argent Street was crowded. A brass band was playing on the kerb, with a red-faced bass drummer who was a partial beat out of time and unsteady on his feet.

'He looks like he fell into a barrel of rum,' said Sam.

'And swallowed half of it while he was there,' agreed Denny.

They stopped also to listen to a street orator, who seemed to have also fortified himself before his performance. 'We are part way there, comrades,' he cried, 'but the chains of oppression are heavy—'

Then, heading across to the Grand Hotel, a juggler had set his skittles afire, and was managing to keep three or four in the air at once.

After a brief appreciation of the juggler's skills, they threw down two pints each at the Grand, then two more at the packed Duke of Cornwall. Conversation formed a wall of sound, with a blue mist of cigar, pipe and cigarette smoke drifting through the gas lights.

One more beer then let's hit the hay,' said Denny finally, unable to stop yawning. 'Then back to Sydney we go.'

★★★

'Already I am regretting the adjournment,' growled His Honour, Sir Avery Lanistone of the Chancery Division of the High Court, 'for it seems to me that the plaintiff's case is no better organised than it was three months ago. Who is running this circus and are you ready to proceed?'

Forgill's lead attorney stood from his carved chair. 'I am Thomas Brachard, of Donald and Associates, and I appear on behalf of the plaintiff. 'We are ready to proceed, your honour.'

'Then please do so.'

'Our first witness is Mr Moon, sir. Chief Engineer of the Forgill Works from 1846 until 1889.'

Moon took the stand in an air of huffy indignation, with a brief stabbing glance at Frederick as if he had been personally offended by him.

One of the juniors on the Forgill bench led the man through a verbal resume of his skills and experience, before Brachard himself stood to handle the meatier aspects of the interrogation, asking Moon whether he knew anything of Frederick Morton working on a special project.

'Yes, sir. I do know for a fact that Lord Forgill Senior asked Morton to work on a superheated steam engine.'

'Very well. How long did this project take?'

'Oh, four or five months Morton worked on it, and he was paid to do so – every hour of it.'

'Now you have examined these original plans and those of the Morton Fortis. Would you say that they are very similar?'

'They are one and the same thing. Apart from some minor changes, Morton is building and trying to sell the engine he was paid to design for Forgill's.'

'Why did Forgill's not build this engine?' asked Brachard.

'We would have, I believe, were it not for the untimely death of Lord Forgill.'

Moon finished his testimony with another smirk aimed and fired at Frederick.

Wallace, however, was standing for the cross-examination, looking intimidating. His wig sat somewhat awry, and his jaw was as rugged as an exposed beam.

'Is it true, Mr Moon, that you embarked on a campaign to discredit the superheated engine design?'

'I did not, sir.'

'I put it to you that you pursued a policy of low-pressure engines on the prejudice of safety.'

'Low pressure engines *are* safer,' said Moon. 'But I did not stand in the way of our company founder wishing to explore a new technology.'

'But you managed to convince several board members that the planned engine was a mistake?'

'I did not.'

'I allege that you did, and I have witnesses to back the allegation. I ask you again, did you lobby board members to vote against Frederick Morton's design?'

Moon's face turned a violent shade of red as he went on the attack. 'Even if I did, how on earth does it matter. The question here is whether Forgill's owns the industrial design that Frederick Morton completed on our payroll. As far as I'm concerned, that's where the matter rests.'

After the morning recess yet another consulting engineer, appeared, at a fee approaching five guineas per hour.

'Sir, you have had the opportunity to examine both designs.'

'I have.'

'Your opinion on the matter?'

'The engines share many features, yet I can see nothing proprietary in the Morton design. The superheater was based on the work of Wilhelm Schmidt in Dortmund, Germany ...'

The defence witnesses came and went swiftly. Vic Jones gave evidence that Frederick Morton had spent hundreds of hours at the Morton factory, working on the designs for the Fortis engine. He had never seen him so much consult any other, older plans, and did not appear to possess them.'

The judge took in the room with one pass of his eyes and a gulp of water from his glass. 'It seems to me that this case should never have been brought to this court. Frederick Morton has combined existing technologies in a very clever way. I declare the case for the defendant, and the plaintiff must pay costs for both parties.'

The Forgill team were on their feet in a moment, with a chorus of, 'Your honour!'

'Sit down, if we allowed this kind of case to proceed, no engineer in the country would be able to design anything at all.'

★★★

In one of those strange twists, where the hand of fate loves to throw good on good or bad on bad, when Frederick called in at the factory on the way home, he was given a telegram that had just arrived from Australia.

He read it out to Clare with trembling hands.

'Three thousand pounds in deposits – fourteen engines. It gives us a chance,' he said. 'Denny has given us hope – and now we can sell the Fortis in the UK again as well.'

Clare hugged him. 'We have such clever children.'

Chapter Forty-eight

The Carlton Club was busy for a Tuesday luncheon, and the general hum of conversation set Percy's teeth on edge as he took the last mouthful of his lemon savarin and looked around at the other diners.

'How did you get on with the Australian situation?' the Small-Arms-Factory owner asked Percy.

'Not too well,' Percy said. 'My man has been found, drowned in a damned river, and Morton's son has snatched a deal worth upwards of twelve thousand pounds by the time the engines are delivered.'

The Banker shrugged, 'You did not deploy sufficient resources, dear boy.'

'It seems so,' said Percy. 'But I have another man on the way – one whom I trust absolutely to get the job done. This is not the end of the matter.'

BOOK FOUR

THE MORTON STEAM COMPANY LIMITED

PUBLIC SHARE OFFER

Manufacturers of Stationary Steam Engines, boilers and associated apparatus

CAPITAL - £1 000 000

Divided into 250 000 Cumulative Participating preference Shares of £1 each. (Conferring the right to a fixed cumulative preferential dividend at the rate of 7 1/2 per cent, per annum.

AND

750 000 Ordinary Shares

This Company has been formed for the objects stated in its Memorandum of Association, and in particular to secure and extend the business of designing and manufacturing Stationary Steam Engines, boilers and associated apparatus. The Company was formed as a private Company in 1870 by Frederick Morton. As well as home trade, the Company enjoys a considerable export market across America, the colonies and Europe.

PROFITS

The following is a copy of a certificate by Messrs. Harmitage and Norton, Chartered Accountants of Huddersfield, London, in regard to the profits of the company.

GENTLEMEN.

We certify that the trading profits of your Company for the four years ended 31st June 1893, after allowing for depreciation and for Director's renumeration, but before deducting Excess Profit Duty and Income Tax, have been as follows:

£1890 11'

£1891 79'

£1892 13'

£1893 12'

Applications for shares must be made on the accompanying form and forwarded with the amount due on application to:

Lievere and Co.

49 Cheapside, London

Applications open on April 17, 1894 and close on April 19, 1894 at which time all allotments will have been made.

Chapter Forty-nine

One passenger on the SS *Vesuvius* was even more isolated than Eadie. Peter Craven, with his scarred face, hands and neck, was the subject of stares and whispers. He ate alone, and his cabin-mate arranged to transfer to an empty bed elsewhere, a move that suited Craven well.

Having never been aboard a passenger steamer, he had rarely seen so much wealth in a confined space. Yet, strangely, he had little interest in stealing pocket watches, or slipping into unlocked cabins to pick through jewellery boxes.

Sometimes he looked at young couples, in love and attentive to each other, and he found himself wishing that he too could have had such a life.

Yet he knew it could not be. Craven was a carnivore; a predator, living a life outside of the herd, patrolling on the edges and seeking out weakness. Now he was on his way to kill a man, and from that time on he would be hunted by the forces of law and order. Of course, Percy Forgill would hide and protect him, but would it be enough?

The ship's doctor, catching sight of him in the dining room one day, took an interest in Craven's terrible scars, supplying him with an ointment, and recommending that he took a good dose of sunlight each day.

Following these instructions, Craven took to sitting on the promenade deck around noon, watching the sea, observing other passengers. He loved to hate those who were very different to himself. The ones most lavishly endowed by the fates: the young men of around his own age with exceptional good looks, breeding, and the kind of confidence that comes from privilege.

Most interesting of all, however, quite early on in the voyage he spotted a young woman familiar to him. He had been asked, several times over the years, to watch members of the Morton family as they went about their business. He had noticed this young woman on several occasions.

Though very attractive, she looked different than he remembered, but one night in the dining hall, watching her eat from a distance, he realised who she was – Denny Morton's woman. He experienced a moment of grim pleasure at the realisation. It was obvious that she was going out to the colony to meet her man. This was a positive development. Locating his target in a new country was always going to be difficult, but now all he had to do was keep track of this female and she would lead him to his target.

More than once he picked the lock of her cabin when all four of the women who slept there were out, going through drawers and trunks. Her name was Eadie Harris, or Eadith, he discovered.

He took nothing, but read what his poor language skills allowed him of her letters, learning a little about Denny Morton's plans, last time he had written. He took to sitting near her on the promenade deck when she came out to take in the sun and air. It seemed that she scarcely noticed him, absorbed as she was in her embroidery.

On one such day two small boys were also present, running around, causing trouble. One was dark-haired and the other fair. Both wore sailor-suits complete with ribboned hats.

These brats were usually restrained by the presence of their mother, but today she was distracted, in deep conversation with one of the stewards. The fair boy spotted Craven, then, fascinated, walked up close.

'What happened to your face, Mister?'

'Why lad, the same thing what 'appened to yer manners.'

The boy danced back a few yards. 'You look like you was skinned wif a skinning knife.'

The other brat had been distracted by a fallen penny he had spotted on the deck. Once it was buttoned into his pocket, he joined in. 'Maybe the poor beggar was born all scarred and ugly.'

'Get out of 'ere,' growled Craven. 'Or I'll skin you both, and I means it too.'

The boys giggled. Life on board was tedious, and the danger of this game only made it more fun. One turned to the other, still safely out of reach. 'I seen a plucked turkey one time, looked just like this fellow.'

Craven lumbered up from the seat and pursued the boys, yet they were fast, scampering out of reach.

'Plucked turkey, scalded with boiling water,' the dark boy called from a safe distance.

At this point the mother ceased her conversation, gathered her two charges and left the deck. As soon as they were back under her wing the boys' rascally faces turned angelic, and they followed obediently. Craven glowered as they went. The mother, he saw, looked right through him, as people do to the disfigured and maimed.

Then, as he sank miserably back into his seat, Eadie Harris said, 'What a frightful pair of boys. It was very rude of them to say those horrible things.'

Craven looked at her curiously. 'They're right, more's the pity. I do look like a scalded turkey.'

'You do not,' she scoffed. 'Lots of people have scars. How did it happen?'

Craven grinned at the thought of truthfully explaining the events of that night in the Morton factory. Instead, he said simply, 'I was burned, love. Burned in a fire.'

The young woman had a kind face, and her words were kind too. 'I do feel for you – and I don't know why people have to be so cruel.'

Craven smirked. On a day not too long from here, he thought to himself, she would see Denny Morton beg for mercy, but she was not to know that just yet. Let it be a surprise.

★★★

After dealing with quotations arising from his site visits in Johannesburg and the Kimberley, Matthew spent much of his time pursuing a government contract. The process was fraught, with multiple bureaucrats involved in design and supply decisions. This fact did not deter the inexperienced but enthusiastic Matthew.

Weary of purchasing electricity for lighting in Central Cape Town from a third party, the Cape Colony Parliament entered the planning stages of building their own utility, the Graaff Electric Light Station, near the main wall of the Molteno Reservoir, with a view to eventual hydro power.

Scanning the back pages of the Cape Times, Harriet had spotted the call for tenders for a stationary steam engine to run a pilot direct-current alternator. After submitting a time-consuming and detailed tender, the Morton company was now on the short list.

In an intense exchange of letters and telegrams with London, Frederick had encouraged Matthew to quote on the forthcoming Imperium engine, designed for electricity generation, rather than the Fortis. This would give Frederick an opportunity to address the coupling requirements of the alternator and the brand-new engine, the main shaft of which was five inches in diameter.

Since the submission of the tender, the purchasing committee had requested constant fine revisions that required updates to the quotations. The Imperium was not quite ready yet, Matthew made it plain, but with a delivery timetable of twelve months the Cape

Parliament would be running the most advanced engine in the world. This fact did appeal to them.

Still, Matthew was not prepared to sit around waiting for more minor revisions. 'They might not be ready to sign for another month,' he said to Harriet, 'and I need to chase sales where I can.' Armed with a South African Railways timetable Matthew booked himself on a journey that would take him to many regions of interest, from a sales point of view, and all in a mere two weeks.

'So many hours of travelling time,' said Harriet. 'Are you sure this isn't just a way of sitting on trains and reading?'

'That's certainly a side benefit,' said Matthew.

★★★

While Harriet kept the office open, with Jules assisting if he needed to, Matthew arrived in Stellenbosch, where he walked down rows of vines, already a century old. There he tasted fine wines that danced on his tongue and sparkled in his mind. He saw the engines that drove the presses in the major vineyards, some of which bought up production from many smaller farms. He was surprised at a strong anti-English sentiment, but he disarmed this with his natural earnest charm, and a few lines from the great Dutch writer, Isabelle de Charrière.

'One of my favourites,' he said, many times. 'One of the greats, even in translation.'

The cane farmers of Durban, on the east coast, welcomed this limping and intense young man. The sugar industry required steam power for several stages of processing and refining, and while Matthew made no sales, he generated strong interest.

In the dry Paroo he opened negotiations with bore-sinkers, for the Mobilis engine was a near-perfect machine for drilling and drawing water out of the earth. Morton engines were built to last, using less coal than any competitor.

★★★

In London, the benefits of the BHP order were beginning to flow through. Nothing gave Frederick more pleasure than the opportunity to re-hire the men he had been forced to let go. Some had found other employment in the industry, but most were back on Monday morning, to a chorus of back-slapping.

'If you open the Times to the business pages today,' said Frederick to his augmented work force, holding up a copy of the paper, 'you'll find an article with the headline, "Morton's lands lucrative contract in New South Wales." Lifting the paper, he began to read, "The Morton firm has snatched a tender out from under the noses of rival stationary engine firms, signing a contract to supply fourteen of their Fortis engines. Brokers have reported an increase in interest in the upcoming public share offer in the company."'

Within the hour Frederick was up at Bosun Benson's office, arranging the lease of an existing brick warehouse adjoining the factory, so they could start assembling the new Imperium engines there – every inch of the existing bays would be needed to complete the BHP order.

'Bravo,' Ned Baring told him later. 'You're expanding. Potential shareholders will love it.'

'It's a race against time. If the float fails, then Percy gets the company and everything else we own. If we go broke now, he gets it anyway.'

The new facility's design incorporated the latest overhead lifting equipment and electric lights – a feature Frederick also added to the rest of the factory. Vic Jones smiled more often now than he had for some time, and Frederick noticed the change. Vic was becoming even more capable with age, his own impeccable standards of workmanship becoming a company ethos, and it showed in the excellence of every engine that left the factory.

Chapter Fifty

Harriet was a morning person, an early riser who woke with the sun. She ate breakfast on the balcony before the last stars had faded into white. There was a magic in that time of morning, hearing the seabirds' cries as they sailed over the bay, making her smile as she ate her small bowl of oatmeal and milk, sweetened with a teaspoonful of molasses.

It became her habit to take the first tram into the office, opening up and making a list of tasks needing completion by the end of the day, ticking items off, deleting and adding where necessary. With Matthew away, however, there was not so much work to do, and by mid-afternoon Harriet had a clear desk, stifling a yawn and stiff from sitting, missing her sibling's company. Her work completed, Harriet began what had become a weekly task – writing a letter to the editor of the Cape Times, bashing it out on the typewriter, backing up when she made a mistake.

Twice she had posted her letters, and twice they had failed to see print.

> I am writing to highlight the disgrace that is occurring in the shanty town of Woodstock, under the noses of authorities, with nothing being done to assist them ...

The letter went on for three paragraphs, and she signed it with her own name. This time, however, she did not post it, but rather carried the letter around to the Times office, just a couple of blocks away.

'I need to give this to the editor.'

The clerk barely looked up, 'I'll see that he gets it. He's a very busy man.'

'I insist on delivering it in person.' Harriet rounded the counter and set off down the corridor with the clerk struggling to keep up. The editor's door was at the end of the hall, wide open with a bearded man inside, at a table so crowded with paper and open books that the surface was not visible.

'Who on earth are you?' cried the editor.

'My name is Harriet Morton. Why won't you print my letters?'

'No one wants to read about shanty towns and slums.'

'So everyone can ignore it? These people need food.'

The editor smirked, 'If you care so much why don't you go and feed them?'

'That's what I intend to do,' said Harriet, stamping her foot.

After storming from the office, she headed to the grocers, where she purchased a sack of rice and a bucket of vegetables. At the butcher shop she asked for ten pounds of cheap cuts of beef.

This was too much to carry on a tram, so Harriet co-opted Roundhead Jimmy to take her home. As she took her seat up on the box next to the driver she said, 'I wonder, Jimmy. I know it's Saturday tomorrow, but will you come at seven in the morning to pick me up?'

'Every day is the same as the next, and the last, as far as I go,' he said. 'If you have a paying fare fer me, Miss, then I'll be where'er you want me to be.'

The next morning, at five minutes before the appointed hour, Harriet was out on the footpath helping Jimmy load the cart with a folding table, chair, and a huge pot of still-warm curried beef and rice.

'Where to, Miss?' he asked.

'Woodstock, please?'

'I beg yer pardon?'

'You heard me the first time. Woodstock. The place everyone pretends doesn't exist.' Harriet had done some research. There were other slums: Coffee Lane on the waterfront, Waterkraut Street, and the tenements of Horstley Street, but none rivalled the size and scale of Woodstock.

'Now why would a young lass want to go to such a place?'

'That's my business.'

The older man shook his grizzled head sadly, then flicked the reins. 'So it is.'

Most of the trip passed in silence, but Harriet was never bored, looking out at the awakening city – the good and the bad – the smell of chamber pots emptied into the sewers; workers hurrying from their homes, many of them indentured servants, working for a pittance in the homes of the rich.

Finally, reaching the settlement, a frown touched Harriet's face. They had entered a narrow thoroughfare that appeared to be a centre of sorts. There were a couple of shops, shanties really, further along.

'Where do you want me to stop?' the driver asked, not commenting any further on her choice of Saturday morning activity.

Harriet noticed a patch of clear ground where some children were chasing each other with sticks, round and around, laughing all the time. 'Here looks fine.'

'D'you want me to wait?'

'If you think I'm going to pay you to sit and watch me,' she said, 'you're mistaken.'

Harrumphing with disapproval, the driver flicked his reins, effected a U-turn, then disappeared back towards the town, leaving her quite alone.

The difference between London's slums and those of Woodstock was that the former occupied old buildings dating back centuries, many gutted by fire and partially rebuilt. Here in Woodstock only a minority of the slum-dwellers lived in structures with solid walls.

In between glass and brick factories, and with Devil's Hill a brooding presence in the background, families lived in mere sketches of huts. These flimsy dwellings were cobbled together out of scrounged materials, with no sewerage or water. A line of women, balancing jugs on their heads, walked half a mile from the nearest supply.

Children played in puddles that were foetid with waste. Lines of people waiting their turn at government-built privies stretched for hundreds of yards, with some wailing with need, others giving up and heading for patches of bush alongside putrid pools.

The smell of the slums sat like acid in Harriet's nostrils, and she was a little frightened of the people who started to appear and stare as she set up her trestle. Some were big-framed Bantu, others leaner Hottentots. She also saw smaller-framed Malays, and a few Europeans, usually older men.

As always, the children were the first to arrive, their galaxial eyes torn between hunger and distrust of strangers. Most of the crowd held back in curious silence until a confident, tall woman with a child riding on her hip strode up boldly.

'What are you doing?' she asked Harriet in a strong voice, as deep in timbre and musical as church bells.

'I've brought some food.'

The woman laughed, as if it was the funniest thing she had ever heard. She turned and called back towards the nearest shanty. The occupants, five thin children, came out reluctantly, the eldest a teenager, accompanied by a Cape hunting dog that sniffed and snarled at the smell of cooked food.

'Why do you come here with food for us, nice white girl like you?'

'Because I want to help you.'

The woman shook her head, as if trying to understand why someone would behave like that. Then, taking up one of the empty bowls, she held it out for Harriet to fill, receiving a ladle of rice and stew. She moved nearby to eat, sharing some with the child on her hip.

The rest of the crowd watched expectantly, as if waiting to see if she would drop dead from poison. When, after a while, nothing happened, a near-toothless old man approached, saying not a word, but Harriet could see the hunger in his eyes, surrounded as they were by radiating lines, telling the story of years of sleeping hard.

Harriet took up a plate and ladled in rice and stew before passing it to him, affecting an offhand manner, as if it were nothing. He moved away, squatted and began to eat with his fingers, ignoring the spoon she had given him.

When the first two had eaten, suffering no ill effects, the trickle became a stream. In half an hour flat Harriet's ladle was scraping the bottom of the pot and she had nothing else to offer. A good crowd of hopefuls had gathered by then, staring as she packed her things inside the pot and prepared to leave.

The crowd watched in silence as Harriet approached the woman with the baby. 'This table,' she said. 'Will you mind it for me?'

'Mind it?'

'Keep it safe for me. You can use it if you like, as long as I can have it when I bring my stews.'

'If you wish, miss, yes I will.'

Then, burdened with the large pot and ladle, Harriet set off for the two mile walk back to Cape Town. Three hundred staring eyes watched her go.

★★★

Later, after putting the next day's batch of stew on to simmer, it seemed to Harriet that the day had been quite arduous. On the lounge, reading a few pages of a novel, she found her eyes closing and head nodding forward. For perhaps ten minutes she surrendered, at which point there was a light knock on the door. Coming fully awake, she opened it to find Jules standing in the entrance.

'Oh hello, Monsieur D'Marnier, I'm sorry but Matthew is still away.'

'I know. I came to see you, not him.'

'Indeed?'

'Yes. I brought you something.' He unfolded a sheet of paper and extended it. 'Someone has been putting these up in town.'

Harriet looked. It was a poster.

AUDITION CALL FOR NEW DRAMA. SUNDAY 4 PM.
THEATRE ROYAL, BURG ST.

Jules pulled a face, 'Matthew told me that you are quite the actress.'

'Oh ... just silly school productions,' Harriet said, waving her hand airily. 'Ages ago, it seems. Besides, I won't have time. After church I have things to do – I set up a little store at Woodstock today and intend to do the same tomorrow.'

'A store?'

'Well not really a store. There's no charge for the food I give away. I have another big batch of stew on the cooktop now.'

Jules flared his nostrils, inhaling the aroma. 'The slum dwellers are lucky to be given such a meal. It smells delicious – and what a splendid thing to do. So, are you going again tomorrow?'

'I am.'

'I'd like to come and help if I might – and then you will be finished in time for the audition.'

Harriet glanced at him in surprise. 'Your help would be

appreciated,' she said. 'But I don't even know what play is being performed.'

'That doesn't matter so much, you are an actress, and therefore you need to act,' said Jules. His eyes widened with enthusiasm, and he took and squeezed her left hand with his right. 'Oh Harriet. You draw people to you. I have seen how you affect others and I feel it in myself.'

'I'm sure that's not true, and even if it was, it doesn't mean that I have to inflict myself on every audition that comes along.'

'This is not London. There are not so many auditions to pick and choose from here. To have a talent – to entertain, to make people feel things, is a privilege and a gift – to waste it is an affront to God. Go to the audition and see what happens.'

'I'll think about it,' she said at last.

Jules looked at her intensely. 'Can I come inside?'

Harriet felt a tightness in her chest. 'Not just now, sorry. I'm very tired.'

Disappointment crossed his face. 'That's fine, really it is. I'll see you tomorrow.' He started walking backwards away from the door. 'I'll find you at Woodstock, then I will come and watch you audition.'

Harriet watched him go, relieved when he had moved off down the street.

***

The next morning, she had been at work in the slums of Woodstock for ten or fifteen minutes, having already fed an army of slum urchins and their parents, when Jules arrived in a cab, tousle-haired and sleepy.

'Sorry, I'm later than you probably expected.'

'I didn't expect anything. Now shush, here comes the next bunch. I'll spoon the rice and you can ladle the stew.'

Many of the waiting people had been there the previous day, and

Harriet recognised a number of them. Their names were so different to the ones she was used to, however, that she found them almost impossible to remember.

The woman who had been her first customer the day before, tall and regal, brought her a bracelet made of smoke-hardened seeds traced onto string.

'A gift, for you,' she said.

Harriet was touched, and on impulse she leaned forward and hugged the woman briefly, before slipping the bracelet onto her wrist. 'Thank you. I'll treasure it.'

A couple of times during the morning, a white man came out of one of the few substantial buildings in the area, a long stone's throw up the track, and stared down at them. He was very stout, with a black beard so thick that it seemed to cover all but his eyes and nose.

'I wonder who he is,' said Jules.

'Oh, he was glaring at me yesterday. Don't worry about it.'

Just as they were packing up, however, the man marched down towards them. 'What in the name of thunder do you think you're doing?'

'I'm helping the starving people of this settlement,' said Harriet.

'Over my dead body you are. That is my shop just there, and I have not sold a thing all day.'

'I don't care if you sell anything,' said Harriet. 'The people tell me that your food is overpriced.'

The man's face turned red. He picked up Harriet's pot and threw it out onto the road where it spun, overturned then lay still. 'Get out of here and don't come back.'

Jules ran to collect the pot, holding it by one of the handles as he approached the angry storekeeper. 'Did you go to church this morning, Mijnheer?'

'Of course I did.'

'Did the pastor speak of Jesus helping the poor?'

'Not today. Not one word,' the man said smugly.

'Well surely you have read Saint John: "But if anyone has the world's goods and sees his brother in need, yet closes his heart against him, how does God's love abide in him?"'

The storekeeper swallowed, 'I do not read it in such a way. And are you not familiar with Thessalonians? "If anyone is not willing to work, let him not eat".'

'Are these people unwilling to work, or are there no jobs for them?'

Harriet broke in, hands on hips, 'Many do work, and work hard, but still do not earn enough to feed their families.'

Jules continued smoothly, 'What would Jesus have done, Mijnheer? Would He have sent away a woman who seeks to feed the poor, just to allow a storekeeper to profit from them?'

'I am not Jesus. I am a businessman.' He raised a finger and wiggled it threateningly. 'Don't come back here again after today.'

When the storekeeper had gone Harriet dissolved into giggles, and clasped Jules's arm. 'Oh, that was precious, thank you. I can just picture him heading home and getting stuck into his Bible, looking up quotations that justify keeping these poor people down.'

'I'll do the same,' Jules declared, 'and next time I'll be ready for him.'

Harriet smiled. 'Now we'd best pack up and get home. If I'm going to have time to change for the audition, I'll have to hurry.'

★★★

At four o'clock that afternoon Harriet stopped outside the theatre entrance to brush down her top. Jules had wanted to accompany her, but she had told him a firm no, and caught the tram into the city alone. Telling herself that this was not important, anyway – just a whim – she attached herself to the rear of a small group and walked inside. There, amongst the smells of floor polish and perfume, a woman was standing with a clipboard addressing each new arrival in turn.

'Are you here for the auditions?' she said to Harriet after dealing with those in front.

'I am, yes thanks.'

'Name please?'

'Harriet Morton.'

The woman added the name to her list with a pencil. 'Thank you, Miss Morton. Go in, and the director will start things off in a minute.'

The theatre was dim inside, lit by a single gas light on either side of the stage. The first three rows were populated with a group of heavily made-up women and well-dressed men. Harriet felt a pang of inadequacy – her makeup was perfunctory, and her dress more suited to a morning in the office than a stage production.

As several of the women turned to look at her, Harriet felt like giving up and going home. It was ridiculous, she didn't even know what she was auditioning for.

Yet, Harriet had never been inclined to quit once she had committed herself to something, so she took a seat on the edge of the third row. The woman beside her was perhaps forty-five, with her hair piled high, and held fast with an out-sized comb. She leaned over towards Harriet.

'I don't think I know you, do I?'

Harriet shook her head. 'Not as far as I'm aware.'

'Oh, well the scene is quite small in Cape Town, and everyone knows everyone. Fresh out from England?'

'Yes, I am actually.'

'Well, that might turn out to be a good thing. You're very pretty, and this is a smaller pond.'

'I didn't come out here specifically to act – I'm working as assistant to my brother. Business, you know.'

The conversation was cut short by the arrival of the director. He was of medium height, with jet-black hair, and a bohemian taste in clothing. His jacket would have looked well on a Romanian shepherd, but he carried it off, affecting an air of casual disregard. He walked from a side door, onto the front of the stage, reading from a paper as he came.

Then, turning to scan the assembled actors from left to right, he hoisted himself onto the edge of the stage, where he sat, legs dangling, a formidable presence.

'Greetings,' he said. 'You may have heard of a little play called *A Doll's House*, by Henrik Ibsen. Originally written in Danish, but the English language version of the play is selling out night after night in London and New York right now. My objective is to do the same thing, here in Cape Town.' He looked out, and through some artifice seemed to lock eyes with each and every person in the hall. 'You and I are going to make it happen.'

Someone started to clap, and the others followed. It was an act of sycophancy, if not hero worship, but it seemed fitting, so Harriet joined in. When it died down, the director spoke again.

'I,' he said, 'am going to sit down over there.' He pointed to a seat in the middle of about the fifth row. 'I will call the parts starting with the more minor roles. Miss Klassen and I,' he waved at the woman who had been out the front collecting names and was now walking down the aisle, 'have chosen scenes for each character, and she will pass the relevant speech out now, so you can study. Please form a line, and we will apportion potential roles.'

There followed a rumble of conversation as the line opened up, and the first actor fronted the director.

'This one looks like a possible Torvald, what do you think, Miss Klassen?'

'A little old perhaps,' she said, 'but he can try that first, otherwise Dr Rank?'

The next in line was the woman Harriet had been speaking to. 'The nanny?' Miss Klassen ventured.

'Yes, I think so.'

When Harriet's turn came, she raised her chin and let the pair scrutinise her. 'Is she too young and pretty for Nora, do you think?' asked Miss Klassen. 'Or might she play Kristine?'

The director held his lips close together. 'I've never seen you before,' he said to Harriet.

'No, I recently arrived from London.'

'Have you any major productions to your credit?'

'Only at school,' she said, and there was a ripple of laughter at this.

'Let her try out for Nora,' he said. 'Might as well throw her in the deep end.'

Back in her seat, Harriet had barely enough light to read the script. She had a vague idea of the storyline, and the chosen scene, she guessed, was somewhere in the middle.

Meanwhile she half-watched the auditions. Most of the actors, she realised, were accomplished actors. Most were very good, though some were thin-voiced or overly dramatic, too fond of gestures and repetitive mannerisms.

The first attempt at Nora, the main part, held Harriet's attention. The woman was a tall brunette, in her early twenties, the right age for a young mother with small children. Her voice projected well, and she read the lines with just the right amount of emotion. The director and his assistant seemed impressed, making some notes before bringing the next contender forward.

'Harriet Morton,' called the director.

Harriet felt a pounding in her chest as she climbed the stairs leading up to the stage. Taking her stance in the centre, she composed herself, then began the speech. During a pause, however, she heard the sound of voices, and she looked down, past the director, to where three middle-aged men were walking in single file down the aisle and into the theatre.

Harriet froze. One of the men had been on board the *Ormuz* when they sailed from London. He was the one who had seen her without clothes in a photograph in a filthy shop. Heat burned in her forehead and neck. She could think of only one thing, leaving the theatre as fast as possible.

'What's wrong dear?' said the director's assistant. 'Don't let them distract you. They are the money men, the funders. They love to come and watch the auditions.'

Harriet hurried down the steps and ran towards the side door, leaving her *savoir faire* behind her like Cinderella's shoe. Even before the door had closed behind her, and she was into the outside air, she was crying, blundering her way down the street where she hailed a cab and gasped out her address, unable to breathe until she was at home, in her bedroom, with the door closed and Betts knocking on the door asking if she was alright.

Chapter Fifty-one

As the *Vesuvius* crossed the Indian Ocean; day after day of deep blue and benign seas, Eadie began to feel a little better. The slight bulge of her tummy when she looked down as she dressed, both delighted and shamed her at the same time.

More than once, when taking the sun on the boat deck, she ran into the young man with the burned face and neck. Sometimes they spoke. It was difficult for her to look at him, initially, but avoiding doing so made her feel guilty, so she learned to do it without flinching. He reminded her of an injured young tom cat, angry at the world, and doomed to meet his end from a slingshot-propelled stone, or a stronger, angrier cat. The scarred man didn't eat in the dining room, or go to the library, but he did spend time in the sun. He was doing so, he said, because the doctor had told him that tanning might help to hide the scars.

That evening Eadie began knitting a scarf from the softest wool she could find amongst the store she had brought with her to make baby things. It took three days to finish the item, and she carried it around until she happened to see him.

Seeing him arrive in a deck chair one day, she took the package from her bag, then walked across and placed it in his hands. The scarf was wrapped in tissue paper, like a real gift should, with a ribbon made of brown string.

She said, 'I thought you might wear it at supper.'

The scarred young man tore the package open like any child on his birthday. He stared up at her, touched the soft blue fabric, then stood up and went inside, something terrible and strange in his face. He didn't say thank you, just glared and left.

A week passed before she saw him again, and he was wearing the scarf around his neck, staring out at the sea. She had almost walked past when he addressed her.

'I'm wearin' the scarf if it makes you 'appy.'

'You didn't say thank you,' she said.

He stared back at her. 'Well thank you Miss, that you might take pity on a wretch such as I.'

'You are not a wretch, and pity is better than disgust.'

'I don't want pity. I was a big man, just a short while ago, I drank respect like other men drink ale. No one crossed me. Now I only frighten children.'

Eadie reached out and gripped his arm. 'You are not nothing. Don't ever think that.'

Craven narrowed his eyes. 'I know what you are,' he snarled. 'One of those bleeding 'earts oo adopts sick birds and dogs that 'ave been hit by wagons. Well, I don't need your type – keep away from me, right?'

Eadie looked into his eyes, saw he meant every word, and backed away.

★★★

When the *Vesuvius* steamed into Columbo, Ceylon, with a full day in port for coaling, Eadie was eager to set foot on dry ground. Over the gangplank and onto the jetty, she mingled with the other passengers from both her own ship and another larger one, inbound from Sydney.

A young man pressed her to allow him to take a photograph of her with the harbour as a backdrop. The camera was the smallest one she had seen, no larger than a shoebox, set on a sturdy folding tripod.

She stood, with the water of the harbour behind her, dotted with sails, the commerce fleet of the East, and a smile on her lips. Her body still felt the rise and fall of the ocean, despite the hard ground beneath her feet, and she swayed like a piece of flotsam.

'Bravo,' cried the photographer. 'Now hold still, as still as you are able.'

The shutter clicked, and the man thanked her, before wandering off to find a new subject. She followed the press of passengers towards the Colombo foreshore, past the ships in dry dock, chocked up with heavy timber props while workers scrubbed the hulls, or painted them with tar.

The waterfront streets were crammed with businesses trying to make the most of the wandering travellers. Taverns, restaurants, souvenir shops, street sellers and cafés were crowded into ramshackle rows. Finding a vacant place was no easy matter, for the other steamer in port had twice as many passengers as Eadie's, and many of those had come ashore, seeking respite from the journey.

Finally, at a small, clean café she spotted an empty spot, but she wasn't sure if sitting down was polite, for two tanned and attractive young ladies were seated on the other side of the table. Their accents were recognisably Australian.

One of the pair noticed Eadie looking. 'Oh, please do join us — the seat is free, and we love company.'

'Thank you so much,' Eadie said, accepting the offer gratefully, 'there are other cafés, but they seem to be a little less — salubrious.'

'Quite right ... I saw one where a dog was licking plates clean on a table.'

Eadie laughed. 'Sounds like something you'd see in the East End, back home.'

'London you mean?'

'Yes. Where are you from?'

'New South Wales, and we're sisters. I'm Kate Sweetman, and this is Agnes. You are from London? This is our first trip Home. We're beside ourselves with excitement.'

A waiter arrived, and Eadie ordered a cup of tea and a small fruit tart. Both items arrived promptly. The tea was fresher and more aromatic than it was at home.

'At least the weather shouldn't be so bad. What part of the colony are you from?'

'Sydney.'

Eadie's eyes lit up, 'Oh really, my brother and his friend arrived there a few months ago, Sam Harris and Denny Morton.'

'Really?' Kate enthused. 'They aren't in the business of selling steam engines, are they?'

'Yes, that's them. You really met Sam and Denny?'

'Yes, we did. We attended a charity dinner at the Town Hall, and Father introduced us.'

'Denny Morton's ever so handsome,' said Agnes.

Eadie swooned at the memory of him, 'He is, yes.'

'Bad luck for us though, he's already taken,' Kate confided, as if telling an old friend a secret.

'Yes, he's getting married,' Agnes added.

Eadie stared, 'Is he?'

'Yes.'

'Who to, may I enquire?'

'Some society lady I believe,' said Kate, eager to embellish the story.

'Her name is Elizabeth,' said Agnes, 'or something like that.' The sisters smiled over their imperfect memories.

Eadie felt her face turn pink, burning with confusion, 'When is he to be married?'

'Soon, I think,' said Agnes. 'I imagine that we would have been invited, had we been in Sydney on the date.'

'Forgive me,' said Eadie. 'I'm not feeling so well.'

Eadie stumbled to the counter, her fingers shaking so badly that it took her several tries to unclasp her purse and pay. A hammering sound began in her ears, and her feet might have wandered anywhere, heading back towards the ship by mere luck.

***

In the weeks after their first meeting, May had corresponded with James Washington of New York regularly, but once the reality of the distance separating them sunk in, the letters became sporadic. Still, she found herself thinking of him at odd moments. She would remember something he had said in regard to engineering or politics – or recall his respectful nature fondly.

Then, in the midst of the busiest period of her life, with looming examinations as well as double shifts keeping the factory going around the clock, a letter arrived from New York. James was very sorry for the short notice, but he was in London for a symposium, and would she mind if he called on her?

It was bad timing, but still her heart gave a little jump.

May fashioned a reply at her desk, using one of her few luxuries – high quality stationery, thick rag paper, that showed her jet-black India ink beautifully. She wrote that she welcomed his visit, and of course she would make time to show him the sights.

***

Having never been on a dinner date in her life, the décor, staff and food at Sweetings in the City impressed May a great deal. James, also, was a pleasure to be with – even more thoughtful than she remembered, asking searching questions about her university studies but avoiding probing too deeply about the Morton business.

'What about you?' she asked. 'What's this symposium you're attending?'

'Nothing too interesting, especially not for you mechanical engineers – it's as much architecture as engineering, all about the design of high-rise buildings – my field, really, but I have a secret ambition to get more involved in the architecture side of things. I have my secret file, but no one has seen it.'

'I'd love to see your designs,' she said.

'They're at home, but New York is less than a week's voyage away. I'll expect you over for a visit soon.'

'It's very tempting.'

'Then it's settled,' said James.

'Not settled, but I'll come over as soon as I can,' she promised.

As the dessert – a spicy pear strudel – arrived, James asked, 'So have you turned your hand to any designs of your own yet?'

'Not really, only projects I had to complete for my studies. I have a few ideas though.'

'Get them down on paper, don't wait.'

May smiled, 'I'll do that.'

After the meal they strolled down to Grosvenor Bridge, looking down on the river, watching small craft pass by, small steam launches with glowing fireboxes and sparks flying from the stacks. It was a cool evening, and James let his left arm creep over her shoulder and held her warm and close.

'I didn't know it could be like this,' May said.

'What do you mean?'

'Just being with someone, standing on a bridge. I didn't know it could feel like this.'

James drew her closer. 'To be honest, Miss Morton, I didn't know it could feel like this either.'

★★★

When the cab dropped May back home, she was feeling much too alive to go to bed. Despite the hour, she lit a lantern, went to her desk in her bedroom, settled herself onto the chair while allowing herself a final sparkling memory of the night, then took out some drafting paper, a pencil and a rule, and began to work on the first personal design she had ever attempted.

Until then she had not articulated her ideas, but they were all there, compartmentalised in her mind. It seemed that all she had to do was bring them forth, and they would be transferred to her drafting pencil.

The drawing she began was little more than a concept. The sizing was important. Her first engine had to be powerful enough to slot into the most common industrial applications – she knew the importance of sales potential better than most engineers. An hour passed, then two, and May had to force herself to put down the tools of her trade and go to sleep.

Two days later when May accompanied James to Southampton for the journey back to New York, he kissed her cheek and embraced her politely.

'Keep your eye out for positions for me,' he said.

'What do you mean?'

'I mean that I have a strange feeling I'd like to live in England.'

'Don't toy with me,' she said.

'I'm an engineer. I don't toy with anyone.'

After he had boarded, she felt the rumble of the ship's engines transmitted through the earth and sea, and watched him waving from the rail. She was surprised to feel a tear in the corner of her eye, melting like ice, becoming warm, trickling and tickling until it left a wet drop-stain on the material of her dress.

★★★

Harriet was at work in the little office. She had missed Matthew every moment since he left, but today more than usual.

A heavy knock on the door was unusual, and she opened it to find the man from the theatre in the door frame.

'Do you have to follow me? Haven't you hurt me enough.'

'I came to apologise, may I come in?'

Harriet stared at him, 'I'm busy, as long as you are quick.'

She turned away and he followed her into the tiny office.

'I thought you were a different kind of girl,' he said. 'Now I understand that you are not. I'm very sorry for the things I said on the ship.'

'How did you find me?'

'I made it my business to learn who you are, and your little operation here is listed in the Business Directory.' He lowered his eyes. 'Your secret is safe with me, I promise, and I think you'd make a superb Nora.'

'It's a bit late now, isn't it?'

'No. They didn't settle on an actress to play the main part, and Richard, the director, asked where you had gone.'

'I'm a little too young to play Nora anyway.'

'Not at all, a little make-up will add a year or two. Just say the word, tomorrow at noon perhaps? I'll make sure you get a proper audition.'

★★★

The following day, Harriet walked into the theatre. The gaslights were again burning on either side of the stage. She could hear the director's assistant talking, 'It's hardly fair – she's had more time to study the script than the others.'

The director saw her coming, 'Come on up, Miss Morton. Horace told me that you and he had a misunderstanding of some kind on the ship. His presence obviously gave you a start. That's understandable. You are auditioning for Nora?'

'Yes, if I may.'

'Certainly.'

Harriet ascended the side steps. She no longer needed the script but kept it to hand in case.

On the stage itself she took a moment to compose herself, then seemed to transform. She slouched and relaxed her lower back. Her stomach changed from one that was flat and smooth, to one more pliable – that had known the pain of childhood. Her face became that of a woman who has lived with disappointment.

Harriet's lips were dry, and she felt a pounding in her chest. She was conscious of the heat of the lights on her cheeks. The director waited until she had settled herself.

'If you are ready, Miss Morton, I will read the part of Torvald.' Harriet let the magic happen; felt herself transform into what she already knew of the play, and her brief reading of the character.

When she spoke, it was with the voice of a woman a little older, to a husband she could no longer love. 'That is just it,' she began. 'You have never understood me. I have been greatly wronged – first by Papa and then by you.'

The Director kept his voice flat – backgrounding himself and his part. 'What! By us two – by us two, who have loved you better than anyone else in the world?'

Harriet shook her head, delved inside her heart for pain and indignation. 'You have never loved me. You have only thought it pleasant to be in love with me.'

'Nora, what do I hear you saying?' The director's voice was clear and true, filled with the entitlement that a real-life Torvald would have felt.

Harriet drew herself up, seemed to grow in stature. 'It is perfectly true, Torvald. When I was at home with Papa, he told me his opinion about everything, and so I had the same opinions; and if I differed from him, I concealed the fact, because he would not have liked it. He called me his doll-child, and he played with me just as I used to play with my dolls. And when I came to live with you—'

'How unreasonable and how ungrateful you are, Nora! Have you not been happy here?'

'No, I have never been happy. I thought I was, but it has never really been so. And you have always been so kind to me. But our home has been nothing but a playroom. I have been your doll-wife, just as at home I was Papa's doll-child; and here the children have been my dolls. I thought it great fun when you played with me, just as they thought it great fun when I played with them. That is what our marriage has been—'

The director raised one hand and snapped his finger. 'Stop there,' he said.

Harriet came out of her character with difficulty, still overrun with Nora's outrage.

'You were right,' said Miss Klassen. 'She's perfect. A little make up will give her the couple of years she needs to play the part.'

The director addressed Harriet directly. 'Would you like to be Nora in our play?'

Harriet felt as light as air. 'Will you really give me the part?'

'No, Miss Harriet Morton, I do not give you the part. You have seized it for yourself.'

Chapter Fifty-two

When Matthew climbed aboard the train for the long trip south, he was feeling rather pleased with his progress. He had taken two more firm orders, and several other companies had asked for detailed quotes, that would keep him busy back in Cape Town.

When Harriet collected him from the station, and they set off down Castle Street with Roundhead Jimmy holding the reins, she grinned at her brother. 'I've got two bits of news,' she teased.

'Both good?' he asked.

'I think so. The first is that I have the lead role in a play – a professional production here in Cape Town.'

Matthew's heart skipped. He knew how much this must mean to her. 'Congratulations, that's beyond … anything. How did it happen?'

'I auditioned, and they selected me.'

'I can't wait to hear all about it. What's the second item?'

'There's a letter for you back at the apartment,' teased Harriet. 'Not from family either.'

'Oh?' he asked. 'Probably from one of the fellows at Oxford.'

'I doubt it – the postmark indicates that the letter is from, oh somewhere in Europe.'

'You horrid tease!' he cried. 'Where is it from?'

'Prague.'

'Really?' Matthew said, then nothing more. This was a private anticipation, not one that he wished to share with his sister. 'Now, please, tell me how you got this part.'

When they arrived back at the apartment that was starting to feel like home, he dropped his bags through the threshold and turned on her. 'Where's the letter?'

Harriet picked up an envelope from the sideboard, making a pretence of examining the back flap. 'Someone called Miss Pattinson, would you happen to know her?'

Matthew felt a jolt like a kick in the chest. 'Please can I have it?'

'I suppose … unless you want me to read it aloud to you?'

'Absolutely not.'

Matthew took the envelope from Harriet, walked to his room and closed the door. He used a letter opener to slice open the flap. There were four pages inside, all with a faint, feminine scent. It was strange, as if the wonderful Miss Pattinson had just arrived in the room with him.

Dear Mr. Morton

Or may I call you Matthew? I do detest the stuffiness of English manners, though Prague is just as bad. Of course, I remember you; such a bright young man with the eyes of a poet.

I loved reading the stories of your adventures. I mean it too. I remember you told me that you want to be a writer one day. I hope you do; you are very talented.

I am looking forward to corresponding with you, and it will be fun to both be in Oxford again in twelve months' time …

Miss Pattinson went on to lampoon the previous few months in Prague, bringing aristocratic drawing rooms, imperious military barons, and gossiping aunts to life in Matthew's mind. He finished reading, then started again at the beginning. His heart was as light as a bird. Nothing seemed as important as the wonderful, smart, special, beautiful Miss Pattinson, and the chance of seeing her again in the future.

★★★

Later, when he strolled on the beach in the company of Jules and Harriet, Matthew prevailed on his friend to walk at a distance from his sister, all the while extolling the virtues of the object of his affections, and the literary merit and emotional nuances of her letter.

'I think she likes me,' he exclaimed.

'No doubt she does,' said Jules. 'What kind of fool would not?'

Walking on, they saw a man swimming face down in the shallows of the bay, never coming up for air. Matthew opened his mouth to pour forth another superlative on the subject of his obsession, before he noticed that Jules had stopped.

'*Mon dieu*,' said Jules. 'This is quite the extraordinary thing.'

The man in the water appeared, incredibly, to be breathing through a hollow tube. Jules stood, watching as the man swam back to shore and stepped out of the water. On his face was a rubber contraption with a clear pane of glass, like a window. It covered his eyes and nose. A bent tube extended from his lips. The man's hands held a spear, and from the point dangled a small fish, still kicking feebly.

'How ingenious,' said Jules, striding across to make the swimmer's acquaintance. The man was, it turned out, a midshipman on a Royal Navy tender at the naval yards, who had made the underwater apparatus himself. Jules insisted on studying the water mask, turning it over and over in his hands, marvelling at the ingenious simplicity of the device.

For the rest of their stroll Jules waved away any further discussion of Miss Pattinson. Instead, he enthused about the navy man and his ability to see underwater.

'It's incredible. Divers wear a suit weighing two hundred pounds, and have to be fed air through a hose. With the bent tube and mask a man can swim around with a never-ending supply of air, doing whatever he likes!'

'Quite a lark,' said Matthew, but he was disappointed that the conversation had moved on.

★★★

By the following evening, Jules was on the balcony with Matthew, working with a knife, evil-smelling glue, and a circular pane of glass the size of a demitasse saucer, cut for him by a local glazier.

'I'm getting there,' Jules told Harriet. 'The idea is so simple it's a wonder it hasn't caught on before this.'

Over the following days, the trials and triumphs of the process were almost comical. Jules with his head in his hands: 'It leaks so bad I cannot seem to stop it. There is no way to shape the rubber to my face.' Jules smiling, and the smell of cooking fish: 'It works, Harriet. It really does. The mask still leaks, but I could see well enough to spear a sea bream.' Jules dripping wet and freezing cold: 'I stayed in a little too long,' he said. 'I just wanted to get used to the tube and the mask together.'

The fish he dropped into the kitchen sink were welcome, as were the deep green crayfish, boiling to a brilliant orange in the pot. Over time, as Harriet grew busy with both rehearsals and work, however, she started to find Jules's obsession tiresome. 'When are you going to do something productive?' she asked one evening when he arrived at the theatre to walk her to the tram stop, 'Like find some work.'

'I help you with feeding the poor at Woodstock.'

'You spend most of your time arguing biblical quotations with the shop keeper, and that's only once each week.'

Jules broke a long silence with, 'Your brother is a very special person.'

'I know.'

'So are you.'

'Thank you.'

'You are the most beautiful girl I have ever seen.'

Harriet lifted her hand as if to push his words away. 'Please, don't say that. Now hurry ... the tram.'

'Why should I hold back from saying the truth?'

'Stop now, please.'

Jules lowered his head. 'Very well, I will do as you say. But I must tell you, that I'm not so easily deterred.'

Harriet strode at a pace her father would have been proud of. 'Well, I am not prone to succumb to pestering.'

★★★

The encounter niggled at Harriet's consciousness for a day or two, but she was busy, and somewhat distracted by the appearance of one of her letters in the editorial section of the Cape Times. She was rather pleased with it, and even Matthew told her that it was 'well written,' and she took this as high praise.

Three days later the paper printed a response from another reader, calling her several unflattering names. Another was published in support. This one was signed by a Jasmine, President of the South African Equality League. The title intrigued her a great deal.

★★★

May would accompany Frederick to the factory most mornings, but on Wednesdays she had an early start at university, and he made his way in alone, with Jenkins making polite conversation beside him.

Inside, the night shift were finishing off, and the day crew were starting to arrive, shrugging into their work gear, including leather aprons and gloves. With the work of building so many engines, Frederick had to pull his weight in the factory, and he headed for the assembly bay where two unfinished Fortis assemblies sat on a low platform. Taking up a spanner and half a dozen Whitworth-thread bolts, he began to join the lower housing onto the frame. The activity both warmed and absorbed him, yet his mind was on other things.

The monthly payment to Percy Forgill fell due on Friday the twenty-ninth, and Clare's file of invoices at sixty and ninety days was half an inch thick. Frederick kept his hands busy, but his mind was prioritising these bills, thinking through the ramifications of late payments for each.

Unfortunately, gearing up for the BHP order was proving to be more costly than anticipated, and whichever way Frederick looked at it, the best solution was to pay suppliers and employees, and hold off on paying debt.

After stewing about the situation for most of the morning, Frederick retired to his office and wrote a letter to Ned Baring asking for advice. He sealed the communication in an envelope and sent it off with an apprentice for posting.

> I'm sorry to report that the situation is again difficult. The only thing I can do is sell the shares we obtained as part of the Australian deal.

The last mail of the day brought a scrawled note from Ned Baring.

> Don't sell those BHP shares, whatever you do! They're worth twenty pounds each and heading skyward like Chinese rockets. Borrow against them if you must but DO NOT SELL.

★★★

Two of Eadie's cabin mates were English women, themselves on a long and uncertain journey to marry men they scarcely knew. They huddled together and spoke in low voices, knitting clothes for babies that existed only in their minds.

Eadie's third cabin-mate occupied the top bunk against the stern wall. She was a little older – a prim Devonshire widow with a small income, heading out to join an elder brother and his family in the

Adelaide Hills. She was pinched of face and small of mouth, relishing gossip and any opportunity to demonstrate her moral superiority.

Yet, those three had become close over the voyage, and had for some time been aware of Eadie's 'condition'. The bulge in her stomach was noticeable when the young woman was dressing, as was the way her seasickness had been most acute in the morning.

After days of whispering behind palms, and secret conferences in the passage, the three 'concerned passengers' informed the steward that Eadie was hiding a pregnancy, and they were worried for her health.

Soon afterwards, a written message instructed Eadie to present herself to the ship's doctor for an examination. The Devonshire widow insisted on escorting her down the corridors past the row of cabins.

The doctor was a forty-five-year-old man with red veins in his nose and cheeks, and clammy hands. He asked Eadie to disrobe and lie prone while he listened to her heart with his stethoscope, moving the drum around near her breastbone. With his hands and fingers, he probed her breasts then stomach, all with a serious, inquiring expression on his face.

Finished at last, he sat in his chair. 'You are between two and three months pregnant,' he said.

'I know that,' she said, and since he did not ask to her to start dressing again, she took it upon herself to do so.

'Since you are not married,' he said. 'I take it that you are on your way to Australia to rectify the situation. The father is there?'

'The child's father is there, yes,' she said, but she could not prevent a stricken look.

The doctor winced at her reaction. 'May I then conclude that a wedding is by no means settled?'

Eadie said nothing. The words smacked of judgement, snide paternalism, and they wounded her.

The doctor dipped his quill in an inkwell and scribbled on a pad.

He tore off the page and passed it to her. It was a woman's name. 'This lady runs a house in Balmain. She will feed and clothe you until your baby comes, at which point a fine adoptive home will be found.'

'May I leave now?'

'Yes, of course.'

Eadie left the doctor's cabin and walked out onto the boat deck, which was a quiet area at this time of day. She had set off, in good faith, to join a man who was no longer hers, in a foreign country. No doubt everyone on board now knew she was single and pregnant.

The thought of returning to her cabin, and the company of disapproving females was unsupportable, and she wandered the deck, staring at the sea as if it were an implacable enemy, the force that had borne Denny away from her, and brought on an endless nausea.

★★★

Later in the day a light rain began to fall, accompanied by strong pulses of cold air.

A figure appeared at the rail beside her. A brief sideways glance confirmed her first thought – it was the man with the scarred face, wearing the grey scarf she had knitted for him.

'What 'appened to you?' he asked. 'I 'aven't seen you much.'

Eadie ignored him.

'So now you won't talk to me?'

Still, she said nothing.

'I heard people gossipin'. They say that you're in the family way.'

Eadie felt the tears slide down her face. 'The man I thought I was going to marry, is marrying someone else.'

'Denny Morton is a bleeding, God-forsaken idiot.'

Eadie turned. 'You know him?'

Craven shook his head. 'Not personally. I know of 'im, but I can't tell you 'ow or why.'

Chapter Fifty-three

'Percy and Sophie grew up with no mother – they were wild, and mixed up with all manner of nonsense,' said Eve Simpson, as she fussed with the teapot, pouring cups for Clare, Eleanor and herself, offering milk from a jug and a bowl filled with lumps of sugar. 'The worst job I ever had, I don't mind saying, and I had high hopes, with them being nobility an' all.'

Percy Forgill's former nurse was around sixty-five years, Clare decided, and appeared to have abandoned any regard for fashion, wearing a yellowed calico dress like a rhino's hide. The house itself had a buttery smell, and a brown pigment defined the room. From the wallpaper to the interior doors, brown was so dominant that even the fine teak furniture – heirlooms surely – took on that shade.

The window, however, admitted a blaze of light, dazzling from the saltings below the village of Leigh-on-sea, the flats littered with boats on the hard, fallen to one side while they waited for the tide. It was a calming view for Clare as she listened to the nurse speak, letting loose a torrent of thoughts and observations that must have been bottled up for a long time.

'Lord Bartholomew married badly. His wife was a social climber, who had got her hooks into him with the help of a conniving mother, and she was addicted to laudanum. She died when she was just twenty-nine – drowned at night in a lake on their country property. Then, when the boy died—'

'The police told me that you made the original allegation that Percy killed his brother,' Clare said.

Eve cocked her head at a funny angle. 'That's what they told you, is it?'

'Isn't it the truth?'

'Well in part, Mrs Morton, but my allegation concerns more than just Percy. He wasn't the worst of them.'

'No?'

'I think Percy pushed his twin down the stairs, but only after Sophie had beaten the poor boy around the head.' Her voice shook. 'I saw with my own eyes the chair leg that had been unscrewed from a small table that she did it with.'

'You think Sophie did the actual killing?'

'I cannot be sure, but that is what I believe. Oh, she was such a beautiful but cruel girl! When she was a mere tot she would pinch me to see if she could make me cry. When I complained to Lord Forgill, he would make her apologise, but it meant nothing. His children were his weakness, but in all other respects he was a wonderful man. He paid for this house. He gave it to me before his death – it had been in the family for a long time, he told me. Out of consideration for him I maintained my silence, but once he was dead, I went to the police.'

Clare stared silently at first, then, 'You are like Frederick, my husband. Lord Forgill did the same; helped his career and gave him a house.' She paused, 'Have Sophie and Percy been in contact with you?'

Eve Simpson's eyes darkened. 'She hasn't changed. After the police investigation they both came here, and threatened me. Sophie herself has been back twice more over the years, raving and carrying on.'

The former nurse lowered her teacup, walked to the mantle and took down a wooden box. 'When my father died, this was among his things.' When she opened the lid, Clare saw that it contained a revolver with a wooden grip and blued-steel cylinder and barrel. Six brass cartridges nestled in holes drilled in the wood.

'If Sophie comes back again,' she said. 'If she tries to hurt me. I will kill her.'

★★★

With rehearsals taking much of her time, on a rare free evening Harriet would sometimes walk to Mouille Point where Jules liked to spear-fish. Taking a seat on the grass, she would read a book or watch the surf smashing against the cliffs below – with Robben Island standing clear from the sea in the distance.

Far from shore Jules would fearlessly swim, with a spear in one hand and a netting fish bag tied around his waist. There would always be a flutter of worry in Harriet's heart as she watched him, and the words on the page would diminish in importance until she saw him step out of the water, turn to acknowledge her, drop his bag of fish and pose in the sun like a cormorant drying her wings.

Today, having worked until three-thirty, Harriet spent half an hour shopping for the weekend's stall out at Woodstock, dropped the goods off at home then headed off down to her favoured seat on the grass with a copy of Washington Square by Henry James. She read a page or two, then, with the music of the words still dancing in her head, watched for Jules to appear on the rocks below.

It was near five when he came, swivelling his head to see if she was there, then giving her a cheery wave. She watched him pick his way down to the water, cleaning out his mask then pushing out through the shore-break with his fish-spear extended in front. On each occasion he ventured further out into the water, diving more deeply, staying down longer. Today was no exception, and Harriet divided her time between keeping an eye on Jules, reading her book, and pausing to scan for creatures, both in the sea and aloft. Before long she spotted a pod of seals working a bait shoal along the coast a little, then a majestic sea eagle.

When she saw a black fin rise through the surface not far behind Jules, at first she dismissed it as a porpoise, yet there was something brutal about the blunt shape, at least the length of her forearm.

The first jolt of alarm came with the realisation that the fin seemed to be following Jules, zig-zagging through the light wind chop behind him. Harriet's breath caught in her throat. Henry James fell from her hands to the grass, closing in the process. The breeze was in her face, as she opened her mouth to call her friend's name.

A man fishing on the water's edge, cat-gut line between his fingers, turned at the sound of her shout. Holding her skirts away from her ankles, she ran down the hillside of broken rock, yet even when she had run as close as she dared, just above the surge of swell and spray, he was still quite a distance out.

The fin disappeared, and she worried this meant that the shark had submerged in order to attack. She waved both hands and shouted for Jules with all the breath in her lungs. By sheer accident, or some trick of breeze and water he seemed to hear her, raising his head momentarily. After a short hesitation he started to swim back. Harriet watched his progress; every kick of his legs and every stroke of his arm.

Finally, he scurried up the rocks between breakers, still carrying his fish bag. He plodded towards her. 'What's wrong?' he asked.

'You fool,' she stamped, and turned away, swallowing the tears of desperate worry that dripped down her cheeks.

★★★

Back in Sydney Denny found that there was more to do than there were hours in the day. The most important business, apart from hunting up new orders, was preparing for the transport of the Broken Hill engines.

Delivering them to Sydney, it seemed, was not the best option, and Denny advised his father that the engines would best be shipped to Port Pirie, South Australia, from whence they could be carried by rail to Cockburn, South Australia, then transferred on the Silverton Tramway to Broken Hill. The last mile or two would be dependent on a bullock team.

'The trains carry ore to Port Pirie, and the cars are damned near always empty on the trip back – we should be able to negotiate an excellent rate,' said Denny, and set about writing letters.

Written correspondence, followed by site visits, was proving to be the best way of selling engines in such a big country. Denny and Sam sent one hundred letters in two weeks – sawmills, big sheep stations and mining companies.

The replies were few, but they were followed up rigorously. 'We'll need another trip,' Denny declared, 'just as soon as Eadie is here and settled.'

★★★

Suffocating heat, heaving seas, and seasickness caused Eadie's mental state to disintegrate further. She hardly left her bed, where she bathed in tropical sweat. Soon she developed boils in her armpits but did not notice them until the swelling grew so bad it interfered with her ability to change positions in bed.

She began to think about the sea, about the somnolent beauty of the waves, the coolness – an escape from the incessant heat. She imagined what a relief it would be to fall over the side in the darkness, there to be cushioned and cooled by the waves.

In the sea there would be no more hot sweats. No more images of Denny and the society girl he would marry. She had known that the Morton family were moving upwards in an economic sense, and this had seemed to be a good thing when he had been in love with her. Once they were apart, however, it appeared to have been their undoing.

Sitting up in bed, she stood and reached for her robe.

'Where are you goin', Eadie darlin'?' crooned the Devonshire widow.

Eadie shuddered. In recent days her cabin mates had become patronising, and sometimes called her 'Our Eadie,' or even 'Our poor Eadie.' It made her feel like she was dying, and that thought had become a compelling one.

'I just need a little air,' she said, then turned the door handle.

Out on deck, she walked through a patch of air that made memories and feelings flood her system – some interaction of motion and crosswind, air that twined shipboard smells with those of the vast ocean. Something there reminded her of childhood; family trips to the sea.

At the rail she stared down at the black water, full of mystery and the promise of an ending, or a new beginning. Out here, God alone knew how far from the vast coast of Australia, survival would not be possible. The thought comforted her. She did not want to end up on some foreign beach, just the embrace of cool nothingness forever.

Lifting her nightdress, Eadie climbed over the rail, standing with her heels on the very edge of the deck. Tears streamed down her face, but they were tears of joy and relief.

'Hey! Don't be a duffer,' called a voice, accompanied by the heavy sound of boots on deck. Eadie swivelled her head to see. It was the man with the scars, wearing the grey scarf around his neck.

She turned back to the sea, knowing what she wanted. Before he could reach her, she let herself fall in an untidy tangle. Those moments of emptiness were fleeting, then the shock of hitting the water numbed everything. She landed on her side and the impact was terrible, pain came in heavy pulses. Eadie didn't care. This was for the best. The power from her jump, shattering at first, then drove her deep down under the water surface until her natural buoyancy carried her upwards again.

Bursting through the surface she looked up for long enough to hear a loud shout and see another figure falling from the deck towards the water.

Eadie went under again, for she could not swim. A moment of panic took her in its grip. The pain and shock of being unable to breathe started to replace the solace she had felt at first.

She felt herself sinking, and her arms flailed at the water. Then, however, as her movements began to slow, an arm wrapped around her middle.

'Let me go,' she cried as her head burst through the surface.

She tried to fight him off, but still she sucked at the life-giving air.

'I'm a bad bastard,' said Peter Craven, spluttering at the water in and around his lips. 'But I aren't bad enough to watch an angel like you drown in the fucking sea.'

Eadie gasped, her mind exploding into fragments, but the great bulk of the *Vesuvius* was moving away from them, the stacks belching smoke into the moonlit sky.

★★★

Over time, a new fatalism came over Eadie. She knew that the man who held her was struggling to keep them afloat, though they both observed that the ship was now slowing and turning around, surely to look for them. Someone had heard the shouts or seen them fall.

'I can paddle a bit,' gasped Craven, 'for I've been a Thames-rat since the day I were born, but it ain't easy to swim for two.'

Eadie felt his hands under her armpits, as he sought to lift her up at his own expense, but he was going under periodically, coming up gasping and spitting. Lights began to play across the water surface.

'They've stopped just yonder,' Craven managed to gasp.

'Launching a boat, it looks like.'

But it was far away, and Craven's strength had reached the limit. His head was slipping beneath the waves more and more as he fought to keep Eadie elevated.

'H'aint it funny that Denny Morton will live, and I'll die,' he managed once.

'They're coming for us,' Eadie managed.

'Too late Miss Eadie. I'm fucked.'

He went under, releasing her then, sliding beneath the boiling surface, and she sank also, reaching out for him. But her lungs were filling with water.

New hands grasped her, dragging her up into the lifeboat. 'Please save him,' she tried to say, but they were turning her on her side. A torrent of seawater and vomit came from her mouth.

She tried to sit up. 'Help him, please.'

Two men dived again and again, before gripping the sides of the boat and heaving aboard.

'I'm sorry miss, but he's gone.'

Eadie was crying, streaming tears. A man was dead, and her actions were the cause.

★★★

When Harriet left the office, she found Jules waiting on the street. The first thing she noticed was his appearance: neat black trousers, polished shoes and starched shirt.

Harriet stifled a giggle, 'Where are you off to, a court appearance?'

'No. Harriet, I need to talk to you.' Jules was fidgety, and gravity tugged at the usual upturn of his lips.

'You are not heading down to the water this afternoon?' she asked.

'No, Harriet. It's time for me to leave.'

'Oh,' she said. 'You intend to fly back up over the continent?'

'No, I will take my balloon folded and stowed. I'll catch a steamer to Marseilles, and travel home from there by train and coach. Can I talk to you? Shall we have tea, or coffee?'

Harriet's expression was a little guarded, if not suspicious. 'If you want to.'

They sat in a nearby cafe, drinking tea, and sharing an apple tart which he halved neatly, offering her a portion.

'I don't really need it,' she said. 'Yet how can I resist?'

When they had finished eating, he leaned across the table towards her, 'I don't understand how you reconcile your social conscience with playing parts on a stage.'

Harriet bestowed on him a look of pity. 'Art,' she said, 'is humanity. It is kindness, empathy, and understanding – a serious business.'

'So, comedy cannot be art?'

'Only if it has empathy at its core.' She paused. 'Jules, why are you being like this?'

'I told you I must go, yet you seem oblivious.'

'I'm not oblivious. But Jules, some people are not as open about showing what is in their hearts as others. I'll be sad, not least because our show opens in two weeks, and you won't be here to see it. After all, you were the one who suggested that I should audition in the first place.'

He reached out for her hand. 'I love you, Harriet Morton. I want to take my balloon, return to France, and establish myself. Then I'd like you to visit me and allow me the opportunity to woo you.'

'Oh Jules, I'm very flattered that you would want to do that.'

'I want to show Paris to you,' enthused Jules. 'They have just built a tower of iron there that reaches to the sky. The workers on the tip, on some days, could not see their hands in front of their faces because they were in the clouds. And Paris is the home of great theatre – you could be an actress there – amongst the very best.'

Harriet made a face. 'I've already been to Paris, with my mother, and my French is not good enough to act on the stage there. Besides, like London, Paris is a city built on the blood of poor colonies. The grandiose monuments of empire leave me cold.'

'It doesn't matter where the money to build Paris came from. The Eiffel Tower and Arc de Triomphe are like the pyramids. The blood spilled to construct them is lost in time, but the structures will stand forever in memoriam. Paris is a gift to the world, a gift to the ages. Around each corner is a new wonder. I want to kneel with you at Notre Dame where you can almost see God. Walk the halls of the Louvre and feel the strivings and passions of past generations.'

Harriet squeezed his hand. 'You need to find someone else to do those things with you.'

'I will not give up.'

'Would you want me if I could not return your love?'

He did not answer, just looked pained.

'I'm sorry Jules. My priority now is my family. In a matter of days, we will be involved in the public float of the company. I cannot give what you ask of me. My answer must be no.'

When he had gone Harriet burst into tears, loneliness closing in on her like a curtain. She was on a path to something that could not be reconciled with the life she would need to live with him or any other man.

It was not egotism driving her towards a career in the theatre. It was a deep recognition that had begun with Jules's own words of a few months earlier: the realisation that she must serve her talent, and let it take her as far as possible.

★★★

When Eadie opened her eyes, she was lying in a bed, in a cabin with white walls. She saw strange details: rust and flaking paint hanging off the pipes running along the ceiling, a steel bench and sink, and a semi-enclosed shelf holding bottles of various sizes. Her body rolled slightly with the motion of the ship.

Minutes passed before she realised that she was not dead, but back on the ship, in the infirmary. The memory of the rough, scarred man who saved her life came to her like a lightning strike.

'Oh God,' she cried, then prayed under her breath that her memories were only nightmares. It was a vain hope, and she knew it. 'Did they save him?' she burst out finally.

The doctor came through from the other room, dabbing at his face with a handkerchief.

'No, I'm sorry to say that he was lost. Now please stay still, and don't excite yourself. You've swallowed a lot of water.'

Eadie was sobbing, 'It's not fair, he died to save me.'

By evening her forehead was burning and her breathing laboured.

'Pneumonia,' she heard the doctor say to the steward who had come to check on her, 'and a fever with it.'

Those days were an ordeal. The beast of shame and guilt crawled inside her, raked its claws through every organ, and every vein. Saharan heat followed Arctic chills. Time slowed and sped. The doctor's voice was gentle and his face kind. In the worst times she could not hear him, only feel the texture of his hand as it held hers, imploring her to fight.

In this way the dark hours passed. One of several clergymen on board was summoned, murmuring ancient words that gave her scarce comfort. Reality too, became elusive. Images of herself as a younger soul. Childhood days. Mangled truths. Dark thoughts and memories.

'I killed him,' she said aloud, many times.

Late in the darkness of a frightening night, while the ship plunged and tossed, the door to the infirmary opened. The doctor stumbled in and sat on the bed beside her, breathing whisky fumes. For a time he held her hand, tears in his eyes.

'Don't leave me, Maggie, my darling.'

And Eadie knew that he was as lost as she was.

★★★

When the fever broke, she felt a strange sense of calm. The doctor was bleary eyed but sober as he examined her.

'God wants this baby to live,' he said at last. 'If He had wanted you to lose it you would have.'

'Who is Maggie?' she asked.

The doctor looked up at her. 'I'm sorry that I said her name, sometimes it's all a bit much for me.' Their eyes met, an understanding deeper than pain. 'Maggie was my daughter … my wife and I … our marriage didn't survive the loss … I should have been able to save her. That's why I came to sea.'

Chapter Fifty-four

In those last days of wild Southern Ocean swells Eadie fought the *most* virulent illness of her life, and her own fear of the future. Then, in the relative calm of Australia's east coast, she recuperated somewhat.

The sound of cheering from the decks drew her out of her cabin and onto the deck. The cliffs lining the twin massifs of the Sydney Heads reminded her of fortress towers, set against the grey sky of a southerly weather system.

As she stood at the rail, her arms crossed over her chest for warmth and comfort, two desires conflicted in her head. One was to run as far and fast as possible – to book a ticket back to London and the safety of her Lewisham house – yet the thought of two more months of illness and melancholic seas was too much for her to bear. Her other instinct was to see Denny – even if it was just once before he disappeared from her life.

Sam was also in her thoughts. He might soon be ready to go home and perhaps they could leave together, once Eadie had gathered her strength sufficiently to face the voyage again.

The *Vesuvius* docked at Circular Quay, where rows of warehouses, steam cranes, barges and freighters filled the foreshore. Despite herself Eadie scanned for Denny in the waiting crowd, standing with a bunch of flowers on the concourse, looking smart in a dark suit. Sam was beside him, smiling, and she felt a little better. For a moment it seemed like nothing had happened in the intervening time. No pregnancy, no news of Denny's betrayal, not the insanity of her leap over the rail, and the death of a man who had saved not just her life, but that of the child inside her.

The sun beamed down, strengthening the lift in her spirits. Denny had come to see her, indicating that there was something left of their love and friendship.

As she walked down the gangway he spotted her and began to wave. She saw that he had changed too: his skin brown and his hair a little fairer. His hands seemed to have grown.

Sam had to come first. Their relationship was much older, less complicated, and more direct. They embraced and she felt strength flowing into her – his strength bolstering hers.

'Eadie?' Denny asked, and as soon as she had released Sam he moved to her with that fluid way he always had, taking her face in both hands and looking with a serious expression. 'What's wrong, why are you crying?'

When she said nothing, he took her hand. 'Let's not stand here all day. I've taken a room for you where Sam and I are staying. Let's get your things and we'll talk when we get there.'

★★★

Once into the city the traffic was light, and the journey passed swiftly. Despite the weather, however, Eadie's hands were cold and clammy with sweat as she looked out at the streets. The city was lively but frightening, and it seemed that the harbour lay in all directions, shimmering blue.

When they reached Wynyard Square Denny helped Eadie out of the cab. He and Sam collected her things. The room he had arranged for her was in the single women's area, a different set of stairs to Denny's.

'Just take her things up and then leave,' the landlady warned. 'You can do your consortin' somewhere else.'

When they had carried everything in, Denny hesitated. 'When you are washed and refreshed will you come out and eat with me?'

'Of course.'

★★★

Sam did not go with them, when they met downstairs and walked out into Martin Place. 'I'm no genius,' he'd said to Denny, 'but I'm thinking that you two need to talk.

When Denny tried to take Eadie's hand she shook it free. 'What's wrong?' he asked.

She stopped walking. 'How can you ask that? When I found out about you ... and that you are marrying someone else, I was in despair. I still am.'

Denny's brows knit together, as if trying to understand what she was saying. 'Marrying someone else? Why on earth would I do that, and what made you think so?'

'It's not true?'

'Of course not. I have been true to you, in every way. Heart, mind and body. What on earth gave you that idea?'

A sunbeam was starting to break out from Eadie's heart now. 'I was told you were soon to marry, by some young women I met in Colombo – they were on their way to England.'

'I think I know who that must have been, and I did tell them I was getting married – to you.'

Eadie's face showed her confusion. 'They said you were marrying a society girl.'

'Those were their words, not mine. You know how silly some people can be.'

Eadie threw her arms around him. 'Oh God, I've been a fool. Will you forgive me?'

'There's nothing to forgive. I'm the fool.'

Eadie drew back, touched the slight moistness under each of his eyes, then dropped her hands to the tight muscle in his shoulders.

'I met those girls at a ball. I told them that I had decided to get married – to you, dear Eadie, but I did not say your name, in fact, as I recall, they were trying to guess.'

She folded him into an embrace, weeping happily into his neck. Afterwards they resumed their stroll, now hand in hand.

As they walked down towards the harbour he asked. 'Do you still want to marry me?'

Eadie grasped his hand so tightly that if she had the strength, she would have crushed it like a nut. 'More than I want to breathe.'

★★★

Just in time to boost publicity for the float, on the afternoon of September the third, 1894, after years of work, life, planning, living, testing, and hope, the prototype Imperium engine was assembled and made ready to run for the first time. Frederick, brimming with pride, announced that all workers should down tools to watch the test.

The men unlaced their aprons, removed heavy gloves, washed their hands and faces and gathered on the factory floor. They applauded as the regulator was opened for the first time. Frederick stood back to watch this moment, with Clare beside him.

The Imperium was a beast of an engine, almost twice the size of the Fortis. The turbine blades spun in a blur of movement, and could be felt in a hum, transmitted through the ground and the air of the room.

'It looks like a winner,' Ned Baring enthused. He had been unwell, and now leaned heavily on a stick. 'I congratulate you.'

Cheers rang from fifty throats, and the landlord's boy arrived from the Joiners' Arms with a barrel of ale on a trolley. This he tapped on the factory floor. Before long, he was passing full pots around for the floor workers.

Nothing could wipe the pleased smile from Frederick's face. The

Morton Imperium was a special engine – perfect for the age of electricity. As soon as the trials were finished, they could begin selling, and some of the costs of development would finally flow back into the coffers.

★★★

Lord Percy Forgill left his coach and sailed past the driver with an arrogant stride. He stomped up the steps to the second floor and snubbed the *maître d'hôtel*. He took his seat at his table and accepted a drink with a snarl.

His distress at the news of the death of Peter Craven manifested itself as indignation, but deep down he was bereft. Craven was the first and most loyal of his boys, who had now thrown his life away to save some woman on a ship.

At the same time, it looked like the Morton float was gathering momentum. The thought of Frederick extracting himself from debt and impending foreclosure filled Percy with rage.

'Look out,' said the Barrister. 'Old Forgill is riled up.'

Percy's eyes focused on the speaker. 'And well I might be. Damn Morton and this float business.' He took a long sip of his brandy and soda then cleared his throat. 'I need your help, gentlemen. We must ensure that this public share issue does not get traction. We can allow Morton the small-time investors, but when it reaches the stock exchange this thing must drop like a stone.'

The Financial Adviser held up his thumb and forefinger an inch apart. 'From what I hear Morton is this close to the wall – in arrears all over the place. He's playing a dangerous game.'

'I can help get negative information out into the city,' said the Newspaper Owner. 'If you feed me the details.'

The Stockbroker patted his jacket pocket, found the tin he was looking for, removed it and took a pinch of snuff. 'I'll spread the word among the other brokers and jobbers. I'm sure I can influence enough of them to make a difference.'

Percy Forgill took another long sip of his brandy and exhaled slowly, the combination of the spirit and his friends' words beginning to allay his anxiety. He smiled for the first time that day.

It was like being back at school. The bedrock of their friendships had not shifted. He relaxed somewhat, with his comrades rallying to the cause, forming like a rugby scrum around him.

'Would anyone care for a hand of whist?' he asked.

★★★

Frederick returned from the tram stop to find a brougham parked outside the factory, and Vic Jones hovering in the entry, looking very stressed indeed.

'Who's here?' Frederick asked.

Jones jerked his head in the direction of the office. 'A woman you probably don't want to see. In there waiting for you.'

Strangely, a man's first crush stays with him through the years, so that even when things have turned bad later, he retains some fondness, if not for the person, then for the memory.

Sophie Forgill was sitting on the visitor's chair, a cigarette between the fore and middle fingers of her right hand. Frederick was surprised – yes, her lips were red with lipstick, and she wore a morning gown which would have cost more than all the furnishings in the room – but there was an older, harder look to her now.

'Hello Freddie.'

'What are you doing here?'

'Am I not allowed to visit an old friend?' she asked, taking a draw of her cigarette and blowing the stream between pursed lips towards the window.

'We were never friends,' said Frederick, and he rounded the desk to take a seat in his chair, feeling the need to place a yard of heavy mahogany between himself and his visitor. 'Therefore, you must have a reason to be here.'

'I want to warn you to mind your own business, or things are going to get worse for you.'

'What on earth do you mean?'

'Don't fox with me Freddie, you've never been very good at that. We know you've had your little mademoiselle and the dreadful hag who lives with you digging into things that they should not.'

'I don't know what you're talking about,' said Frederick. 'And I'll thank you not to speak about my family in those terms. I'm busy, so if that's all you have to say then it's best you get in your carriage and leave.'

'Do not cross us, Freddie. We've been playing nicer than you deserve. Now is the time to come to an understanding.'

'I want nothing from you and Percy, not even an understanding.'

Sophie leaned over and stubbed her cigarette out into the ash tray, surely aware at how this pose made her breasts bulge over her bodice. 'Ah Freddie, but there was a time when you wanted something from me, wasn't there?'

'That's enough,' Frederick said, coming to his feet. 'It's time for you to go.'

'Fine,' said Sophie, then waggled her finger. 'But don't go telling stories and making trouble. If you do, we will respond in a very unpleasant manner.'

'Everything Percy does is unpleasant,' said Frederick. He walked to the door and held it open until she passed through, with the rustle of clothing like a snake on stone.

***

When Frederick returned home at the end of the day, Clare was in the fernery, re-potting lemon button ferns. She was wearing a canvas apron, trowel in one hand and a smudge of dirt on her nose.

'Oh hello *cheri*,' she said when she saw him.

'Hello.' He bent to kiss her cheek. 'Can you please tell me what is going on?'

'With what?'

'I had a visit from Sophie Forgill – turned up in a red carriage like a madame from Haymarket. She threatened us with trouble unless you and Eleanor stop digging into things. Now what on earth does she mean by that?'

Clare put down the clipper. 'I'm sorry Frederick. I should have told you – and I was going to when I got to the very bottom of it all. Let's go and have a cup of tea and I'll tell you everything.' Then, as they walked down the passage she went on. 'I have some exciting news too, though a little sad we can't be there to share this special time.'

'What is it?'

'We got a letter from Denny today. He and Eadie are getting married – in fact, just a few days away now.'

Frederick stopped in his tracks. 'Was she—'

'I assume so,' said Clare, 'and don't get all moral about it, or have you such a short memory you can't remember fronting up to the Vicar and trying to get married as a matter of urgency?'

'This is not an occasion for tea,' said Frederick as they reached the drawing room. 'Eleanor,' he called, 'do we have champagne? Where's May, does she know yet?'

They were on their second glass before Frederick realised that Percy and Sophie Forgill had slipped from his mind.

★★★

Six days before the float of the Morton Steam Power Company, Eadie and Denny married at Sydney's St Philip's Church, off York Street, with half a dozen old pew warmers, along with the last-minute inclusion of Henry Lawson.

That night, Denny took Eadie back to the boarding house as his wife. They ate dinner with the rest of the guests, then went up to the room he had once shared with Sam. He lay back on the bed, with Eadie beside him, her head on his chest, hair spilling out so that it tickled his neck.

'I have some news for you,' Eadie said. She drew his hand down over the small bulge in her abdomen, then opened his fingers so they splayed over her skin. 'If you were a little more observant, I wouldn't have to tell you, but inside there,' she said, 'is a big part of you, a big part of me.'

At first he looked at her, not comprehending, then tried to sit up. 'You're ... having a baby?'

'Yes, that's why I came over here, but I didn't want to tell you until we were married, I didn't want you to feel pressured.'

Denny turned to face her, his face pressing wetly against hers. 'I never thought I'd be holding my bride, both crying our eyes out on my wedding night,' said Denny.

'They're tears of joy,' said Eadie, 'and that's permitted.'

Chapter Fifty-five

The *Standard* began a series of articles, scurrilously questioning the integrity of the Morton Steam Company float, and the part played by Baron Revelstoke, the disgraced banker, as they called him.

'We knew that Percy Forgill would start pulling strings,' Ned Baring said. 'We have to weather the storm, and we can play the same game.'

The Saturday before the issue date, the London Times carried a small article in the business pages. The journalist was 'in possession of information that Morton Steam shares were in demand at a one-and-a-half times premium.'

This sponsored snippet would not sway Stock Exchange insiders who knew how such things worked. It was intended to encourage the small-time investors who believed that reading the Times made them experts. Every broker in the city knew that the price of this innocuous little editorial was the placement of a large advertisement on the page, featuring an image of the new Imperium engine.

MORTON STEAM. Public share offer opens tomorrow. Don't miss your chance to be part of a global industry with a big future in delivering power to industry, agriculture and mining. One million shares with an issue price of one pound, expected to sell fast.

There was also an unsolicited article in the Tattler.

> Some readers might remember the steam engine maker who, in his younger days often moonlighted as a professional walker, winning the London to Leeds event under controversial circumstances. It has come to our attention that this week his company is floating on the London Stock Exchange. We wish Frederick Morton, along with his family and staff, the best of luck with this venture.

Three days before the float, the *Financial News* ran an article, accusing Frederick of stealing workers and designs from Forgill's, and linking him with the failed Barings Bank.

It was a putrid piece of journalism, and through Wallace a libel suit was threatened. The newspaper printed a retraction on page fifty-three the following day, but the damage was done.

★★★

On the last night before the issue began, Frederick slept badly, sweating through the early hours of the night. Clare took him in her arms and kissed his forehead. 'You need sleep, my love.'

'I've thrown the dice high. Everything, even this house is riding on the outcome – I fear for us, Clare, I really do.'

She gripped his hand. 'I have faith in you, and Ned Baring is a special breed of man. All will be well.'

Frederick wished he could share her faith.

★★★

On the Fifteenth of December, Frederick, Clare and Ned Baring travelled to Cheapside and the broker's office, the front counter of which was open at nine a.m. to accept share applications from the public.

There were no crazed scenes, stone-throwing or police barriers as had apparently happened years earlier for the famous Guinness float, but there was a tidy line of teachers, bookkeepers, retired professionals and fund managers all wanting to buy into the company. Clerks began opening the mail, taking cheques and sorting. Five days of similar scenes followed, demand slowing as time went on, at the end of which some fifty per cent of the available shares had been taken up.

'Not quite as much as we'd hoped for,' said Lievere, 'but the market is cautious. We knew that.'

'What now?'

'Tomorrow we go public, and God alone knows what will happen.'

★★★

The Royal Exchange, incorporating the Sydney Stock Exchange, occupied a Victorian Mannerist block on Bridge Street between Pitt and Grisham. Denny was pacing the roadway outside before it opened, still some twelve hours before London would begin trade.

Finally, when the doors swung wide, Denny joined a rowdy mob heading into a room with chalkboards covering the walls. He recognised the names of hundreds of companies, with scrawled prices underneath. Shouts rose over a general hubbub of talk.

'New issue,' came a voice. 'We've got Morton Steam, based in London. Market capitalisation of a million pounds. One pound a share. Fresh on the news of the deal of the century with the Broken Hill Proprietary Company, sitting on more silver than King Midas, or was that gold? Never you mind, they're a good thing.'

The initial buying, however, was cautious, and Denny found himself standing next to a man in a top hat and dress coat, who saw his nervousness.

'You're Denny Morton, aren't you?'

'That's correct.'

'I recognised you from a photo in the *Herald* yesterday. Don't fret. There'll be no real action until London opens late today. They're sheep around here. Encouraging start though. All the best with it.'

'What was your name, sir?'

'Anthony Myer.'

'And what do you do?'

'I'm a shopkeeper.'

'A noble profession,' said Denny. 'I do hope we'll meet again.'

With an embossed card in his hand Denny went back to the board, watching the sales trickle in.

★★★

At the long sweep of South Pier, jutting like a crooked finger into Table Bay, the officer-of-the-watch blew a whistle and passengers began to stream up the gangway.

Harriet took Jules in her arms, loosely at first, then clung to him. 'I will never forget you.'

'Nor I you,' he said.

'Forgive me Jules. There is not only one kind of love in the world. There are many.'

He pulled back from her. 'I understand that, but I have not given up.'

'Come back soon,' said Matthew as they clasped hands. 'I'll miss your company.'

Something extraordinary happened. Jules, the brave adventurer, burst into tears, then turned and ran, stumbling up the gangway. Reaching the deck he went below, and they did not see him appear at the rail until the ship sailed, long after the lines had been cast off.

★★★

Soon afterwards, Matthew and Harriet arrived by cab at the Commercial Exchange on Addersley Street, Cape Town. This low, classical structure, adorned and supported by rows of white columns, was the hub of mercantile life in the colony.

There was no true stock exchange in the building, but

telegraphic communications linked it to the four-year-old facility in Johannesburg. As they entered the commodious Exchange Room, some of the men looked askance at Harriet's presence. This was a male domain, though there were more than a few women present also.

As in Sydney, stock prices, major sales and new issues were displayed on boards across the walls. Brokers were in evidence, but transactions were placed remotely through Johannesburg and London.

It was a vibrant and exciting place, with men in suits, lads running for coffee or tea, gentlemen in top hats rubbing shoulders with managers and speculators.

The Morton siblings waited half an hour before there was any word of the share issue. Then, without any fanfare, a chalkboard was placed with the word MORTON neatly printed, and an English voice called out. 'We 'ave Morton Steam Power selling at nineteen shillin's in Jo'burg and Sydney. Not to be traded in London Town for a couple 'a hours hence.'

Matthew turned to look at Harriet. Her eyes were everywhere, taking it in, her cheeks flushed with excitement.

'You're enjoying this,' he said.

'Yes. I think I am. After all, this is a new chapter in the history of our family business. I'm sure you read Father's last letter – every worker in the factory will be a small shareholder. It's the beginning of a new way of doing things – not capitalism, not communism, but the best of each.'

'I hope you're right,' said Matthew. 'Shall we have a cup of tea while we await developments?'

'Why not?' agreed Harriet.

Leaving the Exchange Room, they settled into one of several cafés, allowing the waitress to lead them to a table with views through the window to Adderley Street, the view dominated by the Standard Bank.

With scones, cream, and cups of tea on the table, Matthew enthused about the float, and how perhaps, if all went well, he might be back at Oxford in a few months. After all, hadn't their father asked for only one year of their time?

Harriet dropped a dollop of cream over a smear of jam, replaced the spoon in the jar and lifted her scone between thumb and forefinger. The float was just one thing on her mind – on the cafe window she could see a playbill advertising opening night – that coming Saturday, when she would take the stage as Nora in the first South African production of *A Doll's House*, by Hendrik Ibsen.

★★★

The London Stock Exchange occupied a full block at Capel Court, Bartholomew Lane. After fire gutted the seventeenth century Royal Exchange, architect William Tite had been commissioned to design and build the new premises. Prince Albert had laid the first stone in 1842, and Queen Victoria herself cut the ribbon. Crowded to capacity, in 1885 a new wing had opened, with piers of granite and a central dome. The cheese-like texture of the marble linings gave rise to the nickname 'Gorgonzola Hall.'

Frederick was both frightened and enlivened as he walked with John Lievere through this new section of the complex. The subscription room was fascinating – a foreign country inside a city he thought he knew well, where jobbers shouted, clerks hurried, and indecipherable numbers seemed to fall from the sky. Cigar, pipe, and cigarette smoke hung in a grey fog over it all.

For all that, it was a grand place, with mahogany fittings, and ceilings stretching to the heavens as if high-level commerce was a religion. The murmur of voices was constant, with humour infusing the words and phrases, many of them unique to these rooms. A 'turn' was a profit, and a 'rasper' was a 'good turn'. The 'jam tart' referred to the current price on the market.

Even the stocks themselves had nicknames. 'Beetles,' were

Colorado United Mining Company shares. 'Bulgarian Atrocities,' referred to the recent Varna Railways issue. 'Matches' were shares in Bryant and May.

Thankfully, John Lievere was on hand to interpret this strange cultural world. 'Morton Steam opened at one pound and has fallen to eighteen and sixpence,' he said. 'Not good news I'm afraid.'

Frederick felt the sick slide of fear. Fear that the last five years of endeavour might be lost in a puff of financial chicanery. Fear that he might lose his profession – his delight in the form and function of machines – the smell of a freshly turned part, still hot from the lathe.

Investors were reticent, however, and the Morton shares fell to just over fourteen shillings by the end of the second hour. Looking around for an ally, Frederick saw Ned Baring enter the subscription room, and begin to limp his way across. Slipping into the seat beside Frederick, the banker squeezed his forearm. 'It's not going well?'

'No, not so far.'

'A disastrous start,' agreed John Lievere glumly, 'now just twelve and sixpence. We've thrown everything at it, but I fear that if there is no momentum soon, we will close under-subscribed and at junk value. Now, if you'll excuse me, I'll do the rounds and see if I can scare up some interest.'

Time passed. Ned Baring also wandered off somewhere, and to Frederick the great hall that had seemed so exciting a few hours earlier now appeared to be noisome, immoral and even malevolent.

Minute by minute, the Morton shares continued to fall.

Percy Forgill and Wilkins arrived, and could be seen across the floor, waving dismissively at the brokers, and smiling distantly at Frederick.

'You dog, Percy Forgill,' Frederick hissed under his breath. 'You and your damned friends have sabotaged me.'

When the hour seemed darkest, John Lievere hurried back and sat down next to Frederick, edgy and agitated. 'Encouraging news. Someone just bought a block of fifty thousand shares.'

Frederick sat up in shock, 'Fifty thousand shares, who?'

'I don't know.'

Ned Baring also arrived back in his seat. 'Frederick, have you heard?'

'Yes. Do you know who is buying the shares?'

'Someone very wealthy,' Baring said, then turned to Lievere. 'Not Natty Rothschild do you think?'

'I doubt it, picking up blocks of random industrials on launch day isn't his style.' He paused. 'Look at the price? Whoever's doing this, it's getting people interested.'

For ten minutes the price rose – eighteen, nineteen shillings – then it began to stall, dropped a little, back down to seventeen.

'Whoever it was might have lost heart,' said Frederick.

Then, a minute later a hundred thousand shares went in one block. This was a green light to the market – the fence-sitters who knew only enough to follow. By the time this sale went through, the jobbers had nicknamed the Morton shares, 'Pedestrians,' in deference to Frederick's history in the sport.

'That's a good sign,' said Lievere. 'It means that the jobbers think the float is going somewhere.'

'Buy five hundred pedestrians at four-fifths,' came the shout. The manner in which the shares had so quickly become part of the stock exchange scenery gave Frederick a warm feeling.

Lievere was grinning, 'I've never seen anything like it. Someone's trying to help the float along and is purchasing a sizeable stake in the process.'

The price continued to climb. Within an hour the shares reached thirty shillings, and the ache in Frederick's heart began to ease. One thought did concern him, however, 'You don't think this might be Percy Forgill trying to buy out the company?'

'Unlikely. Lord Forgill's best chance of doing so would be to let the float fall on its face then come in and buy up the corpse. This buyer is driving the price up – ensuring the success of our little venture. Anyway, I've found out a little more – the shares have been purchased in the name of a Hendrik Golding. He's a broker with a firm a few blocks from here – he's what we call a nominee shareholder. I could ask him who he's representing, but I doubt he'll tell me. I think we just have to accept that someone with a lot of money wishes you well.'

Before the market closed for the day, at five in the evening, John Lievere extended his hand to Frederick. 'Congratulations, Mister Morton. Your company's shares are fully subscribed and holding at a price of two pounds, ten shillings and sixpence. You have made a lot of money today. Welcome to the world of big business.'

★★★

When Percy Forgill alighted from his carriage, walking through heavy mists to the front door, he sought only silence. Meeting the butler, ignoring questions about arrangements for the evening meal, he escaped to the smoking room, where he poured for himself a single malt from a boutique distillery near Alness.

Sinking into a leather armchair with a glass in his hand, Percy fought to overcome the bile in his throat, and the bitter taste of disappointment. He allowed himself to accept the result. That Frederick Morton was as exceptional as he was lucky.

He wondered who had purchased so many shares and pushed the Morton Steam float to a full subscription. He cursed them with every sinew, cell and nerve ending in his body.

★★★

For the second time, that charming old Lewisham house hosted a genuine baron of the realm, and a number of others besides. Eleanor was ready, with a bottle of Bollinger, a haunch of venison and even the sweet smell of lobster boiling in a foaming pot.

'A toast,' cried Ned. 'To Frederick Morton and the most rewarding public float of my career – and that includes the great

Guinness float. I was on top of the world then – and now I've been brought low, but the events of this day have made me feel like I'm fighting back.'

After they had downed the first toast, Frederick raised his glass again. 'To the unknown, but much-appreciated party who bought one-fifth of our little company. You saved us, sir.' Now, he reflected, the sweetest thing would be to pay back his debts to Percy Forgill in full. Also, to set his children free from family business obligations, to choose the path they desired in life.

While they ate, the clock in the alcove stopped for the second time Frederick could remember. With the comings and goings, and the business of celebrating Morton Steam's arrival as a business force, it wasn't easy to tell. Ned's driver had taken him away in a brougham when Frederick noticed that the comforting tick had ceased. Investigating, he found that the hands had frozen at a quarter past eight.

Frederick wound the mechanism fully, and still the pendulum failed to swing. Clare joined him, no less concerned than her husband. She rapped on the side several times and still nothing happened.

Then, for no discernible reason, the ticking resumed, as if it had never faltered, and again Frederick had that feeling of alignment. The river tides, the pendulum, the piston of a steam engine and his own heartbeat.

Feeling elevated, but somehow humbled, Frederick took Clare's hand, and they climbed upstairs to bed.

Chapter Fifty-six

Harriet's nerves, in the hours before the curtain rose for the first time, quickened her heart, reddened the skin at the base of her neck, and made her feel nauseous. Yet, she knew her lines, and even more importantly she felt Nora inside her, bursting to tell her story. The insiders who had seen the rehearsal had enjoyed the show, and complimented Harriet on her part.

'The audience will enliven you,' said the director. 'You will feed on them and rehearsals will be just a pale imitation of what we will see tonight. Don't be nervous, but instead revel in the moment.'

Harriet took the stage, feeling a swoop of adrenalin as the curtain rose. Yet still the shock of the audience, arrayed before her – each individual staring back, wanting entertainment, wanting pathos, clever sets, wanting an experience – unnerved her. The first scene, even to her own ears, felt a little wooden, as if she were merely reciting words, parrot-fashion.

'Hide the Christmas Tree carefully, Helen,' she began. 'Be sure the children do not see it until this evening, when it is dressed.'

Then she turned to the porter, played by a funny, short man who had once been a merchant seaman. 'How much?'

'Sixpence.'

'There is a shilling. No, keep the change.'

Harriet began to worry that her performance had started off a little thin, but then Torvald, her stage husband; played by a man as condescending and patronising as his character, came through from a side-door in the set.

'Is that my little lark twittering out there?' he called.

Harriet, becoming her character, felt herself bristling. 'Yes, it is!' she retorted.

'Is it my little squirrel bustling about?' he continued.

And when Harriet gazed out at the audience she looked with Nora's eyes and felt their investment. These women, she knew, understood condescension, how pet-names belittled them, dismissed their every thought and action as having no consequence. How dare he!

The mood carried her into the story, and at the finale, when Nora decided that she must leave her husband, she uttered the telling words of the final scene, near shaking with emotion.

'I see, I see,' said Torvald grimly. 'An abyss has opened between us – there is no denying it. But, Nora, would it not be possible to fill it up?'

Harriet's Nora was utterly convincing, because she had convinced herself. 'As I am now, I am no wife for you!'

When the last word had been uttered, and Torvald sat, shattered at her supposed betrayal, the audience came to their feet for a round of applause as the cast assembled in a line on stage, bowing together. Harriet's eyes were filled with tears as she smiled at Matthew, sitting transfixed in the third row, and she could read the pride in his face.

She had made people feel the emotions she had projected. Not only a rare gift, but the greatest moment of her life.

★★★

A few months after the float, on a Sunday, the du Brice family arrived from Saint Laurent, with tears of joy in their eyes at the reunion.

At a luncheon in the back yard, under the sycamore tree, Eleanor sat uncomfortably – so out of place that she could not help but attract some questioning.

'And Eleanor – you are a family friend?' asked Madame du Brice.

Eleanor fondled her clay pipe in the pocket of her smock with one hand, wanting a smoke more than anything, but aware that lighting and blowing cheap tobacco smoke around the table might confound her guests.

'I don't know what we would do without her,' said Clare, placing her arm around the older woman's thin shoulders.

'Eleanor lives here,' added Frederick. 'I've known her since I was a boy.'

All in all, it was a successful visit, and later, Frederick strolled with his father-in-law down towards High Street, ostensibly to allow him the taste of a good local British ale, but also to give Clare and her mother some time together. In the front bar of the Joiner's Arms, the two men drank three porcelain mugs, one each of dark, mild, and India pale, then finished with a small brandy.

Before leaving, Frederick bought a bottle of stout to take back for Eleanor, and the two men walked homeward, relaxed and friendly.

'I'm going to ask you a question,' said Frederick, 'and I'll be obliged if you'll answer it.'

'I can't promise, I'm afraid,' teased du Brice. 'Ask me the question first.'

'Was it you who started buying large blocks of shares, saving my company when we listed on the Stock Exchange?

Du Brice grinned devilishly. 'I was wondering if you had worked it out. Yes, it was me. As I've said before, I believe in you, I believe in your engines, and in your company. Not only that, but I suspect those shares will prove to be a very good investment.'

Frederick stopped walking. 'I don't know how I can thank you.'

'You already have. You have welcomed Noelle and I into your family.'

'But you own a good portion of the company. You could have a seat on the board if you wanted.'

'Not so easy from our little corner of France, and you know how busy I am.' He clasped Frederick's shoulder and they both continued walking. 'I will leave the running to you and the very capable board you have assembled. If ever you need any further help, please say the word.'

★★★

That afternoon, when the du Brice family had returned to their room at The Savoy, May walked into the kitchen to find Eleanor coughing into the sink. When she stood up May saw the stricken eyes, and blood on her chin.

For a moment they stared at each other, while Eleanor dabbed at herself with a handkerchief.

'Have you lost a tooth?' May asked, leaning on the bench with one hand to look at Eleanor's face. But the older woman broke into a paroxysm of coughing – a hacking bout that bent her body sideways, and culminated with both hands over her mouth, and May's hand around her bony back.

'Eleanor, you need a doctor.'

'Don't fuss, me love,' she croaked out at last. 'There's nothing that can trouble an 'ard old thing like me.'

But May called for Clare, who insisted that Eleanor go to bed while May fetched Doctor Ellis. He was busy at the infirmary with a difficult birth, but May waited for his return, her mind filled with thoughts of the woman who had been cook, nurse and friend since her earliest days. It was late afternoon before the doctor arrived back at his rooms, and he travelled with May on his cart to the house.

The doctor asked Eleanor a series of questions, felt the glands in her neck, then listened to her chest at front and back with his stethoscope. Finally, he asked her to cough onto some paper. He examined the sputum. May and Clare watched as he proceeded with the examination.

His diagnosis was both immediate and dire. The black thief – cancer – was clogging her lungs, eating into the soft tissue.

'You have only weeks – or months, if you are lucky.'

'Don't tell Freddie, please,' Eleanor begged, after the doctor had gone.

'Why not?' Clare asked. 'He needs to know.'

'I don't want 'im to pity me again, like 'e done all them years ago. I'll tell 'im meself, but give me a day or two to get used to it.'

★★★

Sophie Forgill knows how to travel anonymously, on an omnibus; down through Dagenham and on past the lights of Tilbury, nursing her anger.

Oh, Percy has the Yard in his pocket, of course he does, and it didn't take long to find out that Freddie Morton's little mademoiselle has been digging up the past. It's time to warn the damned old nurse to keep her mouth shut.

Sophie opens her bag a little so she can see the knife blade shining inside.

Three husbands have left Sophie with more money than she will ever need. No room in the city is locked to her. Few men refuse her, at least not if they are certain their wives will not find out. Yet, the past is the wolf pursuing her, threatening to swallow her up, and now and then it is necessary to turn and fight it off. Like that night when the wolf came for Monty again, and she and Percy had done what they needed to do.

The omnibus stops along the road below the hill with its neat rows of houses, and the saltings, shining in the moonlight. Sophie knocks on the door, and at length it opens.

'You old bitch,' Sophie hisses.

Only then does she drop her eyes and see the Webley revolver in the woman's hands. She barges forward, summoning all the strength in her legs and shoulders.

BOOK FIVE

Chapter Fifty-seven

One foggy morning there was a knock on the front door and Clare opened it to see Inspector Gerard Hatfield standing on the drive in a black trench coat, looking grave and serious. Few things disturb the equanimity of a person more than the arrival of a policeman at one's front door.

'Oh, hello,' said Clare. 'Can I help you?'

'Possibly. I have some news.'

'Come in, please, it's icy out here. I'll make you a coffee or tea.' Once they were settled inside, with mugs at the elbow, the policeman brought his eyes to bear on Clare. 'Eve Simpson was found dead yesterday morning, by local police, after a neighbour reported sounds in the night.'

'Oh dear.'

'That's not all, there was another body as well. Shot through the heart.'

Clare reached out for the wall, looking for support. 'Was it Sophie Forgill?'

'Yes,' said the policeman. 'It was her. You were one of the last people to talk to Miss Simpson about her relationship with the Forgills. Do you feel that you can help at all?'

'In any way I can.'

The policeman produced a calf-bound notebook, and a pencil. He asked probing questions that made Clare think deeply, but in her mind all she could see was Eve Simpson's body, in the house overlooking the saltings.

When he had finished, Inspector Hatfield put the notebook away in his jacket. 'I doubt I will have need to call on you again about this matter. It's a bad and sorry business.'

When he had moved out the drive to where his carriage waited on the street, Eleanor moved up beside Clare. 'One Forgill gone,' she hissed. 'One to go.'

Clare said nothing; she was still processing the news.

★★★

The public listing of the Morton Steam Power Company Limited ushered in a new era of monthly board meetings, stress over share price fluctuations, press coverage and new attention from competitors. The public float was not just a boost to the company's liquidity, but to its expertise, transparency, and its importance to London's industrial scene.

The Steam Manufacturer's Association could no longer dismiss Frederick Morton as a small or inconsequential manufacturer, and his membership was nominated by Antony Grimmen from Thames Ditton and seconded by John Chadwick of Manchester.

During the first Morton Steam board meetings, Frederick quite naturally became chairman, while the company secretary was a man called John Ovens, a former stockbroker and solicitor, with a strong loyalty to Ned Baring and the underdog quality of the Morton Steam Power Company.

Clare, as a shareholder and director, could have opted to give Frederick her proxy. She insisted, however, on taking a seat on the board, her experience with the du Brice estates in France invaluable. She believed that a company's good name was its greatest asset, and that maintaining the Morton Steam Company's reputation, along with ensuring profitability, should be the board's main concern.

★★★

In those early days of the publicly traded company, Denny planned another trip into the 'outback' to generate sales.

With two and a half months of her pregnancy remaining, Eadie was happy enough to stay at the boarding house until his return.

'I'll miss you of course,' she said. 'Just be sure you'll be home for the baby.'

Five days later Sam and Denny boarded a train on the North Coast Line, visiting sawmills in settlements amongst the tall trees with names like Gloucester, Wauchope, Tamban and Bowraville. The young businessmen guaranteed owners that Mobilis engines would turn power saws better than any other engine on the market.

From Bellingen they caught a Cobb and Co express coach, climbing the winding track up to Dorrigo, with the coastal plain laid out below, lit by the moon's white lantern.

Their first big sheep run was at Saumarez Station near Armidale. Most of the family and staff, apart from a cook and roustabout or two, were out on the run. A teenage girl of no more than about fifteen, but as confident as most adults Denny had known, met them at the grand house and took them on a tour of the outbuildings and the woolshed, which was already fully mechanised.

'We've shorn twenty-two thousand sheep this year,' she told them proudly, freckled cheeks shaded by a felt hat. We finished last Monday.'

Denny studied the shed itself carefully. It was powered by a compound steam engine with Cornish boilers turning a gin connected to Wolseley machinery. It was the first chance he'd had to study the mechanics of a working system. The gin connected through a set of gears to an overhead shaft along one wall, higher than a man's head, with wheels at each shearer's 'stand.'

Here, leather pipes contained a twisted length of gut, which was geared to spin at some 1600 rpm. These cables transmitted power to the shears, which would cut with the action of a sharp knife against the comb.

Denny gave the girl a card. 'Pass this on to your pa and let him know that if he ever needs engines, talk to me first.'

★★★

From Armidale they changed coaches, rolling past dry grass hills. The stops were regular, every twenty miles or so, the horses being changed at that interval. The place names were exotic and interesting: Gunnedah, Narrabri, and Wee Waa, or others longer and more difficult, constructed from languages neither Sam nor Denny understood.

By the next dawn they were sprinting west in a landscape of huge skies, over a land of stones. The colours were earthy and rich, clouds rare and pure white. And all the time the horses ran on, fresh and eager. The coach startled mobs of kangaroos, emus, and the occasional dingo. At times they spotted the flame of a drover's campfire, or travellers bivouacked on the side of the road.

The coach reached Tibooburra late on the fourth day, pulling up outside a pub with 'Downie's Family Hotel,' painted across the front, where Denny booked he and Sam a room for the night.

Sam, however, was feeling poorly, and Denny had several ales on the veranda alone, listening to conversations around him, watching minor arguments that flared into chest-shoving and even, once, a full-blown fist fight out in the dust. Denny was starting to understand a lot of things about the outback he had so longed to see.

The men of the Australian Frontier were hard characters, almost savage. They worked with muscle and brawn and fought the same way. Some were the illiterate sons of British education's failures, and others were running from crimes, disgrace or both. Empathy was not their strong point. They were unwitting, blunt weapons of the British colonising machine.

In the background, and at a distance, wealthy businessmen used these men like chess pieces and vast tracts of land as squares on a board. And the system was complicit in the whole arrangement. As soon as the hard men had cleaned out a new area, and subdued any resistance they found there, surveyors went in and planned towns – divided riverbanks and hunting grounds into neat squares.

In such a manner, 'civilisation' arrived, and other hardy souls could get down to the business of extracting profit from the land, whether from minerals, the fleece of sheep, or beef.

These were troubling thoughts, and Denny went to bed wondering whether he was making himself part of the problem.

★★★

The next morning Denny and Sam were on the mailman's cart, heading out to Mount Wood Station, where they had their first experience of a shearing shed in full swing, the unshorn sheep backed up in the holding yards, bleating and carrying on, pushed forward by a couple of boys and dogs. On the other side, freshly shaved animals clambered and scurried down a ramp, clumps of wool that the shears had missed still clinging to their skin. Most bled from multiple cuts, smeared with tar, on the back and flanks. Inside was an atmosphere of industry and concentration. The smell of greasy lanolin deepened. Ten men were at work to a rhythm of clicking shears – grabbing a sheep, trimming wool off the brisket, belly, hind legs and tail. Then, adjusting his position, the shearer would clip off the neck, head, shoulder, side and back. The tar boy hurried forward to dab his harsh ointment onto any nicks or cuts (and Denny saw that there were almost always cuts). This done, the shorn animal was pushed down a chute. While roustabouts brought up fresh candidates for the blades, tar boys took a breather and the boss of the board smoked his pipe, calling out orders here and there, bad-tempered and missing nothing.

All the while the manager gave the Englishmen a commentary on exactly what was happening at each stage of the process. Denny marvelled at the skills on display – not just the shearing itself but the way the classer examined each fleece on the table, before it was carried away to be baled.

Heading outside again, into the relative quiet, Denny asked, 'Have you thought about mechanising the shed?'

The manager scratched at his beard. 'We have. Maybe in a year or two.'

'My family owns the Morton works in London, and my legal representative and I are in the country to sell steam engines. We've just done a deal with the Wolseley firm of Sydney to partner with their shearing machinery.'

'Everyone's talking about machine shears,' the manager agreed. 'The big advantage is that it takes the whole fleece on one go, whereas the hand shears chop, no matter how sharp they are. More wool means greater profits. You're in the right place at the right time.' He went on to give Denny a lesson in the economics of sheep shearing. 'Some of the sheds up in Queensland are ten times this size – the biggest ones have already installed machine stands, but many haven't.'

Denny gave him a business card. 'When the time comes, send me a letter. Our Mobilis is the right engine for you. Compact, self-contained and powerful.'

'I'll bear it in mind,' said the manager. 'Now, did you want to buy some neddies?'

'That's right, we do.'

'Come out to the horse yards and we'll see what we can do.'

★★★

On the other side of a dry creek, they leaned on the rails and talked, while a couple of stockmen ran a mob of about twenty horses into the yards. They were a mix of colours, predominantly greys or chestnut, but there were a couple of bays, some very dark brown, one white and some mottled.

Denny perched up on the rail, Sam beside him, and studied the horses.

'I like the chestnut mare,' said Sam.

'Yes, me too,' agreed Denny, 'and look at the barrel on that grey.' He couldn't take his eyes off the horse.

'Not quite a grey,' said the manager. 'He's roan, actually, but it's hard to tell the difference with him.'

'I stand corrected,' said Denny, liking the nuances of colour description. He hopped down from the rail, and called to the nearest stockman, 'I want to have a close look at some of these, can we cut them out please?'

Denny walked through the dusty yard, making his picks in consultation with Sam. When he selected each horse a rope halter was fixed in place and the animal tied to the rails. The other horses were chased out while Sam and Denny went over each, checking teeth, eyes, and searching for signs of lameness.

Looking on in approval, the manager said. 'You haven't been out from Blighty long, but it looks like you know your horses.'

'Thanks, but they're bred differently here.'

'That they are lad. Very different, yet you've chosen some nice horseflesh there. How far do you plan on going?'

'Up into Queensland, all the way, as fast as a horse will canter, is the plan.'

'Half yer luck.'

'I don't think I want that roan fellow there. Nice and straight, but I'm worried he might be a bit wild.'

The manager chuckled. 'Take those six for fifty quid and I'll throw the roan in for free. He's got some interesting breeding, and you might find that he outstays the rest when the going gets tough. Now come and grab some tucker.'

At a table on the verandah they ate cold mutton, with slabs of butter on home-baked bread for lunch, then they set about saddling up the new horses. Just when they were ready to leave, the manager came up again, and with him was an Aboriginal girl in stockman's gear.

Denny looked at her curiously. She was slight of build, ignoring the flies on her face, looking away from him, anywhere but his eyes. Her lips were full, with strong cheekbones, almost gaunt, and with wild, glossy-black hair.

'Who's that?' Denny asked.

'Just a young lubra I'll chuck in for free. She'll go along and tail the horses for you. Cook your tucker. There's always a few hanging around that someone's got tired of – they don't cause trouble. Not like the bucks.'

Denny looked at the girl, at Sam, then back at the station manager. 'We don't need another travelling companion, and she's another mouth to feed.'

'I doubt she'll eat much, and she's from up north somewhere – since that's your planned route I think you'll find she's worth a bit of tucker to have on hand.'

'What's her name?' Denny asked.

The manager pointed to her. 'Hey you, whassyername?'

'Missy,' she said.

'There you go,' he said. 'That's as good a name as any, wouldn't you think?'

★★★

At the August board meeting of the Morton Steam Power Company Limited, Frederick delivered a full sales report, including new pending orders for the new Imperium turbine engine from the Witwatersrand, New York and Chicago.

'The Imperium is, I believe, one of the most talked about machines in the world right now, and the Fortis is still the best choice for hundreds of industrial applications.'

There was a genteel clap of hands, then a murmur of conversation as the meeting started to wrap up – chairs scraping back on the floor, a few side-questions from the members to others. The company secretary, John Harris, stood up and spoke. 'Before we adjourn, Mr Chairman, I'd like to speak on a matter of importance if I may.'

The chatter ceased, and Frederick answered smoothly. 'Of course. Please go ahead.'

'There seems to be an attempt afoot to take over the company – it's very slow moving but determined. It may have been ongoing for some months. This morning I received a "substantial holding notice" from a Cheapside broker by the name of Hauss, who is the nominee for one or more buyers. The threshold for such a notice is five per cent of total shares, but I suspect that the holding may already be higher at this stage.'

Frederick shook his head. 'Do we know who's behind it?'

'Not yet.'

'Why start buying shares by stealth? Wouldn't the interested party simply launch a bid for the company?'

'Not necessarily, they may be seeking to acquire a pre-bid stake. Not only does it make their bid more powerful when it comes, but it demonstrates to us that they are serious about the acquisition.'

This news sat heavily on Frederick through the morning, and when he returned to the factory, he engaged a couple of foundrymen in polite conversation before asking if they might have been approached about selling the twenty ordinary shares each employee had been issued during the float.

The two men traded shuttered glances, before one answered. 'Well as a matter a' fact, sir, I was offered a price above the rate by a bloke six or eight weeks ago.'

'Did you accept?'

'I'm sorry Mister Morton. I were offered forty pounds – more than I've ever held in me hands in me life sir.'

Frederick exhaled slowly. Of course it was. There was no denying that it made sense for them to sell. He walked around the factory, talking to the men in ones and twos.

'Have you been approached by someone who expressed an interest in buying your shares?'

He was rewarded with guarded looks, evasions, and the occasional obvious lie. Almost all of them had sold out.

Frederick was bitterly disappointed. The shares had been issued to make them feel part of the company – to feel like owners, and most of them had sold.

Chapter Fifty-eight

There were surprises around dusty corners and in the corella-lined trees of the waterholes as Denny and Sam investigated the big shearing sheds of Northern New South Wales, then set sail for the sheep stations of Queensland's Channel Country. Now the skies were endless, and the rivers mere chains of waterholes.

In deference to Sam's aversion to darkness, they lit lanterns and kept the fires high at night, the waters of wild rivers reflecting the flames like mirrors. In daylight they urged their horses up orange dunes, fetlock-deep in sand, looking out over the landscape with the bloody sun arcing towards the horizon.

And while the inclusion of Missy the horse tailer had at first mystified Denny, he soon saw her worth to a pair of new-chums such as he and Sam. She was so skilled, so adept in the arts of the bush, that he wondered how they might have managed without her. Not only did she care for the horses as thoroughly as any royal groom, she appeared to smell water at a great distance, knew the best firewood, and could handle hazards such as snakes, spiders and centipedes with brutal aplomb.

As a rider she had a natural ability that far outstripped her travelling companions. Bareback or saddled made little difference. 'If we shipped her back to England,' said Denny, as they watched her ride effortlessly off to catch a couple of bolters, 'I swear she could ride the winner in the Grand National.'

Near Windorah they saw their first mechanised shed in operation, amazed at the difference it made. When the shearer brought a sheep to his stand, he pulled a handle on the wheel, positioned his chosen animal and started to shear, in fast long strokes, starting with the brisket, just as his hand-shearing comrades would have done, and finishing with the sides and back. But what a difference in the execution! The number of cuts was minimal, and the wool came away as a true fleece, which could be thrown onto the table – just an iron frame, really – where the classer could skirt it in half the time.

When Denny viewed the partially constructed Tinnenburra shed near Cunnamulla he was awed by the sheer size. 'Sorry mate,' said the owner. 'You needed to be here three weeks ago, I've ordered an engine through Sharps in Brisbane and it'll be here before we shear again.'

Yet, there were other sheds. One on the Barcoo was the biggest yet. 'We'll shear twenty thousand sheep a year in forty stands,' boasted the squatter. Denny's head for figures was a boon as he sat down at a scratched table in the office and compared efficiencies with other competing engines.

'How much will coal cartage cost you?'

'Twenty quid a ton.'

'And running an engine four months of the year you'd use five hundred tons on one of these old designs. With the Fortis engine, you'll cut that down to three hundred. That's two thousand pounds a year in savings. You'll pay for the price difference in just a couple of years.'

Denny would then run through pricing, and delivery times, for the Wolseley machinery. 'We can organise the timing to fit in with the engine. We'll give you specifications for a concrete pad, and the engine and boiler can be rolled off the dray and bolted down, then the shearing machinery assembled by the Wolseley team.'

The squatter took a chequebook from his pocket and poised with his quill over the paper. 'How much is the deposit?'

'Ten per cent.'

The man dipped his quill and wrote the cheque, holding it up to dry close to the candle flame, then passing it to Denny. 'Then for God's sake get this miracle on the way for me.'

There was no bank nearby, and no telegraph office, so getting news of the sale to London would have to wait until they hit town. The cheque and sales agreement went deep into a leather folder in the saddle bags and Denny smiled more often – this experience of the outback was being justified by real sales. He was learning a lesson: that every business needs to find a sweet spot – the perfect markets for its products, and remote areas seemed to be purpose made for the Mobilis, and the Fortis as well, with its 'lift onto a pad' design.

Denny was not the only one experiencing new things. One day, camped on the Barcoo, he had been looking for his horse, which had broken her hobble strap and wandered. He came back into camp and heard laughter from down at the river. It was Sam and Missy, sitting on a bank in shallow water, splashing each other and laughing. He backed away, without betraying his presence.

It occurred to him that Sam had not complained of the dark or his fears for at least a week.

★★★

Yet, when they rode up to each new station, Missy drifted into the background. Sam looked wistful as she, as custom demanded, headed off to the 'black's camp' on the nearby creek or waterhole.

★★★

In the town of Longreach, Denny banked two cheques and sent a cable to report the sales. Around this time, however, they heard mutterings of dark days ahead. Camped on the Thomson one night, they shared a fire with three wiry shearers, all members of the Australian Shearer's Union.

'Big things is coming,' said one of the men. 'It's time to show the damned Queen that Australian blokes won't be pushed around. What we want in this country is a revolution and a republic. If the amalgamated miners will back us, we are prepared to take the colony.'

Denny and Sam shared the shearers' fire, while they read aloud from Marx and Engels, culminating with the leader firing his revolver into the air and shouting, 'The squatters are cutting wages, and when our members refuse to work for a pittance, they're hiring scab labour across the country. It's up to us to stop the rot.'

The next day, as Sam and Denny continued their journey, they ran headlong into a troop of Queensland police: forty mounted men with rifles, meaning business. At the rear of the procession, amongst the pack horses, was a wheeled Gatling Gun. The sergeant at the head of the party challenged Denny.

'You're not shearers, are you?'

'No sir,' said Denny. 'Businessmen.'

'Well, I'd be making my way east, if I were you,' said the sergeant. 'This area is a powder-keg.'

'We need to keep going north.'

'Well, keep your wits about you, there are armed camps of strikers going up, and we won't be able to protect you.'

★★★

Sam had been aware of Missy as a woman from the first day they rode together. She moved like no other, on strong legs, muscled and balanced.

Missy was brave. He saw her pick up a hissing-angry snake by the tail and crack it in the air like a whip so the head flew away. She would charge down a scrub bull, or whistle at a curious dingo until it padded silently away from the camp.

Sam loved her smell of the sky and the earth, of muddy waterholes and dry red sand. He was falling in love with her, falling into something that would never do on High Street Lewisham.

The first time he touched his lips to hers she did not understand what he was doing. Sam realised that other white men's interests had all been further down. When he tried again her mouth opened at last, and he was pleased that he was the first one to give her this pleasure.

At each night's camp Sam would lay sleepless in his swag, conscious of Missy moving to her own bedroll, away from the fire and near the horses. He wanted to go to her but cared too much of what Denny might think.

★★★

On Isis Downs Station the owner had a daughter in her mid-twenties who invited Denny to ride out across the run with her, and she made no secret of her admiration. They raced tough stock horses across dry parched plains, and stood together in the shallows of muddy billabongs, boots off and trousers rolled while their horses drank.

'You would suit this life,' she said. 'If you were to stick around.'

Denny did love this horseman's paradise, a huge country under huge skies, but he had a wife he loved, and an important job to do. 'I'm sorry, but I can't do that. I'm married – and happily so.' He paused. 'Someone special will come along for you.'

'Perhaps,' she said, though she looked down sadly. 'Not many men like you come along at all.' She paused. 'Your friend, Sam. I saw him slipping down to the black's camp. He's with your horse tailer, isn't he?'

Denny addressed that troubling question in his own mind. 'I think so.'

'Don't worry, that's usual around here, though everyone pretends that it's not. Many of the stockmen have their 'boy' who's really a girl.'

'I think for Sam it might be more than that. He likes her.'

'Things are going to be difficult for him,' she said, then spurred away.

★★★

Near the town of Winton, the two travellers came to a roadblock. Ten shearers stood across the road, holding an assortment of rifles and knives.

'Scabs or workers?' demanded the leader.

'Workers. Let us through.'

'We'll see if you pass muster first.'

Denny and Sam sat in the shade, while a kangaroo-court of shearers fired questions at them. When one started searching through the travellers' saddle bags, Denny stepped forward with a resolute look in his eye. 'Now you listen,' he said, 'we're not so different – but I wouldn't rifle through your belongings, and I don't expect you to start going through mine.'

The man looked back at the leader, who nodded. 'Yeah, fair enough. Get on your way then.'

'I hope you win this fight,' said Denny.

'We have to mate, or our bloody poor families will starve.'

★★★

The primary market for the Imperium, was not mills and factories, but city councils and power companies. This was an all-new direction for the company and Frederick found it necessary to change his approach, hiring a clerk whose sole task was to scour major newspapers for upcoming tenders across the United Kingdom, the United States and the Empire.

It was a busy period, with Frederick and his team scrambling to solve small teething problems, ensuring that when Imperium engines went out into the world, they would be as maintenance-free as possible.

★★★

Three months after the successful float, news arrived that Ned Baring had died during the night at his Membland estate at South Devon. Frederick was sick with grief, taken back through the years to when Lord Bartholomew Forgill had passed away. Ned Baring was the second great mentor of his lifetime – a mover and shaker and fixer of deals, with a rare nose for a viable enterprise no matter how many years down the track profits might take to arrive.

When Frederick went home, he drew comfort from the roses in their neat beds, and the tidy stone house. Inside, he savoured Clare's terrariums of green that made the house so welcoming, and Eleanor bustling in the kitchen, for she still, despite her advancing illness, ran the kitchen with efficiency and skill.

Clare was in the drawing room, putting down her embroidery to stand and take him in her arms.

'I heard, *cheri*,' she said. 'You must be upset.'

'I am,' Frederick admitted. 'I will miss him in so many ways.'

Later he took his old model steam engine from the wooden case and set it up on the kitchen table, filling the boiler and burner, cycling the small engine on the table while smoke puffed, and steel hissed on steel. Tears fell from his eyes as the model ran: this miracle that lay at the centre of his existence.

Clare saw beauty in the puffs of steam, romance in the sound, and symmetry in the engine's geometry. But it was May who shared her father's passion, looking on it with the eyes of an engineer, understanding the magic of the parts working together, how each was machined or cast to precise dimensions in order to fulfil a role. No part was redundant, and each one was engineered to last as close to forever as possible.

★★★

Uprooting the family, apart from Eleanor, who was too sick to travel, to the village of Noss Mayo, in South-West Devon, where Ned

Baring would be buried, was a major expedition, but Frederick was determined to pay his respects. The Mortons travelled together in the family carriage, driven by Jenkins. It was a three-day journey, with nights in sleepy inns along the way.

At the Church of St Peter, a structure Baring had funded to replace the Thirteenth Century ruin that preceded it, the funeral began with whimsical grace, a small crowd of diehard supporters from London in attendance. Sitting with Clare and his family on the fifth pew, Frederick paid his respects to the man who had helped him break down the walls of privilege that guarded the rooms of power, and assisted in the creation of three very special engines.

There were tears in Frederick's eyes when, at the concluding moments of the service, he took his place as a pallbearer, walking down the church aisle, scarcely feeling the weight of an old man who had been so much more than the body within.

The funeral meant a week away from the factory, but it was worth every moment. Frederick felt very grown up – after all he was no longer young – and his shoulders squared to accept just a little more of the weight of the future.

Chapter Fifty-nine

While Harriet thrilled audiences, playing Nora in her first major production in Cape Town, Denny, Sam, and the quiet, hard-working horse-tailer struck the Cloncurry River near McKinlay. From there they followed the watercourse in its perambulations, encountering storms that drenched the earth, thickening the air with steamy moisture, and populating the night with hordes of mosquitoes. 'Bloody weird it is,' said Sam. 'We haven't seen a drop since Sydney, and now it's raining every evening.'

'We're getting closer to the coast again,' said Frederick, pointing a finger to the north. 'And it's the rainy season into the bargain.'

Having left sheep country behind there were no longer striking shearers to worry them, but often now, they saw black men chained to stirrup irons, or with heavy brass plates around their necks proclaiming them as 'king' something-or-other. They saw punitive troops riding out, and native police in their cheap saddles, expensive Martini rifles, the scalps or ears of dead men tied to their saddles as trophies.

★★★

The town of Cloncurry was a series of rectangular blocks set between the river and a small creek, running brown. The settlement was surrounded by hills topped with russet-coloured crags, the southern approaches dominated by an open-cut gold and copper mine with the tailings piles resembling, to Denny's mind, the spoil heaps dumped by Thames River dredgers. The mine's founders must have had high hopes for it, for a sign at the access track announced the site as THE GREAT AUSTRALIAN MINE, CLONCURRY,' in large block letters.

As they walked across the Coppermine Creek bridge the track developed into a broad, beaten-earth main street, signposted as Sheaffe Street, shimmering in a languid late afternoon heat. Despite the high temperatures and harsh environment, the town had a picturesque charm in the deep red light of sunset.

It seemed, from the activity and signage, that there was currently a race meeting in town, and travellers with their plant were camped all along the river and creek. Denny was hopeful, however, after nights of bush camping, and Sam's failing health, to take a room at a hotel.

The first pubs they tried, the Prince of Wales and the Royal, both backing onto the creek, were booked out and an overflow of campers spread out on adjoining lots. The Imperial and Palace, further into town were likewise over capacity. Lastly, they tried the Front Hotel facing Sheaffe Street. The owner, an Irishman called Patrick Brady, clearly happy with the flow of cash running through his tills, had one double room and space for a swag on the floor.

So it was there they took a room, while Missy slept in the stables with the horses. That evening they sat on the covered porch, really just an extension of the street, frosted beers in their hands, 'I swear this one won't touch the sides,' Sam said.

Keeping to themselves, Denny was on the third beer when he became aware of a lanky, dusty ringer beside him. Being near sunset Missy had emerged from the stables, taking the horses past the front of the pub, two at a time down to the water to drink.

'Is she yours?' asked the man.

'Yes, she's ours,' said Denny, with a glance at Sam.

'Nice lookin' lubra,' said the ringer. 'And good with horses too. How much do you want for her?'

Sam's face reddened, 'She's a person,' he said, 'not a horse, and as such, she is not for sale.'

The man guffawed, showing a mouth full of missing teeth. 'You're not the first new chum to fall for a lubra. You'll learn better habits before long, I can promise you.'

'You need to learn better manners,' said Sam.

The man turned to the rest of the shaded verandah, his voice cutting through the mutter of conversation. 'These new chums want me to learn better manners 'cos I offered to buy their gin.'

Sam moved fast. Standing, pushing his stool aside, he thrust at the centre of the man's chest, sending him stumbling backwards across the room, taking out two tables and a couple of chairs in the process, before landing on the earthen floor.

The crowd was buzzing with expectation of what might happen next. Sam and Denny resumed their seats, but Sam's hand was shaking as he sipped his beer. Missy had disappeared into the stables, as if she knew that she was the subject of the current trouble.

'Good work,' warned Denny, 'but that fellow won't have liked being humiliated.'

The ringer, having picked himself up off the ground, spat in their direction, then worked his way through the tables and chairs and down the street.

Nothing happened for a minute or two, at which point there came the sound of jangling spurs, and the man appeared on the roadway with a stock whip coiled in his hands. A moment later it stung through the air and exploded an inch from Sam's ear.

Sam came out of his seat and charged, all in the same movement, eyes fixed on the man who was preparing for the next stroke. Despite the man's partial dodge, he was soon too close for the whip to be deployed again.

Taking the man around the middle with all his weight behind a shoulder, Sam sent him crashing to the dust, then manoeuvred his body so he was on top of his assailant. Wrestling was Sam's thing, though his foe was strong. They went from hold to hold, coated in dust from the ground.

The stranger tried to throw punches, but Sam hampered him with arm and foot, bringing pressure to bear in every way. Finally, he managed an arm-lock, applying more pressure until the other man's face took on the same red tinge as the dust on which they fought.

'Had enough?' Sam asked.

'Yeah, enough.'

After releasing his foe, Sam walked with Denny back to the table, but there were rumblings from the injured man's friends, so the two Englishmen drained their glasses and headed upstairs.

'You love her, don't you?' said Denny when the door had closed.

'I think I do.'

'What now?'

'Our work is done here. We need to get back down to Sydney, to follow up on enquiries by mail, and start thinking about Victorian gold mines and South Australian copper. Not to mention a certain young lady and an imminent arrival. The quickest way home is by sea – we ride north to the river port of Burketown, then a steamer for Sydney.'

'Sounds good,' grinned Sam.

Denny inclined his head back at Missy. 'It's not going to be easy for you.'

'I know that. She won't come with us – if I want to be with her, I'll have to stay.'

Denny felt a jolt. He had not considered that he might lose his best friend and right-hand-man. 'Are you prepared to do that?'

'Jesus Denny, I don't know. I'll have to let it sit for a few days and see what happens.

From Cloncurry onwards the heat became oppressive. Sam, Denny and Missy followed the picturesque Gregory River north, and there was an urgency to their ride.

They rode side by side, or in file when the track narrowed. Missy, as always, rode behind with the spare horses and packs. Denny had been conscious of the need to travel as fast as possible back to Sydney.

The landscape, however, was an endless source of fascination to him: plains of yellow grass as high as a man's chest, rivers flowing with green clear water amongst pandanus, paperbark and palm. Large, bronzed and silver fish hunted in the shadows, and gum trees grew as if in defiance of their surroundings, twisted and tortured things, as beautiful as the land itself.

They camped in wide clearings, using plentiful firewood to light the bush and propel sparks skywards until the glow from the flames lit the trees. Yet, Sam had no recurrence of the terrors of the darkness, and Denny knew that it was strong, quiet Missy who kept them at bay.

After three more days along the Gregory, including a stop at a pub known as Beame's Brook, a change came over Missy. She walked taller and spoke often to Sam. Denny was amazed at how much of the language his friend had picked up.

'This is her country,' Sam explained, 'she was taken from here by a drover a couple of years ago, though she travelled with several different fellows before she reached Tibooburra.'

Denny narrowed his eyes and looked ahead. 'Is that a lake I can see?'

As they rode on, the trees drew back, and the wide expanse of water revealed itself. It wasn't a lake, but the place where the Gregory flowed into the Albert River – in full spring high tide. Tongues of brown water thrust in bitter channels that had to be skirted, and the small group was forced to slow their mounts and pick their way through.

The two Englishmen saw their first truly large saltwater crocodile, his armoured head forming a colossal obstruction in the current, a stone's throw from the bank. Missy laughed at their consternation at the sight.

They rode for ten more minutes – before the ground rose sufficiently to be dry enough – and safe enough – to camp. While Missy saw to the horses, the two men gathered a stack of firewood. Much of it was old driftwood that had caught against tree branches and trunks like piles of ivory. And as evening turned the sky to the bloodiest red they had ever seen, the heat did not abate, only seeming to become more humid, and the mosquitoes arrived like tiny minions of hell, a continual high pitched whine in the ears. This last menace forced them to fossick for heavy clothes, far too hot to bear but their sole protection against the needle-sharp stings.

Soon they had a fire leaping skyward, and together they drank the last of their whiskey. Denny watched the orange flare on Sam's face, the light comforting him. On the other side Missy was staring up at the stars.

'We've done well,' said Denny. 'Thousands of miles, and we've sold a lot of engines, kept Father going. We're bloody marvels, really.'

'It's all due to you, Denny. I'm just the hanger-on.' Sam turned to Missy. 'Come and sit with me.'

The young woman came with them into the full flame and sat beside Sam. Their hands twined together, black and white.

'Denny, we've been best friends for quite a time, haven't we?'

'Years and years now.'

'Would you hate me if I stayed here while you go back to Sydney?'

'Here?' asked Denny incredulously, waving an arm at the shining river. 'What are you talking about?'

'It's not a matter of what's here for me, but more a case of what might become of this dear woman if I leave her here. Can I allow her to stay and be picked up by the next desperate who comes along? Or worse, be burned on a pyre like those unfortunates we saw.'

'But Sam, this is a wilderness, how will you survive?'

'Not exactly here, but in Burketown itself. I asked a couple of fellows in Cloncurry. There's a district court, and one in Normanton too. I can maybe get my old job as a clerk back – I'm quite good at it – to earn a few bob and be with Missy here.'

Denny felt breathless with anger. 'Why would you throw your life away like that? Missy has been good for you, but when we sail off you'll soon forget her and she'll move on to someone else.'

'I understand that you're angry, but I've found someone who makes me happy. She can't leave her country again, so I have to stay. It's as simple as that.' Sam paused, then, 'How can I go back and marry some tame English girl after knowing her? This is a different life mate, it's real. In England it's been washed out of us.'

'And what about me?' asked Denny. 'I need your help.'

'You have Eadie.' Sam's eyes filled. 'You'll have each other – and I've found my love here.'

Denny shook his head sadly. 'I can accept your reasoning – I don't agree, and it makes me sad, but I do accept it.'

And later, lying in his swag while the soft sound of lovemaking came from his best friend's swag, Denny stayed close to the fire, swathed in cloth to stave off mosquitoes. His eyes stinging with smoke, Denny missed the calmness of Home. He missed the smell of hot metal from the foundry and the rough camaraderie, the fire of union rallies and most of all his family and their close-knit love that had never faltered from the day of his birth.

Most of all he missed Eadie, and he swore he would never leave her for so long again in his life.

★★★

The next day they rode into Burketown, a sparse sort of place: a wide brown main street with sun-washed buildings on either side. One store carried a huge sign along the facade, identifying it as belonging to the steamship company, Burns and Philp. There, Denny booked passage on the steamer lying at anchor in the river, for thirty-two pounds, all the way to Sydney.

This done, the small party walked on past the Commercial Hotel, and a couple of banks. The river was a distance away on the left, wide and brown, warehouses in a cluster near the jetty.

Sam and Missy rode off to find somewhere to camp along the river, while Denny walked into the Commercial Hotel. The proprietor, busy washing pewter tankards at the bar, introduced herself as Missus Lynott. She looked Denny up and down as if trying to work out what kind of man he was.

'I'm sailing on the *Truganini* tomorrow,' said Denny. 'I need a room, a hot bath, and a big feed.'

'Then you're in luck. A shilling for the room, another for all the beef and veg you can eat, and sixpence for the bath.'

'Done,' said Denny.

A few minutes later he dropped his bags in his upstairs room and went down into the public bar to order dinner. It should have been the best meal of his life, after months of living rough, but it tasted like cardboard in his mouth.

Missus Lynott was behind the bar, working a couple of barmaids hard with a mixture of scowls and sarcasm. As soon as Denny had eaten the last forkful he put on his hat and walked off to find Sam.

★★★

Sam and Missy had set up camp overlooking the river, and they must have visited the store, for the young woman was fishing with a length of cat-gut wound on a bottle, and as Denny approached, she pulled in a fat fork-tailed catfish and threw it unceremoniously on the coals.

'I wish you'd come up and take a room,' said Denny. 'That bath sure felt good.'

'I'm happy here,' said Sam, 'and we'll soon find a place to live.'

Denny coughed, 'I want to make you a gift of the horses, and packs, I'll take my saddle and bridle, the rest of it is yours.'

'Thank you,' said Sam.

'Will you come and see me off in the morning?'

'I wouldn't miss it,' said Sam.

★★★

The next morning the *Truganini*, a little tramp steamer built by Black and Noble, arrived at the jetty. At two hundred and three gross tons and with a beam of just twenty feet, she was nothing like the *Ormuz* had been, but still, she looked seaworthy and in good shape.

'Goodbye old friend,' Denny said, shaking Sam's hand. 'Eadie and I will be back to visit when we can.'

The expression on Sam's face showed his understanding that such a visit might be many years away. 'I'd ask you to look after Eadie,' he said, 'but I know you will.'

'Of course.' Denny embraced Missy. Sam was right, there was much to admire about her.

Just before he boarded, a lad hurried up with an envelope. 'Mister Morton sir, here's a telegram for you.'

Denny put this in his pocket, boarding the steamer and finding a seat on one of the two wooden benches on either side up at the bow, watching as the lines were thrown off and the screw took the vessel into the tide.

A final wave and they passed downstream, out of town, the helmsman heading for the other side, presumably where they might face a less strenuous current.

At times they diverted around snags piled up on a mud bank, or even once the wreckage of something that looked very much like a barge. The helmsman smoked his pipe in silence, though after a while another passenger, a young policeman heading south for the sake of his health, took a seat next to Denny and asked polite questions about his home and travels.

Alone again as they passed through the mouth and into the Gulf of Carpentaria, Denny lowered his head, not to hide his tears, but so he could pretend he was not leaving his best friend behind in one of the most remote corners of the Empire. He fumbled in his jacket pocket for the half bottle of rum he had purchased over the bar before his departure.

It was only after the second mouthful that he took out the telegram.

YOUR WIFE IN LABOUR THIS AM RETURN ASAP ENDS

Chapter Sixty

Frederick had noticed, recently, that Eleanor was not, as usual, bustling away in the kitchen. The household chores were being performed by two replacements. There seemed to be a conspiracy afoot – Clare and May were prone to whispering together, and sometimes disappeared on unknown missions.

Despite these observations, his mind was too fixed on the attempted buy-out of his business to investigate further. The Morton share price had risen, leading to a slowing of growth in the mystery-buyer's stake, but substantial pressure to sell had been brought to bear on principal shareholders, and Chadwick, the company secretary, had written to Frederick on Friday intimating that a tender offer for control of the company might be forthcoming.

By Sunday a note had arrived via private messenger, asking Frederick to attend a meeting the following morning at the offices of John Lievere. It was an important day and Frederick knew it.

He roused Jenkins and headed over to the river before nine, finding that Lievere and Chadwick were already in conference.

'Morton Steam Power has just received a tender offer,' Chadwick explained.

'Who's it from, and what does it mean?'

'Lord Percival Forgill, and it's a takeover bid. In parcels of fifty, a hundred shares, at times even paying a little above par for the shares, Forgill has gathered to himself around twenty percent of the issued shares of the Morton Steam Power Company Limited.'

Frederick stared at the letter as if it were poisoned. The words brought up the bile in his gut. The thought of Forgill bringing his contempt of the working class, his arrogance, hatred and bitterness to the boardroom table, to control the company Frederick had built, filled him with anger.

He wished that Ned Baring had never suggested the public company. He wished that after all these years Percy Forgill could forget the past and leave him alone.

'So, what happens now?' he asked.

'We meet with the board and, provided Forgill hasn't managed to sway any of the board members, then we vote to refuse the offer. Then the fireworks begin – an Extraordinary Shareholder's Meeting. I hope you are feeling strong, Mr Morton.'

'Strong enough to face the bastard one last time,' said Frederick.

★★★

When he arrived home that evening, Eleanor was on the front porch, a cloud of smoke emanating from pipe and lips. She seemed peaceful, and he took a seat on the step beside her, watching her smoke, pausing to cough.

At length she said, 'You seem lowly, this afternoon Freddie, and it aren't like you to be like that.'

'Is it unfair of me to be angry at a dead man?'

'I'd say that the 'ating of corpses is more commoner than you would think, Freddie. 'Oo is it you're angry at?'

'Ned Baring,' said Frederick. 'He talked me into the whole public company thing – life was so much simpler before that.'

'We can't go back an' alter things,' said Eleanor. 'But why a change of mind now?'

'It's that damned Percy Forgill – he's trying to buy my company.'

'Percy Forgill 'ates you for your cleverness. It's a canker in 'is 'eart.' She coughed again, and this time it went on for a long time.

When it was over she put down the pipe and covered her mouth with a handkerchief.

Frederick saw the pain in her eyes. 'You need a doctor,' he said.

'I already seen one, Freddie.' She stared at him. 'I didn't want to tell you, but it's best you know. Cancer, it is. I'm not long fer this earth.'

'That can't be true. Can it? We'll take you to another doctor. The very best.'

'There's no use Freddie, an' I won't be the cause of you wasting money. Sometimes, when the ebb tide goes too long, a person forgets how to swim. That's me, Freddie.' She squeezed his arm. 'But now is not the time for me to unload me troubles, not when ... Percy Forgill an' 'is tribe are cooking up mischief.'

Frederick stood up, 'Are you coming inside?'

'Not just yet, gi'us a minute will you, Freddie?'

'Of course.'

When he had gone Eleanor remained on the step, picking up her pipe and repacking it with tobacco. Striking a vesta, she took another draw of the burning hot smoke.

★★★

One of the busiest weeks of Frederick's life followed: sending and receiving letters, setting up meetings, and sitting with small investors in poky drawing rooms. In general, sympathy remained with the board, but some had seized on phrases such as 'economies of scale' – becoming part of a bigger company appealed to them. By Thursday night, Frederick was both exhausted and dispirited. Clare sat with him while he talked, drinking a little more brandy than usual, his eyes red with strain. New lines appeared on his forehead and around his face.

'People trust you,' she said, 'and with good reason. All will be well.'

Frederick wasn't so sure.

★★★

The extraordinary shareholders' meeting took place at the Corn Exchange building in Mark Lane, London. Before the meeting started, John Lievere met Frederick at the colonnaded entrance. 'Be prepared for a fight. It seems to me that Forgill has some high-profile shareholders in his pocket.'

The board distributed themselves along a row of seats fronting the stage, along with three representatives of Forgill's legal team. Pockets of small talk rippled around the hall while the last of the crowd entered, filling at least half the available seats.

Frederick asked the secretary if he was ready then walked to the dais. Looking out at the assembled crowd, he felt humbled by the faces he saw looking back at him. Most were ordinary people, with modest savings to invest, but he also saw fund managers, brokers and jobbers – all of whom had put their faith in he, Frederick Morton, and his managers, to grow a company, build beautiful engines and return a profit.

'We,' he began, 'have had no choice but to convene a shareholders' meeting to consider a tender offer of one pound, sixteen shillings per share—' He stopped cold, staring at the rear door, for Lord Forgill had just arrived. He walked by leaning heavily on a cane, his head a grey-fuzzed skull spread with skin. He was followed by Wilkins, now at least seventy but still spry. The pair proceeded into the room, taking a seat just behind the board.

Now, finally, Frederick took a deep breath and went on. 'The offer comes from one of our competitors, and the Articles of Association of this company dictates that rejecting or accepting this offer is not up to me, or any one person, but to a full shareholders' meeting such as we have convened today. Some of you know of my journey to this position. I started out in Stepney—'

Percy came to his feet, and his voice filled the room like thunder. 'Frederick Morton was a slum boy. Little more than a beggar when my father found him.'

The hall hushed at this, heads swivelling and eyes widening. They had come to vote on the takeover, few had expected entertainment.

Chadwick also rose, 'Excuse me Lord Forgill, but would you please sit down. You will have your opportunity to speak shortly.'

Forgill sat, but on the edge of his seat, as if ready to rise at any moment, while Frederick summarised his experiences at the Ragged School.

'Some of you may be aware that Lord Bartholomew Forgill was my sponsor. He sent me to school and employed me as an engineer at his factory. He was a great man, and I will be forever grateful—'

Again, Percy rose to his feet. 'Morton was dismissed from Forgill's – on my orders.'

Frederick turned on the man, the anger rising in his bloodstream. Yet he sensed that Forgill was baiting him, that a reciprocal response from the dais would not be to his benefit. Slowly he controlled his emotions and returned to his speech.

'The Morton Steam Power Company produces three of the best steam-powered engines available anywhere. We are negotiating with governments and industry across the world. Our designs are more advanced than those of any of our competitors. At this point he could not resist a tiny barb, 'including Higginbottom's and Forgill's.'

Percy Forgill eased himself to his feet again, but Frederick continued at high volume, drowning the other man out.

'We have a partnership with one of the fastest growing mining companies in the world, and the biggest player in the French flax industry. Our Mobilis engines power shearing sheds, potteries, sawmills and bore pumps across the remote parts of Australia, Africa and the Americas.'

For some quarter hour he enumerated the company's

achievements, the skills of its staff, the fully owned and favourable location on Deptford Creek, the work ethic of the current management and future plans.

'Why would we allow this vibrant young company to be absorbed by a much larger and older corporation – one which has fallen behind the times? One that would take our tooling and designs and put a different badge on them.' Frederick cast a glance towards a smirking Lord Forgill. 'They are not looking to buy Mortons as a going concern. They will take our engines and close us down. That is what they will do.'

The crowd hissed in disapproval, and Frederick felt their goodwill. 'I urge you,' he continued, 'to reject this offer and to keep Morton Steam under its current management.'

He stepped down from the dais, receiving a congratulatory nod from Chadwick, standing ready to introduce Percy Forgill, who had also left his seat and was heading up the stairs. Forgill appeared to consult his notes for some time before speaking.

'I thank Freddie Morton for his words, and one must admire his efforts to cling to the illusion of independence. He and I go back a long way, and I think it's fair to say that we know each other's faults intimately.

'I first met him at one of the schools my father funded. I admit to feeling bemused when he was singled out for elevation to Charterhouse, when there were more deserving pupils at the little ragged school he attended.' Grumbling broke out from the board, and Lord Forgill waved it away. 'Yes, I do digress. Let us talk about the here and now – the offer on the table for Morton Steam – a very small player in the industrial scene. Three engines? Forgill's produce four times that number of models. Companies like Robey even more.

'If our offer is accepted, Morton Steam will keep its own identity, but I add to it a tried and tested distribution network across the world. I give it the industrial strength of a fifty-year-old manufacturing base. We will not just take these engines, as Freddie puts it, but with our team of experienced engineers – we will improve them.'

For twenty more minutes he piled argument on argument, a light sweat breaking out on the skin of his face. 'In the final analysis, you are voting to either continue to own shares in a minor player on Britain's industrial scene, or vote to enliven and strengthen the company, to see it through the difficult years ahead.'

There was some scattered applause. Frederick turned and scanned the faces in the room. Percy Forgill's speech appeared to have made an impression.

Frederick watched as Chadwick stood and walked up the steps to the dais, where he cleared his throat. 'I thank both speakers for their words. I do support the chairman's position that we should not sell out to this company, but I also bow to Lord Forgill's right to make the attempt, and to argue his case. This is a most important matter – the most important that has come before us in the life of the company. According to the articles we will now vote by simple show of hands.' He raised his voice. 'All in favour of accepting Lord Forgill's offer?'

Frederick stood to watch, as some twenty or thirty hands went up.

'Those *against* accepting Lord Forgill's offer?'

The vast majority – hundreds of hands – rose into the air.

Clerks' hands, teachers' hands, labourers' hands, and bookkeepers' hands. The hands of honest people who had put their trust in Frederick Morton and his skills. A building, crashing wave of applause broke out.

When it had died down Chadwick said. 'The result is overwhelming.' He turned to address Lord Forgill. 'Your offer has been rejected by this Extraordinary Meeting. Good day to you sir, and I'm sure I speak for all our shareholders when I offer you my best wishes for the future.'

Percy Forgill's face had turned as red as a postman's livery as he reached his feet, shot Frederick a look of pure venom, then stood and headed for the aisle.

★★★

For three days Percy Forgill did not leave his home. He walked in bitter circles in the grounds or reread the same pages of the same books in the smoking room.

Finally, he gathered the vigour to dress in tails and top hat and order his driver to take him to the club for lunch.

Yet, from the moment Percy reached the top of the stairs and entered the Carlton Club's upstairs dining room, he felt uncomfortable. Unusually, part of the great dining room had been screened off for a private function, leaving the room at about half of its capacity. This made it seem more crowded than usual, and it forced him to approach the table from an unusual angle.

It was a strange thing, but as he rounded the bar area, he heard his own name mentioned loudly, then a rumble of laughter. He stopped to listen to the conversation for a moment or two, then started forward again. He heard someone shushing the others as if they had seen him coming.

Percy gathered himself, then walked closer. The chair in which he had sat, for almost every weekday luncheon for all his adult life, was occupied. For a moment he was lost for words, then, 'Excuse me,' he spat, 'but are you fellows laughing at me?'

The Banker, who had taken Percy's chair, puffed his chest out. 'It's rather funny, you must admit, old boy, that you have been so busy watching Morton that you've let his little company leap ahead of yours. Now you have tried, belatedly, to swallow him up, but little Freddie Morton has beaten you again.'

Percy gritted his teeth. 'Don't speak of things you don't understand. Furthermore, you're sitting in my chair.'

'Oh, there are plenty of empty chairs, Forgill. Take one. As far as I remember the Lord God did not ordain that you had to sit in the one particular place, year in and year out; did he?'

Percy sat down. The unfamiliar seat made him uneasy, yet he wasn't sure how he could take the initiative without causing a scene, and causing a scene was unforgivable at the Carlton Club.

The Banker warmed to his topic. 'You must see the funny side of things, Forgill. I've heard you, so many times, sit in this chair and boast of how efficient you've made Forgill's Engine Works, yet you forgot all about engineering. When was the last time your factory released a new model?'

'I do think that's quite enough—' started Percy, but the other man had not yet finished.

'You've made yourself look foolish, failing at this eleventh hour bid to acquire Morton's company in order to obtain the modern machines that he himself has designed.' The Banker raised his chin like a pugilist inviting a blow. 'It must be quite uncomfortable with all that egg on your face.'

No one dared laugh now. Every man sensed that this was the moment when the rival bull elephant had come from the jungle and confronted the herd male. The rival, it seemed, had won.

Percy Forgill had never in his life stormed out of anywhere, but he stood and ran his eyes around the table, focusing on the lack of respect, if not outright scorn. He stood, and in a quiet and dignified fashion he turned and walked from the room.

As he left, his rage at the Banker and the others in that room funnelled itself into one thing. Hatred of Frederick Morton.

★★★

Later that same week, Frederick walked from the front door of the factory, heading towards the tram stop on Carson Lane. He had many things on his mind, but the defeat of Lord Forgill's takeover bid had been such a relief, that even the worst of the hurdles now in the company's path seemed surmountable.

As he walked on, he heard the soft whir of a bicycle on the road behind him, and he turned to look as the rider came alongside, then swung to his feet, continuing to push the conveyance by its handlebars.

Frederick recognised Wilkins, so very thin now – just skin and bone. It seemed strange that he had the strength to balance on and power the bicycle.

'What do you want?' Frederick demanded.

'I want to talk.'

Frederick increased his pace. 'That desire is not mutual. I'm no longer interested in intrigue from your master. He has become irrelevant to me.'

Wilkins spoke through his teeth. 'Lord Forgill ain't me master anymore.'

This news was a surprise. 'He sacked you?'

'Nah. I took the jump meself.'

Frederick scoffed. 'I hope you don't think I'll give you a job.'

'Given the history between us I wouldn't expect you to. I came to warn you. Lord Forgill is in a proper rage – lost 'is mind I reckons. I fear that 'is next step will be murder – not something I will be party to. My dealin's with him is over, and I told him so. But there's others who will be eager for the extra ready – Lord Forgill will find 'em.'

'Thank you for the warning,' said Frederick. 'I do appreciate it, but while I know Percy is angry, and that he has no love for me, I don't believe that he would follow through with such a plan.'

'Ordinarily sir, I'd agree with you, but if Peter Craven hadn't drowned on 'is way to Sydney he would have killed your Denny, on Percy's orders, so murder is within 'is capabilities. Now it's you in his sights. He's unhinged sir, and hittin' the bottle. Anyway, I'd best be gone, but at least you know. Take steps, won't you, Mister Morton?'

Frederick watched as the cyclist ran alongside his bicycle for a few paces, mounted the pillion, then turned around in a wide arc.

He could scarcely believe what he had heard – that Percy Forgill had plotted to kill Denny, and now he, Frederick, was in the firing line.

Chapter Sixty-one

The SS *Truganini* was no greyhound, and the journey around the tip of Cape York and down the east coast to Townsville, where Denny changed ships for a Sydney-bound packet, took more than a week – far too much time in which to imagine the things that might have gone wrong with Eadie and their child.

All down the East Coast, he wrestled with guilt that he had not been in Sydney for the birth. He had left Eadie alone in a strange city, travelled too far, and had received no word since the telegram in Burketown. To make matters worse, on his arrival he would have to break the news to her that Sam was not coming back.

When the *Corel* steamed into Sydney Harbour, he was on deck, gripping the rail with white knuckles, packed and ready, and he was first down the gangplank at Circular Quay.

Within the hour he was stepping out of a cab with his gear, and approaching the door of the Belmont Family Hotel. Hovering at the desk inside, watching him come, was the proprietor, Mrs King.

'Well sir, you've taken your time,' she said. 'Missed all the action, as it were.'

'Is she here?' Denny stammered out breathlessly, 'or still in a hospital somewhere. I've got the cab waiting.'

'Oh she's here, and a bit of a surprise package as well, I might say.'

His luggage forgotten, Denny was in the entry and up the red carpet of the stairs in an instant. He knocked on the door of their room and heard Eadie's voice in response.

Opening the door, Denny saw Eadie in the chair, and in her arms was a babe as healthy and chubby as any he had seen. Her eyes filled with tears as he came to them, went down on one knee and took his family in an awkward embrace.

'I'm sorry I took so long.'

'It doesn't matter,' Eadie said. 'You're here now. Would you like to hold him?'

'Both of you,' said Denny. He had never seen Eadie so much in control, and so happy. 'Just let me keep on holding both of you.' He looked down to study his son's face. 'He's so beautiful, have you thought of a name for him?'

'Yes,' she said. 'I've already called him Peter, if that's acceptable to you.'

'Peter is a fine name.' He paused for a moment, eyes swimming with tears. 'Peter, my son.'

Chapter Sixty-two

Later, when Frederick informed Clare of what Wilkins had told him, and they talked of hiring security at the factory and to protect Frederick personally, he did not see Eleanor, listening around the corner, the last of a red sunset passing through the blinds, casting shadows on her face. The cancer in her lungs was spreading, she knew, for she now had lumps under her arms like cricket balls. It was a sign that Doctor Ellis had asked her to look for, but dying in a bed in some crowded hospital was not the way she wished to go.

As she listened, she thought of smug Lord Percy Forgill, secure with his wealth and title, understanding that his enmity for her Freddie had turned to thoughts of murder. Taking herself away, out to the front porch to sit, smoke and cough she muttered to herself, 'Don't you bloody touch my Freddie, not an 'air on 'is sweet 'ead – not when I won't be 'ere to stand at 'is side against you.'

Filling her pipe, and striking a vesta, Eleanor's mind drifted back through the years, to the inexhaustible list of kindnesses bestowed on her by a boy who was clever with tools, who she had once met on a riverbank.

★★★

Through a sleepless night Eleanor could feel her strength slipping away. The next morning, fighting the pain of every movement, she dressed in the nicest clothes she owned, took her savings from a hiding place under the drawers of her wardrobe, then went to Frederick's office.

He no longer kept the double-barrelled pistol he had made so long ago in the briefcase, but in a box in a cupboard. She found it there, still well-oiled and lacking any trace of rust. She broke the action, and loaded it with the heavy, powerful cartridges. Now she placed it in a small carpet-bag Clare had once given her.

Eleanor found herself unable to leave without saying goodbye. She started with May, the only one of the three Morton children still at home, working at her desk on a series of schematics.

Eleanor bent to kiss the side of her head, almost giddy with the memories that the two of them had shared, since May had first appeared as a baby in Clare's arms.

'I'm goin' away, me best love,' said Eleanor.

May reached an arm up to encircle the old woman's neck. 'You shouldn't be going anywhere, sick as you are.'

'I 'as to, this time, my love. You are a daughter to me, 'an you'll 'ave a good life. I do know it.'

May crinkled her eyes suspiciously. 'Where are you going?'

'I won't answer that, but it's what I 'as to do. Please don't make a fuss or try an' stop me.'

When May began to cry it nearly broke Eleanor's resolve. It would be so easy to stay, lie down on the bed and take her destiny passively. Instead, she bent again and kissed the place where the girl's hair parted, inhaling the beautiful clean smell of her. 'Say farewell to your brothers and sister for me, when you see them,' she said, then walked from the room.

Eleanor found Frederick at his desk, the care on his face obvious, the changes time had wrought. Instinctively she knew he would read her, that she could not afford to say goodbye. Instead, she laid a hand on his shoulder, and said the words inside her head.

Goodbye, me lovely, clever, gentle Freddie, oo I 'ave loved all these years.

I cannot leave that mongrel dog in this earth to keep maulin' you.

Clare was in the kitchen, and Eleanor used a little half-truth. 'I'm going to see my dear Juliet one last time. Alone.'

'I'll get Jenkins to take you.'

Eleanor took Clare's hand and squeezed it, 'Not today,' she said. 'Let me make my own way.'

'You shouldn't be walking anywhere … and travelling so far …'

'I'll only walk so far as the train, my love. Please just let me preference on the matter be.'

And if Clare thought the old woman unusually intense, she gave no sign, apart from a long stare as Eleanor shuffled out the door, paused to cough and light her pipe, and went down the drive, clutching the carpet bag under her arm.

★★★

Leaving the house, Eleanor walked up to High Street, caught the train from Lewisham to Waterloo, where she changed for Woking, to the southwest of London, where the Sisters of the Community of St Peter had a grand new facility and a larger hospice.

Eleanor spent more than an hour with her daughter, brushing aside Juliet's tears and desire to admit her mother to an infirmary room where she could be nursed.

'I ain't one for closed rooms and routines,' said Eleanor. 'Let's instead say goodbye and allow yer old mother to leave this earth on 'er own terms.'

★★★

Late that afternoon Eleanor was back at one of her old haunts, the Old Swan Wharf, descending to the lowest level, and waiting, leaning against a rail until she saw a passing ferryman in his skiff, his merry face familiar to her, his skin as weathered as the shell of an old tortoise.

'There's a face I ain't seen for a while,' he called, using his blades to bring the skiff to a stop beside the dock timbers.

'A face fairer than the likes of you deserves to see,' Eleanor croaked, stepping onto the thwart seat before settling down. 'Now tell me, 'as you seen me old china, the Lineyham?'

The ferryman began to pull away from the dock. 'That I 'as. Just a short time past. Shall I take you to him for ha'penny?'

'I would like that, very much.'

'Well, Miss Eleanor, if you 'as a butchers in the chest in the bows you'll find a quart o' Seagrams to sip an' enjoy on the ride.'

★★★

Along a mile of river, the oarsman making smooth progress against the tide, Eleanor sat, smoking, drinking sparingly from the gin bottle, and spitting bloody phlegm over the side at intervals. The Lineyham was indeed in residence at the Cherry Garden Wharf, across the river from the Wapping Basin. He was half asleep in his own boat, a near-empty bottle under his armpit.

He sat up, a look of surprise on his face. 'Well if it aren't old Eleanor?'

'One an' the same,' she grinned, pleased to see him. An old partner in crime, he would help with her requirements. No man on the river had a better sense of humour, and the plan that Eleanor intended to put to him would appeal.

Within a minute or two they were sitting next to each other on the edge of the dock, swigging gin together and talking softly. The Lineyham cackled when he understood what she planned to do and what his involvement must be.

'Now take me across the river an' up to the Embankment,' she said, 'and we'll get cracking.'

He was still smiling when, with her depleted purse clutched in her hand, she walked up from Temple Wharf towards the street and hailed a cab.

A moment of vertigo, when she swooned and almost fell, saw the driver curse and start driving off before she recovered and shouted at him to stop, threatening curses as fluidly as any waggoneer. Still, he did not help her up, and she was struggling now, the gin and exertion not having helped.

Finally, swinging into the seat and gripping the handle like a lifeline, she snarled, 'Park Lane, you rude young cock, an' be quick about it.'

The cabbie raised his eyebrows at such a low woman, albeit a reasonably-garbed one, requesting a genteel address, and gave voice to his feelings. 'Park Lane, for the likes a' you? You must be joking.'

'I aren't joking. You'll take me there, an' if all goes well there'll be another man wif us when we head back to the river. It'll be a pretty fare you'll earn today, if you keep yer trap shut.'

As they travelled, Eleanor continued to hold her bag and watch the passing streets as if she were counting them down. Finally, however, the cab reached Park Lane, off Hyde Park, a broad street of the grandest houses Eleanor had ever seen: marble façades, huge windows, gentlemen and ladies strolling and fine carriages on their way in and out of gravelled drives.

Greedy bastards, Eleanor hissed to herself. It seemed nonsensical to her that some people were able to display such vast wealth, and she wrinkled her nose as if at an unpleasant taste.

Finally, the cab stopped on the road outside a high-walled gate. Stepping down from the cab and taking the path, Eleanor was not surprised to see a guard on duty. She turned to the cabbie, 'Wait 'ere. As I sayed before, there'll be a kingly fare paid when your work is done.'

Stepping down, she approached the guard, who glared at her as she walked, folding his arms across his chest. 'Excuse me, missus, what on earth do you think yer doing here?'

Eleanor scowled a mighty scowl, 'You 'igh class servants think yer better than everyone else, jes' like the families ye slave for. Be off an' tell your lord and master I need to see 'im – that I 'ave certain information regardin' Freddie Morton 'e must hear from me own lips and no other.'

The guard narrowed his eyes. 'Why should I do what any old piece of baggage that turns up from the street tells me?'

'Because 'is Lordship will string you from one a' them turrets there if you don't do as I say. This is a matter of importance to 'im.'

'Stay here,' said the man, who then walked down the path. He was back before Eleanor had time to get her pipe drawing properly. Lord Forgill was at his side, walking with an outraged stride. Instructing the guard to return to his post, he proceeded through the gate, and approached Eleanor, his lips twisting into a snarl.

'What do you want?'

Eleanor looked at him slyly. She had not been sure he would answer her summons, but now she understood his madness. He was also more than a little drunk, not enough to slur his words, but it was there in his eyes and the callous lack of feeling in his voice. The drink would help, she decided.

'Freddie Morton wants to talk to you,' she said at last.

'He wants to talk with me about what exactly?'

'That's not my business, but use yer imagination, sir. 'E is a clever man, Freddie is – so very clever – but 'e 'as problems no one else knows about. He wants to talk to you where no little pitchers might be lurking.'

Percy Forgill seemed to be pleased, levering his body up and down with his toes, both hands in his pockets. 'You're the crone who lives with Morton, correct?'

'Me name is Eleanor Demsie, an' I 'ave lived under the roof of Freddie Morton, for these many years.' She pointed towards the waiting cab. 'Now come with me, 'urry up or 'e may not wait an' I would 'ate to see this opportunity slip through yer 'ands.'

'I'll get my coat.'

When Percy Forgill returned, one of his footmen was walking a discrete distance behind him.

'No one else comes,' cried Eleanor, 'not even one of yer lackeys, or the meetin' is off.'

Percy Forgill made a face, as if he were swallowing a mouthful of something bitter. Turning to the footman he said, 'Go back. I have nothing to fear from her.'

★★★

The cabbie followed Eleanor's instructions, the horses clip clopping in the gathering darkness. The two passengers said not one word to each other, as the cab continued down Belgrave Road and Saint George. Yet, she could smell the brandy on his breath, and his hands never stopped moving, delving into each other like mating eels.

When they reached the riverfront above Pimlico Pier, Eleanor pressed every last coin from her purse into the cabbie's hand, then turned to Percy. 'We walk from 'ere,' she said, stepping down from the cab, waiting for him to follow suit, then leading the way.

A series of close passages led to a foetid and crowded dock, where a couple of ferrymen in oilskins, smoking clay pipes, were playing dice in the light of a gas lamp while they waited for clientele.

Eleanor led the way along a boardwalk, at the end of which the Lineyham waited, wide across the shoulders from years of plying the oars, nodding in greeting but saying nothing.

'We're here,' Eleanor said simply, then hauled on a painter hung with strings of green river slime, bringing in an old clinker dinghy with oars ready in the rowlocks.

'You expect me to go out on the river in that?' Percy spat.

'You will if you want to see Freddie Morton. It's just a short ride.'

'And who will row?'

'I will,' said Eleanor, 'for there were a time when I could best most men with the oaken blades in me 'ands.'

The gaunt ferryman held the gunwale steady while first Eleanor, then a reluctant Percy Forgill stepped aboard, the boat lowering appreciably with their combined weight.

The Lineyham flipped the painter off the bollard and Eleanor took up the oars. Then, with the Thames dark, and stinking of the city's waste, she propelled them out into the stream.

The fog was thick over the black water, and when Eleanor looked at Percy Forgill, his face was white, his eyes staring back at the gas lights on the northern bank. Twice she held the oars to let a steam launch slip by. Once they passed a ferryman unfamiliar to her in his boat, two young women in the bows.

'Out of me way, ye scale-eyed old cock,' cackled Eleanor.

'Ye're the one blockin' the damned current, get off with ye, and take yer poxy smell with it.'

All the time there was the gentle slap of water against the hull, the groan of the rowlocks and swish of the oars. Soon, there was the added sound of Eleanor's hoarse breathing, for each stroke was gained at great cost.

Things floated in the water – foul-smelling flotsam that could only be excrement, and once, a dark shape that made Eleanor laugh when she nudged it with her oar. 'A fucking dead dog. Ripe barsted too, for it just fell in 'alf when me oar struck it.'

A choking, rotting smell climbed aboard the boat, sliding into Percy Forgill's gullet, making him dry retch. 'You foul thing,' he cried. 'End this charade now and take me to the bank.'

'Not fond of a little Thames soup are you?' she roared. 'There's worserer n' that in 'ere … some things a body don't even see, even if your eyes 'appen to fall on them.'

'I demand that you turn back. You're up to something. You're not taking me to see Freddie Morton at all, are you?'

But Eleanor was now engrossed with cutting into the racing ebb in the middle of the channel, dodging other boats and heading downstream. The fog thickened again, and the boat went barrelling along in the current.

'I'll pay you,' he said, begging now. 'Just take me back to shore and I'll pay you … twenty guineas.'

With a wicked grin Eleanor stopped rowing, then lifted an oar. 'Not for a thousand,' she cried, throwing the implement away from the boat, repeating the process with the oar from the other side, letting the tide carry them downstream.

'What are you doing? Fifty guineas, I promise you. A hundred.'

Eleanor sat and watched him in the gloom. 'It's time for you to leave Freddie Morton alone, you've hounded him all these years. No more, my lovely, fine, special Lord.'

'I will. Just take me ashore. I'll leave Freddie alone and do much for you besides.'

'I don't care what you can do for me. I got what I wanted from life – and it ain't nothin' you 'ave the power to give. I know how you gathered to yourself orphans – boys oo would do your bidding. Well, I am Frederick Morton's orphan, and I am doubly powerful, for I was suckled on kindness and care, and I will gladly end my life protectin' 'im from you.'

Eleanor delved into her bag, removed the pistol and held it with both hands. Percy's eyes reflected fear like gas lamps.

'You hag,' he snapped, 'how dare you?'

Eleanor lowered the muzzle and pointed it at the floor of the boat. Then she pulled the first trigger, and the night exploded with a starburst of light and sound. The stink of gunpowder invaded her nostrils, and a hiss like summer rain filled her ears.

Eleanor was no stranger to guns, and she had braced herself well, but still the recoil was cruel to her wrists and elbows, pushing them back to bruise against her ribs, yet she maintained the tight grasp of her fingers on the grip.

Percy Forgill cowered back against the side of the skiff, and stared down at where the water was already beginning to rush through the hole made by the bullet.

'You're mad,' he cried. 'The boat will sink.'

Eleanor could hardly hear him with the ringing in her ears. She gathered herself and raised the pistol so the barrel pointed at his chest. She could feel water lapping around her ankles. It was ice-cold, but the blood in her veins seemed to be already dropping to the same temperature.

'Freddie made this gun to kill you,' shrieked Eleanor. 'He made it to kill the wolf. You *are* the wolf. You and your damned sister, and now it's time for you to join 'er in the underworld.' These words were the last thing Percy Forgill heard, save for the gloating cry of an old woman at the moment of her triumph.

Eleanor jerked the second trigger and again there was a flash of light and a terrible thump of sound. The force of the kick and smoke made it hard to see what had happened, but a dark stain appeared on Percy's chest, and he slid into the Thames water which was by then filling the little craft.

Eleanor looked out into the river, as if she were searching for that little god who lived in the tides and the light mist over the water, in the night airs and the river smells and the creatures which dwelt within it. She scampered to the bowsprit, and there she leaned, standing like a bizarre figurehead. 'Ye can take me now,' she shouted. 'I'm comin' 'ome to the tides an' the sea.'

★★★

Far downstream, three nights later, when the Thames began its second ebb of the day, farming families living close to the river between Erith and the marshes of Crayford Ness were woken before midnight by a dreadful smell, borne on a very light northerly breeze. Lantern light appeared in windows, and men gathered on laneways, muttering and wondering.

Soon after, equipped with torches, a group of ten or so fanned out on the exposed banks. There they found the body of a man rotting on the shore like a fish.

They carried the stinking corpse on an old door up to the village while a lad rode to Erith for the constable.

The body of Eleanor was never found.

Chapter Sixty-three

Over the coming months and years, despite the sadness of Eleanor's passing, it was as if a dark cloud had cleared away. A steady procession of Fortis and Imperium engines rolled out of the factory's rear dock and onto barges floating in Deptford Creek.

Encouraged by Clare, at fifty-three years of age, Frederick joined the 'Lewisham Rambler's Club'. The members of this tight-knit little organisation were not strictly pedestrians. They believed in walking tours for sheer entertainment. Some of the members also saw themselves as hill-climbers, cavers, mountaineers and amateur archaeologists. Most of the walks, usually undertaken on a Saturday, were from five to ten miles in length, and Frederick realised just how much he loved this activity.

The joy of placing one foot in front of the other led him, despite his mature age, to enter the relatively new 'Long Distance Championship of the World,' event, which was held in London's Agricultural Hall over six days. He placed fifty-second overall, and first in his age group, but it would be his last formal pedestrian event.

Soon afterwards, May graduated as an engineer from the University College, London.

For Frederick, this was a proud and special moment, and it felt very much like the next stage in the founding of a dynasty as he and

Clare escorted their first-born across the lawns of the college, the portico and ornate dome of the octagon building a dramatic backdrop. James Washington, who had travelled from New York for the occasion, hovered nearby.

Hundreds of young people, predominantly men, stood in dark gowns and mortar-board hats, surrounded by family members. Photographers with tripod-mounted cameras were doing brisk business capturing graduates in front of the rose gardens.

While Frederick smiled proudly, a tall, older man in an academic gown, looking doddery and unsteady, made his way over to May, doffing his hat with a flourish. 'Congratulations, young lady.'

'Thank you, Professor Harlburton.'

'You have done well, Miss Morton.' Then to Frederick. 'Sir, your daughter is a gifted engineer, and I know for a fact that she has taught me more than I have taught her.'

★★★

That night the family dined at the luxurious Langham Hotel in Regent Street. Despite the presence of the Prince of Wales and more than a few key players of the City of London, the mood remained light-hearted.

'I have an announcement,' Frederick said. 'Let's charge our glasses.' A waiter appeared, lifting the bottle of Bollinger and splashing a little into each of their glasses. 'Now,' he continued, his gaze falling on his daughter. 'I must tell you that I have created a new position in the factory. It's called Chief Electrical Engineer. Will you accept it?'

May looked up in surprise, then a tear formed in the corner of her eye. 'I suspect that the pay will be not as high as I would expect elsewhere.'

Frederick grinned back. 'I suspect so, too.'

'It doesn't matter, and I accept. But I have news for you too. I've been doing some designs of my own.'

'Can I see them?'

'I'd love to show them to you.'

The next morning May laid a series of pages on the dining table of the Lewisham house. They were blueprints, beautifully drawn machine designs. Yet, these were not steam engines.

Frederick did not say a word until he had picked up and examined each of the pages in turn. The side, front and top diagrams. The component lists, and even estimated costs of manufacture.

'Your work is near perfect,' he said.

'I'm hoping that this will be the first Morton alternating current induction motor,' she said. 'If my calculations are correct, it will develop fifty shaft horsepower from less current than anything on the market. Can we build one?'

'No,' said Frederick, and his voice dropped to a whisper. 'We will not build one. We will make and sell five thousand of them.'

May teased, 'You might have to change the company name to the Morton Steam and Electric Power Company.'

Frederick reached across to take his daughter's hand. 'How about, the Morton *Family* Steam and Electric Power Company?'

★★★

By early 1895 Matthew was back at Oxford, and Harriet was playing Teresa in a Lyric Theatre production of *The Mountebanks*. The Cape Town office was still in the same building – small but busy, with a young man in charge, an excellent rugby player who was selling engines and establishing the brand.

While Matthew set himself on a path of finishing his arts degree with honours and commenced a PhD thesis on 'Continental Influences on Major Nineteenth Century English Literary Styles,' there was one great sadness in his heart.

Miss Pattinson had returned to finish her degree, but had commenced a life of travel, journalism and scholarship that was more like a sailing skiff being pushed by restless winds than a lifestyle. Their letters continued, but on one of her rare visits she made it plain that she was not looking to start a relationship.

'We're friends,' she said, patting his hand after a meal at the Bear Inn, a six-hundred-year-old Oxford fixture. 'I don't have time for anything more. There's too much to do and see. I feel like I'm making up for lost time – not just for me but for women everywhere.'

Yet, when Matthew was promoted to a junior professorship, she was there in the audience, still unmarried, yet unattainable in the way he wished to attain her. He consoled himself with the knowledge that to cage her in an Oxford house would be like caging a wild thing with the world as her territory.

★★★

When Frederick planned another overseas journey, there was no question but that Clare would accompany him. May also decided to come along for the first leg, to make good her promise to James Washington, who had not yet found a suitable position in London. The journey was exhaustively planned, with passages booked on the best and fastest steamers, and reservations made at well-regarded hotels.

This time, also, there was a juggling of activities selected for personal and professional reasons. Clare intended to use the trip to further her collection of ferns and other exotic plants, while Frederick made lists, not only of potential customers, but of engineers he'd like to meet, and factories he wanted to visit.

Central to Frederick and Clare's itinerary was the commissioning of a new type of borehole pump, coupled to a standard Mobilis engine. These were not yet for sale but were being sent out to selected sites across the world, places where poverty was so pervasive that people could not obtain fresh water.

Cholera had been determined by pioneer physicians like Filippo Pacini and Robert Koch to be caused by contaminated water, not bad odours. Clean water might have saved Frederick's own mother, and this became a special passion.

The first of these systems was destined for the vast slum of Woodstock, South Africa, where a crew were already boring into the water table, preparing for the machinery's arrival.

★★★

Frederick, Clare and May steamed across the Atlantic in a First-Class cabin, spending time in New York, where the Fortis was becoming a preferred engine, still tagging along on the skyscraper revolution. James Washington was there to meet them, and May burst into tears when he kissed her hand.

Leaving their daughter with the Washington family at their home in Queens, Frederick and Clare headed down to East Pittsburgh, Philadelphia. There, as a guest of George Westinghouse, Frederick was inspired by both the candour with which the company founder shared his experience, and the advanced processes he had initiated within the company.

Westinghouse was working with budgets beyond the dreams of even the largest British industrial companies, and Frederick made pages of notes when he returned to their room at night, his mind buzzing with new ideas.

After an enlightening few days, the couple retraced Frederick's long-ago journey across America, this time enjoying the luxury of a Pullman sleeper. For the first time in a while, Frederick felt the energy of youth, and he devoted himself to Clare, making the most of this special time together.

From San Francisco they boarded the RMSS *Zealandia*, one of a new breed of steamship: three-hundred-and-seventy feet long and of almost three thousand tonnes displacement. By the second day Frederick had inveigled his way into the engine room, viewing the 2400-horsepower engines that would drive her to Australian shores in just eight days.

Far out in the Pacific Ocean, Frederick's imagination was challenged by the sheer distance involved. He enthused to Clare about giant ships, with hulls so long that their displacement speed would allow turbine engines to drive them from San Francisco across the Pacific at even faster speeds.

The *Zealandia* docked in Sydney where Frederick and Clare stayed with Denny, Eadie and young Peter in their new home overlooking Rose Bay, for two weeks. Father and son held a series of talks with the City Council about power generation using Imperium engines.

In South Australia, Denny and Frederick had meetings with the managers of flour mills, a cannery, a steel works, and finally the manager of a copper smelter who travelled down from Burra to meet them.

On their last day in the City of Churches they travelled by hired coach, out along Northeast Road, through the straw-coloured hills of Tea Tree Gully to Newman's Nursery. This was one of the biggest such facilities in the world – hundreds of acres of orchards, centred on a series of exquisite stone buildings, in Water Gully below Anstey's Hill. Here Clare purchased more than eight dozen plants, including some unique Australian ferns, to add to her collection, arranging for their despatch via the next fast ship.

The party of four caught a coastal steamer up the Spencer Gulf to Port Pirie, then a train on the narrow-gauge railway through the South Australian outback and onto the Silverton Tramway to Broken Hill, where Frederick and Denny were greeted heartily by the BHP board.

Over a week of negotiations, Frederick and Denny nutted out another major tender – this time for one of the largest industrial electricity generation plants in the state of New South Wales. The deal they signed allowed for the BHP company to purchase three Imperium engines, all running Westinghouse alternators, to power a new smelter design.

Frederick celebrated by taking Clare to one of the town's excellent silversmiths and purchasing a heavy solid silver chain, on the end of which hung a stylised pickaxe.

'Silver from the source,' she said, 'from mines powered by Morton engines. Nothing could be more appropriate.'

A week later, travelling from Perth to Kalgoorlie meant yet another overland journey: this time to the newest and richest gold rush on earth. Together Clare and Frederick walked the Golden Mile, where Fortis Engines with their winding gear were already popular.

Mining towns were exciting places, with wealth and despair in equal measure, deals in front bars sealed with beery handshakes and rough men carousing after weeks of hard labour. Frederick was enjoying himself, but he also knew that the pace of this frenetic journey was wearing Clare down.

'Now Cape Town,' he said, 'where we will commission the new Woodstock pumping machine, then Egypt, and finally France to visit your family. Can you cope with that?'

Clare smiled wanly, 'I can – I'll be with you, and I've heard there's a delightful little nursery just near Bloemfontein ...'

They returned to London to find May wearing an engagement ring, and James Washington negotiating with a firm of civil engineers, having also submitted an application to study architecture at the University College.

By 1900 Frederick and Clare had three grandchildren, two in Australia and one in London, and May had long since supervised the design and production of the first Morton alternators.

★★★

As the years passed Frederick was, on balance, happy enough. He and Clare grew ever closer, their marriage melding them into the kind of close-knit unit that only couples who stay together through thick and thin, through many years, experience. A state arising from the realisation of how few people are truly on your side, from the joys and despair of shared experiences, and the secret things that no one outside the marital unit can know.

Yet there were times when the tide's sweet pull was no longer seductive, and Frederick spent time in the eddies, suffering from a strange broodiness that was all the more unwelcome for being without any real basis. Yet, later, when he traced the beginnings of this difficult period, he could point to four events. Each affected him a great deal.

The first was an accident. It was strange, but despite having lived through the Boer War, the death of a monarch, and numerous other tragedies, the sinking of the RMS *Titanic* on her way to New York in 1912, with the loss of more than fifteen-hundred souls affected Frederick deeply.

Every engineer took this failure seriously. It was a symptom of the hubris growing in scientific and engineering circles. An overall design that did not foresee the flooding of multiple compartments, weaknesses in the frame strength that led to the ship splitting open, and the possibility of brittle fractures of iron in freezing conditions.

The second cause of Frederick's listlessness was the rapidly changing nature of technology. The Mobilis engine had been all but replaced in new installations by small diesel, petrol and electric engines, and even the Fortis sold in only small numbers, despite several upgrades and redesigns.

The Morton Company's new electric engines were now waiting on dozens of pallets in the despatch bay, ready to be taken to their new homes across the world. They were made to the highest possible standards, ready for a maintenance-free life of hundreds of thousands of hours.

The Imperium turbine engine, now available in three sizes, was still the industry standard for power generation, at least in Britain and the Empire, but Frederick did not love it as much as he loved the others. He missed the action of the piston in the cylinder, the power of direct-action steam, and he spent more time with the Fortis that still ran the factory, than he needed to.

Sometimes, at home, he would sit at his desk with his model engine, watching it cycle and puff steam, enamoured anew with the forces that combined to make it work. The direct-pressure steam cycle was in his blood and always would be.

The third cause of Frederick's general discontent was the sense that he had not yet fulfilled the future Lord Forgill had expected of him.

Frederick wondered if he had done enough. Yes, he had several hundred contented workers; well-paid and cared for. He was a fair and empathetic employer. He had installed pumps in slums around the world and was developing power generation for some of the same locations. Yet had he truly helped anyone else to make the jump from working class drudgery to life as a professional, as Lord Bartholomew Forgill had done for him?

While he had always been able to talk to Clare about his feelings, some months passed before he was ready to discuss this with her. When he did, he was surprised at her reaction.

'Of course, you can do more, and you should. Will you let me help?'

'I would value it, certainly. Education is the key, yet things have changed since the days of the Ragged Schools.'

This was an understatement. The Elementary Education Act of 1870, pushed through by the efforts of that visionary Member of Parliament, Mr William Forster, meant that every child in England now had access to a school. The Act's successor, made into law six years later, made school attendance compulsory and a further update in 1891 abolished fees at government schools, making them free for all students.

Clare studied Frederick's face. 'The things that Lord Forgill did for you changed your life, but is pulling talented children out and sending them to expensive schools still the best way to go forward?

God knows Harriet and Matthew have done well enough, but I suspect that he, at least, was not happy at the Charterhouse. May did very well at the government school here – combined with university it's given her a chance at a profession she would not have had even twenty years ago.'

Frederick grasped her argument as if it were a clever engineering idea requiring development. 'You're right. In that case we could do two things, the first of which is to try to improve the system itself.' He stood and began to pace. 'The first way to do that is to lobby the government—'

'There are already groups doing that,' said Clare.

'There are, I agree,' said Frederick. The Times often carried articles detailing the activities of committees such as the *National Society for Promoting the Education of the Poor in the Principles of the Established Church*. Most, however, had a particular angle or agenda, and starting a new one seemed to be adding to a crowded field. 'Perhaps,' he mused, 'we would be better off providing funding directly to schools – for books and writing materials.'

'I agree. What's your second idea?' Clare asked.

'Elementary education is now free,' said Frederick. 'University is not. We could initiate a series of scholarships in various professions for talented students.'

Clare squeezed his arm. 'That, Freddie, is a perfect idea. Shall we make a list?'

For the first time in years, Frederick felt the fire glow bright inside. The initial recipients of Morton scholarships, in Medicine, Law, the Arts and Engineering were selected from the Stepney government high school.

This, Frederick knew, seeing these shining faces, was just the beginning, with plans for endowments over some thirty-eight schools in the poorer districts of London and the surrounding boroughs.

By the time the scholarship scheme was well advanced, however, the fourth cause of Frederick's discontent was beginning to rear its head – the inexorable drift towards war with Germany.

Chapter Sixty-four

In December 1914, at the age of 43, Matthew announced that he would enlist in his local infantry battalion, the Oxfordshire and Buckinghamshire Light Infantry. He was by then a tenured professor in English literature, and no one thought joining up was a good idea. Oh, one or two of his fellows professed their admiration and a desire to do the same. Others were dismayed at Matthew's confidence. 'Without being indelicate, old man,' someone said. 'They won't take you with a gammy leg.'

'They will when they get desperate enough,' he said.

'But why? I'd rather move to Tasmania or Timbuktu and wait the whole show out.'

Matthew could not explain why. Glory. Self-punishment. Escape. Self-hatred. A lifetime of stories that, in the Greek tradition, glorified the hero. His mind was incomplete and did not yet know itself. From such clay are soldiers made.

And at polished tables in Clubs and War Rooms, men in tailored suits and hand-tooled black leather shoes made decisions that propelled a generation into a nightmare, tore families apart, and turned entire French provinces into black holes of terror, steel and high explosive.

'Don't do it!' wrote Miss Pattinson. 'You're a man of beautiful thoughts, of prose and poetry. Your hands are made to hold a pen, and not the tools of war.' Yet she had abrogated her hold over him many years earlier. That was the price she paid for freedom.

Six months after Herbert Asquith's declaration of war, Matthew presented himself at the Oxford recruiting station, a crippled man in early middle age looking for meaning, staring at the banner and colours for the Oxfordshire and Buckinghamshire Light Infantry. Men in uniform – perfect specimens placed to entice youths to want to imitate them – stood nearby, straight and manly, laughing and talking, tanned and confident.

The corporal at the table seemed happy enough to sign Matthew up, talking of the coming 'show,' sending him down the hall to the line waiting for a medical.

The doctor rejected Matthew reluctantly. 'I'm sorry, was it polio?'

'Consumption.'

'Stick to Oxford,' said the doctor, 'for I can't pass you through.'

Matthew fought his disability. He began to practice walking – spending hours perfecting an even stride – even strengthening his leg by strapping on weights and swinging his afflicted limb from a table.

In early 1916 he tried the recruiting lines again, and the doctor did not meet Matthew's eyes as he certified him as fit for active service. 'There, you've got what you want, God help you.'

Three days later Matthew donned battle dress for the first time, smelling carbolic soap and feeling the coarse wool against his skin, touching the neatly-stitched patches that the RSM told him were old bullet holes suffered by the uniforms' previous owners.

Shipped by special train to Salisbury, Matthew took to basic training with relentless keenness, if not the natural skills of some of the others. He felt as if he was part of something important. That he could make people proud.

Over the next months, Matthew learned a new rhythm of life: reveille at 0600, marching drill, breakfast, obstacle courses, pack drill, digging sullage pits, lunch, rifle drills, forced marches, supper, retreat and bed.

Nothing the corporals and sergeants dished out, however, could match the pain of Matthew's first years at school, especially since many of the other soldiers were university men also – after the first few days books began to be passed around, and pages could be read in snatches during the day.

The recruits were issued rifles – brand-new weapons, straight out of the crate from the Royal Small Arms Factory in North London. The walnut stocks felt good to the touch – having been sanded smooth and oiled. The bores required only a first range-ready clean with gun oil and the supplied pull-through, then a hundred rounds or so for the barrels to settle into minute-of-angle accuracy.

Matthew was enough of his father's son that he appreciated the fine engineering of the Lee-Enfield SMLE, the best infantry rifle in the world at the time. He understood the efficacy of the charging clip and the rapid rate of fire it allowed. At the range he found an activity not dependent on agility, but concentration, good eyesight, a steady hand and an understanding of the weapon which fitted so snugly against his shoulder. Matthew qualified at 'marksman' level. He was prouder of the badge with its crossed rifles than anything else in his life.

At the end of basic training Matthew was assigned to the 8th Service Battalion, and after rumours of being sent to France they were loaded on a troop steamer and shipped to Salonika.

'We'll be fighting the damned Bulgarians,' someone explained, and Matthew wished he had paid more attention to this country in his reading. This lack he was able to remedy by borrowing books from the ship's library, which was also stocked with current periodicals.

The Balkans theatre was a scarcely known corner of the Great War, one that many Britishers knew little about. Yet, the Bulgarian army was numerous, armed with hard-hitting Mannlicher rifles, and were bolstered by elements of the German 11th Army. The landscape itself, Matthew found, was not so different from home.

The night before the Battle of Horseshoe Hill, an attack against a fortified position, well defended by Bulgarian troops backed with German regulars, Matthew wrote a poem.

Only Tomorrow Knows
by Matthew Morton

The sound of voices,
illiterate men dictating letters, to scribes in battle grey.
Will these brave men return? Only tomorrow knows.

Artillery shells; the 'softening up,' erupts on the fire-
struck plain.
Ghostly wailing in the night.
Which of my comrades will these cruel shells take?
Only tomorrow knows.

My weapon gleams, bayonet with razor edge,
in the darkness growing. 'Tis here I may bid goodbye.
Shall I wilt or show courage in the field of fire?
Only tomorrow knows.

When the battle started, Matthew found something strange: he was not afraid. Perhaps it was because the enemy were some distance away, but he did not fear the bullets that whizzed and whined through the air, and the artillery shells that landed nearby.

Instead, he took careful aim and sent clip after clip of .303 rounds down-range into the ranks of the enemy, through clouds of cordite smoke and the thump of landing artillery shells. At the end of the battle his platoon lieutenant commended him personally.

'Iced water in those veins of yours, Morton, well done.'

Despite being proud of his bravery, Matthew was horrified by the sight of the dead and dying. He felt that he had been transformed to a different state of being, by the dragging-back of corpses, the screaming of wounded from the nearby field hospital, and the knowledge that he had most likely killed and badly wounded other men.

Three months later, at the battle of Doiran, a bugler sounded the advance from a set of fortified trenches. Matthew was in the process of coming to his feet when something struck him a hammer-blow in the side of the face. He came back to consciousness on a stretcher, hearing voices and feeling himself manhandled through a void of strangeness.

The 8mm lead projectile had impacted the sloping side of his cheekbone, shattering it, then deflecting around his skull, emerging near his left ear, taking half the lobe with it.

After initial treatment at a field hospital in Salonika, Matthew was shipped home, where his convalescence was long and difficult. He had learned the habit of cigarette smoking, and he smoked in endless chains, lighting one from the relic of another.

He slept so badly that his eyes sank deep into pits, and when Frederick took him to the factory, he could not raise the enthusiasm to walk through the bays and greet the workers he had, in the main, known for all of his life.

'I feel like I'm no longer your son,' he told Frederick. 'Rather, I belong to something dark and horrible – the living who will die and the already dead.'

'The war will end,' said Frederick, 'and I pray that in time you will no longer feel this way.'

★★★

In May 1917 Matthew was judged fit for active service and sent back to the front. On July the sixth, a telegram arrived at the Lewisham house, delivered by the vicar and the local militia commander.

Matthew had been shot through the chest and killed during a determined series of attacks, pursuing the Bulgar forces into the Strumica Valley. Clare wrote to Matthew's commanding officer and asked if they had any further information, if they knew of any other personal effects, or if he had said any last words. Weeks later a package containing a leatherbound diary and a locket holding the image of a woman, arrived in the mail. There was also a worn and faded jeweller's case, and inside it an engagement ring set with a perfect blue-white diamond. A folded certificate of authenticity from Kimberley, South Africa, was nestled underneath the padding.

The diary was a treasure to a grieving mother. On the inside pages Matthew had written poetry, observations, and some notes.

> On a Macedonian field, with dawn a predator below the horizon,
> you see the advance of men, in troubled darkness.
> And on that Macedonian field there is no honour;
> only the spilled blood,
> of good men, dying for no good cause.

For Frederick the loss of his second son was a trauma from which he would never recover. It was the greatest blow of his life, leaving a yawning emptiness in his heart that the gentle boy had filled.

Worse, his emptiness was not just the loss of one man, but of many, for there were empty spaces in the production bays. Dozens of leather aprons hung unused on their pegs. Morton scholarship places went unfilled. So many young men would no longer learn professions at Oxford, Cambridge, Durham or London, but had instead died violent deaths in France, the Dardanelles, or North Africa. For no tangible gain to anyone, and an insufferable loss to millions.

Frederick drew the remnants of his family close, and at every opportunity, watched Harriet on the stage, her presence enlarged by her own grief. May was his chief support at work, her talents continuing to transform the company. By the middle of the nineteen-twenties Morton Steam Power had a life of its own, now beyond his control, and he did not argue when the board wished to change the company name to the Morton Electric Motor and Turbine Company.

When Clare asked her husband if he minded, he replied; 'Ned

Baring told me once that I would know I have succeeded when my own company does not need me anymore. He was a wise man. It's time for me to step away.'

Epilogue

In the winter of 1919, Frederick noticed a tremor which started in his hands, spread up his arms and entered his upper body. Clare became solicitous, helping him out of bed and down the stairs. He still attended board meetings, and frequented the factory, but he arrived late and left early.

The doctor diagnosed a palsy known as Parkinson's Disease. Frederick hated the nodding, shaking, and weakness, but strangely, he did not shrink. He grew. He grew not in stature, but in kindness, grace, and wisdom.

With his responsibilities to the company diminished, he spent more time expanding the scholarship program. He attended graduations, interviewed prospective scholars, and encouraged those who showed aptitude on the sporting field or track.

When he spoke, people listened. When he stopped walking to look at something as if at a new angle, others stopped with him, trying to catch the nuances that he homed in on with his still erudite mind. In this growth of his spirit, he found time to sit with his daughters, and the grandchildren who came to visit, filling the house with laughter. They were drawn to him like elephant calves to their patriarch.

On the morning of his eighty-second birthday, with his wife and daughters fussing over their preparations for the day, Frederick walked into the kitchen, where a cake was being baked.

'I don't need a party, or a cake,' he said.

'What do you want then?' asked Clare. 'If you want ten dancing girls with banana-peel hats on their heads I'll find them for you.'

Frederick felt gratefulness well up in his chest. His wife still knew how to make him smile. 'I've been thinking a lot, lately, about the river – near where I grew up. Could we go there?'

Clare raised her eyebrows, 'If that's what you want, so we shall.'

***

With Jenkins at the reins, they made it an outing – crossing on the Tower Bridge, then a sharp right along river streets to the Limehouse Basin – diverting past the slum-terraces of Frederick's childhood and ragged children hunting pennies in the streets, past costermongers and their wares, down to the mud banks, where Frederick insisted on hobbling from the embankment to the vast exposed flats.

'Father, what are you doing?' cried Harriet. And they stood on the bank, watching him.

Frederick did not answer – but he walked on, all the way into the water, up to his thighs, heedless of the mud and cold, just so he could feel the strength of the ebbing tide against his thighs, while tears dripped down his face. This was the force of forever. Of history and time – greater by far than any human life or engine made of iron.

Looking down along the river he could see mudlarks grubbing trinkets from the flats. An occasional steam-powered vessel passed by, but most of the Thames craft were now driven by internal combustion engines, with their stink of oil and foul exhaust.

The glory days, Frederick thought to himself – the spring tides – were gone, and the long ebb was nearing its nadir. Clare reached him, wet skirts winding around her legs and thighs. She gripped his hand so very tightly, knowing in her heart that soon she would lose him.

There was a sense of time slipping, water running out of reach. Visions of a Parisian hotel room, children playing on creeping-fescue lawns festooned with toys between flower beds in full summer bloom, the open road with a knot of pedestrians ahead and more behind, and the competitive spirit driving his feet onwards.

Frederick smelled oiled steel, and molten iron. He heard old Eleanor's cackle, and the voices of his lost son and living offspring.

Clare softened her grip, placed her free hand on his shoulder and looked into his eyes. 'We glimpsed unknown splendours, celestial fires. Do you remember?'

Something beautiful came into his eyes. 'I remember,' he said, and they turned together, making for the embankment.

★★★

Across the river, in the Lewisham house, the clock in its alcove at the foot of the stairs hesitated. One minute, two minutes passed, until the movement resumed. In the Deptford Creek factory, a steam engine continued to cycle.

The clock, the engine, and the tides in the river merged with the beating of Frederick's heart, until they became one. The swinging of the pendulum. The cycling of the piston. The tread of a walking man. On and on, changing, pausing, but never stopping completely, into forever.

Acknowledgements

This novel was written, on and off, between 2017 and 2023. Being trapped in an apartment in East London during the Covid pandemic helped, as I could write or edit for six or eight hours at a stretch, then wander along the streets and canals where Frederick spent his childhood.

As was the case for many years, my now-retired agent Brian Cook was the first to read the manuscript and offer his usual insightful advice. Thank you, Brian, I'll never forget what you did for me and my writing. This would be a poorer book without your input.

Technical help from stationary steam engine experts David Davies and Naomi Cornish was a wonderful boost for me. Thanks for your time and knowledge. (Needless to say, the blame for any remaining technical errors rests with me, not them).

A strong creative team worked on this book. Thanks to Brad Connors for your exhaustive edit (I'm sure it must have worn you down), and to talented artist Angus Crowley who is a one-of-a-kind book cover designer who never fails to delight and surprise me.

Thanks to my family, who are far more important than any fictional story. Writing can be self-indulgent, and it's certainly time consuming. Thanks for putting up with it.

To my test readers, who made valuable contributions. Catriona Martin, Bob Barron, and Bob and Anne Martin. Your suggestions and comments helped enormously.

To my writer friends: Peter Watt, Karly Lane, Lily Malone, Favel Parrett, Jenn J Macleod, Fiona McArthur, Don Douglas, Dick Eussen, Rusty Carrington, Annie Seaton, Desley Polmear, Tamara McWilliam, Roby Aitken and Chris Allen. Even when we don't talk much, you inspire me to do better and try harder.

Finally, to my readers. Thanks. The real magic is in you.

Crime, history, and international politics are all passionate interests of author Greg Barron. He has lived in North America, New South Wales and in and around Katherine, Northern Territory. He once crossed Arnhem Land on foot and has a passion for outback landscapes.

Published by HarperCollins Australia and Stories of Oz Publishing, Greg's books are gutsy page-turners that have won a wide readership and critical acclaim. The Pedestrian is his twelfth full-length novel.

Gjbarron@outlook.com
Facebook.com/storiesofoz
Facebook.com/gregbarronauthor
Twitter.com/gregbarronauthor

ALL BOOKS AVAILABLE AT OZBOOKSTORE.COM

www.ingramcontent.com/pod-product-compliance
Ingram Content Group UK Ltd.
Pitfield, Milton Keynes, MK11 3LW, UK
UKHW041259020126
9870UKWH00059B/1278